AF352474

THE PLEASANT NIGHTS

Volume 2

THE DA PONTE LIBRARY SERIES

Giovan Francesco Straparola

THE PLEASANT NIGHTS

VOLUME 2

Edited with Introduction and Commentaries by
Donald Beecher

Translated by W.G. Waters
Thoroughly Revised and Corrected by the Editor

UNIVERSITY OF TORONTO PRESS
Toronto Buffalo London

ISBN 978-1-4426-4427-4

The Lorenzo Da Ponte Italian Library

Library and Archives Canada Cataloguing in Publication

Straparola, Giovanni Francesco, ca, 1480–1557?
The pleasant nights / Giovan Francesco Straparola; edited with introduction
and commentaries by Donald Beecher; translated by W.G. Waters, thoroughly
revised and corrected by the editor.

(The Lorenzo Da Ponte Italian library series)
Translation of: Le piacevoli notti.
Includes bibliographical references.
ISBN 978-1-4426-4426-7 (v. 1).   ISBN 978-1-4426-4427-4 (v. 2)

I. Beecher, Donald.   II. Waters, W.G. (William George), 1844–1928.   III. Title.
IV. Series: Lorenzo Da Ponte Italian library series.

PQ4634.S7P513 2012   853'.3   C2012-902024-9

Publication of this book assisted by the Istituto Italiano di cultura, Toronto.

This book has been published under the aegis and with financial assistance of:
Fondazione Cassamarca, Treviso; the National Italian-American Foundation;
Ministero degli Affari Esteri, Direzione Generale per la Promozione e la Cooperazione
Culturale; Ministero per i Beni e le Attività Culturali, Direzione Generale per i Beni
Librari e gli Istituti Culturali, Servizio per la promozione del libro e della lettura.

University of Toronto Press acknowledges the financial assistance to its publishing
program of the Canada Council for the Arts and the Ontario Arts Council.

University of Toronto Press acknowledges the financial support for its publishing
activities of the Government of Canada through the Book Publishing Industry
Development Program (BPIDP).

Contents

THE PLEASANT NIGHTS, VOLUME II

The Greetings of Giovan Francesco Straparola of Caravaggio   3

[The Nights and Their Fables with Commentaries]

The Sixth Night
VI.1   Two Friends Who Held Their Wives in Common   7
VI.2   Castorio's Welcome Castration   29
VI.3   The Widow's Broken Promise   39
VI.4   Who Will Become Abbess?   47
VI.5   The Virtue of Stones   56

The Seventh Night
VII.1   The Wife, the Courtesan, and the Witch   67
VII.2   Malgherita Spolatina's Death at Sea   93
VII.3   Flogged at the Pope's Court   101
VII.4   Share and Share Alike   113
VII.5   The Three Brothers   123

The Eighth Night
VIII.1   The Three Idle Rogues   149
VIII.2   The Right Handling of Wives   169
VIII.3   The Priest and the Image-Carver's Wife   192
VIII.4   Lattanzio and the Secret Arts of Sorcery   212
VIII.5   The Donkey's Skin and the Doctor's Apprentice   236
VIII.3A   The Woes of an Old Gallant   245
VIII.3B   The Merchant's Monkey   254

The Ninth Night
IX.1   King Galafro's Vain Precautions   263

vi   Contents

IX.2	Rodolino and Violante, or the Broken Hearts	276
IX.3	Francesco Sforza's Narrow Escape	293
IX.4	Papiro Schizza's Pedantry and the Scholar's Revenge	305
IX.5	Of the Bergamasques and the Florentines	318

The Tenth Night

X.1	Madonna Veronica Recovers Her Stolen Jewels	333
X.2	The Lion and the Ass Named 'Brancaleone'	343
X.3	Cesarino the Dragon Slayer	361
X.4	The Diabolical Testament of Andrigetto di Valsabbia	394
X.5	Rosolino's Confession for Love of His Son	406

The Eleventh Night

XI.1	Costantino and His Wonderful Cat	417
XI.2	The Grateful Dead, or Bertuccio and Tarquinia	446
XI.3	Wind, Water, and Shame, or the Gluttony of Dom Pomporio	475
XI.4	The Buffoon and the Stolen Veal	483
XI.5	Frate Bigoccio Takes a Wife and Leaves Her	491

The Twelfth Night

XII.1	How Florio's Wife Cures His Jealousy	503
XII.2	The Simpleton's Blackmail	508
XII.3	The Language of Animals and Pozzuolo's Wife	515
XII.4	Of the Sons Who Disobeyed Their Father's Testament	527
XII.5	How Pope Sixtus IV Made His Servant Rich	532

The Thirteenth Night

XIII.1	The Huntsman and the Madman	549
XIII.2	Diego, the Hens, and the Carmelite Friar	558
XIII.3	On the Liberality of Spaniards and Germans	569
XIII.4	The Servant, the Fly, and the Master	573
XIII.5	Vilio Brigantello, the Robber, and the Fateful Sack	584
XIII.6	How Lucilio Finds the 'Good Day'	589
XIII.7	Giorgio Hales His Master before the Tribunal	604
XIII.8	Midnight Feast and Famine	611
XIII.9	Of Filomena the Hermaphrodite Nun	617
XIII.10	The Judgments of Cesare, Doctor of Laws	630
XIII.11	The Novice's Night in the Barn	638
XIII.12	The Healing of King Guglielmo	648
XIII.13	How Pietro Rizzato Finds a Treasure and Becomes a Miser	655

THE PLEASANT NIGHTS

Volume 2

THE PLEASANT NIGHTS
(Le Piacevoli notti)

VOLUME II
Nights VI–XIII

THE FABLES AND ENIGMAS OF
MESSER GIOVANNI FRANCESCO STRAPAROLA DA CARAVAGGIO

To All Gracious and Lovable Ladies,
from Giovanni Francesco Straparola, Greeting

Dear ladies, there are many envious and spiteful men who are always and everywhere attempting to fix their fearsome fangs in my flesh and scatter my dismembered body in all directions, claiming that the entertaining stories that I have collected and written in this and the previous little volume are not of my making, but materials which I have feloniously appropriated from others. It's true, I confess, that they are not mine; to have said otherwise would be a lie. Nevertheless, I have set them down faithfully in the manner in which they were recited by the ten young ladies who had gathered for their recreation. So if I bring them to light now, it's not to gratify my own pride or to seek honour and fame, but simply to please you all, and particularly those of you who may rely on my service and to whom I owe continual devotion. With smiling faces, then, dear ladies, accept the humble gift proffered to you by your servant, paying no heed at all to those snarling whelps who, in their currish fury, would cling to me with their ravenous teeth, but read my book now and then, taking such pleasure in it as time and place will allow and give honour to God from whom all blessings flow. May you be happy, always keeping in mind those who have your names graven on their hearts, among whom I do not count myself the least.

Venice, Sept. 1st, 1553 (in the edition of 1555)

Here Begins the Second Book of the Fables and Enigmas of
Messer Giovanni Francesco Straparola da Caravaggio

The Sixth Night

The shadows of a night sombre and overcast had spread themselves
everywhere around and the golden stars no longer shed their light in
the spacious heavens, while Aeolus, sweeping over the salt waves with a
long-drawn moan, was stirring a tempestuous sea and obstructing the
efforts of mariners, when our noble and faithful band of companions,
indifferent to the blustering winds and the cruel cold, made their way
to the customary meeting place and sat down in due order, once they
had paid their respects to the Signora. Soon after, she ordered the
golden vase to be brought to her and therein she placed the names of
five young ladies. The first to be drawn was that of Alteria, the second
Arianna, the third Cateruzza, the fourth Lauretta, and the fifth Eritrea.
This done, the Signora directed these five to sing a canzone, a command
they obeyed at once, beginning with the following strains in soft and
melodious tones:

Song

O Love! if faith rose with thee at thy birth;
    If ye, twin flowers of earth,
Should twine around my lady's name
And deck the presence I adore,
    Then never more
Should they divide, or time let sink my loyal flame.

She feels your power indeed, but not enough
    To let your onslaught rough
Sway all her nature, and release
Her passions kept so well in hand.
    And thus I stand
With failing hope, while my desire doth aye increase.

When the singing of this sweet and most pleasant song was ended, Alteria, who had been chosen to tell the first story, laid aside her viol and plectrum and began her tale as follows.

VI. Fable 1
Two Friends Who Held Their Wives
in Common

ALTERIA

Two men who were comrades and close friends dupe one another and in the end have their wives in common.

Many are the tricks and deceptions which men practise upon one another nowadays, but among them all you will find none comparable in craft and knavery to those which friends and relatives will play against each other. Since the lot has fallen upon me to begin this evening's entertainment with a story, I've decided to give you an account of the subtlety, cunning, and treachery that a certain man employed in deceiving his closest friend. Yet even though his knavish trick, for its cleverness, was entirely successful in duping him, in the end, he found himself tricked by craft and ingenuity equal to his own. If you'll kindly hear my story, all of these things will become clear.

In the ancient and famous city of Genoa there lived in times past two friends, one of whom was called Messer Liberale Spinola, a man of great wealth and an easy life, if a little excessive in his pleasures, and the other Messer Artilao Sara, one of the leading and busiest merchants of the city. The friendship between these two was very warm and close – an attachment so great that they could hardly endure to be apart. If by chance either one needed something that belonged to the other, he could obtain it without question or delay. Because Messer Artilao was engaged in numerous merchandising ventures and had a hand in many affairs, both his own and others, he one day had to set out on a journey to Soria. Wherefore, he sought out his dear friend, Messer Liberale, and addressed him in the same spirit of sincerity and benevolence he had always felt towards him. 'Well you know, my friend, just as it is known to all men, how great the love and affection is between us, and how I've always relied upon you, as I do now, both by reason of the friendship we have had for each other for so many long years, and of the vow of brotherhood that exists between us. Because I've settled in my mind to go to Soria, and because there is no other man in the world I trust as much as I do you, I come to you in boldness and confidence to ask a favour of you – something that, although it may cause some disturbance to your own affairs, yet I beg you to do for me out of your goodness and for the sake of our mutual good will.'

Messer Liberale, who was entirely disposed to do his friend any kindness he might ask for, without further words on the matter said, 'Artilao, my dear friend, the love we have for one another and the bond of fellowship which our sincere affection has knitted between us render all further discourse on the matter unnecessary. Tell me freely what you desire and place me at your command, for I'm ready to discharge whatever duty you may place upon me.'

Messer Artilao then said to his friend, 'My desire and request of you is that, for as long as I shall be away, you take charge of the governing of my house and of my wife, calling to her attention anything that may be needed. And whatever sum of money you disburse on her behalf, I'll repay you in full upon my return.'

Messer Liberale, as soon as he understood all that his friend desired, first gave him hearty thanks for the high opinion he had of his probity in holding him in such esteem. Then he promised, to the best of his poor abilities, to discharge the task which had been placed upon him.

When the time came for Messer Artilao to set out on his voyage, he loaded the merchandise aboard his vessel. His wife Daria, then three months pregnant as it happened, he recommended to the care of his friend, then boarded ship and departed from Genoa with his sails spread to a favouring wind and with good fortune to aid him. No sooner was Messer Artilao embarked and on his way than Messer Liberale went to the house of his well-beloved neighbour, Madonna Daria, and said to her, 'Madonna, Messer Artilao, your good husband and my dearest friend, before he set forth on his voyage, urged me with his pressing entreaties to take charge of all his affairs, together with your good self, Madonna, and moreover to keep you mindful of all the things needful and beneficial to you. For the sake of the affection that has always existed between us and still does, I promised him to perform any duty he might lay upon me. So I have come right over to let you know that you may employ me in any way that occurs to you.'

Now Madonna Daria, possessed of the sweetest and most gentle nature, warmly thanked Messer Liberale for this speech, begging him to be as good as his word if ever she found herself in need of his offices. To this Messer Liberale made his promise. Thereafter, he visited his fair neighbour most regularly, taking great care that she lacked for nothing. In the course of time it came to his knowledge that she was with child, but this he feigned not to know, one day saying to her, 'Madonna, how are you feeling? A bit strange, perhaps, what with Messer Artilao's departure?'

To this Madonna Daria replied, 'My good neighbour, you can be sure that I feel his absence for many reasons, but above all on account of my present condition.'

'In what condition do you find yourself?' asked Messer Liberale.

'I'm going to have a child,' Daria replied, 'and there's something strange about this pregnancy of mine. I've never felt myself so ill at ease before.'

Upon hearing this, Liberale rejoined, 'But my good neighbour, are you really in the family way?'

'My friend, I wish it were you instead of me!' said Daria, 'and that I had kept on my fast.'

Messer Liberale kept up the banter for some while with his fetching neighbour until by degrees he fell under her charm, seeing how pretty, fresh, and engaging she was. Soon enough he was consumed by his luxurious desires and could think of nothing else night or day except how he could satisfy them. For a time his longings had been deterred by the esteem he held for Artilao, but spurred on by the violence of his passion, which melted away all his noble resolutions, he one day went to Madonna Daria and said, "Alas, my dear friend, how deeply grieved I am that Messer Artilao has gone away like this and left you pregnant, because on account of his sudden departure, he may very well have forgotten to complete the child that he began and that you now carry in your womb. Perhaps this is the reason that your pregnancy has left you feeling ill at ease.'

'Oh, good sir,' cried Madonna Daria, 'do you really believe that the infant which I'm carrying may be lacking one or another of its members? Is that the cause of my worries?'

'To tell you the truth, that's my opinion,' replied Liberale. 'In fact, I'm certain that my good friend Messer Artilao has failed to give it the proper number of limbs. It happens often, in these cases, that one child is born lame, another blind, one in this fashion, another in that.'

'Ah, my dear friend,' said Madonna Daria, 'what you're telling me troubles my mind. Where should I look for a remedy to keep this disaster from happening to me?'

'My dear neighbour,' replied Messer Liberale, 'be cheerful and don't worry yourself over nothing, for I'm telling you that everything has a cure, well, everything except death.'

'I beg you, for the love you bear your absent friend,' said Madonna Daria, 'that you'll provide this remedy, and the sooner you can let me have it the greater will be my debt to you, for then there'll be no danger that the child will be born imperfect.'

Seeing that Madonna Daria was now in a mood favourable to his aims, Liberale said to her, 'Dear lady, it would be great baseness and discourtesy in a man if he didn't stretch out his hand to aid a friend in danger of perishing. Knowing that I'm able to correct the defects which currently afflict your child, I'd be no less than a traitor and malefactor to refuse to come to your aid.

'Then my dear friend,' said the lady, 'hurry up and do what has to be done to perfect the child; if you don't, it would be mean and downright sinful.'

'Have no doubts on that score,' said Liberale. "I'll do my duty to the full extent of my powers. Give orders, then, to your waiting-woman to prepare the table, for the corrective measures must begin with a nice meal together.'

So while the maid was setting out the table, Messer Liberale went with Madonna Daria into the bedroom, and once the door had been locked, he began to caress and kiss her, giving her the most loving embraces any man ever offered to a woman. Madonna Daria was nothing less than astonished when she realized the nature of the treatment and said to him, 'What does this mean, Messer Liberale? Is it right that we should do such things as this, even though we're good neighbours and the best of friends? What a pity it's such a great sin, for if it weren't the case, I'm not sure but what I'd consent to your wishes.'

Liberale replied, 'Tell me, then, which is the greater sin, to sleep with your friend, or let this child come into the world maimed and defective?'

'Surely the greater sin,' replied Madonna Daria, 'would be to let an infant come misshapen into the world through the fault of the parents.'

'Then you'd be committing a monstrous sin not to let me supply what your husband has left undone,' rejoined Messer Liberale.

Greatly desiring that her offspring should come into the world perfect in all its members, the lady credited her neighbour's words. So despite the close ties between him and her husband, she acquiesced to his desires, so that many times over in subsequent days they took their pleasure together. In fact, the lady found this method of restoring the child's defects so pleasant that she kept on begging Messer Liberale to take special care not to fail her as her husband had formerly done. Seeing that he had fallen in with such a dainty morsel, both day and night he did his best to make up anything that the child lacked so that it might be born perfect in every way. At last, when Madonna Daria had gone her full term, she was delivered of a lusty boy, who was the perfect image of its father, Messer Artilao, exquisitely formed and lacking nothing in any of his parts. As you might guess, the lady was overjoyed and full of gratitude to Messer Liberale as the cause of her good fortune.

Little more time passed before Messer Artilao returned to Genoa and headed straight for home where he found his wife healthy and beautiful. Full of joy and merriment, she ran to meet him with her baby in her arms and they embraced and kissed one another most eagerly. As soon as Messer Liberale got news of his friend's return, he went right away to see and greet him, congratulating him on his happy, safe, and prosperous return.

A few weeks later, as he sat at table one day with his wife playing with the child, Messer Artilao said by chance, 'O Daria, my wife, what a beautiful child this is. Have you ever seen one better made? Look at his pretty face and sweet mouth and bright eyes that shine like stars!' And thus, feature by feature, he went on praising the handsome boy.

Then Madonna Daria answered, 'It's true what you say, there's not a single feature missing, through no thanks to you, my good man, because, as you know well enough, I was only three months along when you went away, leaving the baby I conceived with members not fully furnished, and seriously endangering my pregnancy. Therefore we have great reason to thank our good neighbour Messer Liberale, who was most eager and diligent in supplying all the child was lacking out of his own strength, making good all those parts where your own work had failed.'

Messer Artilao listened carefully and knew exactly what his wife was saying – enough to turn him white with rage inside. It was as though he had a sharp knife in his heart, for he was not slow in understanding that his sworn friend had played the traitor to him and had debauched his wife. But like a sensible man, he pretended not to understand the meaning of what he heard, held his peace, and when he spoke again turned the conversation to other matters.

After leaving the table, Messer Artilao began to reflect upon the strange and shameful conduct of his friend, whom he had loved and esteemed far above any other man in the world. Day and night he brooded and planned by what fashion or means he might best avenge himself for so great an offence against his honour. Thus enraged, the poor man devoted himself constantly to these projects, hardly knowing what course to take. Finally, however, he resolved to do something that would satisfy a very particular desire, saying then to his wife, 'Daria, make sure tomorrow that our table is furnished more generously than usual, because I want to invite our good neighbours, Messer Liberale and his wife, Madonna Propertia, to dine with us. But if you care for your life, you have to keep quiet about all the arrangements and patiently endure everything you see,' to which Daria agreed. Then leaving the house, he went to the public square where he met his neighbour, Messer Liberale, bidding him, together with his wife, to dine at his house on the following day. Messer Liberale gratefully accepted the invitation.

At the established time, the two invited guests repaired to the house of Messer Artilao, where they were most graciously met and received. When they were all gathered together and conversing about this and that, Messer Artilao said to Madonna Propertia, 'Dear neighbour, while they are getting the food ready and setting the table, you should have some toast and a little wine to sustain you.' Then he led her aside into a chamber and there poured her a glass of drugged wine and gave her some biscuits, both of which she accepted without any fear whatever, eating the biscuits and empting the glass. They then returned and seated themselves at the table and so the dinner began.

But long before the meal had come to an end, Madonna Propertia began to feel a drowsiness stealing over her so that she could scarce keep her eyes open. When Messer Artilao perceived this he said, 'Madonna, would you like to go and repose yourself a little, for perhaps last night you didn't sleep very well.' With these words he conducted her into a bedroom where, as soon as she tossed herself down on the bed, she fell asleep. Worried that the strength of the potion would wear off and that time might fail him for carrying out the project he secretly had in mind, Messer Artilao called Messer Liberale and said to him, 'Neighbour, let's go out for a while and let your good wife sleep for as long as she needs. Perhaps she just got up too early this morning and is in need of rest.'

Then they both went down to the piazza. But once there, Messer Artilao gave the impression that he was in a hurry to dispatch certain matters of business. So bidding farewell to his friend, he returned secretly to his own house and stole silently into the bedroom where Madonna Propertia was lying. Going up to the bed, he saw that she was sleeping quietly. Then, without being seen by anyone in the house or being noticed by the lady herself, with the utmost lightness of hand he removed the rings she wore on her fingers and the pearls from about her neck and left the chamber.

The effects of the potion had entirely dissipated by the time Madonna Propertia awoke. But when she rose up to leave the bed, she noticed that her pearls and her rings were missing. Jumping up, she searched here, there, and everywhere, turning the room upside down without finding a trace of them. Mightily upset, she rushed out and began to question Madonna Daria whether by chance she might have taken her pearls and rings, but she assured her friend that she hadn't seen them. With that, Madonna Propertia was not only aggrieved but frantic. While the poor lady stood there anxiously, having no notion of where to look next, who should come in but Messer Artilao. When he saw his friend's wife so painfully agitated, he said, 'What has happened to you, dear friend, that you are in such trouble?'

Madonna Propertia told him the whole misfortune, whereupon, making as though he knew nothing of the matter, he said to her, 'Search very carefully, Madonna, and try to remember, and perhaps you'll find them. But if not, I promise you on the faith of our old friendship that I'll make such an investigation of the matter that whoever has taken these things of yours will be made to regret his deeds. But first, before we've put our hands to the business, I urge you once more to search in every corner.'

Then the ladies, and the serving-women as well, ransacked the house from top to bottom several times over, turning everything upside down, but they found nothing. Messer Artilao, taking note of their ill success, began to make an uproar through the house, threatening punishment first to this person and then to that, but they all solemnly swore that they had no knowledge of the matter. Then Messer Artilao turned towards Madonna Propertia, saying, 'My dear neighbour, don't be overcome by this trouble, but keep a light heart, for I'm at your service to see this matter through. And you should know, my dear friend, that I'm in the possession of a secret of such great virtue and efficiency that, by its working, I will be able to lay my hands on the man, whoever he is, who has taken your jewels.'

On hearing these words, Madonna Propertia said, 'Oh Messer Artilao, I beg you to make use of these powers so that Messer Liberale will have no cause to suspect me.'

Seeing that the time was now come when he might work his vengeance for the injury that had been recently done to him, Messer Artilao called his wife and the serving-women and firmly commanded them not to come near the room for any reason whatsoever unless he called them. When his wife and the women folk had disappeared, Messer Artilao closed the door of the chamber and began drawing a circle on the floor with a bit of charcoal, into which he set certain signs and characters of his own invention. He then said to Madonna Propertia, 'Dear heart, lie down on that bed and make certain that you don't move. Don't be afraid on account of anything that you may feel, because I'm determined not to leave here until I've found your jewels.'

'You needn't fear a thing,' said Madonna Propertia, 'for I won't budge an inch, or do anything at all without your express command.'

Then turning towards the right Messer Artilao made certain signs upon the floor, then turning left he made other signs and conjurations in the air, pretending all the while to be conversing with a multitude of spirits by uttering all sorts of strange noises in a false voice, all of which left Madonna Propertia somewhat bewildered. Anticipating this, Messer Artilao reassured her with comforting words, telling her not to fear. After he had been inside the circle some seven or eight minutes, he began to sing these lines in a harsh and growling voice:

> What I've not found and you're seeking still,
> Lies hidden, deep in a hairy vale;
> The one who holds it now is the one who lost it then,
> So take your fishing-rod and you'll win it back again.

Hearing these words, Madonna Propertia was no less happy than amazed.

When the incantation was finished, Artilao said to her, 'Well, you have heard all that was said. The jewels that you lost are somewhere inside you. So keep up your spirits and with God's good help we will find them. But it's essential that I'm the only one who tries to find them in the place my art has revealed to me.'

The lady, who was very desirous to get her jewels back, eagerly answered, 'Good friend, I fully comprehend all this. So don't delay, I'm begging you, but begin your search right away.'

With that, Messer Artilao came forth from the circle and prepared for his sport by lying down beside her on the bed. She didn't move a bit. Then he removed her outer clothes and her undergarments and began his angling in the hairy vale. As he made his first cast, he drew a ring out of his shirt pocket without the lady seeing him and he handed it to her, saying, 'Look, Madonna, what a good fisherman I am, and how at the first cast I've recovered your diamond.'

When she saw her diamond, Madonna Propertia was delighted beyond measure, 'Ah, my kind and excellent friend, please do the same again. Perhaps you will get back all the other jewels I've lost.'

Messer Artilao pursued his angling with manly vigour, bringing out one jewel after another, working so well with his tackle that at last he recovered and handed back to the lady every article that had been lost. For this service, Madonna Propertia was highly grateful and most satisfied with the outcome of the whole affair. Having gotten back all her precious jewels, she said to Messer Artilao, 'Dear friend, just look at all the valuable things you've recovered for me with your line. In the same place you might win back for me a beautiful little bucket that was stolen from me some days ago and which I prized very highly.'

'Most willingly,' he replied, and resumed his thrusting with his instrument into the shady valley, struggling to make contact with her little bucket. But despite his efforts, he couldn't pull it out. At last he became so worn out that he was forced to confess, 'Well, sweetheart, I found your bucket and even touched it, but it was bottom side up, so I couldn't hook it with my rod and haul it out.'

Madonna Propertia, still longing for it and finding the game most pleasing, would have persuaded him to go on with his fishing. But our hero had no more oil in his lamp. With his wick completely extinguished, he confessed, 'Alas, my sweet, the fishing rod has a broken tip and is out of commission, but be patient for now. Tomorrow I'll take it to the blacksmith and have the tip repaired. Then at our first opportunity, we'll go fishing for the little bucket.' Madonna Propertia was fully content with his proposal and so, bidding farewell to Messer Artilao and Madonna Daria, she took her jewels and went home with a light and merry heart.

As it turned out, the next night, when the good lady was in bed with her spouse and he was fishing in the same furry vale, she said to him, 'Dearest husband, would you try through your fishing to find that little bucket that we lost a while back, because yesterday, I have to say, when I missed certain of my jewels, our good neighbour Messer Artilao was kind enough to go fishing down in the valley and pull them all out again. But when I begged him to try another cast to find the bucket, he told me that he could touch it, but couldn't snag it because it was upside down, and that with so much angling he had broken the tip off his pole. But hopefully you can hook it instead.'

After he had heard this speech, Messer Liberale understood perfectly well the manner of repayment his neighbour had made him for his own trick. But he kept his peace and patiently pocketed the affront. The next morning the two neighbours met in the square, where they each looked the other narrowly in the eyes, but neither of them had the courage to broach the subject. So nothing was said on either side, nor did they take their wives into their confidence. Given such an outcome, their course of action was to establish for the future a common right for either one to take his pleasure with the wife of the other.

Alteria's story was so much to the taste of the company that it seemed they would have gone on for the rest of the evening remarking over it and discussing the craft and dexterity with which the one friend had duped the other. But the Signora, when she saw that the laughter and repartee promised to go on longer than time allowed, gave the word that the merriment should stop and that Alteria should follow the established custom of reciting her enigma, which she delivered without further deliberation.

> A useful thing, firm, hard, and white,
> Outside in shaggy robe bedight;
> Hollowed within right cleverly,
> It goes to work both white and dry.
> When after labour it comes back,
> You'll find it moist and very black;
> For service it is ready ever,
> And fails the hand that guides it never.

Alteria's enigma aroused as much pleasure among her auditors as her story had. Notwithstanding the fact that certain features seemed an affront to modesty, the ladies didn't refrain from discussing it, because they had on another occasion heard the same thing. But Lauretta, pretending to have no inkling of the meaning of the enigma, asked Alteria to explain it. So she, with a merry countenance, replied, 'Signora Lauretta, it's superfluous work to carry crocodiles to Egypt, or vases to Samos, or

owls to Athens. Still, to please you I'll unfold my riddle. I declare that
the instrument, perforated at one end and shaggy at the other, is simply
a pen of the kind used in writing, which, before one dips it in the ink-
stand, is white and dry, but that when it's withdrawn, it's black and moist-
ened and ready to serve the writer holding it in whatever way he wishes.'
With this explanation given, Arianna, who was sitting next to her, now
stood up and began to tell her story.

VI.1 Commentary

This story begins with the betrayal of a perfect friendship and concludes
with a perfect commune among the two friends and their wives. The
defiance of social mores is even more pronounced in the original with
the use of 'comare' and 'compare,' here rendered as 'friend' or 'neighbour,' for these terms signify a special relationship of trust pertaining
to family members, the equivalent of godparents or cousins. The tale's
leading thought experiment is the open sexual arrangement at the end
hinting of the victory of utopian ideals over instincts, customs, and institutions in a de facto solution to a de jure dilemma. If another man
shares in your property with your permission, it is a sign of mutuality,
generosity, and reward. If another man shares in the favours of your wife
without your permission, it is cause for revenge, violence, and compensation, unless power on the side of the seducer brings enforced temporiz-
ing. Under practical consideration, in this story, is the appropriate rigour
of justice in light of past friendship and whether something more tem-
pered might do in the place of bloodshed. At issue is the sense of injury
and the craving of the ego for satisfaction counterbalanced by a cost
analysis and the potential for a quid pro quo. The genius of this story is
that in settling scores in kind – the enjoyment of your wife in exchange
for your enjoyment of mine – justice is served according to the principle
of talion reinterpreted as reciprocity, allowing the bond of friendship to
be extended merely by adding the wives to the communal formula.

Readers may amuse themselves with the 'meaning' of such a tale on
the assumption that writers frame their stories in ways that control the
process of inference and extrapolation through pattern reduction down
to a maxim or precept from which the story presumably begins. There
is a folk hermeneutic at work insofar as readers are inclined to treat all
such stories as allegories through which precepts are enacted at a literal
social level. Yet the matter remains unclear whether, through the celebration of a harmonious *ménage à quatre*, the story proposes an ironic utopia,

a viable alternative life style, or merely a mental fantasy. In effect, two close friends agree upon institutionalized wife-swapping because it is already a fait accompli, because the ideal of Renaissance friendship takes precedence over the ideal of Renaissance marriage, and because, after all, the parties are consulted and the arrangement is discovered to be entirely mutual. Such a story is bound to divide the sceptics from the dreamers over a question of interest to all eras: whether jealousy and an instinct for exclusive enjoyment of sexual partners can be overcome through social engineering.

At the heart of the tale are two inordinately naive women. Their acquiescence to two of the most implausible rationales (ostensibly) for intercourse with extramarital partners ever dreamed up is a precondition to 'belief' in the story's world of representations. In fact, 'perfecting babies' and 'fishing for lost articles' were favourite motifs with raconteurs in Straparola's time and thought to be worth recycling like a good joke, appealing as they do to the same level of humour as the one about the child whose parents' mysterious parts were euphemized as a flashlight and cave, leading to the inevitable speleological proposal we laughed about when I was young. At the end of the tale, both men, upon hearing the innocent confessions of their wives concerning the wonderful favours they had received, knew in a trice that they were made cuckolds by reciprocal deception. Yet the story can work only if the schemes are not entirely preposterous for their time, which is the source of their particular spice, much as Jonson's gulls in *The Alchemist* fall prey to the scientific jargon and posturing of Face and Subtle, even as members in the audience compliment themselves for their superior understanding of things pertaining to alchemy as a pseudoscience.

How indeed were children formed? Why were some born monsters? Could it not be due to some aspect of the coupling that might account for the variables at birth? By the same token, necromancers specializing in the black arts might well offer as a benefit the location of lost articles through the omniscience of demons. A lengthy essay could be interpolated here to explain the range of mentalities and equivocal beliefs that characterized the Renaissance mind in its many echelons of knowledge and understanding. Such stories, in fact, contribute to the evolution of mentalities simply because readers wish to align themselves with those 'in the know.' Both schemes – that children might be perfected through post-conceptual fertilizing, and that lost objects accidentally 'ingested' into the body might be dislodged and recovered by the piscatorial operation of a male appendage – are preposterous as science, but effective folk analogies or misguided similes: that children and plants are alike in their need of maintenance; and that fishing by sexual intercourse gives exploratory access to bodily recesses. By a subtly different process of reasoning, Daria deliberates over her choices, knowing that adultery is a sin, but that not doing all to ensure a healthy and whole child is an even greater sin; the argument from the genes overwhelms the argument from morality. She would rather have a healthy baby. That order of debate was not unknown even in medical circles, as when Christian doctors contemplated the moral implications of therapeutic coitus to cure love melancholy or erotomania – according to the universal teachings of the best Arabic physicians such as Avicenna and Haly Abbas. Jacques Ferrand demurred in his *Treatise on Lovesickness* in protest against the immoral recommendations of fellow practitioners, but the physician in the final act of Shakespeare and Fletcher's *The Two Noble Kinsmen* overrides the girl's father's moral misgivings with his medical rationale that coitus alone could save her life.

The story idea of exchanged seductions involving two friends and their wives leading to an extended family is at least as old as Boccaccio's *Decameron*, dating to the mid-fourteenth century, indebted in its turn to the French *fabliaux*.[1] Still to come is the linking of this Boccaccian plot

---

1 See, for example, 'Le meunier d'Aleux,' by Enguerrand d'Oisy in the *Recueil général et complet des fabliaux des XIIIe et XIVe siècles imprimés et inédits*, ed. Anatole de Montaiglon and Gaston Reynaud (Paris: Librairie des Bibliophiles, 1879–90; reprint, New York: Burt Franklin, 1964), no. 33, vol. II, pp. 31–45. In this story, Marien d'Estrée goes to the mill to have her flour ground. Jakemare the miller agrees with his assistant to set the girl up for seduction in his house in exchange for a fat little piglet. Closing down the mill for the night before the girl's flour is ground, the miller offers her lodging at his house, where his wife would take care of her and feed her well. But the wife suspects something and the girl is afraid, so they agree to exchange beds. Before turning the girl over to his assistant, Jakemare decides to have a bout with her himself. Only then does he send in his boy to repeat the exercise. But from comments made by the girl the following day as she collected her grain, the men come to realize that they have shared the miller's wife between them – five times each no less – for which reason the assistant demanded the return of his fat piglet. There is high irony in the ensuing legal confrontation, which is over the pig rather than the wife, and further irony that the bailey declares the animal forfeit to the court because the miller had failed in his promise while the assistant had enjoyed the wife, thus voiding both their claims. Enguerrand was from Douai and lived in the thirteenth century. Hence this or similar *fabliaux* of that era might well have served as models for the trickery that led to the Italian double seduction plots.

with the seduction ploys of perfecting babies and fishing for jewels. There were, in fact, several stories in the fifteenth and early sixteenth centuries making progress in this direction, chipping away at Straparola's originality, while underscoring another substantial truth: that these story ideas were passed along as common literary property, or were, themselves, appropriations from potentially hundreds of variant renditions of the story type through the channels of popular culture. It would seem that Straparola is now working from written sources, insofar as this story shows few or none of the traits of oral transmission. But that all the motifs of the present tale occur in diverse literary versions predating Straparola is not, in itself, decisive. From the Straparolan perspective, four, nevertheless, stand out as paradigms of the several components that make up the Straparolan tale: the eighth story of the eighth day of Boccaccio's *Decameron*; a story from the *Lozana* of Francisco Delicado; no. 223 of Poggio's *Facetiae*, and the third story of *Les cent nouvelles nouvelles*, first published in Lyons by Antoine Vérard in 1486.

Boccaccio's story of double seduction is concerned with moderating revenge, with finding a milder but equally satisfying form of justice.[2] Spinelloccio and Zeppa are, after all, like brothers, and have been for a long time. But then the crisis of desire sets in like a force of nature hardly to be denied in light of the familiarity maintained between the two households. When Zeppa is accidentally on hand to witness Spinelloccio's coupling with his (Zeppa's) wife, a fact she could now hardly deny, his first negotiation is with her, arguing that her infraction not only provides him with a sexual entitlement to Spinelloccio's wife, but that she must participate in the plot. She must set up a new assignation with Spinelloccio, agree to Zeppa's well-timed intrusion, lock Spinelloccio in a chest, and

---

2 Giovanni Boccaccio, *The Decameron*, trans. James M. Rigg, 2 vols. (London: The Navarre Society, [1922]), VIII.8, vol. II, pp. 230–4. There are many imitations of this *novella*; several are listed by A. Collingwood Lee in *The Decameron: Its Sources and Analogues* (New York: Haskell House, 1966), p. 265. It is presented nearly verbatim in Martin Montanus's *Gartengesellschaft*, by D. Mahrold in the *Roldmarsch Kasten*, 1608, by Frey in *Gartengesellschaft*, in *Le courier facetieux*, and in *Divertissements curieux de ce temps*. Lee also includes no. 120 in Nicolas de Troyes's *Le grand parangon des nouvelles nouvelles*, entitled 'De deux voisins qui se entr'aymoint comme frères dont l'un fut amoureux de la femme de l'autre' (Of the two neighbours who loved each other like brothers, but one of whom was in love with the wife of the other). This is not in the Mabille edition, and Lee does not say where he read it. Also worth consideration is no. 142 in this same collection and its relationship to *Decameron* III.6.

then occupy herself elsewhere while Zeppa convinces Spinelloccia's wife, within earshot of her husband, to submit to his desires on the top of the very chest where he is hidden. The reader is invited, by sheer dint of the situation, to think more of each party's thoughts than the writer chooses to share or confirm. What we know is that Spinelloccio exits the chest in agreement with himself that justice has been served and that they will be better friends for it in the future, while his wife chimes in, with a laugh, that tit has been had for tat. Boccaccio is generally credited with providing the narrative source for all the stories to follow featuring this generic design – at least among the Italian *novellieri*.

Early in the sixteenth century, a modified version is included in Francisco Delicado's *Portrait of Lozana, the Lusty Andalusian Woman* which contains all the Straparolan features.[3] His principal innovation is to make Lozana the trickster mediator who masterminds both sides of the seduction plot, having the fishing after lost jewels come first and the perfection of the child's ears come second. As a procuress, Lozana looks for beautiful women on behalf of her clients. Among her customers is a physician to whom she promises a virtuous, pregnant, married Lombard woman, whose jewellery she steals from the public bathhouse to place her under obligation for its recovery. The physician is then invited to carry out the necessary angling, pretending all along to be removing the rings from her body. We pay particular attention to the lady's additional request to restore a copper pot and chain that have fallen down the well by the same means, a clear anticipation of the request made in Straparola's tale to continue the fishing in order to find a tiny bucket. (This motif turns up concurrently in Cinthio degli Fabritii's *Libro della origine delli volgari proverbi*, Venice, 1526, described below.) When the naive wife explains her happy adventure to her husband, he knows that Lozana is behind it all and thus he goes to her to compel her to arrange for his revenge in kind. It is she who convinces the physician's wife that her child will be born without ears or fingers and that the remedy was urgent and couldn't wait for her husband's return – a husband who had, in any case, failed in his duty. The seduction is carried out, and true to form, the receiver of these benefits complains to her husband of his neglect upon his return and celebrates the corrective measures, thus completing the circle of

---

3 Francisco Delicado, *Portrait of Lozana, the Lusty Andalusian Woman*, ed. Bruno M. Damiani (Potomac, MD: Scripta Humanistica, 1987), pp. 259–61. For further information on Delicado, see Augusta Espantoso Foley, *Critical Guides to Spanish Texts* (London: Grant and Cutler, Tamesis, 1977), vol. 18, 'La Lozana Andaluza.'

understanding. There the matter ends with the physician gently reproving his friend Lozana, who has become the centre of the narrative. Delicado has disguised the story well by integrating it within a great deal of other matter, but its affinity with the tradition under study is clear; he too is recycling a story, a version of which was already in circulation fifty years earlier in *Les cent nouvelles nouvelles* (description to follow). That *La Lozana Andaluza* was first published in Venice in 1528 holds the prospect that it came to Straparola's attention. But that it was derivative also allows for common sources and traditions.

Meanwhile, Poggio Bracciolini's tale 'Of the Friar Minor Who Creates a Child's Nose,' dating to the 1470s, is indicative of the formerly independent circulation of the 'child perfection' motif incorporated into the tales of Delicado and Straparola. A friar instructs one of his jolly parishioners that on the authority of a witch he has learned of the imminent misfortune of her unborn child.[4] By degrees the expectant mother, in a panic, worms out of the cleric that the child will be missing his nose and that only the friar can repair the defect by having sex with her. Despite her distaste for such a procedure, she acquiesces, not once but several times, in order to firmly implant the missing feature. When the child is born without defect, the friar claims the credit and the husband, duped along with his wife, expresses his entire satisfaction with the procedure. In the moralizing epilogue, we are told that great ills are performed under the cover of friendship, and that by abusing a husband's confidence the wife had been raped (*violer*), yet the story is offered up for laughter, because seduction of the ignorant is somehow comic at the same time, on the assumption that she might have known better. Poggio's story reveals the currency of the foetus-perfecting motif and its stand-

---

4 'De fratre minorum qui fecit nosum puero' in *Les facéties de Pogge Florentin,*
ed. Pierre des Brandes (Paris: Garnier Frères, [1853]); also *The Facetiae or jocose tales of Poggio,* 2 vols. (Paris: Isidore Liseux, 1878), no. 223, vol. II, p. 152; no. 156, vol. II, p. 57. There is a later variation on this motif in the *Contes nouveaux* of Jean-Baptiste Willart de Grécourt (Amsterdam: Mortier, 1745) entitled 'Les cheveaux' (hair), in which young Alix gets herself pregnant, but when an officious party accuses her of not having the job finished properly and offers his services, she says it's none of his affair, that the baby is only missing its hair, and that she intends to have them planted one at a time [presumably by the appropriate party]. This or a similar story recurs, apparently, in the *Delictae poeticum Italie* of Gerardus Dicaeus, published in Lisieux, no. 223, 'Partus imperfectus,' vol. II, p. 152, but I have not identified or located this work.

alone potential. There were a goodly number of these in circulation during the years predating the *Notti*.

In the third tale of *Les cent nouvelles nouvelles* (1486), the story tradition is reduced nearly to a farce, yet it contains many of the future directions the story type will take, including persuasion on the grounds that sexual intercourse alone will repair a serious physical defect.[5] In this version, however, the husbands are not friends, or even of the same social standing, and there is no indication that the miller's wife is pregnant. The local *seigneur* merely informs the attractive wife, in the absence of the miller, that her front (*devant*) is about to fall off, which the woman understands in the specific sense of her private parts, which the lord offers to 'do up' (*retaper*). The job is done several times to ensure its success and the wife proudly informs her husband upon his return of the fine service their *seigneur* has rendered them, and for which they must be grateful. The miller keeps private counsel but yearns for revenge. We must accept that on the pretext of presenting a pike for the *seigneur*'s table, the miller gains secret access to the lady's bath where he finds and steals a precious diamond ring. The chatelaine, distraught, sounds the alarm, the miller falls under suspicion, avows his innocence, but promises to find the missing jewel. By divination he comes to know that the ring has entered the lady's body. He then demands a private audience to resolve the mystery and prevails upon the lady to allow him to carry out his fishing. The narrator emphasizes the equivalence between the two modes of seduction. Similarly naive, this wife too informs her husband of the favour rendered her in the location of her ring. Now wise to each other, both men agree to let the matter remain eternally in silence for all the strategic reasons pertaining to honour, scandal, and the turnabout that constitutes fair play. By how much this begins to approximate Straparola's tale some sixty-four years in advance is clear,

---

5 'Un prêté pour un rendu' (Tit for tat) in *Les cent nouvelles nouvelles*, ed. Roger Dubuis (Lyons: Presses universitaires, 1991), no. 3, pp. 40–5; or 'La pesche de l'anneau' (Fishing for the ring). A similar double trickery of wives occurs in Henri Estienne's *Apologie pour Hérodote*, ed. Paul Ristelhuber, 2 vols. (Paris: Isidore Lisieux, 1879), chap. 16, vol. I, p. 313. A doctor seduces the corset-maker's wife with a medical trick; the corset-maker seduces madam the doctor's wife while measuring her for a corset. It is the same basic story with the usual consequences.

without necessarily declaring this *conte* a direct source.[6] Just who made the adjustments whereby this story, in relation to Delicado's, turns into the present rendition remains typically moot, whether Straparola himself or the raconteurs of popular culture.

In the years leading up to the mid-sixteenth century and the decades following, there are a goodly number of related tales that involve intended bed tricks that miscarry and thus bring about the symmetrical seductions. Masuccio of Salerno's *novella* no. 36 of his *Novellino* (1476) offers inventions of its own on the familiar model.[7] A miller and a cobbler

---

6 Giuseppe Rua in his *Tra antiche fiabe e novelle: Le 'Piacevoli Notti' di Gian Francesco Straparola* (Rome: Ermanno Loescher, 1898), p. 57, cites Leroux de Lincy on Straparola's debt to *Les cent nouvelles nouvelles*, giving primacy of place to this work in the creation of the present story. Rua concurs, stating that Boccaccio is not the main source. Celio Malespini, in his *Ducento novelle*, first published in Venice in 1609, takes up his version of the story from *Les cent nouvelles nouvelles*. It is the same asymmetrical exchange of seductions in social terms, for the first to be approached is a miller's wife by the local lord of the manor; he is an aristocrat who presumes upon the naivety of a commoner by convincing her that her front is falling and that he knows how to repair and pin it up again. In the second part, the miller retaliates by gaining access to the palazzo, entering the lady's bath, and stealing one of her jewels. This tale offers the same enactment of quid pro quo by means of pleasure for pleasure rather than injury for injury. Ultimately, the nobleman is reduced to silence when he is told of the fishing party, given that he has to admit the justice of the miller's act and his wife's own gullibility, so that when the two men meet later in the streets they merely hail each other by the names of their respective ruses and promise never to mention the matter again.

7 Masuccio Salernitano, *The Novellino*, trans. W.G. Waters, 2 vols. (London: Lawrence and Bullen, 1895), vol. II, pp. 187–93. The story is also told by Aloyse Cinthio degli Fabritii, *Libro della origine delli volgari proverbi* (Venice, 1526), no. 16, 'Chi non ha ventura non vada a pescar' (If you're not lucky, don't go fishing), pp. 228–36; by Celio Malespini, in his *Ducento novelle* (Venice: al Segno dell'Italia, 1609), I.45, pp. 119*ff*; and by Franco Sacchetti, *Trecentonovelle*, ed. Emilio Faccioli (Turin: Einaudi, 1970), no. 206, pp. 621–7, about the miller Farinello de Rieti who had eyes for Monna Collagia, but ended up with his own wife after the women made arrangements between them. Others to consider in this general category include 'I tonfi di San Pasquale' by Domenico Batacchi (1800), in which a priest seduces the Countess Isabella by having her maid enact San Pascuale. The act is revenged on the priest's sister by a ruse using a special charm to recover a lost item; *Le novelle*, ed. Ferdinando Giannessi (Milan: Feltrinelli, 1971), no. 10. See also Reinhold Köhler, *Kleinere Schriften*, ed. Johannes Bolte (Weimar: E. Felber, 1898–1900), vol. III, pp. 163–4.

have been friends from youth and live in close proximity, as in Boccaccio. When the cobbler takes a fancy to his friend's wife, he approaches her simply and frankly, and her reaction is to report his behaviour to the cobbler's wife. The women agree to an exchange so that the cobbler will find his own wife in bed with him, first accepting his ministrations and then berating him. But a preliminary meeting between the men spoils the plan, so that each enters his own house and performs in the dark with the woman he finds in his bed. In effect, the cobbler enjoys the wife he dreamed of, but doesn't know it, while she bears it with patience and a show of pleasure in order to make him believe she was his wife – which doesn't make entirely logical sense, but convention dictates – while the poor miller, after an innocent performance, finds himself berated with pure vitriol by a woman thinking to have taken her own husband red-handed. The high irony of this misplaced tongue lashing is the apex of the drama. Paradoxically, it is the miller, the man more sinned against than sinning, who proposes that the malice of wives had produced their better fortune and that what seemed a prejudice might be accepted as a blessing. It is the cobbler who thinks through the private benefits as opposed to the esteem of the world, which, in their time, he concludes to be a thing of little worth. From that time forward, all would be in common so that the children would know for certain only the identities of their mothers. This is almost a different tale, given the centrality of the bed trick, but it serves to create the Straparolan *ménage à quatre* without the logistics of crime and punishment.

Bonaventure Des Périers includes in his *Nouvelles récreations et joyeux dévis* (written by 1536 but first published in 1544), the story of the man who finished the baby's ear for his neighbour's wife, involving a rationalization that almost resembles a medical anecdote. This tale does not contain a retaliatory counterpart. André banters with his neighbour's pregnant wife about her baby's unfinished ears, but she takes him seriously and he sees his opportunity by elaborating that if the ears are unfinished for one child, then all those to follow will also be born without them. Revealingly, the seducer employs a phrase reappearing in Straparola, that 'there's a cure for everything except death,' suggesting its place in the line of influence. So André offers his services, claiming this as a real favour to the lady, given his many other pressing affairs. But he visits so often, in fact, that the wife fears the child will end up with five or six ears. When her husband returns, she teases him about leaving his work undone, and the penny drops concerning what had taken place, although after a few vain threats against André there was little more to be done.[8] It is likewise included in Noël Du Fail's *Contes et discours d'Eutrapel*.[9] Another, closely related, appears in *L'élites des contes du Sieur d'Ouville* (1641), which involves a king and a gentleman neighbour who are excellent friends. The comic seduction strategy is absent and, given the king's status, his social inferior must endure his majesty's visitations with patience, but not without seeking a repayment in kind. His seduction of the queen is slow and delicate, but ultimately persuasive when she understands the king's conduct. The arrangement continues for years, and while the gentleman is known abroad as the king's cuckold, the king never discovers the truth of his own situation and thus the revenge is enjoyed entirely in private.[10] These stories are, of course, all derivative, in their respective ways, from the now common legacy.

Jean de la Fontaine redevelops the story out of Boccaccio's *Decameron*, but includes, in keeping with the tradition, the story of the incomplete ears whereby the protagonist imposes upon a close friend's gullible wife.[11] When she relates all to her husband as a meritorious service, the husband broods upon his revenge, offering a great deal more rage and anger in dealing with his own wife than with his one-time friend. As in Straparola's tale, under her husband's instruction the lady must lure her lover into her bedroom one last time and send him into hiding when he arrives. Then she must go next door and tell the man's wife that her husband is

---

8 Bonaventure des Périers, 'De celui qui acheva l'oreille de l'enfant à la femme de son voisin' (Of the man who finished the baby's ear for his neighbour's wife) in *Les nouvelles recreations et joyeux devis* in *Oeuvres françoises* (1558) (Paris: P. Jannet, 1856), no. 9, vol. II, pp. 46–50. See James Woodrow Hassell, *Sources and Analogues of the Nouvelles Récréations et Joyeux Devis of Bonaventure des Périers*, 2 vols. (Chapel Hill: University of North Carolina Press [1957], 1969). After 1601 the work was known as *Les joyeuses adventures et nouvelles récréations*. This work is known in English after 1583 as *The Mirrour of Mirth and Pleasant Conceits*, now in a modern edition, ed. James Woodrow Hassell ([Columbia, SC]: University of South Carolina Press, 1959).
9 (Rennes: Noël Glamet, 1586), pp. 142*ff*; (Paris: Librairie des Bibliophiles, 1875).
10 Antoine Le Métel, Sieur d'Ouville, 'Un roy de Naples, abusant de la femme d'un gentilhomme, porte enfin luy même les cornes' (A king of Naples, taking advantage of a gentleman's wife, in the end wears the horns himself) in *L'élites des contes*, ed. G. Brunet, 2 vols. (Paris: Librairie des Bibliophiles, 1883), vol. II, pp. 47–53. Another version of the story is also to be found in Antoine de Saint-Denis, *Les comptes du monde aventureux* (Paris: Estienne Groulleau, 1555).
11 'The Ear-Maker and the Mould-Mender' ('Les qui pro quo' or 'Le faiseur d'oreilles'), in *The Complete Tales in Verse*, trans. Guido Waldman (New York: Routledge, 2001), pp. 37–42. See also *Tales and Novels by J. de la Fontaine*, 2 vols. (London: The Society of English Bibliophilists, ca. 1895), vol. II, pp. 177–84.

about to be maimed. When she arrives, she learns that, tit for tat, she is about to have her children's noses repaired as well as the mould, thereby remedying the defect in all future offspring. The woman is relieved that her husband will escape with such a light punishment, and allows the seduction to take place on the very bed under which her husband is hiding – a man content to wear horns so long as he can keep his ears. That the story echoes Boccaccio and Bracciolini combined may point to Straparola, or to La Fontaine's own confectionary skills.

Thomas-Simon Gueullette, perhaps the greatest appropriator of materials from the *Piacevoli notti* after Mme. d'Aulnoy, may have made selective use of this tale in a complex fantasy about two friends betrayed by women who later recover their friendship upon discovering the many coincidences that continue to unite them. The story is, in effect, 'orientalized' and is called 'Of Al-kuz, Tahar, and the Miller.' Despite their friendship, Tahar falls in love with his companion's bride, Liva, and flees with her.[12] Al-kuz, in his grief, becomes a wanderer, settling down with a girl named Solle whom he rescues from a fire, only to be jilted by her as well. When the two men meet again, Tahar offers a long and abject confession and the two embrace, so desensitized have they both become by the perfidy of women, for Liva had also abandoned Tahar. They then discover that Tahar had taken up with the girl rescued from the fire and found himself trapped in a marriage with a pregnant wife who is, in fact, carrying Al-kuz's child. The two men now consider themselves quit, having received injury for injury. But Gueullette desires to multiply the effect by having the two men form a *ménage à trois* with a miller's wife. They then encounter the miller in a similar *ménage* with the two unfaithful wives, Liva and Solle. The entire creation becomes a study in plot symmetry, betrayal, and accommodation, creating a comedy of coincidence rather than an investigation of psyches. The story is entirely cynical, particularly about the fidelity of women, yet paradoxically idealistic regarding male friendship and the ability to overcome possessive instincts. The wives are pardoned in a gesture of reconciliation, and each is returned to her rightful husband; there is no talk of a communal solution. Given Gueullette's unacknowledged employment of Straparola's tales throughout this *oeuvre*, we are invited to think that this story too,

---

12 Thomas-Simon Gueullette, *Thousand and One Quarters of an Hour* (1723), trans. Leonard C. Smithers (London: H.S. Nichols, 1893), pp. 181–209. Straparola's story is transcribed or adapted by Sansovino in *Cento novelle*, VII.2, and by Chappuis in *Facetieux journées*, VII.2.

despite the many substitutions and the orientalization of names and circumstances, may have found its origins in the *Piacevoli notti.*

As a little coda it may be mentioned again (as in a footnote above) that Cinthio degli Fabritii, in his prolix collection of tales in illustration of proverbs, gives a version of the present story in which he includes the angling for a 'secchielletto,' the equivalent of the little bucket in Straparola.[13] This is the object which Madonna Propertia requested her fisherman to find after he had located all her 'missing' jewellery. This idea may owe something to Cinthio, adding him to the list of potential sources, all of which Straparola may have had ready to hand in order to compound the present version. The passage also gives rise to another of Straparola's playful metaphors for sexual conduct. Waters, in his translation, faithful in all matters except these, has Artilao say 'Most willingly would I do this, were I not somewhat wearied just at present over what I have already done.' But Straparola speaks of lamp oil, a dull point, and blacksmith's tools to sharpen it, all of which Waters, no doubt, found pointlessly excessive. This story also appears to have had an afterlife among the folk, if it did not exist in a folk tale from which all of the above-mentioned authors derived their materials – a now familiar dilemma with regards to stories and their origins. In a Russian folk version, the fisherman says he found the little bucket the lady so desired to retrieve, but that it was 'upside down, so that his instrument couldn't quite get hold of it and draw it forth.'[14] On the strength of this story's resemblance to Straparola's, the adventurous scholar may wish to give everything back to the oral culture of Straparola's time, as so many previous stories have invited us to do. That would appear to be somewhat too adventurous in this case, but that such tales existed in parallel folk cultures even as far back as the sixteenth century appears more probable, in light of Straparola's early registry of so many others.

---

13 Aloyse Cinthio degli Fabritii, *Libro della origine delli volgari proverbi* (Venice, 1526), no. 16, 'Chi non ha ventura non vada a pescar (If you're not lucky don't go fishing),' pp. 228–36.

14 *Kryptadia*, vol. I, *Contes secrets traduits du russe* (Paris: H. Welter, 1883), no. 43, pp. 60–1.

VI. Fable 2
Castorio's Welcome Castration

ARIANNA

Castorio, desiring to grow fat, had Sandro cut off both of his testicles and very nearly died from it. But at the last, by a merry jest of Sandro's wife, he is relieved of his trouble.

The fable Alteria just told us with so much grace and discretion puts me in mind of a certain drollery as comic as hers which I heard told, a short time back, by a merry dame of the nobility. But if I'm not able to set it forth with the same distinction and elegance it was told to me, I ask to be held excused, seeing that nature was stingy with me when it came to the fine qualities so liberally granted to the lady I mentioned.

Not far from Fano, a city of the Marches situated on the shore of the Adriatic, there is a small town called Carignano, including in its population many lusty youths and fair damsels. There among the others lived a peasant named Sandro, one of the wittiest and most rollicking fellows nature ever produced. He hadn't the slightest concern for what happened, but let things go as they would for better or for worse. He grew so fat and ruddy that his flesh resembled nothing more than a piece of fresh-cut larded bacon. Now this chap, when he came to the age of forty, married a woman as good-humoured and fat as himself [...] A week never went by without this good woman carefully shaving her husband's beard so that he might look more handsome and frolicsome.

By chance, a certain Messer Castorio, a rich, young gentleman of Fano, although not very bright, purchased a farm for himself in the commune of Carignano. A moderate-sized house stood there, where he would spend the greater part of the summer with two of his servants and a lady whom he entertained for his pleasure. One day, as was his custom, Castorio was walking through the fields after dinner when he noticed

Sandro, who was turning up the earth with his plough. Seeing what a fine, fat, ruddy fellow the peasant was with his smiling face, he said, 'Good neighbour, how is it that I'm so lank and lean, as you can see, while you're so ruddy and well rounded? Every day I eat the best food and drink the finest wines. I lie in bed as long as I please, and there isn't anything I need. Nobody in the world longs to grow fat more than I do, but the more effort I make, the thinner I get. All winter long you eat only the coarsest food and drink watered-down wine. You rise up to your work when it's still night and all summer long you don't have an hour's rest. Still your rosy face and your well-covered ribs make you a pleasure to behold. So given my desire for a bit of girth, can you help me put on some pounds, the best way you know how, or show me how you've managed to get so fat? I'll give you fifty gold florins up front, and beyond that I promise to reward you in such a way that, for the rest of your life, you'll bless me and call yourself happy.'

Now this Sandro was a cunning rogue by nature, being a red-haired type, so at first he refused to teach Castorio the way. But after a little while, listening to Castorio's prolonged pleading, and keen to finger the fifty gold florins, he consented to show him how. Then he left off his ploughing for a time and sat down beside him, saying, 'Signor Castorio, you say you're astonished by my rotundity and your own lean condition, thinking that a man gets fat or thin by reason of what he may eat or drink. But in this you're entirely wrong, for any day of the week you can see diners and drinkers in great numbers who gulp down their food and yet they're as thin as lizards. But I can tell you, if you want to do for yourself what I've done, you'll be as fat as I am.'

'And what is it that you did?'

Sandro answered, 'Why, about a year go I had my balls removed and from that very moment on I grew as fat as you see me now.'

'Well, I'm amazed you didn't meet your death in the process,' replied Castorio.

'What do you mean death?' cried Sandro. 'The practitioner who did the business for me had such a skilled hand that I didn't feel a thing, and since that time, my flesh is like that of a child. To tell you the truth, I've never felt myself as well and happy as I do right now.'

'So then, tell me the name of this fellow who slices off testicles with so much skill that you don't feel any pain,' said Castorio.

'Ah, he's dead,' replied Sandro.

'Too bad! So what can we do, seeing he's dead?'

Sandro then answered, 'Not to worry, because this great practitioner who died taught me the art and from that moment I mastered it. Since then I've removed the nuts of countless calves, poultry, and other animals, all of which became remarkably fat. If you'll leave all this business to me, I pledge my word you'll be entirely satisfied by my handiwork.'

'But I'm afraid I may die under the operation,' said Castorio.

'What do you mean, die? Look at the calves and the capons and the other animals with their balls cut off. Not one of them ever died,' cried Sandro. Now desiring more than any man alive to get fat, Castorio began to consider the matter.

Once he had fully made up his mind, Sandro told him to lie down on the fresh grass and open his legs. As soon as he did that, Sandro, who had a knife with him as sharp as a razor, pulled on his scrotum, took his cods in hand, and with an oil to soften things up, carefully made a cut, stuck two fingers in the incision, and with all his skill and dexterity he extracted them both. Once done, he took some sweet oil and the juice of certain herbs and made a dressing which he applied to the wound, and then helped Castorio up on his feet. Now he was as proper a capon and eunuch as there was anywhere in the world. Putting his hand in his pocket, Castorio then took out the fifty golden florins and gave them to Sandro before taking his leave and heading back to his house.

But before he had known an hour's experience of life as a gelding, Castorio began to feel the greatest pain and anguish that any man has ever known. He couldn't get a single moment's rest and daily his suffering increased. The wound became so infected and gave off such a fetid stench that those around him could hardly endure it. When this news came to Sandro's ears, he was terrified and heartily began to wish he'd never played such a scurvy trick on Castorio. What if his victim should die of his injuries? Castorio, meanwhile, found himself in a most lamentable state, enraged by the pain he suffered, not to mention the disgrace he would soon endure, and so made up his mind then and there that he would kill Sandro, whatever the risk. To carry it out in the manner he judged most fitting, he went to Sandro's house, accompanied by two of his servants, where he found him at supper. 'Sandro, nice work you've performed on me to cause my death. But before I die, I swear I'll make you pay the price for this wickedness of yours.'

Sandro replied, 'The business was your own choosing, not mine. You're the one who begged and talked me into doing it. But let me show you that it's not the fault of my skills, and that I still deserve the reward, and that I won't be the cause of your death. Meet me early tomorrow morning in my field and then I'll help you out, and stop worrying about dying.'

No sooner was Castorio gone than Sandro broke into bitter weeping, certain he'd better flee the country that very moment into some foreign land, for all he could imagine he heard was the footsteps of the law right at his heels about to place him in jail. Knowing nothing of the cause, but seeing how grief-stricken he was, his wife asked him why he was in such a tragic mode. Then he told her the whole story, word for word. As soon as she fully understood the cause of his dismay and had taken stock of his stupidity and the chance that he might die, she didn't know what to do – well not at first – except berate her husband for his folly in running into so much danger. But afterwards, when she had calmed herself down, she comforted him, telling him to keep up hopes and that she'd set to work to arrange matters so that he would escape the risk of death.

The next morning at the appointed hour, the wife took her husband's clothes, put them on her back, pulled a cap down over her head, and went into the fields with the plough and oxen. There she set to work with the furrowing, watching all the while to see whether Castorio would meet his appointment. Sure enough, before long he appeared, and taking Sandro's wife for Sandro himself at work ploughing his field, he said, 'I'm a dead man certain, Sandro, unless you help me. That incision you made is still not closed and the flesh of those parts is so festered, and the stench of it so strong, that I fear for my life. Unless you give me the needed remedy, you'll see me die at your feet.'

Then the crafty dame in her Sandro disguise asked him to let her look at the wound, saying that she'd take charge of curing it. With that, Castorio took off his shirt and showed the wound, which was all putrid. After a brief inspection, the woman said with a laugh, 'Castorio, my good man, you're just scared because you think your case can't be cured. But you're totally wrong, because the cut that I got is a lot bigger than yours. It still hasn't healed up and stinks like you wouldn't believe compared to yours. Still, you see how fat I am and plump and fresh as a lily. What's more, so you can trust me in what I'm telling you, you can see the open wound for yourself.' Saying that, she planted one leg firm on the ground and the other on the plough, pulled up her clothes, let fly a hidden rocket, and put his head down to show him the gash. Once he saw Sandro's cut to be much larger than his own, still gaping, with a stench that went right up his nose, and saw that he'd lost his pecker into the bargain, his spirits rallied, making him determined to endure all of his own reeking and pain. Not long thereafter, his skinny physique was transformed; Castorio grew fat, just as he always wanted to be.

The ladies laughed merrily at Castorio, thinking about how he was bereft of his gear. But the hilarity among the men was greater still when they saw how Sandro's wife, disguised as her own husband, showed him her great amen, making him believe that both pebbles and prick had been amputated. Seeing that no one in the company could restrain their laughter, the Signora, clapping her hands, called for silence and urged Arianna to keep the protocol by reciting her riddle. Not to seem less obedient or obliging than the others, she recited the following:

> My friend, I bid you, if you please,
> To lay you down, and for your ease
> I'll take the thing and hold it fast
> Betwixt my hands, and at the last
> I'll clap it in the gaping place.
> Then pushing two and fro apace
> With heedful look I'll force along
> A liquid thick and warm and strong.
> You cry enough, and sore complain,
> I'll kill you quite, but still amain
> I work and work with all my might.
> No stopping now till wearied quite
> We both call truce and stop the fight.

Arianna's enigma wounded the ears of her audience, which they found more than a trifle immodest. The Signora rebuked the damsel sharply, making her displeasure most plain. But the gentle maid, all smiling and merry-hearted, excused herself with a frank and open face, saying, 'With your permission, Lady, there's no just reason to be angry with me, for my riddle is meant only to move your mirth. It isn't the least immodest, as you might think, and here's why. When anyone administers an enema to a sick man, doesn't he ask him to lie down? Then afterwards, doesn't he take the instrument between his two hands and insert it in the hole? And seeing that the patient generally dislikes the operation and complains, doesn't he ask him to be brave and take it well? Moreover, doesn't the person administering the enema push the pump back and forth to fill the place full of injected liquid? This done, doesn't he stop, now weary with the pains he has taken over his patient? So you see, most noble friends, my enigma is not so foul and evil as you thought it to be at first.' Hereupon the Signora, after hearing and duly weighing this subtle interpretation of the merry riddle, relaxed her severity, saying that from then on each lady would be free to say what she liked without fear of rebuke. Hearing that full freedom was accorded her to say whatever came to her lips, Cateruzza, whose lot it was to tell the third tale, began it in the following manner.

VI.2 Commentary

In placing this scatological tale after a story about double seduction, Straparola appears determined to launch the second volume of the *Piacevoli notti* in a far naughtier vein than the first. This tale is little more than barnyard humour based on the principle that if capons may be fattened by castrating them, the same operation performed upon a dumb townsman by a wily peasant will have the same effect – and did. It is outrageous enough that Sandro performs the operation on the spot with a pocket knife and botches the job rather badly, but it is doubly so when the farmer's ludicrously unsavoury wife, by impersonating her husband, places her own nether anatomy on exhibition as evidence of Sandro's own unhealed castration-cum-amputation, thereby convincing Castorio that he had nothing to complain about. The tale begs its redemption only on the grounds of wit, for it was deemed so smutty by Waters, its late Victorian translator, that he left the entire scene of the impersonation in the fields in the French of the Larivey translation. Such a tactic suggests that only those with a talent for languages are fit to read this immodest fare, or worse, that French was the natural language of *grivoiseries*. For him, at least, this story was the first to cross a line regarding taste, followed immediately by that of the three nuns (VI.4), most of which Waters also preserved in sixteenth-century French. It would seem that Straparola had fallen under the tutelage of Morlini, in the process redefining his readership and the little society to which these stories are told.

The hermeneute may find some enjoyment in teasing out the underlying assumptions upon which this story is based with regard to its particular brand of humour, the fears it may express, the class distinctions it registers, and the region in which it is set. Straparola makes it specific to the market town of Carignano, near Fano (south of Rimini) on the Adriatic coast. Messer Castorio – the choice of names says it all (perhaps with overtones of *castoro*, the beaver, which, according to Pliny and his sect, was thought to castrate itself to escape its pursuers) – has a naive longing to become fat and for that reason falls afoul of Sandro, the crafty peasant who is offered a handsome reward to make it happen. Contrasting town and country mentalities, and the tricks put upon one by the other, was a staple of the medieval tale; that theme, as represented in the Italian *novelle*, has come under recent investigation, this story serving as a prime example.[15] A special kind of humour pertains to the triumph of peasant cunning over the presumed intellectual superiority of high culture, epitomized by the half-millennium long tradition of *The Dialogue of Solomon and Marcolphus* in which the world's wisest man is repeatedly outwitted by a deformed local rustic.[16] That formula finds new expression here.

Concerning castration as a 'complex,' the less said the better, insofar as this story has none of the interrelationships that could give such an analysis meaning. Nevertheless, the story inevitably evokes the primal fear of injury to that region and all that pertains to anatomy and the masculine condition. The foolish indifference to such concerns on the part of Messer Castorio for the sake of putting on a little weight profiles this ultimate booby and establishes the grounds for Renaissance laughter. Apart from that, Castorio is simply young, well-to-do, not very bright, and concerned about his appearance in relation to an overactive metabolism about which he knows nothing. It is a mystery to him how a hard working peasant on meagre rural fare could have such girth. When putrefaction sets in following the 'operation' and complaints arise, Sandro panics, but his more level-headed wife devises a scheme to put off the threat of arrest by using her private parts to rhetorical ends. Messer Castorio makes but little of the fact that he still has a penis, she not, and forgets that Sandro had already claimed that his operation was an entire success. But such cavilling is merely to spoil a good joke, which everyone in the audience seemed ready to enjoy, the women laughing at the prospect of a man who had lost his manliness, and the men laughing at the size of the woman's wicket. What aspect of psychology or of humour

---

15 Marie-Françoise Piéjus, 'Le couple citadin-paysan dans les "Piacevoli notti" de Straparola,' in *Ville et campagne dans la littérature italienne de la Renaissance*, ed. Anna Fontes-Baratto (Paris: Université de la Sorbonne nouvelle, 1976), p. 160, from which I take the suggestion about the beaver.

16 *The Dialogue of Solomon and Marcolphus*, English translation of 1492, ed. Donald Beecher (Ottawa: Dovehouse Editions, 1995).

does this entail?[17] One thing certain is that the story will be of little help to those wishing to make of the Renaissance an age in the fashioning of sex and gender. Those in the audience sniggering over a man's willing abandonment of his gonads and of a woman pretending to be a castrato by just being a woman can hardly get more essentialist; men and women, monstrous or mutilated, are male and female still.

Alteria is willing to play the hoyden in telling this tale, brazenly and without apology, for the sake of a laugh. It is related, moreover, not quite as an old wives' tale – which it undoubtedly was in fact – but as an anecdote recently picked up from a noblewoman as something more akin to gossip. The story is told as remarkable because it also purports to have happened. Alteria regrets only that she cannot tell it with the same spirit of elegance and distinction as her high-society source, which is merely part of telling her immodest tale as refined parlour fare. Such posturing is part of the storytelling sport, and part of Straparola's own campaign to bring folk stuff to the elite through print. Safely through this exercise, Alteria comes to her riddle and proposes something equally *risqué*, to the point of exasperating the hostess who was ready to discipline her for smut. The name of that game, however, is to lead the imagination through the gutter and then to come back with an innocent gloss that places the responsibility with the auditors. Once again, the hostess is satisfied, insofar as the enigma signifies merely an enema rather than intercourse, despite its administrator playing with the bottle and working the tube in and out; do we ask why a kinetic clyster is more acceptable to socialite sensibilities than a sexual cluster? Thus, in coming to book 6 and the inauguration of the second volume of tales, Straparola has progressed from clean family fun to brown wrapper entertainment, turning his coterie readership into a huddle of sniggerers, at least as an overture. But more tasteful tales will follow.

---

17 The answer to that rhetorical question is perhaps best supplied by François Rabelais
   in the fifteenth chapter of 'Pantagruel,' in which he discusses how Panurge
   demonstrated a very new way of building the walls of Paris. Along the way he
   concocts the fable of the lion, the fox, and the old lady who had fallen over
   backwards and revealed her old wound that went from her backside to her navel,
   no doubt the result of a hatchet blow, which the lion asked the fox to wipe continually with his tail to keep off the flies. Meanwhile, he went for moss to stuff the
   wound, while the old woman 'pooped and blew, and stank like a hundred devils,'
   making the poor fox rather uncomfortable. So much for masculine innocence
   and gynaecological hyperbole. *Gargantua and Pantagruel*, ed. J.M. Cohen
   (Harmondsworth: Penguin [1955], 1970), pp. 220–1.

That Alteria attributes her anecdote to an aristocratic lady with an earthy sense of humour may be but a rhetorical ploy. Yet her attribution may also harbour a truth: that the story was in local circulation. Its potential history is now a rather familiar profile, consisting of scattered Eastern analogues and scant traces in early sixteenth-century European storytelling. For an Eastern source, Somadeva's eleventh-century *Katha sarit sagara* again provides an early prospect. A Brahmin allows a demon to heal his injured leg, only to be threatened by death if he fails to bring in further wounds to be healed. The Brahmin thinks of his daughter, whose vulva might impress the demon as a wound worthy his attention but hardly subject to healing. The demon becomes discouraged by the failure of his arts, particularly when he discovers a second wound underneath the first from which the young lady lets fly a timely fart.[18] Surely we are in the right territory, although half a millennium away. Yet the story does not turn up in Europe in a form resembling Straparola's before 1531 (unless we include Rabelais's 'The Lion, the Fox, and the Old Lady,' recounted in a footnote above). Hans Sachs, bless him, tells the one about the farmer who, at the request of a bear, cuts off his testicles so that he might become a monk. The bear, discomfited beyond measure, threatens the next day to emasculate the farmer in revenge. But true to the version we know, the farmer's wife, dressed in her husband's clothes, assuages the bear and gives him encouragement to endure by showing him her 'tear' before frightening him away with a fart.[19] This story is related to ATU 1133, 'The Gelding of the Bear and the Fetching of the Salve.' Again, from slight records we can infer a circulation adequate to have made the story known in Germany and Italy at the same time, and that Straparola worked from a version in the vicinity, thereby providing the second telling in the European literary record – a place that might easily slip to third or fourth with the discovery of other early renditions.

Of related interest, but presumably not connected to the implicit stemma linking Sachs to Somadeva, is Jacques de Vitry's sermon exemplum based on the foolish and malicious man who, to get even with his wife, mutilated himself and thereby deprived her of all future pleasure,

---

18 *The Ocean of Story, being Tawney's translation of Somadeva's Katha sarit sagara*, ed. N.M. Penzer, 10 vols. (Delhi: Motilal Banarsidass, 1968), vol. III, pp. 32–5.

19 Hans Sachs, *Sämtliche Fabeln und Schwänke*, ed. Edmund Goetze & Carl Drescher, 3 vols. (Halle: Max Niemeyer, 1900), vol. III, no. 25.

forgetting that in the process he would be harming himself.[20] There is
another by Poggio Bracciolini about the man so jealous of his wife that
he castrated himself so that if his wife ever became pregnant he could
prove her an adulteress.[21] Or consider the following by Bonaventure des
Périers in which a priest, carrying on with his landlady, came under the
suspicion of her husband, so that at the lady's request, he put out the
news of his forthcoming castration, as though this served for proof of
his disinterest in things sexual. He goes so far as to inform his family
and friends and pays Master Peter a significant sum to feign the procedure. But the landlady's husband, seeing through the ruse, paid Master
Peter double the sum to turn it into a reality, and thus the priest endured
in earnest the unkindest cut of all.[22] The topic of castration under a
variety of guises and motifs was a popular one and seemed always good
for a laugh in those hearty days of cock fights and public executions.
What all these stories confirm, including Straparola's, is that *couilles* are
synecdochic for the man, the 'witnesses' (testari) to an essential virile
condition upon which all further social credibility of a masculine persuasion depends, and that any man foregoing them lightly is deserving
of ridicule.

---

20 'On Self-Mutilation to Spite His Wife' in *The Exempla or Illustrative Stories from the
    Sermones Vulgares of Jacques de Vitry*, ed. Thomas Frederick Crane (London: Folklore
    Society, 1890), no. 22, pp. 7–8.
21 *Les facéties de Pogge* (Paris: Garnier Frères, ca. 1900), no. 225, pp. 277–8.
22 This story originated, no doubt, in the sixty-fourth tale of *Les cent nouvelles nouvelles*,
    ed. Roger Dubuis (Lyons: Presses universitaires de Lyon, 1991), pp. 252–5. It is
    concerned with a clergyman who was a practical joker, so that when a castration
    specialist came to town, he proposed that they set up a false operation in which he
    would spin about at the last moment and avoid injury. But the host plays the better
    joke by paying the specialist double to whack them both off before the *curé* could
    execute his manoeuvre. The news of the castrated priest travels quickly thereafter,
    to the alarm of a few women but the universal delight of the men.

VI. Fable 3
The Widow's Broken Promise

CATERUZZA

Polissena, a widow, has several lovers. Her son, Panfilio, reproves her, whereupon she promises to mend her conduct if he refrains from his scratching. He agrees to this, but his mother dupes him, and finally they both go back to their original ways.

Once a woman is thoroughly wedded to a certain practice, whether it is good or bad, she finds it hard to abstain, because the habits learned from sustained usage she will keep to the end of her days. I propose now to tell you the story of a young widow who could not break off the wanton life she had for some time been living. Even when in loving kindness her own son reproved her, the crafty dame played a wily trick upon him to carry on with her evil ways. You'll hear about all this in the course of my tale and fully understand.

Gracious ladies, not long ago in the splendid and renowned city of Venice, there lived a pretty widow named Polissena, still young in years and exceedingly beautiful in person, but of a very low estate. To her husband, who is now dead, this woman had borne a son named Panfilio, a youth of good parts, a virtuous life, and praiseworthy manners, and who by trade was a goldsmith. Because Polissena was young, handsome, and graceful, there were many gallants who cast amorous eyes upon her and wooed her persistently, among them some of the principal nobles of the city. Because in her earlier days she had tasted freely of the pleasures of the world and of the sweet delights of love, she was not slow in giving assent to the solicitations of her wooers and so delivered herself up, both body and soul, to all those who would have her. Her temper was so hot and amorous that in no wise would she confine herself to the endearments of just one or two – which in a woman so young and widowed so early in life would have been but a venial fault. But she granted her favours to all comers, having no regard whatsoever for her dead husband's honour or her own.

Panfilio, enforced to witness her shameful behaviour, was tormented nearly to death by it and suffered greatly, as may well be supposed. Living from day to day with his soul vexed by these displeasures and often feeling that the burden of his disgrace was more than he could bear, the wretched youth took counsel with himself whether it wouldn't be better for him to slay his mother outright. But when he remembered that she had given him life, he abandoned such a cruel intent and resolved instead to see if he could prevail upon her with words and induce her to adopt a more proper style of life. One day he seized an opportune moment. Sitting down beside his mother, he addressed her affectionately, 'My beloved and honoured mother, it's with the greatest grief and distress that I bring myself to speak, and I'm certain you'll not refuse to listen carefully to what I have to say. It is something I've kept closely hidden in my own heart until this moment. Formerly I believed you to be wise, prudent, and circumspect. But now, to my great sorrow, I know too well that you are none of these things, which makes me so grieved that I wish to God I were as far from you as I am near to you now. As I see it, you're involved in the most scandalous life imaginable, one that stains your own honour and the good name of my late father. But if you won't have any regard for you own reputation, I beg you at the least to show some consideration for me, seeing that I'm your only son and the only person you can depend upon as a firm and faithful support in your old age.'

His mother, hearing him talk like this, fell to laughing and went about her business. Panfilio, seeing that she wasn't in the least affected by his entreaties, resolved not to waste any more breath over it, but to let her go on as she pleased. Then a few days later, by a stroke of ill fortune, Panfilio became infected with the itch and in so malignant a form that he was almost like a leper. Besides, the weather was then very cold, which prevented him from finding relief. In the evenings poor Panfilio would sit near the fire, its heat inflaming his blood all the more, aggravating the itch tenfold and causing him to scratch non-stop, working him nearly into a frenzy. One evening, sitting in front of the fire tenderly rubbing his scabies, one of his mother's lovers came to the house and the two of them carried on their love banter for a long time right in front of him. The miserable fellow, besides being annoyed by his irritating scabs, was saddened at heart by the sight of his mother's dalliance. When her lover finally left, Panfilio, still scratching his lesions, said to her, 'Mother, some time back I exhorted you to restrain your lust and abandon this evil and ill-mannered life, which not only shames you, but injures me, your son. Still, like the wanton wench you are, you turned a deaf ear to what I had to say, preferring to carry on with the guilty indulgence of your carnal appetites rather than hear my counsel. Ah, my dear mother! I entreat you to have done with this disgraceful way of living. Keep that honour which is your duty to preserve and cast this shame from you to avoid killing me with grief and shame. Don't you realize that you could be called to account at any moment, inasmuch as death is always by our side? Don't you hear what evil things are said of you at every corner?' And all the while he spoke, he kept up the chafing.

Polissena, when she heard his preaching and saw his scratching, then and there planned a joke to play on him, hoping thereby to put a stop to his complaints about her conduct. She did it so adroitly, in fact, that it had exactly the outcome she predicted. Turning to her son with a mischievous smile, she said, 'Panfilio, you're forever grieving and complaining to me about the evil life I lead. Well, I confess that my life is not entirely upright and that your caveats and counsels mark you out for a good son. But I ask you now whether you'll do one single thing to please me as proof that you're as jealous of my honour as you protest. If you'll consent to this, for my part I promise to place myself in your hands, to have done with all my lovers, and to lead a good and holy life. But if you fail to gratify me in this one respect, well then I'll pay no more attention to your wishes and give myself up to practices more vicious than any I've indulged in before.'

Longing to see his mother return to an honest way of life more than anything else in the world, he made her this answer, 'Mother, command anything of me you want, for even if you asked me to throw myself into the fire and be consumed to ashes I'd gladly do it for you if that would free you from the shame and infamy of the life you're now leading.'

'Listen carefully then to what I'm about to say,' said Polissena, 'and consider my words, for if you carry out diligently the injunctions I lay upon you, everything that you wish for will be fully granted to you. If not, the turn of affairs will only increase your scorn and damnation.'

'I bind myself to observe and perform any duty or task you may put upon me,' said Panfilio.

'Then,' replied his mother, 'I'll tell you what I require, which is nothing more arduous, my son, than that you promise not to scratch yourself for three whole evenings, and then I'll promise to satisfy your wishes.'

Upon hearing his mother's proposition, Panfilio sat for some time thinking it over, knowing full well, with his itching craze, that her conditions would not prove easy to keep. Nevertheless he accepted them and, as a token of good faith, shook hands with her to seal the bargain. When the first evening rolled around, quitting his workshop, Panfilio went home, threw off his cloak, and began walking up and down the room. After a little, finding himself somewhat cold, he sat down in a corner of the chimney close to the fire, and then, provoked by the heat, the troublesome itch began to molest him so sharply that he was greatly tormented and longed to scratch himself to get some relief. Cunning jade that she was, his mother had taken care to have a fierce, hot fire on the hearth, warming Panfilio all the more. Now when she saw him writhing and stretching like a snake, she said to him, 'Panfilio, what's the matter with you? Watch out that you don't break your promise. If you keep your word, I'll assuredly keep mine.'

To this Panfilio answered, 'Never doubt my constancy, mother. Make sure you stay resolved yourself, because I'm keeping my pledge.'

All the while they were speaking, they were both of them raging with desire, the one to scratch his itching hide, the other to find herself once more with one or other of her lovers.

So the first evening went by, bringing great discomfort both to mother and son. When the second came, Polissena again caused a large fire to be made. Then with a good supper prepared, she awaited her son's return. Firmly set on keeping his word, Panfilio clenched his teeth and put up with his trouble as well as he could and thus the second evening went by without any misadventure. Polissena, when she saw how steadfast Panfilio was in his determination, and considering how two evenings had already gone by without him once scratching himself, she feared she might lose after all and began to feel some regrets. All this while, her amorous fury greatly tormented her. It was her incentive to find something, anything, to set her son scratching so she could get back to her lovers' embraces. The next evening she prepared a most delicate supper with plenty of costly and heady wine and then waited for her son's return. When Panfilio came in and noticed the unaccustomed luxury of their evening meal, he was taken aback. Turning to his mother, he said, 'Why on earth have you set out such a princely feast as this, mother? Can it be possible that you've really changed your mind?'

To this Polissena made answer, 'Certainly not, my son. I'm more firmly set in my purpose than ever. Yet the thought struck me that you work hard every day at your trade from early morn till nightfall, and beside this I couldn't fail to notice how sorely this accursed itch has worn and emaciated your body, almost leaving no life in you. So I felt compassion for your suffering and decided to make you a fancier dish than we usually have so that you can regain your strength and your nature will be enabled to withstand the torments you suffer from the itch.'

Young and simple as he was, Panfilio didn't detect his mother's cunning scheme, or see the snake hidden among the flowers of her kindness, but sat down to the table with her, himself still close to the fire, and began eating with a zest and drinking his wine with a merry heart. Meanwhile, the cunning and malicious Polissena kept stoking the flames, poking the logs, and blowing the embers to make them burn more fiercely, plying the poor fellow with the delicate and savoury dishes, seasoned up with all manner of spices that would make his blood more inflamed with the food and the heat of the fire, and thereby force him to scratch his itch. And indeed, at the last, when Panfilio had sat for a time close to the hearth and filled his belly to repletion, such a fury of itching came over him that he thought he would die if he couldn't scratch himself. Still, by twisting his body and fidgeting now to this side and now that, he continued to endure the torment as best he could.

But after a while the heat of the food, which had been carefully salted and seasoned, and the Greek wine, and the scorching fire so sorely inflamed his blood that the wretched Panfilio found his torment greater than he could bear. So tearing open his shirt to lay bare his chest and untrussing his hose, then turning up his sleeves over his elbows, he set to scratching himself with so much abandon that the blood ran down like sweat from every part. Turning to his mother, who was laughing heartily to herself, he cried in a loud voice, 'Let each go back to his own trade! Each back to his own profession!'

Although she saw clearly that the game was now hers, the mother feigned her sorrow, saying to Panfilio, 'My son, what folly is this of yours? What is it that you want to do? Is this the way you keep your promises to me? It goes for a fact now that you'll never again be able to throw it in my teeth that I haven't kept faith with you.'

Panfilio listened, scratching himself with all his might at the same time, and answered his mother with a troubled mind, 'Let's for the future just follow the bent that each likes best, mother. You go about your business and I'll go about mine.' And from that hour the son never again dared question his mother about the course of her life, and so she returned to her usual marketing, now trading brisker than ever.

All the listeners were mightily pleased with Cateruzza's fable, and after they had spent a while laughing, the Signora called upon the damsel to propound her enigma, and she, being disinclined to interrupt the accustomed order of the entertainment, smilingly gave it in these words:

> What is the thing we ladies prize:
> Five finger's breadth will tell its size;
> Divers fair nooks you find inside;
> No outlet, though the gate is wide.
> The first attempt will give us pain,
> For free access is hard to gain;
> But later it will grow long and straight,
> Or large and short, t'accommodate
> The shape of him that doth employ
> His pains to work this pleasant toy.
> It's always ready to oblige
> The user's taste, whate'er the size.

Cateruzza's obscurely worded enigma gave abundant details for the ladies and gentlemen to consider. But no matter how carefully they debated it from every point and turned it over and over in their minds, they were not able to hit upon its real interpretation. Wherefore the prudent Cateruzza, seeing that they were all still wandering in obscurity and unable to grasp the meaning of her riddle, said promptly, 'So as not to keep this honourable company any longer in suspense, I will forthwith give the interpretation of my enigma, while submitting myself also to the judgment of others who may better understand and interpret it than myself. My riddle signifies nothing other than the glove you wear to protect your hand. This, you know, will sometimes cause you slight hurt when you first put it on, but once on soon accommodates itself to your pleasure.'

The explanation was held to be quite satisfactory by the honourable company, and when Cateruzza had ceased speaking, the Signora gave sign to Lauretta, who was sitting at Vicenza's side, to take her turn in the storytelling. Then with a pretty boldness of manner and speech, Lauretta turned her fair face towards Bembo, and said, 'Signor Antonio, it were a great shame, kindly and gallant gentleman as you are, if you, with your usual grace and talent, did not tell the company some fable. For my part, I would willingly relate one, but just now I can't call one to mind that would be pleasing and funny at the same time. Therefore, I beg you, Signor Antonio, that you perform the office in my place, and if you grant me this favour, I'll ever consider myself beholden to you.'

Bembo, who had no thought of telling a story that evening, answered, 'Signora Lauretta, although I feel myself most unfit for the task, yet because a request from you is as powerful with me as a command, I will accept the charge you lay upon me, and will strive to satisfy your wishes as much as I possibly can.' And the Signora, having given her gracious permission, he began his story in these words.

VI.3 Commentary

This story has no known sources. Rather, it is a vignette or a social anecdote, putatively true, and in fact, in a more mundane way, it could have been so. It does not have the properties of a folk tale, but illustrates, instead, a real or imagined proverb about the necessity of scratching that which itches. As in the tale of Modesta and her collection of shoes, the material counterparts to her sex life (V.5), in this story Panfilio's itch from scabies or the scurf becomes the graphic counterpart to Polisenna's 'itch' for sexual partners. In that regard, the story turns on the semantic plurality of the word insofar as any compulsive craving for the pleasures of the flesh may be referred to metaphorically as an itch, arising from the evolutionarily selected propensity for irritated or infected skin to signal a relentless need for chafing as one of the body's adaptive features. Such was the birth of a metaphor and a verity – that what itches is a manifest destiny to seek release through friction. The story arises in pitting one instinct to fricative satisfaction against another in a contest of abstention, of mind over matter, or will over instinct.

By these terms, the conflict arising over a widow's gaiety and her son's offended sense of modesty and decency will be resolved according to the logic of a game or contest. The mother, unwilling to give up her lovers, and the son, outraged by her shameful ways, had come to an impasse. Best to let the conditions of a contest determine the outcome by both agreeing to a set of rules. The first to acquiesce to the itch, she in dalliance, he in scratching, would cede to the wishes of the other. The rest of the story is about the cheating, or surreptitious advantage, taken by Polisenna whereby, in showing her son the utmost of consideration, she exacerbates his instinct to scratch to an irresistible level of intensity. Her ploy is predicated on medical knowledge then current, that foods and wines are calibrated according to their degrees of heat, flatuosity, and venereal incitement. Rich meats and spicy wines were provocative, inflammatory, aphrodisiac, and prickly. Thus, under guise of comfort and joy, she warmed her son, both within and without, with food and fire, driving him to frenzy. The *peripeteia* of the entire tale is a scratch fest that draws blood, with the simultaneous acknowledgment of defeat and the concession that from thenceforward his mother could follow her will. From three days' abstinence she gained a widow's licence.

The social and legal circumstances of this vignette are insufficiently drawn to make of it a sociological document pertaining to the family, the mores of widows, a male code of honour, or legal regulations. Quite simply, Polisenna was determined to have her lovers to the chagrin of her son, and the son was determined to curtail her activities for the sake of his deceased father, the reputation of the household, and by extension his own place in the mercantile community. Nevertheless, it allows for questions about a son's lien on his widowed mother's sex life, legally, socially, or psychologically, and about a woman's right to ignore him. In Calderón's Spain of nearly a century later, the issue was vitally alive in such plays as *La dama duende*, in which a widowed sister's capers provoke a narrowly averted bloody showdown between her high-strung brothers exercising their rights over her person and an innocent friend staying in their house. Honour underwrites Straparola's story, but lacks the martial force of a revenge culture, even though the thought of murder passes through Panfilio's mind. There is, nevertheless, a sense of honour that pertains even to the minimalist of nuclear families: that what a mother does reflects upon the son; that her life is in violation of a son's emotional investment in her purity; and that both their lives are under the invigilating scrutiny of a censorious community. Ultimately, however, the tale is about a trick played on an unsuspecting son by a mother determined to resist all constraints upon her social life. By the terms of the story, we are brought to champion her cunning in securing her pleasure and autonomy. The story goes no further, so that what Polisenna may represent as a destabilizing social force in casting her glances at all manner of men in a potentially closed community, or as the catalyst to a son's sex nausea, or the cry for widow's rights are not demonstrable parts of the story.

VI. Fable 4
Who Will Become Abbess?

ANTONIO BEMBO

A dispute having arisen between three sisters of a convent as to which of them would fill the post of abbess, the bishop's vicar general decrees that the office should fall to the one who gives the most eminent proof of her worthiness.

Modesty lends a great charm to all who possess it, yet judgment I rate even higher when it is in the possession of a man who knows himself. With the permission of the gracious ladies around me, I propose to tell a story no less witty than beautiful, although in certain ways it's silly and indecent. I will hence do my best to relate it to you with as much modesty and propriety as is due and proper. But if by chance any part of my discourse affronts your chaste ears, I would now forestall your pardon for the offence by entreating you to hold back your censure for another time.

In the noble city of Florence there is a certain convent with an illustrious reputation for holiness of life and pious practices. The name of it I will not reveal just now for fear of marring its glorious name with a spot of scandal. It came about some years ago that the abbess of this house, afflicted by many grave infirmities, came to the end of her days and rendered up her soul to her Creator. She being dead and her body buried with all the solemn rites of the Church, the surviving sisters called a meeting of the chapter by the ringing of the bell, so that all who had a voice in the matter should be called together. The vicar general of the bishop, a prudent and learned man who desired that the election of the new abbess should be carried out according to the strict letter of the law, gave word to the assembled sisters to be seated. Then he spoke, 'Most respected ladies, you know well enough, I'm certain, that the sole reason for gathering you here today is that you may make choice of a new head over you all. In such a case, it behoves each of you, at the bidding of the conscience which is in each of you, to elect that one who seems to you the best fitted for the office.' All the sisters agreed that such was the course they were minded to follow.

As it came about, there were three nuns in the convent among whom there was a very keen competition as to which of them should become the new abbess, because each had a certain following among the sisters, each had the respect of other superiors, and each had a great desire for the title. While the sisters were preparing themselves to elect their new head, one of the three nuns just mentioned, Sister Veneranda, rose from her seat, turned towards the other sisters, and addressed them: 'My sisters and my children whom I hold in such high affection, you are all aware of the loving zeal with which I have bestowed my best energies in the service of the convent, not only growing old but veritably decrepit in the performance of my duties. Therefore, on account of my long devotion and my advanced age, it seems only just and proper that I should be elected as your head. If my long-continued labours, the vigils and prayers of my youth fail to persuade you to choose me, at least let my old age and infirmities appeal to your consideration, which should compel your reverence above every other thing. It must be apparent to you all that I can expect to live but a short time longer. Assure yourselves that before long I will leave my place to another among you. For this reason, my well-beloved daughters, I beg that you will give me this brief season of ease and pleasure, keeping foremost in your hearts the good counsels I have always given you.' In this manner she ended her speech and burst into a fit of weeping.

The appeal of the first sister concluded, Sister Modestia, a woman of middle age, rose from her seat and spoke in this manner: 'Mothers and sisters of mine, you have heard and understood the claims openly stated by Sister Veneranda, who happens to be the most advanced in age among us. But this fact, in my estimation, does not give her a special claim to be chosen as our abbess inasmuch as she is now come to such a time of life that senility has diminished her powers of counsel, so that before long she will herself require control and care instead of controlling us. But if you, in your mature judgment, give proper consideration to my good estate, to the trust you can place in me, remembering my ancestry, surely you cannot, in all conscience, choose anyone but me to be your lady abbess. As every one of you knows, our convent is greatly harassed by legal suits and procedures and is much in need of support and protection. What greater defence could you provide to our house against its adversaries than the endorsement and patronage of my family, who would give not only their wealth and goods in your defence, but their very lives if I were elected your head.'

Hardly had Sister Modestia resumed her seat before Sister Pacifica rose to her feet, and with a show of deep humility, she spoke in the following way: 'I am well assured, most honoured sisters – in fact, I take it for certain that you all, for the prudent and well-advised ladies that you are, will feel no little astonishment that I, who came as though it were but yesterday to abide among you, should now desire to put myself on the same level, or to even supersede the two most honoured sisters who have already spoken. On the score of age and experience these ladies are far above me. But if you consider carefully, with the eyes of your understanding, how many and great my qualifications are, surely you will rate the freshness of my youth over the decrepit age of the one and the family claims of the other. As all of you must well know, I brought with me here a very rich dowry that has enabled our convent, very nearly fallen into ruin through the passage of time, to be rebuilt from foundation to roof-tree. I won't mention as well the houses and farms that bring to our convent every year such vast sums in rents. On account of these, along with my other qualifications, and in recompense for the many great benefits you have received from me, it is your bounden duty to choose me for your abbess, seeing that your food and raiment depend upon my endowment and upon no other.' Having thus spoken, she sat down.

With the discourses of the three sisters brought to this conclusion, the vicar general summoned all the nuns into his presence one after the other and asked them to write down the name of the sister they wished to be raised to the dignity of abbess according to their conscience. When this was done, and all the sisters had recorded their votes, it was discovered that each was equal to the others in the votes cast – there was no difference between them. Then a most acrimonious dispute arose among the sisters, some championing the first, some the second, and some the third for their head. Nor was there any means found to pacify their contention. The bishop's vicar could plainly see how doggedly obstinate each faction was, and he realized, in light of the special qualifications presented, that each of the three sisters might be promoted to the honourable office of abbess. Thus he tossed about in his mind to find ways and means for retaining one for the post without causing undue offence or disaffection to the others. He then ordered the three contending sisters to be summoned into his presence and there he addressed them: 'Well-beloved sisters, I comprehend fully your many virtues and qualifications, and I must say that any one of you would be in the highest sense worthy to be chosen abbess of this convent. But among you three honourable sisters the contest for election has been incredibly rigorous and the votes cast have produced a deadlock. For this reason, and to the end that you may continue your peaceful lives in love and tranquillity, I hereby propose to you what I hope will be a means of election that will end this contention to the complete and mutual satisfaction of everyone. The method I propose it this, that each of you three sisters who have made a bid to succeed to the office of abbess will take the next three days to prepare some particular feat, one that is praiseworthy in itself and worthy of remembrance, to be performed in the presence of us all. Whichever of you shows herself able to perform a work of the greatest glory and virtue by the good consent of all the sisters shall duly be chosen Lady Abbess, to whom shall be accorded all the honour and reverence belonging by right to the said office.'

This proposition of the vicar general won the approbation of all three sisters, who with one accord promised to observe the conditions laid down. When the appointed day had come for the trial and all the nuns belonging to the convent were convened in the chapter house, the vicar general called before him the three sisters aspiring for the high post of abbess and questioned them individually as to whether they had given due thought to their affairs by performing some noteworthy feat as he had ordained. They all answered that they had. So as soon as all were seated, sister Veneranda, the oldest of them all, took her place in the middle of the floor. She then drew from her hood a little Damascus needle which was fastened there, lifted up her clothes and her undergown in front, and raising one leg to the side, in the presence of the vicar and the entire sisterhood, she pissed so delicately through the eye of the needle that not a single drop fell to the ground without first passing through the hole. Seeing this, the vicar general and the nuns all thought for certain that Veneranda must become the abbess, for it seemed impossible that anyone could do a more cunning feat.

When this was over, Sister Modestia, who was the second eldest, rose from her seat and sat herself in the centre of the chapter house. She drew out a die and laid it on a bench with the five-point side uppermost. She then took five little grains of millet seed and placed one in each of the five points of the die. Baring her backside and bringing her buttocks near the bench on which she had placed the die, she let fly so great and terrible an explosion that the vicar general and nuns took fright. Now although the fart flew out of the hole in a giant puff, yet it was passed with such adroitness and dexterity that the grain that was in the middle spot stayed in its place, while the other four entirely disappeared and were nevermore seen.

The entire assembly considered this feat as wonderful as the first, yet kept their peace, waiting to see what sister Pacifica would so. She presented herself in the middle of the chapter house to perform a feat too agile for the aged, but possible for a young hoyden like her. Pulling from her pocket a solid peach-stone, she tossed it in the air, and then instantly baring her backside and pointing it up, she caught the stone between her buttocks and there she squeezed it so vigorously that she crunched it up smaller than the finest dust.

Then the vicar general, sage and well-counselled man that he was, forthwith began in all sobriety to confer with the sisterhood and duly consider the performances of all three sisters. But finding within a short time that there was little prospect of a consensus, he took time to deliberate over what the final decision should be. Inasmuch as there was nothing in his learned books that might guide him in making his judgment, he abandoned the matter as insoluble. Even to this day the dispute is still pending. Therefore, I call upon you, most learned and prudent ladies, to disentangle this question which, by reason of its importance, I would myself never dare approach.

This story of Bembo's proved to be more a source of mirth to the men than to the ladies, seeing that for the shame of it all, the ladies hid their faces in their laps and dared not look up. But the men discussed first one incident and then another of the story they had just heard, finding great diversion in the matter, until at last the Signora, disapproving such unbecoming laughter, and aware too that the ladies sat as though they had been transformed into so many marble statues, commanded silence and so put an end to their profligate mirth, in order that Bembo might follow the rules and give his enigma. But he, having already said more than was appropriate, turned towards the fair Lauretta and said, 'It's now your turn, Signora Lauretta, to set an enigma. I may have satisfied you in one matter, but that is no reason why I should satisfy you in another.'

Having no wish to put up resistance because he wouldn't do his duty, cheerfully she began.

> My comrade awaits me for the bout,
> With open'd legs and arms stretched out.
> I mount atop, my mate below,
> And getting ready, off we go.

> Then something long I take in hand,
> And temper it with an unguent bland,
> And place it where it ought to go,
> Then work it featly to and fro,
> And swing and sway it up and down,
> Until success my efforts crown.

Everyone declared that the enigma proposed by Lauretta was no less entertaining than Bembo's story, but insofar as few of the company could fathom its meaning, the Signora directed her to give the interpretation. Then Lauretta, in order not to impose further delay, spoke up, 'My riddle means that there were two men who set to work to saw a huge beam of wood in pieces. One of these took in his hand the saw, which is a long thing, and went up above, while the other remained in the sawpit beneath. The first then smeared the saw with oil and placed it in the fissure of the beam, and then the two companions working together ran the saw up and down in order to accomplish their task.'

This ingenious interpretation of the enigma gave the greatest pleasure to all the company and, after the talk had died down, the Signora gave word to Eritrea to begin telling her fable, which she delivered as follows without any further need for persuasion.

VI.4 Commentary

Straparola's choice of a tale for presentation by Antonio Bembo is a *conte mignon* about nuns in competition for the leadership of their community who, after making solemn appeals tainted by a hypocritical show of humility replete with the pious rhetoric of 'my sisters and my children,' 'high affection,' and 'loving zeal,' arrive at an impasse in the democratic process verging on acrimony. In order to assign this indivisible prize, the presiding vicar calls upon each candidate to perform a deed that is praise-worthy in itself and meritorious of future fame. Each, with ceremonial solemnity, performs a feat of precision, whether in pissing, farting, or dexterity with the gluteus maximus. This *pince-sans-rire* convent humour is hardly anti-clerical, really; the point is to have those in the society deemed models of propriety and discretion perform these remarkably scatological feats. There is nothing to suggest that anything of its kind had ever transpired or was in any way typical of convent life (although the invention is worthy of Swift in his Lilliputian satire on the assigning of offices in the British parliamentary system). This is mere inventive fantasizing. If there is satire, it is in the three opening campaign speeches, the second of which is about entitlements based on ancestry, legal skills, and family patronage as opposed to piety, service, and seniority, while the third admits that she has neither age nor experience, but reminds the community that their material well-being is entirely due to the largesse of her family. They are depictions of convent politics and a reminder that these institutions were often beholden to the world of wealth and power.

Bembo presumably achieved his desired effect upon his audience, for the story is a social provocation of a particular kind. The men laughed openly, exclaiming over the merits of the respective talents presented, while the ladies, in show of real or feigned embarrassment, looked down into their laps in shame and confusion, until the Signora halted the guffaws and restored them to activities in which the two genders might negotiate with equality and propriety. The story, with its delicate indelicacy and calculated immodesty, had sundered the group, exposing differences according to gendered predilections. Tellingly, the ladies' reaction was prescient in terms of the future of the story, for it was among the first to be suppressed in subsequent editions of the *Notti*. Moreover, the present story is listed in the *Biblioteca Scatologica* and was among the works to elicit the attention of the nineteenth-century critics pioneering in the field of historical pornography.[23]

All of Straparola's former editors are in agreement that this story has no known written sources and that it does not correspond to any story types circulating among the folk in the nineteenth century, so that by right or default, Straparola may enjoy authorial credit. There is slight evidence, however, that a model may have been in circulation, for Pietro Fortini retells the story as no. 18 in his *Giornate delle novelle dei novizi* in a manner similar to the present tale, although the victory in the end is assigned to the elderly nun who urinates through the eye of a needle without spilling a drop – a decision that once again sets the convent wrangling and causes the two losers to quit the community in a huff.[24]

---

23 Pierre Jannet, Jean-François Payen, Auguste Veinant, *Bibliotheca Scatologica* (Scatopolis [Paris]: Les Marchands d'aniterges [P. Jannet], [1845], 1850).

24 *Le giornate delle novelle dei novizi*, ed. Adriana Mauriella, 2 vols. (Rome: Salerno, 1988), no. 18 (III.4), vol. I, pp. 321–36. The three sisters are named Contessa, Agnesa, and Cecilia, upon whose respective natures Fortini elaborates considerably. The tale is set in Bologna. When the convent divides up its loyalties into thirds, the bishop is called in and Cecilia, as in Straparola, recounts how the entire church had

The doubt arises because Fortini's chances for reading the story in the *Piacevoli notti* are rather slight, thereby necessitating a common source. (He was a member of a noble Sienese family and died in 1562.) His *novelle* are traditionally assigned to his younger years and were unquestionably written before 1557 (the year in which events culminated in the fall of the Sienese republic). Thus, the period is indeed limited during which Fortini could have lifted and modified the story from Straparola. Inversely, Fortini's work was not published in his lifetime, precluding imitation by Straparola. As in the case of Machiavelli's 'Belfagor,' thought must be given to a common folk tradition known simultaneously in Tuscany and the Veneto. But there are further considerations.

Straparola's debt to Morlini for some twenty or more of the stories to follow is well known, although this story is not among them. Nevertheless, mention must be made here of his story of the three women who find a precious pearl (no. 81), because it too concerns an indivisible prize contested by three women and the appointment of an arbiter who will make his decision based upon an outrageously scatological contest.[25] They agree to abide by the decision of Palemon who proposes that the jewel be awarded to the one who had experienced the most ridiculous or disagreeable misadventure. As can be imagined, his plan becomes the pretext for three remarkably salacious vignettes. The confession of so much ignominy for a pearl carries an irony all its own. The first woman tells of embracing a statue resembling her deceased husband and finding herself riding a priapus from which she could not descend even when, after many hours, a great crowd had assembled to watch. The next and younger tells how she was caught by her husband as she was being mounted horseback style with a bridle in her mouth by a servant boy with a hyperbolical phallus. The third and youngest was pleasuring herself with a rotund leek when her husband entered. She got her skirts down in time, but was made to follow him through the streets with the

---

been restored at her family's expense down to the beds and dishes. In Straparola's leaner version, the events are reversed and no ruling is deemed possible. Fortini's bishop is likewise confused by so much virtue, and later by so much craft and skill. The tricks are performed only for him and not for the community. But in the end, he is able to decide, and Cecilia, with her precision pissing, becomes the abbess. Arguably, Fortini took his tale from the *Piacevoli notti*, but equally plausible is that both found it in versions current among the popular tales in their respective parts of the country.

25 Girolamo Morlini, *Novelle e favole*, ed. Giovanni Villani (Rome: Salerno, 1983); *Les nouvelles*, trans. Fernand Caussy (Paris: E. Sansot, 1904), no. 81, pp. 184–7.

instrument still in place until she fell down, in full view of all, her skirts over her head, and the vegetable, bloodied by her erotic diligence, was extracted as forage by a passing donkey. Indecision overcomes this judge as well, leaving the reader to determine which is the greatest calamity (or howler) of the three. The analogous structure could have served Straparola as a frame for his invention and Fortini's imitation might have followed as a compliment to our author's wit. The alternative, as stated above, is a common source, not currently known, which would render the Morlini template extraneous. The delicate decision in these matters must likewise be turned over to the judicious reader.

VI. Fable 5
The Virtue of Stones

Father Zefiro works a spell on a youth who was eating the figs in his garden.

It has often been said, dear ladies, that mysterious powers reside within words, herbs, and stones. But stones assuredly may be thought to excel both herbs and words in persuasive virtues, as you will come to understand from this little tale.

There once lived in the city of Bergamo a miserly old priest called Father Zefiro, who, by common report, was said to be possessed of as much wealth as any man of the cloth. This prelate had a garden located beyond the city walls near the Penta Gate, itself surrounded by walls and ditches in such a way that neither man nor beast could get in. It was well planted with fruit trees of every kind, among which there was a great fig tree with branches spreading on all sides. Every season it was laden with beautiful and excellent fruit, which the priest not only enjoyed himself but shared with all the gentlemen and notables of the city. These figs were of a mixed colour between white and purple and they dropped tears of juice like honey. They were so precious that they were guarded every night by a watchman.

When by chance one night he forgot to send the watchman, a youth clambered up into this fig tree. There he chose out the ripest of them and silently set to work to stow them away, skins and all, just as they were, in the storehouse of his belly.

Suddenly, Father Zefiro remembered that there was no guardian in his garden and rushed back, only to see straightway the fellow sitting in the tree eating figs at his leisure. The priest began by begging him to come down, but the boy paid no attention to his words. Father Zefiro then threw himself upon his knees and conjured him by heaven, by earth, by the planets, by the stars, by the elements, and by all the sacred words written in the scriptures to come down from the tree, but still the youth ate steadily on. Father Zefiro, seeing that he made no progress whatsoever by these solemn appeals, now gathered certain herbs that grew round about in the garden and once more conjured the rascal by the virtues that dwelt therein to come down, but he only clambered up higher so that he could fill himself up more easily.

Then the priest said, 'It is written that "in words, herbs and stones there are secret virtues." I have conjured you by the first two and they have been to no avail in bringing you down from the tree. Now by the virtue of the third I once more conjure you to come down to the ground.' Having said this, he began to hurl stones at the thief with great rancour and fury, smiting him now on the arm, now on the leg, now on the backbone, so that in a short time, all swollen, clobbered, and bruised as he was from the frequent hits, the youth was obliged to come down from his perch. Then he took to flight, dropping all the figs he had stowed away in his shirt. Thus, stones proved themselves superior in power and virtue than either words or herbs.

No sooner was Eritrea at the end of her brief story than the Signora asked her to follow it up with her enigma, which she presented without further delay.

> Gallant knights and ladies gay,
> Tell me truthfully, I pray;
> Answer quickly my behest,
> Which bedfellow you like best?
> One that's bound close and tight,
> One that makes you writhe by night,
> Or one that in the evening grey
> Drives you from your bed away.
> If my speech you fathom well,
> Tell me, gentles, quickly tell.

All the listeners were greatly perplexed by Eritrea's cunningly made riddle and none knew what answer to make. But the Signora pressed each to give an opinion, so that one finally gave preference to the trim, tight, and closely clad one, another to the hot, ticklish one that makes you writhe all night, and another to the gay, tricksome one that will not let a man rest in his bed. Yet none of them understood the true signification of the enigma. So Eritrea, seeing their bewilderment, said, 'I think it not good that this gentle company should be left longer in doubt, so I'll say

it outright, that the one which is tight and closely tied is the scurf, which
to be cured must be doctored and tied up tight with bandages. The quick,
tricksome one is the flux, which constrains a man to rise from his bed at
all hours to relieve his belly, while the hot, ticklish one signifies the itch,
which towards evening and in the night so heats and enflames a man's
skin that he is inclined nearly to tear his flesh with his teeth, as the
widow's son did in the tale so elegantly told by Cateruzza a short time ago.'

The pleasant interpretation set forth by Eritrea to her knotty riddle
gave general satisfaction, and when the listeners had all taken leave of
the Signora, the hour now being late, they went their several ways under
promise to return next evening to their customary place of meeting.

The End of the Sixth Night

VI.5 Commentary

Straparola's source for this sketch – it is hardly more than a single episode
in demonstration of a proverb turned upside down – is incontestably
no. 61 of Girolamo Morlini's *Novellae, fabulae, comoedia*, published in
1520 – a book concerning which there will be more ado in the commentaries to follow.[26] The vignette, that of the wealthy priest who seeks by all
the virtues invested in words, herbs, and stones to bring a fig thief down
from his precious tree, employs a saying of unknown antiquity, one
attributed to the wise Solomon himself, as the basis for the tripartite
attack on the felon. The efficacy of stones redeems the dictum when
beseeching words and the power of herbs fail. The joke depends upon
the recognition of a paradigm shift in which the occult power residing
in precious stones is exchanged for rocks as simple projectiles. The
reversal, in effect, represents a peasant's or pragmatist's deflation of erudite learning, for according to the original dictum, 'In verbis, herbis, et
lapidibus sunt virtutes' (or 'magna est virtus'), all three have great powers, herbs in their pharmaceutical virtues, precious stones in their occult
powers through the principle of correspondences or by innate properties,
and words through their magic significations, as well as through prayers,
curses, and spells. But always among these, whether according to science,
magic, or the Scriptures, the greatest was the word, including that 'which

---

26 Girolamo Morlini, *Novelle e favole*, ed. Giovanni Villani (Rome: Salerno, 1983),
   pp. 292–5; *Novelle*, trans. Fernand Caussy (Paris: E. Sansot, 1904), pp. 134–5.

was made flesh and dwelt among us.' Thus, while there is a vignette to be imagined in the mind's eye of a recalcitrant poacher and an irate priest trying in incremental fashion to bring him down, the humour turns on the reversal of this bit of official learning. For that reason, the story type must have belonged initially to scholastic culture, featuring a schoolboy send-up of the famous maxim by granting to stones the greatest virtue, as with the proverbial apples that distance doctors when they are aimed right. It is the same joke because the virtue of the fruit suddenly becomes its efficacy as a missile. Such schoolroom spoofing of proverbs provides the opening segment of *The Dialogue of Solomon and Marcolphus*, in which Solomon and the German peasant hero (cited by Luther on more than one occasion) have a contest in which the peasant deflates high wisdom. When Solomon warns, 'Woe to that man that hath a double heart and in both ways will wander,' Marcolphus replies, 'He that will two ways go must either his arse or his breeches tear,' or again, 'Of abundance of the heart the mouth speakest,' to which Marcolphus replies, 'Out of a full womb the arse trompeth.'[27] The genesis of the present story resides in the same cultural nexus.

Those interested in tracing the proverb's history should consult Hans Walther's *Proverbia sententiaeque latinitatis medii aevi: Lateinische Sprichwörter und Sentenzen des Mittelalters*.[28] There, among the several entries, will be found one by an earlier Walther: 'Christus vim verbis, vim gemmis, vim dedit herbis: Verbis maiorem, gemmis herbisque minorem,'[29] again confirming on the grounds of the Scriptures that of the three, gems and herbs come in second. The proverb was known to John Gower who, in his *Confessio Amantis* (last quarter of the fourteenth century), wrote:

> In ston and gras vertu ther is
> Bot yet the bokes tellen this,
> That word above alle erthli thinges
> Is virtuous in his doings
> Wher so it be to evele or goode.[30]

---

27 Ed. Donald Beecher with Mary Wallis (Ottawa: Dovehouse Editions, 1995), p. 151.

28 (Göttingen: Vandenhoeck & Ruprecht, 1963), vol. II, nos. 11787, 14224, 7310, and 2748 (the Walther quotation).

29 Christ gave power to words, gems, and herbs, the most to words, the least to gems and herbs.

30 *Confessio amantis*, bk. VII, in *The English Works of John Gower*, ed. G.C. Macaulay (London: Oxford University Press, 1901), vol. II, p. 82.

The phrase appears in a more comic setting in Henry Chettle's *Kinde-hartes Dream* (1592) embedded in a tooth-drawer's little charm to ease the pain of his patient. First he must write the name and age of the patient on a piece of paper, on top of which he writes 'In verbis, et in herbis, et in lapidibus sunt virtutes,' followed by such 'Chaldean' gibberish as 'Ab illa hurs gibella,' allegedly representing the name of blood devils causing pain that are expelled when the paper is burned with a little frankincense. The very words, still attributed to Solomon, like those of the Mass itself, have become magic.[31]

In the sixteenth and seventeenth centuries, the saying remained in wide circulation as a commonplace, an incantation, and a scientific nostrum.[32] Straparola and his predecessors could count on its familiarity as the prerequisite bit of cultural literacy for chuckling at their vignettes, but it remained, at the same time, an operative principle and the subject of heavy philosophical speculation, as in Johann Rudolf Glauber's *Explicatio oder Auslegung über die Wörten Salomonis: In herbis, verbis, et lapidibus, magna est virtus*, in two volumes, published in Amsterdam by Joannem Janssonium in 1664. For in effect, the dictum holds in résumé the underlying principle of every lapidary and herbal and all that pertains to the secret nature of things with which God has invested the world; it is a preamble and mantra to the pursuit of science bent upon discovering those mysteries for the benefit of mankind through the unfolding of the laws of nature and of the universe.[33] It may well be asked, as it was during the Middle Ages, whether words, through their power to name, capture, emblematize, and create, do in fact hold pre-eminence in the philosophical

---

31 H[enry] C[hettle], *Kind-hartes Dream* (London: William Wright, 1592 [1593]), p. D4. See also Keith Thomas, *Religion and the Decline of Magic* (London: Weidenfeld & Nicholson, 1971), p. 180.

32 Giordano Bruno, writing his *Il candelaio* (The Candlebearer) in 1582, assumed that the phrase was familiar to his audience of readers. At the beginning of the third act, Bartolomeo states, 'When philosophers discuss the essence of things they usually begin with the old division: *in verbis, in herbis et in lapidibus*.' It was something like the categories of things represented in 'animal, vegetable, or mineral.' Bartolomeo, ultimately, laments that the saying did not also include 'metals,' for as a pseudo-alchemist he was interested in their value and transformation. *Renaissance Comedy: The Italian Masters*, ed. Donald Beecher (Toronto: University of Toronto Press, 2009), vol. II, p. 377.

33 The magic associated with herbs in their occult pharmaceutical actions, in words through incantations and spells, and in precious stones through their semiotic properties corresponding to elements within the body were a part of the mentality of magic that invested all aspects of medieval science. Edward Peters studies related

firmament. When Father Zefiro conjures the youth to descend in the name of words and herbs, he is in fact conjuring in the manner described in such works as the *Clavis* or *Clavicula Salomonis* in which the practitioner in the first conjuration calls upon the demons by the waters and by the sea, by the winds, the whirlwinds, and the tempests, by the virtues of words, herbs, and stones, by all that is in heaven, earth, and hell, and by the holy names of God, for it is in the magic configuration of these incantations that the secret forces may be commanded. This, the greatest of all the medieval grimoires, pretends to have been written by Solomon himself, and to have been rediscovered by Byzantine scholars while repairing his tomb.[34]

Morlini's source would appear to be Lorenzo Abstemio in his *Hecato-mythium*, or Franco Sacchetti's Novella 67, the latter related as an event in the life of Messer Valore de' Buondelmonti (d. 1357), in which he explains that he has found greater virtue in a little pebble than in a millstone, or in precious stones, or words, or herbs, and that experience has taught him in which of the three God has placed the greatest virtue. There was once a young man who had gotten into his fig tree. Messer Valore began by testing the power of words in commanding him to come down. Failing that, he proceeded to herbs, but to no greater effect. Then he launched a stone, telling him to get down, and when he started to pick up the second rock the boy descended from the tree in haste.[35] This story dates to the third quarter of the fourteenth century, confirming both the long-standing history of the anecdote and the tradition of writing comic fiction in illustration of proverbs. Alternatively, Morlini's vignette may be an elaboration upon the story as it is told by Abstemius, writing less than thirty years before the publication date of the *Novellae, fabulae* ... He tells in a page how a boy pillaging apples made light of the old man's words and mocked his herbal powers, but scampered down

---

matters in 'The Medieval Church and State on Superstition, Magic and Witchcraft: From Augustine to the Sixteenth Century,' in *Witchcraft and Magic in Europe: The Middle Ages*, ed. Karen Jolly et al. (London: Athlone Press, 2002), pp. 173–245.

34 *The Key of Solomon the King* (Clavicula Salomonis), trans. Samuel L.M. Mathers (London: Kegan Paul, Trench, & Trübner, 1909), chap. IV, the First Conjuration.

35 Franco Sacchetti, *Il trecentonovelle*, ed. Emilio Faccioli (Turin: Einaudi, 1970), pp. 171–2. Undoubtedly one of the most amusing accounts of the virtues of stones is found in Boccaccio's story (VIII.3) in which two men impose upon Calendrino's ignorance by telling him of the remarkable powers of the 'heliotrope' stone to make its bearer invisible. *Decameron*, trans. J.M. Rigg, 2 vols. (London: Navarre Society, n.d.), vol. II, p. 188.

with the hurling of stones, 'lapidesque quibus gremium impleverat, in iuvenem iactens, illum descendere & abire coegit.'[36] There the inquest into the matter of sources must rest, without absolute assurance that Morlini relied upon either, so many were the potential contributors.

It is revealing, nevertheless, that the idea of reversing this proverb in casting stones to efficient ends also circulated outside of Italy, reflecting the pragmatic humour of other times and places. Straparola's story is anticipated in England by a quarter of a century in *C Mery Tales and Quicke Answeres* (1535?), in which an old man conjures a boy out of his apple tree with stones, repeating the same familiar tripartite structure based on the old adage.[37]

Nevertheless, boys in fig trees are largely an Italian matter, while the *böse Weib* is the matter of the Germans, and hence the adaptation of the plot to the taming of a shrew in Pauli's *Schimpf und Ernst* (1522).[38] The prelude explains that in the time of King Solomon, his praise was great throughout the land. He would give audience to anyone, although his answers were short and enigmatic. Those who lingered to question him were conducted to the door. When a man appeared before him complaining of his evil wife, the king replied, 'In words, plants, and stones are great powers.' Although the man was baffled, there was no time for

36 *Laurentii Abstemii Maceratensis, Hecatomyhthium primum hoc est centum fabulae* (Venice, 1520), no. 91, pp. O1r–v. Lorenzo Abstemio (Laurentius Abstemius) wrote Latin fables that were first published by Valla in Venice in 1495. He was born in Macerata around 1440 and was still active in 1505, working in Urbino at the time of Guidobaldo and Pope Alexandre VI. His fables were translated into several vernaculars, including English by Roger L'Estrange in his *Fables of Aesop and other eminent Mythologists* (London, 1692). No. 91 deals with the matter of the present story. See also *L'hecatomythium, ou fables* (Orléans: Gibier, 1572).

37 *Mery Tales and Quicke Answeres* in *Shakespeare jest-books*, ed. W. Carew Hazlitt (London: H. Sotheran & Co., 1881), no. 80, p. 98. See also 'Tales and Quick Answers,' in *A Hundred Merry Tales* (1526), ed. P.M. Zall (Lincoln: University of Nebraska Press, 1963), pp. 301–2. (In the original, fol. Hiir).

38 Johannes Pauli, *Schimpf und Ernst*, ed. Johannes Bolte (Berlin: Herbert Stussenrauch, 1924; Hildesheim, Georg Olms Verlag, 1974), no. 134. See also the story below, 'Conjugal Correction' (XII.3). For further tales on the correcting of wives by throwing stones after the failure of words and herbs, see the list by Johannes Bolte, *Schimpf und Ernst*, vol. III, p. 293, which includes references to Hans Sachs, *Das bös Weyb mit den Worten, Würtzen und Stein gut zu machen* (The evil wife made good by words, herbs, and stones), 1553, *Fastnachtsspiele*, no. 49, vol. IV, p. 125; and Adolf Holtzmann, *Indische Sagen* (Karlsruhe: G. Holtzmann, 1846), vol. II, p. 258.

clarification. He arrived home, still turning the words over in his mind. When his wife flew at him with her evil words, he offered the sweetest answers, but the softer he spoke the more imperious she became. He then went to the market and purchased all manner of greens and herbs, but upon his return she berated him as a fool for wasting his money. Then he went out and fetched stones. 'What will you do with those?' she nagged. The first one hit her on the chest. She began to accuse him of murder. He threw more and she ran for the door. He followed and she thought she was going to die, so she turned, fell on the ground, and began to apologize, promising to improve. Then they lived in peace, and the man wanted to inform the king concerning his riddle, that stones surpassed both words and weeds for power. The Germans merit precedence in this application, although it does occur in Italy at an early date. The *Rosarium sermonum predicabilium ad faciliorem compilatum* of Bernardino de Busti, written late in the fifteenth century, relates the same story of Solomon, his cryptic words, the recitation of the proverb in the managing of wives, the abuse of the wife when the husband begins with his words and posies, and her final submission when stones strike her in the chest and head.[39] This proverb cum riddle, incantation, and gnomic principle of science has also become part of the reverse wisdom of the folk, a cultural mirror for those moments in which force alone will serve where diplomacy fails.[40]

---

39 Da Busti's *Rosarium* is a vast compendium of sermons and exempla the equivalent of 3,000 quarto pages in two parts, but without his name, the city, publisher, or date printed in the copy I consulted on microfilm. It must have been either the edition of Hagenau, 1500, or Lyons, 1513: the Seconda pars, folium CCVI.

40 On the correction of wives by force when all else fails, no commentary would be complete without Boccaccio's *novella* IX.9, on the two young men who seek advice from King Solomon himself. To the one the king says simply 'love' and to the other 'go to the Bridge of Geese.' Both were troubled until time made his wisdom clear. To show love is often to win love and respect (including obedience) in return, whereas at the Bridge of Geese, the defeated husband sees a stubborn mule beaten by its master until it moves, at which point he states, 'This muleteer has shown me what I have to do.' Giovanni Boccaccio, *The Decameron* (London: Privately Printed for the Navarre Society, ca. 1900), vol. II, pp. 302–6. Hans Sachs also tells the story among his *Fabeln*, presumably basing himself on Pauli. Sachs creates an animated domestic spat at the end with running up and down the house before matters are settled. *Sämtliche Fabeln und Schwänke*, ed. Edmund Goetze and Carl Drescher (Halle: Max Niemeyer, 1900), vol. III, pp. 167–9. This dates to the 1550s.

The Seventh Night

As the darkness began to settle over all parts of the cool and distant west and the rays of Pluto's beloved Proserpina penetrated to all the corners of the pitchy night, the honourable and loyal band of gentlefolk returned once more to the palace of the Signora and, hand in hand, took their accustomed seats as they had done on the previous nights. Then Molino, by the order of the Signora, had the vase brought forth, and thrusting in his hand, he drew out first the name of Vicenza, then that of Fiordiana, then Lodovica, reserving the fourth turn for Lionora, and the fifth for Isabella. Having settled the order of the storytelling, the Signora gave the word to Lauretta that she should sing a song. Without demur or excuse, the damsel began at once.

Song

Trembling I burn, and as I burn I freeze,
   I hunger ever for a love
   Which neither time nor fate can move.
      I live bereft of ease,
Because my heart now bids me speak, and then
My courage fails, and I am mute again.

Ah, many a time would I my woes have told,
   To damp the flame that in me burns,
   But aye my courage backward turns,
      Lest by my pleading bold
I should provoke your anger, and instead
Of favour, it should fall upon my head.

Thus fear and my desire are aye at strife,
   And surely fate a woeful end
   To my long martyrdom will send,
      And cut my thread of life;
And for the love which sanctifies my breath,
How transient is the life, how sure the death!

This sweet and tender song concluded, Vicenza, who was designated by lot to take the first turn at storytelling that evening, rose to her feet, duly saluted the Signora, and spoke in this manner.

VII. Fable 1
The Wife, the Courtesan, and the Witch

VICENZA

Ortodosio Simeoni, merchant and noble citizen of Florence, goes to Flanders where he becomes enamoured of Argentina, a courtesan. He forgets his lawful wife, but by magic means she is conveyed to Flanders and from there returns to Florence pregnant by her own husband.

To tell just how great the love of a wife is for her husband would require some time, and above all when she is married with a man to her liking. Contrarily, however, there is no hatred more rancorous than that of a woman who finds herself under the rule of a distasteful husband. For as wise men have written, a woman either loves wholeheartedly or hates without limits. All this you will easily understand if you follow carefully the tale I've chosen for you.

Once upon a time, gracious ladies, there lived a merchant called Ortodosio Simeoni, a man of noble rank in the city of Florence, who had to wife a lady named Isabella, a lady most fair to see, of gentle manners, and of a holy and saintly life. Ortodosio, weary of being so long at home and desiring to embark in foreign trade, took leave of his kinsmen and family, to his wife's no small regret. Setting forth from Florence, he accompanied his merchandise to Flanders, and there, by fate's direction – which at first seemed propitious but that later proved evil – upon arrival he hired a house opposite that of Argentina the courtesan. Soon thereafter he was inflamed with an ardent passion for her and entered into a guilty dalliance, forgetting all thoughts of Isabella his wife and of his former life.

Five years were now passed since Isabella had received any news of her husband. She didn't even know if he was alive or dead, or in what country he was residing. Such was the cause of her affliction, which was the greatest sorrow a woman could know; it seemed that from day to day her life was torn anew from her breast. This unhappy Isabella, who was very devout and attentive to all the ordinances of her religion, went daily to the Church of the Annunziata in Florence and there fell upon her knees in prayer to God, begging with her tears and piteous sighs that He would bring about the speedy return of her husband. But her humble prayers, lengthy fasts, and numerous charities were to no avail. Seeing that neither fasting nor prayer, neither almsgiving nor her many acts of charity to others obtained a favourable hearing, this poor lady resolved to change her humour and follow the opposite course. In the same measure, then, that she had formerly been devout and fervent in her orisons, thereafter she gave herself over completely to incantations and witchcraft, hoping that by such means her state might be improved. Therefore, she went early one morning to seek out Gabrina Furetta, a woman of great renown whose skills corresponded to all her needs. She was the foremost of her age in the arts of magic and could perform such things outside the ordinary course of nature as to amaze all who saw and heard them.

Gabrina, after listening to Isabella's pleas, was moved to pity. With comforting words she promised to help her, telling her to stay cheerful because very soon she would see her husband again and rejoice over their reunion. Most gratified by this favourable answer, Isabella opened her purse and gave Gabrina ten large pieces of money, which she received with pleasure, all the while speaking of strange matters and awaiting the fall of darkness. When the bewitching hour came at last, she took up her little book and drew a small circle on the ground, surrounded with certain mysterious signs and figures. Then she poured out some subtle liquor from a flask, drank a drop of it, and gave the same to Isabella. When the lady had drunk it, Gabrina said to her, 'Isabella, you know that we have met here to work an incantation so that we can discover where your husband is presently residing. It is therefore imperative that you remain firm and that you flinch at nothing that you see or feel, however terrible. Do not let it enter your mind to invoke the assistance of God or the saints, or to make the sign of the cross, because by then there will be no turning back and you will stand in danger of death.'

Isabella answered, 'Never doubt my constancy in any way, Gabrina, for even if you conjured up before me all the demons living at the centre of the earth, they would not frighten me.'

'Undress yourself, then,' said the witch, 'and step inside the circle.' Isabella then stripped herself and stood there as naked as the day she was born, whereupon she boldly entered the circle. Gabrina opened her book and likewise entered the circle, saying, 'Powers of hell, by the authority which I hold over you, I do conjure you that you instantly appear before me!' Then Astaroth, Farfarello, and the other demon princes, compelled by Gabrina's conjurations, instantly appeared before her, shrieking loudly and crying, 'Command us to do thy will.'

Gabrina then said, 'I conjure and command you that, without delay, you truthfully disclose to me where Ortodosio Simeoni, the husband of Isabella, is now residing and whether he is dead or alive.'

'Be assured,' replied Astaroth, 'that Ortodosio lives, that he is in Flanders, and that he is consumed by so fierce a passion for a woman named Argentina that he no longer remembers his own wife.'

On hearing this, the witch commanded Farfarello to change himself into a horse and transport Isabella to the very place where Ortodosio was dwelling. Suddenly transformed, the demon caught up Isabella and with her flew into the air. In all of this she felt neither harm nor fear, and the next morning before the sun was risen, he placed her without being seen in Argentina's palace. Then Farfarello put upon Isabella the form of Argentina, creating a resemblance so complete that she no longer seemed to be Isabella, but Argentina herself. At the same time, he transformed Argentina into the shape of a hideous old woman, invisible to all and untouchable, nor could she see anyone around her.

When the hour for supper arrived, Isabella, in her new guise, supped with her husband, Ortodosio, after which they withdrew together into a rich bedchamber where there was a soft and downy bed. There she laid herself by Ortodosio's side, while he, all along thinking he was in bed with Argentina, was in reality enjoying his own wife. The tender caresses and kisses he bestowed upon her were so ardent and impassioned, and so close were their embraces as they took their pleasure with one another, that on that very night Isabella was gotten with child. Meanwhile, the demon Farfarello contrived to steal from the chamber a rich gown all embroidered with pearls and a beautiful necklace that Ortodosio had formerly given to Argentina. When the following night arrived, Farfarello restored Isabella and Argentina to their proper shapes, and at daybreak, having once more transformed himself into a horse and taken Isabella on his back, he transported her back to Gabrina's house, at the same time handing over to the old woman the gown and the necklace he had stolen. When she had received them from the demon's hands, the witch gave them to Isabella with these words, 'My daughter, guard these things as well as you would the eyes in your own head, for at the right time and place they will be the true testimony of your loyalty.' Isabella took the garment and the fair necklace, thanked the witch, and hastened back home.

After four months had gone by, Isabella began to show signs of her pregnancy. When her kinsfolk noticed this, they were most amazed, having always taken her for a virtuous and saintly woman. Over and over they asked her if she were with child and by whom, to which question she would always reply with a cheerful face that she was pregnant by her husband, Ortodosio. But her relatives all declared this a lie, for they knew well enough that her husband had been absent from her for a long time, that he was at present in a faraway country, and that with matters standing as they were, it was impossible that he could be the father. Then her kinsfolk showed their grief, increasingly afraid of the shame that would come to them all, taking frequent counsel among themselves whether they should not kill her. Yet the fear of God, the dreaded loss of the child's soul, and the murmuring of the world, together with their care for the husband's honour held them back from committing this crime. So they decided to await the birth of this little creature.

When the time came for her lying-in, Isabella gave birth to a beautiful baby boy. But when her kin got word of it, they were plunged into sorrow and straightway they wrote the news to Ortodosio in the following words: 'Without any intent to annoy you, dearest brother, but to bring you the pure truth, we write to inform you that your wife, Isabella, and our kinswoman, to our enormous shame and dishonour, has given birth to a son. Who his father may be we do not know, but we would have said assuredly that he had been begotten by you had you not been so far from her and for such a long time. We would have deprived this child and his brazenfaced mother of their lives long before this had not the reverence that we bear to God stayed our hands, for it is not God's pleasure that we should stain our hands with our own blood. Hence, you must set your own affairs in order to save your honour and not allow this crime to go unpunished.'

When Ortodosio received these letters and the sad news they contained, he lamented sorely, and calling Argentina into his presence, he said to her, 'Sweetheart, necessity calls me back to Florence so that I may take care of certain affairs of considerable import. But as soon as I get them all set in order, I will come back to you with all possible speed. Meanwhile, take good care of yourself, using the store of goods God hath been pleased to give me as though it were your own. Live merrily and don't forget me, who cannot live without the fond memory of our love.'

Thereupon, Ortodosio left Flanders and with a propitious wind sailed for Florence. Arriving at his own house he was joyfully received by his wife. But as the days went on, he was many times seized with a diabolical inclination to kill her and flee the city in close secrecy. But considering the danger and dishonour he would incur, he resolved to postpone his revenge to a more convenient season. So without delay, he let all her kinsmen know he was back and in time sent out an invitation urging them to come to dinner the following day. In response to the invitation, his wife's relatives arrived at Ortodosio's house, where they were received by him with a most gracious welcome before they all dined merrily together. When the dinner came to an end and the table was cleared, Ortodosio began to speak as follows, 'Kind brothers and sisters, I think the cause of our meeting here must be plainly manifest to you all. I hardly need to speak at length over the matter, so I'll come right to the subject of our mutual concern.' Raising his eyes towards his wife, who sat opposite him, he said, 'Isabella, tell me truthfully. Who is the father of the child whom you are rearing up in this house?'

Isabella replied, 'You are his father.'

'Me, you say? Me, his father?' said Ortodosio. 'I have been away now for five years, and from the hour I left you haven't seen me, so how can you say that I'm his father?'

'Yet I declare the child is your son,' replied Isabella, 'and that he was begotten by you in Flanders.'

Then Ortodosio, growing very angry, cried out, 'Ah, woman, lying and brazen that you are! When were you ever in Flanders?'

'When I lay in bed with you,' answered Isabella. And then she told him everything from beginning to end – the place, the time, and the very words that had passed between them on that night. Ortodosio and her brothers, hearing such things, were filled with astonishment, but they refused, nevertheless, to believe her words. Wherefore, Isabella, seeing the stubborn pertinacity of her husband, knowing full well that he didn't believe a word she said, rose from her chair, withdrew into her bedroom, took the embroidered robe and the fair necklace, went back to the room where the company sat, and said, 'My lord, do you know this robe which is so cunningly embroidered?'

Bewildered and almost beside himself at the sight of it, Ortodosio replied, 'It is true that a robe similar to this one went missing and that I could never discover what had become of it.'

'Now you know,' said Isabella, 'for this is the same one that you lost.' Then putting her hand into her bosom, she pulled out the rich necklace and said, 'And what about this necklace?' Her husband could not deny that he recognized it, saying that it too had been stolen from him at the same time as the robe. 'But so that my fidelity may be made clearly manifest to you, I will show you that I'm worthy of your trust,' said Isabella. After saying this, she asked the nurse to bring the child, which she carried to her in her arms, and when she had stripped off its spotless white garments she said, 'Ortodosio, do you know this child?' Then she showed him how one of its feet was faulty for missing the little toe, which afforded a true indication and absolute proof of her marital fidelity, because Ortodosio's foot was likewise naturally missing a toe. When Ortodosio saw this, he was so completely silenced that no word of contradiction came to him. So he took the child in his arms and kissed him and acknowledged him as his own son. Then Isabella took greater courage and said, 'You must know, my beloved Ortodosio, that the fasting, the prayers, and the many good works that I performed in order to gain news of you brought me the fulfilment of my wishes, as I will explain. One morning, when I was kneeling in the holy church of the Annunciata and praying that I might have news of you, my prayer was granted, for an angel carried me invisibly into Flanders and placed me by your side in bed. The caresses you bestowed upon me that night were so close and loving that then and there I became with child. On the following night I found myself again in my own house in Florence, together with the robe and the necklace I have just laid before your eyes.' When Ortodosio and the brothers had seen these trustworthy signs and heard the words spoken by Isabella with such a great show of faith, they all kissed and embraced one another and so in this manner, with general good feeling, they renewed their affectionate relationships.

After some days had passed, Ortodosio returned to Flanders, where, within a short time, he procured an honourable marriage for Argentina. Then, loading his goods into a great ship, he returned to Florence, where he lived long after in tranquil peace and much happiness with Isabella and his child.

As soon as Vicenza had come to the end of this moving tale, all the company applauded her warmly, and the Signora, with tears of pity in her beautiful eyes, signalled to her to proceed with her enigma. Without hesitation or excuse, Vicenza offered the following words:

> I am shining, big and round
> When I am most ardent found;

> They take me and conceal me quite
> Between two tender things and white.
> Here and there I move about,
> Until my strength is all gone out.
> Eyes I have though I see not;
> A fellow bold of temper hot.
> When coldest nips the winter frost,
> Then am I want to warm you most.

Vicenza's subtle and ingenious enigma won the praise of all who heard it, but there was not one of them, however sharp-witted, who was not baffled by it. Therefore Vicenza, perceiving that all were silent, and that her riddle was yet unsolved, stood up, and having obtained permission, thus explained it: 'The subject of my enigma, ladies and gentlemen, is the warming pan, which, after it is filled with burning cinders, is placed between the white sheets. It has eyes, which is to say, the holes pierced into it, wherewith it never sees a thing, and it is used when the weather is coldest.'

Fiordiana, whose turn it was to tell the next story, did not wait for the Signora's command, but with a smiling face began in the following way.

VII.1 Commentary

When is the bed trick not a dirty trick, one may well ask, for what is it to make a man speak and act passionately in the dark towards a person for whom he has no feelings? All stories featuring this ploy put the question to the test, particularly when extenuating circumstances, along with former claims and promises, provide the bed trickster with legitimate entitlements. The trick, after all, when it involves a wife estranged from her husband, entails both rightful claims and a touch of revenge. This question, in the case of Shakespeare's *All's Well That Ends Well*, has generated a classic literary 'he said, she said,' reflected in the thousands of student term papers in which black-and-white stances are taken over the sins or the sanctimony of Bertram and Helena. No one would pretend that Straparola's 'Wife, Courtesan, and Witch' is of the same literary order as the Bard's play, much less that it had any influence upon him, but it is a uniquely crafted representation of the same generic circumstances, with its own terms of motivation and resolution around the central device of switching places in bed with the husband's mistress, getting pregnant, seizing hold of a significant number of material proofs to legitimate the child, and sticking it to the father on a subsequent occasion. Straparola's tale augments the drama, for just when the husband is certain of his wife's infidelity and ready to have her executed by her own clan, she turns the tables. Never has the double standard been so pronounced or the nefarious means of the blood family for maintaining the purity of its line been so patently murderous. Shakespeare does not move into this territory. Moreover, a beloved husband's waywardness drives Isabella to accept not only trickery but the diabolical when heaven refuses to come to her aid. The stakes are high and her determination exemplary, for unlike other heroines in the generic tale, this woman faces the demons of Hell, Astaroth and Farfarello, strips herself to the skin, does not flinch for a moment as she steps into the magic circle and mounts the back of a flying horse to head for unknown parts in search of her husband. Such is her demonstration of the story's declared theme, that women, whether through profound love or deepest hatred of a husband, are capable of extreme and desperate conduct. Despite the curious fantasy component added along the way to a story better known for its novelistic realism, Straparola's interpretation is a worthy and thought-provoking rendition.

One irony in this 'she said' tale is that it is the wife who becomes the guardian of her husband's bloodline when he remains abroad for five years in residence with a Dutch courtesan. We are not told that Argentina has bewitched him, but the extent to which he forgets his wife and loses himself in his passion for a woman who can bear him no legitimate heir, carries thematic overtones. The dynastic factor might have been overlooked were it not so prominent a feature of the early French sources. When, in these, a king abandons his beloved wife precisely because she cannot bear him children, she follows him in one last desperate attempt to get pregnant by exploiting the passion he intends for another, as though the excitement for the mistress might contribute to her own fertility.[1] Such cunning is calculated to arouse moral reservations, given

---

1 The degree to which sex with new partners increases the excitatory effect by comparison with the habituated conditions with familiar partners has been studied in relation to human feelings and emotions. See, for example, Aaron Ben-Ze'ev, *The Subtlety of Emotions* (Cambridge, MA: MIT Press, 2000), pp. 429–33. The quest for sexual variety, driven by hedonic considerations, is potentially adaptive with regard to reproduction alone, but threatens the long-term relationship with a wife and family. The perpetrator of the bed trick, in a counter-measure, reasserts the claims of the stable family environment for the raising of offspring by first masquerading

the other-directedness of the king's imagination concerning his sex partner. In the present application of the bed trick, a wife imposes herself
through right of matrimony upon a husband whose diminished interest
has led to an estrangement simply by usurping the place of a sex partner
more exciting to his thoughts and appetites. The question is whether
such a violation of the husband's emotions will permit eventual reconciliation once the truth is made known; it is one of the classic dilemmas of
this 'problem comedy.'

At the same time, this story is about industry in retrieving something
that is lost, the thematic aegis under which the story is told on the Third
Day of the *Decameron* (III.9). It has always been about the anti-Griselda,
about the woman who does not pine in silence and patience, but who
assumes a proactive role in shaping her destiny – in getting back what
she craves – and who presents her children as seals and guarantors of
her claim to a man who has rejected her. It is a high-risk ploy because,
as in Shakespeare's play, its success depends upon controlling the emotions of the duped party through the careful preparation of a theatrical
finale, as Gabrina warns. In the one story, Griselda's, the wife acquiesces
to the tyranny of the male and is recalled for her submissiveness, while
in the other, the wife enforces the rights that law and unflinching devotion have earned for her. This, of course, is at the root of all discussions
concerning the 'wellness' of such endings, for love cannot be coerced.
What then is left to commend her if not her sheer industry? There are
several answers. There is her *vir*tue, which has been manly in its fortitude,
her craft and skill in deception, and her suffering, which, as an act much
like penitence, earns merit or deserving. The gamble is that such skill,
suffering, and merit, once demonstrated to the wayward partner, will
serve as credits to be ratcheted up to respect, then admiration, and then
something akin to love. Helena, through her gathering of evidence and
sudden resurrection, counts on as much from Bertram, and Lafew's

---

as an excitingly novel sex partner. It is a way of short-circuiting one of the leading
discontents of civilization, which is that the male must forgo sexual promiscuity in
the interests of dynastic continuity. Such matters pertain to the degree to which
sexual excitement is a matter not of physical reality but of the imagination. The
'Coolidge effect,' namely, that sexual desire and familiarity are negatively corre-
lated, is here offset by trickery, but at a considerable risk. The bed trick thereby
becomes an experimental instrument in the management of the family by
addressing the asymmetry between desire and domesticity. Much of the 'deep
meaning' of the story resides in these negotiations.

weeping gives encouragement to think she has succeeded. That is common to all the renditions. Meanwhile, the riddle-solving feature of *All's Well*, the terms of which Helena is invited to meet on a contractual basis, does not figure in Straparola as it does in so many cognate versions otherwise related to the present story. It is a significant omission, for Isabella is not challenged to complete an 'impossible' task by her husband at the time of his departure in order to win him back. Rather, Ortodosio is confronted by the simple fact of a child born to his wife – a wife he then seeks to exterminate for having placed him in an embarrassing and contradictory situation. Hence, much of the psychological energy of their story is taken up with the implicit negotiations between the angered husband and the shamed relatives over who would carry out the deed, each party seeking retaliation while attempting to avoid the jeopardy of the law. The merriment of the banquet preluding Ortodosio's sinister announcement is a macabre bit of counter-theatre to Isabella's intended scenario. The departure from riddles and play is a major bifurcation in the history of the story type and a major separation from the Boccaccio-Shakespeare tradition. This distinction also anticipates the reasoning to follow concerning Straparola's source.

Especially important is Straparola's employment of demons, conjuring, and transvection in actualizing the story, the sum of which may be far greater than the 'unhappy imitation of the second part of the story of Giletta di Narbone told in the *Decameron*' for which this story has often been taken, and as such has reaped this condemnation by Marc Landau.[2] Devils were believed in as efficient agents in the material world who get things done, usually at the cost of the soul of their beneficiaries. Isabella takes that risk to accomplish what she later styles a miracle and the work of angels. That white lie is a nice touch, but it establishes the miraculous either way, and where the act is divine, the moral lien is all the greater. She grants her achievement to the intervention of angels, making her reunion the work of Providence. It is a smart move. Straparola's novel solution for locating the missing spouse and conveying the wife to his bed incognito may also be a reference to the practices of urban witches, according to Giuseppe Bonomo.[3] It provides a conjuring scene based on

---

2 *Beiträge zur Geschichte der italianischen Novelle* (Vienna: n.p., 1875), p. 128.

3 'Motivi magico-stregonici in una novella dello Straparola,' *Rassegna della letteratura italiana* 62 (1958), pp. 365–9. Bonomo holds that hints of magic were already slightly intimated in the mood of Boccaccio's tale, and that given the many fifteenth-century resources concerning witches, the modification was a natural

the generic procedures involving circles and signs, incantations, and secrecy, although it hardly pretends to any form of documentary originality. For the story to function, even so generic a representation demands a level of credence on the part of readers and characters alike. Convention demands that we accept devils, transvection, and metamorphosis as real because they are a part of the story's phenomenal world, much as Ortodosio is compelled to believe in his wife's presence in Flanders as a precondition to her escape from a death sentence. The story is thus a special form of science (fiction) that simultaneously, in the contemporary world of inquisitors and witch tribunals, represents tangible realities in the real world.

Stories built around the bed-trick motif are very old, but they never lost favour. The Boccaccio-Shakespeare corridor alluded to above provides one of the best known examples. Straparola's, by contrast, has no king seeking to enforce a marriage and no 'faint hope' clause in the form of a written dare to the estranged wife to fulfil seemingly impossible conditions. Isabella is an abandoned wife, but there is no indication that she was initially an unwanted wife. The Giletta-Helena (*Decameron* III.9 and *All's Well That Ends Well*) tradition, moreover, entails bartering and bargaining with a prospective mistress and her mother for access to the bed, whereas, by magic, Isabella simply becomes Argentina, while the courtesan is made old, ugly, and invisible and has no active part in the negotiations. Helena both wins and loses points for staging her own death and resurrection, a ploy that, for many readers, holds adverse connotations.

---

development, although this goes entirely against the counter-movement in which folk tales were turned into contemporary stories in local settings about real people by the *novellieri*, as though they were 'news.' This may have been a concerted effort on Straparola's part to align the ethos of this story with the supernatural agencies that characterize, in particular, the first twenty-five tales – those published in the first volume in 1550. Bonomo's principal point is that this story is a further testimonial to the interest in witches in Italy in the second half of the sixteenth century (p. 369). But his thesis gets the best of him when he proposes that Straparola's tale, by allowing the heroine to succeed through conjuring and diabolical transvection, becomes 'uno stumento di propaganda della 'religione del diavolo'' (an instrument of propaganda for the religion of the devil, p. 369). Interdictions against necromancy did not stop the circulation of Faustus stories in Germany in both Protestant and Catholic circles, a moral tale to be sure that nevertheless represented conjuring and black magic, in turn brought to the English stage by Christopher Marlowe in his *Doctor Faustus*. But it is an old debate, whether the representation of any sort of evil practice is not a form of propaganda. If so, literature can only deal in 'safe' and 'permitted' evils.

Isabella, upon her return, is less empowered and far more vulnerable, hardly aware that her very life is in the balance. Her situation is more precarious, despite her employment of demonic powers, than that of her Shakespearean counterpart. These differences are the beginning of an argument concerning the story's provenance.

Boccaccio's *Decameron* is traditionally cited as the source of the present tale, but if Straparola is working as a literary imitator plying the art of remaking, or *rifacimento*, he does so in a remarkably eccentric way. The departure from Boccaccio's social narrative through the addition of supernatural agents and the restructuring of the story in the image of a folk tale is conceivably his literary invention, but more plausibly, that which resembles a folk tale is far more easily accounted for as a product of oral culture. That assessment depends largely upon the origins of the supernatural elements and the demonstrated existence of structurally similar tales. In general, the design of the narrative appears to be the result of the retention and shedding of materials typical of the folk tale in accordance with the habits of memory in the processing of paradigmatic structures and expendable or variable details. This would account for the diagrammatic and formulaic units of plot and characterization. Nevertheless, a clashing literary feature is the witch, Gabrina, who is certain to have been inspired by the old crone in Ariosto's *Orlando furioso* – the Gabrina driven away by Orlando (12.92), who takes on Zerbin as her escort only to have him condemned for murder (23.39), and who is hanged by Odoric (24.45).[4] If the witch comes from Ariosto, the combination of Astaroth and Farfarello surely derives from Pulci's *Morgante* (canto 25), in which Malagigi calls on Astaroth, as in the present story, to tell him in which country Rinaldo and Ricciardetto are to be found, after which the two devils serve as a mode of transportation to Roncesvalles.[5] Their interpolation into the present story is very likely Straparola's principal contribution to its presentation. But they need not be taken as additions to a reworking of Boccaccio. The several antecedent literary tales and subsequent folk tales closer in design to Straparola argue, instead, for yet another narrative tradition disseminated through

---

4 Ludovico Ariosto, *Orlando furioso*, trans. Guido Waldman (Oxford: Oxford University Press, 1974), pp. 271, 287.

5 Luigi Pulci, *Il Morgante*, ed. George Benson Weston (Bari: Laterza & Figli, 1930), vol. II, pp. 274*ff.* Farfarello originates in the *Inferno* of Dante, one of the thirteen Malebranche who claw evil businessmen trying to escape the pitch of the Fifth Bolgia.

popular storytelling. For a start, several Eastern tales have come to light that possess all the narrative parts of the present work. Their existence challenges us again to imagine a continuous evolution over centuries of a story type originating in the East, one that provided a series of templates from which writers (including Boccaccio) might take inspiration as it pursued its own destiny within the oral culture. Arguably, the survival of that tradition during the Renaissance likewise supplied Straparola with a version closely resembling the one he recorded in the *Notti*. His story, in effect, represents the earliest rendition of a divergent stream of stories within the tradition that distinguish it from the tale taken up by Boccaccio, making the present tale a comparative cousin to the better-known versions.

As stated at the outset, bed-trick stories have an intrinsic interest as fantasy and psychodrama and they take on a kaleidoscopic range of meanings in relation to the quality and condition of the participants and their motivations, their respective degrees of sinning and being sinned against, and the levels of determination and cunning of the actors. The trick need not always require negotiations between a wife and a mistress, but may simply entail the donning of a disguise that enables a wife to seduce her own husband. This is true of most of the Eastern renditions, versions of which were clearly known in the West by the twelfth century. Moreover, they too, in their later literary versions, often reflect the kinds of deterioration or reconfiguration that come about through long phases of oral transmission. One such is 'The Clever Wife, included by Maive Stokes in her *Indian Fairy Tales*.[6] One day, this

---

6 (London: Ellis and White, 1880), no. 28, pp. 216*ff*. Behind this story is a substantial tradition of Eastern tales involving a wife abandoned by her husband, who then meets up with him without being recognized and who, in the end, brings about reconciliation by producing a ring or some token of her secret presence. An important prototype appears in Dandin's *Dasa Kumera charita or The Adventures of Ten Princes* (eleventh century), ed. H.H. Wilson (London: Society for the Publication of Oriental Texts, 1846). This reappeared as *Hindoo Tales or the Adventures of Ten Princes*, trans. Philip Whittington Jacob (London: Strahan and Co., 1873), pp. 274–82. The tale resolves the moral dilemma of the bed trick by proposing that 'love is only imagination' precisely because a man may fall in love with a princess who is his first wife in disguise, live with her in bliss for many years, and even tell the world that she *is* his first wife to avoid scandal. The wife's trouble begins on her wedding day, as it does for Helena, because her husband takes a sudden unaccountable dislike for her. She too, as in the present story, seeks the counsel of an old woman mendicant, hoping for a love charm. Her strategy is to pass herself off as the daughter of a rich neighbour by using the old lady as a go-between. Meanwhile, the wife and the

domineering wife's husband announces that he has business to carry out that would keep him away for a year. Semi-jokingly in parting he declares, in mockery of her self-proclaimed sufficiency, that during his absence she can build a well and get him a son, too, if she is so damned clever. It takes two to get children, and he knows where he'll be. The well turns out to be a matter of money, which she gets through trickery, and the child is a matter of finding her husband, getting up a disguise, and seducing him. This story has the riddle design, which may therefore be deemed a primitive feature of the type and hence shed by Straparola's source branch. The husband falls for her cowherd daughter's get-up and even marries her – how embarrassing will that be? After three months he abandons her to return home, while his new wife gets a hat and a picture and then races him back to become his old wife. When he arrives, he isn't too happy about the child, but when she produces the picture and the hat, shows him the new well to boot, and makes no mention of his infidelities, that's as 'well' as it gets, in reference to Shakespeare's title. The story doesn't require bloody-minded kin to settle the affront. Once again East apparently meets West in the generation of a story tradition, the direction of influence presumably travelling with the sun, for it is indubitably the same story. The hesitation is due only to its late date and the chance of Western contamination.

A more complex version appears among tales from the Turks – complex because it weaves together a variety of causes and motifs that usually appear singly, as though it were a compound résumé of many versions.[7] A prince is so impressed by the cleverness of his vezir's twelve-year-old daughter that he marries her. But it was to be a battle of wits between them of a kind reflected in the Western versions in which an estranged husband refuses to take his wife back, no matter how clever she is, until she apologizes – which she always refuses to do. Here is an entirely new yet familiar construction put upon the separation – rivalry for control

---

woman next door arrange matters between them so that she can use the other's garden as a rendezvous. There, love ensues and they elope. The bed trick lasts, in fact, for as long as the husband loves and is deceived, having never met the girl next door. For Dandin in French, see Hippolyte Fauche, *Tétrade, ou drame, hymne, roman et poème traduits pour la première fois du Sanskrit en français*, 3 vols. (Paris: A. Durand, 1861–3), vol. II, p. 220.

7 'Die kluge Wesirs-Tochter' (The clever vezier's daughter) in *Proben der Volkslitteratur der nördlichen türkischen Stämme*, ed. Vasilij Vasilevic Radloff (St Petersburg: Kaiserliche Akademie der Wissenschaften, Eggers & Schmitzdorff, 1866), vol. VI, pp. 191–8.

within the marriage, the husband outclassed by his wife's perpetual
stratagems. The girl, at her tender age, refused to consummate the marriage until the prince supplied her with a white elephant and a man who
had never known sorrow. Because, after three years, the prince still
couldn't find such a man, he left for the hunt, saying to her, essentially,
'If you're so smart, fill up the locked chest with money without breaking
the seal (the equivalent of digging a well), find horses that will produce
a foal identical to my black stallion, then give birth to a child who is sent
to me on the horse.' Here is riddle for riddle. But he isn't gone long
before the wife goes after him in male attire, attracts his attention, becomes a friend, plays gambling games, beats him at checkers, wins the
necessary horse, then intentionally loses a wager over supplying a bed
partner. This loss allows her to change from male companion to slave-girl
sex object, who so takes the prince's fancy that he sleeps with her until
she puts an end to it by boxing him on the ear – the eternal shrew that
she was. This story inaugurates or retains the model for her becoming
her husband's valet-de-chambre or squire in certain of the medieval
romances, as well as the gambling games by which the husband loses his
land in betting on his wife's chastity, which is falsely impugned by a villain, leading to their estrangement. In the Turkish tale, the husband is
away for nine years, during which time their early-begotten child grows
up. The riddle conditions are still to be met as the child rides to meet
his father on the horse, the wife shows the filled chest, and she tells her
marvellous story. This prince is at last reconciled to her intelligence and
industry, admires the well-schooled child that he acknowledges as his
own, and now cherishes this wife above all his others. It is the riddle
structure that dominates in an economy of valued cunning, along with
the episodes of the wife as male companion. Wives who intellectually
dominate their husbands wear scissors as well as trousers, and it is her
fantasy to be a slave girl to restore the sensuality, even while she desires
to reign over the harem. That dimension of the bed trick is worth record-
ing for there are subtle truths therein concerning the dynamics of the
couple.[8] This story, moreover, is rather compelling evidence for its wide
circulation in the oriental world.

---

8 Just how ancient this tale may be is suggested by a cognate version in the
  Bragtha-Magus Saga, which was circulating in Iceland by the thirteenth century;
  it was based on materials borrowed from the French *trouvères*. Hlothver, king of
  Saxland, is to marry Ermenga, but when he arrives to fetch her, she meets him with
  her face painted and then takes him a roasted chicken to divide up between her

Coming to the Occident, the four following versions from the twelfth, thirteenth, fourteenth, and fifteenth centuries respectively may be considered paradigmatic. Gabriel Dupréau, reading in the Chronicles of the Kings of Aragon, tells the putatively historical legend of King Pedro II, who did not fancy his queen at all and couldn't perform with her, even though she wasn't bad looking, yet maintained his potency in his relations with many other women.[9] The matter was serious because he had not supplied the kingdom with an heir. Through the help of a chamberlain, the queen negotiates with one of the king's mistresses to be placed secretly in his company. When the morning approaches, however, and the king tells her for his honour's sake to retire, his wife declares herself and says she isn't about to leave before reliable witnesses are called in to testify that she had spent the night with him. That way, if she became pregnant there would be no question concerning the child's legitimacy. When the king saw 'l'honneste tromperie' (the honourable trickery) of his wife, he was pleased, called in the witnesses, and abstained from

---

father and two brothers. This riddle he treats as an insult and when he is later off to the wars, he sets one for his wife that she has three years to accomplish: build a castle as fine as her father's, procure a horse, sword, and hawk as fine as his own, and produce a legitimate son. She then sets up an elaborate ruse with the help of her kin. Pretending to be a captive maiden in the clutches of Jarl Iring, she calls upon Hlothver to free her. When the king sends for Iring, she plays that role too and promises to give up the girl for his stallion, sword, and hawk. She then changes back to women's clothes to spend three nights with the king, coming away with his ring. Returning to Saxland, she gives birth to a son and awaits the day of reckoning. This is a tale of spousal competition in which the king is compelled to capitulate. It shows kinship with several others in the bed-trick family. Gunnlaugur Thordarsson, *Bragtha-Magus Saga* (Kaupmannahöfn [Copenhagen]: Utgefandi, Pall Sveinsson, 1858). There is another entitled 'Ehestand, Tod und Hochzeit' (Marriage, death and wedding) in which a husband hates his wife and wishes her dead. An old woman counselling the wife suggests she feign her death and burial while hiding out with the old lady. Later, when she is no longer recognized, the old woman arranges to have her remarried to her own husband. Friedrich Heinrich von der Hagen, *Gesammtabenteuer*, 3 vols. (Stuttgart: Cotta, 1850), vol. II, p. 171.

9 *Histoire de l'estat et succes de l'Église dressée en forme de chronique générale et universelle … depuis la nativité de Jésus-Christ jusques en l'an 1580* (Paris: J. Kerver, 1583), 'l'an 1196,' pp. 508v–9r. The story of Pedro de Aragon becomes the substance of the *Romance del engaño que usó la reina doña Maria de Aragon para qué el rey don Pedro su marido durmiesse con ella* (Romance of the trick used by the lady Maria de Aragon by which the king, Don Pedro her husband, was brought to sleep with her), in Ferdinand Wolf, *Über eine Sammlung spanischer Romanzen in Fliegenden Blättern* (Vienna: Braumüller, 1850), p. 52.

further extramarital affairs. The story is a tale of dynastic continuity by subterfuge, managing wayward male desire by re-exciting the king. Who can say whether history has been rewritten according to fiction, or whether through life at court a new form of fiction was born. To be sure, there are no framing circumstances or riddles to solve, but the bed trick is complete, the exchange is a negotiated one, and at the centre is a motivated and industrious queen. History is apparently rewritten here in the guise of an oriental tale.

Among the stories originating in thirteenth-century France is the romance of *Le Roi Flore et la belle Jehanne*.[10] Paradoxically, for our purposes, the wife does not trick her husband sexually, but this story provides the narrative substance from which *Le roman du Compte d'Artois* emerged two centuries later, and which is thought to have been derived from a fourteenth-century manuscript that served Boccaccio as his source for 'The Tale of Giletta of Narbona.' These are troubled questions and the editor of the romance has largely exploded such claims from the perspective of the origins of the *Compte d'Artois*. More safely, it can be said that the intervening two centuries between *Le Roi Flore* and *Le Compte d'Artois* allowed for the maturation of the motifs characterizing the earlier story that eventually came to include the sexual encounter between a husband and his wife in disguise in the latter work. *Le Roi Flore* features two stories in parallel. The king is married to the beautiful but infertile daughter of the prince of Brabant. This woman is pious, loves God and the Church, and the Holy Spirit is in her. He goes off to tournaments and travels in foreign lands, but the good queen does not follow him. Meanwhile, the twelve-year-old Jehanne is married to Robin or Robert the squire. Robert keeps his vow to leave his marriage unconsummated until he completes a pilgrimage, but not without making a bet over the incorruptibility of his wife with the traitorous knight, Raoul, wagering land for land. Faithful she was, even when an old crone betrays her to the villain, but while she is scratching his face and kicking out his teeth, he manages to get a glimpse of the birthmarks near her privy parts that become the proof of her dishonour. When her husband returns and her case is heard before the king's tribunal, her husband loses his land, scorns his calumniated wife, and sets off to fight in the tournaments. Jehanne is so discredited that she has no choice but to disappear disguised as a boy and hope to

---

10 *Nouvelles françois en prose du XIIe siècle*, ed. Louis Émile Moland and C. Héricault (Paris: P. Jannet, 1856), pp. 85–157.

meet her husband along the way to become his squire, much as Viola enters the service of Orsino. Robert and Jehan (the male equivalent of her name) go through a series of privations, sell their horses, settle down near Marseille to become bakers and hostel owners and slowly recover their losses as the best of male friends. Raoul ends up in their auberge, Jehanne recognizes the scar she left on his face, and before he leaves to visit the Holy Sepulchre in penitence for his sins he entrusts them with all his land. The two then return to their place of origin and Robert, in possession of the truth, sends out a missing-persons report on his calumniated wife. Jehan then disappears. Raoul meanwhile returns reclaiming his land, but is challenged by Robert, who has subsequently learned of his treachery. The fight confirms the side of right, Jehanne is discovered by her father, the lovers are united, then Robert dies, Jehanne is taken by King Flore as his third queen, and she bears him children. It is a shaggy tale insofar as key features are divided between the two parts. The infertile queen, instead of resorting to the bed trick, is replaced by a fertile heroine, while the accused wife follows her husband in disguise through years of exile in expiation for a deed she did not commit.

The template tale from the fourteenth century must be Giovanni Boccaccio's story of Giletta (*Decameron* III.9), who, for curing the king's fistula, wins Beltramo in marriage against his will. He scorns her, leaves for Florence, and takes a mistress. The outline of the story is too well known to merit rehearsal, if not from Boccaccio, then from Shakespeare's adaptation of it in *All's Well That Ends Well*. He had been her childhood flame and when he went off to live at court in Paris, she was wild with worry that he would marry someone else, meanwhile rejecting many eligible suitors of her own; she had set her cap. Better than her Shakespearean counterpart, Giletta comes up with twins from her few nights' stand with her husband. She completes his parting conditions – the ring and the child – both of which are remembered as tangible tokens in Straparola, but without the inaugural dare. She, like the offended males in the French versions, promises to go on a pilgrimage from which she would not return, which is reduced to Isabella's piety in the present story, 'Wife, Courtesan, and Witch.' Back in Roussillon, Giletta delivers her boys, who look like their father, and she confronts Beltramo on a feast day with sons, ring, and a good explanation in which his honour is conflated with his shame. According to the story, she had overcome his pride and prejudice and had demonstrated her own admirable mettle, which brought Beltramo back to the marriage with his full consent. Fortunately, we can leave aside all the wrangling over Boccaccio and Shakespeare compared, a polemic that is epitomized on the one side by Harold S. Wilson's view that Boccaccio's effort was 'a folk tale by a master of rapid narrative with the simplicity and emphasis upon action to the disregard of motivation or psychological probability that is characteristic of the kind,' and on the other by Howard Cole's more positive appraisal of Boccaccio's ingenious 'mischief' in the creation of Giletta. In Mariella Cavalchini's conciliatory approach, she sees 'due versioni *ugualmente geniali* di un medisimo tema' (two equally ingenious versions on a single theme).[11] Cole relies on the contextualizing subtleties gained through an examination of all the stories and their tellers of the *Decameron*'s Third Day to show how many more insights are provided by each individual story, the final effect of which is merely to add nuance to the roles played by each partner in this representation of the gender wars. What is germane to our purposes is Boccaccio's novelistic elaboration of an ancient tale belonging to the generic type that received modification in the direction of a wonder tale either before or when it fell into Straparola's hands.

The story later evolved from the wife in disguise pursuing and seducing her own husband to the wife of an enforced marriage pursuing her husband to replace a mistress.[12] In the fifteenth century there is a new

---

11 Harold S. Wilson, 'Dramatic Emphasis in *All's Well That Ends Well*,' *HLQ* 13 (1950), pp. 222–40; Howard Cole, 'Dramatic Interplay in the *Decameron*: Boccaccio, Neifile, and Giletta di Nerbona,' in *The All's Well Story from Boccaccio to Shakespeare* (Urbana: University of Illinois Press, 1981), pp. 12–32; Mariella Cavalchini, 'Giletta-Helena: Uno studio comparativo,' *Italica* 40 (1963), pp. 320–3.

12 This situation is brilliantly deployed by Giovan Maria Cecchi in his *L'assiuolo* (The horned owl), in which two students in love with the same woman discover that her older and obstreperously jealous husband is nevertheless in love with Madonna Anfrosina. So one of the students arranges to have him sent to the Madonna's house under false expectations, there to be locked out in the cold. Madonna Oretta, his wife, meanwhile, is informed of the old man's intentions and is led into the bed trick arrangement with Madonna Anfrosina to teach her husband a lesson. But she is tricked instead, for the person who comes to her in the dark as her husband is the young student, who enjoys her and endures the berating intended for her husband before revealing his identity and hanging on to her by force until she consents to his love. Cecchi claims in his prologue to have taken this story from a recent event in Florence, but the models of *Les cent nouvelles nouvelles* and Poggio, described below, may prove to be a bit too close to leave Cecchi entirely in the comfort of his conviction. Trans. by Konrad Eisenbichler in *Italian Comedy: The Italian Masters*, ed. Donald Beecher (Toronto: University of Toronto Press, 2009), vol. II, pp. 222–98.

twist in which the trickster wife, in substituting the mistress, is also pandered by her husband. That cynical turn of events, in the spirit of the *fabliaux*, or the trickster tricked, was an idea waiting to be grafted upon the ancient tale as a narrative opportunity. In *Les cent nouvelles nouvelles*, from the mid-fifteenth century, the writer tells of a noble knight in love with his wife's first lady-in-waiting, who refuses him valiantly.[13] When the wife gets wind of it, she tells her to accept and that she would take her place. Meanwhile, a friend comes visiting who expresses an interest in finding a village girl for a bit of night fun. The lord of the household offers a share in his mistress after the first round, during which he culminates some three or four bouts with the lady before ceding the bed. The wife unwittingly then takes on the friend and the next morning accosts her husband with the news that in the night she had stolen from him what was hers by right. In reckoning up the tricks and realizing his error, the husband faced the choice of revealing the double dealing to his wife, identifying the lady to his friend, or, more plausibly, keeping his folly as a dark personal secret. As may be seen, all these stories share in a common identity, but the current tale is a departure now in the direction of the mutual trickery tales and double bed crossings that lead to the *ménage à quatre* sexual utopias explored in the commentery to VI.1, 'The Two Friends Who Held Their Wives in Common.'

The two following works are essential to an understanding of the bed trick as it was employed in the romances of medieval France. There are many complex questions regarding these works in need of more erudition than can be offered here regarding their precise dates, provenances, and cross-fertilizations. The first is *Gérard de Nevers*, which is the prose version of the *Roman de la Violette*; it is from the second half of the fifteenth century, as far as I can make out from reading Lawrence F.H. Lowe's study of the work, but he mentions a verse version of the story in

---

13 'Bawd for His Wife' in *The Hundred Tales*, trans. Rossell Hope Robbins (New York: Crown Publishers, 1960), no. 9, pp. 35–8. See also *Les cent nouvelles nouvelles*, ed. Roger Dubuis (Lyons: Presses universitaires de Lyon, 1991), no. 9, pp. 60–3. A most similar story is told by Philippe de Vigneulles in his *Cent nouvelles nouvelles*, ed. Charles H. Livingston (Geneva: Droz, 1972), no. 39, pp. 179–82. The master desires the servant, who tells her mistress, who takes her servant's place in bed, then berates her roaming husband in the harshest of terms, to which he replied, 'By my faith, my prick is smarter than I am because he knew you on the first thrust and that's why he wouldn't stay up, but I didn't have a clue who you were.'

Picard dialect dating to 1284.[14] In this delicate and expressive work, attributed to Girbert de Montreuil, there is to be found the same story that constitutes *Le Roi Flore et la belle Jehanne*. Liziars, conte de Forés et de Beaugoloys, makes the same wager with Gérard over his beloved Eruyant's fidelity, bringing the girl to grief.[15] Liziars had discovered by fraud the violet mark on her right breast which he claimed to have seen while sleeping with her skin to skin. Exiled, sans terre, he takes the girl with him, intending to behead her in the Forest of Orleans, but a serpent monster comes to her rescue. She is found and attempted by the Duc de Metz while Gérard rides all over northern and central France pursuing his semi-historical exploits. He plays the jongleur at the court of Liziars and discovers the truth. When Melyatir frames Euryant for the murder of Ismaine, Gérard has two scores to settle on her behalf upon his return. But at no point, in spite of constant expectation, does she join her estranged husband on the road, nor does she have a role in frustrating the designs of the several smitten women Gérard must deal with along the way. This story merely holds the promise that is realized by a version of the famous trick in the anonymous *Roman du Compte d'Artois*, dating to the mid-fifteenth century (ca. 1453–67). The abandoned wife finds her husband in Spain and enters his service as Philipot, gains his confidence, and thereby learns of his love for the daughter of the king of Castile. She, like Viola in *Twelfth Night*, is even sent as a proxy wooer. But after the arrangements are made, she takes the place of the princess, gets pregnant, and receives as her reward for faithful service as Philipot the diamond and the horse that together fulfil the 'impossible' conditions for reconciliation set by her husband before his departure, conditions of a kind familiar from *All's Well That Ends Well*. The denouement follows in the reunion of husband, wife, and child. This work, once thought to have been Boccaccio's source, was also thought to have originated in a French verse source dating from 1338–60. With that prospect now called into doubt, and with the first translation of Boccaccio into French in 1414 by Laurent de Premierfait, it would appear

---

14 *Gérard de Nevers: A Study of the Prose Version of the Roman de la Violette* (Princeton: Princeton University Press, 1923), p. 18.

15 *Gérard de Nevers: Prose Version of the Roman de la Violette*, ed. Lawrence F.H. Lowe (Princeton: Princeton University Press, 1928; reprint, New York: Kraus Reprints, 1965). See also Gerbert de Montreuil, *Le roman de la violette ou de Gerart de Nevers*, ed. Douglas Labaree Buffum (Paris: Champion, 1928).

that the influence may have run in reverse direction from Boccaccio to the French romance.[16]

Apart from the famous mining of Boccaccio by Shakespeare, whether directly or through the interpretative translation by William Painter in *The Palace of Pleasure*, perhaps the imitation of *Decameron* III.9 the most worthy of mention is the *Virginia* of Bernardo Accolti, if not written for, at least performed for the wedding of Antonio Spannocchi of Siena in 1494.[17] Virginia, based directly on Boccaccio's Giletta, is even more conniving and crafty in exploiting her wiles in tracking down her man, and in her use of religion to disguise her own appetites and cravings 'con pietoso inganno.' As a daughter of Salerno, famous for its ancient school of medicine, she carries the credentials to heal Alphonso, while in setting her sights on the Prince of Salerno she is even more ambitious and calculating than her counterparts.

Poggio Bracciolini in his *Facetiae* tells the same tale recounted in the *Cent nouvelles nouvelles*, this time of a married man having an adventure with a servant girl. The wife offers to take her place, whom the husband enjoys before passing her on to one of his apprentices. When his wife confronts him and mentions the number of bouts, of which the husband could have no doubts, he can only blame himself and suffer his disgrace in silence.[18] Mention may be made in passing of the story by Masuccio

---

16   *Le roman du Compte d'Artois: 'Roman' anonyme du XVe siècle* has been recently edited in
    modernized French by Roger Dubois (Paris: Champion, 2007). Dubois allows that
    Boccaccio's story of 'Giletta' may well have been an influence on the design of this
    amateur work written for the Burgundian court of Philippe le Bon, whereas
    Jean-Charles Seigneuret, editor of *Le roman du Compte d'Artois* (Geneva: Droz, 1966),
    is sceptical of the Boccaccian associations. However that debate is resolved, this
    romance remains in the tradition of the Turkish tale described above, along with its
    many cognate versions, in which a scorned wife, abandoned at home, is presented
    with a departing wager by her wanderlust husband, in this instance to get herself
    pregnant by him, and to receive from his own hand his favourite horse and his
    diamond ring. That fundamental story may have been in circulation as part of the
    oral culture. There was also a nineteenth-century edition of *Le livre du très*
    chevalereux comte d'Artois et de sa femme, ed. J. Barrois (Paris: Techener, 1837).
17   *The Palace of Pleasure*, trans. William Painter, ed. Joseph Jacobs, 3 vols. (London:
    David Nutt, 1890; reprint, New York: Dover, 1966), no. 38, vol. I, pp. 171-9. Accolti,
    La Virginia (Florence: [n.p.], 1514); ed. Marina Calore (Bologna: Arnaldo Forni,
    1983).
18   'Of an English Dyer who had an Adventure with his Wife' in the *Facetiae of Poggio*,
    trans. Edward Storer (London: George Routledge, 1928), no. 96, pp. 142–3. Jean de
    la Fontaine provides a spirited version of the story in 'The Quid Pro Quo or the

of Salerno in which the miller and the cobbler, friends from childhood, end up with their wives and goods in common as the best solution to a terrible mistake. When one falls in love with the wife of the other, the women confer and come up with the bed trick as the best solution. The wives make the switch, but the miller's early arrival home interrupts the cobbler's plan, so that each returns to his own house to make love in the dark, each to the other's wife. When the miller, in complete innocence, is awakened to a tongue lashing by the cobbler's wife, the error comes out, thus inducing the ménage à quatre as the best of all solutions.[19]

Mistakes,' *Tales and Novels in Verse*, 2 vols. (London: Society of English Bibliophilists, ca. 1900), V.8, vol. II, pp. 215–22. A young aristocrat has eyes for his wife's maidservant, who tells her mistress. The exchange is arranged between the two women, but a young friend of the master comes to town, they chat, the friend offers to pay half, and they toss dice to see who goes first. Both husband and wife are aware of the situation in the end, but amidst a great deal of speculative moralizing they all keep silence given the circumstances, and the author teases the reader about how he or she would have handled the same situation. (This edition is possibly the same as that published in Paris in 1884, trans. Charles Eisen.) An English play on a similar theme is James Shirley's *The Gamester*, in the tradition of *Le meunier d'Aleus* as well, which deals with Mr. Wilding's wooing of Penelope, who is an honest girl and reports all to her mistress, Mrs. Wilding. The women decide to exchange places, but meanwhile, Mr Wilding decides to pay off his debt to his friend Hazard by offering to him the joys of the rendezvous – the bed trick that backfires for both husband and wife. James Shirley, *The Gamester* (London: John Norton, 1637); the work was rewritten by Charles Johnson in the eighteenth century as *The Wife's Relief, or, The Husband's Cure* (London: J. & R. Tonson, 1736).

19 Shakespeare's *All's Well That Ends Well* has been intentionally passed over for summarization because the plot is so well known and for our purposes does not vary significantly from its source in Boccaccio. These two stories, however, are not the only instances of the bed trick in the works of either author. In *Decameron* III.6, Boccaccio tells the story of Ricciardo Minutolo, who was in love with the wife of Messer Fighinolfi. His ploy was to set up a misguided bed trick by telling the jealous wife that her husband was in love with his own wife and had made a rendezvous with her in the bathhouse. By degrees the jealous wife comes to the idea of the exchange. Thinking to meet her husband, she in fact finds herself in a dark room with Ricciardo, who takes his pleasure, after which the lady goes into a tirade against her husband until Ricciardo finally identifies himself and she is prevailed upon to keep silence. An even stranger employment of the ruse occurs in *The Two Noble Kinsmen*, jointly written by Shakespeare and John Fletcher. It is Chaucer's 'Knight's Tale' enlarged, in which the Jailor's daughter is so in love with Palamon that she is like to die of her love melancholy. The disease once diagnosed, the doctor recommends therapeutic coitus, considered among physicians a sovereign cure of the condition, thus arranging, with the father's anxious complicity, that she

Two stories by Pietro Fortini in his *Giornate delle novelle dei novizi* appear to divide up the respective features of Straparola's story. In his second, an Italian from Siena falls in love with a Flemish courtesan in Venice, learns her language, forgets his own family and country, and in the end is brought to shame, but not through the clever ruses or usurpation of the bed by his own wife. In Novella 47, however, the wife is altogether more proactive in reclaiming her wayward husband. A Sienese gentleman takes a fancy to a widow, and when his wife finds out she goes to the widow's house, enters into an agreement with her and her brothers, performs in a bed-trick arrangement, and later confronts her man to his shame. This requires no more than might have been suggested by Boccaccio in his *Decameron* III.4, or by Sacchetti in his *Trecentonovelle*, no. 206. But the exhibition of a jewel taken from the husband as proof of their coupling aligns the story more closely to Boccaccio III.9 and ostensibly to Straparola. There is a very particular description of the old lover preening himself in the street like a youth of twenty. The widow imposes conditions that prevent the wayward husband from seeing his own wife in the room. She arranges for the exchange of the ring and her brothers are involved in setting up the old man's arrival, meanwhile barely able to contain their laughter. With Fortini, not only is embarrassing evidence produced once the protagonist is back at his own house, but he must confess his entire exploit to his confessor.[20] That Fortini relied upon Boccaccio or Straparola, or an intermediary (folk) source, is difficult to demonstrate. Clearly the story type was in circulation, its various parts in fluid arrangement. Again, the departures from the principal literary sources may strengthen the theory of an extensive diffusion of the story type in the popular culture.

In a somewhat different vein yet still within the generic tradition of the Eastern tale, Basile elaborates a story based simply on temperamental incompatibility in 'La sappia Liccarda' (Liccarda smart and clever).[21]

---

should be put to bed with a rejected suitor, informing the girl meanwhile that she would embrace her Palamon. The girl is thus cured by the trick as a form of medical subterfuge. Ed. G.R. Proudfoot (London: Edward Arnold, 1970), especially V.ii, pp. 111–18.

20 Ed. Adriana Mauriello (Rome: Salerno, 1988), vol. I, pp. 47–57 and vol. II, pp. 825–39.

21 'The Wise Woman' in the *Pentamerone*, trans. Sir Richard Burton (New York: Boni & Liveright, 1927), V.6, pp. 426–30. A further early Italian version appears in Giovanni Sagredo, *L'Arcadia in Brenta, ovvero la malinconia sbandita* (Venice, 1667); ed. Quinto Marini (Rome: Salerno, 2004). Reinhold Köhler studies many further

This is a delightful set of variants that make light of the entire situation. The king has a blockhead son who refuses to learn anything, so he sends him to be brought up with the quick-witted daughter of a baroness who by the age of thirteen was already known as 'Sapia.' When Sapia, in a snit over his dullness, boxes him across the ear, he determines to master his lessons and become wise, but he never forgets the indignity. So to settle scores, he marries her merely to abuse her, locking her up and starving her in expectation of a full apology. But the girl is too stiff-necked to give in and so the contest is prolonged to absurd lengths. When she reproaches him for his former ignorance, his anger increases. He therefore leaves without her to claim his crown, but the baroness equips her with a coach and fine clothes and sends her ahead. When the new king sees her, he courts her as another, gets her pregnant, and gives her a necklace. Upon his return, he expects Sapia to be dead, but she is in health, with a son, and sassier than ever, calling him an ass. Leaving a second time, she repeats the same ruse, and a third time as well, until the family grows to two sons and a daughter. Basile is having a good time. Then the baroness reports her daughter to be dead and buried, but hides her at home. A new marriage is then arranged for the king and at the most dramatic moment Sapia arrives with all three progeny in tow, along with the jewels, telling him not to rob the children of their rights. The king has to admit to her artful tenacity and so makes his peace with her, even though he never gets his apology. The very existence of this tale is of considerable historical importance, for it supplies further corroboration of the circulation of the story type already familiar from the Eastern sources outlined above, both Indian and Turkish. The bed trick, the implicit departing challenges, the struggle for dominance, the dramatic denouement orchestrated in advance by the triumphant wife, and the securing of the husband to domestic ends – all features in common with Boccaccio and Straparola – testify to a generic story type that had been subdivided into variant forms within the oral tradition. Moreover, it remains closer than the others to the Eastern type of the sassy wife and the fleeing husband who never gets his apology, a type still in circulation among the folk three centuries later when it was independently collected in Sicily by Laura Gonzenbach and Giuseppe Pitrè.

---

analogues pertaining to Boccaccio's 'Giletta of Narbonne' on a geographical scale reaching from Norway to the Valley of the Nile, and includes many further references, in *Kleinere Schriften zur erzählenden Dichtung des Mittelalters*, ed. Johannes Bolte (Berlin: Feiber, 1900), vol. II, pp. 650*ff.*

Sapia is now Sorfarina, who also gives a slap to the man she eventually marries and refuses till the last moment to offer an apology. Her husband travels to Rome and Naples by sea, but she always precedes him on land. In Genoa he threatens to take another bride and Sorfarina in disguise says, 'Take her.' That evening she wishes for her three children and they appear, and then for a gown, which is delivered to her in time for the ball. The prince is trapped and has to send his new bride away, but he doesn't get his apology until he thought he had killed her. This is a story not only about the cunning and tenacity of women in keeping the fathers of their children under their control, but about their stubbornness.[22] With that, the survey comes to an end. All such tales contribute to a sense of yet another story tradition originating in the East that remained in continuous transmission in the oral culture from the Middle Ages down to modern times, one distinct version of which Straparola appropriates for the *Notti* and relates, presumably much as he found it, with the addition of the devils and witches. Straparola's collection, meanwhile, continues with another story of family honour affronted by sexual transgression, only this time the retribution is carried out to tragic ends.

---

22 'Die Geschichte von Sorfarina,' *Sicilianische Märchen*, no. 36; *Beautiful Angiola: The Great Treasury of Sicilian Folk and Fairy Tales collected by Laura Gonzenbach*, trans. Jack Zipes (New York: Routledge, 2004), pp. 1–8. Pitrè's version is entitled 'Catarina the Wise'; the heroine runs a school so renowned that the prince attends and has his ear boxed. He marries her to get an apology, and while he thinks she is locked up in a cellar, she actually travels the world just ahead of him, marries him as a different woman each time, gives him three children named Naples, Genoa, and Venezia, and on the eve of his marriage to an English princess, turns up with the children, the 'next slap' she had all along promised, and still no apology. Nevertheless, they all live happily ever after. *The Collected Sicilian Folk and Fairy Tales*, trans. Jack Zipes and Joseph Russo (New York: Routledge, 2009), vol. I, pp. 59–65. Pitrè cites a variant tale in vol. II, pp. 811–12. There is an Egyptian version of this tale in which a commoner marries a prince who then refuses to live with her. She assumes disguises on three occasions and each time comes home with a new child. In the end, he too acknowledges her cunning and loyalty as the basis for reconciliation and future happiness. S.E. Yacoub Artin-Pacha, 'La fille du menuisier' (The cabinet-maker's daughter) in *Contes populaires inédits de la Vallée du Nil* (Paris: J. Maisonneuve, 1895), no. 20, pp. 239–45.

VII. Fable 2
Malgherita Spolatina's Death at Sea

FIORDIANA

Malgherita Spolatina falls in love with Teodoro the hermit and swims to his island where he lives. Being discovered by her brothers, however, and tricked by a false signal, she dies miserably by drowning in the sea.

Love, as it has been described by wise men, is nothing more than an irrational desire or passion of the heart engendered by wanton thoughts. Among its ill effects are the squandering of worldly riches, wasting the strength of the body, infatuation of mind, and loss of freedom. It knows no order or reason, nor is it steadfast in anything. It is the father of vice, the enemy of youth, the destroyer of old age, and seldom or never does it lead to a good or prosperous outcome. Proof of this is the fate that once befell a woman of the noble Spolatina family who, being conquered by love, ended her days most miserably.

Ragusa, noble ladies, is a famous city of Dalmatia situated on a bay of the sea. Not far offshore is a small island commonly called Middle Island upon which there is a strong and stately castle. Between this island and the city is a rock uninhabited by reason of its corrupt and unhealthy air and the barrenness of its soil. No buildings are to be seen there except a little church and a wretched hut, half roofed over with dried herbs, moss, and planks of wood. A poor hermit named Teodoro is confined there in order to look after the shrine and to wipe out the guilt of his sins before God. Insofar as this man had no other means of sustenance except the alms and gifts of the pious, he was accustomed to go begging, sometimes to the city of Ragusa and sometimes to the Middle Isle. One day it happened, after going in his usual way to the island to seek his bread, that Teodoro found something he never expected to find – a fair, young maid named Malgherita who, after noting his handsome shape and gentle, pleasing face, thought to herself that he was a man better suited for love and pleasure than for imprisonment and a life in perpetual solitude. There and then the poor child took his image so fondly to heart that she dreamed of him and only him both day and night. The beggar hermit, knowing nothing of the girl's passion, wandered from house to house, and particularly to Malgherita's, asking for charity. This girl, for the great and perfect love she felt for him, always gave him alms with the best will in the world, without ever daring to reveal her love to him. But love is the buckler to all who willingly serve under his banner and never fails to show the way to reach the desired goal. At long last, this love gave Malgherita the courage to confront him with these tender words: 'Teodoro, my only love and sole pleasure of my heart, the passion that torments me is so great that unless you have some pity on me and rescue me, I will soon put an end to my sad and forlorn life. I am consumed away by a love so ardent that I can no longer resist the fierceness of the flame that burns my soul.' Having uttered so much, she was hindered from saying more by her own sobbing, sighing, and the flood of tears that fell from her eyes.

The hermit stood like a man out of his wits, having never suspected the maid's love until then. But pulling his thoughts together, he began to speak to her, and such was the outcome of their mutual discourse that all celestial things began to fall from his thoughts as love made its entry. There was nothing left but to find a way of coming together to accomplish their longing desires. Not short on cleverness, the young girl said, 'My love, don't be afraid, for I'll show you the means we must take. Here is the plan I think will best serve our ends. Tonight at the fourth hour, place a lighted torch in the window of your hut, and as soon as I see it, I'll come right over to you.'

To this Teodoro replied, 'Alas, my sweetheart, how will you cross over the sea, given that neither you nor I have a boat to carry us, nor can we entrust ourselves to the hands of others, which would be perilous both to honour and life.'

The girl spoke up, 'No, I'm telling you once and for all not to be afraid, but leave the care of this matter to me, and I'll find a way of coming to you without fear of death or dishonour, for when I see the light burning I'll swim over to you so secretly that no one will know of our deeds.'

But Teodoro replied, 'We'll rue the day, so great is the danger that you'll be drowned in the sea, for you're so young, and weak, and short of breath, and the journey is long.'

'But I have no fear that my strength will fail me, for I can swim as well as any fish.'

Seeing her firm resolve, the hermit was satisfied, and when the night came, according their plan, he lit the torch and awaited the maiden's coming, whom he longed to see with the greatest joy. When she saw the light, the guiding star of their love, she was filled with delight. She then shed all her clothes and, clad only in her shift, went barefoot to the seashore. Once there, she pulled her shift from her back, wrapped it about her head, then committed herself to the sea, making such skilful use of her arms and legs that in less than a quarter of an hour she had reached the hut where the hermit was waiting for her. He took the maid by the hand and led her into his poor shelter, and taking a fine linen cloth as white as snow, he gently dried her entire body. Then kissing her most amorously, he led her to his little cell and laid her down on his narrow bed, and there beside her he received from her a thousand fond embraces and soft caresses before culling the supreme fruits of love. Two hours they spent in sweet conversation and the damsel delighted in every attention of her monk so that when the time came to leave, she was full of resolve to return. She would grow accustomed to his sweet sustenance, seeking him out each time she saw his lamp aglow across the waves.

But blind Fortune, the destroyer of kingdoms, the maker of all mutability, and the enemy to human happiness, would not permit the girl to enjoy for long the soft embraces of her lover, but would suddenly shatter all their plans as though jealous of the happiness of others. One night, when the sky was overcast with dark, black clouds, Malgherita, noting the flame was alight, threw herself into the sea to cross over, but as she swam it happened that she was seen by certain fishermen casting their nets nearby. Taking her for a great fish swimming past, these fishermen began to watch her intently. Soon they discovered her to be a woman, and moreover observed with wonder how she entered the hermit's hut soon after. Astonished by this, they took their oars and rowed towards the shore, there lying in ambush until the girl came out of the hut to swim back towards the Middle Island. The poor child could not hide herself sufficiently to keep from being seen by these men. And when they discovered who she was, considered the dangers she ran, and had noted the signal of the torch, they were of half a mind for a time to keep it all secret.

But when they considered the disgrace that might fall upon an honourable family and the risk of death to the girl, their minds altered and they determined to reveal the entire matter to her kinsmen. Going to the house of Malgherita's brothers, they told the story from beginning to end. When the brothers heard and understood this sad news, they were as though turned to stone, and were determined to witness the matter with their own eyes. And once the facts were made clear, in their minds they marked her for death, and taking full counsel among themselves, they set out to achieve their ends. When the darkness of night began to fall, the younger brother climbed into a little boat and alone went quietly to the hermit's hut, begging him for shelter for that one night inasmuch as something had happened to him that placed him in danger of capture and execution if he fell into the hands of justice, stating that if he would grant him this favour, he would be indebted to him for the rest of his days as the one who had saved his life. Recognizing this man as Malgherita's brother, the hermit received him charitably and embraced him, all that night remaining with the young man, discussing many questions with him and disclosing all the miseries of humankind, as well as the grave sins that corrupt the soul and render it a servant of the devil.

While the younger brother remained with the hermit, the other two secretly left their house, took a sail-yard and torch, embarked in a boat and rowed towards the hermit's hut. When they had come near, they set the sail-yard upright, tied the lighted torch to the top of it, and waited to see what might happen.

No sooner did the girl see the light than she swam out boldly into the sea in her customary manner, striking out in the direction of the hut. The brothers, keeping total silence, as soon as they heard the movement that Malgherita made in the water, took their oars in hand and silently rowed away from the hut, carrying with them the burning torch. They rowed so gently that she heard no sound, nor could she see them on account of the darkness. The poor creature saw nothing but the lighted torch burning in the boat, and following this, she swam on and on. But by degrees, the brothers advanced further and further from the land, leading her at last out into the high seas where they dropped the sail-yard and put out the light.

The unhappy girl was completely bewildered, no longer able to see anything, entirely lost, weary, and exhausted with too much swimming. Finding herself beyond all human help, she gave herself up for lost, and like a wrecked ship was swallowed up by the cruel sea. Seeing that her situation was beyond all remedy, the brothers abandoned their unfortunate sister in the midst of the waves and returned to the house. The next morning, the younger brother also appeared, having left the hermit after duly thanking him for his night's lodging.

Already the sad news had spread throughout the Castle how Malgherita Spolatina had disappeared, for which the brothers feigned the greatest grief while secretly rejoicing immeasurably in their hearts. The third day had barely passed when the dead body of the girl washed ashore near the hermit's hut. There, when he had cast his eyes upon her and recognized her, he very nearly died of grief. Shedding a great flood of tears, he drew her fair, amorous body out of the water that once had been his joy and contentment. He bore it to his chamber and throwing himself upon her dead face he wept over it for a long while, bathing her white bosom with abundant tears and calling out to her many times, but all in vain. After he had wept his fill, he resolved to give her an honourable sepulchre, and to hasten her soul along with his prayers, fasting, and other good works. Taking his garden spade, he made a grave in his little church, and after closing her eyes and mouth, he made a garland of roses and fresh violets that he placed on her head. Then he gave her a last benediction, and kissing her a thousand times, placed her in the grave, which he covered first with earth, and the earth with flowers. In this way, by her untimely death, the honour of the brothers was saved, as well as her own, and nothing was ever discovered of her love and her unhappy end.

Several times during the course of this sad story the ladies had been moved to tears and had been obliged to wipe their eyes with their kerchiefs. But the Signora found herself overcome by grief on account of the sad ending of Fiordiana's fable, so she gave order to Molino to give them a merry enigma in order that some new pleasure might temper their present pain, which he provided without demur.

> Nurtured in the kindly nest
> Of a maiden's glowing breast,
> There I take my birth, and soon,
> As reward for such a boon,
> I labour hard by day, by night,
> To bear her offerings rich and bright.
> But as the moving stars fly past,
> I'm shut within a prison fast,
> Freed therefrom, I seek my mate,
> And, bound to her by hidden fate
> That life may more abound thereby,
> Embrace my doom and willing die.

Few or none of the company were able to fathom the meaning of Molino's learned riddle, and he, seeing them all perplexed, said: 'The true interpretation of my enigma is this: in the month of May it is the custom of young maidens to place in their bosoms the eggs of the silk-worm, which there come to life, and in return for this boon the worms give the silk that they spin. Then the worm is shut up in the cocoon, and when it issues forth, it is united with its mate, which lays more eggs and then dies voluntarily.' The solution of this intricate riddle appeared to the company to be no less clever than beautiful, and won unanimous praise. Then Lodovica, to whose lot it fell to relate the third story, stood up. Bowing deeply to the Signora and craving her permission to speak, she told the story that follows.

VII.2 Commentary

This story implants a particularly concrete image in the mind's eye of an island with chapel and hut inhabited by a beggar hermit who lights a lantern to guide Malgherita across the water to his bed. The story unfolds with great economy in relating the girl's persistent courtship and the hermit's conversion from ethereal to earthly interests, followed by her tender and rhapsodic reception and the betrayal by her brothers. The manner in which she is misled into the open sea and there abandoned by her kin in the blackness of night as they fold sails, keep silence, and put out the light can only produce a shudder of primal fear. Only two scenes follow: the covert jubilation of the brothers in the name of family honour as they feign to mourn her loss; and the tender, almost erotic, burial after she washes ashore on the hermit's island. The rest is mere innuendo on all sides; the story has no place to go. It follows the arc of tragic love as a destructive imperative that fixes a young girl's affections on a mendicant, while Fortune ensures that no state of bliss will last for long and death will seal up all in oblivion.[23] Yet the story endures, a marker and a monument to the rapture of pure erotic desire that the world of clans, mercantilism, and patriarchal values seeks to destroy. Hence, the opening moralizing about the uselessness, waste, shame, and

---

23 W.G. Waters noted that 'in the whole of the seventy-four fables there are hardly half-a-dozen which can be classed as tragic in tone, but of these one, the story of Malgherita Spolatina, is the finest of the whole collection. It is rarely one meets with anything told with such force and sincerity; yet, in placing before his readers this vivid picture of volcanic passion and studied ruthless revenge, Straparola uses the simplest treatment and succeeds *à merveille.' The Nights of Straparola*, 2 vols. (London: Lawrence & Bullen, 1894), vol. I, p. xxii.

counter-productivity of love falls far short of the story's pathos, leaving the familiar divide between ethical demands and insistent passions. Young love and a precious child are pitted against the demands of the family, raising once again the ancient question of kin and their right to discipline unto death in the name of honour. The story in this regard is powerful in its atavistic compulsions and timeless in its juxtaposing of life and death.

The story evokes thoughts of Musaeus's 'Hero and Leander,' to be sure, in which a lantern guides a swimmer motivated by love to a death by drowning, but there the resemblances cease.[24] Was it enough to have a classical template around which so many variables might be woven: a Dalmatian setting, a female swimmer, Renaissance family honour, and death by treachery rather than by adverse weather conditions? Such a means of genesis appears remote. Thus, without a literary source or comparative folk versions, the story must be granted local currency in a form only to be imagined from the present tale. Or for those favouring Straparola's inventive genius, it is a rare instance in which little remains to gainsay his authorship except the lack of custom. But the story is so finely conceived that it becomes implausible that its author left no more in kind. Inclination thus favours a tragic legend collectively generated that Straparola first and alone captured for posterity, or a contemporary bit of Venetian colonial news that caught his imagination and died with the following few imitators.

The work enjoyed a short new lease of life in the pages of *Les facétieuses journées* of Gabriel Chappuys, but therein it constitutes no more than an indirect transcription of the tale in the *Piacevoli notti*.[25] It had come to Chappuys through its replication as IV, no. 10 in Sansovino's *Duecento novella scelte*.[26] Chappuys's is a faithful translation of Sansovino, but the latter had given the original a more moralized and elegiac turn, being less moved by the girl's destiny than scandalized by the monk's erotic lapse. Larivey, in his translation of Straparola, is even less faithful through his addition of moralizing sentiment. A noteworthy borrower of this poignant tale is the German romantic poet Clemens Brentano, whose library

---

24 Musaeus, *Hero and Leander*, ed. Edward Henry Blakeney (Oxford: Basil Blackwell, 1935); Musaeus was a sixth-century B.C. grammarian. The work was imitated in the Renaissance and Romantic periods by, among others, Christopher Marlowe, George Chapman, Leigh Hunt, and Thomas Hood.
25 Ed. Michel Bideaux (Paris: Champion, 2003), IV.4, pp. 435–40.
26 (Venice: Sansovino, 1561), followed by editions in 1562, 1563, 1566, 1571, and 1603.

contained copies of the *Piacevoli notti* in Italian and French as well as German. Reinhard Hosch made the connection between Malgharita and Brentano's history of the beautiful beggar in his *Urchronica*.[27] Strangely, the story may have left no greater literary legacy.

The setting for this story is a small island about fifteen kilometres north-west of Dubrovnik. It was near Lopud (Middle Isle), which was a prosperous mercantile city and fortress at the centre of the Elaphites cluster, then a small republic under Venetian protection. The hermit's island, Skupielli, known to the Italians as Donzella, 'damsel,' was some 800 metres south-east of Lopud. It is charming to think that the name of the island inspired, or was inspired by, the story, and that perhaps a local legend gave rise to the present work.

This story is not devoid of Straparola's characteristic verbal borrowing. Giuseppe Rua first detected the Boccaccian diction of the story's opening thoughts concerning the risks and hazards of love. Straparola begins: 'Amore ... niuna altra cosa è che una irrazionabile volontà causata da una passione venuta nel cuore per libidinoso pensiero.' His inspiration from the *Filocolo* is patent, for there it reads: 'Questo amore niun'altra cosa è che una irrazionabile volontà nata da una passione venuta nel cuore per libidinoso pensiero.' Their common reflection is that 'love is nothing other than an irrational desire caused by a passion of the heart aroused by libidinous thought.' The balance of the proposition is taken nearly verbatim from the *Corbaccio*.[28] Not only does this passage provide further insights into the conflationary stylistics of the Renaissance imagination, but it reveals the curious disparity between such pedestrian morals and the story's tragic vision. The design reflects the persistent double construction of the readership in terms of empathetic suffering and pathos and the desire to learn sententious and precautionary values through exempla. Those two criteria were often incompatible and addressed in contradictory ways, as though the work's meaning could be reduced to vilifying love or shaking the head over distracted monks and disobedient children. The dissonance between precept and tragic *récit* remains one of the striking aspects of the story's presentation.

---

27 'Eine unbekannte Quelle und biographische Hintergründe zur Geschichte des schönen Bettlers in Brantanos "Urchronika,"' *Jahrbuch des Freien Deutschen Hochstifts* (1986), pp. 216–33.

28 Giuseppe Rua, *Tra antiche fiabe e novelle: le 'Piacevoli notti' di Messer Gian Francesco Straparola* (Rome: E. Loescher, 1898), p. 101. Boccaccio, *Filocolo* (Venice, 1530), p. 73; Boccaccio, *Corbaccio*, in *Opere minori* (Milan: E. Sonzogno, 1879), p. 277.

VII. Fable 3
Flogged at the Pope's Court

LODOVICA

Cimarosto, a jester, goes to Rome and there, confiding a secret to Pope Leo, he procures a beating for two of his household guards.

Gracious and lovesome ladies, the fable so elegantly told by Fiordiana has given occasion for the shedding of many tears by reason of its woeful nature, but as this is a place better suited for laughter than for weeping, I have decided to tell you one that I hope will give you no small pleasure. It concerns the buffooneries performed by a certain Brescian who went to Rome in expectation of becoming a rich man, but who, failing in his schemes, ended his days in poverty and misadventure.

In the city of Brescia, situated in the province of Lombardy, there once lived a jester named Cimarosto who was a very cunning fellow. Yet he was held in mean repute by his neighbours not only for his avarice – a vice that mars everything it touches – but just because he was a Brescian, for no prophet is well received in his own country.

Cimarosto felt indignation in his heart that his witty sayings were not fully appreciated for the merit he saw in them. So without making his intentions known to anyone, he departed from his native city and made his way to Rome in expectation of amassing a great sum of money there. But things did not fall out for him according to his wishes, for as time would prove, that great and famous city of Rome cares little for the sheep who have no wool.

The supreme pontiff of Rome in those days was Leo, a German by birth, who, although he was a man of great learning, was prone at times – in the manner of great lords – to take delight in buffooneries and other such diversions. But it was rare that jesters received from the pope any rewards for their efforts. Cimarosto, who had no acquaintances in the city and had no idea how he might bring himself to the notice of the pope, made up his mind that he would go to His Holiness in person and display before him some proof of his wit. Wherefore, he made his way to the palace of St Peter's, the residence of the pope. But as soon as he arrived at the outer door, hoping to slip in with the crowd, he was suddenly stopped by a private bodyguard, a stout, sturdy fellow with a black beard who called out to him, 'Heh, where are you going?' And putting his hand on Cimarosto's chest, he pushed him deftly backwards.

When he saw the guard's annoyed manner, Cimarosto said with a humble tone of voice, 'Ah, my brother, please don't deny me entrance, I beg you, for I have some very important questions to discuss with the pope.'

'Get away from this place as quickly as you can,' replied the guard, 'for otherwise you'll be rewarded in a manner not to your liking.'

Cimarosto insisted nevertheless on entering the palace, declaring over and over again that the business he wanted to discuss with His Holiness was of a most important nature. The guard, at last persuaded by Cimarosto's pertinacity that some weighty business was afoot, and thinking furthermore that an affair of this magnitude would bring to Cimarosto a liberal reward out of the Holy Father's purse, agreed to let him in. But before opening the door, he struck a bargain with him, namely, that upon his return from the pope's presence, Cimarosto must hand over half of what had been awarded to him. With alacrity, Cimarosto promised to abide by the terms.

Having passed over the threshold, Cimarosto entered into a second chamber, likewise in the custody of a young man of the pope's guard more gentle than the first, who, upon seeing him, rose from his chair to meet him, asking, 'What do you want here, my friend?'

To him, Cimarosto replied, 'I would speak with the pope.'

'But you can't speak with him right now,' the young man answered. 'He's engaged in other affairs, and heaven knows when it will be convenient for you to have a word with him.'

Cimarosto spoke out, 'Ah, don't hold me back, for the things I have to tell him are of the highest importance.'

When the young man heard these words, the same notion came into his mind that had suggested itself to the other guard, so he replied, 'If you wish to go in, you must promise to hand over to me half of whatever the pope may give you.' Cimarosto readily made a vow to keep this promise as well.

When at last Cimarosto made his way into the sumptuous papal chamber, his eye fell first upon a German bishop standing in the corner of the room at some distance from the pope. Going up to this prelate, he began talking to him. The bishop, who spoke no Italian, answered in German, then in Latin, to which Cimarosto feigned to answer in German, in the manner of a buffoon, blurting out any nonsense that happened to come to his lips, each speaking in such a way that neither the one nor the other understood a word of what was said. The pope, who was at the time occupied in talking to a cardinal, said to the latter, 'Are you hearing what I'm hearing?'

'Yes, Holy Father,' replied the cardinal.

And when the pope, who knew all languages perfectly, saw plainly that Cimarosto was playing a joke on the bishop, he was greatly amused and laughed out loud at the pranks that were going on. But in order not to spoil the sport, he turned his back upon them and pretended to talk to the cardinal on other matters.

So Cimarosto and the bishop carried on with their jargon for some time without a word of understanding – the pope all the while laughing heartily at the jest. At last the buffoon said to the bishop in his mock Latin, 'What city do you come from?'

The bishop answered, 'I am from the city of Nona.'

Cimarosto replied, 'Monsignor, it is no wonder that you can't understand my language, nor I yours, for you come from the Nones whereas I come from the Complines.' When the pope heard this prompt and witty answer, he began to laugh so heartily with the cardinal whom he held in conversation that he nearly burst his sides. Then calling the fellow to him, he asked him who he was, where he came from, and what his business was. Cimarosto, throwing himself down upon the ground before the Holy Father and kissing his feet, told him that he was a Brescian named Cimarosto, and that he came to Rome to obtain a favour from His Holiness.

The pope said, 'Ask me whatever you desire.'

'I ask nothing else of your Holiness,' said Cimarosto, 'than twenty-five of the sharpest lashes of the whip that can possibly be had.'

When the pope heard this foolish request, he was mightily astonished and laughed outright, but Cimarosto went on begging persistently that this favour and no other should be granted to him. Seeing that he was firm in this wish, and fully persuaded that he really meant what he said, the pope asked that a stalwart young fellow be called in to whom he gave orders then and there to lay upon Cimarosto's back twenty-five good sharp cuts with a whip. At the pope's command, he immediately stripped Cimarosto as naked as the day he was born. Then he took a tough lash in his hand and prepared himself to carry out the pope's command. But with a loud voice Cimarosto cried out, 'Ah, but hold up my man and don't beat me.' The pope, who realized this was part of the fellow's antics, burst into loud laughter and ordered the youth to hold his hand.

When the fellow had lowered his lash, Cimarosto, all naked as he was, knelt down before the pope and said with pretended tears, 'Holy Father, there is nothing in all this world more displeasing to God than broken faith. For my part, I will keep my pledge if your Holiness will give me aid and countenance. Much against my will, I promised to hand over, first to one of your guards, and then to another, half of whatever your Holiness might be pleased to give me. I asked you for twenty-five sharp cuts with a lash, and you, in your natural kindness and courtesy, have consented to let me have them. Will you, therefore, in my name, give twelve and a half blows to one of the said guards and twelve and a half to the other? By this means you will be granting my request, and I shall be making good my promise.'

The pope, who as yet hardly understood the drift of this matter, cried out, 'What is the meaning of this?'

Then Cimarosto said, 'Holy Father, when I wished to come in here and present myself to your Holiness, I was forced most unwillingly to chaffer and bargain with two of your household guardsmen, who made me bind myself by oath and promise that I would hand over half of whatever your Holiness might grant me of your beneficence. Wherefore, because I do not wish to fail in my plighted word, I feel myself bound to hand to each of them his due share, and I will myself forego any part of the reward.'

When the pope heard what Cimarosto said, he was greatly angered. Straightway, he caused the two retainers to be brought before him and commanded that they should be stripped and beaten according to the terms of the bargain made between them and Cimarosto. This order was promptly carried out, and when the young man had given each one of them twelve stripes, there yet remained one more lash due to somebody to make up the full number of twenty-five. Wherefore, the pope gave order that the guard who had been flogged last should have thirteen. But Cimarosto interrupted him, 'That would hardly be fair, for in that case he would get more than I promised him.'

'What shall we do, then?' asked the pope.

Cimarosto answered, 'Have them both tied together on one table with their backsides uppermost, and then let the young man lay on to them together a single stroke, a really sound one, that will include the two of them. Thus, each one will receive his share, and then I'll be free to go.'

When Cimarosto had left the pope's presence without any reward whatsoever, he was soon surrounded by a crowd of people. A certain prelate, a good and merry fellow, having come up to him, said, 'What is the latest news?'

And Cimarosto replied forthwith, 'Nothing less than that tomorrow we shall hear cries of peace.'

Unable to give any credence to the matter, the priest replied, 'You don't know what you're saying, for the pope has been at war with France for a long time, and until now we have not heard a word about peace.'

After they had held a long dispute together, Cimarosto said to the other, 'Messer, are you willing to make a wager with me of a good dinner that tomorrow there will be no cries of peace?'

'Yes,' answered the prelate. So in the presence of several witnesses they each deposited ten florins with the understanding that the loser would cover the cost of the dinner. Then the cleric took leave of Cimarosto in a merry humour, thinking that the next day he would hold high revel at the other's cost. But Cimarosto, who was by no means asleep, went to his lodging, and having found the master of the house, he said to him, 'My master, I'd like you to do me a favour that may turn out to be both to your pleasure and to my profit.'

'What do you wish me to do?' said the landlord. 'You know you only have to ask me.'

'Well, I ask nothing else of you,' said Cimarosto, 'but that tomorrow you dress up your wife in that old suit of armour you have in your chamber. You need have no fear that any dishonour or injury will come to her; just leave the rest to me.'

It turned out that the landlord's wife was named 'Peace.' And the armour Cimarosto had spoken of was that of a powerful man, very rusty, and of such great weight that anyone dressed in it and stretched out on the ground couldn't possibly get up without help, no matter how valiantly he tried. This landlord was a merry soul and well liked, and he knew that Cimarosto was full of tricks – reason enough for him to comply with the request.

When the next day came, the landlord dressed up his wife in the full suit of armour and had her stretch out on the floor of her room. Then he said to the woman, 'Stand up now, up on your feet,' and several times she tried to get up, but couldn't move.

Cimarosto, seeing that his plan was in a fair way to work out as he desired it, said to the landlord, 'Lets be off.' Having closed the door of the room, which faced out on the public street, they departed. The landlord's wife, when she perceived that she was shut up alone in the room and unable to rise, greatly feared that some misfortune was about to happen to her and began to cry out with a loud voice. The neighbourhood, hearing the outcry and the clash of arms, ran to the landlord's house.

Cimarosto, when he heard the tumult made by the men and women who had flocked together, said to his host, 'Don't move or speak, but leave everything to me, for the laugh will soon be on our side.' Then he went down the stairs and into the street and asked first one man and then another, 'Who is doing all the yelling?'

And with one voice, they replied, 'Can't you hear, it's Peace who's screaming.' Having these words repeated to him two or three times, he called several men to bear witness that they had heard the cries of Peace.

When the hour of compline was past, the prelate came and said, 'You have lost your wager of a dinner, brother, for so far we have heard no cries of peace.'

'I take it to be otherwise,' said Cimarosto. So between them there arose a sharp contention, and it became necessary to find a judge to decide the case. Now this judge, when he heard the reasoning of one side and of the other, and listened to the witnesses, who roundly declared that the whole neighbourhood had recently heard the cries of Mistress Peace, sentenced the priest to pay for the feast.

Two days had hardly gone by when Cimarosto, as he was passing through the city, encountered a Roman lady who was very rich, but ugly as the devil. This woman had managed to get a handsome youth for a husband, to the astonishment of all those who knew her. It happened that at the same moment a little she-ass was passing by, and Cimarosto turning to her said, 'Ah, poor little thing. If you had as much money as this woman, you could easily get married.' By chance, a gentleman, one of the ugly woman's kinsmen, overheard this saying, took up a stick and gave Cimarosto such a blow on the head that he had to be carried back to his landlord's house by his arms and legs.

In order that he might more easily dress his wounds, the surgeon had his head shaved. His friends, when they came to see him, said, 'Cimarosto, what have they done to you? Your head's as smooth as silk.'

'Quiet, all of you, and don't mock me,' he said, 'for a head of shaved satin or hairy velvet would still be worth half a florin, but this one's not worth a damn.'

When the last hour of his life was approaching, a priest came to give him extreme unction, and when he was come to his feet, Cimarosto said, 'Alas, good sir, don't oil me anymore. Can't you see my life is running off the reel fast enough as it is?' All the bystanders, when they heard this, began to laugh, and so Cimarosto died jesting even to the last moment of his life. So it was that both he and his buffooneries came to a miserable end.

Lodovica had no sooner ended her tale than the Signora ordered her to continue the established order of things by reciting her enigma, whereupon, with a smiling face and obliging demeanour, she did as she was commanded.

> Old was I before my day,
> For when in infancy I lay
> I was a man-child strong and bold.
> First was I plunged in water cold,
> Then racked with torture fierce and fell;
> Next scorched with heat, then, truth to tell,
> Again with irons torn and rent,
> Then out on homely service sent.
> Useful my lot, though scant my fame;
> Now if you can, declare my name.

This subtle riddle commanded great admiration from all the noble company, yet no one was able to interpret it. Whereupon, the wise Lodovica, seeing her enigma was likely to remain undeciphered, said with a smile, 'It's not that I'm keen to teach, but because I don't want to leave you longer in suspense, allow me to explain the meaning of the enigma I just recited. Unless I'm mistaken, this can only be flax, which is brought forth by its mother, that is to say the earth, of the male sex, then it is placed in cold running water to be steeped, then dried by the sun, next spread on the floor and heavily pounded with a mallet, and finally torn to pieces with the iron to rid it of the little sticks still left in it.

Everyone was marvellously well pleased with this explanation and held it to be most apt. Then Lionora, who was seated next to the speaker, rose to her feet, and having made due salutation began her fable.

VII.3 Commentary

The simple logic of the story is that if you are owed a large reward and another is unjustly claiming a share, ask for something punitive or deleterious and endure your own portion in order to bring the bounder to torment, or negotiate to have your own quota assigned to the other as an ostensible act of good will. That is the defining trait of the story type. It is a perverse form of trickery, originating in the ready wit of one willing to suffer in order to turn tables, foster irony, and inflict justice. The delight for the reader, meanwhile, is in the simple cunning of the invention, as though devised on the spot, just when the blackmail of a bully seems inevitable. The principle is open to many interpretations and medieval storytellers delighted in searching out all the possible changes. About as remote as they get, but still within the tradition, is Jacques de Vitry's story of two men, one avaricious and the other envious, who were allowed to ask for anything they desired on the condition that the last one to ask would receive twice as much.[29] This story no doubt originated in Avianus's fable of 'The Greedy Man and the Envious Man' (early fifth century).[30] Working through all the permutations in hypothetical fashion creates a splendid mental exercise in the logistics of human intentionality processed through the lenses of these two temperaments: greed and envy. Each one, whether for the one motive or the other, is unwilling that the second should receive a greater benefit and thus refuses to make a first request. At last, the envious man asks to have one of his eyes torn out so that, according to the agreement, the avaricious man would lose both. The story thereby reflects the logic of accepting a partial loss as a condition to inflicting a complete loss upon another.

After de Vitry, this vignette was disseminated widely throughout the following four centuries. Among them is no. 647 in Johannes Pauli's *Schimpf und Ernst* (Amusing and serious), published in 1522 and forty times thereafter, in which three servants are called in by their lord, one of whom is avaricious and another jealous. The *Seigneur* offers to them whatever reward they desire as long as they agree that the second should receive a double portion, and the third a portion double that of the second. After some discussion of the matter, the jealous one, because he

---

29 Jacques de Vitry, *The Exempla: or Illustrative Stories from the Sermones Vulgares*, ed. Thomas Frederick Crane (London: David Nutt, 1890), pp. 81–2.
30 *The Fables of Avianus*, trans. David R. Slavitt (Baltimore: Johns Hopkins University Press, 1993), p. 30.

was compelled to make the first request, asks to lose an eye so that the second would lose both, and the third his ears into the bargain. So it was done.[31]

A story far closer to Straparola's in design and content appears in Juan de Timoneda's *Buen aviso y portacuentos el sobremesa*, the third of the 'Cuentos de Joan Aragonés.' This story is in direct line insofar as it tells of a countryman who had given many gifts to the king, but was not allowed to enter the palace unless he promised to pay half of his rewards to the keeper of the door. An agreement was struck, but little to the door-keeper's liking, for the peasant asked for no other payment than five hundred lashes of the whip.[32] Another in this precise tradition appears in Thomas Wright's *A Selection of Latin Stories from Manuscripts of the XIIIth and XIVth Centuries*: 'De janitore imperatoris Frederici' (Emperor Frederic's porter). This version alone is all that is required to account for Straparola's creation, for all the critical parts are there in the briefest of forms: the offering of fruit, the doorkeeper who insists on having his part of the reward, the request for 100 blows, the emperor's enquiry, and the full sum of the lashes meted out to the porter.[33] The

---

31 *Schimpf und Ernst*, ed. Hermann Österley (Stuttgart, 1866; reprint, Amsterdam: Rodopi, 1967), pp. 356–7. There is little point in offering more in this vein because they are not directly in the Straparolan mode, but the interested reader is directed to the cryptic list of analogues in Österley's annotations, p. 546, which includes references to *The Panchatantra*. A list nearly as extensive and less cryptic appears on p. 212 of Crane's edition of Jacques de Vitry cited in note 29 above, including Bromyard, *Summa praedicantium*, 'Invidia,' I, vi, 19 (see MS Reg. 7 E iv, fol. 249r); Juan de Timoneda, *Libro de los enxemplos* (Barcelona: Dirección y Administración, 1885), no. 146, the first of the *Tre novelline antiche*, published in Florence in 1887; and another half-dozen or more collections of medieval exempla including Robertus Holkot's *In librum sapientiae Regis Salomonis* (Basel: s.n., 1586), Lectio 29, p. 104. Another occurs in Jean Gobi's *La scala coeli*, ed. Marie-Anne Polo de Beaulieu (Paris: Centre nationale de la recherche scientifique, 1991), no. 594, p. 418, the source for which appears to be Jacques de Vitry. A similar episode is found in Giovanni Sagredo's *Arcadia in Brenta*, ed. Quinto Marini (Rome: Salerno, 2004), pp. 432–3, in which a fisherman catches a fine fish that he seeks to present to the Duke of Mantua. But before he can gain entry he is blackmailed by the porter. He requests fifty hits with a stick, alerting the duke to the avarice of his servants. This one too is in line with Straparola's.

32 Joan Timoneda, *Buen aviso y portacuentos el sobremesa*, ed. Pilar Cuartero and Maxime Chevalier (Madrid: Espasa-Calpe, 1990), pp. 317–18.

33 (London: The Percy Society, 1842), no. 127, p. 122. The story allegedly occurs as well among the *Mots et facéties du Curé Arlòtto*, but it was not found in this collection as published in *Conteurs italiens de la Renaissance* (Paris: Gallimard, Pléade, 1993).

story was adapted by the author of 'The Ballad of Sir Cleges,' in which the impoverished knight, in offering a gift of cherries to his liege, is abused and insulted by the porter, the usher, and the steward. The knight asks for twelve blows, sharing them three ways with the porter and the steward.[34] The motif is much adapted and modified in a *fabliau* from this same period entitled 'Le villain au buffet,' in which a wicked seneschal finds himself sharing in what he least desired.[35]

Franco Sacchetti found this little trickster plot by the end of the fourteenth century and gave it, perhaps, its earliest novelistic elaboration in a story about the court of Philippe of Valois (1428–50).[36] The king's favourite falcon, during a hunting expedition, returns to the wild and remains lost for a month before it is coaxed back to the fist of a peasant farmer. A reward of 200 francs had been posted meanwhile and the peasant makes his way to Paris with the bird to collect his money. There he encounters a pesky doorman blocking his entry and demanding half the promised reward. The peasant attempts to stand his ground but accedes in the end to gain entry. When, in the king's presence, he asks for fifty blows or lashes of the whip, the king's curiosity leads to an explanation, the invocation of the porter, and the administration of the unexpected reward, while the peasant goes home with new resources for his family. There are many more such examples, including the elaboration upon the theme by Voltaire in *Ce qui plait aux dames* (That which pleases the ladies), but the principle of the exchange that characterizes each of the above admits of little variation, making a proliferation of examples supererogatory, particularly because none promises to lead

---

For more on this entire tradition, see Johann Georg Theodor Grässe, *Die grossen Sagenkreise des Mittelalters zum ersten Male historisch entwicklung* (Dresden: Arnold, 1842), p. 251.

34 Oxford MS Bodleian 6922, fols. 67b–73a. It has been edited by George H. McKnight in *Middle English Humorous Tales in Verse* (Boston: Heath, 1913), pp. 331–53; it is also included in *The Medieval English Breton Lays*, ed. Anne Laskaya and Eve Salisbury (Kalamazoo: Medieval Institute Publications, 1995). For an account of this story motif, see John R. Reinhard, 'Strokes Shared,' *Journal of American Folklore*, 36 (1928), pp. 380–400.

35 *Nouveau recueil complet des fabliaux*, ed. Willem Noomen et al. (Assen: van Gorcum, 1990), vol. V, pp. 283–312. A similar tale entitled 'Le brochet du Florentin' appears in *Nouveaux contes à rire*, 2 vols. (Cologne: R. Bontemps, 1722), vol. II, p. 39.

36 Franco Sacchetti, *Il trecentonovelle*, ed. Emilio Faccioli (Turin: Giulio Einaudi, 1970), no. 195, pp. 581–5.

us closer to the precise version that Straparola employed for his inspiration.[37] This too was a story 'in the air,' circulating among the folk at the same time that it attracted the attention of the writers of *exempla*, *fabliaux*, and *novelle*. That this motif does not seem to have been widely represented among the folk raconteurs of the nineteenth century suggests that Straparola created his modestly 'novelized' version from a written source, although here, as elsewhere, the point is uncertain. It is conceivable that the anecdote had historical origins, for it has been associated with Cimarosto, the buffoon of Cardinal Trentino, who appears to have played this trick on the doorkeepers at the court of Pope Leo IX (1049–54).[38] But whether its origin was historical or literary, it became a travelling motif in the prank literature of the late Middle Ages.

In the present story, the sharing of lashes with the doorman is but one trick among the scant few that constitute a miniature jest cycle conceived in Cimarosto's name. Just how old and extensive that micro-trickster biography may once have been is uncertain, but in the minimal form in which it appears in Straparola, it is either seriously eroded or seriously stunted as a literary creation. The remainder of the present hero's career consists of a free supper gained by having peace cried by the landlord's wife, Madonna Pace, or 'Peace,' and by playing on words to provoke laughter in those who attend him in his dying moments. Such *momento mori* foolery and nonchalance was a standard feature of the jest cycles conceived in the name of a hero. Till Eulenspiegel, at the time of his death, famously made a mockery of his last communion, made smutty jokes about beguines, prepared a jar full of excrement with a few coins over the top into which he invited the greedy priest to thrust his hand but not too far, and ultimately expired leaving a mere stone in the coffer that was to have contained all his worldly wealth, thereby causing the

---

37 Ed. François Bessire (Arles: Actes Sud, 2008), p. 53.

38 See Ortensio Lando, *Sette libri de cathaloghi a varie cose appartenenti non solo antiche ma anche moderne* (Venice: Gabriel Giolito de Ferrari, 1552), bk. VI, p. 502. The point, however, is unclear. Arturo Graf in 'Un buffone di Leone X,' the final study in his *Attraverso il cinquecento* (Turin: Ermanno Loescher, 1888), p. 375, is convinced that Straparola made an error in referring to the 'German' Leo IX when he meant instead Leo X, the Medici pope, 1513–21, who had an interest in buffoonery. His article (pp. 364–94), in fact, covers the topic thoroughly, particularly with regard to Fra Mariano and his caprices, along with Cardinal Bibbiena, a famous jokester of the time, but Graf knows no more of Cimorosto than what is attributed to him by Straparola.

beneficiaries to accuse each other of theft.[39] Marcolphus's actual death is unrecorded, but when he was slated for execution by King Solomon, he begged and received one final request, which was to choose the tree from which he was to be hanged, and then began a long march during which he never found a tree to his liking.[40] Cimarosto's deathbed joke takes up the word 'raso' (shaved) in reference to his own head following a medical procedure and puns on 'raso' (satin), a smooth fabric contrasted with velvet, both of which had value, while his own life was now worthless in death. The three jests that constitute this tiny jest cycle, offered in the name of this elusive court buffoon, are minimal, conventional, and arbitrary. But how much greater this cycle once might have been I have been unable to determine. It appears to be the remnant of a tradition. Such motifs, in any case, belonged to popular culture and were typically recycled in many directions. The point to be made is that the present tale bears a small-scale resemblance to the design and substance of the trickster-cycle biographies of his more famous counterparts: Bertoldo, Marcolphus, and Faustus.

---

39 *A Pleasant Vintage of Till Eulenspiegel*, trans. Paul Oppenheimer (Middletown, CT: Wesleyan University Press, 1972), pp. 224–31.

40 *The Dialogue of Solomon and Marcolphus*, ed. Donald Beecher (Ottawa: Dovehouse Editions, 1995), p. 199.

VII. Fable 4
Share and Share Alike

LIONORA

Two brothers were living together in great amity. After a time, one of them demands a division of their goods. The other consents, but only if the first does the partitioning. When this is done, the second remains discontented because he expects to have a half-interest in the other's wife and children, as well.

Great indeed, beloved and gracious ladies, is the tender love that a father bears towards his children. Equally great is the affection of close and faithful friends for each other. Great too is the attachment that a loyal citizen feels for his beloved country. But in my estimation, the love between two brothers who cling to one another with sincere and perfect affection is fully as great as any of those I have named above. Occasionally it falls out otherwise, but love of this kind gives rise to the most blessed and happy results, bringing sweet fulfilment to the projects of men beyond their most sanguine hopes. I could produce numerous examples of this truth, although I will pass them over in silence in order not to weary this noble and gracious company. Yet to the end that I may duly fulfil the promise I made to you, I'll give to you, as an example, the case of two brothers who lived only a short time ago, a story that I hope will provide both pleasure and profit to you all.

In the justly celebrated and famous city of Naples – one abounding in lovely women of virtuous carriage and rich in all good things that one can imagine – there resided, not long ago, two brothers, one of whom was called Hermacora and the other Andolfo. These two men were of noble lineage, being scions of the great family of Carafa. Both were blessed with good parts and lively wits. Moreover, they were both men of considerable wealth, acquired through large-scale merchandising and trade. Now these two brothers, rich, of noble parentage, and bachelors, shared, as loving brothers should, the common expenses of their living. So great was the attachment between them that neither would dream of doing anything that would not please the other.

As time went by, the younger brother, Andolfo, with Hermacora's consent, married a beautiful gentlewoman of noble blood named Castoria. As was becoming of a wise and high-minded woman, she loved and reverenced Hermacora, her brother-in-law, as much as Andolfo her husband, while each of them, alike, reciprocated her affection – filling the household with concord and peace the likes of which are seldom seen. It pleased heaven to give Castoria numerous children, which, as they grew in number, brought an increase in affection and welfare. At the same time, their riches daily increased, and because they were always of one mind and heart, no discord ever arose between them. But when the children had grown and come of age, blind Fortune, always jealous of the happiness of others, interposed, attempting to sow discord and strife where before there had been such perfect union and peace.

Moved by an immature and misguided desire, Andolfo was captured by the idea of parting company with his brother, to section off his share of their common fortune, and to live elsewhere on his own. So one day, he accosted his brother with these words, 'Hermacora, we have now lived most happily together for a long time, sharing all our belongings, and without passing a single word in wrath between us. But now, so that fickle Fortune, like the wind among the leaves, cannot come and blow up discord between us, causing disorder and dissention where there has always been peace and concord, I have decided to take my share of our wealth and go my own way. It's not that you have ever done me any form of injury that I propose to leave, but merely to be able to spend my wealth according to my own pleasure.'

When Hermacora heard this explanation of his brother's foolish desire, he felt deeply offended, because he couldn't really see what the cause might be that motivated him to leave on such frivolous grounds. So in words as gentle and loving as he could muster, he began to advise and beg Andolfo to put this evil counsel out of his mind as quickly as he could. But no matter what he said, Andolfo grew more obstinate and persistent in his stubborn desire, giving no thought whatsoever to the losses that would inevitably ensue. At the end he exclaimed most vehemently, 'Hermacora, you know the common saying well enough that there is nothing to be gained by arguing with a man whose mind is made up. So there's no point in coming to me with your wheedling speech to try to deter me from following the course I've set my mind upon.

Furthermore, I don't see that you have any right to press me further for the reasons why I might want to separate myself from you. I'll only say that the sooner the division is made and we go our separate ways, the better pleased I'll be.'

Seeing how strongly his brother was bent on carrying out his scheme and how little he might be moved by gentle speech, Hermacora said to him, 'Brother, seeing that it is your pleasure that we now divide our goods and part from one another, although not without deep pain and considerable displeasure, I'm ready to satisfy your wish and do your bidding. But there's one favour I must ask you, which I beg you not to refuse me, for should you turn me down, it'll be a mortal blow.'

Andolfo replied, 'Speak your mind, Hermacora, for in all other matters besides this one we've been discussing, I'll do whatever you like.'

Hermacora then answered, 'There's no doubt by all that's right and reasonable that we should divide our possessions and go our separate ways. But given that this partitioning has to be made by someone, I demand that you be the person to settle the two parts in such a way that neither of us will have any cause to complain.'

To this Andolfo replied, 'Hermacora, it is hardly right that I, as the younger brother, should be called upon to make this division. Surely that duty belongs to you, who are the elder.'

But in the end, Andolfo, keen to get on with the division and fulfil his wish, and unable to hit upon a better way to end the matter, undertook the task himself, giving to his elder brother the choice of taking whatever share he would. Now although Hermacora saw that the apportioning was well done, he pretended, nevertheless, that the two parts were not equal, saying, 'Andolfo, the division that you've made here no doubt seems fair to you and so you assume that neither of us has grounds for complaint, but it seems otherwise to me. So I'm asking you to make another attempt to divide it more fairly, so that neither one of us has cause for discontent.'

When Andolfo saw that his brother was dissatisfied with the division he had made, he took away certain things from one of the shares and added them to the other, asking Hermacora whether the parts were made equal by these changes, and whether he was now content. Hermacora, who in his heart was all kindness and love, still cavilled at his brother's work, feigning his displeasure, although the portions, in truth, were perfectly just and right.

Meanwhile, it seemed uncanny to Andolfo that his brother refused to accept his work, so that with an angry look upon his face, he took the paper upon which the reckonings had been made and tore it to pieces. Then, turning towards his brother, he said, 'Go and divide our goods according to your own will, for at any cost, I'm determined to get this business over with, even if it is determined to my own disadvantage.'

Despite his brother's impetuous anger, Hermacora continued to answer him in a kind and mild manner, 'Andolfo, my brother, put aside your scornful bearing; don't let your indignation get the better of your reason. Restrain your anger, temper your wrath, and learn to know yourself. Then in all wisdom and prudence, consider carefully whether the parts into which our substance has been divided are truly equal. If you discover them not to be so, divide them once more, and then I'll most certainly be content, taking the share allotted to me without complaint.'

Andolfo still didn't comprehend the thoughts hidden in the breast of his kind-hearted brother, nor did he perceive the artful net that Hermacora was casting over him. So, growing even more angry, in wrath he yelled at his brother, 'Hermacora, didn't I tell you at the beginning of this business that you were the elder brother and that it was your responsibility to make this division of our wealth? Why didn't you make it yourself? Didn't you promise to be satisfied with any apportionment that I might make? Now you fail to keep faith with me.'

Hermacora answered, 'My dearest brother, if, after you've divided our goods and given me my share, I find mine isn't equal to yours, what wrong do I do you by complaining?'

Andolfo replied, 'What thing is there in all the house of which you have not been allotted your due share?'

But Hermacora went on insisting that he had not been fairly treated and they fell to wrangling, the one saying 'yes' and the other 'no,' until finally Andolfo said, 'I'd very much like to know how I've failed to make the parts equal.'

And Hermacora replied, 'My brother, you've failed in the most important part.' But after he had said this, Hermacora could see that Andolfo was only growing more enraged and that if the matter were drawn out further, it would bring scandal and harm to the honour of their household and possibly even place their lives in jeopardy. He then heaved a deep sigh and continued, 'You tell me, my dearest brother, that you have given me the full share which by right belongs to me, but this I deny and I will prove this to you in the clearest way, so that you may see it with your own eyes and touch it with your hands. Now, putting all anger aside, tell me whether, from the day when you led Castoria, your beloved wife and my dear sister-in-law, home to our house, we have not all lived together in fraternal affection?'

'Assuredly we have,' answered Andolfo.

'Then,' asked Hermacora, 'has Castoria not striven to do her best in governing the house for the benefit of us all?'

'Certainly,' said Andolfo.

'Is she not the mother of all these children whom we have now around us?' asked Hermacora. 'And haven't this mother and her children lived at our common cost.'

While Hermacora was speaking in this tender and loving strain, Andolfo grew more and more astonished, failing to see to what end his brother might be driving.

Hermacora went on, 'My brother, you have divided our goods, to be sure, but you have not divided your wife and children, giving me my share of them. Shall I no longer have any part in their love and care? How am I to live without the society of my dear sister-in-law and my beloved nephews and nieces? Give me, therefore, my share in the love of these, and then go in peace, for I shall be well content. But if you can't do this, I'll never consent to the division being made. And in the event you won't agree to this proposition of mine, may God forbid, I swear that I'll summon you before a human tribunal on earth and there claim justice of you. Or, indeed, if I can't obtain it in this world, I'll cite you before the tribunal of Christ, to whom all things are most clear and manifest.'

Andolfo listened attentively to his brother's words and was most amazed by what he heard. Then for the first time he began to understand the great tenderness of heart that stirred the deep well of love in Hermacora's bosom. Overcome with shame and confusion, he could no longer venture a word in reply. At last, he felt the justice of his brother's thoughts, thereby softening his formerly hardened heart, so that, prostrating himself on the ground before him, he said, 'Hermacora, truly my ignorance has been great and my fault as well. But greater still is your gentleness and humanity. Now I clearly see my wretched error and foolish blindness. Only now do my eyes pierce through the baffling mist that formerly dulled and obscured my understanding. Honestly, I deserve the swiftest and sharpest punishment the public tongue can pronounce against me and I confess myself worthy of the severest chastisement that can be devised. But seeing your heart has always been full of clemency and love towards me, I'll venture to draw near you as to a fount of living water, begging you to pardon my heinous fault, promising never to forsake you, but only to remain ever in affectionate union with you, together with my wife, and to allow you to dispose of my children as if they had been born to you.'

Then the brothers embraced one another with tears of love and reconciliation falling from both their eyes. In this manner, they found perfect reunion one with the other, and from that time on there never arose another word of discord between them, leaving their children, nephews, and nieces richly provided for after their deaths.

This pathetic story of what had passed between the two loving brothers greatly pleased the entire company and proved to be so moving of pity that not only the ladies, but the men as well, shed tears. For who could resist, when the fullness of their love was revealed, together with the gentleness with which Hermacora appeased Andolfo's obstinate humour and in the end defeated the attack of evil fortune? When the prudent Signora saw that the men as well as the women were wiping away the tears flowing from their eyes, she made a sign that everyone should cease their weeping, commanding Lionora to finish her story with an enigma, which she offered in humility and obedience:

> When we look on all around,
> Many beauteous things are found.
> Once I was a virgin fair,
> Now a mother's part I share,
> Giving life so full and free
> To him who once gave life to me.
> And my mother's mate I feed,
> Mother to my sire in need.
> Tell me who is she who gives
> Life to him through whom she lives.

When Lionora had ended her riddle, which won the praise of all present, one of the company rose up and proffered an interpretation, thinking it was the right one, but which turned out to be far from it. Wherefore, Lionora burst out laughing and explained it in the following words: 'Once upon a time there was an innocent old man who, contrary to all law and equity, was unjustly thrown into prison and condemned to death by starvation, and was in consequence kept without food. But his jailers allowed his daughter to visit him, and she nourished him with the milk from her own breast, suckling him as though he were a babe. Thus from being a daughter she became a mother, giving life to him that had given life to her.'

The enigma told by Lionora proved no less interesting to the company than her piteous tale. In order that the last of the damsels might complete the storytelling of the night, she sat down after she had made due salutation to the Signora, and Isabella, who had been chosen to fill the last place, rose from her seat and thus blithely began her fable.

VII.4 Commentary

This relation is perhaps not quite a 'story' for want of developmental complexity, although there is conflict and resolution through strategic negotiation concerning the nature and possibilities of brotherhood. The ménage arising from their shared interests is unusual but plausible. If one of them chooses to marry and raise children and the other does not, yet given their mutual ties to the younger generation, it is not so extraordinary, in a theoretical sense, that they might want to live together and to share alike in the care of the younger brother's wife and offspring. It is conceivable, too, that the advantages for the entire family from such avuncular attention might well inspire the sister-in-law to accept and foster the arrangement in the absence of competition for her sexual favours. (Fear of such competition enters into cognate versions of the story.) The arrangement is, in a sense, utopian and constitutes the novelty of the anecdote. But the less tangible factor is the nature of the underlying emotions and values that join Hermacora and Andolfo – two younger brothers and leading merchants from the famed Carafa family (itself representing a unit of cohesion and motivation for nepotism). In brief, the story, merely by dint of its exceptional arrangement of facts, explores the possibilities of kinship combinations in which the blood ties between male siblings are linked to kinship ties with a wife and children and, ultimately to the extended family as a unit within the clan. Opposite these claims is the natural desire for individuality and autonomy. The story tests whether unity in the face of such potentially conflicting emotions can long endure.

Despite the emotional bonds that cement fraternity, the younger brother decides, by a twist of fortune (for lack of clearer motivational explanation), to divide the household and to strike out on his own simply to gain control over his material destiny. What he fails to take into consideration is not only the older brother's loss of community, but his emotional as well as material involvement in the extended family, something that the elder brother attempts to express in quantitative terms as an entitlement that must also be divided with the parcelling out of the household. Much of the felt quality of the conflict may be summed up in the word 'brotherhood' or *fraternité* – a word often borrowed by group promoters, politicians, and religionists, but that has its only real meaning in the fellow feeling for a biological brother. The logic of the genes speaks through that sense of mutuality that can arise only when siblings cease to battle over parental resources and attention and cooperate in the interest of their own offspring.[41] In the reunion of this extended family, despite the cost to individualism, there is a sense in which the emotional ties of brotherhood are seen to redefine the nuclear family. That too has thematic potential.

The diligent social historian, in following the Carafa lead, might attempt to find historical bedrock beneath this story. But its connection to that great Neapolitan family, one of whom became Pope Paul IV in 1555, may be little more than an idealizing compliment superimposed upon a traditional tale. More perplexing is why Straparola maintained the allusion, presumably drawn from his now indeterminate source. His practice, in any case, was to assign proper names and places of his own; in which case, who were the Carafa to him? Even more perplexing is why Rotunda classified it as the only story under the heading J2246, 'Fool claims share of brother's wife and children,' which is in turn placed among the stories based on an 'absurd lack of logic.'[42] The sole reason is that the story bears a relation to those in which the equitable division of goods entails the literal severing of a living person to settle a dispute. That detail may tell us something about the story's origin in the Eastern tales in which this motif prevails. One of the earliest of the surviving 'division-of-goods' tales is found in the *Katha sarit sagara*, a collection with roots going back to the middle of the first millennium. Two brothers,

---

41 Male friendship has its terms, conditions, and thresholds in real and simulated families. But the duty to the genetic imperative may carry an adaptive edge. Richard Dawkins would argue hére, no doubt, as he did throughout *The Selfish Gene*, that the interests of progeny, through the evolutionary predispositions of our brains, are hard wired. The final line of the story confirms that even the material concentration of goods by the father and the uncle becomes the ultimate legacy to the offspring, even as their concentrated nurturing while alive, through the directives of powerful hedonic desires, trumps the breakdown of the clan.

42 *Motif-Index of the Italian Novella in Prose* (Bloomington: Indiana University Press, 1942), p. 74.

disputing their inheritance in terms of exact equivalents, go so far as to have the female slave also cut in half, anticipating the present discussion over the divisibility of wives. In their case, however, the presiding judge becomes so enraged that he confiscates everything and leaves the two fools destitute.[43] The interim literary record is relatively slight, but we may nevertheless be tempted to posit a story type reaching back from the Renaissance to this Eastern prototype and beyond.

The contemporary tale closest to Straparola's is to be found in the *Heptameron* of Marguerite of Navarre.[44] Its outcome is very different, but the story opens with a situation in common. Two men who are close friends live in perfect amity, sharing all they have, even when one of them weds and brings a wife into the household. She is kind to the friend, as she is instructed to be, and on occasion all three even share the same bed, with the husband appropriately in the middle. But in the course of time, the husband grows uneasy, suspicious, and must fight his incipient jealousy. The two then have an open confrontation, the friend protesting in a state of consternation that friendship trumps all other things, that he never has or ever would betray the trust they share, and that if in the future such suspicion should return, though it is not his accuser's fault but a natural vice, it would constitute a breach of that sacred bond between them. So much openness and transparency, however, is to no avail; the jealousy returns, the wife is instructed to keep her distance and not speak to the friend, and so the denouement follows, that where there was once mutuality and trust, the friend now vows to bring to fact what the other feared. In that spirit he removes himself and his goods from the household, thereafter cuckolding his friend in revenge.[45] The differences

---

43 *The Ocean of Story*, trans. C.H. Tawney, ed. N.M. Penzer, 10 vols. (Delhi: Motilal Banarsidas, 1984), no. 123, vol. V, p. 114. This matter arises in sharp relief as well in all the stories in the tradition of 'the grateful dead,' represented in this collection by the story of 'Bertuccio and Tarquinia' (XI.2), and the offer by Bertuccio to have his bride severed by sword to honour the pact with his benefactor to divide all his gains and spoils equally.

44 *The Heptameron*, trans. P.A. Chilton (London: Penguin, 1984), no. 47, pp. 410–13.

45 Margarite's story illustrates the principle of psychological reactance. The person who is accused of sexual predation by a jealous man interprets that suspicion as a limitation of his freedom, his ability to act, which, paradoxically, can be restored only by doing precisely what that jealous person most feared, even if the thought of doing so would never otherwise have entered his mind. Emotion is behind the deed, spurring a self-fulfilling situation, inspired by the false appraisal of his intentions. In the words of Marcel Proust, 'once the jealousy has been discovered, the person

between the two versions are marked, but the stories may be pendants all the same, diverging from a common popular font. Straparola and Marguerite compared (the *Heptameron* was first published in 1558) is unfruitful in terms of direct influence, but a challenging exercise in imagining just how the common features came about through the dissemination of affiliated tales in the oral tradition independently recovered by these two authors. The question is whether they are sufficiently cognate to necessitate such a tradition that might then be attached to remote Eastern sources. Allowing for such a tradition necessitates, in turn, that it broke into two groups, those featuring sexual rivalry and jealousy as the grounds for dissension and those that did not.

---

who is its object views it as a challenge that authorizes the infidelity.' *À la recherche du temps perdu* (Paris: Gallimard, 1954), vol. III, p. 150. For a further discussion of 'psychological reactance,' see Jon Elster, *Alchemies of the Mind: Rationality and the Emotions* (Cambridge: Cambridge University Press, 1999), p. 267.

VII. Fable 5
The Three Brothers

ISABELLA

Three brothers, poor men, go out into the world in search of a livelihood, and in the end return to their own house again rich and prosperous.

I have often heard it said that wit is always the master of force, and that there is no undertaking in the whole world, however difficult and arduous, that a man of ingenuity cannot perform. The truth of this I'll prove to you in the short tale to follow if you'll lend me your attention.

In this city of ours there once lived a poor man who had three sons, but by reason of his great poverty he could find no means to feed and rear them. Thus pressed by need and aware of the cruel poverty and decaying strength of their father, these three youths consulted among themselves and resolved to lighten their father's burdens by going out into the world to wander from place to place with scrip and staff in search of sustenance and means to keep themselves alive in the coming days. Kneeling humbly before their father, they begged him to give them permission to go out into the world in search of a livelihood, promising at the same time to come back to their city at the end of ten years' time. With this purpose in their minds they set forth, travelling until they came to a certain place where it seemed best that they should part from one another.

The eldest of the brothers happened to find his way into a camp of soldiers marching to the wars, and straightway he agreed to take service with the head of the brigade. In a short time he grew highly expert in the art of war, a powerful man-at-arms and a doughty fighter, so much so that he took a leading place among his fellows. He was so nimble and dexterous that he could scale the walls of the highest keeps with a dagger in each hand.

The second brother came to a certain seaport where many ships were under construction. Establishing himself with one of the master shipwrights, a man greatly skilled in his craft, he set to work with such diligence that in a little time there was no other workman equal to him in his calling, and the good report of him spread throughout the country.

The youngest brother, as it chanced, one day came to a certain place where a nightingale was singing most sweetly. He was so charmed and fascinated by it that he went in pursuit, following the traces and the song of this Philomela by shady valleys and thick woods, lonely forests, and regions forlorn, deserted, and uninhabited. The sweetness of the bird's song took such a strong hold over him that he continued to dwell in these wild woods, forgetful of the way that led back to the world of men. There he lived ten whole years in this solitary state, becoming, as it were, a wild man of the woods. During such a long period of time, and by his uninterrupted habitation of this place, he became skilled in the tongue of all the birds to which he listened with the keenest pleasure, understanding all they had to tell him and becoming more familiar to them than the god Pan was to the fauns.

When the appointed day had come for the brothers to return home, the first and second went to the meeting place and there awaited the third. As he approached, naked as he was and all covered with hair, they ran to meet him and, out of the tender love they had for him, they broke into tears, embracing and kissing him a thousand times over while getting him back into some clothes. Next they went to an inn to get food, and while they sat there, what should appear but a bird which alighted upon a tree and as it sweetly sang, it said, 'Be it known to you, O men who sit and eat, that near the cornerstone of this inn a mighty treasure is hidden, kept there through many a long year for you,' and so having spoken, the bird flew away.

Then the brother who had come last to the place of meeting explained to the two others the meaning of the bird's words, and right away they began digging in the place described and removed the treasure they found there. In this manner, they all became men of wealth and means, and returned to their father.

After receiving the paternal embrace, there followed a magnificent feast. Then in days following, the youngest brother heard the song of another bird, which spoke as follows: 'In the Aegean Sea, some ten miles from the land, there is an island by the name of Chios, whereupon the daughter of Apollo built a massy castle of marble. At the entrance lies a serpent, its guardian, spitting out fire and venom from its mouth, while upon the threshold there is a chained basilisk. There Aglaea, one of the fairest ladies in the entire world, is kept a prisoner with all the treasure that she heaped up and gathered together, along with a vast store of coin. Whoever goes to this place and scales the tower will become the master of the treasure and of Aglaea as well.' When the bird had concluded its words, it flew away. Once their meaning had become clear, the three brothers resolved to go to this place, the first promising to scale the tower by the aid of two daggers and the second to build a swift-sailing ship.

Their vessel was completed in a very short time, allowing them to set forth. After crossing the sea with good fortune, carried along by the favourable breezes, they found themselves one morning close to the isle of Chios just before the break of day. Then the man-at-arms, aided by his two daggers, climbed the tower, there seizing and binding Aglaea with a cord before handing her over to his brothers. Next, after he had removed all the rubies and precious stones as well as the heaps of gold from their hiding places, he descended, elated at heart, and so the three adventurers, leaving naked the plundered land, together returned to their fatherland safe and sound.

But with regard to the lady, seeing that it was impossible to divide her into three parts, there arose a sharp dispute among the brothers as to which one should have her, a dispute both heated and drawn out. At last, the case was taken to a court of law, but for its decision we will have to wait for a very long time, thereby leaving the matter entirely up to us.

When Isabella had brought her short story to an end, she put her hand into her pocket and drew out a scroll upon which her enigma was written, and read out the following:

> A proud black steed, with wings of white,
> The earth ne'er touches in its flight;
> Behind it bears the rein which guides,
> And wearies oft the man who rides.
> Great store of wealth within it brings,
> Now flaps its plumes and now its wings,
> Now midst the strife of battle lies,
> Now peaceful fares; has two great eyes,
> But naught can see; runs to and fro,
> And bears man where he would not go.

This enigma, so cleverly set forth by Isabella, was in a certain sense understood by all the company, for it could be held to describe nothing other than a stately ship with its white sails but its hull made black by pitch. It ploughs the sea and flees the shores in order not to be shattered on the rocks. It has its rudder at the rear that directs its course, and rows of oars on either side resembling wings. In times of peace it is taken up with traffic, and in time of war it goes forth to battle. In front it has two great eyes that nevertheless see nothing, and sometimes by hazard carries men onto reefs and into strange regions where they would rather not go.

Now, because the hour was late, the Signora requested the torches to be lit, and gave leave to all the ladies and gentlemen to return to their dwellings, at the same time directly charging them to reappear upon the following evening to take their accustomed places ready to continue the entertainment. By one accord, they all promised to obey her command.

The End of the Seventh Night

VII.5 Commentary

Straparola recounts here the tale of the three brothers who, given the complementary skills they have acquired, form the perfect team for rescuing a desirable young woman before coming to words or blows over which of the three merits her most. It is a story of ancient standing that maintained an uninterrupted history from the time of the early Sanskrit writers down to the folk raconteurs of the nineteenth century. The versions in the *Novelle antiche*, the *Paradiso degli Alberti*, the *Novelle e favola* of Morlini, the *Piacevoli notti*, and the *Pentamerone* of Basile may constitute all the evidence that remains of this story's passage through the Renaissance, but they will suffice to demonstrate that it was in circulation in the West at least as early as the late thirteenth century and that it was known to the Renaissance in multiple forms in parallel to the extensive oral tradition that carried this story type from its Western origins down to the early twentieth century.

This tale, despite its brevity, has three principal parts, each of which is subject to considerable variation. The first part, a late addition, features the departure from the parental abode, whether for reasons of poverty, or to learn a trade, or for adventure. Typically, the protagonists are brothers, as in the present tale, and they will come to a parting of the ways, striking out on their own during an apprenticeship period, but with an agreed-upon rendezvous date. Sometimes one fails to return and must be sought, or one lingers and causes concern. But once together, they either go back to the paternal hearth before setting off in quest of a lost princess, or they go in search of her straightway. The second part of the story entails a set of skills requisite for liberating an abducted heroine from a castle, rock, dragon, or ogre. The important point is that the abilities acquired in the first part are now called upon to effect the rescue. In the final section a dispute ensues over the relative merits of each contribution, amounting to a riddle that, in the present story, remains unresolved. But in other tales, the brothers slay one another, or cede the girl to their father, or see her given away to an independent suitor, or allow her to choose for herself. The tale has many potential resolutions and yet it is always the same tale, for the skills acquired or assigned at the outset contribute first to a collaborative search and rescue and then to a showdown over who will possess the girl. The story may appear here for its resemblance to the preceding story, in which adjudicants and audiences alike are unable to discern winners and losers in contests among three contestants.

Worth mentioning in passing is the story's proximity to a 'rising' tale in which a protagonist from an impoverished background, through the rescue of an aristocratic maiden, is destined not only to win her for his bride, but her considerable wealth and inheritance into the bargain. The present tale sets up those narrative expectations, yet forestalls the 'fairy tale' potential by leaving the contention unresolved, thus undermining the order of heroic initiation and bride winning. Arguably, Straparola is the first author to have recorded (or written, according to Ruth Bottigheimer) such rags-to-riches wonder tales, including 'Constantino and His Wonderful Cat' (XI.1) and 'Adamantina's Astonishing Doll' (V.2), both of them rather strange and ironic representations of the genre. The present tale inaugurates but frustrates those arriviste aspirations.

Speculation is always free as to why some tales endure while others die out or modulate into different stories. Concerning the present tale, Valentin Schmidt made much of the opening voyage into the world and the emblematic significance of the respective apprenticeships, the one becoming a soldier, the other a shipbuilder, and the third a wild-man communicant with the creatures of the woods.[46] He perceived in these callings the estates of man, the soldier fighting to protect the common

---

46 *Die Märchen des Straparola*, vol. I of *Sammlung alter Märchen aus dem Italianischen* (Berlin: Duncker and Humblot, 1817), pp. 353–4.

good from foreign influences, the second representing the material production of the working classes, while the third pursues the eternal word or the hidden secrets of life through the forces of nature. If there is resistance to this romanticized symbolism, it is because these profiles change from story to story within the narrative tradition, diluting any sense of an archetypal social order. What are we to understand, for example, when the story features a thief or a man who specializes in catching falling objects? The trades are merely a function of the rescue. Nevertheless, there is a kind of allegory embedded in the design: three young men embark upon a life road, choose professions, labour collaboratively in a common endeavour, yet ultimately come into competition for the universally desired woman. In short, men may cooperate in work, yet use that work prowess to qualify for females. Moreover, the heroine is given an emblematic name, Aglaea (originating with Hesiod), better known as Charis, thereby suggesting radiant brightness, purity, or splendour, being the youngest of the three Graces and married to the god of Fire. She is complete desire for whom all men compete in accordance with their endowments and skills. Thus, the story responds to a symbolic glossing that reflects certain large truths about the *Bildungs* and mating processes. In a less archetypal vein, it is a problem tale in which three men contribute to a common goal, the liberation of a princess or goddess, who then becomes an indivisible prize (as in the preceding story). The reader, meanwhile, is challenged to arbitrate in choosing the most deserving – a veritable koan. Inversely, the story reveals the simple truth that with regard to bride selection, societies must have their means to determine winners and losers while avoiding hostility, vengeance, or disaffection in the community. Contenders may be sent on quests, required to perform great feats, or offer superlative gifts, all in the hopes of establishing a clear order of merit, as the many following stories in this tradition will reveal. But where due process is followed and no natural choice emerges, allies may become enemies and the raw combative instincts of the race may come to the surface, tragically even among brothers. A vague perception of such truisms must have contributed to the longevity of this thematic group.

In the simplest structural sense, the story may be compared to that of the three nuns in competition for the title of abbess who are to be adjudicated according to their performances of remarkable and memorable feats (VI.4). This was a contingency measure to break a tie vote in a serious matter, but of course sets up the conditions for one of Straparola's most outlandish tales, one that, like the present story, arrives at an impasse that is passed along to the reader. Equally, it follows the pattern of 'The Three Idle Rogues' (VIII.1), in which a precious ring is claimed by all three, each of whom had a small and relatively equal part in its discovery. They too fall to blows and are stopped by a passer-by who offers to arbitrate, this time by staging a laziness contest which leads to performances of such equal merit that the impasse remains at the story's conclusion. Embedded in all three is the common pattern of the contest as a means to dispute resolution that in the end solves little, but provides occasions for fanciful and hyperbolical skills, adroit feats with the privy parts, or remarkable manifestations of laziness and stupidity. The story is a reminder, as well, of the circumstantial fact that jewels, leadership positions, and wives entail exclusive enjoyment; they are indivisible, without justice for all.

The origin of the story type is something of a puzzle. The shortest answer is that Straparola took it nearly verbatim from Girolamo Morlini's 'De fratibus qui per orbem pererrando ditati sunt' (Three brothers who, after wandering the globe, became rich).[47] There is little to be said about this essentially unmodified appropriation in terms of literary adaptation and development; it is the same story and there the matter ends, unless something remains to be settled on the score of plagiarism. There can be little doubt that Straparola had pages to fill and turned to this rather rare Latin work (rare because nearly all copies had been destroyed by the authorities immediately after its publication in 1520) to swell the girth of his second volume. Of greater interest is the constitution of the Morlini-Straparola story in the larger context of the history of its motifs. Noteworthy are the association of the third brother with the wildman and the presence of a basilisk guarding the forlorn girl. The role of the seer figure for locating the missing girl is now taken over by the Western wodewose, a variation that crept in along the way, while the basilisk, in telltale fashion, is forgotten when it comes to rescuing the girl from her monster guardians – a little like forgetting the dragon in the story of St George. There is reason to think that Morlini found his prototype among the folk in a decayed and simplified form in which this feature had atrophied.

The story of the King of Jerusalem and his four sons in the Codici Panciatichiano-Palatino 138 (being an early manuscript version of *Le*

---

47 From *Novellai, fabulae, comoedia* (Naples: Pasquet de Salo, 1520); *Les nouvelles de Girolamo Morlini*, trans. Fernand Caussy (Paris: E. Sanson, 1904), no. 80, pp. 181–4. See also *Novelle e favole*, ed. Giovanni Villani (Rome: Salerno, 1983), pp. 374–9.

novelle antiche that contained stories not included among the 100 that became *Il Novellino*), is perhaps the oldest surviving Western form of the tale. The king's four sons are handsome and courteous. They divide up to visit Paris, Sicily, Catalonia, and Genoa, where each learns a specific skill. The first could study and learn all things, the second became an expert with the crossbow, the third a subtle thief, and the fourth a master shipwright. After ten years they were to meet and return home. Upon their arrival their father threw a great feast (a feature retained by Straparola), gave them high positions, and asked for an account of their years abroad. The second part of the story entails an island guarded by a serpent. The scholar locates the princess, the shipwright crafts a vessel, the thief rescues the girl from the dragon, and the marksman protects them from the pursuing beast by shooting out its eyes – at which point the story breaks off (due to the loss of manuscript pages). It is, in fact, defective throughout, but at this juncture we can only assume that a dispute breaks out concerning their respective contributions and that some measure is taken to break the tie. What we have of the story is important, however, in establishing the link between Eastern and Western versions and in representing the state of the tale in the Latin West by the mid-thirteenth century.[48] The material makes another early appearance in *Il paradiso degli Alberti*, a romance by Giovanni Gherardi (da Prato), who, in an early section, associates the founding of his city with the Eastern folk tale of the 'I Quattro fratelli artefici' (the four clever brothers). In Giovanni's version, the girl is turned into a hawk by a witch. She nearly drowns in a river, but is rescued by four friends who fight for her and in the end come to a dispute over their respective contributions to the group endeavour. The crisis is resolved when the girl is allowed to choose for herself by order of the council of the gods. The work dates to 1389 and is yet another witness to the circulation of the Eastern tale among Western writers.[49]

---

48 *Le novelle antiche dei codici panciatichiano-palatino 138 e laurenziana-gaddiano 193*, intro. Guido Biagi (Florence: G.C. Sansoni, 1880), Biagi no. 156 / Papanti no. 23, pp. 201–4. This manuscript was discovered by the Russian scholar Alessandro Wesselofsky, bearing the title 'Fiore di Filosofi'; it contains 120 stories, but has been much damaged by humidity over the years. This is the last story in the 'Panciaticiano-Palatino' section.

49 *Il paradiso degli Alberti*, ed. Antonio Lanza (Rome: Salerno, 1975). Extensive annotations tracing the story to Eastern sources may be found in Giovanni da Prato, *Il paradiso degli Alberti: Ritrovi e ragionamenti del 1389, romanzo dal codice autografo e anonimo della Riccardiana*, ed. Alessandro Wesselofsky (Bologna: G. Romagnoli,

Turning now to the Eastern prototypes, it may prove that the story originated in a myth about the resuscitation of dangerous beasts through the unwise use of fanciful or magic gifts. In the *Panchatantra* account, four young friends form a micro-society, of whom three had learned very particular skills, while the fourth was merely intelligent, but had no 'science.' They thought of dropping him from their quest for riches because he could do nothing to win the favour of a king, yet they kept him out of loyalty. Along the way they find a dead lion and make it the object of their skills. One would assemble the bones, another the blood and flesh, and the third would bring it to life (in anticipation of the many tales in which craftsmen would fashion a woman and a physician would grant her life). But the intelligent one, who could contribute nothing, nevertheless understood the consequences of such brilliant craftsmanship and hied himself up a tree, whereby he alone survived the ferocity of the resuscitated beast.[50] There is a moral in that. Thereafter, the principle was extended to the risky creation or resuscitation of a winsome and desirable woman. The archetypal overtones of that intervention I leave to the reader's musing. Three brothers contributed to her fashioning and painting as a machine doll. The fourth brother alone had the power to animate her with life, whereupon he falls in love with her and 'claims her by right of invention, because I breathed into her a soul that could be loved, nor was there any enjoyment in her but for me.' The question was, of course, who deserved her most (a further account will be given below).[51] The story of the princess and the three Brahmin suitors in the

---

1867), vol. I, pt. 2, pp. 239–70; vol. II, pp. 102–71. Four Etruscan youths riding out together see a beautiful sparrowhawk entangled in a thorn bush and nearly drowned. The first sees its danger, another saves it by warming it on his breast, another remembers the forgotten bird (?), while the fourth gives it a balm or medication, whereupon it suddenly recovers its original life form as Melissa, daughter of Odysseus under the spell of the jealous Circe. All four now seek her in marriage and repair to the temple of Jupiter for a decision. The male gods wisely defer to Venus and Minerva, but given the harmony between those two, the matter remained unresolved. This is the folk tale in humanist guise with a mythological overlay, proof of its passage in Italy around 1400.

50 *Pantschatantra*, ed. Theodor Benfey (Leipzig: F.A. Brockhaus, 1859), vol. I, pt. 104, pp. 290*ff*; 'Les Brahmanes et le lion' in the *Pañcatantra*, trans. Édouard Lancereau (Paris: Gallimard [1871], 1965), bk. V, no. 4, pp. 321–2.

51 This story is undoubtedly very ancient, having a close affinity with the tales from the Vikramaditja tradition. It reappears in *The Saga of Ardschi-Bordschi*, ed. Rachel Harriett Busk, *Sagas from the Far East; or Kalmouk and Mongolian Traditionary Tales* (London: Griffith & Farran, 1873), p. 301, which is the Mongolian

Vetalapanchavimsati (Twenty-five tales of a demon or vampire) may serve as a point of departure from which the present story may be said to have evolved during its gradual migration towards the West.[52] In this, the fifth tale, the princess Somaprabha (Moonbeam) tells her parents that the man she marries must possess either great heroism, advanced learning, or magic powers. Three Brahmins independently seek her hand and through different members of her family she is promised to each. The first has the power to create a magic flying chariot, the second is an expert in weapons and missiles, while the third is a man of great knowledge and insight. (In these three we may imagine the man of arms, the master builder, and the man of insight and intuition.) All three grooms arrive on the wedding day and the king must confront the problem, for each has a legitimate claim; justice is a precious principle, yet there can only be one victor. Meanwhile, Somaprabha disappears and the king

---

Vetalapanchavimsati. It is also the fifth tale in the Persian *Tooti Nameh or Tales of a Parrot* (Calcutta and London: J. Debrett, 1801), pp. 49–53, in which a goldsmith, carpenter, taylor, and hermit quarrel over a wooden woman they have respectively carved, clothed, embellished, and brought to life. The hermit accuses the others of taking his lawful spouse and hails them before the Cutwal. Then the judge says she is his brother's wife, whom they have killed. The hopeless dispute continues until it is suggested that they go to the 'Tree of Decision.' As they argue, the tree opens, the woman enters and returns to wood.

52 'The Story of Somaprabha and Her Three Suitors,' included in Somadeva's *Katha sarit sagara* (The Ocean of Streams of Story), trans. C.H. Tawney (Calcutta: Munshiram Manoharlal [1880], 1992), vol. II, pp. 258–60. In the 10-volume edition published in Delhi by Motilal Banarsidas in 1923, it is chap. 80, no. 163G, vol. VI, pp. 200–8. This story is closely related to 'The Three Young Brahmins Who Restored a Dead Lady to Life,' *Ocean*, vol. VI, pp. 179–81. All three are in love with the same girl and argue over her before she dies of a fever. One builds his hut on her grave, another washes her bones in the Ganges, and the third becomes an ascetic. When the ascetic learns the art of resuscitation and she is brought back to life, the quarrel revives concerning who has rendered her the greater service, but the king ultimately favours the one who built the hut and attended her ashes. Essentially the same story ('The Three Young Brahmins') was translated by the Baron Daniel Lescallier in his *Trône enchanté, conte indien traduit du persan* (New York: J. Desnoues, 1817), vol. II, pp. 200*ff.* Among Penzer's annotations to the *Ocean of Story* is a variant in which the maiden is claimed by six young men who, failing to come to a decision among themselves, agree to cut her into pieces, shouting 'Strike! Strike!'; vol. VI, p. 264. In a Burmese version, the one who restores her to life is adjudged the most deserving. *The Precedents of Princess Thoodama Tsari*, trans R.F. St. A. St. John, *Folk-Lore Journal* 7 (1889), pp. 309*ff.* See also Sudhamma-Chāri, *The Precedents of Princess Thoodamma Tsari*, trans. Christopher J. Bandow (Rangoon: C. Bennett, 1881), pp. 53–5. (Both spellings are used.)

demands her whereabouts. Only the man of knowledge could say, for he understood that a rakshasa had taken her to a place in the forest. The man with magic powers offers to build a flying chariot capable of carrying all three of them to the house of the demon-witch. When the rakshasa appears in a rage, only the Brahmin skilled in arms could sever her head (the forgotten basilisk). The princess is rescued and together they return. Then the dispute begins, the king is vexed, and no obvious solution is in sight, but the king ultimately chooses the man of arms, the 'dragon slayer,' insofar as the strategist and the engineer are merely placed at his disposal. In this decision the military takes precedence over both halves of the university.

The story reappears in the Persian *Tooti-Nameh*, where the beautiful daughter of a rich merchant of Kabul declares that she would marry only the wisest or the most skilful man to be found.[53] Three young men respond to the invitation and make their bids to her father. One could find lost objects and foresee the future, another could make a horse of wood that floats in the air, while the third was an archer able to pierce any object. (Both archers and flying animals enter into some of the later Western versions.) During the night, the daughter disappears. Upon consulting the youths, the merchant discovers from the clairvoyant one

---

53 Ziya al-Din Nakhshabi, *The Tooti Nameh or Tales of a Parrot* (Persian and English) (Calcutta and London: J. Debrett, 1801), no. 22. There are subtle differences between the versions in the Persian and Turkish recensions of this work. See Nakhshabi, *Das persische papagaienbuch* (Tuti nameh), trans. Karl Jacob Ludwig Iken (Berlin: Hegner, [1905]), p. 93 and [The Turkish] *Tuti-Nameh, das Papageianbuch*, trans. Georg Rosen (Leipzig: Insel Verlag, [1912]), vol. II, p. 165. An important variant version described by W.A. Clouston exists in the unique Persian MS. of the 'Sindibad Nama' in the India Office Library. A demon carries the princess away to his cave in the mountains of Yemen. The king promises her in marriage, along with half the kingdom, to anyone who could retrieve her. Four brothers volunteer and their trades are of some interest; one is a world traveller and guide, the second is a crafty robber, the third is a man of arms, and the last is a physician. New to the formula are the physician and the robber, both of whom will reappear frequently in subsequent versions in the West. The guide serves as seer and obviates the need for a supernatural means of transportation supplied by a builder; he simply guides them to the cave. The warrior liberates her while the demon is away, the physician heals the damsel, who has fallen ill, while the fighter dispatches an army of club-wielding dívs. Information concerning the outcome is not provided, but clearly they must all return, each seeking favour for his part in the rescue. But how the impasse is broken is beyond guessing. *Popular Tales and Fictions*, ed. Christine Goldberg (Santa Barbara: ABC Clio, 2002), p. 127.

that she had been abducted by a fairy and taken to a mountain top. The carpenter then makes a wooden horse and the archer ascends the mountain to shoot the fairy and fetch the girl. Each one then claims her and the dispute breaks out. In this version, the merchant actually makes his choice, which falls on the archer, who, in his estimation, had shown courage and enterprise, whereas the others showed merely skill. The story is now entirely familiar and the patterns confirmed, despite the alterations accommodating local times and cultures. This is of a girl who establishes her criteria for marriage, but who implicitly defers to her father in making the final choice. Fundamentally, it is about male competitive strategies for anticipating what a girl seeks most in a man: protective prowess, material production, or spiritual insight. This girl's father chooses protective prowess, hence brawn over building and brains. The three categories of choice are themselves instructive in a game that allows for no compounding: football hero, engineer, or literary critic.

A parallel tradition originating in the East that tells of the wanderings and exploits of the three sagacious sons of a king lends a certain structural support to the present story. In its principal form, King Gaiffer had three sons whom he raised up in wisdom under the tutelage of the finest teachers. He first tested them by offering them power, which all three refused. He then sent them out into the world, where they demonstrated their acuity through close attention to detail. They are, for a start, able to determine the exact nature and condition of a missing camel – that it was blind in one eye and carrying a pregnant woman – by examining the evidence that remained after its passage. As advisers to King Beramo, they are sent after the stolen mirror of justice, which they are able to recover. During their absence the king falls in love, has a falling out with the beloved, exiles her to the forest, and then plunges into a state of remorse. Through careful management, the three princes cure his insomnia and distract him in appropriate ways until news of the missing girl is received and reconciliation can be brought about. Ultimately, these three brothers who go into the world to prove their great wisdom receive kingdoms, two of them through romantic connections.

The story tradition suggests structural affinities with the tale of the three princes who seek to discover the most wonderful things or to perform the wisest feats in order to win the hand of the princess with whom all three are in love. This story begins as the *Hasht Bihisht* (Eight stories of paradise) written in 1302 by Amir Khusrau of Delhi. It was first translated in the West by Christoforo Armeno as the *Peregrinaggio di tre giovani figliuoli del re di Serendippo* (from the Persian Sarendib), first published in

Venice by Michele Tramezzino in 1557.[54] A variant by Béroalde de Verville appears in his *Voyage des princes fortunez*. Horace Walpole read the work in 1754 as *The Three Princes of Serendip* (Sri Lanka or Ceylon), and thereafter enriched the English language with the word serendipity, the faculty of happening upon or making fortunate discoveries when not in search of them. This, however, is a byway to the principal narrative tradition.

The Western folk tale of the three princes must have derived its substance and design from the Eastern story of the princess who chooses her husband according to the skill, wisdom, or sacrifice employed on her behalf, as in the version in the *Sindibad nama*. The history of this link, however, is perplexed by the tale of 'Prince Ahmed and the Peri Banu,' Nights 644–67 of the *Arabian Nights*, which might offer itself as a prospective channel of transmission, were there greater certainty that it was available in the pre-Straparolan literary world.[55] This is the eternal problem with the later tales in the *Nights*, because Galland, who finished his assembly of *Les mille et une nuits* only at the beginning of the eighteenth century, appears at times to have taken more liberties than are supposed in generating his oriental tales. Particular to this version is the figure of the physician, known from the *Sindibad nama* and represented by Basile in the *Pentamerone*, who must heal the dying princess with his magic herbs, potions, or fruits. The tale's adherence, whether early or late, to this alternative tradition, diminishes its direct pertinence to Straparola, in any case, and for that reason need not be retold in detail. Instructively, however, it is the same generic tale. Three princes, all of them in love with their cousin, are challenged by her father to travel and see the world first and bring back the most wondrous objects they can find. This detour resembles the apprentice section of the present tale, but the prize is already in sight and the men are already in competition. The king is concerned that the issue be resolved amicably and equitably because he fears the feud that might otherwise ensue between the brothers. According to formula, they come to a tripartite division of the road and agree to meet in a year. One purchases a flying carpet for an exorbitant price, the next an ivory telescope (or spy tube) with which he felt certain to win the princess, while the third purchases a healing apple, the scent of which

---

54 Ed. Renzo Bragantini (Rome: Salerno, 2000), esp. pp. 9–53.
55 *Tales from the Arabian Nights*, trans. Richard F. Burton, ed. David Shumaker (New York: Avenel Books [Crown Publishers], 1977), pp. 766–823. A tale similar to this appears in Jón Arneson's *Icelandic Legends*, trans. Erikr Magnússon (London: Richard Bentley, 1864), pp. 348–54.

had the virtue of revitalizing those on the verge of death. It was an expensive shopping spree to impress their cousin. When the girl goes missing, the far-sighted one locates her, the carpet carries them to her bedside far away, and the apple heals her. Upon their return, the king is unable to decide, for the contest is no longer over the intrinsic value of the objects as wonder purchases, but their roles in the rescue. He then proposes a shooting contest, the outcome of which is rejected by the two who lose, leading to the famous Peri Banu story that lies outside our present purposes. Clearly, these initial episodes belong to the 'Three Brothers' tradition, but they appear to be a later Oriental or Occidental adaptation, possibly influenced by Western developments in the tradition. The tale as we have it in the *Arabian Nights* seems pitched to the tastes and aesthetics of the French salon, but that is a question for others to resolve.

The story was also in circulation in the West in a form associated with the philosopher Bidpai and the textual tradition of the *Kalila wa Dimna*. This is a novel version insofar as the four suitors are no longer brothers, nor do they go into the world with special skills or in search of trades or occupations. Rather, they are distinguished by social class and innate traits or defining beliefs, for one is a king's son, the second a merchant's son, the third a beautiful nobleman, and the fourth a peasant's son. The first is a fatalist who believes that all is determined by God's will, which demands patience, whereas the second believes in prudence, the third in beauty, and the fourth in labour. They come to the city of Methrun (Sanskrit: Mathura) and there take up activities around the city until they all become involved in the rescue of a merchant's wife, which tests each of their qualities. This work was known in German as early as 1474 in a translation by Anton von Pforr, made from the Latin *Directorium humanae vitae* of Giovanni di Capua under the general title *Das Buch der Beispiele der alten Weisen*.[56]

Giambattista Basile's *Pentamerone*, appearing in print in 1634, tells of a dead princess who must be restored to life by the juice of a herb squeezed directly into her mouth.[57] Hence, there can be little doubt that a parallel version of the basic design was in circulation in Renaissance

---

56 'Der königssohn und seine Freunde' (The king's son and his friend) in *Das Buch der Weisen in lust und lehrreichen Erzählungen des indischen Philosophen Bidpai*, trans. Philipp Wolf (Stuttgart: Scheible, 1839), bk. 14, pt. 2, pp. 108–22.

57 'I cinque figli' (The five sons), Day Five, Seventh Pastime (V.7) of *Lo cunto de li cunti*, 5 vols. (Naples: Ottavio Beltrano, 1634–6); *Il Pentamerone or The Tale of Tales*, trans. Richard Burton (New York: Boni & Liveright, 1927), pp. 431–5.

Europe that called for a physician suitor and the healing of the abducted girl. There are, nevertheless, points in common with the Morlini-Straparola group. The story begins with a father overburdened by the care of his five sons, for which reason he sends them away for a year to learn a craft. This apprenticeship phase is a contribution added during the Renaissance (the Eastern tales begin directly with the rivalry over the prospective bride). One becomes a master thief, eliciting the father's disapproving irony that he will end up on the gibbet. The second learns boat building, as in the present tale, the third is an ace with a crossbow, as in the earliest versions, the fourth knows a herb that can raise the dead, from the Arabic tradition, while the fifth learns the language of the animals, known to this story tradition from as early as the *Katha sarit sagara*.[58] Upon their return, they are questioned and evaluated by their father, as in all the tales in which a numbskull son, who learns only such a useless skill as bird talk in school, earns his father's anger and must go forth destitute into the world to prove himself. In Basile's tale, this skill leads to the discovery of the abducted princess who had been carried to a remote rock, followed by the proclamation concerning her rescue. The brothers agree to go as a team, the shipbuilder making a craft to sail them all to Sardinia. There they find her with her head resting on the breast of a sleeping ogre. The thief places a stone on the monster's stomach and steals the girl (thereby avoiding immediate combat). The giant wakes up, turns into a black cloud and pursues them. After the princess gives a warning she drops dead, the marksman shoots out the ogre's eye, and the girl is returned to her lamenting father. But one son remains, he who can find the herb on the shores of Sardinia that will restore her to life. Such rapid episodic inventions suggest an oral rather than a written source, a further indication that the story type had already diversified

---

58 A strangely truncated version of the same story described above from the *Vetalapanchavimsati* occurs four stories later, chap. 83, Vetala 9, 'Story of Anangarati and her four suitors,' in which the second is gifted with an understanding of the language of animals. *The Katha sarit sagara*, trans. C.H. Tawney (Calcutta: Munshiram Manoharlal [1880], 1992), vol. II, p. 276. These brothers are a tailor, one who knows the language of animals, a strong man, and a physician-magician who can resuscitate the dead. Each competes for the girl, but the choice is given to the king, who decides that the tailor is beneath his daughter, the language of animals is useless, and the fourth is just a boasting magician, so he chooses the strong man as her social equal. In the 10-volume edition, trans. C.H. Tawney, ed. N.M. Penzer (Delhi: Banarsidass, 1923), bk. VII, chap. 83, this story is in vol. VII, pp. 1–4.

itself throughout Italy among the folk. A final twist is that to avoid a bleak outcome from the wrangling over their respective claims, the sons all agree that the girl should be awarded to their father, who practically regains his youth at the prospect.

The story is rewritten by Clemens Brentano in *Das Märchen von dem Schulmeister Klopfstock und seinem fünf Söhnen* (The tale of the schoolmaster Klopfstock and his five sons).[59] The author recreates the tale in a German milieu with Germanic names. After a long discussion, the sons agree that old Klopfstock should have the girl, but in fact she is allowed to choose, and she takes the poet, as Romantic sensibilities might well dictate. To avoid strife, the king then divides his kingdom in half, one portion of which he subdivides between the remaining sons.

By the nineteenth century, the story was known throughout Europe and collected by folklorists in Greece and Albania as well as in Spain and Germany. Some of them are remarkably close to Straparola's tale in order and ethos, while others vary, but the matter of actual influence remains moot. J.G. von Hahn collected a variant in Greece that combines the apprenticeship motif with the skills and implements from the Arabian tradition.[60] Three youths fall in love with the same girl. The winner, however, will be selected, not for his marvellous purchase or great wisdom, but for his power to provide. All are sent into the world for three years to learn a trade. One becomes an astronomer (the counterpart to possessing an ivory telescope), the second can raise the dead (the counterpart to the physician or the smelling apple that restores life), while the third can run with great speed and go anywhere he desires. It is then a matter of how these diverse accomplishments achieve equal esteem for their contribution to the girl's rescue. The astronomer reads her sickness in the stars, the physician prepares the saving potion, and the third runs to her bedside to pour it down her throat. The point of the story is the

---

59 *Das Märchen von dem Schulmeister Klopfstock und seinem fünf Söhnen* (Heidelberg: Schneider [orig. ca. 1815], 1948). Earliest among the German versions is that to be found in Everhardus Guernerus Happelius, *Der ungarische Kriegs-Roman* (Ulm: Wagner, 1685), pp. 537–41. The story is in two parts. In the first, three skilled boys reveal their arts in the presence of a nobleman, while in the second they make a long sea journey to rescue an abducted daughter from a demon. The number of versions of the basic fable type is staggering, not only in German-speaking regions, but in Greek, Serbo-Croatian, Bulgarian, Albanian, Czech, and Russian.

60 Johann Georg von Hahn, *Neoellenica paramythia* or *Contes populaires grecs* (Copenhagen: A.-F. Høst, 1879), no. 2, pp. 98*ff*; also ed. Jean Pio (Athens: Verlag D. Karavia, 2002).

challenge presented to the young lady in the everyday situation of having to choose between her doctor, lawyer, merchant, or chief.

Three twentieth-century versions of the generic tale may be mentioned in passing. Elizabeth Jamison Hodges republished *The Three Princes of Serendip* in 1964, which incorporates the now famous story; Eric A. Kimmel, in *The Three Princes*, tells of the princess who sends off her three suitors to find the most wonderful thing in the world; and Isaac Asimov provides yet another version in *Magic: The Final Fantasy Collection*, 'The Fable of the Three Princes.' Of the three, that by Kimmel is the most akin to Straparola.[61]

A third potential point of entry of the story type from the East is through the Mongols – the matter is much contested. But for the record, a story in outline from the Kalmuks with its fantastic variations, brings further matter to a comparative approach.[62] The age of the story is difficult to estimate; there is a tendency to add years to works from such remote cultures, but the disposition of the story appears rather modern. In this complex tale there are now six adventurers: a rich young man, an astrologer, a mechanic, a painter, a physician, and a blacksmith who travel the world together. They go their separate ways when they come to the estuary channels of a great river. Before parting, each plants a tree of life, the state of which reflects the life condition of the planter. The feature is common to many folk tales, including cognate tales in 'the truth-speaking bird' group (IV.3). They too agree to make this their rendezvous point at a given time in the future. The rich young man marries a beautiful girl, but she is abducted by the Khan, while the hero is killed and buried under a rock. When the others meet, they note the withered tree of their absent colleague. The astrologer discovers the body, the smith breaks open the rock, and the physician restores him to life. This is a telling variant employing the otherwise familiar skills and places. The young man tells his story and they all agree to go in pursuit of the maiden without further mention that she is his wife. The mechanic fashions a flying wooden bird, decorated by the painter, which functions

---

61 Elizabeth Jamieson Hodges, *The Three Princes of Serendip* (New York: Atheneum, 1964); Kimmel, *A Tale from the Middle East* (New York: Holiday House, 1994); Asimov, *Magic: The Final Fantasy Collection* (New York: HarperPrism, 1966).

62 Siddhi Kür, *Sagas from the Far East, or Kalmouk and Mongolian Traditionary Tales*, ed. Rachel Harriette Busk (London: Griffith & Farran, 1873), no. 9, 'Five to One,' pp. 105–14; or Bernhard Jülg, ed., *Mongolische Märchen Sammlung. Die neun Märchen des Siddhikür ... des Ardschi-Bordschi Chan* (Innsbruck: Wagner, 1868), no. 1, p. 55.

by pegs in the manner of the horse from the *Arabian Nights*. The young man climbs inside and hovers over the palace.[63] When the Khan sees the bird, he desires it for his wife. The motif is redolent of all those stories in which the hero gains access to the lady by enclosing himself inside a wonderful statue or chest that is taken into the palace as a gift. When the bird descends, the girl recognizes her man, embraces him lovingly, and leaps inside the bird; the pegs are turned and they make their escape. The debt to the *Arabian Nights* at this point is patent. (See the commentary to III.2.) When the companions reunite and discuss their relative contributions, a knife fight breaks out and all five are slain.

In 'Le Pou,' an Albanian tale, the princess is abducted by the devil and the king offers a reward for her safe return.[64] The number of initial collaborators has grown to seven, and the special skills have been further diversified: hearing sounds, causing the earth to open, stealing without the victim's knowledge, throwing objects, creating impregnable towers, shooting arrows, and catching things that fall from the sky – all very convenient for the adventure to follow. Tracing the cumulative order of these abilities in relation to the dating of the stories grows more complex with each added example. They find the sleeping fiend and liberate the girl from his breast precisely as in Basile's tale, now replacing her with a toad. Next they hurl the devil's shoes away to slow his pursuit. When he wakes up, his annoyance is manifest. He manages to follow them to their newly made tower, where he snatches the girl through a tiny hole and flies with her into the air. The marksman shoots him, the girl falls and is caught, and so they all return. In this story, the heroine is allowed to choose and she takes the one who caught her, not for the superiority of his feat, but because he was the youngest and best looking. There is a nice twist. This story has traits in common with 'Il negromante' (the

---

63 There are, however, older stories of flying birds in or on which the protagonist transports himself to the palace of his beloved. One such is the 'Story of Rupinika' in which Lohajangha rides upon a great bird with shell, discus, and mace, back to the abode of his beloved, hovering in the air over her house. *The Katha sarit sagara or Ocean of the Streams of Story*, trans. C.H. Tawney (Calcutta: Munshiram Manoharlal, 1992), vol. I, p. 79. In the 10-volume edition, published in Delhi by Banarsidass (1923), 1984, the story is found in vol. I, pp. 138–49.

64 From *Albanian Tales*, trans. M. Dozon, no. 4 as transcribed by W.A. Clouston, *Popular Tales and Fictions*, ed. Christine Goldberg (Santa Barbara: ABC Clio, 2002), p. 125. The reference is to *The Tricks of Women and Other Albanian Tales*, ed. Paul Fenimore Cooper, Auguste Dozon, and Holger Pederson (New York: W. Morrow and Co., 1928); the original French edition is entitled *Contes albanais* (Paris: Ernest Laroux, 1881).

necromancer) collected by Pitrè in Tuscany, which also features a queen married allegedly to a handsome king, but who is abducted by a magician and incarcerated in a tower, chained to her bed. A dove from her father reaches her and her plight is made known, calling for volunteers to rescue her. A father appears with seven sons, each endowed with a special gift. One could put his ear to the earth and determine that the necromancer was sleeping. The next was to scale the walls of the tower, the third was to approach the princess with so much stealth that the magician would not be wakened, another was to raise a great river, while the first with his universal knowledge continued to monitor actions inside the tower. Thus, step by step, the girl was rescued and rewards distributed. She becomes the ruling queen when her father dies.[65]

Of the many modern versions of the tale, there is room here for only two more, one from Italy and one from Germany. Jacob and Wilhelm Grimm published 'Die vier kunstreichen Brüder' (The four skilful brothers) in their *Kinder- und Hausmärchen*.[66] In this tale a poor father sends

---

65 Giuseppe Pitrè, *Novelle popolari toscane*, ed. Laura Regina Bruno (Palermo: ILA Palma, 2005), no. 10, pp. 433–9.

66 (Göttingen: Dieterich, 1857), no. 129; *Grimm's Complete Fairy Tales* (Garden City, NY: Nelson, n.d.), pp. 572–5; *The Great Fairy Tale Tradition*, ed. Jack Zipes (New York: Norton, 2001), pp. 342–6. Bolte and Polívka in their *Anmerkungen* or Annotations to the Grimm tales provide a profile of analogues as well, in vol. III, pp. 45–58, in relation to the story 'Die vier Kunstreichen Brüder.' Other German versions occur in Josef Haltrich, *Deutsche Volksmärchen aus dem Sachsenlande in Siebenbürgen* (Hildesheim: Olms, 2007), no. 42; orig. published as *Sächsische Volksmärchen aus Siebenbürgen* (Hermannstadt: Krafft, 1885). See also Ulrich Jahn, 'Glück und Verstand' in *Volksmärchen aus Pommern und Rügen* (Norden: Soltau, 1891; Hildesheim: Georg Olms, 1973), no. 15, pp. 83–90 in which the tale of the three skilful craftsmen who make a woman is an inset tale with which the little clockmaker makes the princess speak. In bringing her to break her silence, he becomes like the third in the story who breathes life into the statue; and Eberhard Werner Happel, *Der ungarische Kriegs-Roman ... mit allerhand nutz- und ergötzlichen historischen, politischen und dergleichen lesenswürdigen Sachen angefüllt* (Ulm: Wagner, 1685), in which the story is retold with peasant sons in the leading roles. The story is also told in full in 'Der Vogel Phönix' (The Phoenix bird), in which the king's three sons set out to find the magic bird to heal their father. The first two reject the offer of the bear to help them, but the third accepts and is led to the sacred object. Through errors in following instructions, however, the quest of the third son is prolonged. He must now steal a magic horse and return to the princess's father from whom he had stolen the bird. On his way home with the princess he ignores advice and is treacherously betrayed by his jealous older brothers, who steal both bird and girl. But the bear, who turns out to be a prince liberated only when the animal is

his four sons into the world to learn their trades. At a crossroads they part, vowing to meet in four years. The oldest becomes a master thief, the second an astronomer who is given a telescope, the third is a hunter and marksman, while the fourth is a tailor with a needle able to stitch up nearly anything. When they return home, their skills are demonstrated before their father by finding, stealing, shooting, and sewing eggs so well that the birds will later hatch. When a dragon steals the local princess, star-gazer finds her, the king supplies the ship, and the lady is found on a rock in the middle of the sea with the dragon's head in her lap (Arthur Rackham illustrated the story). The thief steals her, the dragon awakes and flies after them, the huntsman shoots it in the heart, it falls on the ship and smashes it, the tailor sews the planks of the wreck back together, and so they all arrive home. The quarrel ensues over their merits. This is a tale of apprenticeship and a potential rising tale as one of the brothers is entitled to a princess. But the king hits a dead centre, awarding the princess to none, although he does offer to each one-eighth of his kingdom, keeping the other half for himself.

Gherardo Nerucci collected the following tale in Montale Pistoiese called 'I tre regali a la novella de' Tappeti.'[67] A king with a beautiful

beheaded by the hero, rescues him again. This is the magic helping animal who, like Biancabella's snake sister, and the cat in the 'Puss in Boots' tradition (in some versions), is enchanted. This tale also parallels the services rendered by those among 'the grateful dead.' The boy's return is, of course, triumphant, leading to a father's healing and his own marriage. Johann Wilhelm Wolf, *Deutsche Hausmärchen* (Göttingen, 1851; Hildesheim: Olms, 1972), pp. 230–42.

67 *Sessanta novelle popolari montalesi*, ed. Roberto Fedi (Milan: Rizzoli, 1977), no. 40, pp. 335–40. This story was scaled down by Italo Calvino, with all vestiges of the Peri Banu part of the story suppressed that were still evident in Nerucci's version, no. 65, 'L'uva salamanna' (The Salamanna grapes), *Italian Folktales*, trans. George Martin (New York: Pantheon Books [1956], 1980), p. 229. See also Laura Gonzenbach, 'Von den sieben Brüdern die Zaubergaben hatten' (The seven brothers and their magic skills) in *Sicilianische Märchen*, 2 vols. (Leipzig: W. Engelmann, 1870), no. 45, vol. I, pp. 305–7, and no. 74, vol. II, p. 96. These seven possess very particular skills such as knocking down iron doors with a fist or raising the dead with a guitar, just two that will be required to rescue an abducted princess. When they allow the pursuing giant her little finger, they must virtually start over. In shooting the giant dead, they also kill the girl but bring her back with the guitar. For his vital service, the king chooses the guitar player as her husband and they all live together in the royal palace. Sebastiano Lo Nigro provides a study of the type with its variants in *Racconti popolari siciliani: Classificazione e bibliografia* (Florence: Leo Olschki, 1957), pp. 132–4. See also Pietro Pellizzari, 'Lu cuntu di li persi,' the story of five prodigious young men in *Fiabe e canzoni popolari del contado di Maglie in Terra d'Otranto* (Maglie:

daughter tells the three princes hankering after her from the neighbouring kingdom to go out and see the world; he who comes back with the finest and most spectacular gift will win her. They separate at the dividing of the road. One purchases a carpet, the second a telescope, and the third nothing but Salamanna grapes, noted for their healing powers.

Collegio Capece, 1881), p. 89; Hermann Knust, 'Der Kaufmannssohn aus Livorno' (The merchant of Leghorn's son) in *Italienische Märchen* (Berlin, 1867), no. 10, a version with six brothers, one of whom has the ability to locate persons by placing his ear to the ground; Georg Widter and Adam Wolf, *Volksmärchen aus Venetien* (Leipzig: F.A. Brockhaus, 1866), no. 6, 'Die vier kunstreicher Brüder' (The four clever brothers), whose trades are carpenter, hunter, magician, and thief; and Isaia Visentini, 'L'uccellino miraculoso' (The miraculous little bird) in *Fiabe Mantovane* (Bologna: Forni, 1968), pp. 60–8, a story of three brothers who seek adventure, one of whom brings back a princess; but this is a tale of rivalry and treachery among the three and resembles far more the three-brother versions of 'the grateful dead' motif (see XI.2 commentary). The story was also collected in Spain by Aurelio M. Espinosa, no. 15, 'La cosa más rara del mundo' (The rarest thing in the world) in *Cuentos Populares Españoles* (Stanford, CA: Stanford University Press, 1923–6), vol. I, pp. 360–4. These three protagonists, in love with the princess in the next kingdom, go in search of objects of great value. The first bought a floor carpet (alfombra), the next a spyglass (canuto), and the third a healing apple. The victory was awarded to the man with the spyglass, but the girl preferred the one with the apple, so he was the one who led her home. Espinosa's commentary follows in vol. III, pp. 83–9, where he offers references to cognate versions from Jewish, African, Antilles, and Indian sources. One overlooked is that collected by Consiglieri Pedroso, in which a maiden, equally in love with three princes, sends them on a mission to bring her keepsakes – the donor of the choicest among them winning her love. They find a universal portrait mirror, a resurrection candle, and an all-destinations rug. When they meet again at the crossroads where they had earlier parted ways, they discover in the mirror that the princess is dead, fly to her on the rug, and raise her with the candle. Unable to decide which operation was most meritorious, she immured herself in a tower. *Portuguese Folktales*, trans. Henriqueta Montiero, intro. W.R.S. Ralston (London: Folk Lore Society, 1882), no. 23, pp. 94–7. Other versions appear both in the Haute- and Basse-Bretagne. See François-Marie Luzel, *Contes populaires de la Basse-Bretagne* (Rennes: Presses Universitaires de Rennes, 1996), vol. III, pp. 217–25, and Paul Sébillot, *Contes populaires de la Haute-Bretagne* (Paris: G. Charpentier, 1880), vol. I, no. 8. The first of these is a tale of classic proportions, with six lazy sons sent out to learn trades. The first climbs buildings, the second repairs things broken, the third shoots arrows at tiny targets, the fourth makes even cadavers dance with his violin, the fifth builds buildings that travel on land or sea, and the sixth divines the location of lost objects. Their collaboration is in liberating the princess with the golden hair by slaying a serpent. The princess is given the choice of a mate, but can't make up her mind. Representative among them is 'La langage des bêtes,' in Jean Fleury's *Littérature orale de la Basse Normandie* (Paris: G.-P. Maisonneuve & Larose, 1967), pp. 123–35. In this tale, a father sends his sons

Immediately this story is recognized as a scaled-back, formulaic, folk reduction of the tale from *The Book of a Thousand Nights and a Night* (The Arabian Nights). There is no doubt a local joke in the fact that the grapes were so expensive that the boy could afford only three of them. When it is discovered that the princess is dying, they fly in on the carpet and put grapes in her mouth. When they later fight over her, the king gives her to a fourth suitor, who had done nothing at all.[68] The story adds little to the historical narrative, but confirms the circulation of the story type in a world much influenced by the work of Galland.

The language of the animals, mastered by the third brother, constitutes a motif with an equally ancient ancestry, one that was defined and

---

to school hoping to make them brilliant, but one of them majors in dog talk (literature instead of law or medicine), which annoys his father no end. 'That's not what I sent you to school for!' With each new master he learns but another animal language, that of the frogs and the birds. Now the father wants the boy dead and has him sent to the woods with murderous-minded neighbours. But they show their compassion by taking the heart of a slain dog to represent the boy's, and tell the kid to scram for good. He travels with two priests, and in the first inn he overhears the dogs talking about thieves digging a tunnel into the basement. The boy's stock rises when that turns out to be true. In each instance he is in his room with a candle burning that brings in the maid, who sees the boy at his divination, takes him for mad, and reports him to the host. The next episode deals with the host's daughter, who has been mute for years because on her confirmation day she had let a piece of the host fall into the mouth of a frog. This fact, too, the boy overhears and uses frog talk to get the wafer back, thereby curing the girl. Moral: if you want people to understand you, you have to speak to them in a language they understand. Finally, he becomes pope and receives his guilty father for confession before revealing to him how a degree in the humanities is not a bad qualification after all. This story is closely related to the Grimms' tale of the 'Drei Sprachen' (The three languages), that of dogs, frogs, and birds. This boy too becomes pope, but the intervening episodes are quite different. *Grimm's Complete Fairy Tales* (Garden City, NY: Nelson Doubleday, n.d.), pp. 366–7.

68 The story was particularly popular in Sicily. See Sebastiano Lo Nigro's 'I sette fratelli fatati' (the seven wonder-working brothers) in *Racconti popolari Siciliani: Classificazione e bibliografia* (Florence: Leo Olschki, 1957), no. 653, pp. 132–4, which provides the generic profile of a king who learns from an astrologer that his daughter has been carried off by a giant. The reward of marriage is announced and the mother of seven remarkable sons offers their services in finding the tower and breaking through the seven doors, each brother offering an essential service as the giant throws up new obstacles. All the brothers claim her and the king awards her to the one who resuscitated her. He cites the versions in Gonzenbach and Pitrè, examines the variants, and points to the studies by Bolte and Polivka (III, 45) and Espinosa (III, 83).

epitomized in an independent stream of tales.[69] Typically, in this story tradition, a boy becomes pope because he knows the language of the animals, but only after being spurned by his father, even sent out to be killed by servants for the shame his stupidity and scholastic ineptitude had brought upon the family. In some versions, it is the animals who tell him that he is about to be slain, although this may be an enhancement by Italo Calvino. In a version collected by Isaia Visentini, the travelling boy understands from the animals that the daughter of his host has been ill for six years because at the beginning of that period she had tossed a consecrated host into a ditch where the frogs had continued to play with it throughout the interim period.[70] Ultimately, he makes his way to Rome, where the dove of the papal election alights upon his head. He, of course, becomes one of the best popes ever, and his father puts in an appearance to confront the results of his cruelty.

What seems clear from this sprawling sampler of tales is that a type of narrative, although subject to great variation in its details, persisted

---

69 Sebastiano Lo Nigro's 'Il linguaggio degli animali' in *Racconti popolari Siciliani* (see preceding note), no. 67, pp. 134–5, profiles a different story type popular in Sicily, that of the young boy who eats a serpent in error and acquires an understanding of the language of animals. The story follows a course entirely unrelated to the present one, but demonstrates the extensive development of the language-of-animals motif. Jean Gobi mentions the learning of the language of animals in *La scala coeli*, which he traces to the *Book of the Seven Wisemen of Rome*; ed. Marie-Anne Polo de Beaulieu (Paris: Centre nationale de la recherche scientifique, 1991), no. 520.

70 'Il linguaggio degli animali,' in *Fiabe Mantovane*, ed. Isaia Visentini (Turin: E. Loescher, 1879; reprint, Parma: Astrea, 1993), no. 23, retold by Italo Calvino in *Italian Folktales* (New York: Pantheon, 1980), no. 23, 'Animal Speech,' pp. 68–71. An investigation into the story type was made by Emmanuel Cosquin in his annotations to the *Contes populaires de Lorraine*, 2 vols. (Paris: F. Vieweg, 1887), no. 42, vol. II, pp. 84–8. There are many stories in this tradition. See Carolina Coronedi-Berti, *Favole bolognesi* (Bologna: Monti, 1883), no. 12. Another entitled 'Il linguaggio degli animali,' a tale from Monferrato, was collected by Domenico Comparetti in *Novelline popolari italiane* (Turin: E. Loescher, 1875), no. 56, pp. 242–3. In this last, a boy who is a knucklehead at school nevertheless masters the language of birds, dogs, and other animals. Scorned and driven out by his father, he becomes a wanderer. He first hears the dogs discussing the arrival of one hundred assassins, and thus he is able to inform the treasurer of a foreign court, for which favour he wins the treasurer's daughter. Later the birds are overheard saying that one of the three pilgrims under the tree will become the next pope, and then the dove lands on his head. From relative rags to astonishing riches, the boy can at last invoke his father and let his situation speak his 'I told you so' on his behalf. We do not ask what happened to his wife once he became pope.

throughout centuries, its formulaic ordering of events undoubtedly contributing to its core stability. Morlini provides Straparola with a literary source, which may have been dependent upon another literary version. But all such are derivative creations drawn from a story type disseminated through an unbroken continuum of oral transmission beginning in the West at least as far back as the High Middle Ages and persisting down to the nineteenth century. In this case, Straparola was not the first to provide the literary transcription, but the effect is much the same, for the story still preserves the narrative ethos of its popular origins and confirms the intermittent parallel existence of the type in written form. It is another of his major contributions in the category of the Western wonder tale with its oral styling and folkloric design.

The Eighth Night

The fair-haired and radiant Apollo, son of Jove the Thunderer and Latona, was now departed from the world, and the fireflies that fly in the night, quitting their dark and obscure hiding-places, were sporting abroad, gleaming in the thick gloom of darkness that was now spread everywhere. Entering the spacious salon with her group of damsels, the Signora graciously welcomed the honourable company, which had just arrived in a happy state. Then, as on the preceding evening, she commanded the instruments to be brought in and, after a time of dancing, a servant appeared with the golden vase. Out of it a child drew five names, the first being Eritrea, the second Cateruzza, the third Arianna, the fourth Alteria, while the last place was reserved for Lauretta. But before the lively Eritrea was allowed to begin her fable, the Signora desired that all five of them should sing a song together to the music of the instruments, whereupon the damsels, with joyful faces, and looking as fair as angels, began their madrigal.

Song

Ah, cruel and ruthless fair!
How often from your eyes is sped the ray
That gives me life, that takes my life away.
My flowing tears will gain for me, I ween,
If not thy mercy, yet at least thy ruth;
Nor care nor credence hast thou for my truth.
And in your face serene
I read a doom more dire to me is given;
An outcast I from Love and Death and Heaven.

The song, with its cadence so divinely soft, gave great pleasure to all who listened, but especially commended itself to Bembo, touching him to the quick, wherefore, in order not to divulge the secret thought he cherished within his breast, he did not join in the laughter, but turned towards the gracious Eritrea and said, 'It must be time now for you to favour us with a delightful tale, for you were the first chosen to recite.' So without waiting for a further command from the Signora, she joyfully began.

VIII. Fable 1
The Three Idle Rogues

ERITREA

Three lazy rogues journey together to Rome. On the way they pick up a jewel and then break into an argument over who should have it. Meeting a certain gentleman, they ask him to arbitrate, and he decides it should go to the idlest oaf of the three. But in the end, all three prove themselves so arrantly lazy that no decision can be made.

I have carefully considered, most excellent ladies, the very great number of unfortunate conditions under which mortals presently live, and of these I find the most wretched and miserable to be that of a lazy rogue, because men of this sort, given their mean-spirited idleness and obstinacy, are the most singled out for denigration and scorn. More often than not, they prefer living in rags and poverty to giving up their disgraceful conduct. This contention I'll prove in the clearest fashion in the course of recounting my story.

No more than two years ago, there lived in the territory of Siena three fellows, young in age, but as old in the arts of roguery and laziness as anyone might imagine. One of them was called Gordino, being more addicted to gluttony than the other two. The second, because he was a good-for-nothing wimp, was called Fentuzzo by everyone who knew him. The third, his pumpkin devoid of all sense, went by the name of Sennuccio. It happened one day as they came to a crossroads that a discussion broke out.

Fentuzzo said, 'Heh, brothers where are you headed?'

'I'm on my way to Rome,' replied Gordino.

'And what are you aiming to do there?' asked Fentuzzo.

Gordino continued, 'I'm on the lookout for some good adventure that will bring me a living so I don't have to trouble myself about anything in the future.'

'Ah, then we'll go along with you!' he replied.

'Sure, if it meets with your pleasure,'

'I'll happily join in the enterprise,' chimed in Sennuccio.

So all three joined in fellowship, making a vow among themselves that they wouldn't part company on any account until they had arrived within the city of Rome. As they went along the road talking together of this thing and that, it chanced that Gordino cast his eyes down on the ground and there espied a fine gem set in a gold ring shining so brilliantly that it dazzled his eyes. Prior to this, Fentuzo had pointed out the jewel to his two companions, which became an issue when Sennuccio picked it up and put it upon his finger. No sooner done than a violent dispute sprang up between the three of them as to who had the firmest claim to it.

Gordino stoutly maintained that it was his because he had seen it first. Fentuzzo replied, 'Surely by rights it's mine because I pointed it out to you.'

'Rather than to either of you, it belongs to me,' said Sennuccio, 'because I picked it up from the ground and put it on my finger.' So the three knaves kept up their wrangling – no one willing to give up his claim in favour of the others – until at last they went from words to blows, cuffing each other's heads and faces with their fists till the blood on all sides ran down like rain.

Just at that hour a certain Messer Gavardo Colonna, a Roman noble and man of high office, was on the road back to the city after visiting one of his farms. Catching sight of the three rogues from afar and hearing the uproar they were making, he slowed his mount, entirely confused and fearful that they intended to attack and slay him. More than once he felt the urge to curb his horse, even double back the way he had come, but at last he plucked up courage and continued on till he came to the three companions, addressing them thus: 'Ho, fellow travellers! What means all this hurly-burly among you?'

Gordino answered, 'May God save you, good sir, here's what we're arguing about: we three set out from our different houses and by fortune met upon the road. So we agreed to travel in a company to Rome. But as we were making our way and chatting the while, I saw on the ground a very fair jewel set in gold, which by every claim of reason most assuredly should belong to me, because I was the first to see it.'

'But I first pointed it out,' declared Fentuzzo, 'and on this account it appears that it ought to belong to me, not them.'

Then Sennuccio, who certainly wasn't asleep, cut in, 'Well sir, my view is that the jewel should be awarded to me because, without any signs made to me, I picked it up from the ground and placed it on my finger. Anyway, that's how it happened that we started to fight to the peril of our lives; nobody here is willing to give in to the other.'

Now when Signor Gavardo fully understood the cause of their dissention, he said, 'Tell me, my good fellows, whether you're inclined to refer the decision to me so that I can bring you all back to one accord?' All three of them accepted these terms and pledged to abide by any decision in the matter that this gentleman might make.

When messer Gavardo saw that they were all disposed to act fairly, he said, 'Since by common consent you have placed yourselves in my hands, making me the sole adjudicator of your dispute, I request of you only two conditions: first that you place the jewel in my hands and second that each of you seeks to demonstrate proof of the greatest laziness. At the end of fifteen days, the one who shows himself to be the meanest, laziest rascal will become the undisputed owner of the jewel.'

The three companions straightway agreed to the terms, and having given over the jewel into the gentleman's keeping, they set out on their journey to Rome. When they arrived in the city they went their separate ways, one going here and the other there, each determined to do his solemn best at performing some feat of sluggardliness that would surpass all former accomplishments.

Gordino at once found a master whose terms of service he accepted. One day in the piazza this man bought a lot of early figs – the kind that ripen by the end of June – and gave them to Gordino to hang on to until they returned to the house. Not only lazy by nature but a glutton, Gordino, following in his master's steps, extracted a fig and ate it secretly bit by bit. The taste of it so tickled his palate that he went on, the lazy glutton, covertly eating fig after fig. He continued to gorge himself until finally he stuck in a fig so large that he began to fear his master would catch him out. So he thrust it into the corner of his mouth in the manner of a monkey and kept it there. Suddenly the master turned to look back, and seeing Gordino, he fancied that his left cheek was somewhat swollen. Looking him steadily in the face, he became fully assured of the matter, and when he asked Gordino what had happened to him to cause such a swelling, the rascal stood there like a dumb man, answering not a word.

When the master took all this in, he was astonished and said, 'Gordino, open your mouth so that I can examine what's the matter with you and then maybe I can come up with a remedy.' But the wretched fellow would neither open his mouth nor utter a word. In fact, the more his master tried to make him open up, the tighter and closer the rogue clenched his teeth. So at last, after the master had made several tries at getting Gordino's jaws apart and failing in each attempt, he took him to a barber who lived nearby, afraid that some dire mishap had come to him, and showed him to the blood-letter, saying, 'Master, a very foul accident has just come over my servant. As you can see, his cheek is so swollen that he can no longer speak nor even open his mouth. I'm really worried he might choke.'

The surgeon then deftly touched the swollen cheek and said to Gordino, 'What do you feel, good brother?' But he got no response. 'Open your mouth,' he went on, and the fellow didn't move in the least. Finding it hard to hit upon a cure by verbal means, he picked up one of his instruments and began to make trial to see whether he could get the mouth open, but there were no means by which he could induce the lazy rascal to move his jaws.

The surgeon now imagined that the evil must arise from an imposthume that had gathered little by little and that was now mature and fit for treatment, so he made an incision to allow the area to drain. Still, this lazy rascal, Gordino, although he had heard all that was said, refused to move a muscle or utter a sound, standing as still as a stone tower. Having done this, the surgeon began to press the tumour in order to examine the discharge issuing therefrom, but in place of pus and putrefaction he found nothing but healthy blood mixed with the flesh of the fig that Gordino still kept closely shut in his mouth. When his master saw that all this turmoil had arisen over a fig and that his servant was but a lazy rogue, he asked the surgeon to dress the wound, telling Gordino meanwhile that as soon as it was cured, he was to be gone and may ill luck go with him.

Fentuzzo, who was no whit less given to slothfulness than Gordino, soon squandered the few coins that he happened to have in his pocket. Witless as he was, there was no one he could convince to play the sponge, so he went about begging from door to door, sleeping now in this portico, now in that, and sometimes even out in the forest. By chance one night our vagabond came upon an old building fallen to ruin. Inside he found a heap of dung and a little straw upon which he lay down, disposing himself as best he could with his torso on the dung heap and his legs stretched out beyond until weariness came upon him and he fell asleep. Before he had been there long, there arose a violent wind accompanied by a downpour of rain so great that it seemed as if the world were coming to an end. All through the night the rain and lightning never ceased. The roof covering was so old and rotten that rainwater came down through a hole, a drop of it falling into Fentuzzo's eye which awoke him and put an end to his quiet rest. Yet he was such a lazy lout that he had no inclination at all to remove himself from the place where he lay or to elude the danger that was threatening him. There he stayed in the same spot, dogged in his obstinacy, his eye still exposed to the falling drops as though it were a hard and lifeless pebble. The drops turned to streams that endlessly fell from the roof, striking upon his eye, water so bitterly cold that before morning had come the sight of the poor fool's eye had been destroyed.

The next day, after stirring for a time plotting how he might gain some food for his belly, he realized his eye was damaged. Imagining he was but half awake, he put his hand over the other to shade it, thereby discovering the blindness in his eye. Once assured of this condition, he lapsed into a fit of joyfulness, thinking nothing luckier or more favourable could have befallen him, for he was fully persuaded that so remarkable a feat of slothfulness could not fail to win him the coveted jewel.

Sennuccio, meanwhile, had adopted an equally indolent way of life, having taken to wife a woman named Bedovino, who was his match for sluggardliness. One evening after supper, the season being warm, the two of them were sitting near the door of the house to catch a bit of breeze. Sennuccio said to his wife, 'Bedovina, shut the door, for it's time to get to bed.'

To this she replied, 'Shut it yourself.' They went on disputing like this with neither tending to the door. Then Sennuccio said, 'Bedovina, let's make a deal that the one who speaks first will shut the door.' Lazy by nature and obstinate by habit, she agreed to this. So Sennuccio and Bedovina just went on sitting there, slothful as they were, neither one uttering a word for fear of losing the match and having to shut the door. In time, growing weary of the sport, the good woman, now heavy with sleep, left her husband sitting on a bench, took off her skirt and went to bed.

A short time later the serving man of a certain gentleman was passing through the street on his way back home when suddenly the candle in his lantern went out. Seeing that Sennuccio's house was still open, he entered and cried out, 'Hello there, is anyone home? I need a light for my candle.' But no one answered him. Advancing further into the house, the servant spied Sennuccio sitting there with his eyes wide open on the bench and took up courage to ask him for a light. But the lazy fellow offered no word in reply. Deeming that Sennuccio was fast asleep, the servant took him by the hand and began to shake him, saying, 'Good brother, what's the matter with you? Answer me, right now.' But Sennuccio was not asleep. He was merely keeping silent in order not to incur the penalty of having to shut the door. So the servant went on a bit further and noticed a faint light on the hearth where the embers were still alive, and when he entered the inner room he found no one except Bedovina, who was lying alone in the bed. He called to her and shook her roughly more than once, but like her husband, she too would neither speak nor stir in order to avoid losing the wager and having to shut the door. The servant, after taking a closer look at her, found her attractive enough, though stingy with her words. So he climbed in bed beside her, took his rod in hand, which was fairly rusty, and stuck it into her forge. Bedovina remained dead silent the while, easily enduring it all, while the young man followed through to a climax, right before her husband's eyes.

After this chap had gone on his way, Bedovina got out of bed, went to the door, found her husband wide awake, and set about chiding him. 'A fine husband you are. You left me lying all night long with the door wide open, giving free access to any lewd fellow wanting in, without even lifting a hand to keep him out. May you never drink again except from a rotten shoe.'

With that, the lazy rogue got to his feet and made her the following answer, 'Now go and shut the door yourself, you little fool. Haven't I proven myself to be your match? You really thought you were going to make me shut the door, but I've out-tricked you right properly. This is the only way to keep the headstrong in submission.' Seeing that she had truly lost the wager, but that she had enjoyed a merry night at the same time, Bedovina shut the door and went to bed with her cuckolded knave of a husband.

After the appointed fifteen days had passed, the three fools went looking for Gavardo. When he had been fully informed of the feats of the three companions just related, and had given consideration to their several arguments, he was unable to come to a decision, for it seemed to him that under the vast canopy of heaven, other poltroons to match these three could never be found. So he took the gem and threw it back on the ground, saying that whoever picked it up first could have it.

At the end of this amusing story there arose a great dispute among the auditors. Some held that the gem belonged by right to Gordino, while others awarded it to Fentuzzo, and still others to Sennuccio, all the disputants giving excellent reasons for their particular views. But the Signora, observing that time was fast flying, urged that the question be reserved for some future time, asking them all to be quiet so that Eritrea could keep the custom by telling her enigma. Smiling merrily, the damsel pronounced it in these words:

> By the drear and swampy seaside,
> Gazing o'er the brackish tide,
> Sits a bird of plumage gay
> On a rail the livelong day,
> Watching for the fish that swim
> In the shallows under him.
> Should a large one come that way,
> Too lazy he to seize his prey,
> Neglects it, hoping to discover
> One bigger; but when day is over,
> The lazy sluggard now must feed
> On worms that in the marshes breed.

This enigma by Eritrea proved vastly pleasing to all the company, but no one fathomed its meaning except Messer Bembo, who declared it to be a certain bird, very timid in its habits, which men called the 'perdigiornata' or 'time-waster.' It dwelt, he affirmed, only in swampy places because its favourite food was carrion, and so great was its sloth that it would sit all day long on a stake watching the fish swimming about. If it happened to see one of fair size it wouldn't move, but would let the fish go by while waiting for a bigger one, and so from morning till evening it would go without food. And then, when night had fallen, it would be driven by hunger to descend into the mud in quest of marsh worms to make up its meal. Eritrea listened to this clever solution to her enigma and saw clearly that Bembo had guessed it. Although she was a little annoyed about it, she didn't let on, but resolved to wait patiently for a time and place to flout him in return. Cateruzza, when she saw that the enigma no longer engaged the attention of the company, chose not to wait for further direction, but raised her voice and began her fable in the following fashion.

VIII.1 Commentary

This story is a delightful foray into the counterintuitive and the absurd. The protagonists are artists in sloth, men made remarkable simply by their inactivity when all others of the species, placed in similar situations, would react vigorously out of self-interest and instinct. At face value, the compound narrative is little more than a pretext for presenting three inane acts, arranging them in incremental order from the boy who has his cheek cut for refusing to open his mouth to the man too lazy to prevent an intruder from seducing his wife. The writers who invented these novelties sought merely to outdo themselves in the creation of imagined scenarios of extreme and costly laziness.

But other analyses constantly intrude upon this innocent reading insofar as the anecdotes are produced, not by constitutional indolence, but by a cost analysis in the interests of capturing a greater good. These are, in fact, calculated gestures of demonstrable laziness in relation to a contest, with its agreed-upon rules, conditions, and time frame. In order to settle a dispute over a jewel discovered while the three were en route together – a dispute that had turned into a bloody brawl – they accepted an arbiter who imposed a laziness contest as the means for determining the winner. Given these circumstances, each act of sloth becomes but a sham of indifference calculated by opportunity and executed as an act of discipline, if not perverse will and unrelenting stubbornness. Ultimately, sloth is an illusion created by an exertion of self control out of all proportion to the expected gain, leaving readers gaping after an explanation of those competitive acts in which high loss or suffering is sustained for the sake of token prizes. In that regard, the entire anecdote is about the power of the game in which the conditions of victory are played out against gains and losses in the real world, as well as about the peculiar psychological victories that make those sacrifices worthwhile. The examples given in the stories are hyperbolical extravaganzas, but sensible men have, nevertheless, been known to forego an entire day's wages to appear in court for the prosecution of a thief who had been apprehended for stealing an inexpensive watch. The human perception of gains is not always driven by material logic, at least not proportionally so, as the madman demonstrates of the hawker, who spent lavishly on gear and training to catch a few game birds (XIII.1). An assessment of that cost-benefit exchange against the background of human nature is the most challenging feature of this narrative and the crux that no doubt fostered the propagation of the story type throughout centuries.

The nature of their respective performances is homogenized to a manifestation of laziness on the assumption that torpor itself might be quantified in order to determine winners and losers. In fact, the adjudicating party was unable to resolve the matter and thus could do no more than cast the contested ring on the ground, in the manner of a hockey face-off, and let the powers of desire, dexterity, and luck take over – or worse, the resumption of the inaugural combat through which men settle their disproportionate claims by disproportionate violence in the tooth-and-claw tactics of fitness. As the unresolved contest is passed along to the reader, it then challenges our own sense of categories and intuitions, for we are invited to choose from among an act of self-control in the face of inflicted pain, a refusal to protect the body's most vital yet most vulnerable organ, the eye, and a stubborn struggle for supremacy and power within the domestic couple. Being three rather different orders of achievement, these call for an exercise in category comparison that may be impossible, for how is the laziness motivated by gaming and its rewards by self-destructive indifference to be compared to marital hostilities and the struggle for control? The extremities of pure inactivity draw upon too many social and instinctual variables to leave them comparable in computable terms. The story has become a riddle in the byways of cognition that defeats the value of the game as an intrinsic self-regulated medium for selecting winners and losers according to its own rules of play. We simply do not know whether the willed endurance of pain, the loss of a sense organ, or the loss of honour represents the greater sacrifice. We cannot even decide whether these are acts of sloth or of stubborn will, although there is no doubt agreement on the part of those outside the game structure that these are supreme acts of stupidity.

Tales of excessive sloth reach back to the ancient world. Somadeva, in the *Katha sarit sagara* (The ocean of the streams of story) relates the one about the Takka who was such a miser that he was fearful of incurring even the slightest cost in receiving guests. One day, as a very special treat, he allowed his wife to make a milk pudding, and just as it was to come out of the oven, a friend dropped by. To avoid sharing it, he arranged with his wife that he would play dead. The visitor caught on early and played along, inviting friends in to mourn and requesting the funeral pyre to be prepared. Call it avarice or extreme sloth, this miser allowed himself to be burned rather than share a bite of his pudding – the ultimate sacrifice for the banal and trivial.[1] In a related vein, it was said of Pliny the emperor, according to the author of a vignette preserved in the *Gesta Romanorum*, that he decided to award his realm to the most slothful

---

1 Trans. C.H. Tawney, intro. N.M. Penzer, 10 vols. (Delhi: Motilal Banarsidass [1923], 1984), no. 150, vol. V, pp. 165–7.

of his three sons.[2] We must pause to ask if there is some form of hidden wisdom in such a proposal. Here again, the winner among combative siblings must actively perform a memorable display of indolence. The first burns his legs in the fire because he is too lazy to remove them. Of the second it is merely reported that with a rope around his neck and a sword in his hand, he would forfeit his life rather than trouble himself to cut the cord. The third endures a downpour of water whereby he is blinded in one eye, precisely as in Straparola's tale. The kingdom is assigned to the third. Whatever the merits of this version of the story, it is early confirmation that Straparola was writing in relation to an established literary tradition with separable and identifiable parts. The *Gesta*, dating to the late thirteenth century, predates Straparola by two-and-a-half centuries, and may itself reflect a story type already widely known in the West. The story is closely related to a version told in the Latin *Aesop* of the father and his three sons, and of the mill, the pear tree, and the goat that had to be divided equally among them.[3] Various means for determining the most meritorious included the performance of the most evil deed, the telling of the greatest lie, and the greatest act of torpor. The first was he who was too lazy to avoid a stream of foul water by which he was blinded and his flesh made to rot. The second was too lazy to eat unless the food was placed directly into his mouth, even after years of fasting. The third would die of thirst while standing in water up to his neck to avoid the exertion of bending his head. These were merely inventive boasts, which also constituted lies at the same time. The judge in the matter concluded that the entire procedure was nonsense and that they would have to figure it out among themselves. It was just such material as this that found its way into the treatments by Sercambi, Morlini, and Straparola.

The device of the discovered ring appears to have been taken over from the *fabliau* 'Des III dames qui trouverent l'anel' (Of the three

---

2 *Gesta Romanorum*, ed. Charles Swan and Winnard Hooper (1876; reprint, New York: Dover, 1959), no. 91, pp. 163–4. A similar anecdote is related by Jean Gobi in *La scala coeli* of the five sons whose inheritance would be determined by the inventiveness and persistence of their laziness, feats including danger to the sight and the burning of feet in the fire for lack of will to remove them. Ed. Marie-Anne Polo de Beaulieu (Paris: Centre nationale de la recherche scientifique, 1991), no. 25, p. 174.

3 The story 'Of the fader and of his thre children' first made its way into English in the Caxton translation of 1483, *Here begynneth the book of the subtyl histories and Fables of Esope*, ed. Joseph Jacobs (London: David Nutt, 1889), bk. V, no. 13, vol. II, pp. 172–5.

women who find the ring).[4] The opening of the *fabliau* is brief. Three women find a ring, dispute its ownership, and accept an outside judgment. Victory will be assigned to the one who plays the cruellest or wittiest trick on her husband. Accordingly, they must perform their inventions within a set period of time, as in the present story. The first gets her husband drunk, dresses him as a monk, and with the help of her lover deposits him at the entrance of the local monastery. It has the surprising effect of entirely disorienting his sense of identity, for when the husband comes to, he considers his transportation a miracle and a vocation, and thus asks for admission into the order. Amusingly, the wife shows up to second his candidacy.[5] The second goes to a neighbour to

---

4 *Recueil général et complet des fabliaux des XIIIe et XIVe siècles*, ed. Anatole de Montaiglon and Gaston Raynaud, 6 vols. (Paris, 1880; rpt. New York: Burt Franklin, 1964), vol. I, pp. 168–77. It is also to be found in a modernized version in *Fabliaux ou contes du XIIe et du XIIIe siècle*, ed. P.J.B. Le Grand d'Aussy, 5 vols. (Paris, 1781; rpt. Geneva: Slatkine Reprints, 1971), vol. IV, p. 163. This comes, in fact, from *Steinhowel's Asop* (1501), ed. Hermann Oesterley (Tübingen: L.F. Fues, 1873), bk. V, no. 13, 'De patre et tribus filiis.' 'Of the fader and of his thre children' was also translated by Caxton in his *Fables of Aesop*, ed. Joseph Jacobs (London: David Nutt [1484], 1889), V.13. Of interest regarding its structure is Jean de Bove's 'Des trois larrons' in *Fabliaux*, ed. Le Grand d'Aussy (Geneva: Slatkine Reprints, 1971), vol. III, pp. 308–22, in which two master thieves stage a contest to show their remarkable skills. The first steals and replaces eggs in a bird's nest without disturbing the mother, while the second imperceptibly steals the first thief's pants. Their peasant friend, witnessing such a show of craft, is dissuaded from joining them, returning to his wife and homestead. When, later, the two show up looking for him, his wife is frightened by the way they case the place and inhospitably sends them away. The returning husband relizes he is in for a thieving contest over a slaughtered pig because they had not been properly invited in. A series of impersonations follows by which the thieves and the farmer manage to steal the creature back and forth several times before the peasant gives up, realizing it would continue interminably unless the master crooks were simply invited in to share the feast. The thieving contest over a few helpings of bacon – their efforts out of all proportion to the value of the prize – tells much about the psychology of ritual combat and the medieval frame of wit that gave rise to the present Straparola tale. This *fabliau*, also known as 'De Barat et de Haimet,' can be found in *Fabliaux des XIIIe et XIVe siècles*, ed. de Montaiglon and Raynaud, no. 97, vol. IV, pp. 93–111. The story is also retold in Giovanni Sagredo's *L'Arcadia in Brenta*, ed. Quinto Marini (Rome: Salerno, 2004).

5 The earliest version of this story as an independent narrative may well be Exemplum 231 of *The Exempla: or Illustrative Stories from the Sermones Vulgares* of Jacques de Vitry, ed. Thomas Frederick Crane (London: David Nutt, 1890), p. 96, assembled in the second quarter of the thirteenth century. He tells of a woman who so hated her husband that she got him drunk and then sent for some monks to inform them that

roast some eels, spends a week with her lover, drops by the neighbours to do the cooking, and then turns up at home trying to convince her angry husband that she had been gone only a short time. As the dispute flares up, she calls in the neighbours as witnesses, for indeed she had been at their house only recently. It is another example of contradicting the targeted gull's basic knowledge of self, place, or time through arranged evidence, a form of trickery favoured by the writers of farce. The third, already wed, proposes nevertheless to marry her lover by disguising herself in such a way that her own husband presents her at the altar. These brio performances likewise defeat the powers of choice, leaving the ring unassigned at the end. It may be said, in effect, that Straparola's story was a recycled thirteenth- or fourteenth-century *fabliau* using three rogues who re-enact the sloth contest featuring episodes drawn from a variety of sources, including the *Gesta* already cited. Others of these sources can be provided, but precisely how they all arrived on Straparola's desk remains open to speculation. Either he assembled these motifs on his own to reconstruct the story type or, more credibly, his source was configured for him by the oral tradition that either furnished or drew upon these early *fabliaux*. This tale, in effect, is an excellent example of the potential for exchange in both directions between literary and popular cultures.[6]

A related question is just how the laziness contest in the form of the silence game came to the West from its Eastern origins; this too invites

---

her husband was dying and wished to take the habit as a final act of contrition. Because the man was rich, the monks were pleased to oblige. They tonsured him, dressed him in the habit, and then his wife set up a loud lamentation that brought in all the neighbours. The monks took him away in a cart to the monastery so that when he awoke he found himself a monk in a cloister, at which point shame and fear of being declared an apostate prevented him from returning home. Clearly, this became one of the tricks played on husbands that attached itself to the story cycle of the three wives and the precious object. Felix Liebrecht mentions its history in *Zur Volkskunde, alte und neue Aufsätze* (Heilbron: Henninger, 1879), p. 124. Examples occur in *El libro de enxemplos* of Climente Sánchez de Valderas (Vercial), ed. Pascual de Gayangos (Madrid, 1860), no. 236, as well as in *A Selection of Latin Stories*, ed. Thomas Wright (London: T. Richards for the Percy Society, 1843), p. 65, from British Library, MS. Harl. 463, fol. 18b, col. 2.

6 Philippe de Vigneulles (1471–1528) tells a similar story, opening upon the same question of origins involving both literary and oral options. In this compound story, he includes the wager among the three women to determine which of them would keep the precious object they had simultaneously discovered. Each one persuades her husband to believe an illusion in a sequence of incremental credulity. The form

further investigation because the dating of some of the principal vehicles, such as the *History of the Forty Vezirs or the Story of the Forty Morns and Eves*, remains problematic. The creation of this Ottoman work (from an Arabic source) goes back to the reign of Murad II, 1421–51, and thus came late to Europe.[7] Nevertheless, 'The Lady's Fourteenth Story' provides persuasive proof of the motif's Oriental origin. A group of opium eaters finds money on the ground that enables them to buy food. They then retire to the area of a tomb enclosed by a wall. Neglecting to close the gate to keep out rival drug heads, they fall to arguing about who would do it. This brings them to the silence wager as the means of selection: the first to speak closes the gate. Meanwhile some fifteen dogs appear, enter, eat all the food, lick the men's faces, and chew off one of their lips. When the injured man makes an inward moan, he is declared the loser and is ordered to close the gate. He instead pronounces the futility of it all, now that everything is eaten, and so they all go their own ways. There in sum is the third part of Straparola's tale.

That the story, among its Eastern representations, also included domestic contests between husbands and wives in which the struggle for sovereignty is brought down to infantile stubbornness over trivialities is testified to by Abbé Jean Antoine Dubois in his *Description of the Characters, Manners, and Customs of the People of India*.[8] He relates the story entitled 'Four Simple Brahmins,' in which W.A. Clouston recognized the form closest to the oikotype that we are ever likely to possess. Accused of being a chatterbox, the first Brahmin's wife counter-accuses and the husband proposes that the matter be settled by seeing who will be the first to speak thereafter. Relatives appear, gain no response, and break down the doors. Seeing them speechless, they attribute it to demons and price out the cost of exorcism. Finding that too high, they begin to place heated gold all over the husband's body, which he endures patiently – forgetting apparently that he only had to remain speechless, not immobile. At that point, the wife tosses down the betel leaf they had wagered (a trivial

---

is similar to Straparola's, but the particulars, each known from its own folk or *fabliau* version, form a unique configuration of the tale. *Les cent nouvelles nouvelles*, ed. Charles H. Livingston (Geneva: Droz, 1972), no. 91, pp. 349–59.

7 Sheykh Zada, *History of the Forty Vezirs*, trans. E.J.W. Gibb (London: George Redway, 1886), pp. 171–3.

8 *Description of the Characters, Manners, and Customs of the People of India*, trans. from the French (London: Longman, Hurst, Rees, Orme & Brown, 1817; reprint, New Delhi: Asian Educational Services, 1989).

object) and stops the procedure. Upon understanding the nature of their contest, the relatives declared them both pure idiots.[9]

William Beloe, in his *Miscellanies consisting of Poems, Classical Extracts, and Oriental Apologues*, reconfirms the story type in the tale of a man and wife arguing over a dry supper and which of the two would moisten it. The ensuing silence contest accounts for their mysterious behaviour when a friend drops by. This tale of mounting concern brings in the police and an appearance before an exasperated judge who orders the husband's execution. The wife is the first to break silence to save his life, at which point he calls her a devil and tells her to prepare the meal properly. Such determination is cause for laughter, but represents an underlying truth concerning the struggle for control juxtaposed with the right training of wives or the tactics for taming a shrew. Straparola's tale is further proof that the motif had come early to Europe, testifying to the presence of the silence wager stories that would enjoy world-wide success in subsequent years.[10] Stith Thompson identified the motif as 'the silence wager' (J2511), stating that in the generic version it is the husband who breaks silence first because he is unable to refrain from scolding his wife. He traces its origins to early Buddhist literature and points to the many oral forms of the story, particularly in Italy, although it is known from Scotland to Japan.[11] The earliest version I have located is in the *Vetâlapañcaviñçatikâ* of Civadâsa, which tells of three friends reduced to penury who put their wives to work and live off the largesse of their in-laws. One of them renounces all eating during the day, but is caught during the night with his mouth stuffed full of rice. Unwilling to

---

9 W.A. Clouston, *Popular Tales and Fictions*, ed. Christine Goldberg (Santa Barbara: ABC-Clio, 2002), pp. 279–80; originally published in 1887 by Blackwood and Sons, Edinburgh and London. A closely related variant is the Arabian story of 'Sulayman Bey and the Three Story-Tellers,' in which a newly wed couple, even before the honeymoon has begun, sits in silence over the responsibility for closing the front door. Straparola's present story featuring this same contest is perhaps by no accident placed in conjunction with the story to follow (VIII.2) concerned with the early disciplining of wives. When thieves enter neither husband nor wife reacts, and when the police inspectors arrive and their silence is taken for insolence against authority, the wife breaks silence only to prevent her husband from being beheaded. The police are baffled beyond measure. Told by Clouston, *Popular Tales and Fictions*, pp. 276–7.

10 This material was translated by Dr. Russell from a MS. from Aleppo. The collection was first published by F. and C. Rivington in London in 1795.

11 *The Folktale* (Berkeley: University of California Press, 1977), p. 195.

make his hypocrisy known, he allows a doctor to be called who treats him with medicinal powders. Another was pleased to hear his wife say in bed that she would never utter another word and he resolved to do the same. Meanwhile, a thief enters the house and, seeing them in their dumb state, proceeds without opposition to sack the place. The story ends by asking which of them was the greatest fool.[12]

The Italian writers preceding Straparola who touched upon these materials are Giovanni Sercambi, Poggio Bracciolini, and Girolamo Morlini. All three are important in demonstrating the transmission of the type and its constituent materials, but paradoxically, none may be said to have provided Straparola with his source, although Morlini's version, however unlike Straparola's in substance, is traditionally taken as his inspiration by former editors. It is a point for debate. Sercambi, the apothecary 'novelist' of Lucca, in his story 'Of Mucchietto and Stoltarella' develops the silence wager as played by a newly wed couple in the full manner of the Italian *novella*, but it is the familiar Eastern anecdote, all the same, gussied up with contemporary detail.[13] Following the wedding feast, the couple retires, but ends up in a discussion over who will clean the 'scudelle,' and they decide that the matter will be settled against the one who speaks first. When the families come calling the next day to see how the newly-weds are faring, they get no answer. Taking them both for dead by vesper time, they break into the house. Finding each on their respective sides of the bed with their eyes wide open but completely mute, a friend begins to whisper in Mucchietto's ear in a way that merely calls

---

12 *Die Vetalapañcaviņçatica*, ed. Heinrich Uhle (Leipzig: commissioned by
   F.A. Brockhaus, 1881), is best known through its incorporation into the *Katha
   sarit sagara*, although the present story was not included. This story was found by
   Giuseppe Rua in *Sei novelle soprannumerarie alla Vetalapancaviņçati* and given in
   résumé in *Tra antiche fiabe e novelle: Le 'Piacevoli Notti' di Messer Gian Francesco
   Straparola* (Rome: Ermanno Loescher, 1989), p. 36. A similar tale, 'Les trois frères
   à l'excessive délicatesse' (The three finicky brothers), from that same collection
   appears in the French *Contes du Vampire*, trans. Louis Renou (Paris: Gallimard,
   1963), no. 8, pp. 80–3. These three brothers are illogically disdainful of certain
   food or beds, one saying that the rice smelled of incinerated bodies, another that a
   beautiful girl smelled of goats, and the third that the bed was contaminated. But in
   each instance they are justified, for the rice was cultivated near a cemetery, the girl
   was raised on goat's milk, while the print on the flesh was caused by a hair under
   seven layers of mattresses. Very sensitive brothers.
13 Giovanni Sercambi, 'De simplicitate viri et uxoris' in *Novelle*, ed. Giovanni Sinicropi,
   2 vols. (Bari: Laterza, 1972), no. 78, vol. I, pp. 341–4.

for nods of the head. He made proposals for the will, the heirs, and the
church burial until Stoltarella forgets herself and blurts out her wishes.
The husband pronounces his victory and the game is explained to both
families, whereupon they enter into the spirit of it all, telling the girl she
would have to get up early to do her work. Sercambi provides even more
dialogue, more detailed settings, and keener motivation of his characters.
But his story is no more than a remake of the Eastern tale, one that had
come to him by the end of the fourteenth century.

Poggio adapts the design to the indomitable shrew who prefers death
over making an apology or admitting error.[14] When she calls her husband
'lousy,' he goes so far as to beat her to make her retract her words. That
tactic failing, he throws her into the well, but even as her head goes under
the water she thrusts out her arm to make the pinching sign of killing
lice. The point in common is the distance married folk will go to score
points against each other in the battle for the last word. This anecdote
has its own extensive history that includes versions by Marie de France,
Lorenzo Abstemio, François Béroalde de Verville, and Antoine le Métel,
Sieur d'Ouville.

Straparola may well have taken his inspiration from Morlini, but if
he did so, he changed every detail, for Morlini's contest among three
women disputing a pearl calls for accounts of their most embarrassing
moments, thereby providing the author with an occasion for retailing
three of the most salacious anecdotes in all of literature. This appears
to be a witty deviation from the stock model. The first mounted a statue
that reminded her of her deceased husband, but when it came time to
descend, a considerable crowd had gathered, and 'non valui marmoreum
illum priapum e vulva extrahere' was made to remain in that position
from dawn till noon. The second was on all fours, naked, and with a
bridle in her mouth mounted by a servant when her husband came in.
The third had been pleasuring herself with a leek, rather violently, when
her husband returned home, and while she disguised her act for a time,
she was told to follow him to her brother's. Out in the streets she fell,
inviting a passing ass 'cernens porri folias mediis coxis meis insurgentes,
fame concitus, illum vastum porrum suis saxeis dentibus e vulva sper-
mate madefactum evulsit atquea exstirpavit,' this too in the presence of

---

14 'D'une femme qui s'obstinait à appeler son mari pouilleux' (De muliere obstinata
   quae virum pediculosum vocavit; The woman who insisted on calling her husband
   'lousy' [lice infested]) in the *Facéties de Pogge Florentin*, ed. Pierre des Brandes (Paris:
   Garnier Frères, ca. 1885), no. 59, pp. 82–4.

many lookers-on.[15] The common structure may be manifest wherein three persons contest a precious object by indulging in or recounting extreme behaviour, but in this instance Straparola did not follow the scatological course, but called upon the stories profiled above or looked to popular sources.[16]

Following Straparola, the many literary representations of the tale include that in *L'élite des contes* of the Sieur d'Ouville, in which the wife stubbornly refuses to shut the front door. In this version of the contest, the husband remains dumb and motionless even when a passing soldier finds them both not only speechless but the wife attractive, pliant, and supine, whereupon he takes his pleasure with her without opposition. When she afterwards accuses her husband of being a lout and a cuckold, he claims the victory and commands her to shut the door.[17] The story was known in Scotland by the mid-eighteenth century, and presumably much earlier, bearing such titles as 'The barrin' o' the door.'[18] During the silence wager all manner of indignities are offered to both the wives and the husbands from kissing and coupling to sea dunking from the yardarm, until circumstances grow so menacing that one or the other forgets the game and pronounces a few words, whereupon the victor tells the other to bar the door. As Clouston points out, dubiously crediting Straparola for their existence, these Scottish ballads testify to the enduring

---

15 Girolamo Morlini, 'De tribus mulieribus quae repererunt pretiosam margaritam' in *Novellae, fabulae, comoedia* (Paris: P. Jannet, 1855), no. 81, pp. 158–61. See also 'De trois femmes qui avaient trouvé une perle précieuse' (Of the three women who found a precious pearl) in *Les nouvelles*, trans. Fernand Coussy (Paris: E. Sansot, 1904), no. 81, pp. 184–7.

16 It can be perhaps only of collateral interest that a story published in 1550, without indication of place and publisher, was entitled *Historia nova di tre donne che ogni una fece una beffa al suo marito per gradagnare uno anello* (The new story of the three women each of whom plays a trick on her husband in order to gain a ring). This is an exactly contemporary published version, thereby linking the early *fabliau* to the Sicilian tale of the nineteenth century, 'The Three Good Friends,' profiled below.

17 Antoine le Métel, *L'élite des contes du Sieur d'Ouville*, 2 vols. (Paris: A. Lemerre, 1876), vol. I, pp. 123–4. A version also very close to Straparola's, perhaps even derived from it, is found in Antonio Guadagnoli's *Gosto e Mea ovvero la lingua d'una donna alla prova* (Florence: Salani, 1879).

18 From James Johnson's *The Scots Musical Museum* (Edinburgh: Johnson, 1787), no. 4, p. 376. The motif is also replicated in Prince Hoare's two-act comic opera written for Drury Lane in 1790, *No Song, No Supper*, ed. Roger Fiske (London: Stainer & Bell, 1959).

tradition of the silence wager, going back to the Brahmins in ancient Sanskrit literature.[19]

The ubiquity of the silence wager and the jewel contest in the folk literature of the nineteenth century suggests the existence of well-established story traditions, their ancestors giving rise to the story with which we are presently concerned. Insofar as Straparola's tale differs markedly from Morlini's, yet resembles so closely those collected three centuries later by the great ethnographers, it further confirms his pre-occupation with the tales of the folk. Two among those recorded by Giuseppe Pitrè in his *Fiabe* have particularly close affinities. In no. 166, 'The Three Good Friends,' the women, during an outing, see a gem that each seeks to recover for herself. At an impasse, they decide to consult a lawyer, who likewise cannot come to an equitable decision. There follows a contest to see who can make the greatest fool of her husband. The first goes so far as to nag him into having all his teeth pulled by harping incessantly about his stinking breath. The second wife turns the house into a trattoria, thereby making it impossible for her husband to find his own address. The third husband is carried to a monastery in his sleep and there seeks to become a monk in the manner already familiar. The lawyer then hears their stories and awards the jewel to the wife of the toothless husband. Another, no. 145, entitled 'The Three Numbskulls of Palermo,' is even closer.[20] Three dullards find a coat and, to avoid a squabble, invite an independent party to judge, who in turn sends each of them away to do the stupidest thing possible. The mother of the first calls in the surgeon to heal her son's inflamed cheeks, when, in fact, they are merely

---

19 W.A. Clouston, *Popular Tales and Fictions*, ed. Christine Goldberg (Santa Barbara, CA: ABC Clio, 2002), p. 275. The story type persisted in France down to the middle of the twentieth century, when several versions were collected by Geneviève Massignon, one of which, 'He Who Speaks First,' is published in her *Folktales of France*, trans. Jacqueline Hyland (London: Routledge and Kegan Paul, 1968), pp. 200–1. This one tells of the newly-weds who needed to return a small kettle, but couldn't decide who would take it. Their silence wager seems to have lasted for days as they sang and whistled at their work, until the king out hunting sent a servant to the door to light his lantern. As the result of their muteness, the king decided to haul them off, beginning with the wife, which prompted the husband at last to break silence to rescue her. It was told by an eighty-five-year-old peasant woman in the Isère in 1959. For a study of the type see W.N. Brown, 'The Silent Wager Stories: Their Origin and Their Diffusion,' *American Journal of Philology* 43 (1922), pp. 289–317.

20 *Sicilian Folk and Fairy Tales of Giuseppe Pitrè*, trans. Jack Zipes, 2 vols. (London: Routledge, 2009), vol. I, pp. 605–11 and 533–5.

stuffed with figs. She beats him for his foolery. The second one, staring at his girlfriend, wouldn't look away even with water pouring into his eye. He not only loses his sight but the girl as well. The third has his feet trimmed to fit his new shoes and in the process loses his *bien aimée*. The story follows Straparola's outline so closely that we are left with two choices: that the Sicilian raconteur was indebted to Straparola, or that Straparola was indebted to the story from which this one is derived.

Neither of the above stories features the silence contest, which has either split off from the Straparola model, or enjoyed its own parallel tradition from which Straparola borrowed his third part.[21] Very briefly, two from the same collection of Sicilian fables assembled by Pitrè demonstrate the presence of the complementary tale. In no. 181, 'The Bet,' a scaled-down folk version repeats the formula of a husband and wife – a cobbler and spinster – who need to borrow a pan to fry fish. We might have expected that the first to speak had to go fetch the pan. But in fact,

---

21 A story type related to the silence contest may be called the annoyance contest, in which two 'players' agree that the first to show exasperation, impatience, or anger with regard to the other must lose a strip of skin or pay a substantial sum. In the Irish story of 'Shan an Omadhan and His Master,' three brothers, in sequence, take jobs with Gray Churl, who demands as a condition for employment that if the boy loses patience he must forfeit a strip of skin from shoulder to hip. The first brother is goaded into anger, forfeiting both salary and skin, and the second as well. But Shan, the third, exacted a counter-arrangement, that if the master ever countermanded an order because he was unhappy with the results, he would have to pay double salary. At first the master had the upper hand and Shan bit his tongue at the privations, but in time he worked matters in his favour. He was granted the right to sleep after supper, so he asked the mistress to prepare his supper at midday, which he then ate immediately, spending the rest of the day in repose. In due course the master explodes and so Shan wins the contest. This is a game of will and endurance combined with cunning in working literal language to advantage. Patrick Kennedy, *The Fireside Stories of Ireland* (Dublin: McGlashon & Gill, 1870, pp. 74–80; new ed. Norwood, PA: Norwood Publishing, 1975). This same motif is developed in a folk tale from Lower Brittany in which two brothers, one after the other, take service on the condition that they never show anger under pain of forfeiting a strip of flesh. The condition applies to both sides, making it a true contest. The master is then free to harass the boy with forced labour, bad food, and added tasks, all without remonstration. The boy Janvier loses, but Février turns the tables first by killing the bulldog, then taking the master's wife and daughter by force. The contract was to end only when the cuckoo sang, marking the year, so that, in desperation, the master puts his wife up to faking the song to rid himself of the pest, only to have her shot. In this way, the second wins and walks with double salary and satisfaction. J.-M. Luzel, *Contes populaires de la Basse-Bretagne* (Rennes: Presses universitaires de Rennes, 1996), vol. III, pp. 155–63.

it was the first to complete the daily work who got all the sardines. Nevertheless, silence is somehow part of the formula, for when a friend appears and gets no response, he breaks in, meets the two mutes, gives up, eats the sardines, and wins the approbation of the community. This fragmented tale never returns to the matter of who first breaks the silence. The story is, nevertheless, similar to the tale of the Brahmins who lose their supper to the dogs. Another, no. 178, entitled 'The Poor Shoemaker,' provides a more elaborate version about taking back the borrowed pan. Neither shuts the front door. This story likewise garbles its own terms of play. Strangers enter, find them awake but silent, and call in the priest. The woman finally protests to avoid an outrage and the husband claims victory by telling her to return the pan. These little much-ado-about-nothing vignettes reveal just how consistently the ancient tales remained in circulation. No. 145 includes a variant version from Messina entitled 'Which Is the Greatest Fool?' It tells about three lazy women, one too indifferent to swallow, another too indolent to save her sight from a waterspout, and the third too lazy to avoid freezing to death by shutting the front door. This one also echoes motifs evident in Straparola's tale.[22]

Thus the present story, with its sources and analogues, poses yet again the intriguing question concerning the actual passage of story memes from the literary to the oral and from the folk to the literati. There is sufficient evidence from the early literary record to allow that Straparola could have devised his story by assembling parts from antecedent *facetiae*, *fabliaux*, and *novelle*, themselves carriers of ancient literary traditions. More probably, however, he collected and recorded a tale already assembled and resembling those that were told and collected in the nineteenth century.

---

22 *Sicilian Folk and Fairy Tales*, trans. Jack Zipes, 2 vols. (London: Routledge, 2009), vol. I, pp. 644 and 639–41. No. 181, 'The Bet,' enjoyed considerable popularity for it is known in many regions. Domenico Giuseppe Bernoni collected one entitled 'The Wager' in his collection of *Fiabe e novelle popolari veneziane* (Venice: Fontana-Ottolini, 1873), no. 95, in which the same shoemaker and spinster compete over a frying pan borrowed from their neighbours. As they do their work, a soldier enters and is provoked by their unaccountable silence. When he offers violence to the husband, the wife cries out for pity, with the usual 'dead pan' conclusion.

VIII. Fable 2
The Right Handling of Wives

CATERUZZA

Two brothers who are soldiers marry two sisters. One makes much of his wife and is ill rewarded by her disobedience. The other mishandles his wife, yet in everything she performs his will. The first one describes the means to make the other's wife obey and teaches it to him. But when he threatens his wife, she breaks out in laughter and in the end this husband is held in derision.

The learned and prudent physician, when he foresees that a certain disease will manifest itself in the human body, adopts those remedies and antidotes that show the greatest promise for preserving life, without waiting for the disease to gain control, because a new wound heals more readily than an old one. Likewise a husband – and here I crave pardon of all the ladies – when he takes a wife should act in the same fashion; he should never let her get the upper hand, for amends attempted later are impossible and the affliction will follow him to the grave. This is what happened to a soldier who waited too long before chastising his wife, for which fault he led thereafter a life of patient endurance down to his dying day.

Not long ago in Cornetto, a castle town near Rome in the patrimony of San Pietro, there lived two men who were sworn brothers. In fact, the love between them could not have been greater if they had been born of the same womb. One of these was called Pisardo and the other Silverio. Both one and the other followed the calling of arms and were in the pay of the pope, and great was the bond between them, although they did not dwell under the same roof. Silverio, the younger of the two, lacking someone to manage his household, took for his wife a certain Spinella, the daughter of a tailor, a very fair and lovely maiden with a vivacious but determined mind. After the wedding was over and the bride brought home, Silverio found himself so smitten and dominated by the power of her beauty that she seemed to him beyond all comparison and worthy to have every desire and whim granted to her without delay. And so it came about that Spinella became so arrantly haughty and domineering that she paid little or no attention to her husband. After a time the doting fool fell into such a state that if he asked his wife to do one thing she would immediately do something else. Whenever he told her to come here, she went there, mocking the while everything he said. But because the silly idiot saw everything through his own foolish eyes, he couldn't pluck up enough courage to reprove her and remedy his mistake. So he let her go on having her own way in everything according to her own good pleasure.

Before a year had passed, Pisardo married Fiorella, the other daughter of the tailor, a damsel no less attractive in appearance than Spinella, nor less sprightly and stubborn in her disposition. When the wedding feast was over and the wife taken home to her husband's house, Pisardo brought out a pair of men's breeches and two stout sticks of equal length, and said, 'Fiorella, do you see this pair of men's breeches? You take hold of one of these sticks and I'll take hold of the other and we'll have a struggle over the breeches to see who shall wear them. Whichever one of us gets the better of the other in this contest will have the honour, and whichever one loses will hereafter be obedient to the winner.'

When Fiorella heard her husband's speech, in a gentle voice and without hesitation, she answered, 'Ah my husband, what do you mean by such words as these? Aren't you the husband and I the wife? Ought not the wife always bear obedience towards her husband? And what's more, how could I ever bring myself to such folly? Wear the breeches yourself, for there's no question but what they will become you much better than me.'

'So then I'm to wear the breeches and be the husband,' said Pisardo, 'and you, as my dearly beloved wife, will always hold yourself obedient to me. Well, take heed that you don't change your mind and go hankering after the husband's part later on and try to give me the wife's, for you'll never drive such a deal with me.'

Fiorella, who was a very prudent woman, confirmed all that she had formerly said, and for his part, the husband handed over to her the entire governance of his household and committed all his goods to her keeping, informing her of the order he meant to have observed in his house.

A short time later, Pisardo said to his wife, 'Fiorella, come with me. I want to show you my horses and point out to you the right way to train them, in case you should need to know.' When they had entered the stable he said, 'Now Fiorella, what do you think of these horses of mine? Aren't they handsome? Aren't they finely tended?'

'Yes, sir,' replied Fiorella.

'But also take note of how docile and serviceable they are.' With that, Pisardo picked up a whip and gave a touch first to this horse and then to that one. 'Get over here! Get over there!' he shouted at them. Then they put their tails between their legs and, all in a cluster, obeyed the master's will.

Now among his other horses, Pisardo also had one that was as lazy and vicious as it was handsome – a beast upon which he placed little value. He went up to this horse and dealt it a sharp cut with the whip, shouting, 'Come here. Go over there.' But sluggish and sullen by nature, the creature took no heed of the whip, refusing to do anything his master ordered, lashing out vigorously first with one leg, then the other, and finally both together. At that, Pisardo, taking stock of the brute's stubborn humour, took a tough, stout stick and began to lambaste its hide so vigorously that he was soon out of breath. More stubborn than ever, the horse just tolerated Pisardo's blows and wouldn't budge an inch. Seeing how persistent it was, Pisardo flew into a violent rage, and grasping the sword he wore at his side, he slew the beast on the spot.

Fiorella, when she saw what her husband had done, was greatly moved with pity for the horse, and cried out, 'Alas, my husband, why have you killed your horse, and such a handsome one to look at? Surely, it's a great pity to have slain him like that.'

To this Pisardo replied, with a turbulent look, 'You must understand that all they who eat my bread but refuse my will must expect to be paid in the same coin.'

When she heard this speech, Fiorella was greatly distressed and said to herself, 'Alas, what a wretched, miserable woman I am. It was an evil day for me when I met this man. I thought to have taken someone of good sense for my husband, but see here if I haven't become this brutal man's prey. Just look how, for little or no fault of its own, he has killed this beautiful horse.' And so she continued grieving to herself, not knowing his ends in speaking in such a manner.

In light of what had passed, Fiorella fell into such a state of fear of her husband that she would tremble all over at the sound of his footsteps, and whenever he demanded any service of her, his wishes were her command. She, in fact, came to understand his meaning almost before he opened his mouth and never a word of anger passed between them.

On account of his friendship with Pisardo, Silverio would often visit his household to dine, and on such occasions he took note of Fiorella's carriage and manners. Amazed, he said to himself, 'My God, why wasn't I lucky enough to have had Fiorella for my wife and enjoy the good fortune of my brother, Pisardo? Look how deftly she manages the house and goes about her business without any turmoil. Look how obedient she is to her husband, and how she carries out his every wish. Miserable me to have married a wife who does everything to annoy me and treat me as spitefully as possible.'

One day, as it happened, Silverio and Pisardo were together and chatting of various things when the former said, 'Pisardo, my brother, you're aware of the friendship there is between us and on that account I'd be pleased to find out what method you followed in training your wife to make her so obedient to you and treat you in such a loving manner. It doesn't matter how gently I ask my Spinella to do something, she always stubbornly refuses to answer me, or worse, does exactly the opposite of what I ask her to do.' Then Pisardo, smiling, proceeded to explain word by word the plan and methods he had adopted upon first bringing his wife home, counselling his friend to go and do the same and to see whether he might not also succeed, adding that if this remedy was ineffectual, that he hardly knew what other course to recommend.

Silverio was greatly pleased by this excellent counsel, so taking his leave, he went on his way. No sooner was he home than he called to his wife and brought out a pair of his breeches and two sticks, following exactly the course recommended to him by Pisardo. When Spinella saw what he was doing, she shrieked, 'What new freak is this of yours? What are you on about, Silverio? What ridiculous fancy have you got in your head now? Have you gone stark mad? Don't you think everybody knows that men and not women should wear the breeches? So what's the use now in trying to do things entirely beside the matter?' But Silverio made no answer and went on with the task he had begun, laying down all sorts of rules for the ordering of his household. Altogether astonished at her husband's humour, Spinella said in her mocking way, 'So, Silverio, maybe you think I don't know how to manage your affairs? Is that what brings on this heated demonstration?' Still the husband kept silence and took his wife with him to the stable where he did with the horses precisely as Pisardo had done and in the end slew one of them. When she saw this work of a madman, Spinella was convinced in her own mind that her husband had truly lost his wits. 'Well for God's sake, husband, what crazy humours are these that have risen to your head? What's the reason behind all this insanity you're up to, without a thought for the consequences? Has some evil curse driven you mad, perchance?'

Then Silverio answered, 'I'm not mad, but I've made up my mind that all those who live at my charge and refuse to obey me will be chastised in the same manner you've seen."

When Spinella perceived the drift of her besotted husband's brutality, she said, 'Well you wretched dolt. It must be clear enough to you that your horse was merely a stupid beast to let itself be killed like this. What's the full meaning of this whim of yours? Maybe you think you can deal with me as you've dealt with a horse? I can assure you that if that's what you think, you're hugely mistaken. The steps you've taken come far too late to change anything of the matter now. The bone is hardened, the sore is now ulcerated, and there is no cure to be had. You should have been more prompt in setting all these wrongs of yours to right. You fool! You brainless idiot! Don't you see what damage and disgrace will come to you through such idiotic deeds? You think you have something to gain? Well, I can tell you what, and that's nothing at all.'

Listening to his wife's sharp words, Silverio knew in his heart that because of the doting affection bestowed on Spinella, his efforts were a miserable failure. So to his chagrin, he made up his mind to put up with his wretched lot with patience until death came to release him. And Spinella, taking note of how little her husband's plan had worked to his advantage, made up her mind that if in the past she had done as she pleased with a finger, that henceforth she would do so with her entire arm, for a woman headstrong by nature would sooner die a thousand times than deviate by an iota from the path she has deliberately laid out for herself.

All the ladies laughed heartily at Silverio's foolish devices, but they laughed even more when they recalled the battle over the pair of breeches, trying to decide who should wear them. Seeing that the laughter was growing louder and longer, and that time was on the wing, the Signora gave the sign for all to cease their talking so that Cateruzza could tell them her enigma according to the order of the revels. Divining the Signora's wish, Cateruzza provided the following:

> Ladies, I will surely die straightway
> If you the name correctly say
> Of this the subject I propound.
> It must surely be pleasant found,

> For all who taste its quality
> Depart commending what they try.
> Within my lips its tongue doth bide,
> And close I hold it to my side;
> And when I down beside it lie,
> All but the blind may us espy.

The enigma posed by Cateruzza gave even greater pleasure to the company than her story, seeing that it afforded ample subject for reasoning, some giving an interpretation after one fashion and some after another. But all these guesses were far wide of the true meaning. Whereupon the discreet Cateruzza, with her merry face all covered with smiles, with the permission of the Signora, gave the following answer to her riddle: 'This enigma of mine simply describes the bagpipes, which lets its tongue, which is the mouthpiece, be put into the mouth of the one who plays it and holds it tight, thus giving pleasure to all who listen.' Everyone was pleased with the solution to this well-made enigma and they praised it a lot. But in order not to lose more time, the Signora urged Arianna to take her turn, and the damsel, with her eyes cast down, made her requisite curtsy and then unfastened her little mouth to tell the following story.

VIII.2 Commentary

Two long-standing motifs are featured in this story, the trousers contest and the slaughter of disobedient animals, each employed to render docile a potentially recalcitrant wife. They replace wife-beating, as recommended by so many antecedent tales of the genre, insofar as the psychological taming of shrews is about the avoidance of domestic violence (see 'Conjugal Correction,' XII.3). The first is based on the principle of the game or contest by which power relations in real life are determined by tournament or combat, while the second is an instance of analogous association whereby the wife comes to understand by inference that what happens to some creatures under the assumed authority of her husband can happen to all, including herself. Both are forms of rhetoric intent upon persuading a spunky, independent, or crotchety new wife concerning her best interests for future happiness on the part of a demanding and perseverant new husband. That the husband imposes the logic of a game – the fight for the possession of the trousers – the outcome of which depends upon his own advantage in matters of physical strength, is an intelligent strategy. But in this story its effects are equivocal insofar as both wives refuse to play, the first conceding the victory in agreeing without contest that wearing the breeches is altogether more becoming of the husband than the wife, whereas the second mocks the very idea of the game, seeing through it as a hollow device from the outset. Game logic prevails only in those instances in which all participants abide by the rules and accept the conditions of winning and losing.

It is for this reason that Pisardo moves on to a greater display of brute power to make his point. Such 'show' violence, despite the subsequent compensations, is a risky form of dominance, however, because the wife is for a time overcome by such fear that she dreads his footsteps and thinks of him merely as a brute. The rhetoric of the gesture, misevaluated, may intimidate rather than generate cooperation. Of singular importance is that Pisardo, once his pre-eminence is established, assigns to his wife the governance of his household and commits all his worldly goods to her keeping, for he is no through-and-through bully. But whether such concessions will satisfy all readers concerning the justice of his dealings is much to be doubted. There are, for some readers, no acceptable means by which wives may be 'tamed'; among them is Sir Arthur Quiller-Couch, who complained of Shakespeare's famous foray into this area, *The Taming of the Shrew* (ca. 1594), that 'the whole Petruchio business ... with its noise of whip-cracking, scoldings, its throwing about of cooked food' to any man must seem 'tiresome,' and 'to any modern woman ... offensive as well.'[23] Such sentiments could apply even more persuasively to the present tale.

This story, in fact, opens upon so many assumptions about the power relations between the sexes fixed to a sliding scale between the nagging shrew and the patriarchal bully that it can hardly fail to arouse strong feelings. From its outset it assumes a necessary hierarchy, not in divine but in human terms: that social order, family prosperity, and domestic tranquillity depend upon male leadership. Such a notion is, of course, fortified by the likes of St Paul who, in Ephesians 5, notoriously teaches that women are to be subject to their husbands, and that the husband is the head over the woman as Christ is head over the Church. The story assumes, moreover, that beautiful women are vain and will take advantage of doting and subservient husbands. That point is strengthened by

---

23 William Shakespeare, *The Taming of the Shrew*, ed. Arthur Quiller-Couch (Cambridge: Cambridge University Press, 1928), pp. xv–xvi.

the pointless assertion that the slain horse was likewise handsome and that somehow its good looks had a part in its recalcitrance and laziness. It assumes that women will fill a power vacuum, that where the husband is weak she will take over. It assumes that male dominance and authority must be displayed from the outset, making timing of the essence. All these givens may be challenged by relativists in the face of the 'laws' of the story concerning male and female psyches and the gender wars. But only a fool will bankrupt the wisdom of the Middle Ages that nothing is quite so aggravating from a male perspective – and they have their stories to tell after all – as a leaky roof, a smoky fire, and a nagging wife. Many have been there; many know. If the story has a fallacy, however, it is a fallacy of wisdom literature in general, that complex and qualified matters are made too simple, as though spontaneous cooperation, love, and mutual respect are impossible within marriage.

The story in its design features a perfect symmetry between two men, both in the military, and their wives, who are sisters, daughters of a tailor, both good looking, and both high-spirited and headstrong.[24] We are led to believe that the only differentiating factor was the post-nuptial strategy for seizing power and control on the part of one man that fails for the other once the critical moment had passed. The story offers an either/ or that pretends to embrace all options. The family structure is an adaptive factor and dysfunctional families play out their tragedies in a world of fitness and survival. Hence, the opposite of a submissive wife is not only a cantankerous and obnoxious one, but an uncooperative and useless one – a wife who diminishes the power of the couple to compete in a world of labour and production. To that end, Straparola's opening analogy concerning preventive medicine and the tyranny of uncontrolled diseases is telling. The social sores that afflict human relations, if allowed to fester, may become fatal. The physician must act in a timely fashion. In respect to such unflattering absolutes, it is telling that the story is told by a woman and that all those present in the audience laugh and enjoy the tale immensely and without criticism. Straparola, meanwhile, through his narrator, in telling this tale of the tamed shrew, has already 'crave[d] pardon of all the ladies.' Such a show of ingenuous laughter and ritual

---

24 Spinella is 'vaga, ma di cervello gagliarda molto,' and her sister is 'né men gagliarda di cervello di Spinella.' A 'gagliarda' brain, according to my dictionary options, is lusty, robust, brave, generous, lively, or forceful; the translator must choose. Pirovano glossed the line as of a person who is 'steadfast, decisive, and difficult,' again applying to both.

apology creates a diminution of the effect among the elite, distancing them from such rough-and-ready ways. But the principle of the story remains without contest all the same, and here the reader's contention with a cloud of witnesses begins, some of which are recorded in the following account of sources and analogues, the presumed wisdom of which is confirmed by the very persistence of the story tradition.

Over two-and-a-half centuries before the publication of the *Piacevoli notti*, Juan Manuel placed into circulation his collection of stories and exempla entitled *El conde Lucanor* (ca. 1335), many of those stories, according to John England, undoubtedly derived from the oral and popular traditions. Among them is 'What Happened to a Young Man Who Married a Fierce and Truculent Woman.'[25] It is as good a place to begin as any insofar as Straparola's story is directly or indirectly derived from this work, or from the oral tradition upon which Juan Manuel based his tale. The author does not name his characters, but he tells of an impoverished young man who seeks a high-born wife in order to improve his wealth and standing. He makes up for the class differences by offering to marry an acclaimed shrew despite the misgivings of his own father and his future father-in-law. But the new groom, on his wedding night, replicates the traditional order of the tale by ordering a dog, a cat, and his only horse to bring water so that he can wash his hands, killing them for their disobedience in the presence of his now terrified wife. Upon hearing the same command, the wife, in a state of mortal fear, brings him the requisite water. The neighbours gather the next morning to see how the new couple has fared, fully expecting the war to be in full swing, but to their general amazement, the wife strives to shush and shoo them away in consideration of her slumbering husband. Pertinently, the bride is the true mirror of her own mother's belligerency, having come by her nature most honestly. When the father-in-law is apprised of his son-in-law's tactics, he too makes his attempt, but slaughters animals pointlessly as his termagant wife mocks his efforts, assuring him that it is now too late. This close analogue confirms the antiquity of the taming motif

---

25 *El conde Lucanor: A Collection of Medieval Spanish Stories*, ed. John England (Warminster, UK: Aris and Phillips, 1987), pp. 217–23. Juan Manuel was a powerful and prominent player in the violent politics of fourteenth-century Spain. The stories in his collection exist within a fictional framework involving an adviser, Petronio, who guides the young Count Lucanor by telling him exemplary stories. The story is also found as no. 35 in *El libro de los enxiemplos del conde Lucanor et de Patronio*, ed. Hermann Knust (Leipzig: Dr. Seele & Co., 1900), pp. 155*ff.*

involving animal slaughter that undoubtedly remained in anecdotal as well as literary circulation throughout the late Middle Ages, as it did right down to the end of the nineteenth century as seen in the folk tales described below.

The struggle for the trousers in the form of a little domestic drama, the literalizing no doubt of a popular saying about who wears the pants in the family, can also be traced back to much these same years. Hugues Piaucelle tells the anecdote in a *fabliau* entitled 'De Sire Hain et de Dame Anieuse,' featuring a tailor and his wife who are constantly at odds.[26] She is simply the worst shrew ever, quarrelling over every detail and always urging the contrary – that is what we are told. Because no form of reason would ever prevail, he one day said to her that the matter had to be decided for good and all by other means. So he takes a pair of trousers, declaring that they would literally fight for them, and that whoever wrenched them away would rule the roost. His wife agrees and two neighbours are called in as witnesses. One of them attempts to make peace, but he is confined to his role as judge. Hands only are allowed and thus the insults and fisticuffs begin as they yank the pants back and forth until they are torn in several pieces and the wife falls over backwards into a rain barrel, from which she is not to be extricated until she confirms her defeat and promises submission. A few days into the new regime, they find their mutual happiness in their newly assigned roles. Clearly, in Straparola's telling, these two motifs are brought together from such independent narratives as these, allowing that, for want of a literary model, he is responsible for their conflation – or that he found them joined in a folk source.

This *fabliau* has a perverse or inverted counterpart in the *Fastnachtspiel* of Hans Sachs entitled 'The Evil Smoke,' in which the battle of the breeches takes place to the wife's advantage. While the husband lays out the rules for combat, she attacks, masters him, and drenches him with dishwater. Seeing the husband in misery on the steps of his house, a neighbour comes along to mediate. He urges the good man to fight for himself, at which point the battleaxe appears to deal with the neighbour in kind, taking her husband's knife and purse. The moral is that it is already too late. This is in fact the second half of the story without the

---

26 Jean Pierre Baptiste Legrand d'Aussy, ed., *Fabliaux ou contes, fables et romans du XIIe et du XIIIe siècle* (Paris: Jules Renouard [1781], 1829; reprint, Geneva: Slatkine Reprints, 1971), vol. III, pp. 175–80.

first. The play (1551) takes up the battle of 'Sire Hain et Dame Anieuse,' while the title, 'Der böse Rauch' (The noxious smoke), refers to the proverb then in wide circulation concerning the three vexations mentioned earlier that will drive a man from his house: a leaking roof, a smoking fire, and a nagging wife.[27] Sachs's immediate source was a poem on the topic by Hans Folz, 'Ein liet genant der poss rauch.' Much could be written about the proverb on nagging wives that occurs, for example, in the Samaritan's sermon in the B text of William Langland's *Piers Plowman* (B. xvii, ll. 317–24): 'Thre thynges ther ben that doon a man by strengthe / For to fleen his owene hous, as Holy Writ sheweth. / That oon is a wikkede wif that wol noght be chasted: / Hir feere fleeth hire for feare of her tongue. / And if his haus be unhiled and reyne on his bed, / He seketh and seketh til he slepe drye. / And whan smoke and smolder smyt his sight, / It dooth hym worse than his wif or wete to slepe.'[28] The antiquity of the proverb and its wide currency are incontestable; it owes its origins to the Book of Proverbs 10:26, 19:13, and 27:15.

On the whole, as this story tradition progresses, authors and raconteurs take steps to mitigate the physical and psychological primitivism of the story so that by the time it reaches Shakespeare, Kate is no longer a doltish or stubborn woman in need of a lambasting, or a woman trained up by her domineering mother to grab power who must be taught her place, but a spirited woman seeking her equal in a mate, or at worst a spoiled girl who had been led to her selfishness by inadequate parents and who could only discover her own better nature by meeting a man who could impose those absent boundaries upon her. Such a retreat from pure pugilism is apparent in rudimentary form in the stories already recounted of a woman who submits to the terms imposed by a game and

---

27 Hans Sachs, *Translation of the Carnival Comedies of Hans Sachs (1494–1576)*, trans. Robert Aylett (Lewiston, NY: Edwin Mellen Press, 1994), pp. 93–107. See also 'Ein Fassnacht Spil mit drey Personen: Der böss Rauch,' in Hans Sachs, *Selections*, ed. Mary Beare (Durham, NC: Modern Languages Series, 1983), pp. 58–70. Also, *Sämtliche Fabeln und Schwänke*, ed. Edmund Goetze and Karl Drescher (Halle: Max Niemeyer, 1913), vol. VI, pp. 77–9. This story is likewise told by Georgius Macropedius, *Petriscus fibula iucundissima* (Cologne: J. Gymnicus, 1540), bk. III, no. 4.

28 Walter W. Skeat in his notes to *The Vision of William concerning Piers the Plowman* (Oxford: Clarendon Press, 1869), p. 393, discusses Langland's sources, citing the *Numerale*, no. 243, of William de Montibus and the *Verbum abbreviatum* of the Parisian Peter the Chanter. Other early English quotations of the proverb are discussed by Nicole Clifton et al. in *The Year's Work in English Studies* 81, no. 1 (2002), sect. III, 'Middle English: Excluding Chaucer,' pp. 171–229.

of a girl made rotten by her mother who bends to the fear tactics of a husband. But the story tradition allows for even less nuanced applications, as in the tale recounted by Boccaccio in his *Decameron* (IX.9) in the form of a verdict delivered by Solomon concerning the controlling of headstrong and intractable wives.[29] A preamble sets the tone in which it is stated without equivocation by the 'queen' of that day's proceedings, that any woman of a sound mind will know that 'we women are one and all subjected by Nature and custom and law unto man, by him to be ruled and governed at his discretion; wherefore she that would fain enjoy quietude and solace and comfort with the man to whom she belongs ought not only to be chaste but lowly, patient and obedient: the which is the discreet wife's chief and most precious possession,' a point of view she goes on to defend according to the laws of nature and custom. Revealingly, too, she recommends 'stern and severe chastisement' for the wayward 'as a salutary medicine for the healing of those of us who may be afflicted with this disease.' And while this does not apply to those who do not stand in need of such physic, nevertheless the proverb remains current among men: 'Good steed, bad steed, alike need the rowel's prick, / Good wife, bad wife, alike demand the stick.' There follows the vignette of Melisso and Giosefo, who become fellow travellers to the court of Solomon, the one seeking to know how he should make himself beloved, the other how he might reduce an unruly wife to order. In the wise king's enigmatic way he answers in koan fashion to the first with 'Love' and to the second, 'Get thee to the Bridge of Geese.' Both men ponder and, in finding little, think they have been mocked. But on the return trip they meet a muleteer flogging a mule that refuses to go forward.

---

29 *The Decameron of Giovanni Boccaccio*, trans. J.M. Rigg, 2 vols. (London: The Navarre Society, ca. 1900), vol. II, pp. 302–6. Ser Giovanni takes up the Boccaccian model a century and a quarter later in his *Il pecorone*, trans. W.G. Water, 2 vols. (London: Society of Bibliophiles, 1898), V.2, vol. I, pp. 185–94. Two Romans, already good friends, travel together to seek the advice of the sage Boethius. Janni's farm and estate are mysteriously wasting away and Ciucolo's wife is intolerable beyond words. Janni is told to get up early, while Ciucolo is advised to pay a visit to the Bridge of San Agnuolo. Both are mystified, but do as they are told. Janni, up early, sees his servants stealing everything that is not nailed down. By firing them and choosing his help more carefully, he finds his estate is soon flourishing. At the Bridge of San Agnuolo, Ciucolo sees a mule-driver not only beating a refractory mule, but forcing it with a stick to trot back and forth over the bridge. Ciucolo, by analogy, follows the model with his wife, including making her trot around the room, after which they too discover domestic tranquillity.

When they intercede, suggesting more docile tactics, the muleteer tells them that they may know horses but not mules, and that he will prevail in his own way, which he does. When asked the name of the place, they discover it to be the Bridge of Geese. Once home, Melisso meets Giosefo's contrary wife, who refuses them both the slightest gestures of hospitality. Giosefo, of course, determines to put his newfound wisdom into action and does not relent in his cudgelling until the lady is reduced to a heap of bruises and broken bones. Then both men await the morrow with interest to see the effect. They are offered breakfast as it was commanded (perhaps an echo of those tales in which the wife acts, but always contrary to her husband's orders) together with a declaration of submission. Inversely, however, Melisso is beloved because he shows love in a world of affective reciprocity. That optimistic turn replaces the failed attempts of a second husband to discipline a shrew now set in her ways and confirmed in her dominance. Boccaccio's spirited retelling, for all that, in the use of the cudgel represents a more 'primitive' attitude concerning the subjection of wives that Straparola leaves behind.

Another outstanding early example in this vein is the *fabliau* 'De la dame qui fut corrigée' (Of the lady who was reformed), in its way complementary to the *fabliau* of Hugues Piaucele cited above. This tale takes for its premise the dishonour and shame brought to a man by a domineering wife. The lord of a manor of delicate and wan constitution has to wife a lady of many qualities whose initial submissiveness by degrees turns to imperiousness. She becomes contrary in all things, so that when a group of hunters arrive seeking shelter, the lord can only explain that his hospitality will be obstructed by his wife, but that if they wish to apply in her presence he will refuse them so that she will invite them in. Then he will say to her that surely she did not intend to waste food and drink upon them, or allow their daughter to make an appearance, all of which will eventuate in the desired results through his wife's habitual contrariety. During the supper, one of the men falls in love with the daughter. Hearing her husband's remonstrations, the mother gives her away. Now this daughter is the spitting image of her mamma, who had been her teacher in everything, and the last advice she receives upon leaving the ancestral home is to impose her will upon her husband without delay and get the upper hand in everything. Being a shrew by nature and training, the contest by rights should have been intense, but the husband's pre-emptive measures are prompt, for upon leaving the wedding festivities he kills two disobedient dogs and a runaway horse in spite of the girl's outcries, asseverating that in all such matters he will brook no sedition. At the chateau she dares to countermand his orders for the supper, causing the servant who obeys her to be beaten and sent away by the husband. Yet all such indirect violence is deemed insufficient, for he thrashes her as well, despite her pleas and excuses.[30]

Two further examples of the story, these from Italy, may be found in *Il trecentonovelle* of Franco Sachetti, whose creations predate Straparola's by nearly two centuries. Fra Michele Porcello, in Novella 86 (of that name), goes to an inn and there witnesses a woman of such contrary nature that the host, her husband, is helpless before her. When the good man dies of an epidemic, and his own wife as well, Michele determines to marry the host's wife in order to revenge her husband for the horrid life he had led. No sooner married than the beatings and humiliations begin. When in her insouciance she had scalded his feet, she receives worse in kind until she could barely walk, all of which he performs in the name of her deceased husband. In due course she recognizes her match and makes peace. The story is still about Mr Stick with a sadistic sense of quid pro quo, but it does not lack for episodes and a forthright denouement.[31] The second example, Novella 138, entitled 'Buonanno di

---

30 Legrand d'Aussy, the editor of this work, which is included in his *Fabliaux ou contes, fables et romans du XIIe et du XIIIe siècle*, 3rd ed. (Paris: Jules Renouard, 1829), vol. III, pp. 204–24, provides in his notes, pp. 224–30, a number of references to stories in which animals are killed in the presence not only of wives but of servants to impress upon them the wages of *indocilité* and recalcitrance by painting their destinies in a living bestiary. The storehouse of literary anecdotes about the beating of non-compliant wives could likewise be extended to impressive proportions. Giuseppe Rua calls another to our attention entitled 'De la male dame' (Of the evil lady) in his first volume of *Tra antiche fiabe e novelle* on *Le 'Piacevoli notti'* (Rome: Ermanno Loescher & Co., 1898), p. 50, in which a man disgraced by a shrewish wife tames her stubbornness by killing a dog and a horse that refuse obedience, then beats the girl before going to work on the mother-in-law in an attempt to tame the whole family. A further study on the disciplining of women in Middle High German literature, the *fabliaux*, and Straparola was written by Ernst Strauch, *Vergleichung von Sibotes 'Vrouwenzuht' mit den andern mittel-hochdeutschen Darstellungen derselben Geschichte sowie dem Fabliau 'De la male dame' und dem Märchen des Italieners Straparola* (A comparison of Sibotes' *Vrouwenzuht* with the other middle-high German representations of the same story, such as the *fabliau* 'De la male dame' and the tale of Straparola, the Italian) (Breslau: O. Gutsmann, 1892).

31 This story is found conveniently in *Tales from Sacchetti*, trans. Mary G. Stegmann, intro. Guido Biagi (Westport, CT: Hyperion Press [1908], 1978), pp. 59–63, but for most by this author, the only source remains *Il trecentonovelle*, ed. Emilio Faccioli (Turin: Giulio Einaudi, 1970), in which is to be found no. 138, 'Buonanno di ser Benzio,' pp. 358–60.

ser Benzio,' is defective and incomplete, but features the battle for the pants for which the husband prepares by arming himself from head to toe and marching through the house crying, 'Viva Buonanno.' It was to be a contest to see who would 'wear the breeches' ever after, but the outcome is unknown. Nevertheless, given these braggadocio preparations, we might expect that his mortification is in the offing and that the wife will take the day by a ruse. Many of Straparola's motifs are in evidence, but the conjunction of strategies does not yet appear: the trouser tussle and animal slaughtering still belong to separate traditions.

In *Les contes* of Bonaventure des Périers there is the tale about the old knight who wanted to take the 'crickets' out of his wife's head. She was young and under her mother's tutelage, taking lessons on how to find out if her old husband would tolerate the priest as her lover. First she must see how he reacts to having his favourite tree cut down, then his best dog slain, and finally to having the banquet tables overturned. His docility and tolerance might be proved absolute, giving her complete freedom. These tactics have been seen in other stories. But when she exceeded his patience, his solution was to have her hot and lecherous blood withdrawn by a barber surgeon. As she grew weaker, she came to understand the magnitude of her husband's anger and thereby learned discretion and obedience.[32] Phlebotomy had been used by medical practitioners in powerfully emblematic fashion to impress consequences of a social kind upon their patients. Even depressed lovers and related melancholiacs were bled to underscore, through a symbolic draining of corrupted fluids, the contamination of their thoughts. Deep-seated conditions of various kinds might be assaulted by the shock therapy of bleedings, vomits, and violent laxatives on the basis of the medical principles by which bad thoughts were believed to correspond to bad humours, which were in turn subject to evacuation.

Doubling back, Albert Wesselski provides yet another late medieval work that is an elaboration upon the model established in *El conde Lucanor*.[33] This tale, in a Moorish setting, tells of the son of an honourable man who, for want of means, must supply his lack through a good

---

32 *Les contes ou les nouvelles récréations ou joyeaux devis* (Lyons, 1558; Paris: Dentu & Co., 1887), no. 60, pp. 197–200. The thirteenth-century *fabliau* to which this story is owing, 'De la femme qui voulut épreuver son mari' (Of the wife who wanted to test her husband), is summarized in footnote 43.

33 'Der Widerspenstigen Zähmung' (The shrew tamed) in *Märchen des Mittelalters* (Berlin: Herbert Stubenrauch, 1925), no. 24, pp. 66–9.

marriage. Against his father's counsel, his choice falls upon a rich man's only daughter, who is reputed to be the most devilish female known to mankind. Even the prospective father-in-law seeks to dissuade him, predicting for him a life of misery or early death. This girl is practically a 'black widow,' a layer-out of corpses. According to Moorish custom, the newly-weds are to enjoy an evening meal together. But the young man makes a hell of the occasion by killing animals, hacking them to pieces, terrifying the girl, and moralizing all along about obedience. She is so horrified that she doesn't know whether she is alive or dead. This is Juan Manuel all over again in a hyperbolical mode. There is blood everywhere and oaths writ large. The next morning the bride's father, mother, and kin all arrive expecting to find the bridegroom dead. When they find the girl alone they suspect the worst, but instead she tells them to keep silence or prepare to die in deference to her husband's desire to sleep in. The story concludes in the prescribed manner with the husband of an older couple seeking to quell his vexatious wife with the ritual slaughter, to which she replies, 'Really my friend, you thought of that a little late, for it wouldn't do you any good even if you killed a hundred horses. You should have begun all that long ago, but still it hasn't been so bad so far.' In all these stories Straparola's materials abound as though all had been assembled from narrative parts to be found in a box entitled 'Techniques for Taming Shrews' – the favoured motifs enjoying the greatest number of representations. But of the many tales to survive, none is sufficiently like Straparola's to be considered a direct source. Once again, the relationship between the literary and the oral also remains fluid and indeterminate.

Two further works in this tradition of singular importance are the 'Frauenzucht' ('Der vrouwen zuht' – Disciplining women) of Sibotes von Erfurt and 'Von einem Rosstäuscher' (Concerning a horse-dealer) by Jörg Zobels. The first is in the more violent tradition of horses and other animals slain, including killing the bride's favourite cat. Many of the features are found again in the *fabliaux* of the French writers. The girl is three times worse than her mother, who had tormented the girl's father for thirty years. But a neighbouring knight takes her in spite of the warnings and the ritual taming begins. Although this work seems to have circulated widely, there is no proof that Zobels was directly influenced by it. In his poem, the girl is the daughter of a nobleman forced to marry below her station, and her father had some concern that she would reject the horse-dealer he had chosen as her husband. His tactics are altogether more tame and gentle, for he slays neither horses nor hounds nor her favourite cat, although the cat makes an appearance, receiving orders to prepare the breakfast as an object lesson.[34]

Likewise, of the many that came after Straparola, none bears the specificity of design necessary to establish a clear line of influence, despite the efforts by Gerhard Simrock to give Straparola his due as part of the background to Shakespeare's *Taming of the Shrew*.[35] There are coincidental motifs, but little to suggest direct Straparolan inspiration.[36] Shakespeare so clearly determines Petruchio's game plan in terms of baiting, depravation, and humiliation as opposed to yanking, beating, and animal killing that he transforms the genre. There is a journey during which Katherina is subjected to unpleasantries and crosses, but Petruchio's method is based rather on falcon training with hoods and food deprivation than on mule training with sticks, for he sees in Katherina all along a loving and compliant mate and a spirited and intelligent woman. He is simply outdoing her in her own humour, acting out her ways so that she sees in him a mirror of her own wilfulness. That is learning by analogy of a different sort. He is as contrary as the wives in the *fabliaux* and insists upon having everything black called white until Kate learns the reversal game. When he knocks over a basin of water and blames the servant, it is she who comes to the servant's rescue. In these ways he erases the adverse conditioning of her upbringing and makes her fit for civil society, as she herself secretly desired. As stated by George R. Hibbard in his introduction to the play, this is work carried out 'in a very different fashion' by Petruchio from what Shakespeare might have known from earlier English works such as *Tom Tyler and His Wife* (ca. 1560), in which the stubborn

---

34 Sibotes's text appears in *Gesammtabenteuer: Hundert altdeutsche Erzählungen*, ed. Friedrich Heinrich von der Hagen, 3 vols. (Stuttgart and Tübingen: J.G. Cotta'scher Verlag, 1850), vol. I, pp. 41–57, and there is a modern edition of the *Frauenzucht* by Cornelie Sonntag (Hamburg: H. Buske, 1969). 'Von einem Rosstäuscher' appears under the title 'Die faule Frau' (The worthless wife) in *Die deutsche Märendichtung des 15. Jahrhunderts*, ed. Hanns Fischer (Munich: C.H. Beck'sche Verlagsbuchhandlung, 1966), pp. 286–93. Gerhard Eis discusses these poems briefly, the latter under the title 'Zähmung der Widerspenstigen' in *Kleine Schriften zur altdeutschen weltlichen Dichtung* (Amsterdam: Rodopi, 1979), pp. 303–6.

35 *Die Quellen des Shakespeare in Novellen, Märchen und Sagen* (Bonn, 1870), vol. I, pp. 334–54.

36 Most immediately in Straparola's wake is the version of the tale in Francesco Sansovino's *Cento novelle scelti da i piu nobili scrittori* (Venice: Francesco Sansovino, 1561), Day III, no. 6, pp. 112r–15r, which may be lightly overwritten from Straparola himself, obviating the need to recount the story.

woman is beaten up by her husband's friend disguised as her husband, or *The Ballad of the Curst Wife Wrapt in a Morell's Skin* (ca. 1550), in which the long-suffering husband hits his limit and goes berserk with his fists.[37]

Something of Petruchio's depravation strategy is anticipated in a story in the *Buen aviso y portacuentos* of Juan de Timoneda, first appearing in Valencia in 1564.[38] In this tale a husband, on the first day after the wedding, asked his wife to prepare the supper. When he returned and saw that nothing was done, he not only cooked it and set the table, but ate everything himself without inviting his wife to join him. In the process he divided the portions, saying this is for the one who earns the money, this for the one who buys the food, this for the one who prepares it, and this for the one who lays the table. This went on for a time until the wife did her part and earned an equal portion. As for the dessert, they ate it together from a single plate. In 'Mujer de estrado y almohadilla' (The woman of parlours and lounges), however, a different tactic is taken. When this woman complained that her husband treated her like a slave, he had a portrait of a slave painted and placed on the kitchen door. Refusing to take the hint, he broke it over her shoulders and beat her with a stick, whereupon she went home to her father, only to be told to do what her husband demanded of her.[39] Once more (as in Sacchetti), direct and indirect measures are represented in contrasting stories.

Giovanni Battista Basile in *Il pentamerone* (IV.10) tells the story of King Bello-Paese and Cintiella, which is his own version of the taming of a

---

37 Shakespeare, *The Taming of the Shrew*, ed. G.R. Hibbard (Harmondsworth: Penguin, 1968), p. 18. As he points out, the nagging wife in English literature goes all the way back to Mrs Noah in the Wakefield mystery play of the flood (p. 16). It also prevails in other plays from the Shakespearean period. Chough, for example, in Thomas Middleton and William Rowley's *A Fair Quarrel*, states, 'I am to marry shortly, but I will defer it a while till I can roar perfectly, that I may get the upper hand of my wife on the wedding-day; 'tmust be done at first or never' (IV.i.175–9), ed. R.V. Holdsworth (London: Ernest Benn [1615–17], 1974), p. 84. The commonplace about timely taming was a well-established bit of the collective wisdom of the age. Shakespeare's treatment goes back to the Continent in modified form in such variations on his play as *Kunst über Künste. Ein bös Weib gut zu machen* (Out-tricking the arts [of a woman]; making a bad wife good); ed. Reinhold Köhler (Berlin: Weidmann, 1864), based on a seventeenth-century original (Rapperschweyl: Henning Lieblern, 1672).

38 Juan de Timoneda (1520–83), *Buen aviso y portacuentos el sobre mesa*, ed. Pilar Cuartero and Maxime Chevalier (Madrid: Espasa-Calpe, 1990), pt. I, no. 15, pp. 86–7.

39 *Buen aviso y portacuentos el sobre mesa*, pt. I, no. 28.

shrew. The king, scorned and humiliated as Cintiella's suitor, returns home vowing revenge. His tactic is to go back as a peasant gardener and tempt the princess with irresistible gowns and jewels in exchange for nights spent inside the palace, sleeping closer and closer to her room, until, once inside, he could enjoy her sexually, get her pregnant, and arrange to take her away into the country where she might give birth in secret. The destination, in fact, is his own palace where she is kept in the stables, invited to work at menial tasks, encouraged to steal by her peasant accomplice, then find herself repeatedly accused of theft by the king, who switches regularly between the two personalities. She is taken into the house for the childbirth, fed well, attended, and gives birth to two handsome princes. Only then does the queen mother tell her son that Cintiella has endured enough, that her pride is broken, and that she is ready to be his wife.[40]

Molière, along the way, turns the entire situation on its head in *L'école des maris* (1661). Sganarelle handles his ward Isabelle in the strictest way, but she makes a fool of him by using him as an unwitting go-between with her forbidden beau, Valère. Nevertheless, it is his design to show his

---

40 'Pride Punished,' in the *Pentamerone*, trans. Richard Burton (New York: Boni & Liveright, 1927), pp. 371–7. This story is similar in nature and design to 'King Thrushbeard' in the Grimms' tales, discussed below, for the manner in which a king must disguise himself as a peasant to break a haughty girl's pride. Another story, collected in Bologna in the late nineteenth century, is part of this same tradition in which the princess who refuses suitors is at last pawned off on a peasant who is a prince in disguise, introduced to misery, and at last tamed. In this version, Princess Stella is so whimsical and proud that she would settle on no one to marry, finding fault with every candidate, one after the other. The only one she liked was a dirty fellow with a crumb in his beard. The prince with the dirty face then disguised himself as the sifter for the bakery and began to sing under the princess's window. In short order, she was flinging herself at the baker's boy and they agreed to elope, all as planned by the two fathers, who were overseeing the whole affair. He takes her to a hovel and tells her that she would now have to do manual labour. Then he induces her to steal clothes, before running to dress as a king in order to accuse her of theft. The next day she must return to the palace to bake and steal dough, and again she is caught and humiliated. Finally, an announcement is made that the king's son is to be married and that she must return yet again, terrified, and against her will. Dressed in rags, the king prods her in the midst of the festivities and hits the pot of broth hidden under her skirts. Her humiliation is now complete and she faints away with shame. At last, the queen mother, as in Basile's story, pronounces the moral, reveals the plot, and the fallen princess is kissed, embraced, and welcomed by all the parents present, including her own. Ed. Carolina Coronedi-Berti, *Novelle popolari bolognesi* (Bologna: A. Forni [1874], 1983), no. 15.

far more liberal-minded brother, Ariste, how strictness produces finer results than liberality in the bringing up of young women. In this misguided enterprise, Sganarelle mistakes the identities of eloping lovers and then pressures Ariste into authorizing Isabelle's marriage to Valère. The debate over the training of wives is thus concluded in favour of indulgence, because the demand for extravagantly submissive behaviour merely provokes deception.[41] The work is very far in spirit from Straparola's, as is the work acknowledged to be its source, Paul Scarron's 'The Useless Precaution,' in which Don Pedro raises the daughter of his once beloved Seraphina and in the end marries her thinking that her simplicity and sheltered upbringing was a guarantee of her honour, while in fact her naivety led her into the embraces of a passing amour without any sense of wrong-doing on her part.[42] Spirited and intelligent wives may pose the risk of independence and deceitfulness, but only such women can appreciate and love a husband with full heart and mind.[43]

---

41 *The School for Husbands*, trans. Richard Wilbur (New York: Harcourt Brace Jovanovich, 1992).

42 *The Comical Romance and Other Tales*, trans. Tom Brown, intro. J.J. Jusserand, 2 vols. (London: Lawrence and Bullen, 1892), vol. II, pp. 151–96.

43 At this juncture in the history of the motifs that define Straparola's narrative, a necessary compromise imposes itself, for the story type was widely known. For those wishing to press on, a recommended discussion of further collateral versions may be found in Friedrich Heinrich von der Hagen's *Gesamtabenteuer: Hundert Altdeutschen Erzählungen*, 3 vols. (Darmstadt: Wissenschaftliche Buchgesellschaft, 1961), vol. I, pp. lxxxvii–xc. Some of his sources are recherché, such as the tale of the disobedient son who was improved by example in the shooting of an unruly dog, which he cites as Ebd. 223 from the *Journal de Paris*, 31 July 1777. Härter tells the French tale of a man who, shortly after his wedding, broke his wife's arm and paid the doctor double on the assumption that he was intent upon breaking her other arm as well. This is apparently to be found in Legrand's *Bibliothèque de la cour*, vol. 5, p. or no. 223. Others appear in the stories, recounted below, of Bonaventure des Périers, no. 127, in Clarence Bement's *Les amans heureux, histories galantes* (Amsterdam, 1696, and Paris: Claude Barbin, 1683), p. 123, as well as in Antoine François Abbé Prévost's *Contes, aventures et faits singuliers* (Paris: Veuve Duchesne, 1767), vol. II, p. 13, not to mention the remote analogues in *The Seven Wise Masters* and *The Arabian Nights* to which he alludes without benefit of more specific references. Judging by his commentaries and résumés, none seems to add significant new strategies for the taming process, and none more closely approximates Straparola's tale than those set out above. L'Abbé Prévost's tale is about a contrary wife who, in petulant spite, pulls the tablecloth to the floor during one of her husband's supper parties. He takes her on a trip, pretending to visit a friend, and on the way has her confined for treatment in an asylum for fools. This motif is explored by Barnabe Riche in his *Farewell to Military Profession*, ed. Donald Beecher (Ottawa: Dovehouse

Stith Thompson in *The Folktale* identifies 'the taming of the shrew' as story type 901, giving as a generic profile of the tale the one involving the husbands of three sisters who wager as to which of them is the most docile and obedient. The third is the shrew and thus drastic measures must be employed to bring her to submission before her husband has a chance in the contest. By treating her to tactical indignities, however, and revealing the strength of his will in the slaughter of disobedient animals, he makes her more tractable than either of her sisters. The story is known throughout Europe as a folk tale, particularly in Scandinavia but also in Scotland, Ireland, Spain, and Russia. One such is included among the Danish fairy tales edited by Svend Grundtvig: 'The Most Obedient Wife.'[44] The story offers a representative gathering of motifs. The husbands of three sisters each boast of having the most docile and tractable wife. The father of the three girls is astonished, knowing the third to be a spitfire, but her husband was willing to maintain his claim.

Editions, 1992), 'Of Two Brethren and Their Wives,' pp. 232–59, in which two brothers marry, the first for beauty and the second for riches. The first wife is of a light disposition, while the other is a common scold. The latter responds to no tactics whatsoever. To her husband 'she was such a devil of her tongue and would so crossbite him with such taunts and spiteful quips' that his life became to him a hell. He tried physical force, pinioning her arms, dressing her in humiliating rags, making her out to be a lunatic to the neighbours, until in her 'cursings and bannings' that the devil tear her husband to pieces, he had no choice but to consign her to a real asylum, once her shrewishness had crossed the line into veritable madness. Yet the husband was so ashamed of making her case worse in attempting to tame her that he exiled himself to another country. The stories told by Bonaventure des Périers and by Clarence Bement in *Les amans heureux* turn out to be recensions of the thirteenth-century *fabliau* 'De la femme qui voulut épreuver son mari' (Of the wife who wanted to test her husband), set out above. In brief, an old man marries a young girl, who, in consultation with her mother, decides to take a lover. The mother cautions that she had better test her husband's tolerance, for if he is decisive over little infractions, catching her with a lover would be fatal. The girl begins by chopping down his favourite tree and then kills his whippet, always with pretexts that gain his pardon. But when she thinks she has proved him pliant after pulling the tablecloth and the supper with it onto the floor, he calls in a barber surgeon to purge the bad blood in her veins. She remonstrates to no avail and the blood is drawn from both arms till syncope overcomes her. Pale and ashen, she reports all to her mother, who asks her if she still wants a lover – an enterprise now entirely quelled. The rhetoric of the taming has been conducted in medical terms, much as Renaissance physicians recommended phlebotomy to cure those afflicted with lovesickness, the very treatment serving as a disgust factor. Legrand d'Aussy, ed., *Contes, fables et romans* (Paris, 1829), vol. III, pp. 165–75.

44 *Danish Fairy Tales* (London: G.G. Harrap & Co., 1914), pp. 175–82.

On the way home from the wedding, he took her down from her horse, made impossible demands of the animal, reminded her that he never gave orders twice, and shot it dead. Similar demonstrations followed so that, in the end, to avoid contradicting him, she would agree to patent falsehoods. He had given her for a wedding ring a green willow twig bent to size, an objective correlative to an old proverb about forming wills while they are still pliable as well as to his taming techniques. Needless to say, she performs well in the contest, to everyone's amazement.

Aurelio Espinosa includes two further variants in his *Cuentos populares españoles*, no. 91, 'La mujer mandona' (The domineering wife), and no. 92, 'La esposa desobediente' (The disobedient spouse). The first tells of a woman four times married who buried them all and was never tamed. When another man in the village falls in love with her, his family and associates consider him crazy, because none of her former husbands had the fortitude to endure her. But he takes her to his country house and there kills a disobedient donkey while pronouncing upon his unwillingness to be contradicted, to which she replies 'Haces bien, marido mío. Has hecho muy bien' (You have done well, my husband, very well). Then upon their return he asks her about a pair of young steers he has traded, two fat ones for two old and lean ones, which he induces her to call fat and healthy, whereupon he contradicts her yet again and she enjoins with agreement. It is a variation upon the now familiar story, this one collected in Zamora.[45]

Finally, the story of 'King Thrushbeard,' elaborated by the Brothers Grimm, may bring this essay to a close, for it epitomizes the taming of the proud woman by the gentler means of disguise and disciplining poverty imposed by a loving husband. When the haughty princess made mockery of all her suitors, her father declared that she would be married to a beggar. The suitor king whom the vixen had nicknamed 'Thrushbeard' disguised himself as that beggar, married her, and took her away

---

45 *Cuentos populares españoles recogidos de la tradicion oral de españa* (Madrid: S. Aguirre, 1946), vol. I, pp. 164–9. There is another in the *Sketches of Persia*, rather similar to Straparola's, although it does not contain the battle of the trousers. Sir John Malcolm, *Kisseh-Kühn: Der Persische Erzähler* (Berlin: Nicolai, 1829), no. 29. Thomas Frederick Crane in *Italian Popular Tales*, ed. Jack Zipes (Santa Barbara: ABC Clio [1885], 2001), p. 277n5, provides a number of further references to tales of proud girls who are tamed by princely suitors disguised as commoners. They include the Grimms' 'King Thrushbeard' to follow, as well as others in Norwegian, French, Greek, and Tibetan.

to do menial labour and finally to work in the palace kitchen for scraps of food. In fairy-tale fashion, however, he meets her as himself and invites her to dance, in the process declaring his ruse whereby he had made her a fit wife.[46]

Straparola's story remains its own creation without immediate predecessors or successors – at least none that survives – although it clearly belongs to a long-standing tradition sharing in a common narrative idea and a common repertory of motifs. His version avoids the brutality of the 'primitive' involving physical violence, but maintains something of the schematic naivety of the folk tale, in which merely token gestures are made to explain temperaments, specify personalities, and intimate motivations. The spirit of the story belongs essentially to the medieval *fabliau* and the shrove-tide play in which rustic logic prevails in the negotiations of social life. With the passing of 'primitive' mentalities, such stories should also have passed. But in fact, they treat of eternal questions in a refreshingly forthright manner that continues to claim our amused attention.

---

46 *Grimm's Complete Fairy Tales* (Garden City, NY: Nelson, Doubleday, n.d.), no. 16, pp. 43–7. This tale has much in common in its design with Basile's *Il pentamerone*, IV.10, discussed above. Remote in its tactics, yet very much a tale of shrew taming in extreme terms, is the Indian tale of 'Panwpatti Rani,' which tells of a prince and princess who are married, but descend into the miseries of jealousy. The princess cannot tolerate the husband's friend and schoolmate who had brought them together. When the prince goes to visit him a second time, she sends a gift of poisoned sweetmeats. The prince detects the trick and vows never to return until she has been tamed. Her jewels are stolen, she is wounded with a trident, and she turns cannibalistic until her family disowns her and sends her into the forest, where the two men locate her. Time and suffering ultimately render her docile. Maive Stokes, *Indian Fairy Tales* (London: Ellis & White, 1880), pp. 208–15.

VIII. Fable 3
The Priest and the Image-Carver's Wife

ARIANNA

Father Tiberio Palavicino, expelled from his order but still a secular priest and master of theology, falls in love with the wife of Chechino the woodcarver. With her husband's knowledge, she admits him to the house, where he is discovered and subjected to an ignominious trick from which he barely escapes with his life.

Gracious ladies, if all our churchmen these days – and I'm speaking now of the unworthy and not of the worthy clerics – were zealous in their studies, providing an example to the uneducated, and inclined to live in righteous ways according to their rules, the ignorant rabble would have less occasion to ridicule them and pretend to teach them their duties. For then all humankind would hold priests in high reverence and think themselves blessed of God if they could merely touch the hems of their cassocks. But because our spiritual guides have taken on the manners of secular folk, have given themselves up to the world of luxury and lasciviousness, and do things they would never tolerate from the rest of us, abandoning all reverence for their calling, one hears evil reports of them everywhere both in public and in private. For this reason, I have no scruple in telling you the story of a sinful clerk, and though you may find it a bit long, still it may prove a pleasant diversion to your general satisfaction.

In the fair and ancient city of Florence, there once lived a reverend father named Messer Tiberio. The order he belonged to I can now no longer pronounce, so badly my memory has failed me. Suffice it to say, he was a man well versed in letters, an eloquent preacher, subtle in argument, and held in general esteem. But for some reason unknown to me, he had cast off his monk's habit to become a priest. Once he had thrown away his cowl, his prestige was no longer as great, but still he enjoyed the consideration of many persons of distinction and of the city in general.

Because Messer Tiberio had a good reputation as a confessor, it happened one day that a pretty young woman named Prudence – a name reflecting the modesty of so many women of her age – appeared to confess her sins. She was wife to one Chechino, a carver of images and the premier craftsman of his day. On her knees before Tiberio, this lady said to him, 'Sir, my former confessor, to whom I made known all my secrets, has now passed away, and having heard the report of your holiness and virtuous life, I have chosen you in his place as my spiritual director.'

Messer Tiberio, seeing that she was fair and fresh as a dew-wetted bud, graceful and well made, and in the flower of her youth, fell so hotly in love with her that he scarcely knew what he was saying or doing; the very sight of her beauty drove him half crazy. When he came to deal with the sin of luxury, he asked her, 'And now, my daughter, have you ever felt particular affection or preference for any priest or religious person?'

'Yes, surely,' she replied, quite unaware of his drift. 'For my late confessor, I felt all the love that a daughter has for a father, honouring and revering him as he deserved.'

After this, Tiberio plied her with such subtle words that he managed to find out her name, her condition, and her place of residence. This done, he commended himself to her, urging her to hold him as dearly as her late adviser. Then, as a sign of his charity, he promised to visit her at Eastertide to bring her spiritual consolation. She thanked him for this grace, received absolution, and went her way. After Prudence had gone, Messer Tiberio's brain nearly went off kilter as he called up the fair image of his late penitent, so he began scheming how he might best win her favours. But the affair didn't turn out as he'd planned, for it's easier to sketch your design than to fill in the colours.

Following the Feast of the Resurrection, Tiberio never failed to walk up and down in front of Prudence's house as often as he might, making eyes at her whenever he saw her and saluting her most courteously. But as a woman of modesty, she looked down and pretended not to see him. His comings and goings and salutations became so insistent that Prudence began to fear that his attentions would lead to evil rumours. To prevent this, she was careful to avoid him at all cost – a measure that brought no small displeasure to the priest. Love had so ensnared him that there was no escaping his imprisonment. He sent a young cleric to beg her to let him visit her as her spiritual adviser, but the lady, when she heard the proposal, cautiously refused to reply. At least Tiberio had to credit her with perspicacity and an ability to keep close counsel, and he knew too that one must often knock more than once at a door before it opens, and that a fortification need not surrender before it is valiantly assaulted. So the priest resolved not to give up, but every day sent some fresh messenger to glean tidings of the lady. Noting the priest's resolute humour, Prudence became alarmed for the sake of her honour and felt constrained to speak to her husband. 'Chechino, for many days now Messer Tiberio, my confessor, has sent various messengers to me, and whenever he meets me he salutes me, and what's more pursues me, all along making fanciful speeches, while I shrug my shoulders at his pestering and try to avoid his glances, never lifting my eyes to him or going anywhere that invites his attention.'

'Well, what answer have you given him?' asked her husband.

'I've given none,' Prudence replied.

'You did well, prudent as you are,' said Chechino, 'but I would advise you, should he again salute you or say more to you, to give him a few words in reply – in as sober and discreet a manner as possible – whatever you think suited to the occasion. Then we can watch what the outcome will be.'

Before many days had passed, it came about that Chechino was called away after dinner on affairs to another part of the city and Prudence was left to take care of the shop. Very soon Tiberio appeared, and seeing that she was alone, made his salvo, 'Good day, my lady.'

To this Prudence answered graciously, 'A good day and a happy year to you, my father.'

The priest, noting that she had returned his greetings – something not seen before – assumed that her heart was softened, her pity aroused, and that she would now look kindly upon him. So he entered the shop and there he stayed for more than an hour, passionately expounding to her the object of his desire. But at last, fearing that Chechino would return, he took his leave, begging Prudence to hold him in her good graces, swearing to remain her devoted servant. For this she thanked him modestly and for all else that he had offered her.

Soon after the priest was gone, Chechino came back and Prudence told him everything that had happened. 'Prudent as usual and well done,' he said. 'Now the next time he comes, put on a good face and offer him whatever reception seems honest to you,' and this she agreed to do.

His appetite had been whetted by the sight of the lady, but now Messer

Tiberio had enjoyed her sweet conversation as well and began to send her sundry gifts, all of which she accepted. Then with the sweetest and choicest of words he tendered his love, pleading that she not reject him, for without her favours she would be the reproachable cause of his death.

To this she replied, 'Signor, I would willingly grant your wish, which is my desire too, were I not in dread of discovery by my husband and thereby the loss of my honour and my life.'

These words touched Tiberio so adversely that he was ready to expire. But collecting his thoughts, he begged her not to let him perish when she had it in her power to save him. Then Prudence, pretending to be touched to the heart, seemed to yield to his prayer, saying that she might grant him a rendezvous that very night, since her husband had gone into the countryside to buy wood. The priest was the happiest man alive upon hearing these words and with that begged license to leave.

When Chechino returned home, Prudence told him exactly what she had done, and he replied, 'We must do more than this. We'll play such a trick on him that he'll hightail it straight out of the house and never again think of molesting you. Go and make the bed, move everything else out of the bedroom except the big chest, then clean out the two armoirs so nothing remains there, and I'll fix up the shop and arrange everything. You're going to see a trick I'm planning for him that will bring complete satisfaction to your heart.' Prudence, once she had grasped her husband's intent, promised to do her part by enacting his every instruction.

As for the priest, that day seemed like a thousand years waiting for the night to come that would bring him into the arms of his beloved. He went to the market and bought a fair quantity of the finest meats which he sent to Prudence to have cooked up, assuring her that he wouldn't fail to dine with her at the appointed hour.

When the provisions arrived, Prudence began to bustle about in the kitchen while Chechino hid himself and awaited Tiberio's arrival. As soon as the priest entered, he hastened to give Prudence a kiss while she was busy cooking the supper, but she drew back, saying, 'Sweetheart, have a little more patience, seeing that you've waited till now. It's not the time while I'm all grimed and greasy with cooking.' With that, she began placing the chickens on skewers and putting the veal into the pot. Meanwhile, Chechino kept up his watch through the hidden crack, taking in everything that happened in the room and all that was said, somewhat afraid that the trick might play out to his own cost. At this point in the game, in her dawdling over this and that, Prudence began to tax the poor priest's patience, who, to speed things along, lent a hand with the preparations, only to make her hasten even more slowly. Tiberio began to fear that all the time would be taken up with these operations and that none would be left for the purpose for which he had come. 'Signora, my desire to hold you in my arms is so great that it has taken away all my appetite for food and drink, for tonight I intend to dine otherwise,' and as he spoke he stripped off his clothes and got into bed.

Prudence secretly laughed at the ridiculous figure he made, replying to him, 'What foolishness it is to give up your dinner. You may be silly enough to do without, but it'll be to your own loss, because I can assure you I'm not going to bed without my supper.' All this while, she kept busy with her cookery. The more the priest begged her to get into bed, the more there was to be done outside it. At last, seeing that he was worn out with impatience, she said, to keep him quiet, 'Well, Father mine, one thing is certain, I'll never go to bed with a man who sleeps in his shirt, so if you want to have your will with me, you'll have to take it off, and then you'll see that I'm ready to do all your pleasure.'

Thinking this to be merely a trifling request, Messer Tiberio took off his shirt and lay there as naked as the day he was born. Seeing that he was ready to follow wherever she would lead him, Prudence gathered up his shirt and all his other clothes and put them in the chest and turned the key. Then she made a great show of getting undressed, washing and perfuming herself, and checking on household matters until the poor man between the sheets was half mad with waiting.

Chechino, who had seen all these goings on through the crevice, secretly went out by the back door and, having come around to the front, started knocking loudly. Hearing her husband at the knocker, Prudence made as though she were beside herself with fear. Trembling all over, she cried, 'Alas, what will become of me? Who's that knocking at the door? Surely it's him, it's my husband. Wretch that I am! What shall we do so that he won't see you?'

'Bad luck indeed, but quick, give me my clothes. I'll put them on and hide under the bed.'

'No,' cried Prudence. 'Where will you find the time to do that? No, I see another plan. Go climb on top of the dresser in the right-hand corner of the shop – here, I'll help you up – and stretch out your arms wide open, because when my husband comes into the room and sees you standing there positioned on the cross, he'll take you for one of the crucifixes he's worked on of late and think no more of it.' All the while, Chechino was pounding lustily outside, while Messer Tiberio, without an inkling of the husband's trick, climbed up on the dresser, assumed the shape of the cross with his arms outstretched, and stood as still as he could. Prudence then went down and opened the door to her husband, who bawled her out for keeping him waiting so long. When he entered the room, he gave no sign of seeing Tiberio's presence, but sat down to supper with his wife, and when that was over, they undressed and went to bed.

The tortures poor Tiberio must have suffered I leave to the imaginations of those who have writhed under the jabs of amorous desire, to see the husband gorging himself on the banquet so carefully prepared for his own delectation and recognizing himself the butt of a sly trick.

At last the morning began to dawn and little by little Apollo, rising from the sea, spread his ardent rays. Then Chechino rose from his bed and began to sharpen his tools before settling down to work. But he had scarcely begun when two nuns from a neighbouring convent came to the house and, having entered, said to him, 'Master Chechino, our abbess desires you to send home the crucifix that she ordered from you several days ago.'

'My sisters,' Chechino replied, 'you must explain to the abbess that the crucifix is begun, but that it's not yet completely finished. In two days' time, however, she shall have it.'

'But our Mother told us to say that, finished or not, she wishes it to be sent home, for you have kept her waiting too long already.'

Feigning anger at the nuns' persistence, Chechino replied, 'All right then, my ladies, enter my shop and I'll show you that it's well along but not yet fully sculpted.' When the nuns had entered, he went on speaking and pointing towards Tiberio, 'Look up there over the dresser and tell me whether that one is ready to go or still in need of some endowments; you can report back to the Mother Superior what you've seen with your own eyes.'

The nuns, glancing upward and seeing the crucifix, with the greatest of amazement they exclaimed, 'O maestro, how natural you have made him appear. He seems as much of flesh and blood as we are ourselves. Without doubt he is magnificent and will greatly please the Mother and the sisters. Ah, but there's just one thing you've outfitted that's rather displeasing; it's that nuisance there, right before our eyes and in plain sight, which might cause a big scandal throughout the convent.'

'Well, didn't I tell you it wasn't finished yet? But no need to be troubled by that,' said Chechino. 'I'll give it the finishing stroke in a moment. Would to God I could cure a man of mortal sickness as easily as I can cure this blemish! I can do it while you watch.' Then snatching up one of his sharpest tools, he said, 'It'll be done in a trice. And rest assured, it's no inconvenience to me to remove those offending parts.' Messer Tiberio, who up to this moment had kept as still as a dead man, overheard the entire conversation, and when he saw the freshly sharpened tool that Chechino had taken up, without wasting a moment or saying a word, he leapt from the dresser and, naked as he was, took flight with Chechino in hot pursuit to remove the nuisance he still had in front. But Prudence, fearing lest some scandal should get abroad, grabbed her husband by his clothes and held him back so the priest could make his escape. The two nuns, who watched in astonishment, started screeching in their high voices, 'A miracle, a miracle, the crucifix has come to life and run away,' and couldn't stop.

With all that clamour, a crowd of people flocked around to see what was happening and when they realized the nature of the game, they collapsed into laughter. After Messer Tiberio had put on other clothes, he fled the city, and where he made off to I've no idea. I only know that he was never again seen in Florence.

When Arianna had brought her diverting story to an end, every one of the listeners laughed so heartily that the Signora was compelled to clap her hands together as a sign that everyone should be quiet. Then turning towards Arianna, she asked her to complete her story with a merry riddle. Unwilling to appear less willing and witty than the others, she began as follows:

> A useful thing, firm, hard and white,
> Outside in shaggy robe bedight;
> Hollowed within right cleverly,
> It goes to work both white and dry.
> When after labour it comes back,
> You'll find it moist and very black,
> For service it is ready ever,
> And fails the hand that guides it never.

This enigma set all the men laughing, but not one of them could explain what it meant. Then Alteria, whose turn it was to tell the next story, explained it to them with considerable grace. 'This riddle signifies nothing other than the pen that a man uses to write. It is firm, straight, white and strong. It is pierced at the head and soiled with ink. It is never weary, being swayed to and fro by the writer both in public and in private.' Everyone praised Alteria's wit in explaining this subtly devised enigma, everyone except Arianna, who was more than miffed, thinking that she alone could give the interpretation. The Signora, seeing the vexation that burned in her eyes, said to her, 'Come, come Arianna, be calm. Another time your own turn will come.' Then turning towards Alteria, she commanded her to tell her fable, and so, with a merry gesture, the damsel thus began.

VIII.3 Commentary

This story comes with a moral: that the rabble would have less reason to rail if the monastery men lived according to their rules. But alas – and the court records are there to prove it – many clerics sought all the pleasures of the secular life, often at the expense of the citizenry.[47] Hence, it was deemed no fault of the folk in telling tales of wicked clerks; they deserved the shaming. It is perfectly evident, at the same time, that the moralizing provided a cover for telling saucy and ribald tales, this one popping up persistently over three centuries before going underground early in the seventeenth. Its unique marker is the proposition that castration, if only in comic semblance, is an appropriate expression of anger and justice where philandering priests were concerned. It appealed to the simple logic of talion: injuring those parts by which their wives might have been injured. And if their sadistic impulses could not be satisfied in fact – even the wife in the present story holds her husband back – they

---

47 In England, at the beginning of the sixteenth century, 'priests routinely propositioned women entering the confessional box: absolution was offered in exchange for sex.' Peter Watson, *Ideas: A History of Thought and Invention, from Fire to Freud* (New York: HarperCollins, 2005), p. 458. He is reading William Manchester, who gives statistics on the number of clerics accused of sexual crimes against women in Norfolk, Ripon, and Lambeth; they constituted 2 per cent of the population but accounted for 23 per cent of such accusations. Those statistics might well be generalized to form a portrait of that social age. William Manchester, *A World Lit Only by Fire* (Boston: Little, Brown, 1992), pp. 130–2.

could be satisfied by the sardonic laughter that unites a community against a common enemy through the bite of satiric justice. Monks out of their monasteries and priests out of their chancels had become a sexual fifth column, courtesy of the Church, giving wives not a moment of respite – a truth now treated as an inversion of the social order. Chaucer's friar embodied the secularized cleric wandering the countryside with his gifts for wives and his lisping speech, while the Wife of Bath made irony of the fact that thanks to 'lymytours and othere hooly freres' hiding like incubi under every bush and tree, women were at last free to go about in complete safety from the elves whom they had driven out, but hardly from the priests and friars now lurking everywhere in their stead.[48] Such men had foresworn the use of their sexual organs, so that, in a perverse sense, punitive mutilation was merely the enforcement of their vows. Moreover, by the logic of gene survival instinct, it was the most literal and decisive way to disqualify intruders from spreading their seed. That was one piece of reasoning in the popular mind, without which this story could have no meaning. But in those accounts in which castration becomes actual fact – as when the victim is given the choice of the beaver to disfurnish and divest himself for the sake of survival – the symbolic justice of satire gives way to sadistic fantasies and are altogether less humorous.

Paradoxically, an interpretive inversion sets in when the priest to be punished dissimulates his presence in the guise of a crucifix, for the threat to his manhood is also an assault upon the Christ in relation to the explicit display of his manhood on the cross. Hence, in collateral fashion, readers find themselves thinking about the sexual nature of the incarnate God, for the testicles still attached to the would-be philanderer become the essential part of the double impersonation. In the Christian imagination, the very real body of Christ, its torture and torments in relation to the redemption of humankind, is a matter of concern, of devotion and contemplation, and for some with a baroque bent of mind a veritable fetish. But the sex of the Saviour is troubling territory, a trait to be assumed but rarely iconographically represented as proof of the fullness of his humanity. The pluck of the present tale is to make the matter explicit by bringing the image to life through an impersonator masquer-

---

48 'The Wife of Bath's Tale' (ll. 865–79), in *Canterbury Tales*, ed. A.C. Cawley (London: J.M. Dent, 1975), p. 181.

ading as devotional art. In his own body, complete in all its attributes, he brings the Christ to life as never before. His testicles – those (ir)relevant witnesses of the complete deity, both full God and full man – become the motor to a miracle, for while the Christ of the crucifixion submits himself to piercing and puncturing, he will not give these up to the smiter, but leaps instead from the cross in a 'witness' protection program of his own. The image carver, meanwhile, through his whittling has become a practising hermeneute in determining the representational fullness of Christ's humanity, the Creator of all things. It is the wood-carver as soteriologist who manufactures the visual power of the intercessory image through the representation of Christ's anatomy 'too much in the semblance of nature.' He negotiates the debate concerning the Jesus of history and the Jesus of myth according to the strokes of his knife. (No wonder there was an iconoclastic controversy.) Such cogitations are surely supererogatory to the main thrust of the story, but when the nuns protest the prominance of this member, they do so not in seeing the wayward priest, but in seeing the representation of Christ. The story thus has a double gaze thrust upon us, for when the priest makes his leap, they see a miracle. Our laughter is doubled in a double denouement, and we must wonder if the two laughters can be blended: that of seeing justice brought to the priest; and that of the category confusion in the minds of the bewildered sisters.

To enlarge upon the point, for readers with a robust sense of humour, this inversion of the theological focus is a brilliant narrative coup, originating in some irreverent and witty mind as far back as the twelfth century, and no later than the thirteenth. This audacious stroke of incongruity – the emblematic castration of Christ through an assault on an impersonator – achieved an enduring status no doubt through its representation of an inverted world order, the replacement of the official and pious with the ironic and impious that sets in motion the irresistible reflex of laughter. Just why the brain has been made hostage to this spasmodic response is matter for more precise analysis. It is perhaps good that communities are united by a limbic response to collective subversion, and that the body's reflex signalling is nearly impossible to fake without detection, making that reaction a reliable witness of common feelings. Laughter is a selective trait for building communities of the like-minded or the like-responding, for which reason the derision evoked by the philandering priest spreads throughout the town. Moreover, the catalysts to laughter are very precise; their mastery marks one of the leading skills of gifted narrators, and this story, arguably, is a consummate expression of those insights and talents. Nuns arriving in search of the crucifix commissioned for their convent and objecting to the prominence of Christ's groin for the excitatory effect it would have upon the entire sorority is a stroke of genius. That they should interpret the poseur's escape as a miracle is even better. But that a carver should offer to make an adjustment to please the sisters while executing 'poetic' justice upon the man who attempted to cuckold him is a brilliant doubling of the incitement, for it is the laughter of social escape and the laughter of incongruity combined, touching upon anxiety and interdiction: the fear of castration and the sexual body of Christ. Not surprisingly, this narrative was the first to come under censure, for in all editions after that of 1553 in which it first appeared, Straparola or his publisher saw fit to replace it with two shorter and blander tales, nos. 3A and 3B, added to the present book. (Many others were later deleted, but Straparola's death precluded further replacements.) It was not sexual explicitness, per se, that appears to have offended these humourless critics, but the assault upon priests, the Church, and the sanctity of the family, not to mention, in the present case, the parody of the crucifixion.

A few random points in the story are worth underscoring. Messer Tiberio is attached to a religious order, but the narrator (or Straparola) will not say which, thinking perhaps that by such reticence the story might be shielded from censure. Tiberio hears confessions, having abandoned the habit of his order to become a priest, and his greatest hypocrisy is the manner with which he gradually reconstructs a spiritual relationship into a carnal one, hoping that the lady might acquiesce to his demands as though part of her spiritual duty. That procedure is employed in many a seduction plot involving clerics and innocent, trusting girls. The wife's name is 'Prudence' (Savia in the original), a name she lives up to in every respect. In telling her husband of her plight, she becomes part of a 'Ticco tacco' plot (II.5) in which the husband encourages his wife to invite the lover to a rendezvous in order to lead him into a snare. Besotted by desire, the victim responds without hesitation. Prudence plays her part with aplomb, although the suspense builds when Chechino begins to anticipate the many ways in which the plot could backfire. She plies her pots and pans as a stalling device, then angles to get all of the cleric's clothes, which she locks away in a trunk before inducing him to simulate the astonishing pose. As the victim makes his escape, Prudence creates in interpretational crux in detaining her husband from pursuing his intent with a sharpened knife. Is it for pity of the priest or for fear of reprisal for violence? Would she have acquiesced to the severing of his genitals had immobility kept him in place, as in other versions of the story? Meanwhile, the loiterers in the streets divine the cause of his flight and form an impromptu theatre that erupts in communal laughter (literally, they take or join in the game) – laughter that not only has the power of ridicule but the power of exile, insofar as this monk will banish himself from Florence, no doubt for a very long time. As the story ends, the audience in the primary fiction likewise bursts into uncontrollable laughter, which is viewed as excessive by the Signora; she calls them all back to order. Straparola was perfectly aware of the margins of the subversive he was in the process of establishing, no doubt with considerable relish, by including the carnival laughter that serves up the poetic justice of the entire story. Such laughter is complex, for it acknowledges the cognitive jogs of the narrative that compel by surprise and incongruity, but it is also nervous approbation of the unthinkable, sacrilegious in spite of itself, and a gesture of community. All these features represent for the global history of the story type a set of choices among options. In others, the wives are bad and are caught by their husbands, or the priests are maimed for real. Whether the choices configuring the present story were Straparola's or those of a cumulative source tradition now largely beyond reconstruction, they represent, to my mind, the happiest version of the generic tale with regard to character, episode, lightness of wit, and poetic justice.

The relationship of this tale to its sources is as ambiguous as most in the collection. There can be no doubt whatsoever that it belongs to the 'crucified priest' group, of which there are several examples from the thirteenth to the nineteenth century. But precisely which of the early versions was closest in line to Straparola's model remains unclear. All the Italian renditions predating his are novelistic and compound elaborations of a simpler formula, whereas Straparola's remains nearer in spirit to the originating *fabliaux*, and plausibly to an oral source, the nature of which can be known only through Straparola himself, as well as to folk versions collected some three centuries later. What seems clear is that the present work belongs to a literary tradition that is Western by dint of its aggressive anti-clericalism, even though it bears some resemblance to ancient Eastern tales concerning infidelity or captured lovers subjected to novel forms of punishment. As a literary production, the story loses all momentum in the seventeenth century, with changing tastes in humour and the changing social realities of the new age. Nevertheless, later vestiges in the oral culture indicate the perseverance of the tale in the Italian popular tradition.

The earliest tales of the 'crucified priest' appear among the *fabliaux* of the twelfth and thirteenth centuries. A certain Gautier is credited with writing 'Du prestre teint' (The dyed priest), a tale of extraordinary events that took place in Orléans around the feast of St John in the house of a fat bourgeois. This man feasted his neighbour, the priest, unaware that the cleric was making love to his jolly wife. For a time, on her own, she resisted him for the sake of her husband's honour by chasing him out of the house with a fire poker. Nevertheless, he persisted and found himself dyed red and mounted on a crucifix. It was then determined that his scrotum was too large and his testicles too low for such an office and that the maid should take a knife and trim them. With that, the priest could feign no more and leapt free to run naked through the streets.[49] Perhaps to Gauthier we owe the genius of the story's signature motifs. At the least, his *fabliau*, combined with the following, may be said to form the 'international type' with which all subsequent tales in the group may be compared. (This does not discount the prospect that he too may have been recycling folk materials.) A second, 'Du prestre crucifié,' tells of a crucifix maker who suspected something was going on between his wife and the priest. He feigned a trip and stood watch. When the priest showed up, he terrified both priest and wife with his pounding on the door. The priest is told to strip off his clothes as quickly as he can and to pose himself on one of the crosses in the shop to camouflage himself. But when the carver passes through, he sees an indecent Christ and undertakes to correct it. The priest, riveted to his place, allows himself to be cut and bloodied before the host takes him down and makes him pay fifteen pounds in ransom – double jeopardy.[50] Elements of each tale form

49 *Recueil général et complet des fabliaux des XIIIe et XIVe siècles*, ed. Anatole de Montaiglon and Gaston Raynaud, 6 vols. (Paris: 1872, 1890; rpt. New York, Burt Franklin, 1964), no. 139, vol. VI, pp. 8–23.

50 *Fabliaux ou contes du XIIe et du XIIIe siècle*, ed. P.J.B. Legrand d'Aussy (Paris, 1781; rpt. Geneva, Slatkine Reprints, 1971), vol. IV, pp. 123–4; also 'Du prestre crucifié,' in the *Recueil général*, ed. by A. Montaiglon, no. 18, vol. I, pp. 194–7. In a related *fabliau*, 'Le forgeron de Creil,' a priest is caught by the husband and castrated for real. Legrand d'Aussy, ed., *Fabliaux ou contes, fables et romans du XIIe et du XIIIe siècle* (Paris: Jules Renouard, 3rd ed., 1829), vol. IV, p. 161; and Montaiglon, *Recueil général*, vol. I, pp. 231–7.

the narrative legacy from which Straparola derived his account of the priest, threatened by a husband and wife now working in collusion, who is allowed to escape in the buff to meet his humiliation in the streets. But as will be seen, while there are many reworkings of the materials, there is no linear and stepwise account to be given about how the essential materials reached Straparola and in what form. My own supposition is that the written tale was taken over by minstrels, recited, and thereby became a part of the oral tradition that supplied our author with nearly all his stories.

Many of the details are adopted by Franco Sacchetti, likewise borrowing from the folk tradition or its written sources in his *Trecentonovelle*, a work of the late fourteenth century.[51] In Siena lived Mino the painter with a pretty wife whose wandering eye had brought a warning from Mino's family. When Mino went out of town, his relatives posted spies, and with renewed certainty of her infidelity they travelled out of the city at night to give him the news. Quickly he returned and made a ruckus at the door, forcing the lovers to strategize as best they could. The crosses in his shop were flat on tables and covered with cloths. It was upon one of these under a covering that the lover positioned himself. Mino looked about for him while his wife followed protesting her innocence, but he could not divine the fellow's whereabouts. The next morning, however, he spied two of the man's toes and took out an axe to sever his genitals, sending the man screaming out of the atelier with Mino in pursuit. Nothing came of the chase, so he returned to berate his ever-protesting wife. When she questioned his sanity concerning the ability of crucifixes to break and run, she merely earned for herself slaps and insults until she began biffing him back, making reference to Tessa and Calandrino from the *Decameron* (IX.5). In the end, she managed to convince him that his senses had gone awry, and by sowing such doubt, brought him to beg her forgiveness. Clearly the model of Boccaccio's Calendrino had made

---

51 *Il trecentonovelle*, ed. Emilio Faccioli (Turin: Einaudi, 1970), pp. 218–26. The same story is told by Noël Du Fail among his *Contes et discours d'Eutrapel* (Rennes: Noël Glamet, 1586), no. 20, 'D'ung curé amoureux de la femme d'un painctre, comment il fasoit le crucifix tout nud dessus la croix et de ce qui lui advent' (Of the priest in love with the painter's wife and how he, all naked, made the crucifix on the cross, and what happened to him after that); also edited by Célestin Hippeau, 2 vols. (Paris: Damase Jouast, 1875), pt. II, pp. 87–94.

inroads, inducing Sacchetti to reframe his wronged husband as a cowed cuckold. But the core of the *fabliau* remains intact.

Next in time among the Italian writers attracted to this story was Sabadino degli Arienti (1445–1510), whose *Novelle porrettane* appeared in 1483. In the thirty-seventh *novella*, the wife of Francescotto was so molested by Giovanni da Castel San Pietro, the rector of the church, that she could barely conduct her daily affairs.[52] Her husband, who suffered from jealousy, was ready to kill him on numerous occasions, but instead sought the advice of his friend and patron, the jurisconsult. Here were his recommendations. Prepare a barrel. Have your wife lead her lover along to a rendezvous. Remain hidden. Lock the door. Make a noisy appearance. Once the priest is concealed in the barrel, bring him to me in Bologna. That trip on the following day was intentionally made long and arduous. The poor priest, from jouncing against the lid, had the entire hide from the top of his head scraped off. Once in the city, he was repeatedly doused with water of increasing temperatures until he cried out for mercy and began to offer large sums of money. Niccolò the judge then intercedes, laughing all the while, asking the clerk if he still had any interest in the woman. In the end, he turns serious, preaching him a sermon to which the priest, with his rubs, scalds, and scratches, pronounces the moral. In this *récit*, the familiar order of narrative is clearly visible, but Sabadino has jettisoned both crucifixes and castrations, removing his story from the Straparolan line of succession.

The most perplexing prospect of influence is provided by the writer otherwise relied upon most persistently by Straparola, Girolamo Morlini. Straparola must have known his story. Yet the Neapolitan's elaboration is, of them all, the least like the present tale.[53] In the seventy-third of his *novelle*, a beautiful woman, married to a valiant husband, is pestered to pieces by three priests, not one, so that, in consultation with her husband, they arrange to trick them all. The first is induced to dress himself in women's clothes to sift flour before the promised shaking of the sheets. Meanwhile, the second appears, is talked out of his clothes and hidden in a barrel, as in the Sabadino story. The third is similarly handled and told to position himself naked on a cross. Now with all three in place, the wife hies off to alert her husband, telling him not to let any of the priests

---

52 *Novelle porrettane*, ed. Giancarlo Bernabei (Bologna, Santarini, 1992), pp. 169–73.

53 Morlini, *Les nouvelles*, trans. Fernand Caussy (Paris: E. Sansot, 1904), pp. 156–60; 'De muliere que treis fefellit claricos,' in *Novelle e favole*, ed. Giovanni Villani (Rome: Salerno, 1983), pp. 322–31.

escape without injury. His weapon of choice is a stick, which he lays on the back of the first priest, who gets away barely able to stand. Lighting a lamp before the crucifix, he then feigns devotions, taking up a thorny rod to dust the image which he reduces to bloody scratches. Thereafter, he pronounces the genitals contrary to the Scriptures and proposes to cut them off, at which point this martyr likewise breaks and runs. Lastly, the barrel holding the third is rolled over six miles of rocky ground and sold in the market at a low price. Morlini conflates familiar materials, but once that compound design is made, it becomes the least likely source in which Straparola could have found the inaugural *fabliau* of the priest on the cross, with or without ensuing castration.

Other French collectors and refitters had, meanwhile, launched a parallel tradition that departs from the two 'founding' *fabliaux*, but carries forward the notion of punishment by castration for clerical philanderers. It is the principal point in common with the present tale, with the difference that the *châtiment* is actually carried out. But because these stories lack the motif of the 'priest crucified,' there is less need to dwell upon them in detail. Near the fountainhead is the version in the *Cent nouvelles nouvelles* that inspired both French and Italian imitators.[54] A silversmith's wife finds herself at home alone, bored, and attracted to the priest. Meanwhile, the shop apprentice has his eye on the wife as well, but pre-empted by the priest, he reports the comings and goings of the lover-priest to the master on the promise that he would not be killed. The plot from beginning to end lacks in lightness, invention, and spirit. The priest is merely taken *in flagrante delicto*, strapped on a board, and carried into a shed, where his testicles are nailed down and the shed set on fire. The culprit is condemned to die in the flames or mutilate himself and run

---

54 Ed. Roger Dubuis (Lyons: Presses Universitaires de Lyon, 1891), no. 85, pp. 306–8. Other tales of punitive castration of unwonted lovers even more remote from the present include no. 89, 'Du curé d'Onzain près de'Amboyse, qui se fit chastrer à la persuasion de son hôtesse,' in which the priest agrees to a mock public castration that goes wrong when the lady's husband pays the surgeon double his wages to perform the operation for real. Bonaventure des Periers, *Les contes ou les nouvelles récréations ou joyeaux devis* (Paris: Dentu et Col, 1887), pp. 268–9. In much these same years, Henri Estienne published a version of the story in his *Apologie pour Hérodote. Satire de la Société au XVIe siècle*, ed. P. Ristelhuber (Geneva: Slatkine Reprints, 1969), chap. xv, vol. I, pp. 277–9. The priest subjects himself to this ignominy in front of family and witnesses to remove any doubt concerning a lady's reputation with whom he has been affiliated. In this tale the butcher is given a name: Pierre des Serpens from the town of Berri.

for his life, leaving the offending organs behind. In an approximate resemblance to the present story, he takes the latter option.

Agnolo Firenzuola's *novelle* were published in his collected works a year after his death in 1547.[55] The fourth tells of Don Giovanni's love for Tonia, the wife of Ciarpaglia. He protests that were he not a priest he would do the loveliest things, continually offering the girl gifts. She was twenty-two, a dancer, and very clever, and in time she struck up a bargain with him for a gift that the priest never bestowed. Then she was out to settle scores. Ciarpaglia and his brother are now in the action as well, and after a great deal of cursing and name-calling, the priest is locked inside a trunk and taken out of the room, where the final *coup* is to be accomplished. He is supplied with a knife to perform the deed himself, so that in completing Ciarpaglia's revenge, he ends up a man who is no longer a man. Matteo Bandello tells the same story, perhaps even before Firenzuola, and in greater detail. Bartolomeo Coleone of Bergamo builds a chapel and brings in a priest, who finds himself in love with plump, brunette Bertolina, the wife of Nicolino. The two play eye games and communicate with each other during confession, where the priest tells her that he too is flesh and blood like her husband. They become lovers until the country folk perceive the game and tattle all to her husband. Returning unexpectedly, he finds them 'hiding the devil in hell.' The priest is naked and mute, or reciting his prayers, as the wife pleads for his life. Nicolino promises to spare him, but nevertheless has him place his entire sexual gear, devil and all, on the edge of a chest which he locks shut, telling the priest to remove everything, devil and all, or be killed – supplying him with the knife. He left the house a capon and died a short time later without witnesses.[56] Bandello, himself in holy orders and later a bishop, knew a mediocre story when he saw one.

With no. 93 of Celio Malespini's *Ducento novella* (1609) we arrive full circle with the *Cent nouvelles nouvelles* from which he takes his story. He adds new names and social detail, but tells of the master Oraso, his amorous apprentice, a beautiful wife, and her tailor lover. The tailor, when apprehended, is taken into a little room where his genitals are nailed to a bench and the place set on fire.[57] The story involving crucifixes returns only once in early French literary sources, namely in *Le grand parangon*

---

55 *Novelle* (Florence: G. Barbèra, 1886), pp. 66–80.

56 *Tutte le opera*, ed. Francesco Flora, 2 vols. (Milan: Mondadori, 1952), bk. II, no. 20, vol. I, pp. 839–43.

57 *Ducento novelle* (Venice: Al signo dell'Italia, 1609), bk. I, no. 93, pp. 249v–50v.

des nouvelles nouvelles of Nicolas de Troyes.[58] The work was first discovered
and circulated in 1622, although the earliest surviving manuscript dates
to 1535–7. Nicolas was a borrower, making it fair to presume that his tale
had an earlier source looking much like the present tale. That may be a
reavealing bit of evidence. His story has elements of the pristine *fabliaux*,
of Sacchetti, and of a folk tradition of which he and Straparola are the
most plausible early witnesses. The *curé* falls in love with the painter's
beautiful wife, but she cares for her honour and refuses him. Meanwhile,
clients arrive from the local church seeking a crucifix. They are asked
whether they need one dead or alive and their choice falls on a live one
because if it does not meet with approval it can always be killed![59] The
exasperated wife now reports to her husband the machinations of the
priest and all his proffered gifts. He feigns a trip, she invites the cleric
in, induces him to take off all his clothes, offers a few kisses, procures
the money, and then her husband knocks according to plan. She instructs
her priest to climb up to the attic, where it is freezing cold, and there to
pose himself on a cross for camouflage. After a leisurely breakfast, the
craftsman takes his clients up to see the crucifix and starts blaming his
apprentice for leaving the balls so prominent, whereupon he takes out

---

58 Ed. Krystyna Kasprzyk (Paris: Marcel Didier, 1970), no. 34, pp. 96–103; ed. Émile
Mabille (Paris: A. Franck, 1869), no. 20, pp. 87–94. The motif of purchasing a live
crucifix was known in England in that same year, 1535, in *Tales and Quick Answers*, in
which a live crucifix is the better option because it can always be slain; see also 'Of
them that came to London to buy a crucifix,' in *A Hundred Merry Tales*, ed. P.M. Zall
(Lincoln: University of Nebraska Press, 1963), no. 6, p. 248 (Aiir in the original).

59 This motif is borrowed from a parallel tradition, that of the 'crucifix vivant' (the
living crucifix), which tells of one or more fools who are sent to purchase a crucifix
and are duped repeatedly by a shrewd craftsman who makes them pay extra for the
cross on which to pose the crucifix and finally even more for one that is alive –
deemed the better purchase because if they find it unsatisfactory in any way they
can always kill it. This story has many versions, beginning with Poggio's 'De rusticiis
interrogates an vellent crucifixum vivum an mortuum ab opifice emere' and
culminating in the story of 'Le déndou d'andouille' collected by Paul Sébillot,
Blason populaire de la France (Paris: Le cerf, 1884), no. 34, p. 112. A full list is to be
found in the annotations by Charles H. Livingston to no. 87 of *Les cent nouvelles
nouvelles* (Geneva: Droz, 1972), pp. 338–41. Among them is 'De certains marguil-
liers de village' (Of certain [foolish] churchwardens) in *L'Élite des contes du Sieur
d'Ouville*, ed. G. Brunet, 2 vols. (Paris: Librairie des bibliophiles, 1883), pp. 83–4.
These yokels head to town to purchase a Saint Sebastian, only to be confronted with
a series of questions tending increasingly towards the facetious, until they are lured
into opting for a live statue, which, as they reasoned, could always be tranquillized,
i.e., remartyred, should it not meet with approval.

his knife. In this telling, which is now familiar in so many ways, the priest nevertheless endures the cut before he leaps and runs. The painter declares this act a miracle and his clients now opt for a dead model for fear that their living crucifix might also run, leaving them with little for their expense. Meanwhile, the *curé* has lost not only money, but clothes and testicles, with nothing at all to show for them. Given the textual history of *Le grand parangon*, it is inconceivable that it could have been Straparola's source, but it shares, as closely as any, in the kind of materials from which the present tale was incontestibly built.

If Nicolas's parallel account of the 'prêtre crucifié' adds ambiguity to the quest for sources, the tale entitled 'La monega,' collected in Florence in the nineteenth century, merely extends the enigma. Here is a story of the folk that proceeds in identical terms, whether drawn from a literary source, or more likely representing a late survival of the folk stories, one of which was employed by Straparola. This heroine, pestered by a monk, in collusion with her husband, woos him into a bed and provokes his impatience by her delays. This lover, with the knocking on the door, is gotten into a box, bounced through the streets, and delivered to the convent of the monks of Fottichiate. He is sold to them as a statue of Saint Ignazio (Ignatius) and there is much haggling over the payment. When the box is opened the next day, they find the work beautiful and natural, but marred by a 'coda' (tail) in need of trimming. St Ignatius then leaps from the box, bumping into all the monks, and takes to his heels. They all cry out that it is a miracle and begin their search for him all over the monastery, but to this day he has never been found.[60] There are others scattered about Italy that give further evidence of an oral tradition concerning the philandering priest hidden in plain sight and the miracle of the living crucifix. What are we to conclude but that the narrative 'meme' or motif of the 'priest crucified' maintained its identity through seven centuries of Western storytelling, surfacing from time to time in the creations of the *novellieri*, who borrowed from popular culture. Inversely, it might have been thought that the story was a literary joke too crafted and cynical to have arisen through the workings of the

---

60 Vittorio Imbriani, 'La monega,' in *La novellaja milanese, esempii e panzane lombarde* (Bologna: Fava & Garagnani, 1872), which was published simultaneously in *Il propugnatore, studii filologici, storici e bibliografici*, (Bologna: Gaetano Romagnoli, 1872), vol. V, pt. 1, pp. 146–57. See also Gennero Finamore, *Tradizione popolari abruzzezi* (Lanciano: R. Carabba, 1882), no. 9; Giuseppe Pitrè, *Novelle popolari toscane* (Palermo: Edikronos, 1981), no. 58.

cumulative popular mind, and that any folk manifestations must be derivative. Whatever the case, Straparola's oblique relationship to the prospective literary sources implies that, once again, he turned to the tale's legacy in popular culture. At the same time, enough of what he wrote resided in earlier literary records to deny him founder's status. Straparola was a borrower, but from what he borrowed can best be re-engineered from his own story. And there the inquest must come to a close.

VIII. Fable 4
Lattanzio and the Secret Arts of Sorcery

ALTERIA

Maestro Lattanzio, a tailor, undertakes to train his apprentice, Dionigi, in his craft. But the lad, while learning little of this, nevertheless gains much skill in the secret arts practised by his master, wherefore great hostility springs up between them, Dionigi in the end devouring his master and marrying Violante, the king's daughter.

The judgments of men are varied, indeed, and likewise there are many kinds of desires and wishes. As the sage said, 'Every single man is full of his own conceit': for this reason, concerning the human race, there are some who give themselves over to the study of law, others who cultivate the art of oratory, and others who indulge in philosophical speculations, one being inclined to this thing and another to that. Nature, the mistress of our actions, guides each of our courses, for she, like a kindly mother, impels each man to pursue that which is most congenial to him. This truth will be made clear to you if you'll lend a gracious hearing to what I'm about to say.

In Sicily, the foremost island of antiquity, there is a noble city renowned everywhere for its port, which is commonly called Messina. Therein was born a certain Maestro Lattanzio, a man who put his hands to two distinct crafts and was highly skilled and proficient in both. His trade as a tailor he practised openly before the eyes of the world, but the art of necromancy he kept a secret from everyone.

Now Lattanzio accepted as his apprentice a poor man's son who was to learn the art of tailoring. He was still quite a young lad, this Dionigi, but he was so diligent and clever that whenever something was demonstrated to him he grasped it immediately. One day, while Maestro Lattanzio was locked up alone in his chamber trying out certain experiments in sorcery, the boy, who had developed an inkling of what his master was up to, noiselessly crept up to the chamber door and through a crack got a clear view of his master's operations. No sooner was Dionigi aware of the purpose of it all than he became ardently possessed with the desire to practise this art for himself, so that all day long thereafter he thought of nothing else except necromancy. His interest in the tailor's trade he cast aside entirely, although he dared say nothing of his discovery to his master. When Lattanzio spotted the change that had come over Dionigi, noting how the once skilled and industrious fellow had now become idle and ignorant, giving no further heed to his tailoring work, he forthwith dismissed the lad and sent him home to his father.

Now Dionigi's father was a very poor man and was sorely grieved when his son turned up at home, so he reproved the boy, punished him duly, and sent him back to Lattanzio, begging the good tailor to retain him in his employ and give him his board while keeping him rigorously disciplined. The father asked for nothing more in return than to have him well instructed. Lattanzio, who was quite aware of the father's poor circumstances, consented to take the boy back and to daily teach him how to sew. But Dionigi seemed to have become a total dunderhead who couldn't or wouldn't learn a thing. On this account, a day rarely passed when Lattanzio didn't kick him or beat him by way of chastisement and sometimes cracked him over the head till the blood ran down. In truth, his back was better served with thrashings than his belly with rations. But Dionigi accepted all his punishments with patience while every night, secretly, he made his way to the chink in the door and watched all that was done inside the chamber.

Meanwhile, Maestro Lattanzio, seeing what an addle pate the kid was, and how he couldn't learn a thing about the trade he was being taught, no longer bothered to keep his necromancy a secret, thinking that if Dionigi had a brain too dense to learn the trade of tailoring, he most certainly could fathom nothing of the deep and intractable secrets of necromancy. So Lattanzio no longer kept his apprentice away, but worked his spells openly in his presence. Imagine how pleased Dionigi was with this turn of events, for although his master deemed him a dull-witted simpleton, he found it no hard task to learn the whole art of necromancy. Very soon, indeed, he became so skilled and expert in the business that he was able to work wonders far beyond the powers even of Maestro Lattanzio.

One day Dionigi's father went to the tailor's shop and remarked that instead of working with needle and thread, his son was engaged in carrying the fuel and water for the kitchen, sweeping the floors, and doing other menial jobs. Seeing this, he was mightily disturbed and disappointed, so he took the boy immediately out of Lattanzio's service and led him home. The good man had already spent a considerable sum for his son's clothes and instruction in the tailor's craft. Finding now that he couldn't persuade the boy to learn his trade he bemoaned his plight, saying to him, 'My son, you know well enough how much money I've laid out to make a man of you, but for your part, you've never helped me in the least by the trade I sent you to learn. And now I find myself in desperate straits, without a clue where I'll turn next to find food for you. My only hope, my son, is that you'll light upon some honest calling whereby you can earn a living for yourself.'

To this his son made answer, 'My father, above all I want to thank you for all the trouble and money you've expended on my behalf, while at the same time I'm asking you not to alarm yourself. It's true that I've not learned the tailor's trade as you had hoped, but I've acquired the mastery of another art that will be of far greater service to us in satisfying our needs. So my dear father, don't be downcast or sorrowful, because I'll soon let you see what great profits I can make, and how, with the fruits of my art you'll be able to support your family and maintain good cheer in the household. By the art of necromancy, I'll transform myself into the most beautiful horse ever seen, and you can fit me out with a saddle and bridle and sell me at the fair. Then the day after, I'll resume my former shape and come back home again. But I must ask you to be very careful not to give the bridle to the purchaser, for if you were to part with it, I would not be able to return to you, and by chance you might never see me again.'

With that, Dionigi straightway transformed himself into a beautiful horse that his father led away to the fair and showed off to the many people who were there. All of them were greatly astonished at the wonderful beauty of the horse and at the marvellous feats it performed. Now it happened that at this very same time, Lattanzio was also at the fair, and when his eyes fell upon the animal, he knew there was something supernatural about it. So returning home, he decked himself out in the guise of a merchant. Then he went back to the fair, taking with him a great sum of money. Coming close to the horse and examining it thoroughly, he saw clearly that it was Dionigi, whereupon he demanded of the owner whether the horse was for sale, to which the old man replied that it was. Then, after an elaborate round of bargaining, Lattanzio offered two hundred gold florins in exchange for the horse, a price that fully contented the owner, who stipulated only that the horse's bridle would not be included in the sale. Even so, by cajolery and an additional sum of money, Lattanzio persuaded the old man to let him have it into the bargain, whereupon he led the horse home to his own house and put him into a stall, tying him up securely before savagely thrashing him. This, moreover, he did every morning and evening until the horse became such a wasted wretch that it was pitiable just to look at him.

Now Lattanzio was the father of two daughters, and these young ladies, when they saw the cruel treatment of the horse by their inhumane father, were moved to compassion, so that every day they would go to the stable to fondle it and to bestow many tender caresses upon it. One day it happened that they took the horse by the halter and led it out of the stable and down to the river where it might drink. No sooner had the horse come to the riverbank than it rushed instantly into the water and immediately changed itself into a little fish and sought out the deepest part of the stream. When the daughters witnessed this strange and sudden transformation, they were overcome with amazement and returned home, where they shed bitter tears, beating their breasts, and tearing their fair locks in dismay.

Before long, Lattanzio came back to his house and went at once to the stable in order to beat the horse according to his custom, but he found it was no longer there. In a furious fit of rage, he went in pursuit of his two daughters, whom he found still weeping bitterly. Without questioning them as to the cause of their tears – for he knew enough of their fault already – he said to them, 'My daughters, tell me immediately, and don't be afraid, what has become of the horse so I can try to get it back.' Somewhat reassured by their father's words, the daughters told him exactly what had happened. As soon as Lattanzio heard and understood the situation, he stripped off his clothes and went to the riverbank where he cast himself in, transforming himself at the same time into a great tuna, pursuing the little fish everywhere it went in order to devour it. The little fish, when it knew that the voracious tunny was in pursuit, began to fear that it would be eaten up. So it swam close to the brink of the stream and changed itself into a very precious ruby ring, leapt out of the water, and hid itself away in the basket of the princess's young lady-in-waiting, who, for her diversion, was gathering pebbles along the river's bank. Among these, the ruby concealed itself.

When the damsel had returned to the palace and had taken the pebbles out of the basket, Violante, the king's only daughter, chanced to observe the ruby ring, and taking it up, she put it on her finger, treasuring it thereafter with the utmost of care. Presently, the night having come, Violante withdrew to her rest, still wearing the ring upon her finger, when suddenly it transformed itself into a handsome young man, who, placing his hand upon Violante's tender bosom, found there two little round breasts that were only just beginning to swell. The damsel, who was not yet asleep, was greatly alarmed and would have screamed out, but the young man, setting his hand upon her balmy mouth wouldn't let her cry out. Kneeling down before her, he craved her pardon, imploring her to aid him in his troubles, reassuring her that his presence there was not to shame her or to sully her chaste thoughts, but only because he was driven there by adverse destiny. Then he told her who he was and the circumstances that brought him into her chamber, and how and by whom he was persecuted. Violante recovered her composure somewhat upon listening to these words of the young man. Perceiving by the light of the lamp burning in the room what a proper and handsome figure he had, she felt moved to pity him, and said, 'Of a certainty, young man, you're guilty of great arrogance in coming here without invitation, and your presumption is even greater in touching what you had no right to touch. But now that I've heard the tale of your misfortunes, and because I'm not made of marble nor have a heart hard as diamonds, I'm prepared to lend you any aid that I can give in honesty, provided that you faithfully promise to respect my honour.' The young man offered many words of due gratitude to Violante for her kindly speech. And then, as the dawn was growing bright in the sky, he changed himself once more into a ring, which Violante put away among her most precious jewels. But many times and often she would take it out so that it might assume human form and engage her in sweet conversation.

One day it came about that the king, Violante's father, was stricken with a grave infirmity that none of his physicians could heal. One and all declared that his malady was beyond the help of medicine, and from day to day the king's condition grew worse and worse. By chance this news came to the ears of Lattanzio, who, dressing himself up as a physician, went to the royal palace and gained admission to the king's bedchamber. Then, after enquiring about the king, the nature of his sickness, and carefully observing his countenance and feeling his pulse, Lattanzio said, 'Gracious king, your affliction is indeed grave and dangerous, but be of good heart. You will soon be restored to health, for I know of a certain remedy that will cure the deadliest disease in a very short time. So be of good cheer and fear for nothing.'

Whereupon the king replied, 'Good master physician, if you will rid me of this infirmity, I will reward you in such a way that you may live at ease for the rest of your days.'

The physician replied that he desired neither lands nor gold, but only one single favour. The king promised to grant him anything that might be in his power, to which the false doctor made answer, 'Gracious king, I ask for no other reward but a single ruby stone set in gold that is presently in the keeping of your daughter, the princess.'

When he heard this modest demand, the king said, 'Master physician, if this is all the reward you claim, be assured that it shall be readily granted to you.'

After this, the physician applied himself diligently to work a cure upon the king, who, after the course of ten days, found himself completely free of his dangerous affliction.

So when the king was fully recovered from his ailment and brought back to his former state of health, he one day summoned his daughter into the presence of the physician, and when she appeared, he ordered her to fetch all the jewels she possessed. Obedient to her father's word, the daughter did as she was asked, omitting, however, to bring back with her that one jewel which she held dear above all the others. This doctor, when he had examined the gems, declared that the ruby which he so much craved was not among them, and that the princess would assuredly find it if she made a diligent search for it. But the damsel, who was by this time deeply enamoured of this ruby, denied that she had it. Hearing these words of hers, the king said to the doctor, 'Go away now and come back tomorrow, for in the meantime I will bring such effective pressure to bear upon my daughter that tomorrow the ruby will most certainly be yours.'

When the physician had taken his leave, the king called Violante to him, and the two of them went together into a room and closed the door. There he asked her in a kindly manner to tell him about the ruby that the physician so ardently desired to have. But Violante firmly denied any knowledge of it. Leaving her father's presence, Violante went forthwith to her own chamber and, fastening the door, she began to weep in her loneliness, and took the ruby and embraced and kissed it, and pressed it to her heart, cursing the hour in which the physician had come across her path. No sooner did the ruby behold the hot tears that fell from the lovely eyes of the princess, and heard the deep and woeful sighs that came from her loving heart, than it was moved to pity and immediately assumed human form and spoke in these loving words, 'Dear lady, to whom I owe my life, don't weep or sigh on my account, who remains devoted to you, but rather let us seek some remedy to our calamity. You should know that this physician, who so keenly desires to place his hands on me, is my bitter foe who would take away my life. But you, as a wise and prudent damsel, would never deliver me into his hands. Upon the next occasion that he shall demand me of you, you must hurl me violently against the wall, pretending all along to be angry and indignant, and I will provide for everything to follow.'

The next morning, the physician went back to the king and there he heard again the unfavourable reply, whereupon he grew angry, affirming repeatedly that the ruby was somewhere in the young lady's keeping. Once more the king called his daughter into the physician's presence and said to her, 'Violante, you know well enough that by the skill of this physician I have regained my health, and that, moreover, as a reward for his services, he demanded of me neither great gifts of land nor of treasure, but simply a certain ruby stone that he says you have in your possession. I should have thought that you, by reason of the love you bear me, would have given me not merely a ruby, but even your own blood. Wherefore, because of the love I hold for you, and because of the suffering and trouble your mother has undergone for your sake, I implore you not to deny me this favour that the physician demands.'

As soon as the young lady heard and understood her father's wishes, she withdrew to her chamber, and taking the ruby, along with many other jewels, she went back into her father's presence and showed the stones one by one to the physician. As soon as his eye fell upon the one he so greatly desired to have, he cried out, 'Behold, there it is,' and tried to lay hands upon it. But Violante, seeing what he intended, said, 'Master physician, stand back somewhat, for you shall have the stone.' Then in disdain she took the ruby in her hand, saying, 'If this is the precious and lovely jewel that you're searching for, the loss of which I shall regret for the rest of my life, you'll have it not of my own free will, but only out of obedience to my father.' As she spoke these words, she threw the gem with all her strength against the wall, and the ruby, as it fell to the ground, opened up and became a fine large pomegranate, which in bursting open scattered its seeds all around them.

Seeing that pomegranate seeds were spread all over the floor of the room, Lattanzio immediately transformed himself into a cock, and thinking that he might thus make an end of Dionigi, began to pick up the seeds with his beak. But his intent was entirely foiled by a single seed which hid itself in such fashion that it escaped the bird's notice. Thus hidden away, this seed waited for an opportune moment before suddenly changing itself into a crafty, cunning fox that swiftly and silently crept up to the crested cock, seized it by the throat, slew it and devoured it before the eyes of the king and the princess. When the king saw what was done, he stood as one confounded, and Dionigi, having taken upon him his original form, told the king everything from the very beginning. Then, with full consent, he was united to Violante in lawful marriage, with whom he lived many years in tranquil and honourable peace. The father of Dionigi was rescued from his poor estate and become rich, while Lattanzio, for his envy and hatred, came to this miserable end.

Thus Alteria's pleasant tale was brought to a close, whereupon all the listeners declared that it had given them great pleasure. Then the Signora made a sign to her that she should fulfil her duty with an enigma, which the damsel, with a delightful expression on her face, supplied as follows:

> Of lovers, mine is sure the best;
> He holds me close upon his breast.
> He fondles me; our lips then meet
> With kisses and caressing sweet;
> His tongue my mouth in fondness seeks,
> And with such tender accents speaks,
> That hearts with love are all afire.
> But brief the space of our desire,
> For soon his lips from mine must stray,
> To wipe the dew of toil away,
> And from me gently he doth move.
> Now say, is this the end of love?

This enigma furnished matter for considerable talk and laughter, particularly among the men. But Arianna, who a short time before had suffered somewhat from Alteria's bantering, now said, 'Nay, gentlemen, no longer trouble yourselves, or think in your hearts that there is anything unfavourable about this enigma that my sister has just set for us to guess, for in truth, it can only mean the trombone, which the player slides up and down before drying up the water inside and out to make it sound even better.' When she heard given out the correct interpretation of her riddle, Alteria was greatly annoyed and almost got angry, but after a little, when she remembered that she had only been paid back in kind, she put aside her vexation. Then the Signora asked Lauretta to give them a story, who, without any preamble, launched directly into her fable.

VIII.4 Commentary

In competitive professions based on arcane skills there is a perverse motive on the part of acknowledged and famous masters to subvert the training of their best pupils in order to maintain their pre-eminence. Certain professions, magic and music for a start, are heavily involved in the economy of fame and the marvellous. Hence the mystique that accumulated around the bow and finger work of Heifitz, the illusionism of Houdini, and the wizardry of Faustus. Under extreme circumstances, it is to be imagined that the master who has created a prodigy may also seek to destroy him, or that superiority is to be determined by a contest to the death between the master and his precocious apprentice. In the coterie film *Tout les matins du monde* (All the mornings of the world), released in 1991, Gérard Depardieu plays the role of the young Marin Marais, later to become the greatest violist at the French court. Marais seeks training with the grand master known as Le Sieur de Sainte Colombe, aging and in perpetual mourning over the loss of his beloved wife. Disappointed in his training, the pupil is reduced to hiding under the garden pavilion in order to understand the master's secrets and decode the magic of his playing. The film is a study of intrusion and strategies of exclusion to advance yet obstruct the progress of a gifted and threatening upstart. That contest is, in turn, determined by the fickle opinions of the court and public, who rally to the thrill of technical expertise, raising and quelling reputations. In Straparola's archetypal tale, the master, Lattanzio, attempts literally to destroy his pupil in a *Wettkampf* or contest, each one employing consummate skills in magical self-transformation in relation to a repertory of animate and inanimate objects within their powers to assume.[61] Such combat may be linked to any mythological pattern pertaining to generational conflict or to waxing and waning forces. That the story type conceals a vestige of ancient myth or ritual is plausible given its certain antiquity. Nevertheless, in its present form, the tale has overtones of a fairy tale without fairies, of fantastic wish-fulfilment, as the protagonist on the run becomes a fish, then a ring, then pomegranate seeds, thereby luring the master to become the natural predator to each new incarnation, until Dionigi brings Lattanzio

---

61 For technical studies of these magic contest stories, see M. His, 'Die magische Flucht und das Wettverwandeln,' *Schweizenisches Archiv für Volkskunde* 30 (1930), pp. 107–29, and N. Naumann, 'Verschlinger Tod und Menschenfresser,' *Saeculum*, 22 (1971), pp. 59–70.

down to the vulnerable chicken whose head he can snap off by suddenly becoming a fox – the story had to end somewhere. That the transformations follow so easily and so swiftly seems jejune, even puerile, but may also be part of the charm. More positively, Italo Calvino says of Straparola's tale that it is 'highly entertaining,' and that it comes to us 'from a world so conversant with marvels as to be able to represent the most arbitrary metamorphoses with the swiftness and rhythm of a ballet.'[62]

Moreover, a reticence to hurl critical stones is encouraged by the fact of the story's widespread distribution and centuries-long success. Stith Thompson types the tale under the heading 'magician and his pupil' (ATU no. 325), and reports that it was known not only throughout Europe, with a particular density of occurrences in the Balkans, but also in Turkey, Egypt, Siberia, India, North Africa, the Dutch East Indies, the Philippines, and even Missouri, where it was carried by the early French settlers.[63] Clearly, as a narrative 'meme' the story has invaded consciousnesses around the world on a competitive basis and has confirmed its survival in forms differing less from one another than is usually the case with orally transmitted materials. It has three parts that have remained firmly associated, namely, the circumstances leading to an apprenticeship, the boy's return home, where he shows his father how he can be sold for profit by transforming himself into various costly animals, and the metamorphosis contest that arises as the master seeks to destroy his pupil.

There is a second contest, as well, between the king and princess, the former committed to keeping his unconditional promise to the physician who had returned him to health, the latter to hiding the ruby ring that contained the soul of her beloved. This arises from the romance interest injected into the 'primitive' combat tale, lending a wish-fulfilment perspective that leads to the double denouement of the apprentice over his cruel master and the union of the princess with a pauper who has gained her love through his frighteningly potent magical powers mitigated by his gentility and self-control as a secret resident of the princess's bedroom (an episode parallelling the story of Fortunio in the chamber of a princess, III.4). The confrontation between father and daughter is loosely redolent, as well, of those stories in which kings with maladies make gratuitous promises to their healers that involve the adverse intentions

---

62 *Italian Folktales*, trans. George Martin (New York: Pantheon Books, 1980), p. 741.
63 *The Folktale* (Berkeley: University of California Press, 1977), p. 69.

of third parties, the most famous of which is the promise made by the king of France to Helena in Shakespeare's *All's Well That Ends Well*, that she could have Bertram for her husband in reward for the cure she had performed as a physician's daughter. To be sure, there is no symmetry in the designs of these stories, but the motif is clearly in view and subject to many forms of actualization. These diverse elements indicate a tale made up of early and late motifs, including the rise by unique means of a poor apprentice to a royal marriage – a type of fairy tale not thought to have preceded Straparola by many years. Just when that feature was joined to the metamorphosis contest may prove a subject for engaging debate among folklorists. What seems apparent is that a new *Zeitgeist* was in force that encouraged the superimposing of such romance elements upon the ancient stories to meet with emerging tastes and expectations.

The mainstream design of Straparola's rendering of the folk tale is readily seen in the oikotype outlined by Thompson. Here is his description of the generic story. The son is sent to magician's school and the father can have his son back only if he is able to recognize him in the animal form into which he has been transmuted (not retained by Straparola). The pupil meanwhile learns more than the master intended through stealth and thus can transform himself into nearly any shape imaginable. He escapes and returns to his father's house. Together they engage in the confidence game of selling the boy in the form of various animals. Then the master turns up and insists upon purchasing the boy as a horse, which the father is induced to sell with the magic bridle, leaving the young protagonist disempowered and left to fend for himself. This is followed by the shape-shifting combat, often with a central episode involving a princess and a ring. This ring can become corn, millet, or any sort of seed attractive to chickens, a single grain of which contains the boy's life force that allows him finally to become both the terminator fox and the handsome young man beloved by a princess. Of beast fables, seeds and the life force, loyal princesses, and the triumph of the new generation over the old, little more need be said. It is amusing, however, that in some later versions, the princess is so awed and horrified by the transmutations that she makes it a condition upon her inamorato that he vow never to do such things again and that he burn his book of magic. Straparola's tale is remarkably faithful to this profile, making it one of the earliest survivors of a narrative that achieved nearly global circulation.

Of all the folk story types floating about Europe from the time of the *Forty Vezirs* to the end of the nineteenth century, the shape-shifting contest is among the most difficult to trace in terms of origins. There are no firm grounds upon which Straparola's source can be assigned, for only spotty literary remains predate him, and the later they appear, the more they are fragmented and reintegrated into other tales. But clearly, something close to the prototype proposed by Thompson existed in Straparola's time, presumably in the form of a folk tale. Theodor Benfey (1809–81), the great German philologist, translator of the *Panchatantra* (1859), and author of an influential treatise on the fables and mythologies of 'primitive nations,' held the view that the great stories of the West were in preponderant debt to the Orient, and that moreover, given the stronghold of materials represented by the South Siberian *Siddhi Kür*, much of this material came to Europe from those regions. One of the examples that spearheaded his argument was the framing tale of this Kalmouk epic: the battle of the self-metamorphosing sorcerers. The present story is therefore part of a debate concerning the presence of the Oriental in the Occident. Engagingly, Emmanuel Cosquin (1841–1919), his pupil, took his master to task by arguing against the Mongolian entry theory in favour of a more direct route from the Sanskrit, Persian, and Turkish sources, many of them far closer in design and spirit to the surviving European traditions. This comparative exercise can be conducted by pitting the version in the *History of the Forty Vezirs* against the framing tale of the *Siddhi Kür*. But a fly in this ointment must be dealt with first in the form of the early Greek and Roman inflections of this story and the prospect that its type was initially disseminated from the Mediterranean regions and not from the Indian subcontinent, whether through Turkey or Mongolia.

In a lost work by Hesiod (*Catalogues of Women Fragments*) described by scholiasts, the great shape-shifter Periklymenos, protégé of Poseidon, found himself confronted by the hero Heracles over the future of Pylos. Heracles was powerless against him because of his volatile self-transformations, first into a lion, then an eagle, a serpent, an ant, and a swarm of bees. Heracles finally defeated him, however, when he settled upon the yoke-boss of his horses in the form of a bee, for Athena gave Heracles a sign, and in shooting the bee with an arrow, Periklymenos was overcome.[64] Strategic escape and potential counter-attack through a rapid series of self-transformations into aggressive animals is the

---

64 Hesiod, *The Homeric Hymns and Homerica*, trans. Hugh G. Evelyn-White (London: Heinemann [1936], 1964); see also Apollonius Rhodius, *Argonautica*, trans. R.C. Seaton (New York: Macmillan, 1912), vol. I, p. 156; Pseudo-Apollodorus,

224   Lattanzio and the Secret Arts of Sorcery

principal feature of this story. Ovid also knew the tradition, for in
the *Metamorphoses* he reports that 'Periclymenus had power, through
Neptune's will, and now tried everything and found all changes vain,
and in the end took on the form of [an] eagle, carrier of thunderbolts
... [which tore] the face of Hercules, and soared high to the clouds, but
the unerring bow loosed arrow at him there, and found the joint of wing
and shoulder, a slight wound ... but fatal.'[65] This myth cannot be said to
constitute a direct source for the folk tale under investigation, but the
idea known to Hesiod as early as the eighth century BC could, in a
generic sense, have contributed to later tales specializing in seriatim
shape-shifting as a means of escape and attack. Moreover, Ovid was also
familiar with the other part of the story, at least as a narrative idea – the
lucrative fraud of being sold as an animal that disappears when the magician returns to human form. Erysichthon (one who tears the earth) was
an assertive chieftain who made the error of intruding upon the sacred
woods of Demeter, where he began cutting down trees for his new banqueting hall. Although gently warned, he persisted in hewing down a
sacred oak that bled in protest, causing his own party to retreat in horror.
Demeter then appeared to him in all her terrifying splendour and cursed
him to eternal hunger by sending to the Scythian wilds for the goddess
Famine to steal upon him in his sleep and imprint him with her craving.
In his esuriency, Erysichthon began his avid consumption of food until
his purchasing resources were depleted and he was reduced to beggary.
His daughter, gifted with shape-shifting, was sold at market as a mare, a
heifer, or a bird to many buyers to service his addiction, but in the end
he not only shamelessly exploited his family, but literally consumed his
own body. There must be a lesson here somewhere. Thus, in Ovid, by
chance or borrowing, two of the leading motifs of the Lattanzio story
are apparent, although still in separate tales. These are sufficient fragments, perhaps, of early Western provenance to argue that the shape-
shifters' combat need not have had an Eastern source at all.[66]

Still, there is no interim evidence to suggest that Straparola's tale
gradually emerged from these literary remains, or that a full-fledged folk

---

Bibliotheca as *The Library*, trans. James G. Frazer (London: Heinemann, 1921), I.9.9.
Hyginus, in his *Fabulae*, allowed Periklymenos to escape in the form of an eagle;
ed. Peter Marshall (Stuttgart: Teubner, 1993), Fable 10.
65 *Metamorphoses*, trans. Rolfe Humphries (Bloomington: Indiana University Press,
1961), bk. XII, ll. 560–78, p. 302.
66 *Metamorphoses*, bk. VIII, ll. 736–884, pp. 204–8.

tale was in concurrent circulation in ancient Greece and Rome. What is more certain is that the magicians' combat tale in *The History of the Forty Vezirs, or The Story of the Forty Morns and Eves*, known to Europeans by the fifteenth century, has the three familiar parts and could have served as a template for the Western tales. A woman of Cairo has a worthless son who refuses to learn a conventional trade, but agrees to become a geomancer. Initially, it is his master who becomes the horse sold at market and who cheats the purchasers by returning home as himself. Once the apprentice masters this trick, he goes home to his mother and they repeat the exercise by transforming the boy into a speaking dove placed on sale at a high price. In this form, the master recognizes his truant pupil and sets about to destroy him after the greedy mother sells him the magic key into the bargain, compromising the boy's powers. In time, however, the key becomes a pigeon, the master a hawk, the boy a red rose that falls into the hands of a king, and the master a minstrel who asks for the rose. Then the rose becomes millet seed, which the master seeks to consume as a cock, and the sole surviving grain becomes a man who tears off the cock's head. The love interest is not here, but the involvement of a royal household comes into play.[67] In this brief relation, readers of the tale of Lattanzio can see the resemblances at a glance. There would appear to be no closer analogue to Straparola during the intervening years – at least not on record. To be sure, the vestiges or prototypes of the shape-shifting contest in such earlier works as *The Mabignogion* (a work that survives in manuscripts compiled in the fourteenth century but that represents, in the words of Matthew Arnold, the 'detritus of something far older') casts some doubt that the entire tradition of necromancers, transformation contests, and retail cheating through magic came into Europe exclusively through *The Forty Vezirs*. Nevertheless, for now it must be credited as the earliest literary record in the West of the present tale.

Now compare the form of the tale from the *Siddhî-kür*, a Kalmouk version in which seven brothers who are magicians take for their apprentices the Khan's two sons. The older one, after seven years, learns nothing, much as Straparola's apprentice learns nothing of tailoring, but the younger son becomes a wizard simply by peering through a crack. He turns himself into a horse that the older brother sells to the seven

---

67 Sheykh-Zada, 'The Lady's Twenty-Third Story' in *The Forty Vezirs*, trans. E.J.W. Gibb (London: George Redway, 1886), pp. 253–6.

enchanters. They try to kill the horse, but it escapes as a fish, which the seven pursue as larger fish, then into a dove chased by seven hawks. He then becomes the main bead of a string of prayer beads and is hidden in an aescetic's mouth while the other beads fall and become worms that the magicians peck up as hens. Then the remaining bead becomes the Khan's son himself, who kills the chickens with a stick, which in turn hit the ground as human corpses. For his punishment, the victor, for killing the seven hawks, is sent after the demon (vétala), the Siddhî-kür, who is lured into a sack and begins reciting the tales that become the epic.[68] Variations separate both of these from Straparola, but not by a great deal, although the Turkish tale seems closer. I will say that much in favour of Cosquin, despite the fact that more recently the theories of both have been challenged.

Stated otherwise, insofar as there are no Western works predating Straparola that approach the suggested oikotype, his becomes the first to record the Eastern tale, one that was presumably in circulation among the folk, given its widespread dissemination brought to notice by the nineteenth-century ethnographers. Nevertheless, there are hints of early tales reflecting common narrative designs. Jean de Bove, in the fourteenth-century *fabliau* 'Les trios larrons' or 'De Barat e de Haimet,' creates a candidate in which three brothers, two of them master thieves and one a farmer, engage in stealing a side of bacon back and forth from each other in a series of subterfuges, voice impersonations, and a staged hanging, until they finally agree that the laws of hospitality demand that they share it all around.[69] The contest is fine and witty, but there are no magical transformations, no master-and-pupil relationship, an entirely different opening strategy, a wife who misses all the cues, no selling of trick animals, and no ring on a princess's finger. If there is a debt to the Eastern tale, it has been entirely absorbed.

Altogether more promising is the account in the Welsh *Mabignogion* of the birth of Taliesin. By the time Gwion Bach fled Cardiwen the sorceress for letting the year-long boiling cauldron split before the potion was perfected, he had gained remarkable powers of prescience and shape-shifting from the three drops that, for burning his finger, had

---

68 The *Siddhî-kür*, the Kalmouk version of the *Vetalapanchavimsati*, in Ardschi Bordschi, *Sagas from the Far East, or, Kalmouk and Mongolian Traditionary Tales*, trans. Rachel Harriette Busk (London: Griffith & Ferran, 1873), the framing tale, pp. 1–6.
69 *Fabliaux ou contes du XIIe et du XIIIe siècle*, ed. Legrand d'Aussy (Paris: Jules Renouard, 1829), vol. III, pp. 269–80.

come into his mouth. He made his flight from her in the form of a hare, but she ran after him as a greyhound. He then became a fish and she a female otter, then he a bird and she a hawk who harried him till he dropped down among the wheat kernels on a barn floor. As a hen, she swallowed him, a variation on the now familiar motif, but in nine months he was reborn – his third birth. Too handsome a child to be slain, he was thrown into the sea and was later rescued. The magic contest is the precondition to a miraculous birth of a seer and bard who would become the greatest among his people. There is a sufficient correlation in the order of events here with those of the folk tale to argue for its currency in Europe at any time preceding the fourteenth century, when the earliest surviving manuscripts of the *Mabignogion* were copied.[70]

Back to Eastern influences: 'The Second Kalendar's Story' in the *Arabian Nights* has distinct promise, but again, the date at which these tales entered Europe is a matter of ongoing investigation.[71] In a sense, a demonstrable debt to this tale on Straparola's part could make a contribution to the argument favouring its early circulation (before it was gathered or half invented by Galland early in the eighteenth century). But that likelihood diminishes when it is seen just how much the 'Arabian' story embellishes the prototype, and how much scaling back would be required to rediscover the Straparolan tale. An adventurer who finds his way into the underground palace of an ifrit and enjoys his captive woman is caught as a result of his own misguided bravura. In punishment, he is transformed into an ape and deposited on a mountain top.[72] Many

70 Trans. Charlotte Guest (London: Dent & Sons, 1906), p. 264.
71 In the words of Robert Irwin, 'In most cases it is impossible to determine whether these tales passed into Europe first by word of mouth or in manuscript form.' *The Arabian Nights, A Companion* (London: Penguin, 1995), p. 101.
72 *A Thousand Nights and One Night*, trans. Richard Burton (London: Burton Club, 1885), Nights 12–14, vol. VII, pp. 335*ff*; in *Tales from the Arabian Nights* (from the above) (New York: Avenel Books, 1978), pp. 126–39. Mention may be made in passing of the tale from the *Arabian Nights* entitled 'Julnar the Sea-born and Her Son.' It is the second part of this compound tale that is of interest when Julnar's son Badr Basim finds himself in a shape-shifting contest with Queen Lab with the backing of Abdallah the grocer, who provides him with counter-magic. First Badr transforms Lab into a dapple mule, but the mule is given to Lab's mother. They then gain the ascendancy and transform the young man into a bird to starve him in a cage. He is rescued only when Julnar, his mother, lays waste to the city. In the Burton multi-volume edition of 1979, 'Julnar,' Nights 739–56, is in vol. VII, pp. 264–307; in the Avenel one-volume edition, pp. 462–506. This tale is arguably quite well established, for it also exists in the *Hikayat al-Ajiba al'l-Akhbar al-Ghariba*

episodes follow involving a sea journey, a protective ship captain, winning a writing contest as a literate monkey, and becoming a simian court secretary, until the adventurer is liberated by a princess who is also a skilled practitioner of the necromantic arts. It is she who will become the rival combatant. The ifrit then appears, to challenge not the young man, but the princess who had promised not to intrude upon his professional territory. Then the contest is on. As a lion he charges her, but with one of her own hairs she confects a magic sword with devastating powers. His severed head turns into a scorpion and she becomes a serpent. The scorpion becomes a vulture, the princess an eagle, and so they fight. The devil becomes a black tom cat and the eagle, a wolf. Then the cat becomes a worm and crawls into a pomegranate, which then swells to great size and falls on the palace floor scattering grains everywhere. The wolf (this is the princess) becomes a snow-white cock that eats all but one seed. From the Straparolan perspective, the story is upside down, for in his version the good guy (Dionigi) was the seeds. The one surviving grain leaps into a fountain to become a fish and the princess another. Then the ifrit rises up as a flame and she as a coal, creating a terrible smoke that fills the palace. The fire blinds the hero in one eye, burns the king's beard, and kills the seneschal. (Are you still with me?) The princess is victorious only when the ifrit is consumed in a flame. With the water of life she restores the youth, less his burned eye, and sinks into death beside the jinn in a heap of ashes. That is how the narrator became a one-eyed mendicant. This story is without doubt a reincarnation of the stark tale of combat and transformation, but it has undergone a sea change that has no European sequels before the eighteenth century – if indeed there were any outside the many editions of the *Nights*. That it was known in Straparola's time is a moot point, but it can hardly have been the source from which he rediscovered the 'Ur-tale' from its complex adaptations.

For students of English literature, the most important incarnation of this story is by the actor Robert Armin, entitled 'Phantasmos, or the Italian Taylor and His Boy,' a creation giving every indication that it was drawn directly from Straparola, perhaps through the Louveau

---

(Tales of the marvellous and news of the strange), a single fourteenth-century manuscript copy of which still exists in Istanbul. It appears to be of Egyptian provenance from the tenth century and contains 18 of the original 42 stories, several of them in *The Arabian Nights*.

translation.[73] From the first canto of this work, the tailor's apprentice, having quickly learned his master's alternate trade, is on the run, for his father unwittingly sells him as a horse to his old teacher. The starved creature is whipped and abused, as in Straparola, until the master's children provide some secret relief by leading it to a stream, where suddenly it sheds its saddle and swims off as a fish – Straparola again. The magician takes up the pursuit. Armin even keeps the motif of the sick king and the courting of the princess in her room. The only significant additions are at the end when the fox scampers about the room, then rises on its hind legs to address the court. Armin encircles the tale with an additional framing story about the envious courtier who had slandered a duke and caused his unjust banishment (a motif perhaps taken over from Lord North's translation of *The Fables of Bidpai* as *The Moral Philosophy of Doni*, published in 1570). As it turns out, the fox-apprentice is the son of this wronged duke who seeks, through his exploits, to redress his father's wrongs by taking up magic and necromancy. Then just as this young aristocrat is about to be married to the princess, the narrator himself wakes up and the 'winter's tale' illusion is broken off. This is among the most significant and direct uses of Straparola in England, along with Riche's version of 'The Devil Marriage to Silvia Ballastro' (II.4), and the story in *Tarleton's Newes out of Purgatorie* (IV.4).[74]

---

73 'The Italian Taylor and His Boy,' in *The Collected Works of Robert Armin*, intro.
   J.P. Feather, 2 vols. (London: T. Pavier, 1609; reprint New York: Johnson Reprint
   Co., 1972), vol. II, pp. B2r–H2v. Over 1000 of Armin's lines are not from Straparola.
   He wrote in the ballad style. Such stories from the Italian were popular up to the
   1590s, but less so thereafter. Despite the publication date, this story was probably
   written as early as 1590–5.

74 There are slight traces of the folk tale in the ballad of 'The Two Magicians,' 44.1
   in Francis James Child's *The English and Scottish Popular Ballads* (Charleston, SC:
   Bibliobazaar, 2008), vol. I, p. 436. The five volumes of the original were republished
   by Dover Publications, Mineola, New York, in 2003, and there are many previous
   editions. A lady, threatened by a blacksmith who sought her maidenhead, flew off
   as a turtle dove and he after her. She then became an eel and he a trout, she a duck
   and he a drake, she a hare and he a greyhound. When she became a mare, he
   became a saddle, and the poem grows more erotically symbolic. When she became
   a ship he nailed her to the dock, and when she became a sheet he became a bed
   cover, and so her maidenhead was lost. Freudians have a legitimate claim to
   this story.

Equally reliant upon Straparola, and the most elaborate recreation of the present tale, is 'L'apprenti magician' of Eustache Le Noble.[75] The story was created in those same years that Madame d'Aulnoy, Charles Perrault, and, a few years later, Thomas-Simon Gueullette drew directly upon Straparola for plots to elaborate into the new fairy tales and orientalized adventures fancied by the French salons. The boy, Alexis, has a charming and playful relationship with his grandfather Bonbenêt (Mr Simple-Nice), who puts him to school with a tailor, La Rancune (Mr Grudge), from whom he learns magic by spying through the keyhole. La Noble follows Straparola in all essential details, but adds a great deal of folksy dialogue and some charming details such as the cylinder by which the master spies the boy within the horse. La Rancune's two daughters chat together and assume personalities. When the master goes fishing for Alexis, he catches nothing but carp and goes back home swearing. This princess is more loquacious on the matter of politics and of being a pawn in the affairs of the king. She is tempestuous in her resistance to giving up her precious ring, and Alexis appears to her in his own shape to plead his case in most passionate terms. When the cock pecks up nearly all the grains, the princess wants to see him in a stew. And when the girl is asked by her father, now in Alexis's debt, whether she minded marrying so far beneath her station, she replied, 'Happiness is more important than richness, and with the exception of birth, Alexis is worth a prince.' And so the fairy tale is completed, moralized, and fancified. Yet, as is clearly seen, the story deviates in no essential ways from the full wonder-tale scenario provided by Straparola. Inversely, insofar as this is a representation of the new fairy tale, the Italian is but a few charming conversations away from being a bona fide precursor and practitioner of the form.

There remains to be shown the vast scope of this tale in world literature by reporting on a mere handful of representative survivors from both the literary and folk traditions. Because the diffusion channels of this story are so difficult to determine, it would seem that a comparative approach might begin geographically nearly anywhere. Even the bias of

---

75 Eustache Le Noble, 'L'apprenti magicien' in *Le gage touché, histoires galantes* (Amsterdam: Jacques Desbordes, 1700); in translation in *The Great Fairy Tale Tradition*, ed. Jack Zipes (New York: Norton, 2001), pp. 353–9. This I first read, without benefit of an author's name, in the rare book room of the Archiginnasio in Bologna: *Le gage touché, histoires galantes et comiques* (Paris: Pierre Witte, 1730), Day II, gage 6, pp. 219–31.

starting from the East may be deceptive because the certain antiquity of the stories cannot be demonstrated. A case in point is 'The Story of King Matanakama,' a Tamil folk tale that relates the adventures of two brothers educated by a Brahmin. The master wants to cheat the boys' father by giving back the wrong brother and keeping the one learned in all his secret arts in order to kill him. The boy makes his escape as a parrot, and the story begins as he explains his situation to the princess who has become his owner and protector. His master would soon arrive as a street-juggler and perform feats atop a high pole, hoping to win the parrot as his reward. This parallels Lattanzio's demand for the ruby ring. He explains to her that rather than handing him over, she must snap his neck and then roll the pearls of her necklace on the floor. When all this comes to pass according to his instructions, the pearls crawl away as worms. When the master reduces himself to a cock and the boy becomes a fierce cat, the master calls for a truce and names the apprentice the new master. Even so, the prince holds out until the guru renounces all future stratagems. Only then are the apprentice and the princess married. The story has all the markers of an ancient tale, yet lacks the rigour of the ancient in its final truce, while the feats on a high pole and the romance closure appear to be later accretions.[76] Even European influence cannot be ruled out.

Another, rather unlike Straparola's until the shape-shifting contest, was recorded early last century in Russia, entitled 'The Story of Unlucky Daniel.' Daniel is unlucky, indeed, for he chooses barrels of sand over gold or coal and finds himself exiled, but in due course he is able to liberate a serpent from the flames who becomes his faithful guardian and source of transformational powers.[77] He marries a cruel tsarivna who becomes suspicious of him, and when she finds out, after several false leads, that his Samson-like secret resides in his clothes, she allows him, when naked, to be chopped into pieces. But the serpent restores him and away he goes again to be sold as a horse to the tsar. When the

---

76 *Two Tamil Folktales*, trans. Kamil Zvelebil (Delhi: Motilal Banarsidass & Paris: Unesco, 1987), pp. 26–9. See also *The Dravidian Nights Entertainments, Being a Translation of Madanakamárájanakadai*, trans. Sangendi M. Natesa Şastri (Madras: Excelsior Press, 1986), pp. 8–18.

77 *Cossack Fairy Tales*, ed. Nisbet Bain (London: A.H. Bullen, 1902), pp. 109–21. Another to explore will be found in *Contes populaire de la Russie*, ed. Loys Brueyre (Paris: Chaix, 1874), p. 253, or in *Contes populaire de la Russie*, ed. W.R.S. Ralston (Paris: Hachette, 1874), p. 229.

tsarivna grows suspicious once more and orders his death, the maid takes
pity and agrees to bury the first drop of his blood, which grows into a
cherry tree. When this is cut, the first chip is tossed into a fountain, where
Daniel becomes a drake. The tsar pursues him, but the boy manages to
slay him before having the tsarivna quartered by wild horses, thereafter
marrying the maid who had aided him in her stead. Many parts of the
generic tale remain visible.

In Germany and the Scandinavian countries there are several versions.
In *Kinder- und Hausmärchen gesammelt durch die Brüder Grimm*, it is no. 68,
'De Gaudief und sein Meester' (The thief and his master), a charming,
brief, and efficient recounting in which all the main parts are present,
including a long introit about recognizing the son in animal form and
paying a large sum of money in the event of failure.[78] With help from a
little dwarf the father sees his son in a small bird. The boy is sold as a
greyhound and a horse. Then the master manages to purchase him with
the bridle, which a maid removes when the horse speaks to her. After a
series of contests, the boy escapes and the master dies. Heinrich Pröhle
includes a version in his *Märchen für die Jugend*.[79] In this variation, the
apprentice escapee is sold first as a dog to hunters, then as an ox, and
there is plenty of descriptive detail to charm younger readers. When the
father sells the horse with the bridle, the boy suffers until he makes his
escape, followed by the master as a bird of prey. He too, as in Straparola,
falls to a princess as a ring, and the combat completes itself much as it
does in the *Piacevoli notti* – from which this story may have taken its
inspiration. The most elaborate and romanticized of the German settings is Ludwig Bechstein's 'Der Zauber-Wettkampf,' or the contest of
magic (1856), in which a bookbinder's helper goes wandering into strange
lands and there finds employment with a mysterious man. His only job
is to keep the library books dusted, to read to his heart's content, and
never to touch the one forbidden book, which, to be sure, is a manual
of magic and sorcery. After two fine years of reading and dusting, curiosity overcomes him and he masters the art of self-transformation. Upon
his return home, he surprises his father by flying in the window. Together

---

78 *Kinder- und Hausmärchen gesammelt durch die Brüder Grimm* (Göttingen: Dieterich,
    1857), no. 68; 'The Rogue and His Master,' in *Grimm's Complete Fairy Tales* (Garden
    City, N.Y.: Nelson Doubleday, n.d.), pp. 587–8. See also *The Great Fairy Tale Tradition*,
    ed. Jack Zipes (New York: Norton, 2001), pp. 359–60.
79 'Zauber-Wettkampf' (Halle: Buchhandlung des Waisenhauses, 1854), no. 23,
    pp. 102–5.

they play the confidence game of selling the boy in a series of animal forms until his old master buys him as a pony, even as the poor creature tries every means to signal the danger to his father. At least he is a speaking pony who can instruct a stable boy to remove the rope from his left hind leg. He flees as a swallow with the master in hot pursuit. He too becomes a golden ring, seeks protection from a princess, and scatters into millet seed when the ring falls. This is the princess who, at the end, is shocked by such macho proceedings and compels the hero to burn the book and renounce all such capers forthwith before domesticity could be considered – to all of which he accedes.[80]

The same story was told among the Norse as 'Farmer Weathersky,' in which there is a long opening section dealing with Weathersky the magician who had disappeared with Jack. This version includes the objects dropped behind by those in flight that spring up as forests and mountains to delay the pursuer. There is both the game of false sales and the metamorphosis game until Jack emerges as the master sorcerer by killing his teacher.[81] From Denmark comes 'The Magician's Pupil,' the tale of an apprenticeship in the black arts taught by a wizard in the forest. Once again, the father had to locate his son converted to a dog, the trick taught to him by a shepherd. Straparolan features are in evidence in the abuse of the horse and the maidservant – one who fancied the boy when he was a pupil – serving as his liberator. The story makes its way to the end with little deviation from the plot line of Lattanzio and Dionigi.[82]

Two from Italy must complete the survey, for the tales are much of a kind and number potentially in the scores. Visentini records one with the title 'There Is No Longer Any Devil,' in which a peasant's son kills

---

80 *Neues deutsche Märchen* (Leipzig: Hartleben's, 1856); also known as *Ludwig Bechstein's Märchenbuch*, and *Sämtliche Märchen*, ed. Ludwig Richter (Munich: Winkler, [1965]), pp. 164–8, and many subsequent editions including those in 1977, 1983, and 2003.

81 *Popular Tales from the Norse*, trans. George Webbe Dasent (New York: G.P. Putnam's Sons, 1888; reprint New York: Johnson Reprint Corp., 1970), pp. 285–95. Others to explore include John Francis Campbell, *Popular Tales of the West Highlands* (London: Edmonston & Douglas, 1860–2), vol. II, pp. 423*ff*; Thomas Keightley, *Tales and Popular Fictions* (London: Whittaker, 1834), pp. 123–4 (also modern editions); and Sven Grundtvig, *Fairy Tales from Afar*, trans. Jane Mulley (London: Hutchinson & Co., [1900]), vol. I, pp. 248*ff*.

82 From the *Eventyr og Folkesagn fra Julland*, ed. Carit Etlar (Copenhagen: C. Steen, 1847); in *Yule-Tide Stories: A Collection of Scandinavian and North German Popular Tales and Traditions*, trans. Benjamin Thorpe (London: Henry G. Bohn, 1853), pp. 363–9.

the devil his master in the shape of a hen after many transformations.[83]
A poor family with a son as strong as a bull and as tricky as a wolf wanders
out to place him in service and happen upon a carriage with two black
horses with a man in black – the devil to be sure – who asks for the boy.
These parents, upon his return, delight in selling him at the market in
animal form, until the father fails to retrieve the magic accoutrement
before selling him to the devil in disguise. The horse is destined to die
of privation, but when a servant leads him to a fountain to drink he makes
his escape. With the devil in hot pursuit, the battle ensues, leading to
the final showdown in the palace of a princess. Even more readily to
hand is Italo Calvino's 'The School of Salamanca,' from Apulia. It too
relates the familiar story, but nicely fitted out with mysterious adventures.
Upon the boy's return home, there is banqueting and a month of mer-
rymaking. Then they decide to double the tuition money by selling the
boy as a horse with a star on its forehead at the Fair of St Vitus. But the
master is already there to make the first purchase and beat the horse
bloody all the way to the tavern. Now, with the help of a serving girl, the
hero makes his escape by becoming an eel. But the master is on to him
and pursues as a conger. A feature of this tale is that each combatant
makes a ritual declaration of his new transformation, such as 'Eel I am,
and a dove will I become.' Once the hero becomes the ring, there is time
to charm a princess by becoming himself from time to time, but when
the king falls ill, the master is back in the picture. When he demands
the ring, the final exchange ensues, full of demonstrative energy on all
sides. There is a pomegranate and a fox, as in Straparola, and in the end
a wedding as well.[84] The story, some 300 years after Straparola, could
have been taken directly from his pages. Nevertheless, so widespread
a dissemination suggests that it had all along been part of the pan-
European folk culture, from which Straparola likewise drew his model.
That tales are known to have passed from oral to written and back to
oral forms can inevitably complicate provenance studies. The striking

---

83 Isaia Visentini, 'Non c'è più il diavolo' in *Fiabe Mantovane* (Turin: E. Löscher, 1879;
    Bologna: Forni Editore, 1879), no. 8, pp. 33–7; also to be found in *Les 50 fiabe
    mantovane di Isaia Visentini* (Parma: Astrea, 1993).

84 *Italian Folktales*, trans. George Martin (New York: Pantheon Books, 1980), from the
    edition by Einaudi in 1956, no. 128, pp. 442–6. The story was first collected by
    Pietro Pellizzari, *Fiabe e canzoni popolari del contado di Maglie in Terra d'Otranto*
    (Maglie, 1881). Calvino, in turn, mentions Domenico Comparetti, *Novelline popolari
    italiane* (Turin: E. Löscher, 1875), no. 63.

fact is that so many of the more recent tales perpetuate particularities found in Straparola. For those determined to follow this motif to the ends of the world, a final three may be suggested from Portugal, Russia, and Italy.[85] And as a coda, mention may be made of the potential for contamination with the parallel tradition of 'the sorcerer's apprentice.' In one typical version, a most wise man, learned in all the mysteries of the spiritual universe, keeps the remarkable book from which his knowledge is derived sealed, locked, and chained to an anchored table. His boy in service, taken for a sot, nevertheless develops an insatiable curiosity about such occult operations. But without access to the magic words, his conjuring is to no avail. Then he one day finds the book unlocked and so he begins to read; immediately there are strange effects in the room. He had conjured up Beelzebub. So the boy commands him to water the plants, but he didn't know the words to make him desist. Only the master's return rescues him from drowning.[86]

---

85 'O aprendiz do mago,' in *Contos tradicionais do povo Portugues*, ed. Téofilo Braga, 2 vols. (Lisbon: Dom Quixote, 1987), vol. I, pp. 104–6; bk. VI, no. 49 in *Les contes populaires russes*, ed. A.N. Afanas'ev (Paris: Maisonneuve & Larose, 1988); Angelo de Gubernatis, *Le novelline di Santo Stefano* (Turin: Negro, 1869), nos. 22 and 26. That should do.
86 Loys Brueyre, *Contes populaires de la Grande-Bretagne* (Paris: Librairie Hachette, 1873), no. 69, 'Le maître et son élève' (The master and his student), a story collected in Yorkshire, pp. 289–91.

VIII. Fable 5
The Donkey's Skin
and the Doctor's Apprentice

LAURETTA

This is a tale of two physicians, one of whom was a man of great reputation and riches, but of little learning, while the other, although exceedingly poor, was a man of skill and understanding.

In these days, gracious ladies, higher honours are bestowed upon mere favourites, those of noble birth or the wealthy, than upon men of science. Nevertheless, true learning may lie hidden under modest and humble trappings, yet by its own virtue it shines forth and illuminates like the rays of the sun. This truth will become manifest if, by your courtesy, you'll incline your ears to this brief tale of mine.

There once lived in Padua, city of Antenore, a certain physician who was not only held in high honour, but had also became very rich, although he was little versed in the art of medicine. It came about one day that this man was called to attend a gentleman, one of the chief men of the city, together with another physician residing there, one who was excellently skilled in the practice of his art, but who enjoyed none of the rewards of fortune. One day, the two went together to pay a visit to the sick man, the first of them richly attired like a great nobleman, who felt the pulse of the patient and declared that he was suffering from a violent and trembling fever. Meanwhile, the poor doctor looked under the bed, and seeing there some apple peelings lying about, concluded rightly that the night before the patient had surfeited himself on apples. Then, after feeling the gentleman's pulse, he said to him, 'Brother of mine, I see that last night you must have eaten apples and that's why you have this fever.' Well, the sick man could not deny this diagnosis, given that it was the truth and confessed it was true. So after prescribing appropriate remedies for the distemper, the two physicians took their leave.

While they were walking along together, the physician of high standing and repute was riled up in his heart with envy, insistently demanding of his colleague of low esteem and fortune by what symptoms he was able to determine that the sick man had been eating apples, promising at the same time to reward him with a generous payment. The humble physician, taking note of the other's ignorance, began searching about for some means to shame him, and thus gave him the following instruction: 'Whenever it happens next that you're summoned to work a cure upon a sick man, as soon as you enter into the room, be sure to cast your eye under the bed, for you can be sure that the patient has been eating whatever food you see there. This I tell you is one of the notable experiments of the Great Commentator (Averrois upon Aristotle).' After receiving a sum of money from the rich physician for this information, he went his way.

The next morning it chanced that the rich physician was called out to prescribe a remedy for a certain peasant, albeit well off and comfortably lodged. Upon entering the bedchamber, the first thing the physician saw lying under the bed was the skin of a donkey. After examining him and feeling his pulse, he found him suffering from a violent fever, whereupon he said to him, 'I see plainly, my good brother, that last night you indulged in a great debauch by eating your donkey, thereby putting your life in danger.'

When the peasant heard these foolish and extravagant words, he burst out laughing and cried, 'Sir, I hope your Excellency will pardon me when I tell you I've never tasted donkey's flesh in my entire life, and that for the lasts ten days I have set eyes on no ass but yourself.' With these words he urged this grave and erudite philosopher to go about his business, and sent to find another physician who might be more skilled in his art. This plainly shows, as I remarked at the beginning of my tale, that men put a higher value upon riches than upon skill or learning. But if I have been briefer in my story than seems proper, I beg you to pardon me, for I see that the hour is now late, and that you, by the nodding of your heads, seem to have confirmed as true every statement I have made.

As soon as Lauretta had brought her brief tale to an end, the Signora, who, like the rest, was well nigh asleep, gave the word to her to bring the night's entertainment to an end with some graceful and modest enigma, because the cock had already announced by his crowing the dawning of the day, whereupon Lauretta, without demur, pronounced her riddle.

> Fresh and rosy from your birth,
> Honour of heaven and crown of earth,
> Strong you be for good or ill,
> The round world with your fame you fill.
> Should you plead the cause of right,
> Then darkness flies before the light.
> But if evil be your view,
> Rack and ruin dire ensue;
> The massy glove of sea and land
> Your hostile touch shall not withstand.

'My enigma,' said Lauretta, 'signifies simply the tongue in its good or evil humour. It is red, as we all know, and it is a glorious work of heaven when we praise God with it, thanking Him for His wondrous benefits. It is the glory of the world when it impels men to do good. Likewise, when, by its words, it shows a devotion to evil, it spreads headlong ruin all around. I could provide you with many examples of this were the hour not so late.' And with a little curtsey, she returned to her place.

When this enigma was finished, it was received by the company with generous praise. Then the Signora called for the torches to be lighted, urging that all should return to their homes, at the same time laying strict command upon them that on the following evening they should return to the accustomed meeting place well prepared with a stock of fables. With one voice they all promised to obey her command.

The End of the Eighth Night

VIII.5 Commentary

This is a Renaissance joke, directly from the tradition of the *facetiae* or *facezie* written by the likes of Gian Francesco Poggio Bracciolini (1380–1459) of Florence, who wrote in Latin, and Lodovico Carbone (1435–82) of Ferrara, who wrote in the vernacular. Both wrote versions of the quip about the medical misdiagnosis based on objects under the patient's bed. Poggio's, in particular, circulated widely thereafter in the several French translations of his work. The pleasantry, in fact, is a variation on one of the oldest jokes on record, a repartee surviving from ancient Greece, in which a young man meeting a woman driving a pack of donkeys called out, 'Good morning, mother of asses,' to which she replied, 'Good morning, my son.' The peasant in the present story, misdiagnosed for allegedly dining on donkey's flesh, was likewise encouraged to make a similar disparagement of the doctor in the name of this 'stupid beast.' But there is more to the anecdote in Straparola than calling a pompous doctor an ass, because a smug, rich, imposing, charlatan physician has been set up to make a fool of himself in this manner by a clever, learned, poor, and unimposing practitioner. He, it turns out, is the trickster and maker of comic justice by creating the conditions under which his victim will perform his own humiliation. This is also a trickster vignette.

The simple moral pronounced by the narrator at the outset indicates a further line of satire insofar as 'the people' are the fools, for they are impressed by titles, ceremony, wealth, nobility, pompous accreditation, and charlatanry and thus attribute to such men as this fatuous doctor a level of science and intelligence far beyond their merit. Jonson utters a variation on the theme in *Volpone* (I.i) when his trickster magnifico credits his entire standing among men, whether for fame, courage, or virtue, to his wealth. Bartolomeo makes a similar argument in Bruno's *Candlebearer* (III.i).[87] Both characters are gloating over the power of appearances – one of them already rich, the other planning to become so through alchemy. Grandeur, power, and learning are by definition granted to the wealthy by the impressionable masses. Within the professional sphere itself, the rankling injustice is that patients are drawn to physicians who overwhelm with jargon, exude confidence, dress the part, offer painless remedies, and promise astounding cures, for which the gullible and desperate will pay high sums, while the humble practitioners who conscientiously follow their art and pronounce no more than they can deliver are rendered modest credit. The vignette is, at the same time, an exposé of the abuses of the medical profession. When, in these circumstances, the *bon mot* of a peasant can floor the vain, the vignette is good, and when the honest physician can lure the overrated colleague to a pratfall through his own ignorance, it is even better.

Once the Straparolan rhetoric is firmly in hand, readers may venture to discover buried historical shades and nuances. In the present tale, it

---

87 Ben Jonson, *Volpone or the Fox*, ed. David Cook (London: Methuen, 1962), pp. 61–2; Giordano Bruno, *Candlebearer*, trans. Gino Moliterno (Ottawa: Dovehouse, 2000), p. 105.

is by reading the clues under the bed that the humble doctor makes the better diagnosis.[88] In a related tale, it is the clever but unlearned doctor who tricks patients by making them believe such observations are based on urine samples or taking the pulse, thereby shirking the responsibility for making more pathologically-based diagnoses. In yet another version, it is the first doctor who is clever and observant, and his apprentice who is amazed and asks his master to reveal his secret. His inexperience, likewise, is revealed through the folly of reading the donkey's skin under the bed as a sign of excess ingestion, which gives rise to withering mockery. In still another version, it is laughter alone that will cure the patient, thus prompting the doctor to set up an outrageously false diagnosis. The patient becomes the audience, encounters the epistemic jag, and laughs in salutary fashion. The laughter now becomes a methodical cure, much as Avicenna recommended in the treatment of certain humoral diseases playing upon the patient's fantasies or emotions to a point of shock self-recognition. These variations upon the central plan of the clever and dull practitioners and a particular mode of misdiagnosis can be further illustrated through three paradigmatic sources. Other analogues may then be confined to citations in the footnotes because they are no more than replays of the prototypes set out here.

---

88 As an aside, this is an instance of rule-based training in which attributes, both negative and positive, are taken into consideration in determining membership in categories. Positive attributes are more easily computed, but doctors must also specialize in negative evidence as well by the absence of symptoms or by negative test results. Diseases may often have similar symptoms and can only be distinguished by a greater plasticity of analysis. The rule is that the presence of skins and shells are traces of the patient's recent dietary ingestion. Thus, donkey skin is to donkey meat what apple parings are to apples: *exuviae*. But rote rule application in the presence of negative attributes becomes a marker of limited intelligence. Readers must establish a hierarchy of judgment, the higher level taking in the condition of the patient, the alternative explanations for the presence of large animal skins, and the improbability of such a Gargantuan feast. In failing this logic test, and in such ludicrous fashion, the foolish doctor provokes laughter, which is a complex form of communal judgment based on the recognition of incongruities and normative expectations. Given that such logic belongs to the default cognitive capacities of the species, laughter celebrates a man's diminished chances for survival in a competitive environment, because his computational incompetence threatens the chances of survival of those who depend upon his skills. Satire is born. (Tragedy is the diminished chances for survival that come to those whose computational abilities remain above the norm, but who are overwhelmed by inexorable forms of adversity.)

Without much contest, this story is a nearly verbatim translation, from Latin, of Girolamo Morlini's 'De medico et mediculo.' Morlini had already turned Poggio's model into a story of two doctors, with corresponding reflections upon the ironic reversal of their respective merits. Presumably it was he who redesigned the tale, now having the grand physician manifest his ignorance rather than the inexperienced apprentice.[89] Those changes magnified the satirical potential. The version closest to Morlini's appears among the *facetiae* of Poggio Bracciolini, although to determine whether he appropriated Poggio, directly or indirectly, or relied upon an oral adaptation remains moot. Bracciolini's vignette 'De medico in visitatione infirmorum versuto' is about a doctor's apprentice and his misapplication of the teachings of his master. This well-respected physician makes house calls with his student. He is not really knowledgeable (a hint for Morlini perhaps), but clever and *rusé*. In lieu of more discerning analyses, his tactic is to accuse patients of breaking their regimens and diets by eating quantities of figs or apples, which he detects by the tell-tale signs about the room. Such insights, meanwhile, he attributes to the examination of the pulse or the urine, thereby maintaining his professional mystique. Likewise impressed, the apprentice begs for the secret and is informed of the simple truth. This student, in due course, himself becomes a practitioner, and in his new capacity prescribes for a peasant a certain diet, thinking to return and discover some revealing sign of his failure to observe the restrictions. On the following day, failing to note significant improvement in the patient's health, he makes accusations of gourmandize based on the donkey's skin under the bed and thereby finds himself the laughing stock of both patient and bystanders. Poggio moralized upon the danger to life and limb that might result from such professional nonsense. Computing the changes between this and Morlini's version is a simple exercise, making Poggio, or an imitator, the presumed source of the Morlini/Straparola variation.[90]

---

89 *Les nouvelles de Girolamo Morlini*, trans. Fernand Caussy (Paris: E. Sansot, 1904), no. 32, pp. 86–7.

90 *Les facéties de Pogge, Florentin*, trans. Pierre des Brandes (Paris: Garnier Frères, [ca. 1900]), no. 109. This story had a large circulation in France, no doubt through the influence of the early translation made for King Charles VIII and Anne de Bretagne around 1480 by Guillaume Tardif, for which see *Les facéties de Poge, accompagnée des moralités de Guillaume Tardif*, trans. G. Tardif, ed. Léonce Grasilier (Paris: Garnier, [1919]), no. 61. This work was first published in 1510. A version of 'The Doctor's Apprentice' was also included by Guillaume Bouchet, Sieur de Brocourt (1514–94) in *Les serées* (Poitiers: Par les Bouchetz, 1584), serée 10; there is

This material made its way to England in the sixteenth century to appear in the jest book *Tales and Quick Answers* (ca. 1535) as 'Of the physician that bare his patient on hand, he had eaten an ass.' This doctor had a way of blaming his patients for the state of their health, and particularly by informing them with prescient professional insight that they had over-indulged in eating this or that, merely by looking for the clues about the room. His servant thought to imitate this good trick with a patient of his own. Seeing a saddle, he accused the patient of eating the ass it belonged to and found himself the butt of derision.[91]

A significant variant, albeit more remote from Straparola, appears in the *Schimpf und Ernst* of Johannes Pauli: no. 357, 'Von den artzten' (Concerning doctors).[92] In this tale, a doctor from another town is sent for by an ailing nobleman. After taking the pulse and examining the urine, this medic pronounces that unless the patient breaks out in a joyful fit of laughter he will never recover. He then asks his servant (Knecht) if he knew of a way to make the patient laugh, but the lad could think of nothing. So the doctor planned with his hireling an elaborate trick for the next day, informing the patient that in the next town there was a wise and noble doctor and that he should send for him. He then disguises himself as the rich physician, reappears, and proceeds to examine the urine by holding it up to the light from the window, then exclaiming that it is no wonder the patient is ill insofar as the water reveals that he has swallowed a fool loading manure, two horses, and a servant boy. The incredulous patient is invited to see this for himself by rising from his bed and examining the flask. Seeing that the urine merely conveyed the

---

a recent edition edited by C.-E. Roybet (Geneva: Slatkine, 1969). It appears again as 'Simplicité d'un apprenti médecin' (The simple-mindedness of an apprentice doctor) in *Roger Bontemps en belle humeur* (Cologne: Pierre Marteau, 1670, and Amsterdam, 1670). This work has been attributed, probably falsely, to the Duke de Roquelaure, Doyen des Maréchaux de France, and also to the king himself by the initials L.R. The name Roger Bontemps is fictional and epitomizes the carefree, recreational life; it was derived from Rogier Bon Temps, a character in René d'Anjou's *Le livre de cuers d'amours espris* (1457–77). The story also appears in the *Nouveaux contes à rire* (Cologne: Chez Roger Bontemps, 1713) as 'L'apprenti médecin' (The apprentice doctor).

91 'Of the phisitian that bare his pacient on hand he had eaten an asse' in *Tales and Quicke Answeres* (London, 1535?), pp. Eiiir–v; also in *A Hundred Marry Tales*, ed. P.M. Zall (Lincoln: University of Nebraska Press, 1963), no. 50.

92 Johannes Pauli, *Schimpf und Ernst*, ed. Johannes Bolte (Hildesheim: Georg Olms, 1972), pp. 215–16.

images of those in the courtyard and that the diagnosis was preposterous and falsely founded, he burst out in uncontrollable laughter and in due course found himself healed. In this instance, the absurdity of the diagnosis is intentional, while the helper figure is merely an accomplice in the ruse, all of which the patient takes for gross incompetence. Now the two physicians are the same physician, and the wise and the foolish diagnosis are the same, but the elements of Poggio's generic tale remain evident. An account of the patient cured by laughing at the doctor's ignorance appears, in fact, in the *Facezie* of Lodovico Carbone (1435–82), many of whose short pieces were transcriptions and translations out of Poggio. The collection contains 108, of which this story is no. 106.[93] But that does not explain which tale has the greater claim to antiquity, the laughing cure or the foolish apprentice, for there is reason to think that both were much older.

Among the many potential versions of this tale to be found among later folk tales is the following collected by Giuseppe Pitrè, which is very similar to the tale by Poggio, in which the master doctor teaches his inquisitive but inept apprentice to look for clues in the room. Such evidence may reveal whether the patient has broken his dietary restrictions, as in the present case. Moreover, it is a means for keeping patients in awe by attributing these revealed secrets to the reading of the pulse. With this procedure in mind, in literal fashion, the next day the apprentice notices the straw under the poor patient's bed and accuses him of eating hay, only to find himself mocked for the fool that he was. The story carries a little narrative 'gene' at least half a millennium old with only modest variations in the details. This is not the form consolidated by Morlini and Straparola, but is undoubtedly a survivor of the source on which they built.[94]

---

93 *Facezie di Lodovico Carbone*, ed. Abd-al-Kader Salza (Leghorn: R. Giusti, 1900), no. 106. This is the same tale of the doctor who surprised patients by his knowledge of their eating habits by means of his close inspection of the room for traces of apples, figs, eggs, pears, or peaches (mentioned by Carbone). His assistant applies the technique to a donkey's skin seen under the bed and inadvertently heals the patient through his own laughter (aroused by the assistant's stupidity). Lodovico Carbone de Costacciaro, *Facezie e dialogo de la partita soa*, ed. Gino Ruozzi (Bologna: Commissione per i Testi di Lingua, 1989), no. 84, p. 47.

94 'L'apprinnista di lu medicu' (The doctor's apprentice), from Pitrè's *Fiabe, novelle e racconti*, no. 180, trans. Thomas Frederick Crane, in *Italian Popular Tales*, ed. Jack Zipes (Santa Barbara: ABC Clio, 2001), p. 230.

Straparola's own tale lived on briefly in the collections of Francesco Sansovino, the *Cento novelle scelte* (1561), and Gabriel Chappuys, *Les facétieuses journées* (1584). Sansovino transcribed several tales out of Straparola, with minor variations, and Chappuys translated several of these into French. Both retell the same essential story.[95] Curiously, however, Louveau did not include the story in his translation of Straparola, a translation that, once completed by Larivey, went through a dozen editions in the late sixteenth century.[96]

---

95 *Cento novelle scelte* (Venice: Sansovino, 1561), VIII, no. 9; *Les facétieuses journées*, ed. Michel Bideaux (Paris: Champion, 2003), Day VIII, no. 9, pp. 704–6. Chappuys makes the moral of Straparola's tale even more explicit: that looking the part often impresses more than real science or virtue, and that the rich get richer though they are fools, while the poor but skilled go unappreciated.

96 See Michel Bideaux's introduction to *Les facétieuses journées*, pp. 132–4, where he describes *Les facétieuses nuits du seigneur Straparole*, trans. J. Louveau (Lyons: G. Rouille, 1560).

VIII. Fable 3A
The Woes of an Old Gallant

ARIANNA

Anastasio Minuto is enamoured of a gentlewoman who repulses his advances. He speaks to her spitefully thereafter, for which reason she tells her husband, who, in consideration of Anastasio's age, spares his life.

Gracious ladies, as Cicero writes in his book *On Old Age*, ardent wantonness is always ugly and disgraceful, but in old men it is particularly disgusting and far more blameworthy. Besides being wicked and vile in itself, it saps a man's strength, weakens his eyesight, robs him of his intellect, makes him a disgrace and a laughing-stock, empties his purse, and, given the troublesome and brief period of pleasure it holds out as a lure, entices him into all sorts of evil. If you'll give my fable the kind and gracious hearing that you customarily give, the truth of what I'm saying will all become clear to you.

In this city of ours, which outdoes all others in the world for its abundance of fair women, there once lived a certain gentlewoman who was most graceful and endowed with every beauty, and whose eyes, in their loveliness, shone like the morning star. This lady lived in great luxury and was entertained very delicately by her husband, except where his marital duties were concerned, in the discharge of which he was somewhat slack. For that reason she chose for herself a lover, a well-mannered youth from an honourable family, and made him the object of her favour, lavishing upon him much greater love than she gave to her husband.

After a time it happened that a certain Anastasio, a friend of her husband's and a man far advanced in years, became so violently enamoured of this gentlewoman that day or night he could find no rest. His passion and torment were indeed so consuming that within a few days he wasted all away until there was scarcely any flesh left to cover his bones. His eyes were all bleared and full of rheum, his forehead was ploughed with wrinkles, and his squashed nose was incessantly dripping. When he sighed, his breath was so fetid that he nauseated those around him, while in his mouth there were but two teeth, which were more a hazard than a help. Besides being afflicted with all these ills, he was paralytic, and although the sun might be in Leo and blazing hot as a furnace, in his limbs he felt no warmth.

Ensnared and inflamed by his senile passion, this miserable old dodderer eagerly solicited the lady's favours, offering first one gift and then another. But although the presents he sent her were rich and most valuable, yet she refused them one and all, for she had no need of anything he offered, seeing that her husband was very rich and made certain that she lacked for nothing. Whenever possible, Anastasio saluted her in the streets when she was on her way to or from church to perform her religious duties, imploring her to accept him as her faithful servant and to save him from a lover's death. But wise and prudent as she was, she would always cast her eyes down upon the ground and hasten home without answering a word.

By chance it came to Anastasio's attention that the young man of whom we've lately spoken frequented this gentlewoman's house. He began to keep watch over the comings and goings of this gallant, so that on a certain evening he saw him enter her abode while the husband was absent from the city. That was like a knife in his heart. Maddened by this, he no longer considered his lady's honour or his own, but took from his treasury a great quantity of jewels and money, proceeded to the lady's house, and knocked loudly at the door.

The maid, when she heard someone knocking, went out on the balcony and yelled down, 'Who knocks?'

The old man answered, 'Open the door right now. It's Anastasio and I've certain matters of importance to discuss with Madonna.'

When she knew who it was, the maid ran in haste to her mistress, who at that moment was taking her pleasure with her lover in the next room, and called her aside, 'Madonna, Messer Anastasio is below, knocking at the door.'

To this the lady replied, 'Go down quickly and tell him to go about his business immediately, for it is not my custom to open my doors at night to anybody when my husband is away from home.'

Having heard and understood these words of her mistress, the servant went down as she had been directed and repeated them to Messer Anastasio. The old man, feeling slighted and repulsed, grew angry and began to knock at the door more furiously than before, insisting on being let into the house. The gentlewoman was filled with wrath when she heard this, not only because of the hurly-burly the silly old fool was making, but because of her lover, who was in the house with her. Accordingly, she went to the window and cried out, 'I'm in truth most amazed, Messer Anastasio, that you should come like this and so inconsiderately knock and clamour at the doors of other people's houses. Go to bed, you silly old man, and don't annoy those who have no desire to be disturbed. If my husband were at home I'd open to you without delay. But since he's abroad, I can't and won't do such a thing.' But the old man went on insisting that he had matters of the greatest importance to discuss with her, all the while as they spoke knocking incessantly at the door.

Seeing how persistent he was – the dirty old beast – the lady was afraid that his folly might lead him to speak injurious words against her honour. So she withdrew for a moment to take counsel with her young lover about what she should do. He replied that she might just as well open the door and hear what it was he had to say, and that there was nothing to be afraid of. The old man went on knocking vigorously all the while, so the good lady had them light a torch for her, and then told the maid to open the door. When Anastasio had come into the hall, she issued from her chamber looking as fair and as fresh as a morning rose. She went towards him and asked what business he had with her at that hour of the night. The amorous old dotard, with his wheedling and piteous words, and hardly able to hold back the tears, answered, 'Oh, Signora, you are the only hope and support of my wretched life. Don't let it then be a cause of wonder to you that I should come knocking on your door, no doubt rashly and presumptuously, and to your surprise and alarm. Truly, I haven't come to annoy you, but to reveal to you the great passion I feel for you, and how sharply I'm tormented by it. I hardly need say that the cause of my woe is your surpassing beauty, which renders you the queen of all women. If the fountain of pity in your heart is not entirely sealed up, you will spare a thought for me who, on your account, daily dies a thousand deaths. Ah, soften a little that hard heart of yours! Don't think about my age or my mean condition, but only of my true and devoted mind and of the ardent love that I bear you now and always will, for as long as my sad soul remains joined to my stricken and afflicted body. As a token of my love for you, I beg that of your kindness you will accept this gift and hold it dear, trifling though it may be.'

With these words he drew from his bosom a purse full of golden ducats that shone bright as the sun, and a string of great round white pearls, and two jewels set in most delicately wrought gold. These he presented to the gentlewoman, imploring her in the meantime not to deny him her love.

But when she heard and understood the words of the infatuated old man, she answered him, 'Messer Anastasio, I always took you for a man of better judgment than you're showing now, for you seem to have completely lost your wits. Where is the good sense and prudence expected of a man of your mature years? Do you think I'm no better than a whore that you come tempting me with gifts? You're most certainly mistaken if this is your belief. I have no need of the things you've brought here, but suggest you take them to some profligate woman who will serve your purpose, for, as you should know, I have a husband who provides me with everything I need. So go your way and godspeed to you. And take care that you order your life for the better in the little time you have left on earth.'

When he heard these words, the old man was filled with grief and remorseful indignation. 'Madonna, make it clear to me that you do not speak out of conviction, but for fear of the young man you now keep in your house.' With that he mentioned the gallant by name. 'If you'll not satisfy me,' he went on, 'and yield to my desires, I'll be sure to denounce you to your husband.'

When she heard Anastasio mention the name of the companion at that very moment in her bedroom, she made not the least sign of shame or dejection, but showered the old geezer with the most violent abuse ever to cross human lips. Then she took a strong stick in her hand and would have basted him soundly had he not scurried down the stairs and fled from the house at full speed.

As soon as the old man had departed, the lady went back into the room where she had left her lover. Hardly able to keep back her tears, she told him of the misfortune that had befallen her, fearful that the old villain might reveal everything to her husband. Then she asked her gallant for his advice on the course she should adopt. Now this youth, who was smart and clever, first comforted his lady and urged her to be of good heart, whereupon he sketched out for her an excellent scheme, saying, 'My soul, don't be alarmed or discouraged. Just take the advice I'm about to give you and rest assured that everything will turn out well. As soon as your husband comes back to the house, explain the entire matter to him concerning the old man's intrusion here and just how it happened. Tell him how this wretched old dotard heaped slander on you, accusing you of having guilty relations with one man and another. At that point, call up by name some five or six young men whom you know, naming me as the last on the list. Having done this, we'll leave the rest to fortune, which is certain to work on your side.'

Her lover's advice seemed wise and judicious, and so she did exactly as he had advised her. When her husband came home, at once she presented herself with a sad countenance all stricken with woe and her eyes streaming with tears. Then she began to curse the fate that tormented her so cruelly. When her husband questioned her about her affliction, she answered that she was not free to say. But after a little, she cried out in a loud voice, weeping bitterly at the same time, 'In fact, I don't know what should prevent me from putting an end to this wretched life of mine with my very own hands! I can't accept that so perfidious a traitor should be the cause of my ruin and lasting shame. Unhappy woman that I am! What have I done that I should be slandered and cut to the quick? And do you know by whom? By a very hangman, a murderer, who deserves a thousand deaths!'

Urged by her husband to say more, she continued, 'That headstrong old dotard, Anastasio, who calls himself your friend, that silly, lecherous, and wicked old man – didn't he come to me a few night ago asking me to do nasty and immoral things, offering me money and jewels if I'd agree? Then, because I wouldn't listen to a word of what he had to say, or consent to anything he desired, he began to revile me most shamefully, calling me a harlot and declaring that I brought men into the house, involving myself with one and then with another. When I heard such words, I nearly died of grief. But in short order I collected my wits and courage and grabbed a stick with which I intended to beat him soundly. Fearful that I just might carry out my intent, he ran away as fast as he could, fleeing from the house.'

When her husband heard this speech, he was vexed beyond measure and set about to calm her, promising that he would play Anastasio a trick that he'd remember for as long as he lived. So when the next day had come, the lady's husband and Anastasio happened to meet, and before the husband could utter a word, Anastasio made a sign that he had something to say to him, and the other signalled back that he'd hear him out. Anastasio then spoke up, 'Sir, you know how sincere the love and goodwill has always been between us; there's nothing we could do to improve upon it. That's why I'm determined to reveal something to you out of concern for your honour. Well, let me cut the long preamble and not keep you in suspense. It's that your wife is sought after in an amorous way by a certain young man, and that she, for her part, returns his love and regularly enjoys his favours, which is a great shame and disgrace to you and your entire family. All this I'm telling you is the naked truth. The other night, when you chanced to be away from the city, I saw him with my own eyes going into your house, decked out in a disguise. And I also saw him come out of the house early the next morning.'

The husband, when he heard these words from Anastasio, flew into a violent rage and started piling on the abuse, 'Ah, you villainous bastard, you hangman, you wicked cur! I don't know what stops me from grabbing you by the beard and pulling it out of your chin one hair at a time. Don't I know what kind of a woman my wife is, and don't I also know just how you tried to corrupt her with money and jewels and pearls? Didn't you tell her, you blighted bugger, that if she'd not give in to you and be taken by your lawless passion that you'd denounce her to me and thus inflict sadness and ruin on her for the rest of her life? Didn't you report that this man, and that one, and more after that, had their way with her? Well if it weren't for the pity I have for old age, I'd throw you under my feet and not stop kicking till your soul was plumb out of your body. So go and be hanged, you miserable old dog, and don't ever come into my sight again or let me catch you loitering around my house.'

With that, the poor blighter tucked his bagpipe back into its case and departed like a man struck dumb. As for the crafty and clever lady, under her husband's own protection she spent many a merry hour with her lover in greater security than ever.

[Straparola, here, used the same enigma and ensuing conversation that originally belonged to VIII.3, above.]

VIII.3A Commentary

This effective story, written according to the traditions and conventions of the *novella*, was a late addition to the *Piacevoli notti*. It was the first of two stories that, as early as 1555, replaced VIII.3 above, the salacious and patently anti-clerical story of 'The Priest and the Image-Carver's Wife.' Straparola may have provided them, bringing the total of his stories to seventy-five; Pirovano, however, thought them spurious. Paradoxically, despite this story's ostensibly stock subject matter – that of the married wife and her young lover, combined with the rejection of a Pantaloon amoroso in the person of Anastasio Minuto – it resembles none that comes to mind from the usual *novella* repertory. That is, of course, an invitation to be proved wrong, but for the moment it concurs with the views of all who have commented upon the *Nights*, including Donato Pirovano, who suggested two works by Pietro Fortini, but hastened to clarify that with regard to the intrigue, the characters, and the conclusion, there was but 'una vaga affinità' (a vague affinity).[97] The most novel features are the blackmail attempted by the old lover and the counter-ploy on the part of the young lover, as enacted by the young wife, by which his vengeful (but true) revelations are discredited. This is a 'he said, she said' tale in which the disposition of the offended husband will guide his choice between the rhetoric of his wife's tears and the feigned concern of Anastasio for his friend's honour. These competing claims, neither of them sincere, and the positions readers are induced to take in relation to them, provide the story with its idiosyncratic cachet.

That the author intended a suspension of judgment between them is putatively denied by the story's implicit moral stance against the unnaturalness and folly of geriatric passion. Without disapprobation, the wife is allowed to take a lover because her husband, although a generous provider, has been negligent in his marital attentions. Moreover, we are assured that she has selected a young man of discretion, intelligence, and a good family, as if that would mitigate the wrong. Concerning the *senex amoroso*, however, Cicero is invoked to discredit him. Anastasio is obsequious, obnoxious in his predatory insistence, and stereotyped by his

---

97 Giovan Francesco Straparola, *Le piacevoli notti*, ed. Donato Pirovano, 2 vols. (Rome: Salerno, 2000), vol. II, p. 793. Those works are Pietro Fortini, *Le giornate*, ed. A. Mauriello, 2 vols. (Rome: Salerno, 1988), no. 45, and *Le piacevoli e amorose notte dei novizi*, ed. A. Mauriello, 2 vols. (Rome: Salerno, 1995), no. 14. In the latter there is an attempt on the part of a would-be lover to blackmail an adulterous wife by holding knowledge of her former affair. This wife is also married to a rich merchant, Francescotto de' Bardi, and a similar overall situation pertains. It might be asked if this story takes some inspiration from no. 37, 'La moglie de Francescotto' by Giovanni Sabadino degli Arienti, given the coincidence of names. It tells of the woes of an old gallant, in the person of a pestering priest, who is at last allowed into the house the better to torment him. Upon the husband's planned return, he is bustled into a barrel (*botte*) until the merchant retires. But in fact, he is left there all night, only to be hauled off to Bologna on a cart the following day, to be delivered over to Nicolao, who would force him to cry out by washing the cask in boiling water. After his self-discovery, he is brought to a full and humiliating confession and asked repeatedly about his future plans for visiting the ladies. The story was written in the 1470s and came to print in Bologna in 1483. It predates Straparola, to be sure, but does not proffer a resemblance sufficient to cite as a source. *Novelle porretane*, ed. Pasquale Stoppelli (L'Aquila: L.U. Japadre editore, 1975), no. 37, pp. 232–8.

disgusting attributes: runny eyes, dripping nose, paucity of teeth, and challenged mobility. Every move he makes is accompanied by deprecating words, such as 'inflamed with senile passion.' The stance persists even when some pity might be allowed. Yet even his lean and wasting state, the first sign of the tormented, melancholy lover, merely heads up the list of his loathsome attributes emanating from his antique constitution.

Just how serious Straparola may have been in composing an exemplum on the follies of old men in love as a cautionary tale grounded in the precepts of the philosophers is a moot point, but allowing this to be the case, the position is easily expanded through medical and humanist references. Cicero wrote his treatise 'On Old Age' in 44 BC when he was only 62, but by that moment in his career, although he was still in full possession of his intellectual powers, his place in the affairs of state had been significantly diminished by the imperialistic aspirations of Marc Antony. In the twelfth section, he comes to the matter of old men and love, but his tone is not one of moral dissuasion, as one might expect, but stoic resignation, insofar as the lack of sensual pleasure is considered a charge against old age. Yet the tone turns moral in consolation for that loss, for, in the words of Archytas of Terentum, 'no more deadly curse has nature inflicted on men than sensual pleasure. To gratify it our wanton appetites are roused beyond all prudence and restraint ... Fornications and adulteries and every vice of that stripe are initiated by the enticements of pleasure and by that alone.'[98] For Cicero, it is a boon to the aged that nature removes from them the blemishes and cravings of youth. By inference, then, it might be urged in his name that such passions are foul and disgraceful for all ages, but particularly so for the hoary-headed in that, besides being wicked and unclean, they sap strength, even weaken the eyes, create disgrace, squander resources, and all for an ephemeral moment of pleasure. Cicero is nowhere so particular, but the fame of his essay made it an authoritative reference for the moralist. The comic theatre, both ancient and recent, had specialized in ridiculing pantaloon lovers by contrasting the fresh bloom of youth with the noxious and unsavoury features of old age, and by staging the self-deceiving pretensions of men at the end of their functional virility. Examples abound. Menander is reported to have said, in the words of a Latin translator misidentified by the Renaissance collectors of ancient dicta, 'Senex amore captus ultimum malum' (The greatest danger to an

---

98 Cicero, *The Basic Works*, ed. Moses Hadas (New York: Random House, 1951), p. 141.

old man is to be seized by love).[99] Jean Aubery in *L'antidote d'amour* states: 'Doctors take it as a bad sign when an old man is burning up with an amorous fever, suspecting the scope and violence of the cause in one whose humours are normally icy; it is poor judgment on the part of the old to fall in love, which detracts a great deal from their merit.'[100] Publilius Syrus included the following in his *Sententiae*, 'Amare iuveni fructus est, crimen seni' (Love is fruitful in the young, criminal in the old).[101] Such commonplaces could be multiplied to untold lengths, all of them expressing a normative value that Anastasio had violated in a way that nearly cost him his life, having become peevish and curmudgeonly into the bargain. Renaissance physicians were ready to point out, in chorus, that those with cold and dry natures are in greater danger than the young from hot afflictions, and that love is a downright menace to their health. This is to contextualize as a received idea the bias of the story, but the social dynamics of the narrative remain far richer than a mere lesson in the unseemliness of geriatric philocaption.

99 Jacques Ferrand, *A Treatise on Lovesickness*, ed. Donald Beecher and Massimo Ciavolella (Syracuse: Syracuse University Press, 1990), p. 307.
100 Jean Aubery, *L'antidote d'amour* (Paris: Claude Chappelet, 1599), p. 26v.
101 *Sententiae* in *Minor Latin Poets*, ed. Arnold M. Duff (London: Heinemann, 1934), p. 16.

VIII. Fable 3B
The Merchant's Monkey

ALTERIA

Bernardo, a Genoese merchant, sells wine that is half water, for which reason he is punished by heaven with the loss of half his money.

The tale just told to you by my dear sister puts me in mind of an accident that befell a Genoese merchant who, for selling wine mixed with water, subsequently lost half the money which he had earned for its sale, for which reason he almost died of grief.

In the noble city of Genoa, one in which there is great trafficking in merchandise, there lived once upon a time a certain Bernardo of the Fulgoso family, an avaricious chap, and a man involved in unlawful dealings. Now this Bernardo made up his mind to go to Flanders with a shipload of the finest wines of Monte Folisco, hoping to sell them at a high price. So setting sail one day from the port of Genoa, having good luck on his side, he passed over the sea without meeting any mischance and came within a short distance of his destination in Flanders. Casting anchor there, he brought his ship to her moorings. Once landed, he took in a supply of fresh water, and with that he so miraculously multiplied his wine that from each cask he made two. This done, he weighed anchor and once more set sail. The wind was so fair and fast that, in a short space, he came into harbour in Flanders. Because at that time there was a great scarcity of wine in the country, the people of the place bought up his commodity at a very high price. The merchant was able to fill up two large sacks with the gold ducats he received, and with these he departed from Flanders, thoroughly delighted, and made his way back home.

Now when Bernardo had sailed a good distance from Flanders and found himself upon the high seas, he brought out all the money he had gotten, spread it on a table and began to count it. When he had finished the tally, he put it into two bags, which he tied up by the mouth very securely. Hardly had Bernardo finished his task when by happenstance a monkey aboard ship broke its chain and, having jumped down onto the table, it caught up the two bags of money and nimbly scrambled up the mast of the ship. When the ape had mounted up to the maintop rigging, it began to take the money out of the bags pretending to count it. The merchant almost died from his terrible state of grief and anxiety, unwilling all the while to do anything that might alarm the monkey, or to send anyone in pursuit for fear that from vexation it might throw the ducats into the sea. After remaining in doubt for some minutes, he finally resolved that he would do better to remain quiet and await whatever might ensue from the whim of the beast. The monkey, having untied the bags and taken out all the ducats, handled the coins and played with them for a long time. Then, putting them all back into the bags and tying them up securely, it threw one bag into the sea and the other it threw down to the merchant standing on the deck of the ship, as if to tell the cheating Bernardo that the money that had been thrown into the sea was the price paid for the water that he had mixed with his wine, and that the bag now lying at his feet was the just price for the latter. The water thereby received what was owed for water, and Bernardo received what was due for the wine. Recognizing that this adventure had been brought to pass by the will of Heaven, Bernardo submitted himself to the event with patience, calling to mind the saying that ill-acquired goods are never lasting, and that although he who wins them may enjoy them for a time, they will never be enjoyed by his heirs.

Alteria's ingenious and well-imagined fable won the commendation of the entire company, and when the Signora gave her the signal that she should tell her enigma, she set hers forth in the following words:

> I am featly made, I trow.
> Teeth I have and a tongue also;
> Not a bone in me is found;
> Ever to one spot I am bound.
> I can neither talk nor bite;
> Thus I live with scant delight.
> I beg you look with care on me;
> A hole right in my midst you'll see.
> A man to torture me comes next,
> And through and through I am transfixt;

> Another comes and drags him forth,
> And hangs him up as little worth.

This enigma gave rise to long discussion, but no one of all the company was able to find out the meaning of it, except Isabella alone, who said, 'Nothing can be meant by this enigma except a lock, which has teeth and a tongue, but no bones. It can't eat, and that which fastens it is the key, which also unfastens the box as well. He that draws the key out of the lock will usually hang it up on some nail.' When Isabella had finished her explanation of this most subtle riddle, Lauretta, without waiting for further word from the Signora, launched into her fable.[102]

VIII.3B Commentary

There is little doubt about where this story originated. Straparola or his publisher decided to carry on with the borrowing from Morlini's *Novellae* (1520), of which this is the forty-fifth, entitled 'De mercatore Janvenci qui vinum diultum dendens pecuniam perdit' (Of the merchant J. who sells diluted wine and loses his money).[103] This story was the second to be added in 1555 to replace the scabrous, anticlerical tale of the priest who repents of his sins at the hands of a carver of religious objects (VIII.3). What Straparola does by way of appropriating intellectual property probably never entered his mind as an infraction, given that materials such as these moved freely among writers and collectors; such was the humanist way. Much as he assumed public-domain status for the folk tales he transcribed, he assumed the right to recycle Latin tales in the vernacular with or without elaboration as his fancy dictated. After all, Morlini could no more claim authorship for these vignettes than Straparola. This one can be traced back to the *Dialogus creaturarum* (late fourteenth century), as well as to *Le novelle antiche*, the compositor of which took this story from some such collection as Jacques de Vitry's *Sermones feriales et communes*, in circulation early in the thirteenth century, itself a collection of exempla undoubtedly containing materials derived

---

102 An anomaly is created here by placing this addendum story at the end of Night VIII, rather than in its published position in the revised edition, just before VIII.5 'The Donkey's Skin,' where it was told by Lauretta. This has been done to restore the order of the first edition of 1553.
103 *Les nouvelles de Girolamo Morlini*, trans. Fernand Caussy (Paris: Bibliothèque Internationale d'Édition E. Sansot, 1904), pp. 111–12.

from even earlier sources. Chaucer's wagon wheel may be the only means for distributing the credits equitably.

Needless to say, each new rendition offers modest variations upon a simple narrative that cannot otherwise be altered by much without losing its identity and purpose. There must be a monkey, stolen bags of money, and the animal's 'redistribution' of that money in proportion to the level of the commercial fraud, the performance of which is interpreted by the merchant as a form of providential punishment or ironic justice. At the centre of the tale is the adulteration of commercial goods, half wine and half water, or two-thirds milk and one-third water, and a monkey having a form of advanced intelligence – enough to allow that its handling of the money represents a kind of intuited justice. Inversely, the tale is a beast fable in which a monkey mimicking the merchant accidentally performs an act more meaningful than it can possibly imagine. It is the merchant who brings to bear in his mind the occult or providential interpretation. Without such a world view on his part, shared by readers and auditors, the story is useless to Christian moralizers.

Straparola made his own contributions to the story, modest though they are, that reveal something of him at his desk. He names Morlini's 'Ligurian merchant' Bernardo Fulgoso (Fregoso) and thereby associates him with the leading family of Genoa. He specifies that the wine he sells in Flanders is from Falisco, a region in the direction of Viterbo, that there was a scarcity in Flanders that drove up the price, that the merchant counted out his money in two sacks rather than one, that the monkey imitated him in dividing it up again in its own fashion, and that it does not toss the money down coin by coin, but all at once in the two sacks. Moreover, he remarks that 'the water received what had been paid for water,' and interprets Morlini's 'what is gained by the pipe will be lost by the tabor,' as 'what is momentarily enjoyed by this generation will be lost to the heirs.' These are slight but intelligent additions to a story that had been told formerly in far leaner fashion. Further elaboration could only detract from the spare, emblematic, and anecdotal efficiency required of this apologue.

It would stand to reason that Morlini took the story from *Il novellino* (Les cent nouvelles antiques; or The hundred old tales), and possibly he did, although the work was in limited manuscript circulation before 1525, when one hundred of the tales were chosen by Carlo Gualteruzzi for publication in Bologna. This is some five years after Morlini published his *Novellae*. In this version, the merchant has trick barrels with wine above and below, but water in the middle. Thus, he doubles his profit and quickly sets out to sea. By the will of God, a huge monkey (bertuccio) appears and takes the money to the top of the mast. The merchant attempts to coax it down, but the monkey opens the bag with his mouth and begins to toss down the coins, one on deck, one into the sea, until only that portion corresponding to a fair profit remains. This version, originating as early as 1281 to 1300 (corresponding to the earliest surviving manuscripts), preserves all the economy of a sermon exemplum and may indeed have been the model for many an elaboration, although in its own right it is pared down from a fuller representation that precedes it by almost a century.[104]

By the same token that Morlini would appear to be in debt to *Il novellino*, this anonymous collection, for this particular story, would appear to be in debt to the *Sermones feriales et communes* of Jacques de Vitry (1170–1240), the celebrated bishop of Acre. This collection contains 107 exempla accompanying the sermons that were segmented out in later years and circulated separately.[105] The tale is there represented as an outgrowth of the pilgrimage tradition to the shrine of St James in Santiago de Compostela, for that was the ship's destination. And because the commercial voyage begins in Acre, we may suspect that Jacques de Vitry makes a nod to his own travels while turning the story into a miracle inspired by the famous saint who punishes the merchant for selling adulterated wine to the pilgrims. The monkey makes off with the bags, takes them aloft, then removes coins from the sack and smells them before

---

104 *The Novellino*, trans. Roberta L. Payne, intro. Janet L. Smarr (New York: Peter Lang, 1995), 136, a story attributed, in the annotations, to Jacques de Vitry's *Sermones feriales et communes*. See also *Les cent nouvelles antiques ou le livre du beau parler gentil*, trans. Charles-Albert Cingria (Lausanne: L'Age d'Homme, 2004), 203. This title reflects the name of the work given to the collection for the famous Florentine printing by the Giunti in 1572: *Libri de novelle e di bel parlar gentile*. See also Sebastiano Lo Nigro, ed., *Novellino e conti del duecento* (Turin: Unione tipografico-editrice, 1968), no. 97, 'Come uno mercante portò vino oltremare in botti a due palcora, e come li 'ntervenne,' pp. 207–8.

105 *Die Exempla aus dem* Sermones feriales et communes *des Jakob von Vitry*, ed. Joseph Greven (Heidelberg: C. Winter, 1914), no. 102, 'De symea que denarios proiecit in mare' (The monkey who threw coins into the sea), pp. 60–1. Manuscripts of this work are to be found in Liège, Paris, and Brussels. The story occurs in the thirteenth-century manuscript in the Bibliothèque Nationale, MS. Lat. 18,134, no. 30, 'De symia que denarios projectit in mare' (Of the monkey who throws coins [denarios] into the sea). It can also be found in *Medieval Tales and Stories: 108 Prose Narratives of the Middle Ages*, trans. Stanley Appelbaum (Mineola, N.Y.: Dover Publications, 2000), 56.

throwing them into the sea. (The English translator names the tale 'Stinking Money.') After a time, the sailors chase the creature down and return the bag to the merchant, whereupon, after inspection, he realizes that not one coin remains that he had taken from the pilgrims, for as ill-gotten pelf the saint made them reek in the monkey's nostrils and so be cast away. When this became common knowledge, it was accepted as a miracle whereby the saint reveals his intolerance for dishonest money among those in his service.

Even if Jacques de Vitry was not the source of the three sequels described above, but was himself a borrower from a common folk tale, his story provides evidence of a tradition of some four century's standing by the time it comes to Straparola, a tradition likely to have been far more widely varied and disseminated than these scant few texts would indicate.

A variant upon De Vitry's version appears in a work nearly contemporary with Straparola's, namely, Johannes Pauli's *Schimpf und Ernst*. There the story pertains to a pilgrim to Jerusalem and the Holy Sepulchre.[106] On the return voyage a monkey steals his purse, makes its escape, and tosses one coin out of three into the sea. The man gathers up what remains on deck and recounts his adventure to his wife upon his arrival. It is she who pronounces the miracle, for she recognizes in the monkey's partitioning of their wealth a just punishment for having adulterated the milk she sells with one-third water. God did not desire that the husband should be a pilgrim in an unrighteous state: 'darumb so hat der aff den dritten pfennig in das mer geworffen' (that's why the monkey threw every third penny into the sea).

This story type seems to have exhausted itself by the end of the sixteenth century, although the outline survives in a poem by La Fontaine entitled, in English, 'The Miser and the Monkey.'[107] The miser lives on an island, where he counts his treasure in ostensible security until a monkey gets into the room and begins tossing coins out of the window into the sea. It desists only when it hears the miser's key in the lock. The moral is justly ironic: May God preserve all financiers whose money is handled in this fashion! That was, on the threshold of the Age of Enlightenment, as much of a moral as could be harvested. For Straparola's purpose, the survey may end here. Our author chose out for slight enhancement a

---

106 Johannes Pauli, *Schimpf und Ernst*, ed. Hermann Österley (Literarischer Verein, 1866; reprint, Amsterdam: Rodopi, 1967), no. 375, pp. 228–9.

107 To be found in any critical edition of his complete works or fables. I read it in *Fables of La Fontaine*, trans. Elizur Wright (Boston: Weeks, Jordan & Co., 1839).

popular sermon exemplum that appears to have belonged more to clerics, collectors, and *novellieri* than to the folk, and that carried as its common denominator an intuition concerning justice and punishment during an epoch in the history of mentalities that endorsed occult causes, correspondences among all things in the natural and supernatural worlds, and the mysterious expressions of providence through extraordinary events. For the guilty, mere monkeyshines become an instrument of an ethical universe shot through with hidden purpose.

The Ninth Night

The humid shadows of the dusky night were already beginning to spread over the parched earth and the sweet birds had softly gone to sleep in their nests amid the leafy branches of the trees, when the delightful and honourable company of ladies and gentlemen, setting aside all their troublesome thoughts and cares, made its way to the customary rendezvous. After certain graceful dances had been measured with stately step, the Signora gave command that the vase should be brought out and the names of five of the ladies placed inside. Of these, the first to be drawn was Diana [new to the company], the second Lionora, the third Isabella, the fourth Vicenza, and the fifth Fiordiana. Then the Signora signalled her wish, that before the storytelling began the five of them should sing a canzonetta to the accompaniment of their *lironi*. Hence, with joyful faces and a demure manner, they began their song in these words:

> Forsaken flowerets pale,
> Who needs you now to rise in flowery pride?
> Why are our ladies' looks thus cast aside?
> Our lights decay and fail,
> And dimmed the sun which kills all other ray,
> The blessed sun, which day by day
> Has lighted us by will divine,
> Just as that gracious face of thine
> Has granted to our eyes free course to gaze.
> Ah, hope so fleeting and malign,
> And love, why hast thou barred from us the sight
> Of that sweet face, and changed our day to night?

The innermost hearts of several in the company were touched by the hearing of this amorous song, provoking their sundry sighs. Yet everyone kept hidden from sight whatever secrets of love they held in their breasts. Then the gentle Diana, aware that it was her duty to begin the storytelling for that night, began without need for a second request.

IX. Fable 1
King Galafro's Vain Precautions

DIANA

Galafro, king of Spain, is persuaded by the words of a chiromancer who warned him that his wife would make a cuckold of him. He therefore builds a tower in which to keep her secure, but in the end he is hoodwinked by Galeotto, the son of Diego, king of Castile.

So you see, dear ladies, just as fidelity, which is so much a part of every honest woman's nature, deserves the praise and highest commendation from the mouths of all men, so its opposite, disloyalty, when it dominates a woman's character, merits only censure, universal castigation, and blame. The former stretches out her arms in all directions and is greeted by the entire world with the most cordial welcome and caresses, while the latter, by reason of her feeble gait and defective strength, finds it difficult to advance on her way, and hence comes to misery and is forsaken by all. Because it is my duty to begin the storytelling this evening, it has come into my mind to relate to you a fable that by chance may give you both pleasure and satisfaction.

Once upon a time there reigned over Spain a certain very powerful king named Galafro, a man of a most warlike temper, who, by his valour, conquered many adjacent provinces that he added to his dominions. When King Galafro had grown to be an old man, he took for a wife a young damsel by the name of Feliciana. Truly, she was a very fair lady, very courteous in her manner, and fresh as a rose to look upon. By reason of her gentleness and gracious carriage, the king loved her exceedingly, taking thought of nothing else than how he might please her. One day it happened that the king found himself in idle conversation with a man widely reputed for his skill in chiromancy, and the thought came to him that he might have his hand read by this soothsayer to find out what things fortune held in store for him. Now this chiromancer, when he understood the king's wish, took hold of his hand and examined with the greatest care all the lines he could trace there. After considering them diligently, one and all, he stood silent and his face grew pale. The king remarked that the practitioner had nothing to say and that his face was all white and confused. Something of moment must have been discovered in the lines of his hand – something of a displeasing nature. But collecting his courage, he said, 'Good master, tell me straightway what this thing is that you've seen. Have no fear of any kind, because I'll cheerfully hear out whatever declaration you have to make.'

The chiromancer, assured by these words that he might tell what he had seen, without hesitation said, 'Sacred majesty, truly I'm sorely pained that I should have come here to speak of things that must give rise to sorrow and injury. But because you have encouraged me and allowed me to speak, I will reveal all I know to you. Please understand, O king, that the wife for whom you nourish so ardent a love will one day engraft your brow with horns, and for that reason it is necessary that you keep a very sharp and diligent watch over her.'

As soon as he understood the drift of these words, the king fell into a state more dead than alive, and when he had given strict orders to the chiromancer to keep the matter secret, he granted him permission to depart. In subsequent days the king became so haunted by this distressing thought that he pondered the chiromancer's revelation both day and night, studying the best course he should take to avoid the rocks of injury and ignominy that lay before him. So he made up his mind to shut his wife up tightly in a strong and massy tower, and there to have her carefully secured and watched – this he did without delay. Soon thereafter, the report spread throughout the country that Galafro the king had caused a stronghold to be built in which he placed his wife under the most jealous guard. But no one knew the cause of her imprisonment. This report came likewise to the ears of Galeotto, the son of Diego, king of Castile, who, when he had carefully deliberated upon all he had heard of the angelic beauty of the young queen, the advanced age of her husband, and the manner in which he compelled her to spend her days, keeping her shut up a close prisoner in a strong-built tower, he resolved to make an attempt to put a trick upon this king. In the end, his scheming led him to the fulfilment of his plans exactly according to his desire.

In order to carry out his project, Galeotto gathered together a great quantity of money and a store of rich materials and secretly set out for Spain. Having come to his destination, he took two rented rooms in the house of a certain poor widow. It happened one morning early that King

Galafro mounted his horse and, together with the whole of his court, went off to the hunt, intending to spend several days abroad. When this news became known to Galeotto, he set his enterprise right into motion. He first attired himself like a merchant, then selected many fine objects of gold and silver which were the prettiest to look upon, themselves worth a kingdom's ransom, and went forth from the house to exhibit his merchandise here and there throughout the city. At last, when he had come into the neighbourhood of the tower, he cried out over and over in a loud voice, 'If anyone wants to buy of my merchandise let him come forward.'

Now the handmaidens of the queen, when they heard the merchant shouting so loudly in the street, ran immediately to the window and looking down they noticed all the beautiful cloth he had with him embroidered with gold and silver in such a manner that it was a delight to gaze upon. The damsels ran straight to the queen and said to her, 'Oh Signora, just a short way from here there's a merchant going about with a quantity of the finest fabrics you've ever seen, wares hardly fitting for mere townsfolk, but for kings and princes and noblemen of high estate. Among them we have espied various items that are exactly fitted to your own use and enjoyment, all studded with gems and precious stones.'

With that, being most desirous of seeing these lovely wares, the queen pleaded with the keepers of the place to let the merchant enter. They, however, fearing greatly that they might be discovered and punished, were of no mind to consent to her request. The order placed upon them by the king was a weighty one, which to disregard would assuredly cost them their lives. Nevertheless, cajoled by the soft and winning speech of the queen and by the lavish promises made by the merchant, they at last gave him permission to enter. Having first made the due and customary obeisance to the queen, the merchant spread out the rich and prosperous wares before her eyes. The queen had a sprightly disposition and a rather bold temper, so that in noticing that the merchant was handsome and proper, she began to shoot darts from the crossbows of her eyes in order to rouse his amorous feelings. All the while this trader kept his eyes wide open, and by his looks told her with no uncertainty that he shared her thoughts, and that he was ready to give back love for love. After the queen had looked at a great number of his things, she said, 'Master merchant, your wares are truly very fine; that no one can deny. But among them all, this one pleases me the most, and I'd be happy to know the price you want for it.'

To this the merchant replied, 'Signora, there is no sum of money in the world that could purchase these things, but seeing that you nourish such a great desire to possess them, rather than sell them to you, I'm willing to give them if by such means I could be certain of winning your grace, which I value far above all other things.'

After hearing this magnificent and generous offer, and after considering the loftiness of mind that must have prompted it, the queen was assured that he was of no humble condition, but a man of the highest station. Therefore, turning towards him, she said, 'Good master, this speech you have just made is not the speech of a lowborn man, or of one who is given over to the search for profits, but shows in happy wise the magnanimity that rules over your kindly heart. Wherefore, however unworthy I may appear to be, I offer myself to you so that you may dispose of me according to your pleasure.'

When the merchant perceived how kindly the queen looked upon him, and that the whole affair was likely to come about just as he so ardently desired, he said to her, 'Signora, most truly you are the one firm and enduring support of my life. Your angelic beauty, joined to the sweet and kindly welcome you have extended to me, has bound me with so strong a chain that I find it vain to hope I shall ever again be able to free myself from it. I'm all afire with love for you. All the water in the world could never extinguish the ardent flames that consume my heart. I'm a wanderer come from a distant land for no other purpose than to look upon that rare and radiant beauty that raises you so far above every other living lady. As kindly and courteous as you are, should you take me into your favour, you would thereby gain a devoted servant whom you may employ as though a part of yourself.'

As soon as she heard these words, the queen was wholly overcome, seized with wonder that the merchant was taken by the flames of love. Then when she looked upon him and realized how well-favoured and graceful he was, and when she thought of her cruel wrong in being kept a close prisoner in the tower by her husband, she was entirely inclined to follow the flow of her desires. But before making an open acceptance, she added, 'Good master, the strength of love must indeed be mighty, seeing that it has brought me to such a pass that I seem to belong to you rather than to myself. Yet by the will of fortune, I am under the sway of another, and while I am content that the matter of our discussion should come to deeds, yet I must impose one condition, that the price of my compliance is that I keep for myself the wares that you have brought here.' When the merchant took note of the queen's acquisitiveness, he gathered up his costly merchandise and handed it over to her as a gift. For her part, the queen was overjoyed by the precious wares that the merchant had bestowed, proving that her heart was neither cold as a stone nor hard as a diamond. Then she took the young man by the hand and led him into a little adjoining chamber where she threw her arms around him and kissed and embraced him most fervently, whereupon the youth, drawing her towards him on the couch, threw himself down beside her and, putting aside all that stood in the way of his enjoyment, he turned towards her and in their close embracement they tasted together the sweetest joys known to lovers.

Now as soon as the merchant had accomplished all his desires, he made his way out of the chamber, demanding the queen to given him back the wares he had brought with him. When she heard his request, she was struck with amazement. Overcome with grief and incomprehension, she addressed him, 'Surely it does not become a noble-minded and liberal gentleman to demand the return of anything he has bestowed upon another in good faith. This is the way of children, for given their tender ages, they have no great store of sense or understanding. But to speak the truth, I'm in no mood to relinquish these wares of yours, insofar as you are a man of years and full understanding, being both wary and circumspect, and by no means in need of guidance.'

Much diverted by all this, the young man answered her, 'Signora, if you'll not give me what I ask of you and let me leave straightway, I'll not quit this place at all until the king has come back, and then his majesty, as the just and upright judge that he is, will either have the goods given back to me or pay me the fair price.'

Completely beguiled by the cunning merchant's words, the queen, although much against her will, gave back his wares, fearing that the king would return and find him there. After quitting the lady's presence he was about to escape the castle when the guards blocked his way demanding payment for the good office they had done him in letting him enter. The merchant didn't deny that he had promised to give them something, but the promise was made on the condition that he should sell his merchandise to the queen, or at least some part of it. Now, insofar as he had disposed of no portion of it whatsoever, he didn't consider himself bound to give them any payment, for in fact he was taking out with him the same goods he had brought in. Upon hearing what he said, the guardians became heated with anger and swore that on no account would they let him go out until he had paid his entry.

But the merchant, who was their master when it came to subtlety, answered them as follows, 'Good brethren, if it's your pleasure to stop me from leaving, forcing me to waste time here in waiting, I promise you I'll not budge from here until your king comes back. As a high-minded and just sovereign, he will give judgment on the question between us.'

Hearing that, the guardians threw open the doors of the castle and let the merchant go out at his pleasure, for they were most fearful that the king would return and, finding the young man there, would forthwith have them executed for disobedience. Having gotten free of the castle, leaving the queen inside in possession of more shame and vexation than costly wares, he began to pass through the streets crying in a loud voice, 'I know well enough all about it, but I have no mind to tell. I know well enough all about it, but I have no mind to tell.'

At that time King Galafro returned to the city from the hunt, and hearing the merchant's clamour from far away, he was greatly amused. When he came to the palace he went up to the tower wherein he kept the queen. Upon entering her apartment, instead of greeting her in his accustomed manner, he said in jest, 'Madam, I know well enough all about it, but I have no mind to tell' – words that he repeated several times.

When she heard this speech, the queen was seized by the thought that he spoke in earnest and not by way of jest, and stood as though she were dead. Then, trembling in every limb, she fell down at the king's feet, saying, 'O my lord and master! Know that I have been a false wife to you. Yet I beg you in your grace to pardon my heinous fault, although there is no manner of death which I don't deserve. Trusting in your mercy, I hope to win your forbearance and clemency.'

The king, who understood little of the queen's meaning, was most amazed and ordered her to rise to her feet and give him a full account of what was troubling her. Then the queen, with a trembling voice and copious weeping, like a person out of her wits, told him her adventure from beginning to end. Once he comprehended the matter, the king said to her, 'Be of good cheer, Madam, and stop this pitiful self-torment, for whatever heaven wills to be must come to pass without fail.' Then the king gave orders that the tower should be razed to the ground. Thereafter, he accorded full liberty to his wife to do whatsoever she wanted, and in that state they lived happily and joyfully together, while Galeotto, having triumphed in his scheme, returned to his home carrying all his goods with him.

The fable told by Diana in the words you've just heard greatly pleased everyone in the company, although they were much surprised by the ease and rapidity with which the queen was led to bring her hidden fault to light, holding that it would have been better to suffer death a thousand times than to bring so scandalous a disgrace upon herself. Yet fortune was kind to her, and the king kinder yet by his pardon and by the strength of the love he had for her in setting her at liberty. And now, to allow the other young ladies time to offer their recitations, the Signora gave word to Diana to propound her enigma. Hearing the Signora's commandment, she offered it in these words:

> Flying from their northern home
> Cruel white-clad wanderers come;
> Pitiless they smite to death,
> And rob the sons of men of breath.
> Round head and feet alike they spread,
> And men are whelmed beneath the dead.
> Here and there they take their flight;
> On every hearth the fire burns bright.
> And there men come and safe abide,
> Protected from the foe inside.

Diana's enigma was a source of great pleasure to all the listeners, some of them interpreting it in one fashion and some in another. But very few gathered its real meaning. Then Diana expounded it in these terms: 'This enigma of mine is intended to describe the white snow, which, coming from the north, falls down incessantly in large flakes and alights upon everyone – especially in the season of great cold, when there is no place to be found where men can shelter themselves from it.' As soon as she had set forth the meaning of her enigma with such expertise, Lionora rose from her seat, just beside Diana's, and in the following words made a beginning of her fable.

IX.1 Commentary

Despite the many familiar elements of this story – soothsayers predicting infidelity, jealous husbands, the consignment of wives to towers (or pumpkin shells) for safe-keeping, and the arrival of clever suitors who court them, gain entry, and seduce them – it does not appear to have a 'wholecloth' literary antecedent. Two of its motifs are not formerly associated with the many tales of ladies isolated in towers: the lover who gains entry by posing as a merchant selling his wares (although the motif is known in other contexts, Motif K1349.1.3); and the lover who retrieves the gifts he has bestowed by threatening to remain until the dreaded husband's return (the well-documented and widespread motif of 'the lover's gift regained,' Motif K1581). The creative agency responsible for putting them together may have been Straparola himself, or more probably the collective oral tradition from which the tale was surely derived. The latter supposition is supported by the motivic transitions characteristic of the folk tale and by the survival of the narrative combination among the oral tales of the nineteenth century. Nevertheless, the introduction of the *burla* or practical joke of the merchant-lover who retrieves his gifts into the stock romance of the lady imprisoned in a tower troubles its characteristic ethos of suffering and devotion. Why would the lady liberated by love manifest such an acquisitive nature that her honour appears lost in an exchange for gaudy trinkets? And why would a gallant prince, after so great a show of affection and magnanimity, stoop to take back his merchandise? Either this story is thematically savvy and self-aware, deconstructing its own romantic facade through mutual exploitation and trickery brought to situational blackmail amid hollow and bankrupted sentiments, or the tale, in its impromptu combination of motifs, simply lost track of itself.

The central plot belongs to the generic consciousness of the species – both the construction and the destruction of the prison of love. The male, on the whole, does not wish to share the favours of the woman who has pledged herself to him alone. Perhaps it is a question of pride tending towards right of ownership, or of a biologically engineered disinclination to invest personal resources in raising other men's children. Hence, the tower is the external manifestation of a male psychological state, an objective correlative to jealousy and insecurity, often exacerbated by false reports and gossip, or a wife's innocently flirtatious nature (*The Winter's Tale*), or the indifferent bestowal upon all alike of that special regard the husband would have reserved for himself ('My Last Duchess'). Nevertheless, compulsive jealousy is also an unhappy instinct when it is not mitigated by mutual trust. Comedy may ensue from the destruction of the tower, but it is the rarer denouement. The paradigm of women consigned to towers as a means to enforce purity no doubt correlates to mentalities older than history itself. But it found renewal or confirmation in the medieval European imagination through the very real challenge of securing women in family residences that also served as manned military fortifications. The medieval keep as home, citadel, and feudal headquarters, was a potential prison for women both when the retainers and militia of the liege were in residence and when they were away on missions. That historical reality was a legacy ready-made for literary and psychological interpretation.

One of the inevitable projects of romance was to imagine the energies of desire extended across barriers, carried by looks, gestures, letters, and messengers, if only because there is something that does not love a wall, followed by entry into the guarded sanctum. Nearly all the conventional means are represented in Straparola's own stories: digging underground from castle to castle ('Erminione and Filenia,' IV.2), the lover transformed into a bird who then flies in through the window ('Fortunio, the King's Daughter, and the Mermaid,' III.4), an intruder disguised as a merchant in the manner of Doralice's father – a potential model for the lover in the present story – or entry to the lady's chamber inside a coffer or large work of art ('Doralice,' I.4); or carried out (as in 'The Physician's Wife,' IV.4). These are risky ventures of liberation and self-testing necessitated by destiny and love's imperative. They demonstrate once again that all prophylactic measures are futile, that love will have its way, and that whenever the lady turns wayward in spirit, no tower will suffice, no matter how meticulously contrived, to keep her safe from alien seed. It is an early demonstration of Arnold Toynbee's law that where 'superior' civilizations have built walls to separate themselves from barbarians seeking their wealth and lifestyle, negotiations and exchange always ensue through which the outsiders, in increasing numbers, will establish themselves as insiders until the floodgates are opened. Inversely, the psychological tower of jealousy is deemed so unacceptable to these authors that their sympathy lies entirely with the lovers in opposition to all ethical, marital, and material considerations. In this account, however, although a breach is made and the tower compromised until it is destroyed, love itself falls far short of its affective heights in the purest and most devoted hearts. The aristocrat-cum-merchant lover is something of a cad. That may give hope, after all, to the liberal-spirited husband.

In Marie de France's 'Lai of Yonec' a rich, old man with the intention of begetting children marries a young and aristocratic beauty. The couple proves barren, however, and for safe-keeping the lady is incarcerated in a tower where she is watched over daily by the old man's widowed sister. There she lives a life of misery for seven years until one day, as she laments her narrow state, a bird flies in at her window with the capacity of converting itself into a handsome man. The tale revels in their burgeoning love, the delicate longing, the secret hope, until the lover is caught in a trap set by the cruel and suspicious husband.[1] Johannes de Alta Silva, in his *Dolopathos*, tells the story of the philosopher who takes

---

1 *The Lais of Marie de France*, trans. Glyn Burgess and Keith Busby (London: Penguin, 1986), pp. 86–93.

a wife. Forewarned that women are treacherous and hardly suitable for those determined to live the life of philosophical contemplation, he builds a stone tower with only one door and one small window. There he keeps her in security, carrying the only key 'under his head.' But the futility of his precautions is proved when through that tiny window she makes eye contact with a young lover who reciprocates her desire and honours her need for secrecy. When at last she is able to get the philosopher drunk, she runs off to her lover, but returns too late to prevent her husband from barring the door against her. Mindful of an old trick popular with *Fastnachtsspiele* writers, the wife threatens to drown herself in the well, then throws in a large stone in order to draw her husband out of the house. While he attempts to save her, she runs inside and reverses the circumstances by accusing him of everything of which she had been accused. Seeing the futility of enforced chastity, he too tears down the tower and gives his wife complete freedom.[2] He who would keep a wife by placing her in a tower inevitably learns that desire has no hindrances and the means to union no lets. Therefore, it is wiser to enlist fidelity by showing trust and by razing the walls. In the process of moralizing, however, these tales tell of the erotic imperative, the passion for freedom, and the wiles of lovers to deceive their guardians. Our imaginations are given flight by theirs in a narrative economy that generates empathy for the illicit lovers, justified by the tyranny of jealousy.

The prototype for all of these stories is 'Inclusa' (The confined woman), disseminated to medieval readers in the collection entitled *The Seven Sages of Rome*. It contains a quality of the *fabliau* in its deception of a jealous husband, the *castia-gilos*, when a passing knight sees the lady's plight, befriends her husband, even fights for him in battle, and earns permission to build a keep of his own beside the lady's tower.[3] He gains his access to the sequestered dame by hiring a mason to build a tunnel between the two houses. Thereafter, the two lovers not only disport themselves during regular visits, but grow braver in their appearances together at banquets at which her husband is among the guests. Well may the husband be seized by suspicion and race back to her room, but never

---

2 'The Well' in *Dolopathos, or The King and the Seven Wise Men*, trans. Brady B. Gilleland (Binghamton, NY: Medieval & Renaissance Texts & Studies, 1981), pp. 78–9.

3 This story has already received attention, along with several others in a similar vein, in the commentary above on 'Erminione and Filenia, or the Jealous Husband Outwitted' (IV.2).

does he arrive in time to find her absent, thanks to the secret passageway. Ultimately, he is duped into presenting his own wife in marriage, following which the lovers take flight to his ultimate chagrin. The story type is taken over by the unknown, thirteenth-century, Provençal author of *The Romance of Flamenca*. In this story, an underground tunnel connects Flamenca's baths with William's apartment. He disguises himself as a cleric who preaches to the husband even as he seduces his wife. The work is at once a satire on jealous husbands and a vindication of the troubadour ideal of love. Women are crafty and impossible to control. But the paradox of the work is that the husband tries to protect his wife from an illicit love that the poet approves, as though husbands have no legitimate right to obstruct the goals of *fin' amours*. It is a curious ethic that is also apparent in the present work.

Flamenca was anticipated or closely followed by the romance of *Jouffroi de Poitiers*, in which Lady Agnes of Tonnerre is kept in a tower, from which Geoffrey, in the disguise of a hermit, seeks to liberate her. He tells the Lord of Tonnerre that he must have little faith in God to treat his wife in such a manner. But his solemn preaching is all part of an elaborate seduction plot, for as soon as he gains his point with the husband he enjoys his day with the wife, and for some time thereafter, before remanding her fully to the care of her lord. This is not done, however, before there is a final banquet in which Sir Tonnerre is again deceived in the presence of his lady. These stories, with their origin in the *Book of Sindibad* and *The Seven Sages of Rome*, may serve as prototypes to all such tales of jealous husbands, ladies in towers, determined gallants, and ambiguous denouements, whether in the flight of the lovers or the destruction of the tower. How the story came to Straparola, however, remains speculative. The progression from well-established literary prototypes to transmission among the folk to renewed literary representation in the *Piacevoli notti* is posited largely on circumstantial and stylistic grounds. The exchange between literary and folk narratives had been fluid and frequent for centuries. While the core of the present tale belongs to the literary romance prototypically represented by 'Inclusa,' Straparola's own predilection for oral sources suggests his reliance here upon interim representations shaped by the folk imagination and memory – a supposition confirmed by the absence of literary versions specific to this tale, as well as by the narrative disposition of the story itself.

The oral heritage of this tale is potentially vast, with a regional distribution that has brought folklore specialists to claim its origin for their respective language groups. Teófilo Braga was certain of its Portuguese provenance, while François-Marie Luzel claimed it for the Bretons.[4] At the same time, the central narrative motif of the story, the rapid and secret mobility of the lady from her tower prison to the outside world and back again to the ultimate astonishment of her husband, who had thought to keep her mewed up beyond all recourse, lives on under altered circumstances in the 'Aventures du vieux calender' of Thomas-Simon Gueullette's *Mille et un quart d'heure*. Kalem, illegitimate son of a dervish, is nevertheless watched over carefully by his father, so that when the boy's jealousy of his beautiful wife Dgengiari-Nar renders the girl's life miserable, the dervish employs the same secret tunnel between the convent and the boy's house that he once used to consort with Kalem's mother to effect his cure. The girl is mysteriously conveyed from her bedroom to the convent where, disguised as a visiting dervish, she is presented to her husband. Kalem, tormented by the resemblance, seeing even his wife's birthmark on the young dervish's ear, races home several times only to find her there, always ahead of him by dint of the secret tunnel. Through such excess of feeling, he makes a fool of himself and vows to conduct himself with more measured emotions once the entire plot is revealed. That Gueullette had borrowed so unabashedly from Straparola on several former occasions encourages the supposition that this story was likewise inspired by the *Piacevoli notti*.[5]

The motif of the mean-spirited lover who reclaims his gift was equally widespread and enjoyed a folk and literary tradition of its own quite independent of the liberation of a queen from her tower-prison. The version best known to students of English literature is Chaucer's 'The Shipman's Tale,' involving a merchant, a monk, and the merchant's wife. The wife complains of her terrible life, the monk gives comfort, she borrows of him 100 gold francs out of dire necessity, and pays in the flesh, while the shrewd monk borrows the same sum from her husband and then betrays the wife by telling the husband that he had repaid the francs to her.[6] The poor wife is obliged to pay the sum a second time in the

---

4 Teófilo Braga, *Contos tradicionaes do povo portuguez*, 2 vols. (Porto: Magalhães et Moniz, 1883), no. 3; François-Marie Luzel, *Contes populaires de la Basse-Bretagne*, ed. Françoise Morvan, 3 vols. (Rennes: Presses universitaires de Rennes, 1996), vol. II, pp. 161–75.

5 Thomas-Simon Gueullette, *Les mille et un quart d'heure* (*Contes*), ed. Jean-François Perrin (Paris: Champion, 2010), vol. I, pp. 560–72.

6 *Chaucer's Major Poetry*, ed. Albert C. Baugh (New York: Appleton-Century-Crofts, 1963), pp. 334–40.

flesh, this time to her husband. This is but one version of a folk motif known as 'the lover's gift regained,' which has received considerable study in the names of Chaucer and Boccaccio by John M. Spargo.[7] Albert Baugh speculates that Chaucer's source 'was probably an Old French *fabliau* which has not come down to us.'[8] The story appears concurrently in Boccaccio's *Decameron* as the first story of the eighth day and again in the *Novelle* of Sercambi, no. 19. But the version that most attracts attention here is found in Philippe de Vigneulles, *Les cent nouvelles nouvelles*, a bitter little tale about the merchant who, among his wares, had a 'seriz' for combing hemp and wool that was much desired by a jolly young house- wife, but for which she lacked the means to pay. After some verbal sport, it is made clear by the merchant's hands on her haunches that there was a substitute for cash. To this, the jolly wife acquiesced and the merchant went away, leaving his carder behind. But miser that he was, the pleasure turned paltry as he thought of his lost profits, which thought brought him once again to the hussy's door, there to shout in a high voice audible to her husband that she either had to pay for the carder or give it back. The husband arrives and in an accusatory tone interrogates his wife over such a purchase without payment, putting her in such fear for her honour that she was easily brought to return the instrument and abide her loss.[9] This story, different in its details yet similar in its manner and motifs to the present tale, nevertheless precludes direct literary transmission insofar as the sole surviving manuscript in which it is contained, dating to 1515, was first published only in 1972. Hence, again, the existence of a widespread oral tradition becomes the only explanation for the resem- blances between de Vigneulles and Straparola, the distance between times and places accounting for the story's variants.

---

7 *Chaucer's Shipman's Tale: The Lover's Gift Regained*, no. 91 of the *Folklore Fellows Communications* (Helsinki: Suomalainen Tiedeakatemia, 1930).

8 *Chaucer's Major Poetry*, p. 334, notes.

9 *Les cent nouvelles nouvelles*, ed. Charles H. Livingston (Geneva: Droz, 1972), no. 71, pp. 286–8. Nicolas de Troyes also offers a version in *Le grand parangon des nouvelles nouvelles*, concerning which see Krystyna Kasprzyk, 'Le motif du "don récupéré par l'amant" chez Nicolas de Troyes,' *Kwartalnik Neofilologiczny* 5 (1958), p. 187.

IX. Fable 2
Rodolino and Violante,
or the Broken Hearts

LIONORA

Rodolino, son of Lodovico, king of Hungary, becomes enamoured of Violante, the daughter of Domitio, a tailor. When Rodolino dies, Violante grows distraught by her immoderate grief and falls dead in the church upon his dead body.

If the passion of love is guided by the spirit of gentleness, modesty, and temperance, it seldom fails to run a prosperous course. But when it delivers itself over to the promptings of a voracious and inordinate appetite, it becomes a scourge to men and will often lead them to terrible and disastrous ends. In the final outcome of the brief homily I'm about to relate, you will see the reason for this.

I must begin by telling you, most gracious ladies, that Lodovico, king of Hungary, had an only son named Rodolino, and this youth, although he was still of tender years, was tormented nevertheless by the burning pricks of love. One day it happened, while Rodolino was standing at the window of his chamber and reminiscing upon the many events in which he had formerly taken great pleasure, his eye fell upon a maiden, the daughter of a certain tailor. Because of the girl's beauty, modesty, and gentle manners, he fell passionately in love with her, unable thereafter to find any rest. It was not long before Violante – for such was the maiden's name – found out the nature of Rodolino's love towards her, and on her side was as fired by passion for him as he was for her, so that when a season of time passed without catching sight of him she felt as though she would die. As this mutual affection between the two of them increased day by day, Love, who is always the faithful guide and sure light of every gentle soul, at last caused the maiden to take courage and let herself be engaged in conversation with Rodolino. The prince, by chance near the window and knowing all along that Violante fully returned his love, spoke to her in these words, 'Violante, you must surely know that my love for you is so great that nothing but the coming of a cruel and gloomy death could ever quell it in my heart. Your most laudable and gracious bearing, your sincere and modest manners, your lovely eyes that shine as brightly as the stars, and all the other excellencies with which you are so abundantly endowed, have drawn me on to love you so profoundly that I have resolved never to marry any other woman except you.' Now although Violante was young in years, she was astute in mind, and answered him that even if he loved her as ardently as he declared, yet she loved him even more dearly. Furthermore, she affirmed that her love was not to be compared with his, seeing that a man doesn't love with his entire heart, but is often light and vain in his passions and prone to lead even the most loving and devoted woman to a wretched end.

When Rodolino heard those words he cried out, 'Alas, my soul, don't speak in this way! Most certainly, if you yourself felt even one thousandth as much love as I bear to you, you would never use such hard words. And if you still find yourself unable to believe me, put me immediately to the test and then you'll learn whether I truly love you or not.'

Not long after, it happened that King Lodovico, the father of Rodolino, came to the knowledge of his son's passion for Violante, which grieved him deeply in his heart because he greatly feared some misfortune would follow that would bring reproach and disgrace upon his kingdom. So without giving a hint to Rodolino that he knew anything of the matter, he decided to send him travelling into various far-away countries in hopes that the lapse of time and long distance might cause him to forget entirely this inconvenient love of his. The king called his son into his presence and said to him, 'Rodolino, my son, you know that we have no other children but yourself, and that in the course of nature it is not likely that any others will be born to us, so that, after our death, the kingdom must fall to you as our rightful heir. Now in order that you may grow up to be a prudent and far-sighted man and in due time and place rule your kingdom wisely and well, I have determined to send you for a while into Austria were Lamberico – an uncle on your mother's side – currently resides. There you will also find many learned men, who, for love of us, will give you wise instruction. Under their care and discipline you will become a prudent and lettered man.'

When Rodolino heard these words of the king he was sorely dismayed and stood there as one stricken nearly speechless. 'My father, although it will cause me considerable grief and sorrow to be obliged to leave your presence, thereby depriving me of the company of my dear mother and of yourself, yet, if such be your pleasure, I will at once obey your command.'

When he heard the dutiful answer made by his son, the king wrote a letter soon after to Lamberico his brother-in-law in which he explained the entire matter, commending Rodolino to him as something as precious to him as his own life. The prince, after he had given his promise to obey his father's commands, grieved bitterly in silence. But seeing that he could not honourably go back on his pledged word, he determined to carry it out.

Before taking his departure from the city, however, he found an opportunity to speak face to face with Violante, hoping to instruct her as to how she should organize her life until his return, and how best they might maintain this great love between them. When they met, Rodolino said, 'Violante, in obedience to my father's wishes I am about to separate myself from you physically, but not in my heart, for there, wherever I am, I will always remember you. So I conjure you now, by the love which I've held for you in the past and hold for you now and always will till the end of my life, that you will never allow yourself to be joined in matrimony to any other man. For as soon as I return to this place, without fail I will make you my own lawful wife. In token of my flawless faith, take this ring and hold it ever dear to you.'

When she heard this sad news, Violante was almost ready to die of grief, but recollecting her wandering senses, she answered, 'My lord, would to God that I had never known you, for then I should not have fallen into the cruel situation in which I now find myself! But since it is the will of heaven and my fortune that you must leave me like this, I plead with you to at least tell me whether your stay abroad will be long or short, for supposing that you should stay for a long time, I might not be able to withstand the commands of my father should he wish me to marry.'

To this Rodolino answered, 'Violante, don't make yourself sad, but be of good cheer, for before a year runs its course you'll see me back again. And if, at the end of a year I do not return, I give you full permission to marry.' Having spoken these words with many tears and sighs, he took leave of her, and the next morning early he mounted his horse and set out for Austria, accompanied by a sizeable retinue.

Upon arriving at the end of his journey, he was honourably welcomed by his Uncle Lamberico. But in spite of this kindly reception, Rodolino remained downcast by the sorrow and lovesickness he felt in leaving behind his beloved Violante, nor could he find any solace for his grief, despite the concerted efforts of the young men of the court to provide him with all manner of pleasure and recreation.

Thus, Rodolino remained in Austria with his mind absorbed by his sorrow and the thoughts of his dear Violante until the year had come to an end without him being aware. As soon as he realized that all of the twelve months had rolled away, however, he begged his uncle's permission to return home to see his father and mother, a wish to which Lamberico acceded at once. When Rodolino returned to his father's kingdom, the king and queen made a jubilee of the occasion, but when the celebrations were over, rumours passed around the court that Violante, the daughter of Messer Domitio the tailor, was married. The king was greatly pleased, but Rodolino was plunged into the deepest grief, lamenting bitterly in his heart that he was himself the real cause of this cruel misfortune. The unhappy young man, finding himself the constant victim of misery and sorrow, and not knowing where to seek a remedy for this consuming passion, was on the brink of death.

But Love, who never neglects his true followers and always punishes those who break their vows, devised a means by which Rodolino was once more able to come into the presence of Violante. Without her knowledge, one night Rodolino silently entered the bedroom where she lay in bed with her husband and, having stealthily crept between the bed and the wall, he lifted the curtain, slipped quietly underneath, placing his hand softly on Violante's bosom. Having no thought that Rodolino was anywhere near, when she felt herself touched by someone other than her husband, she made as if she would cry out, which Rodolino checked by placing his hand over her mouth before telling her who he was. When Violante came to understand that the man beside her was truly Rodolino, she nearly went out of her mind, gripped by the fear that he might be discovered by her husband. As gently and discreetly as she could, she pushed him away from her and would not allow him to kiss her. But when Rodolino registered this action of hers, he was persuaded that his beloved mistress had forgotten him entirely, or had come to loathe him. Casting about in vain for some consolation in the dire and heavy sorrow that weighed upon him, he said, 'O cruel and proud one, contentment may soon be yours, for behold I am dying, and then you will no longer be vexed by the sight of me. Perhaps a time will come later when you will find yourself of a more pitiful mind and will be compelled to feel remorse for your present cruelty. Alas, is it possible that the great love that you formerly felt for me is now entirely fled?' While he spoke, he clasped Violante in a close embrace and ardently kissed her whether she wished it or not. Verily, so great was his passion that he began to feel his soul passing from his body, wherefore, collecting all his forces and uttering a deep and final sigh, he yielded up his wretched life as he lay by Violante's side.

As soon as this star-crossed girl knew he was dead, she felt as though her reason had left her, and only after a space of time was she able to deliberate with herself about what she should do to keep all knowledge of this sad mischance from her husband. Without making any disturbance, she let fall the corpse of Rodolino into the alcove beside the bed. Then, feigning to be disturbed by a dream, she shrieked aloud, straightway waking her husband from his sleep, who asked her what it was that caused this alarm. Violante, trembling in every limb and half dead with fear, told him that in her dream it was as though the king's son, Rodolino, had been lying by her side and had suddenly died in her arms. Then rising from her bed, she found the dead body still warm lying there in the alcove. When Violante's husband saw this strange thing that had come to pass, his thoughts were greatly troubled, for he was fearful that he might lose his own life on account of this luckless accident. But tossing aside his fears, he took the dead body of Rodolino on his shoulders, and without being seen by anyone, he went out of the house and laid it down at the gates of the royal palace.

As soon as the sad news had been taken to the king, he was on the verge of ending his own life, so great was his agony and anger. But when this frenzied affliction abated somewhat, he had the physicians called in to examine Rodolino's corpse in order to certify the cause of his death. After they had separately assessed the dead body, the physicians declared uniformly that he had met his death neither by steel nor by poison, but through sheer despondency. As soon as the king heard this, he gave orders for funeral rites to be arranged, directing that the corpse be carried into the cathedral and that every woman of the city, whatever her rank and condition, under pain of his high displeasure, should go up to the place where the bier was standing and kiss his dead son. Many of the city's matrons travelled there and, out of great pity, wept over the fate of the unhappy Rodolino, among whom was the wretched Violante. A desire had come over her to look once more upon the dead face of him to whom, when he was alive, she had refused the consolation of a single kiss. Once there, she threw herself down upon the corpse, feeling certain that he was now lying there dead from the great love he held for her, for which reason she was likewise determined to die. Thus, holding back her breath with all her force she passed away from this life without a word. The other women, when they grew aware of this unlooked-for event, ran to her aid, but all their efforts were in vain, for her soul had already departed from her body to seek out that of Rodolino her lover. The king, who was a party to the love subsisting between Violante and his son, kept the whole matter a secret, but gave orders that the two should be buried in a single tomb.

As soon as Lionora had completed her heart-rending story, the Signora made a sign that she round out her obligations with an enigma, which, without any hesitation, the damsel offered as follows:

> Left in peace I never move;
> But should a foe desire to prove
> His mettle on me, straight I fly
> Right over wall and roof-tree high.
> If driven by a stroke of might,
> I take, though wingless, upward flight;
> No feet have I, yet 'tis my way
> To jump and dance both night and day;
> No rest I feel what time my foe
> May will that I a-flying go.
> No end and no beginning mine,
> So strange my nature and design;
> And they who see me on the wing
> May deem me well a living thing.

The greater part of the listeners comprehended the meaning of this enigma, which, in truth, was intended to signify a ball, given that it is round in form, has neither end nor beginning, is attacked by the players as a foe, and is driven by them now here and now there, being struck by the hand. Then Isabella, to whom had been allotted the third place in the storytelling, rose from her seat and began to speak in the following words.

IX.2 Commentary

The unique quality of this love tragedy, concluding as it does in double death and mutual burial, is the pathological intensity of the lovers' emotions. At the narrative's centre are two catastrophic events that depend upon the power of desire and regret to overwhelm the life force itself. Rodolino will die of grief beside the beloved who is urging him away for the sake of her honour as a married woman. Yet on the following day, this married woman will expire in grief upon Rodolino's body lying in its casket. Such a story is by definition sensationalist, sentimental, and poignant for having conjoined eros with thanatos in a close causal sequence. Love and death now become, not opposites, but closely related drives in the eroticized imagination, and ultimately a single phenomenon when, by mysterious means, death replaces desire in the expiring lover. The 'love me or I die' of the poets, a form of rhetorical hyperbole, becomes fact in this story when Rhodolino whispers 'ecco che io moio,' raising the question whether it is indeed possible to die of erotic grief, for the story clearly illustrates the power of the emotions to destroy the body they have been programmed by selective adaptation to protect. This happens not once but twice during the story, creating the most sentimental of all symmetries, the perfection of love in mutual self-sacrifice. Such fine-tuned emotions, in a sense arriving at a state of eroticized climax, are the legacy of lovers inspired by *amour courtois*, now transferred by the *novellieri* to contemporary mercantile class settings, and most particularly by Luigi da Porto in the most famous of them all: *Giulietta e Romeo.*

Because Straparola's story deals with death by the power of the imagination over the life force, it functions, paradoxically, not only as extreme romance but as a medical 'case study.' Events, in order to be fictionally 'true,' must also be plausible, and for that reason must rely upon some phenomenological rationale. Such an analysis was provided in Renaissance medical treatises dealing with the psychosomatic repercussions of the diseases of the soul. Fear, sorrow, even joy in excess, were included as efficient causes of mortality. Accordingly, Rodolino, after he is deposited upon his mother's doorstep, is examined by physicians. Failing to find signs of violence upon his body, they declare him a victim of grief, thereby acknowledging professionally the notion of sudden death by sorrow. Medical thinkers taught generally that the passions could react as poisons in the blood, as burnt vapours, or as constrictors upon the heart. They explained the role of the humours in corrupting the brain, making excessive love itself a disease of the imagination. In circular fashion, compulsive thoughts could lead to despair and thus to suicide by slow starvation or more violent means. Jacques Ferrand, in his *Treatise on Lovesickness*, spoke of the love that 'gives rise to a pale and wan complexion, joined by a slow fever that modern practitioners call amorous fever, to palpitations of the heart, swelling of the face, depraved appetite, a sense of grief, sighing, causeless tears, insatiable hunger, raging thirst, fainting, oppressions, suffocations, insomnia, headaches, melancholy, epilepsy, madness, uterine fury, satyriasis, and other pernicious symptoms that are, for the most part, without mitigation or cure other than through the remedies for love and erotic melancholy, based on the teaching of Hippocrates toward the end of his book on the diseases of young women and in his book on generation.'[10] But to achieve mortal oblivion by merely lying down beside the unobtainable beloved was an even more occult event.

Searching for the causal link between extreme passion and death, Ferrand speculated that lovers' perturbations resemble those of historical persons who died of excessive joy, 'such as Polycrita of Naxos, Diagoras of Rhodes, Chilo the Lacedaemonian, the poet Sophocles and Dionysius, tyrant of Syracuse; or of sorrow, such as Publilius Rutilius, Marcus Lepidus, and Ely the high priest of the Jews; others of shame such as Homer, for failing to resolve the riddle of the fisherman, and Macrina, the wife of Torquatus, from an ardent desire to see a one-eyed Egyptian or Cyclops passing in front of her house during the absence of her husband.'[11] These are the exceptional but true cases in which emotions are the cause of fatality. But the substance of their explanation is typically sparse and deals in barely concealed metaphors pertaining to the rapid dilation of the heart, swellings, or surgings leading to massive systemic shutdown. Regarding the 'broken heart' as a medical precept, the physicians derived their assessments largely from just such histories as that of Rodolino and Violante.

John Ford, in a play entitled *The Broken Heart*, presents this elusive phenomenon as an act of consummate self-control over the vital force of life – a volitional withdrawal that might be elaborately staged and perfectly timed to full dramatic effect. His play illustrates a palpable

---

10 *A Treatise on Lovesickness*, ed. Donald Beecher and Massimo Ciavolella (Syracuse: Syracuse University Press [1623], 1990). In reviewing the literature, it is remarkable just how the medical philosophers talked around the problem, gave examples, cited the ancients, spoke of passions located in the body, making them subject to the debilities of the regions in which they resided, such as swellings and constrictions of the heart, but offered, in actuality, no substantial explanations for sudden death due to excessive passion, although belief in the phenomenon ran high. This paradox is difficult to avoid, for it is a koan of sorts to explain just how the defence mechanisms of the body can also destroy it.

11 Ibid., 228.

correlation between a devastating social impasse and a physiological disaster, self-administered in an ambience of stoic calm and deliberation.[12] Marguerite de Navarre offers a related example in *L'Heptaméron* of 'The piteous death of an amorous gentleman for want of comfort given too late by his beloved.' This story features a curious conflation of passions, for when the beloved allowed herself to be embraced by the nearly dead melancholiac, 'he caught her between his arms with such force that his feeble heart, unable to withstand the assault, abandoned all powers of movement. In that moment, joy so dilated and stretched it that this seat of the soul abandoned all life.'[13] Now the sudden reversal of passions from an extreme of sorrow to a glut of joy brings perfect consummation in death – the consonance between mind and body making an ultimate rhetorical declaration. Hans Wilhelm Kirchhof, in his *Wendunmuth* (1563), offers a similar tale of a young girl who dies for love when her father refuses to allow marriage to the man of her choice. He too describes how her power and inner spirit fail and her life force is drained from her body.[14] Baldasar Castiglione gives the example of a winsome girl of his own time who loves discretely but intensely a young man who returns that love in equal measure, both desiring to achieve their full happiness in marriage. Once more a cruel and ambitious father interferes, enforcing a marriage upon the girl that she endures for three years in the cruellest anguish imaginable. Slowly she wastes away and abandons her life, like Violante, faithful to her vows and refusing all the secret comforts she might have enjoyed.[15] Geoffrey Fenton was preoccupied more than

---

12 Ford's play epitomizes the conflict between emotional restraint as a marker of civility and political ceremony and the raw drives that motivate love and erotic cravings. Calantha, in the final dance, puts on a bold face of public courage, but is withering internally from her compounded griefs. Meanwhile, the play is shot through with medical references to melancholy and blood letting and 'bubbling life out' (V.ii.107). Calantha literally stages her own death of a broken heart while passing on the power to her successors in a public ceremony. *The Broken Heart*, ed. Brian Morris (London: Ernest Benn, 1965), *passim.*

13 Marguerite de Navarre, *L'Heptaméron*, ed. Gisèle Mathieu-Castellani (Paris: Garnier, 1999), no. 9, pp. 149–57. This story was also translated by William Painter: 'Of a Gentleman that Died of Love,' *The Palace of Pleasure*, ed. Joseph Jacobs (London: David Nutt, 1890; reprint, New York: Dover, 1966), no. 60, vol. II, pp. 107–12.

14 *Wendunmuth*, ed. Hermann Oesterley, 5 vols. (Tübingen: Litterarischen Verein in Stuttgart, 1869), bk. III, no. 224, vol. II, pp. 496–8; new ed. (Hildesheim: Georg Olms, 1980).

15 *The Book of the Courtier*, trans. Charles S. Singleton (New York: Doubleday and Co., 1959), bk. III, 43, pp. 245–7.

ever with the medical dimensions of grief in his rewriting and amplification of Boccaccio's story 'Girolamo and Salvestra' (IV.8). He describes fully how 'a vehement and inward grief of the mind' might 'close the pores and conduits of the vital parts of man.'[16] That one age deems such fatal crises more pathologically plausible than another is a point of interest, no doubt, but hardly intrudes upon our 'folk' appraisal of the remarkable human capacity for suffering and self-denial. Rosalind may well declare that 'men have died from time to time, and worms have eaten them, but not for love.'[17] But the present story reconfirms by example the power of the eroticized imagination to choose death over life in the absence of the beloved. Such 'histories' are memorable because they are rare, yet they invite belief, as with the famous pair from

16 *Bandello: Tragical Tales*, ed. Hugh Harris (London: George Routledge & Sons [1567], 1925), p. 119. A fuller account of the story will be given below. There are several related tales in which lovers sacrifice themselves for each other rather than permit themselves to be compromised by villains. One such is the 98th tale of the *Cent nouvelles nouvelles*, in which the lovers elope, find themselves unprotected and forcefully confronted in a hostel by four brigands intent upon raping the girl. After a valiant fight, the girl's protector is slain and she must either succumb to force or find a way to take her own life. By deceiving her ravisher, she is able to draw a small knife and cut her throat, not so much for love as to preserve her chastity in death and thus bring the tragic and moralized tale to a close. 'The Star-Crossed Lovers' in *The Hundred Tales*, trans. Rossell Hope Robbins (New York: Crown Publishers, 1960), pp. 357–61. That this version differs from the version discussed below, known to have been revised by Antoine de la Salle, provides evidence that he is not the author of *Les cent nouvelles nouvelles*, as has often been asserted. This story type is adapted and varied by Masuccio (1476), *The Novellino*, trans. W.G. Waters (London: Lawrence and Bullen, 1895), no. 31, vol. II, pp. 129–40, replicated by Nicolas de Troyes (1535–6), in *Le grand parangon des nouvelles nouvelles*, known only in MS (Paris: Bibliothèque nationale f.fr. 1510), no. 99, and literally translated by Malespini, *Ducento novelle* (Venice, 1609), I.58, pp. 161v–3v. Its origin is in the early-fifteenth-century tale of *Floridan et Elvide*, written in Latin by Nicolas de Clamanges – based on a historical event in Picardy. It was translated first by Antoine de la Salle's secretary, Rasse de Brunhamel (ca. 1456), then revised and shortened considerably by La Salle himself. Readers interested in the story of this French 'Lucretia' who escapes her fate at the hands of brigands by taking her life should consult the critical edition of the two mid-fifteenth-century versions by Brunhamel and La Salle by H. Peter Clive, *Floridan et Elvide* (Oxford: Basil Blackwell, 1959). In the version by Masuccio, differing from the others in significant ways, Martina and Loisi die at the hands of lecherous lepers, and Martina manages to stage her suicide whereby she will fall upon the body of her dead lover.

17 Shakespeare, *As You Like It*, ed. Alan Brissenden (Oxford: Oxford University Press, 1993), (IV.i.97–8), p. 191.

Verona whose balcony is still said to be there, or another pair whose tombs are seen today in the Church of San Pedro in Teruel.[18]

In this story, Straparola has turned away from his popular sources in the oral culture to reconfigure a 'novelistic' plot bearing a very particular resemblance to Boccaccio's tale of Girolamo and Salvestra in the *Decameron* (IV.8).[19] Both heroines are the daughters of tailors, but Straparola's hero is no longer a Florentine merchant's son brought up by his managerial mother, but the prince of Hungary. The prince is sent to Austria for a year, whereas Girolamo is sent to Paris on shop business. Even such minor adjustments alter interpretations. Boccaccio deals with a mother's

18 Other stories worthy of mention dealing with melancholic retreat, over-refined feelings, and unwavering devotion include Lilio Giraldi Cinzio's 'La leggiadra istoria di Zentile e Fedele' in ottava rima, closely imitated in a folk poem similarly named 'Finita la ligiadra istoria de Zentil e Fidele,' in Erhard Lommatzsch's *Beitrage zur älteren italienischen volksdichtung*, 3 vols. (Berlin: Adademie Verlag, 1950), vol. I, pp. 75–7. Fidele, in love with a married woman, finds himself repeatedly rebuffed and scorned. He retires from Bologna to a little hut in the forest. When this woman goes there in search of her son, she is bitten by a snake, taken to the hermit's hut, there cured, and again confronted by his love. But she stands firm in her resistance. Later, she falls ill and is carried to her house, where a dream of the future causes her to send for Fidele, who hurries back to Bologna disguised as a doctor. Yet the impasse between them lingers into the future as a pretext for exploring the most delicate of feelings on both sides. John Lyly might well have taken a page from this work in his creation of the hopeless love of Fidus for Iffida, faithful in her love for Thirsus, but willing to comfort Fidus in his melancholy lovesickness for her. Even when Thirsus is slain in the wars, she would not break off her devotion to his memory until she dies of a pestilential fever, causing her lover Fidus to withdraw himself from the court and to await his own death in her memory. It is a sustained story of delicate suffering for love and a mutual withdrawal from life into death. *Euphues and His England*, ed. Morris William Croll and Harry Clemons (London: George Routledge and Sons, 1916), esp. pp. 284–5.

19 Boccaccio's sources, and hence indirectly Straparola's, have been much debated. The sentiments of the lovers belong to the delicate turns of emotion associated with courtly love or *amour courtois*, on the presumption that Boccaccio took his story from a tale of love for a married woman that ended in honour for the husband but a double death for the lovers. The closest that might be suggested is the fourteenth-century Middle High German verse tale 'Frauen-Treue' (anon. or perhaps by Jansen Enenkel), which tells of prolonged desire, frustration, the knight's visitation of the citizen's wife in the middle of the night, the rupture of his tournament wounds received while fighting in her honour, his death, and hers to follow. It is generally thought that Boccaccio could not have known this *Minnesang*, but that he must have known something similar. See *Gesammtabenteuer*, ed. Friedrich Heinrich von der Hagen, 3 vols. (Stuttgart: Cotta, 1850), vol. I, p. 257.

interference and her devastating underestimation of love's power, for in breaking off an inconvenient relationship for the sake of her bourgeois aspirations, she cuts the cord of her son's life. Straparola, from the outset, paints a gloomier and more systematic tragedy insofar as Rodolino's first sentence to Violante foreshadows his 'cruel gloomy death,' and her reply expresses a love surpassing his, even 'to a wretched end.' The risk of disgrace is now the concern of a king, and while Straparola implies the father's responsibility, he is slower to lay blame, while styling love as a force of nature too strong to baulk.[20]

Both stories entail an awkward transition from the principled and pragmatic issues of the bedroom scene to the abject drama of the funeral. The refused kiss, the rejection necessitated by honour, the obligation to a loving husband, and the pragmatic concern over the disposing of the body in a way that will avert criminal implication is one ethos; the glut of passion and despair over the deceased and the quid pro quo of death for death on the final day is another. Straparola, more than Boccaccio, leaves that transformation of mentalities to innuendo. His Violante, moreover, does not quite die of a broken heart. She throws herself on the body of the beloved, holds her breath, and so expires. Despite the irrelevant fact that one can no more die from holding the breath than one can be heard while shouting through outer space, this is an act of suicide, although perhaps no less touching. Boccaccio's Salvestra, in this matter, is more nuanced and enigmatic, 'for the heart of this woman, which the prosperous fortune of Jeronimo (Girolamo) could not pierce, now in his wofull death split in sunder; and the ancient sparks of love so long concealed in the embers, brake foorth into a furious flame; and being violently surprised with extraordinary compassion, no sooner did she come neere to the dead body, where many stood weeping round about it; but strangely shrieking out aloud, she fell downe upon it: and

---

20 There is nothing of sufficient particularity about this story to suggest that it relies for its inspiration upon the many Eastern (Sanskrit) stories that tell of mutual suicide for love. One such story is 'Of the Merchant's Daughter Who Fell in Love with a Thief,' in the *Katha sarit sagara, or Ocean of the Streams of Story*, trans. C.H. Tawney, 2 vols. (Calcutta, 1880; New Delhi: Munshiram Manoharlal, 1992), vol. II, pp. 492–7. Seeing the thief on the way to his death by hanging, the girl falls in love and demands him as her lover. When the officials refuse, she immolates herself with his body. The explanation given is that 'creatures are completely dependent upon connexions in previous births' which alone could explain her behaviour: undoubtedly they had been married in their previous lives, for which reason it became her destiny to be his wife again.

even as extreamity of greefe finished his life, so did it hers in the same manner. For she moved neither hand nor foot, because her vitall powers had quite forsaken her.'[21] Boccaccio modulates the moods, creates a spontaneous death, and acknowledges the symmetry imposed by a sense of obligation. Violante resorts to a dream routine as a vehicle for informing her husband that her lover is dead beside the bed, whereas Boccaccio's heroine posits her true situation as a hypothetical one in order to test her husband's response. Assured that she would not be held accountable, she made the truth known by revealing the body. Violante's strategy takes more of that communication for granted.

In one important detail, Straparola makes a significant advance over his source. He interpolates an impassioned speech by Lodovico as he lies beside his beloved – impassioned, yet *sotto voce* to be sure: 'O cruellest proud one, look how I am dying. Be content that soon you will no longer have to look upon this nuisance. Perhaps later you will have more pity and feel compelled to blame yourself for your hard-heartedness. Alas! is it possible that the great love that one time you held for me has now completely fled?'[22] Straparola, with this plaintive note, has ratcheted up the lament. But in this too he appears to have found inspiration, for the passage may be compared with the following from Sannazaro's *Arcadia* in the eighth prose section: 'O most cruel and pitiless more than surly bears, harder than aged oaks, and to my prayers more deaf than the wild murmurings of the swelling sea! See how you win at last, see how I die; rest content that you will no longer have the annoyance of seeing me. But verily I trust that your heart, which my good fortune has not been able to move, will yield to my wretched misfortune; and, all too late grown piteous, you will be perforce constrained to find fault with your harshness, feeling desire at least to view in death him whom living you have not wished to pleasure with a single word. Ay me, and how can it be that

---

21 Giovanni Boccaccio, *The Decameron*, trans. Edward Hutton (1620) (New York: Heritage Press, 1940), p. 224. For a further perspective on the passions expressed in this story, see Valter Puccetti, 'Girolamo, Salvestra e l'inferno degli amori del *Decameron*,' *Studi sul Boccaccio* 20 (1991–2), pp. 85–129.
22 My translation from *La piacevoli notti*, ed. Donato Pirovano (Rome: Salerno, 2000), vol. II, p. 582: 'O crudelissima fiera, ecco che io moio! contentati che più non avrai di vedermi fastidio; e tardi divenuta pietosa, di biasmare la tua durezza a forza costretta sarai. Ohimè! e come può essere che 'l lungo amore che un tempo mi portasti, sia ora in tutto da te fuggito?' These words are drawn verbatim from the longer passage in the *Arcadia*.

the long love that I am certain you bore me at one time should be now altogether fled from you?'[23] The language of pastoral has made an entrance, increasing both drama and feeling, while testifying to the diversity of Straparola's reading. A new discourse of the heart, tender and plangent, generated in the image of the amorous shepherd, was now at Straparola's disposal. That same appeal to the cruel one for pity after the fact is replicated in the canzonet sung by the Trevisan and Molino on the eve of the twelfth soirée.

There is little more to be said of Straparola's tale, once it has been profiled as his 'Romeo and Juliet,' for in the afterlife of the narrative, it is the Boccaccian version that holds sway. Arguably, that afterlife of his source is confirmation of Straparola's choice and tastes, and provides a repertory of analogues for the story type in general. Yet there is need for brevity. Bandello, in part I of his *Novelle*, in the story of Galeazzo and Lucrezia offers a pronounced variation, equally distanced from Boccaccio and Straparola, the latter of whom, in any case, is unlikely to have known or been known to Bandello (1480–1565), given that Bandello composed many of his *novelle* early in his career, yet did not collect and edit them until quite late.[24] The setting is a town in the territory of Milan at the

---

23 Jacopo Sannazaro, *Arcadia & Piscatorial Eclogues*, trans. Ralph Nash (Detroit: Wayne State University, 1966), pp. 82–3. 'O crudelissima e fiera più che le truculente orse, più dura che le annose querce, et a' miei preghi più sorda che gli insani mormorii de l'infiato mare! Ecco che vinci già, ecco che io moio; contèntati, che più non avrai di vedermi fastidio. Ma certo io spero che 'l tuo core, il quale la mia lieta fortuna non ha potuto movere, la misera il piegherà; e tardi divenuta pietosa, sarai constretta a forza di biasmare la tua durezza, desiderando almeno morto di veder colui, a cui vivo non hai voluto di una sola parola piacere. Oimè, e come può essere che 'l lungo amore, il quale un tempo son certo mi portasti, sia ora in tutto da te fuggito?' *Arcadia di Messer Giacomo Sannazaro* (Venice: n.p., 1548), p. E1v.

24 Matteo Bandello, *Tutte le opere*, ed. Francesco Flora (Milan: Mondadori, 1934), pt. I, no. 20, vol. I, pp. 196–200. Part I, no. 33 may be even closer, for it tells of the love of Livio for Camilla, how he dies in her embrace, and how she falls dead on his body. It is the community, touched by their mutual sacrifice for love, which insists on their burial in a common tomb in Casena. This story emphasizes the emotions aroused by an impossible love and their capacity to overwhelm even the instincts for survival. Belleforest translated this story into French and there Geoffrey Fenton found it for translation into English for his *Certain Tragical Discourses*, published as *Bandello: Tragical Tales* (1567), ed. Hugh Harris (London, George Routledge and Sons, 1925), pp. 118–56. Fenton expands the story largely through the creation of drawn-out speeches expressing the most subtle conflicts and transformations of

time of the last great Sforza. A widowed mother busies herself with collecting debts due to her late husband and raising her son to a better future. The boy is sent to Venice on one such debt-collecting mission, and in nearby Padua, while staying with his father's friend, he not only falls in love with his host's fifteen-year-old daughter, but has her abducted by his attendants, while he remains behind to confirm his alibi. She is placed in the care of the boy's old nurse and her husband. Upon his return, Galeazzo regularly slips away to spend time with her in secret for some three years before his mother presses him to marry. Suspecting interference, she then sets spies, has Lucrezia abducted and taken to a monastery, and watches as her son sinks into grief and despair. At last the mother confesses to her deed, promises to bring Lucrezia back and, good to her word, the two lovers are reunited. But because the girl's honour could now be questioned, given the time she has been out of sight, a violent fit of jealousy overcomes Galeazzo – arising indirectly from his mother's meddling. He therefore stabs the beloved on the spot, then stabs himself and falls dead on her corpse – whether for love or justice. The story closes as the proud mother, unwilling to make public the cause of their demise, nevertheless buries them together, yet reports them dead of the plague. The narrative is a splendid exercise in inter-textuality, whether the implicit relationships are due to debt or accidental similitude. Boccaccio's story type seems to linger in Bandello's, despite the displacements, and reveals how something new can arise from some-thing old, whether from true inspiration or to disguise a debt. But the protagonist's murderous pang of jealousy hard upon his grief over the presumed death of his beloved provides a non sequitur that only better hermeneutes can bridge.

There are further sequels to Boccaccio's tale of Girolamo and Salvestra, including John Quarles's *The unfortunate lovers, or the history of Girolamo and Salvestra: A tragical tale*, and no. 38, 'Hieronimus hatte lieb eine jung-frau gennant Silvestra' (Jerome loves a young woman named Silvestra) in the *Schwankbücher* (1557–66) of Martin Montanus, in which the hero grew up with the tailor's daughter but was sent away by his mother to pre-vent so unequal a union. In the end, his body was placed at his mother's

---

feelings that lead by degrees to death. Fenton, paradoxically, surrounds their story with the language of medicine and morality, calling their relationship an 'infection' that leads to 'ruin and decay,' himself refusing in his commentary to acknowledge the terrible beauty of it all. Such madness must be restrained, making of Livio and Camilla a cautionary tale, no doubt in keeping with Tudor expectations.

door, as in the present tale.[25] Add to this Hans Sachs's 'Historia' (1544), Nicholas de Troyes's version in *Le grand parangon*, no. 98, Barnabe Riche's story of 'Livio and Camilla' in *A Right excellent and pleasaunt dialogue, betwene Mercury and an English souldier*, George Turberville's *The Unfortunate lovers, or the history of Girolamo and Sylvestra, a tragical tale* (1587), Parabosco's *Diporti* (I.4), and John Payne's 'Salvestra,' and that should sufficiently top up the Boccaccio legacy for comparative purposes.[26]

But perhaps the most intriguing is the 'prequel' of the two lovers who lived in the city of Teruel in Aragon, where they died and were buried in our Lord's year, 1217. Their names were Diego de Marcilla and Isabel de Segura, both of prosperous merchant families. They were much in love from adolescence, but the hard times that overwhelmed the Marcilla family placed Diego on probation, so that if his fortune was not recovered within five years, there would not be any marriage. The girl held out against her father for the critical period, but when the time lapsed, she was married to Don Pedro de Azegra. Two days later Diego returned in financial triumph, only a tad late, and demanded his due. The miscounted days brought him to immediate sorrow. That night he crept into the couple's room and waited for them to fall asleep before waking Isabel to plead for her love. Unable to prevail or to separate himself from her, he died at her feet. Isabel shivered. Thereafter, she proposed an exchange of stories whereby she informed her husband hypothetically of her dilemma. Reassured – the husband suspecting nothing – nicely she placed his hand on the cold lover's breast. Rather than returning the body to his home, they arranged for a secret burial to avoid suspicion. Yet most equivocally there is also a public funeral, as in Boccaccio, and in macabre fashion Isabel made an appearance in her wedding gown, kissed the man she had formerly refused to kiss, and died. They too were

---

25 John Quarles, *The unfortunate lovers* (London: W.O., 1700; J. Howe, 1706). Copies of either edition are extremely rare. Martin Montanus, *Schwankbücher*, ed. Johannes Bolte (Hildesheim: Georg Olms, 1972), pp. 95–102.

26 Nicolas de Troyes, *Le grand parangon des nouvelles nouvelles*, this story in manuscript only (Paris: Bibliothèque nationale f.fr. 1510), no. 98; Barnabe Riche, *A right excellent* (London, 1574) in *Seventeenth-century Prose and Poetry*, ed. Alexander M. Witherspoon (New York: Harcourt, Brace & World [1963]); *George* Turberville, *Tragicall Tales* (London: Abel Jeffs, 1587), no. 10; *Tragical Tales: and Other Poems* (Edinburgh, Privately printed, 1837); Girolamo Parabosco, *I diporti* (Venice: Giovanni Griffio, 1550), ed. Donato Pirovano (Rome, Salerno, 2005); John Payne, *New Poems* (London: Newman, 1880). The version in Sansovino's *Cento novelle scelte* (1561) is likewise Boccaccio briefly microwaved.

buried together, but, true to Spain, only by permission of the Church. In this historical event there is clear evidence of the birth of a legend that became Boccaccio's source – and Straparola's as well. Moreover, visitors to the tombs of the faithful lovers in the Iglesia de San Pedro are advised not to express audibly any doubts concerning the veracity of their story. Members of the Fondación de los Amantes de Teruel are often within earshot, to the last one devoted to revisionist history. After all, the story of these secular saints has been institutionalized by Pedro de Afrentosa in his *Historia lastimosa y sentida de los tiernos amantes Marcilla y Segura* (mid-sixteenth century), by Andrés Rey de Artieda in *Los amantes* (1581), and by Tirso de Molina in *Los amantes de Teruel* (1635), as well as by Juan Yagüe de Salas in his epic of the same name (1616), down to the quite splendid play by Juan Eugenio Hartzenbusch of the same name again (1837), a work much loved and performed.[27] So substantial a cloud of witnesses can hardly be in error, and where a good legend is also communal identity and good business, let debunkers beware.

But, in fact, their story can be documented no further back than 1555 when a legend sprang up about two mummies found buried in the church, believed to be the two lovers. Just who shaped that legend is uncertain, but there is little doubt among specialists that Boccaccio is owed the lion's share for their storyline. In 1550 the bodies were exhumed and reburied in elaborate tombs still visible today, having touchingly realistic effigies carved on the lids of their sarcophagi, their arms extended towards each other across the intervening space, but not quite meeting in a touch. They are to be found in the Chapel of Saints Cosmé and Damian, where their coffins were again inspected in 1619 and certain 'antique' papers found containing their story – papers not surprisingly no longer extent. A more sober account of their origins can be found in Emilio Cotarelo y Morí's *Sobre el origin y desarrollo de la leyenda de Los Amantes de Teruel*.[28]

---

27 Rey de Artieda, *Los amantes* (Madrid: Taurus, 1971); Tirso de Molina, *Los amantes de Teruel* (Madrid: Taurus, 1971); Yagüe de Salas, *Los amantes de Teruel* (Valencia, 1616 and Teruel, 1951, and other popular local printings); Hartzenbusch, *Los amantes de Teruel*, ed. G.W. Umphrey (Boston: D.C. Heath [1920], and Madrid: Espasa-Calpe, 1935).

28 Emilio Cotarelo y Morí, *Sobre el origin y desarrollo de la leyenda de Los amantes de Teruel* (Madrid: Revista de archivos [as publishers], 1907).

IX. Fable 3
Francesco Sforza's Narrow Escape

ISABELLA

Francesco Sforza, the son of Lodovico Moro, duke of Milan, follows a stag in the chase and becomes separated from his companions. He finds refuge in the hut of certain peasants, who take counsel together as to how they may kill him. But he is delivered by a child who has become privy to the plot of the traitors and the villains are afterwards quartered alive.

The fable just narrated to us by Lionora opens the way to tell you of a very piteous adventure, one that, in fact, may be held for history rather than fable, because it happened to the son of a duke, who, after many tribulations, brought it about that his enemies tasted a bitter punishment for the offences they had wrought.

In our own times there lived in Milan Signor Francesco Sforza, the son of Lodovico il Moro, the ruler of the city. This youth, both during the lifetime of his father and after his death, suffered greatly from the slings of envious fortune. In his early years, Signor Francesco cut a handsome figure with his courtly manners and a face that revealed his upright inclinations. When he came into the full bloom of youthful maturity at the termination of his studies and other becoming exercises, he devoted himself to the practice of arms, to throwing the lance, and following the hunt, taking considerable pleasure in this mode of life. On account of his prowess and expertise in these manly activities, all the young men of the city held him in great affection, while he, for his own part, was equally well disposed towards them. Truly, there was no youth in the entire city who did not enjoy a share in his bounty.

One morning for his pleasure Francesco gathered together a goodly company of young men, none of them yet twenty years old, and, having mounted his horse, he rode away with them to follow the chase. When they had arrived at a certain thicket well known to them as a haunt of wild animals, they surrounded it on all sides, and soon it chanced that, on the side of the wood where Signor Francesco was keeping a close watch, a very fine stag broke forth, but fled away in terror as soon as it beheld the hunters. Now Francesco, with his lion's heart and excellent horsemanship, no sooner marked the stag's rapid flight than he struck the flanks of his horse with his spurs and dashed away in impetuous pursuit. In following it long and far, he outrode all his companions, and in the end also lost his way. The stag now out of his view, he abandoned the chase, having no idea where he was or which way he should go. Finding himself all alone and far from the high road, with no idea how he should make his way back – and now with the dark shadows of night quickly gathering around – he somewhat lost his wits, greatly fearing that some mischance might come to him hardly to his liking. And that is precisely what happened.

Francesco followed dubious paths farther and farther until he finally came upon a small cottage with a straw roof and an ill and lowly aspect. He rode into the yard, dismounted, tied his horse fast to the surrounding fence, and went straight into the cottage. There he found an old man whose years numbered ninety at least. By his side was a young peasant woman, pretty to look at, who held a child of five in her arms that she was feeding. Signor Francesco made a polite salutation to the old man and the young woman, sat down with them and asked them in their kindness, without telling them who he was, to give him shelter and lodging for the night.

The old man and the young woman, his daughter-in-law, took note of his high station and graceful comportment, and willingly made him welcome, all the while making excuses that such accommodation was hardly worthy of a man of his condition. Thanking them heartily, Francesco went out of the cottage to look after his horse and, after seeing to its wants, re-entered. The child being amiable by nature ran up to him, greeting him affectionately and hugging him however she might, which prompted Francesco to kiss the little one and prattle in soft words. Then while Francesco was standing and chatting in a familiar way with the greybeard and his daughter-in-law, Malacarne, his son and the young woman's husband, came home. Upon entering the cottage he espied the gentleman conversing with the old man and caressing the child. He bade good evening to Francesco, which won him a courteous reply, and gave orders to his wife that she should get the supper ready right away.

The master of the house then asked Francesco what he was doing there in so savage and deserted a place, to which the youth replied in explanation, 'Good brother, I'm here simply because I found myself alone in my journey and had no idea which way to go, being ill informed about the features of this country. Then with night falling, I discovered by good luck this little cottage of yours, where I've been invited to enter by the kindness of this good old father and your wife.' Malacarne listened to the young man's speech, sized up his rich attire, took note of the fine gold chain he wore about his neck, and suddenly he conceived a plot, making up his mind, come what may, first to kill him and then take all his possessions. Unwavering in his intent to carry out this diabolical plot, he called his old father and his wife, took the child in his arms, and went out of the cottage. He then drew them aside and made a pact with them to carry out the murder, after which they would remove the man's rich raiment and bury his body in the fields, persuading themselves that when it was done, nothing further would ever be heard of him.

But through the justice of God all their secret designs were brought to light, for He would not allow these scheming miscreants to achieve their desired ends. As soon as the compact was made and their evil plans were set, Malacarne realized that he couldn't carry out the stratagem by himself. Moreover, his father was old and decrepit and his wife had little courage, while the young man, as Malacarne had noticed, was stout of heart and would most certainly put up a good fight for his life, perhaps even escaping out of their hands. So he decided to make his way to a place not far from his cottage and enlist the services of three of the local ruffians, with whose aid he would succeed in his plan. As soon as the three friends comprehended the part they were to play, they joined right in, greedy for all there was to gain. Catching up their weapons, they all headed back towards Malacarne's cottage.

The child, meanwhile leaving her mother and grandfather together, went over to Francesco, greeting and affectionately squeezing him even more than before. He warmed equally to the little one's fond ways, took her in his arms, caressed her tenderly and kissed her again and again. The child saw the glitter of the gold chain around his neck, and as children will do, not only took great delight in it, but toyed with it and expressed her wish to have it around her own neck. Francesco, when he saw the child's fancy, said to her with a hug, 'So my little one, if you'd like, I'll give this to you for your very own.' And with these words he put it around her neck. Now in some fashion the child had become aware of the plot in the making and said to Francesco in her simple way, 'It would have been mine because my daddy and mommy were going to take it away and kill you.'

Shrewd and wary of temper, Francesco soon realized from the child's words the wicked designs being woven against him and didn't let the warning go unnoticed. But prudently he held his peace, got up from his seat, carried the child in his arms with the chain around her neck, and laid her down upon a little bed. Because the hour was late, she fell right to sleep. Next, Francesco shut himself up in the cottage, made the entrance secure by piling two large wooden chests against the door, and courageously waited to see what the desperadoes would do next. Then he pulled from his side pocket a small pistol with five barrels which could be fired one by one, or all together, as he desired.

As soon as the young companions who had ridden out hunting with Francesco that morning discovered that he had strayed off without leaving any trace of his direction, they signalled to him with their horns and their shouting, but they received no reply. Then they began to fear that his horse had fallen on loose rocks and that their lord might be lying dead or was perhaps eaten by wild beasts. While they were standing there stricken with fear, one of the company as last spoke out, 'I followed Signor Francesco in pursuit of a stag along this forest path heading towards the wide valley, but his horse was much swifter in pace than mine and I couldn't keep him in sight or tell where he went.' As soon as the others had taken in this speech, they set out at once on their quest, following the trace of the stag all through the night in anticipation of finding Signor Francesco either dead or alive.

As the young men rode through the woods, Malacarne and his villain comrades were making their way towards his house. They assumed that they could enter without obstruction, but upon reaching the door they found it locked shut. Then Malacarne kicked at it with his foot and yelled, 'Open up, my good friend. Why have you closed up the door of my house?'

Francesco made no word of reply, but kept silent. Peeping out through a crevice, he saw Malacarne with an axe on his shoulder, along with the three other ruffians fully armed. His firearm was already charged, so without wasting any time, he put it to the crevice in the door and fired a single barrel, striking one of the three varlets in the chest so effectively that he fell to the ground dead without a moment to confess his sins. Malacarne, when he saw that, started hacking more violently at the door with his axe, but he couldn't tear it down, so well was it secured on the other side. Then once more Francesco discharged his pistol, and again with such good fortune that he disabled another of the band by shooting him in the right arm. Those who were still alive were now in such a rage that they hurled themselves with all their might to break open the door, making such a clamour that it seemed like the end of the world. Seeing the strait he was in, Francesco was seized with terror, working frantically to further barricade the door by piling on all the stools and benches he could find.

It's a well-known fact that the brighter and finer the night the more silent it is, allowing a single word, although it be spoken a long way off, sometimes to be easily heard. Thus it happened that all this hurly-burly made by these villains came to the ears of Francesco's companions. At once they closed ranks and gave free rein to their horses, arriving at the place of the uproar in time to see the assassins labouring to break down the door. One of the young men asked them the meaning of all this turmoil they were making, to which Malacarne replied, 'Let me tell you right now, you men. When I came back to my cottage this evening worn out with work, I found a young soldier inside, a real bruiser of a fellow, trying to kill my old father, ravish my wife, carry off my child, and rob me of everything I own. I had to flee because I was in no condition to defend myself. Seeing what desperate straits I was reduced to, I went to the houses of my friends and kinsmen and asked for their help. But when we came back to my cottage, we found the door shut and so strongly barricaded that there was no way to get in unless we first broke down the door. Not satisfied with outraging my wife, he has also slain one of my friends with his pistol and wounded another to death, as you can well see. It's beyond my endurance to put up with such brutality, so I'm determined to lay hands on him dead or alive.'

Francesco's companions took pity on him, seeing what had happened, and accepting Malacarne's tale as true because of the dead body lying on the ground in front of them and the other man gravely wounded. Having dismounted their horses, they began to hurl themselves against the door and shout out loudly, 'Traitor, enemy of God, open up the door – now. What are you doing? There's no doubt that you're going to suffer the penalty for your crimes.' To this Francesco made no answer, but with care and dexterity went on fortifying the door from the inside, having no idea that his friends were on the outside. So the men went on battering at the door, still unable to open it, despite the force they used. Suddenly one of them, wandering about, spotted in the yard a horse tied to the fence, which he recognized as Signor Francesco's as soon as he got close to it. Then he let out a shout, 'Hold off, my comrades. Cease your efforts because our master is surely inside,' and in speaking he pointed out to them the horse tied to the fence. As soon as the others saw and recognized the animal, they were convinced right away that Francesco was shut up inside the cottage. Now rejoicing, they called out to him by name. When he heard himself called, Francesco knew that his friends were at hand. Relieved to know that his life was spared, he cleared away his defences and opened up the door. When they heard the reason why he had barricaded himself in so tightly, they seized the two villains, bound them tightly, and carried them back to Milan, where they were first tormented with burning pincers and then, while still alive, they were torn into quarters by four horses.

The little child by whose agency the nefarious plot had been discovered was named Verginea. Francesco gave her in charge to the duchess to raise her carefully and well. When she arrived at a mature age ripe for marriage, as a reward for the great service she had rendered to Signor Francesco, she was granted a generous dowry and given in honourable marriage to a gentleman of noble descent. In addition to this, they gave her the castle of Binasio, situated between Milan and Pavia, but now there is hardly a stone of it left upon another, since in our own time the region has been plagued by continual skirmishes and attacks. In this morbid and terrible fashion, the murderous thieves came to a wretched end, while the damsel and her husband lived in great happiness for many years.

The listeners were equally affected by pity and astonishment in hearing this sympathetic story. But as soon as the happy ending was pronounced, they all regained their felicity and mirth. Then the Signora commanded Isabella to set forth her enigma. This she did in a modest manner, with her eyes still moist with tears.

Good sirs, amongst us here doth dwell
A thing whose seeming none can tell;
Though far away from us it flies,
Secret at home the while it lies.
At last the fatal day doth come,
It leaves for aye its wonted home;
To it the power divine is given
To scan all things in earth and heaven,
Survey the world from place to place,
Within a single breathing space.

> Now who can craftily combine,
> And read aright these words of mine?

Isabella's learned and subtle enigma gave great pleasure to all the listeners, but not a single one of them was gifted with sufficient understanding to disentangle its meaning. So Isabella, in her modest way, thus explained it: 'My enigma means the ever-varying thoughts of men's minds, which are invisible and run into every place, although at the same time they always remain inside the man's brain where they are formed. Thought stays in one place and it wanders around, no one knows where. But though it permeates every sphere of man's intellect, it still remains with him and is the source from which infinite and varied phenomena take their rise.' The solution to Isabella's enigma was weighty and subtle indeed, and there was no one in the company who was not entirely satisfied with it. Vicenza, who knew that it was now her turn to speak, did not wait for a further command from the Signora, but began her fable as follows.

IX.3 Commentary

Giovanni Giustiniani in his *Epistolae* (1554) tells this precise story as an anecdote in the life of Maximilian II of Bohemia, born in 1527, the son of Ferdinand I and later Holy Roman emperor. Moreover, he tells it as a true relation and names his source; it would seem to be authoritative and well established. But if the event took place when the prince was twenty years old, it would have been tantamount to recent 'news' at the time Straparola was composing his second volume of the *Piacevoli notti* for publication in 1553. His knowledge of the event would thus be limited to a brief chronological window of perhaps five or six years. But it is unlikely this story came to Straparola through Giustiniani, thus necessitating a common source. Moreover, without that source in hand (and despite Giustiniani's asseverations), it is a toss-up whether it was about Maximilian or Francesco, because of necessity one of the two must be an adaptation. Straparola's anecdote pertains to the young Sforza, born in 1495. Was this story his own invention, perhaps in relation to the circumstances inaugurating his framing tale, while Giustiniani was the borrower, as he claims to have been?

Then again, insofar as one is an adaptation, both may be. After all, the generic tale of wandering into the forest primeval in pursuit of a prize stag, being caught out by falling darkness, and seeking refuge in circumstances leading to danger may be considerably older. What was new was the application of this tale to a contemporary prince in need of legendary reinforcement of his adolescent prowess in support of his pretensions to power. These two princes – the first destined to rule the German empire as a career-long broker between the Catholic and Protestant forces facing off within his realm, the second chosen by the Hapsburgs to rule over Milan as the last Sforza duke – were in their youths both candidates for the mythologizing that props up reputations. Folk tales with mythic overtones had long been employed to associate the foundations of noble families with heroic or supernatural events. Like Merlin, Richard the Lion-Hearted was said to have been born to a fairy mother; Richard's was Cassodorien, the mysterious daughter of the king of Antioch who had come sailing from the East on a white fairy ship in response to Henry II's quest for the world's most beautiful woman.[29] The family history of Raimon de Chateau Rouset was founded late in the twelfth century when Raimon was crossing a river and there met a beautiful woman who called him by name, agreed to marriage, promised riches and prosperity, and delivered too, until he broke the taboo and discovered her to be a serpent by spying upon her in the bath. Somehow a *mélusine* as the founding mother was thought to have given a special cachet to the dynasty.[30] I recall, too, that the dukes of Berri made similar claims concerning their origins. As the present case will prove, the story was known in the past and was applied to a different ruler in slightly altered circumstances. What is striking in the matter is that two authors should concurrently apply very similar versions of the story to two princes associated with the Hapsburgs and the Spanish court.

To paraphrase the story from *Ioannis Iustiniani Cretensis epistolae familiares ... item memorabilis facti sereniss. Bohemiae Regis Maximiliani commentariolus* is essentially to retell Straparola's story. The setting is Granada and the events take place during Maximilian's sojourn in Spain at the court of Charles V, the acting viceroy. When, towards evening while out hunting, the prince becomes separated from the others in his party, he makes

---

29 *Richard the Lion-hearted and Other Medieval Romances*, trans. Bradford B. Broughton (New York: E.P. Dutton, 1966), pp. 150–5. See also Bradford Broughton, *The Legends of King Richard I, Coeur de Lion: A Study of Sources and Variations to the Year 1600* (The Hague: Mouton, 1966).
30 Gervais of Tilbury in *Les traductions françaises des* Otia imperialis *de Gervais de Tilbury par Jean d'Antioche et Jean de Vignay*, ed. Takeshi Matsumura (Geneva: Droz, 2006), pp. 418–22.

his way to a shepherd's house in a deeply wooded area. This household consists of six persons, including a robust shepherd and his twenty-year-old wife. The youth's rich garments excite their cupidity, but the young wife takes pity on their guest and warns him of the plot. That Straparola assigns this role to a five-year-old child to whom the protagonist has already given his gold necklace is a distinct variation possibly in his source (by definition not the version described here). Giustiniani's prince barricades himself inside his bedroom (not the entire house as in Straparola), prepares his pistol, winds up his spirit of valour, and awaits the assault. The shepherds, their entry obstructed, become violent and the prince kills one of them by firing through the keyhole. Next he opens the door and flees, shouting 'Assassins! Thieves!' as the shepherds prostrate themselves on the ground. A great tumult follows. These too are significant variants. He does not escape, but is seized by rustic neighbours (not quite the isolated wooded area it had seemed) and forthwith reveals his identity, although he is not believed. At dawn they set off to consult the prefect at the nearest castle, but on the way the group is met by the royal hunting party and the prince is liberated. Later the house is burned and the young woman is taken to court, where she is rewarded and treated with great dignity. Giustiniani declares his source to have been one Andrea Mathae, in whom he expresses his entire faith – almost protesting too much in the matter. The story is followed by two full pages of flowery praise concerning a prince deemed temperate in arms and in whose early deeds a true king may be detected.[31]

Presumably Bénigne Poissenot took his materials on the same topic directly from Giustiniani; his 'Faict hardi et courageux de Maximilian, Prince d'Austriche' contains only minor variations and additions. In this version, the hunt is not in the forest but in the mountains. The household is still composed of six persons, including the wife of the shepherd's son. Again, upon the wife's warning, the prince barricades himself inside and waits. The shepherd, at first, asks merely to enter to fetch something he

---

31 *A Commentary on the Memorable Deeds of his Highness, Maximiliani, king of Bohemia* (trans. from the Latin) was included with his *Epistolae*, attached to his *Epistolarum laconicarum ac selectarum farrago altera in qua Latina tantum continentur* (Basel: Joannem Oporinum, 1554), pp. 232–41. Further to this author, his life, and sources, see *Epistolae: Lettere familiari, scolastiche o morali*, ed. Damiano Mevoli (Rome: Vecchiarelli, 2004).

had forgotten. With the dresser blocking the door, the assailant tries to enter by the window. One local is killed by gunfire and now the villagers move in while the women cry over the dead man. This Maximilian withstands them from within the house until dawn. He then tells the peasants that he is their governor and that if they keep it up their village will be levelled – no veiled threat there. Then he allows himself to be tied and delivered to the local magistrate. With his identity reconfirmed, the shepherd's house is torched and the young woman generously rewarded. For our purposes, this is but a reconfirmation of the story tradition in the name of Maximilian II. The legend is still alive.

That Straparola or his source saw fit to bestow the tale upon the young Sforza remains a tease. As a young prince, son of the famous Ludovico Sforza il Moro, he was taken to the court of the Holy Roman emperor, Maximilian I, where he spent his early years. After the death of his father in 1508, he was under the tutelage of the Hapsburgs and destined for a career in the church. But when Milan was taken back from the French by Charles V, Francesco was made duke and remained so until his death in 1535. He was, in fact, no more than a puppet duke under the imperial forces and the last of that dynasty to rule over the city. The implicit moment for this pseudo-historical event is now moved back to 1515. Were we certain that Straparola was responsible for this adaptation, we might presume that it contributes to the Sforza saga of the opening narrative concerning the Signora's widowhood following the death of Giovanni Francesco Gonzaga and the political harassment that forced her to flee Milanese territory to resettle in the Serenissima. That he is the inventor of the Sforza connection is possible, but it is by no means certain, and is all the more to be doubted in light of the undifferentiated handling of the tale within the design of his collection, for if Straparola had been giving any thought at all to the matter, surely he would have devised more comment upon and reaction to the tale than a mixture of general pity and a few latent tears on Isabella's part. This is a Sforza, after all, and the most important of the Signora's living kin. Silence on that score calls into question the entire framing device as a socio-historical plausibility; how could Straparola so readily forget the immediate significance to the Murano set of this singular family-member rite of passage?

As has been hinted, a further possibility remains: that the source common to Straparola and Giustiniani involves neither a Sforza nor a Hapsburg prince, insofar as in 1535 a closely related story is told about St Louis, king of France; it is no. 79 in the MS of Nicolas de Troyes's *Gran parangon des nouvelles nouvelles,* in which the king out hunting near

Fontainebleau lost his way and was confronted by three thieves.[32] The setting was a forest near a little mountain, the king was in solo pursuit of a deer, and the brigands were met at a crossroad. Their intention was to slit the king's throat, having taken him for a rich gentleman worth the assault. The king offered all he had in exchange for his life, but only one of the three agreed, not wishing to harm him. Time passed and still none of the king's many companions came upon the scene. He asked only for a final favour, which was to blow two or three notes on his hunting horn. The first two thieves were in haste, but the third allowed his ultimate wish. Hardly had he sounded a note when in rushed two hundred of his men. In the end, the king granted pardon to the third, but saw the first two hanged. The author does not specify his source.[33] The tale is included among several treating of royal adventures during or following the hunt, for it is then that kings are incognito and thus liable to meet either largesse or injury from the commoners. The origin of the anecdote appears to be French and the materials traditional. If such was the model that ultimately served Straparola and Giustiniani, it was modified by an interim author to a state from which the nearly synonymous but independently generated versions of 1553 and 1554 could be drawn. One can imagine other scenarios even more hypothetical, but here the matter of immediate sources must rest.[34] It is the unique instance in which a written source seems probable, if not necessary, but cannot be identified.

But there is also a sense that this 'historicized' story was once legendary. It tells of young royalty lost in a hostile rural area of outlaw villains, of mountain men representing an antipode to the court. These 'savages,' in the literal sense of the term, wild because woodsmen (*silva*), commit an unpardonable breach of hospitality in their treachery against their ruler incognito. The circumstances make trial of the princely hero's resolve and sangfroid, leading to a personal and moral victory. The parts

---

32 *Le grand parangon des nouvelles nouvelles*, ed. Émile Mabille (Paris: Nogent-le-Rotrou, 1869), pp. 22–3.

33 But we may presume that it is a historicized variation upon the folktale type ATU 958, 'The shepherd's call for help,' in which, typically, robbers fall upon a shepherd in the mountains, who, by subterfuge, manages to get off a last blast of his horn or flute, which is heard in the valley by someone in the village, often a sister or sweetheart, brother or elder, who sends help and thus saves the livestock. The story was widely known among folklore collectors in the nineteenth century.

34 Francesco Sansovino took the story directly from Straparola for his *Cento novelle scelti da i più nobili scrittori* (Venice: Sansovino, 1561), Day V, no. 4, pp. 130r–6r. The copy consulted in Bologna once belonged to the Pontifici Biblioteca.

of the narrative are archetypally direct: the hunting party, the prince alone and unidentified, the request for hospitality, the glimmer of civility in the woman or child who alerts the guest, strategic resistance, deliverance by a rescue party, justice for the demonic, and a fairy-tale advancement for the one who gave warning. The tale carries the structural traits of an ancient existence.[35] But the depiction of the forest-mountain men is emblematic merely in a utilitarian sense. To be sure, there is a symbolic face-off between courtly and rural, urbanity and wilderness, civility and savagery implicit in this tale. Yet in parallel tales there is also the best of hospitality in lowly cottages. Giambattista Giraldi Cinzio rewrites the story in the name of François I, who wanders from his party, seeks refuge among the humblest of the realm, and receives for his supper a turnip and clear water, and for his lodging a bed of hay and fresh clean sheets.[36] The king is charmed by his reception and lavishes upon them a munificent sum of gold in exchange for his turnip, while a peasant daughter, the counterpart to the wife or child who rescues Francesco Sforza, for her simple goodness is introduced into the highest society. It is a fantasy of kingly generosity in mirror relationship to the folk tale of rural treachery.[37]

---

35 Stith Thompson repertories the motif in his *Motif-Index of Folk Literature* (Bloomington: Indiana University Press, 1955–8) as K551–3.

36 Giambattista Giraldi, *De gli ecatommiti ovvero cento novelle*, 3 vols. (Turin: Cugini Pomba, 1853–4), VI.9.

37 Marie-Françoise Piejus includes this story among the Straparolan tales featuring confrontations between city-dwellers and peasants as an example of a Manichean contrast between the brave and civil nobleman and the diabolical peasant, who is to be associated with those who create raids and revolts and resist the rule of law. She speculates that the story may represent a certain fear of these rural poor; 'Le couple citadin-paysan dans les "Piacevoli notti" de Straparola,' in *Ville et campagne dans la littérature italienne de la renaissance*, ed. Anna Fontes-Baratto et al. (Paris: Université de la Sorbonne Nouvelle, 1976), pp. 139–77. In that regard, the story type has a remote cousin in the American thriller *Deliverance* (1972) in which the 'hillbillies' of Georgia and South Carolina are summarily treated as inbred wild men, xenophobic, and murderous.

IX. Fable 4
Papiro Schizza's Pedantry and
the Scholar's Revenge

VICENZA

Pre Papiro Schizza makes pretence of great learning, but in truth knows nothing. Like an ignorant fool, he flouts a certain peasant's son, who, to revenge himself, sets fire to his house, destroying it and everything inside.

Kindly ladies, if with due diligence we were to investigate just how many fools and ignoramuses there are around us, we would soon realize that they are too numerous to be counted. If, moreover, we sought to know all the ills arising from ignorance, we would have to consult that great teacher of all things, experience, who would instruct us like a kindly mother. Now as the common adage goes, if we don't want to leave with our hands full of flies, let me explain that of all the vices, pride is born first among them, for vanity is the foundation of all ills and the root of all human error, because the ignorant man presumes to know all when in reality he knows nothing and seeks to be taken for what he is not. This is what happened to a village priest who gave himself out to be a man of learning when, in fact, he was the greatest dimwit nature ever produced. Cajoled by his imagined knowledge, this fellow in the end lost all his worldly possessions and narrowly escaped with his life, as you'll understand perfectly from the following fable – a story which, perhaps, you've heard before.

In the region of Brescia, a rich, noble, and populous city, there dwelt, not so long ago, a priest named Papiro Schizza, who was rector of the village church of Bedicuollo, not far distant from the city. Although he was as ignorant as a loon, still he liked to play the part of the scholar and exhibit himself as a person of learning to anyone he chanced to meet. The country folk, for this reason, regarded him with great favour, honouring and esteeming him as a man of deep science.

On the celebration day of St Macario, the bishop made a special charge that all the priests of the city, as well as those in the surrounding villages, must mount a solemn and pious procession in Brescia, and that upon penalty of five ducats, they should present themselves *cum cappis et coctis* to do honour to this solemn festival, as was merited by the memory of so pious a saint. The bishop's nuncio, on his rounds, went to the village of Bedicuollo, and finding Father Papiro at home, delivered to him the summons of monsignor the bishop that, under penalty of five ducats, he should duly make his way, *cum cappis et coctis*, to the cathedral of Brescia on the feast day of St Macario so that, along with the other priests, he might appropriately honour the occasion. When the nuncio had departed, Mister Father Papiro began to turn over in his mind what all this might mean – a summons to attend the solemn festival *cum cappis et coctis* – in his dimwitted way beating his brains to figure out the words. After some time, it occurred to him that *cappis et coctis* could only mean cooked capons. Convinced his interpretation was right, the silly fool, without taking advice from anyone else, picked out a pair of his finest capons and ordered his housekeeper to cook them up with the greatest care.

On the following morning at the break of day, Father Papiro mounted his horse, with the capons arranged on a plate, and set off to Brescia, where he made no delay in presenting himself to monsignor the bishop, to whom he gave the roast capons, telling how he had received the command of the nuncio to honour the feast of San Macario *cum cappis et coctis*, which command he had carried out to the letter with this pair of well-cooked birds. The bishop was both wily and astute, and what's more loved a good joke. Seeing that the capons were fat and well roasted, and knowing too what an ignorant fool the priest was, he had to press his lips tightly together to keep from laughing. So with a face full of merriment and good humour he accepted the dish, giving Father Papiro *mille gratis* in return. Now Papiro heard the bishop's words clearly enough, but being so stupid, he hadn't a clue what they meant, concluding at last that by *mille gratis* the bishop required of him a thousand wattle frames. So the stupid loon, falling down on his knees at the feet of the bishop, cried out, 'Monsignor, I pray you by your love of God and the high reverence in which I hold you, that you'll not lay so heavy a burden upon me, for our village is sorely stricken by poverty, and to supply a thousand wattle frames would be too grievous a tax for such poor folk as we are. Yet, if five hundred wattle hurdles would make you happy, I would more than willingly order them for you.' Although he was a man of keen wit, the bishop failed altogether to understand the meaning of Father Papiro's words, but in order not to let on how little he had understood, he simply agreed to the priest's proposal without another word.

As soon as the festival was over, Father Papiro took his leave after the bishop's parting benediction and returned to his own house. When he got home he collected all the wagons of the village, had them piled high with brushwood hurdles, and sent them into the city on the following morning as a present to the bishop. When he saw the wagons laden with hurdles and heard who sent them, the bishop burst into loud laughter and made no scruple about accepting them. In this fashion the lubberly fool of a priest, feigning to knowledge which he lacked, lost both his capons and his hurdles, shaming and dishonouring himself at the same time.

Now it happened that in that same village of Bedicuollo there lived a certain peasant named Gianotto, who, although he was a mere rustic and able neither to read nor write, entertained nevertheless such a profound reverence for scholars of all kinds that, for their sakes, he would willingly have become a slave in chains. This man had a son named Pirino, a youth of goodly aspect, who gave fair signs of growing up to be a man of science and learning. Gianotto held this son in great affection and made up his mind to send the boy to study at Padua, resolving at the same time to supply him with everything a student might require – all of which came to pass. During his few months there, the youth received a thorough grounding in the art of grammar, before returning home – not to stay, but merely to pay a short visit to his parents and friends. Gianotto, anxious to do honour to his son and find out at the same time how much profit he had gained from his studies, invited his friends and relations to a fine feast at his house, including the good Father Papiro, in order to examine Pirino in the presence of them all so that they might judge whether his son had spent his time and labour in vain.

When the day of the feast had come, all the friends and relations of the family, responding to the invitation, came together at the house of Gianotto, and after Father Papiro had pronounced the benediction, they all sat down at the table in order of their ages. When the dinner was finished and the board cleared, Gianotto rose to his feet and said, 'Mister Papiro, I greatly desire, if it is the pleasure of all who are present, that you examine Pirino, my son, to see how much he has gained from his studies.'

To this Father Papiro answered, 'Gianotto, my colleague and neighbour, this burden you would place upon me is nothing at all compared with what I would willingly do for you. It is, in any case, a trifling matter for a man of my capabilities.' Then turning his face towards Pirino, sitting opposite him, he said, 'Pirino, my son, we are all come together here for one and the same end, which is to promote your honour. Hence, we are curious to know whether you have spent your time well at the University of Padua. So for the satisfaction of Gianotto, your good father, and for the contentment of this distinguished company, I will now proceed to examine you in the subjects you have been studying, and if, as we are all hoping, you acquit yourself worthily, it will be a cause of no small gratification to your father, his friends, and myself. Tell me, therefore, Pirino my son, what is the Latin for priest?'

Pirino, who was exceedingly well versed in all the rules of grammar, answered with confidence, '*presbyter*.'

Father Papiro, upon hearing the prompt and ready answer given by Pirino said, 'But how can it be *presbyter*, my son? Of a truth you are mightily mistaken.'

But Pirino, who was well assured of his knowledge, answered boldly that the word he had given was the right one and advanced many authorities to prove it. Then a long dispute arose between the examiner and the pupil. Father Papiro, in no wise willing to give way to the superior intelligence of the youth, at last turned to those who sat at the table and said, 'Tell me, my dear brothers and sons, suppose that in the middle of the night something should happen to you so serious that you wished to confess your sins or call for the Eucharist, or any other sacrament necessary to the salvation of your soul, would you not send immediately for the priest? Most assuredly. So then what would you do first? Would you not knock at the priest's door? Of course you would. Then would you not say, "Hey presto, presto good sir! Get up at once and come as quickly as you can to give the sacraments to a sick man who is at the point of death?"' The peasants sitting around the table could not gainsay Father Papiro's words and declared them to be the truth. Then Father Papiro continued, 'To speak of a priest in Latin you must not say *presbyter* but *prestule*, because he comes *presto, presto* to the sick man's aid. But Pirino, I do not wish to press hard upon you on account of this first mistake. So I will now ask you to tell me what is the Latin for bed?'

Pirino answered promptly, '*lectus*' or '*thorus*.'

When Father Papiro heard this answer, he cried out again, 'O my son, you are once again mistaken. Your teacher has indeed taught you badly.'

Then turning towards Gianotto, he said, 'Gianotto, when you come back home weary from the fields, do you not say right after supper, "I would love now to repose myself?"'

To this Gianotto answered, 'Yes.'

'Therefore,' said the priest, 'a bed is called *reposorium*.' All those present with one voice declared that this must be the truth. But Pirino, although by this time he was starting to mock the priest, did not dare openly contradict him in order not to offend his kinsfolk who were there.

Father Papiro went on with his examination, 'And what is the Latin for the table from which we eat our food?'

'*Mensa*,' replied Pirino.

Then Father Papiro said to the company, 'Alas, alas, Gianotto has laid out his money to little profit. Pirino has wasted his time for he knows nothing of the Latin vocabulary or of the rules of grammar. You must know that the table at which men sit to eat is called *gaudiam*, and not *mensa*, given that when a man is at table he is in state of joy and gladness.' This explanation seemed wise and laudable to all present, so they highly praised the priest, taking him for a man of deep wit and learning. Pirino, although it went sorely against the grain, was forced to give way to Father Papiro's ignorance, because the presence of his relatives cut off all avenues. But when Father Papiro took note of the approbation he had won from the guests, he began to strut about as proudly as a peacock, raising his voice and asking in a loud tone, 'And what is the Latin for cat, my son?'

'*Felis*,' answered Pirino.

'O, you silly gull,' cried the priest. 'Is not a cat called *saltagraffa*, because when you hold out food it quickly leaps up and attacks it with its paws, grips it and runs off?' All the villagers were struck with wonder at the priest's exposition and listened with the greatest attention to the ready way in which Father Papiro posed his queries and gave the answers, judging him to be a most learned man.

When the priest once more began his questioning, he said to Pirino. 'Now tell me, what is the Latin word for fire?'

'*Ignis*,' answered Pirino.

'What do you mean by *ignis*?' cried the priest, and turning towards the assembled guests once more, he said to them, 'Brethren, when you take home the meat which you intend for your dinner, what do you do with it first? Do you not cook it?'

And all the listeners said 'Yes.'

'Then,' said the priest, 'fire is not called *ignis*, but *carniscoculum*. And now tell me truly, Pirino, what is the Latin word for water.'

'*Limpha*,' answered Pirino.

'Alas, alas,' cried Father Papiro. 'What is that you say? A fool you went to Padua, and a fool you have returned.' Then addressing the company, he went on, 'You all know, my good friends, that experience is the mother of everything in the world, and that water is not called *limpha*, but *abundantia*, for if you should happen to go to the river to draw water, or to water your animals, you will never find a lack of water there, and so it is called *abundantia*.'

By this time, Gianotto was like a man almost out of his wits from what he'd heard and began to lament the time lost and the money wasted. When the priest noticed the good peasant's vexation, he said to Pirino, 'I will now ask you one thing more. Tell me what riches are called in Latin and then my questions are over.'

'*Divitiae, divitiarum*,' answered Pirino.

'O, my son, you are wrong again, completely mistaken, for riches are called in Latin *sustantia*, seeing that they are the sustenance of man.'

When the feast and the interrogation had come to an end, Father Papiro drew Gianotto aside and said to him, 'Gianotto, my good friend, you must see by this time how little your son has gained by going to Padua. So if you'll take my advice, you won't send him back to his studies merely to waste his time and your money. In fact, if you do, you'll live to regret it.' Knowing nothing of the true value of Father Papiro's words, Gianotto believed them completely, afterward stripping Pirino of his city-made clothes and putting him back into his homespuns to go out and take care of the pigs. Pirino understood how unjustly he had been overborne by the priest's ignorance, not because he lacked the knowledge but because he didn't want to make a scene in front of the relatives who had come to honour him. Moreover, he sorely felt the distress at finding himself degraded from scholar to swineherd. Then anger and fury inflamed him and he decided to seek revenge for the scorn and ignominy that had been cast upon him, To that end, Fortune worked in his favour, for one day, when he was leading his pigs out to pasture in front of the priest's house, he saw there a cat that he allured with a piece of bread and then caught with his hand. Then, getting a large bunch of flax together, he tied it to her tail and set it on fire and let her go. The cat, feeling something tightly bound to her tail and the fire starting to scorch her rump, fled right into Father Papiro's house. Darting through a crevice in the wall, she ran into the room next to the one in which the priest lay sleeping. Maddened with terror she swooped in under the bed, where a great quantity of linen was stored, and in a very short time the linen, the bed, and the whole room were ablaze. Pirino, when he saw that Father Papiro Schizza's house was on fire and that there was no possibility of extinguishing the flames, he began to scream out in a loud voice, '*Prestule, prestule*, get up quickly from your *reposorium*, take care that you don't stumble over the *gaudium*, because the *saltagraffa* is coming and is bringing *carniscoculum* along with her, and unless you come to the rescue of your house with *abundantia*, you will see the end of all your *sustantia*.'

Father Papiro, who was still lying fast asleep in bed when Pirino began his shouting, woke up and strained his ears to catch the words, but he had no notion as to what Pirino meant, because he had clean forgotten the meaning of the words he had lately used when questioning the boy. By this time the fire was doing its work at all four corners of the house and in a very little time Pre Papiro's own room would also be ablaze. At last, when he smelt the smoke, he got up quickly and found that his house was burning down. Then he went directly to try to extinguish the flames, but it was too late. The fire was burning fiercely on all sides and he barely escaped the house with his life. Thus Father Papiro was stripped of all his earthly possessions and was left with no other cloak than his own ignorance. After having fully avenged himself for his injuries, Pirino quit tending his father's pigs and returned to Padua, where, as best he could, he continued the studies he had already begun so promisingly and at last became of man of great renown.

After Vicenza had brought her comic fable to an end, and was highly praised for it by all the company, the Signora commanded that she waste no time in propounding her enigma, which, amid continuing laughter, the young lady gave in these words:

> Dead to men I seem to be,
> Yet surely breath there is in me;
> Cruel is my fate, I trow,
> Buffeted now high, now low.
> But assaults of fist and heel
> Vex me not, for naught I feel.
> Backwards, forwards, urged and driven,
> Soaring high from earth to heaven,
> Blameless I amid all my woes,
> Yet find all men my bitter foes.

When she saw that no one of the company understood her ambiguous riddle, Vicenza cut the knot in a graceful and dignified manner, 'This enigma of mine, which you listened to with such close attention, signifies the football, which, though it is dead, has breath inside when it is inflated. It is thrown about by the players, now here, now there, now with the hands, now with the feet, and assaulted by everyone as though it were their chief foe.'

Fiordiana, whose turn at storytelling was the last for the evening, rose from her seat and said in a sprightly manner, 'Signora, it would give me no small delight if Signor Ferier Beltramo, kind as he is, would do me a certain favour for which I'll always hold myself in his debt.'

Signor Ferier, hearing his name and the request to grant a favour, said, 'Signora Fiordiana, it is your part to command and mine to obey. So ask me to do whatever may please you, because I'll use my best endeavour to carry out your full wishes.'

When she heard this kindly answer, the damsel first thanked him heartily for his gracious consent, and then said, 'I ask of you, Signor Ferier, only that you assume my place as the next storyteller and recount a fable in my stead.'

When he heard this modest request, Signor Ferier at first began to excuse himself, for such was his custom. But after a little while, seeing that all the company supported Fiordiana's request, he threw aside his show of reticence and said, 'Signora Fiordiana, to gratify your wishes and those of this honourable company, I'm willing to fulfil your request, although don't blame me for what I choose to give you, for I'm a feeble instrument and little versed in such accomplishments, but blame your-selves who are the prime cause.' Having thus presented his excuses, he launched into his fable as follows.

IX.4 Commentary

These two vignettes, rather awkwardly yoked together, expose the ped-antry that was an inevitable by-product of Latin culture. This notoriously difficult language had imposed itself upon the Middle Ages and the humanist Renaissance as the ultimate marker of learning, and hence of intellectual, social, and professional elitism. Inevitably, there were those who pretended to competence merely to enjoy a place among the erudite, a pretence that came with a risk, as the protagonist in the present tale will twice discover: when the bishop detects his ignorance; and when a knowledgeable scholar seeks revenge. That a country priest from the

Brescian outback should be classed among such imposters in fronting neologisms too abstruse for his own retention carries its own satiric weight; priests should have been Latin-literate by definition, but often could not perform so much as 'neck verse' (sufficient Latin to enjoy clerical exemption from legal prosecution). The precise location is the village of Bedicuollo, which, today, is the agricultural town of Bedizzole, about 17 kilometres from Brescia. Straparola may be enjoying a private joke in his choice of settings.

The second part of the present story is a schoolboy's revenge upon a pedantic priest who had humiliated him with his homemade and barely comprehensible Latin. It is the stuff that Giordano Bruno seems to have collected over a lifetime and delivered in an avalanche through the person of Manfurio the pedant in his *Candelaio*. His Latin is all very barren material, set up for show by a man so immersed in his pedagogical world that he speaks no language at all except pieces of his lessons. He is no complete ignoramus, like Papiro Schizza, but has become so impregnated with things Latinate that he loses himself in a discourse of pomposity and obscurity. As for the affectation of using rote Latin tags to impress the plebeians, one may call to the witness stand Chaucer's Summoner, who repeatedly cried out, 'Questio quid iuris' and in a single phrase 'spent al his philosophie.'[38] Because it was by Latin that a man was made, it was by the absence of its true mastery that pretenders were discomforted.

That the shortcomings in the employment of Latin characterizing the two parts of the story are not entirely complementary need not detain the critically inclined. Clearly, Straparola, or the unspecified raconteur who supplied him with the design, saw an opportunity to join materials and make the tale a 'two-for-one' by playing upon the priest's linguistic deficiencies from contrasting perspectives. In the first, the priest is so ignorant that the invitation to participate in the local festival in clerical garb (copes and tunics) is taken as a request for cooked capons (*cappis* as capons, *coctis* as cooked). The bishop, a quick-witted and sporting man,

---

38 *Canterbury Tales*, 'General Prologue' A 646, ed. Albert C. Baugh (New York: Appleton-Century-Crofts, 1963), p. 252. For the *Candelaio* see *The Candlebearer*, trans. Gino Moliterno (Ottawa: Dovehouse Editions, 2000) or *Renaissance Comedy: The Italian Masters*, ed. Donald Beecher, 2 vols. (Toronto: University of Toronto Press, 2009), vol. II, pp. 323–465.

to his own advantage, simply allowed the misunderstanding to run its course. Heaven knows what he did thereafter with five hundred pieces of fencing supplied for his *mille gratis*. There is a kind of logic in Papiro's mistaking of similar words, but not much judgment or reasonable inference in assuming the bishop could have intended capons or hurdles. Language identification is also a matter of context and probability based on social understanding. This is merely an occasion to laugh at a fool who pretends to learning, comprehends little, and reasons amiss. It is a different matter altogether to know enough Latin (as in the second part) to replace the names of things with their attributes, turning cats into rat catchers, but forgetting they are cats. A little philosophical essay might be extrapolated from Papiro's example concerning the origins of Babel and the necessity for a universal coordination between *les mots* (words) and *les choses* (things). The point is underscored when the humiliated scholar creates an emergency by setting the cat's tail on fire while using the priest's own baffle-Latin to warn him of the danger.[39]

The second part, with its signature form of narrative, belongs to an established story type ('extraordinary names,' ATU type 1940) in which the pupil is taught an eccentric nomenclature for ordinary objects. It is known in Germany as 'Die Scheune Brennt' (The barn is burning) and pertains particularly to those featuring a farmer and his farmhand who is taught his master's odd dialectal name for things. A closely related tradition, that of the present story, involves a priest and a scholar. Only in the latter is the cat's tail prepared and ignited, but whether it catches fire by accident or intention, the useless barrage of words that follows produces the same disastrous effect. The story's earliest literary vestige dates to the fifteenth century – to 1479 in the *Diarium* of Johannes Knebel to be precise – but it is undoubtedly older and almost certainly originates in the culture of the medieval grammar school.[40] The frequency of the

---

39 The translation of Straparola's Latin description of the emergency includes only the key words that Father Papiro had used in correcting the student. In the original, the entire message of Pirino, shouted out at the top of his lungs, was in Latin: 'Prestule, prestule, surge de reposorio et vidde ne cadas in gaudium, quia venit saltagraffa et portavit carniscoculum, et nisi succurres domum cum abundantia, non restabit tibi substantia.'

40 Originating in a reference to 'Jakob' Knebel's '*Basle Chronicle*,' 1479, which turns out to be Johannes Knebel's *Diarium*, 1476–9. In his version of 'Die Scheune brennt' (The barn is burning) the fire is accidentally set by the cat, which causes the

tale in later folklore suggests, moreover, that long before the sixteenth century, it had also become a part of popular culture. By the end of the nineteenth century the story was known, whether of priests or farmers, in every language region from the Basque country to Finland.

The only other version of the story predating Straparola's is that of Bonaventure des Périers entitled 'De jeune fils qui fit valoir le beau latin que son curé luy avoit monster' (Of the young son who put to good use the fine Latin taught to him by his priest). It adds to the assurance that Straparola was working with an established popular narrative, for while Des Périers's collection, appearing before 1544, might be cited as Straparola's source, more probably both authors drew upon the same popular folk tale. In 'De jeune fils,' a rich labourer sends his son to Paris and upon the boy's return invites the priest to supper. Keen for a demonstration of the boy's progress, the father asks the priest to test him. Now despite the young scholar's correct answers, the priest insists on finding fault and supplying a foolish construction of his own, seeking to impose his reputation for learning upon all present at the boy's expense. The distressed father was ready to beat the child for his stupidity, leaving the lad with a score to settle. The denouement is precisely as in Straparola: lighting a cat's tail, calling the priest from his bed using his own gibberish, and the loss of all but life in the conflagration.[41] The stories are separated by a decade and their relationship is close. Insofar as they are tantamount to the same tale that appears in later collections collected from the oral tradition, Des Périers and Straparola jointly confirm its early existence and availability for literary transcription in many parts of Europe.

As for authors who more generally satirized Latin pedantry and clerical schools, there are many indeed. Béroalde de Verville makes light of such stuff in his *Le moyen de parvenir* (1610), in which his characters

---

farmhand to shout out the emergency in the periphrastic names taught him by the farmer. The mis-reference is from Kenneth Jackson and Edward Wilson, 'The Barn Is Burning,' *Folklore* 47, no. 2 (June 1936), p. 191. See Knebel's *Diarium* in *Basler Chroniken 2–3*, ed. von W. Vischer (Leipzig: Hirzel, 1887). For further discussion, see S. Prato, 'Una novellina popolare italiana nello Straparola e nel Des Périers,' in *Archivio per lo studio delle tradizioni popolari* 66 (1887), pp. 43–68.

41 *Les nouvelles recreations et joyeux devis* in *Oeuvres françois* (Paris: P. Jannet, 1856), no. 21, vol. II, pp. 95–8.

indulge in an irreverent dismantling of table-talk culture while poking fun at French authors from Rabelais to Montaigne. In no. 26, 'Livre de raison,' a series of questions is posed to school boys about their level of Latin, and in no. 27, 'Parabole,' scholars are constantly correcting one another and the Latin of a priest is put to the test. No. 29, 'Chapitre général,' has more such wordplay as 'coupibus couillibus rasibus du culibus a diabolus,' in which the reader will be pleased to recognize such delicate terms as 'cut, balls, shave, ass, devil,' with syntax to be supplied.[42] To leave the specific story type of the burning barn for satirical humour concerning the pedagogical uses and abuses of Latin is a study of potentially vast proportions.

Centuries later, the tale of jargon, fire, and the victim's payback turns up in Sicily, involving a tiresome husband who replaces plain language with periphrastic names – 'abundance' for water, 'impeders' for chairs – imposing his pedantry particularly on the helpless servant boy. This lad, in collusion with the man's wife, sets the house afire, thereafter announcing the disaster to the master in his own lingo while chaining him into the room where he is engulfed in the flames – rough justice for a palaverer. If the story ever had finesse, it is obliterated here. There are editors of learned journals who would consign scholars for their excessive use of jargon to similar fates.[43]

The list could go on. In Spain, in a story collected by Aurelia Espinosa, the cat becomes a 'cazalorates,' a hunter of rats. The servant, ignorant of such terms, is nevertheless treated with scorn and told that someday he will know the proper names for things such as 'recreancia' in place of 'cama' for bed. This servant attaches oakum to the cat's tail and sets it alight.[44] The pedant is mean-spirited, but always the punishment seems to exceed the crime, to the apparent pleasure of those who entertained

---

42 *Le moyen de parvenir*, ed. Hélène Moreau and André Tournon (Aix-en-Provence: Université de Provence, 1984), pp. 62–72.

43 'Tippiti nnàppiti' in *The Collected Sicilian Folk and Fairy Tales of Giuseppe Pitrè*, trans. Jack Zipes and Joseph Russo, 2 vols. (New York: Routledge, 2008), no. 143, vol. I, pp. 530–2.

44 Aurelio M. Espinosa, 'El agnus dei' in *Cuentos populares españolas*, 3 vols. (Madrid, 1946), no. 57, vol. I, pp. 101–6. For another version in Italian, see Giuseppe Pitrè, ed., 'Vocaboli' in *Novelline popolare toscana* (Palermo: Edikronos, 1981), no. 2, pp. 269–71.

the tale through generations. At this point, because these stories present but variations upon a common theme and design, there is little purpose in offering more than a few further examples of these late renditions in a concluding note.[45]

---

45 Further versions were assembled by Stanislao Prato in 'Una novellina popolare italiana nella Straparola e nel Des Periers.' He added an Albenga version (from the Genovesa) told to him by Gennaro Finamore, in which a cat's tale is lit afire and the cat sent into the house of the pedant priest. Prato adds a substantial list of less specific stories in which cruel schoolmasters are repaid with mayhem by their students (p. 63), as well as tales of ignited cats in the tradition of Samson's incendiary foxes. The high incidence of common words between Straparola and the Albenga tale suggests a direct Straparola influence, as in 'Surge, Prester, quia venit saltingraffa portans carniscoculum inter capillos terrae, ac, nisi venerit abundantia peribit omnis substantia.' Straparola's Papiro employs 'saltingraffa' 'carniscoculum,' 'abundantia,' and 'substantia' for cat, fire, water, and material wealth. *Archivio per lo studio delle tradizioni popolari*, no. VI (Palermo: Luigi Pedone Lauriel, 1887), pp. 43–68. In a version of the story from Nocera, 'El sor Don Dondolo,' the child is beaten, although he answers correctly, because he fails to identify 'il santo arriposagolo' for a bed (p. 45), while in 'Domine-Domine' from Spoleto, a servant mortified by his supposed ignorance sets fire 'dette foco a lu fenu' before reciting the priest's words back to him, who, to save himself, nearly breaks his neck on the stairs (p. 44).

IX. Fable 5
Of the Bergamasques and the Florentines

FERIER BELTRAMO

The Florentines and the Bergamasques convoke their learned men for a disputation, whereupon the Bergamasques, by a certain astute trick, outwit their opponents.

I would remind you, comely ladies, that however great the difference is between men of wisdom and letters and men of duller and more matter-of-fact minds, sometimes it happens that sages are defeated by men of small learning. Is this not clearly set forth in the Holy Scriptures, where we may read how the simple and despised apostles confounded the understanding of those who were full of knowledge and wisdom? I will strive to set this out plainly for you in this little fable of mine.

Some time ago – as I often heard told by my grandsires, and you may have heard as well – it happened that a number of Florentine and Bergamasque merchants were travelling together and, as often occurs, they started discussing all sorts of things. In passing from topic to topic, one of the Florentines said, 'To tell you the truth, you Bergamasques, as nearly as we can judge, are incredibly stupid and thick-headed. Your temperaments are so coarse-grained that if it weren't for this bit of merchandising and trading you do, you'd be good for nothing. And if you have any luck in your business dealings, it's not for your smartness or your skinny wits, but your innate greed and born avarice. I've just never met anyone as lard-headed and dumb as you.'

On hearing these words, a certain Bergamasque came forward and said, 'Well, as far as I'm concerned, we Bergamasques are worth more than you Florentines any way you want to reckon the matter. Maybe you Florentines are more gifted with your smooth talk that pleases the ears of your listeners more than our dialect does, but in every other way you're inferior to us Bergamasques by a long shot. If you'll take the trouble to have a close look around, you'll discover there isn't a man among us, high or low, who hasn't achieved some knowledge of literature. And what's more, all of us are ready any time to carry out noble causes. Nobody can say that such a spirit is met with very often among you Florentines except in the case of the rare few.' That gave rise to a big argument between the two parties in which the Bergamasques weren't willing to cede a thing to the Florentines, nor the Florentines to the Bergamasques, each one up-holding his own side, until finally a Bergamasque merchant got up and said, 'What's the good of all this wrangling? Let's put the matter to the test by providing for a solemn convention, inviting the very flower of our learned men, both Florentines and Bergamasques, to see which side holds the pre-eminent place.'

The Florentines consented right away to this proposition, although there was still the matter to settle of whether the Florentines should go to Bergamo, or the Bergamasques to Florence. So after much discussion, they agreed to cast lots. After preparing two slips of paper and putting them into a vase, they drew one out, which declared that the Florentines should go to Bergamo.

The day for the match was set for the calends of May. This point having been decided, the merchants went back to their respective cities and re-ferred the entire matter to their wise and learned townsmen, who, as soon as they heard the proposal, were greatly pleased by it all and set to work to prepare themselves for long and subtle disputations. The Bergamasques, clever and crafty folk that they were, began to lay plans how they might best beat the Florentines and leave them in a state of shame and confu-sion. Thus, they called together all the learned men of the city, gram-marians, rhetoricians, lawyers, canonists, philosophers, theologians, and doctors of every other faculty. From among these men, they chose those with the keenest wit and told them to keep themselves ready at home and prepared to render service as the rock and bulwark of their city in the dispute with the Florentines. The rest of the learned doctors they dressed in ragged clothes, telling them to go out of the city and to place themselves at different places along the road by which the Florentines must pass, there to accost the strangers at every opportunity, and always to speak to them in Latin. So it happened that these scholars of Bergamo dressed them-selves up in coarse clothes and circulated among the peasants of the plain, setting to work at various jobs, some digging ditches, others breaking up the earth with pickaxes and shovels, one man doing this and another that.

While the doctors of Bergamo were labouring in such fashion that anyone would have taken them for peasants, lo and behold the Florentine delegation came riding past in great pomp and splendour, and when they noticed these men working in the fields, they cried out to them, 'God be with you good brothers.'

Those they took for peasants called back, 'Bene veniant tanti viri.' [Well may the arrival be of such illustrious men.]

The Florentines, thinking they were making some joke, said, 'How many miles have we yet to cover before we come to the city of Bergamo?'

To which the Bergamasques answered, 'Decem vel circa.' [Ten or thereabouts.]

When the Florentines heard this reply they said, 'Brethren, we address you in the vulgar tongue; how comes it that you answer us in Latin?'

The Bergamasques replied, 'Ne miremini, excellentissimi domini. Unusquisque enim nostrum sic, ut auditis, loquitur, quoniam majores et sapientiores nostri sic nos docuerunt.' [Don't be astonished, most excellent lords. Each one of us speaks in this way as you hear because our elders and wisemen have instructed us in this way.]

Having left these men behind, the Florentines, as they continued their journey, saw other peasants who were digging ditches beside the highway and, coming to a halt, they said to them, 'Ho, friends! Ho, there! May God be with you!'

To which greeting the Bergamasques answered, 'Et Deus vobiscum semper sit.' [And may God always be with you.]

'How far is it to Bergamo?' inquired the Florentines.

Whereupon the others answered, 'Exigua vobis restat via.' [There is only a little way for you to go.]

After this reply, they proceeded from one topic to another until at last they began to dispute together on questions of philosophy, concerning which these Bergamasque peasants argued with such weight and subtlety that the Florentine doctors were hard pressed to answer them. Struck with astonishment, they said to each other, 'To be sure, it's truly amazing that these mere rustics, who spend all their time in these menial, rural labours, are so well versed in polite learning.' Then they rode on towards a neat and well-kept inn not far distant from the city. But before they got there, a stable boy went out to meet them and invited them to stop over at his establishment, saying, 'Domini, libet ne vobis hospitari? Hic enim vobis erit bonum hospitium.' [My lords, is it lodging you may be seeking? Here you will find excellent hospitality and accommodation.] Because the Florentines were already worn out from the long journey, they gladly dismounted from their horses. But when they thought to have gone up-stairs to get some repose, the innkeeper advanced and said, 'Excellentissimi domini, placet ne vobis ut praeparetur coena? Hic enim sunt bona vina, ova recentia, carnes, volatilia, et alia huiusmodi.' [Most excellent lords, would you not like to have dinner prepared? Here, most assuredly, there are good wines, fresh eggs, meat, fowl, and many other such things.] Now the Florentines were filled with greater amazement than before and hardly knew what to say, insofar as all the people they had talked to spoke Latin as if they had studied it from their earliest days.

A short time later there came into the room one in the guise of a serving-maid, who, in fact, was a certain nun, a woman of considerable knowledge and learning. She had been well instructed on how to handle herself in this situation, saying to them according to their plan, 'Indigent ne dominationes vostrae re aliqua? Placet, ut sternentur lectuli, ut requiem capiatis?' [My lordships, are you in need of anything? Would you not like to have beds made up for you in order to get some rest?] The Florentines were utterly overcome with astonishment at these words of the servingwoman and right away began to talk with her. After discoursing on many matters, and always in the Latin tongue, she brought up the subject of theology and spoke about it with such universal knowledge that all who heard her were compelled to praise her in the highest terms. While she held the Florentine doctors in dispute, someone dressed as a furnace-man, all black with coal dust, entered the room and, hearing the discussion going on between the maid and the strangers, interposed with a speech of his own, putting forth an interpretation of the Holy Scriptures so learned and erudite that all the Florentine doctors declared that they had never before heard a more excellent discourse.

When this theological debate had come to an end, the Florentines retired to get some rest, and the next day they took counsel among themselves whether they should return to Florence immediately or go on to Bergamo. After much wrangling, they came to the decision that it would be wiser to go back immediately. 'For if such deep learning is found among field labourers, innkeepers, and domestics, both male and female, what must we expect to meet in the city where men are always more accomplished than in the country, devoting themselves to the pursuit of learning throughout the entire year?' As soon as they had come to this decision, without further hesitation and without ever seeing the walls of the city of Bergamo, they mounted their horses and rode back to Florence. On account of this wily stratagem of theirs, the Bergamasques contrived to outwit the Florentines, and ever since that time they have enjoyed a privilege granted to them by the emperor to travel securely in all parts of the world.

As Signor Ferier brought his story to an end, all the listeners laughed heartily, praising the astuteness of the Bergamasques and casting blame and scorn on the cowardice of the Florentines. But because the Signora imagined that such a discussion must cast aspersions upon the honour of Florentine learning, for which she had no small regard, she gave command that everyone should be silent and that Signor Ferier should go on with his enigma. But turning towards Fiordiana, he said, 'Signora, you have laid upon me the burden of telling a fable which can hardly have given much pleasure to any of the listeners, so it would be only right and just that you assume the task of setting an enigma. I have no skill or expertise in such matters, so I'm requesting that you not urge me to it.'

Fiordiana, who never lacked courage, spoke up forthrightly, 'Signor Ferier, I'll not refuse this duty, and at the same time I wish to thank you most gratefully for all you've done for me.' And then, with a merry face, she set forth her enigma.

> I know not why, unfortunate,
> I meet with such an evil fate,
> That although a valiant male I'm born,
> Into a female all forlorn
> I soon am turned. To work this change
> Men fall on me with working strange.
> With grievous heavy blows I'm wrought,
> And made almost a thing of naught.
> And next, a lot more painful yet,
> In burning fiery furnace set,
> To cruel men a boon to give.
> And thus I die that they may live.

Because the hour was late and the grasshoppers had ceased their screeching, and the brightness of the dawn was beginning to shine in the east, the Signora gave the word that Fiordiana should tell the meaning of her riddle right away and that after this, everyone should go home, remembering to return on the following evening according to the established practice. So the damsel cut the knot of her ambiguous enigma in this graceful and pleasing way: 'The enigma I lately gave you to guess, in fact, means only wheat, the name of which is masculine, but which becomes feminine after it is changed into flour. Then, after a sore beating it is made into dough and is finally baked in the fire to serve for the nourishment of man.'

After all the company had warmly praised Fiordiana's solution, they rose from their seats and, having taken leave of the Signora, they went their several ways with eyes heavy with sleep.

The End of the Ninth Night

IX.5 Commentary

Among nations and peoples it is a common practice to choose from among their cities or regions one in particular that, for its harsh accent, odd manners, and backward learning, epitomizes the nadir of their cultural aspirations. The stories of that region's fools, dupes, and numbskulls serve to bolster the snobbery of those who mock them. In Renaissance Italy, that lot fell upon the northern city of Bergamo and the surrounding Lombard countryside, no doubt by a self-fulfilling process, once the nomination had been made. Not only did these folk sport a shocking *patois* and rustic manners, to the discrediting of their intelligence, but they had invaded the cities as emigrant hewers and haulers in search of employment, whether as servants, porters, or stevedores, bringing with them their rough accents, their bluff mores, and their occasionally sharp wit. The stereotype later came to be nuanced by more precise origins: those from the *contado* around Bergamo, and those from the city itself, which was further divided between the upper and lower towns. Of the city, it was said to be like an amphitheatre built on the slopes of the Brentano valley, its lower sector producing the dolts, oafs, and half-wits that came to be epitomized in the simpleton servant Harlequin, and its upper sector producing the crafty and shrewd cronies embodied in Brighella.[46] Thus, out of Bergamo came two of the *commedia dell'arte's* most engaging and enigmatic characters. Both, however, are 'zannis' (from Giovanni), or clowning servants, because Bergamasques, in general, were thought to be fit for little more than servitude. This city and its outlying regions became the choice of the Italians for representing the bumpkin, shrewd at times as wily peasants have always been, but the

---

46 Pierre Louis Duchartre, *The Italian Comedy*, trans. Randolf Weaver (New York: Dover [1929], 1966), p. 124.

opposite of all that constitutes refined learning, urbanity, and elegant speech. Thus, it was spread about as a commonplace that 'I Bergamaschi hanno il becco grosso, ma la ingegno sottile' (Bergamasques have big mouths, but dull brains). Straparola's story plays upon the commonplace by reversing the outcome of the battle of the cultural winners and losers by scoring an ironic victory for the denizens of Bergamo, winning for them a grant from the emperor to travel safely in all parts of the world.

Just as Bergamo came to epitomize bumpkin culture, Florence – the city of Dante, Boccaccio, Ficino, and Petrarch (by adoption), along with other literati – came to epitomize learning, as well as linguistic and social refinement. The Florentine dialect took the lead in the contest for the choice of a regional language most deserving to become standard Italian, and the Florentine scholars were thought to be the finest in Italy. Thus, these two cities emerged as emblems of their attributes, joined forever as opposites in the allegory of learning and culture. Federigo, in his discussion of proper speech and its origins in Castiglione's *Book of the Courtier* (1517), confirms the commonplace contention between the two cities in favouring the Tuscan vocabulary. This is a language of substance and learning, he tells us, as opposed to mere usage through which the faults of speech may prevail among many ignorant persons. To prioritize according to vulgar usage, he argues, is to deny the very real qualities that distinguish between Bergamasque and Florentine, a statement that, for him, required no argument or defence.[47] Pietro Aretino relies for certain strokes of humour on this same cultural dichotomy in his *Cortigiana*. At the heart of the play is the arrival in Rome of a naive and innocent young scholar from Siena, a mere 'studiante in libris' named Maco de Coe; he intends to become a cardinal by first becoming a courtier, but finds himself, instead, the dupe of the 'courtier makers.' The rivalry between Siena and Rome is bolstered by that between Bergamo and Florence. At one point the matter of language arises, for the self-fashioning man must in some sense choose among the many from Bergamese to Florentine. Aretino then tells the little legend about Petrarch's Laura as Calliope's servant, and thus how the girl from Avignon learned the language of Tuscany, which Petrarch thereafter adopted in her honour. He calls the entire play 'The Courtesan,' who, as the daughter of a Tuscan father and a Bergamasque mother, is a mixed form of the highest and

---

47 Trans. Charles S. Singleton (Garden City, NY: Doubleday-Anchor, 1959), bk. I, 30, p. 50.

the lowest formal and stylistic elements, a *métissage* (cross-breeding) that defines his art, for the muses 'eat nothing but delicate little Florentine salads,' while his play also deals in the rude hearty fare of rustics. Elsewhere, he states that the ultimate insult to a scholar's intelligence is to say that his learning would bring him honour among the Bergamasques.[48] The opposition between the two had by then suffused itself into the culture as an allegory of all that is 'high' and 'low.'

Just how saturated Italian culture had become with this idea can only be sketched out briefly. Satire against rustics with reference to those hailing from Bergamo originates, perhaps, in the *strambotti* of the second half of the fourteenth century, which are love songs and sonnets in the rustic manner. The bumptiousness of character, the simple psychology, and the local dialect were compounded together in the word 'bergamasca.' One such collection was entitled *Strambotti d'ogni sorte, Sonetti alla bergamasca*, of which only three copies remain, two in Italy, and the third sold at Christie's in 1996.[49] Many such poems have been collected and anthologized. A new phase emerges in the plays of Angelo Beolco (Ruzante) and Andrea Calmo in his *Il fiorina*. Ruzante, in a play by the same name, had declared his distaste for Florentine usage as entirely unnatural, for those who affect it also try to change their dress and eating habits; his characters, if they are to be themselves, must go on eating their salted cheese, drinking their strong wine, and speaking wholesome Paduan. Calmo goes ever further in deploying the dialects of Venice, Dalmatia, and Bergamo. Two peasants in love with Fiore are kept in a

---

48 Trans. Leonard Sbrocchi and Douglas Campbell, intro. Raymond Waddington, Carleton Renaissance Plays in Translation 38 (Ottawa: Dovehouse Editions, 2003), pp. 55, 53, 54. Donato Pirovano, ed., Straparola, *Piacevoli notti*, 2 vols. (Rome: Salerno, 2000), vol. II, p. 607, mentions as evidence of the Florentine-Bergamasque rivalry the anonymous *Le malatie de Vilani con alquanti Strambotti alla Bergamascha. Et uno contrasto de uno Fiorentino et uno Bergamascho*, to which he assigns as publisher Paolo Danza. This intriguing work I have not been able to examine, but the latter, *Uno contrasto*, is referred to by Carlo Ginsberg in *The Night Battles: Witchcraft and Agrarian Cults in the Sixteenth and Seventeenth Centuries* (1966), trans. John and Anne Tedeschi (London, Routledge & Kegan Paul, 1983), p. 196n38, as 'n.p. n.d. British Library C.57.1 7[3]'; he states that it was widely disseminated. It was also among the items in the Arundel collection given to the Royal Society in 1667, described as a ballad of four leaves published in Venice, 1515, the catalogue published by William Clowes & Sons for the London Royal Society, 1910.

49 *Strombotti d'ogni sorte* (Rome: Eucharius Silber, ca. 1500). Maria Corti edited a number of them for the collection by Carlo Dionisotti, *Tra latino e volgare* (Padua: Antenore, 1974).

steady imbroglio. One of them, Sandrin from Bergamo, speaks the lingo from home while quarrelling vociferously with the other. In the end, Fiore has been so good at playing them off each other that she loses them both and has to accept the old man Coccolin, their union blessed by his dimwitted friend, Allegretto.[50]

This legacy of the *strambotti* and *mascherate bergamaschi* is fused, however, with a growing satire against the effects of the very real appearance of rustics in the workforces of the major cities. Folengo gives a lighter portrait of these singing beasts of burden doing the grunt work of the warehouses and quays, and eating their chestnut-meal cakes.[51] But Tomaso Garzoni is less kind in describing the army of Bergamasques who had invaded Venice, for they work like asses and mules and express their foolish and doltish views on everything in their thick accent.[52] It is to be recalled that Straparola's own Zambù, the third of the three hunchback brothers from Valsabbia (V.3), a part of the Bergamese backcountry, made his way directly to Venice to haul boats at the port, and thereafter to take odd jobs with a variety of bosses, all of whom chase him away for his eccentricity and stupidity. Cinzio degli Fabrizii, in the section of his *Libro della origine delli volgari proverbi* elaborating upon the proverb 'La va da tristo a cattivo' (Going from bad to worse), describes the presence of the Bergamasque labourers as an invasion responsible for the decline of Venetian morals and deserving of his invective.[53] For the emergence of this satiric assault upon the 'villano,' readers will want to consult the study by Domenico Merlini.[54]

The following profile by Teofilo Folengo in his *Il Baldo* (Baldus, 1517, full ed. 1521, final rev. ed. 1552) restates the stereotype of the muscular, thick-headed labourers who, in hard times – like the servants from Asturia on the Madrileno stage – went to the cities on the plains and

---

50 *La fiorina, comedia facetissima* (Venice: Iseppo Foresto, 1557).

51 *Le opera maccheroniche di Merlin Cocai* (Teofilo Folengo), ed. Attilio Partioli (Mantua: G. Mondavi, 1882–8), vol. I, p. 253.

52 *La piazza universale di tutte le professioni del mondo* (Venice: Giovanni Battista Somascho, 1585, 1586, 1588), Discourse 114, [p. 344]. Modern edition, ed. Paolo Cherchi (Turin: G. Einaudi, 1996).

53 Aloise Cinzio delli Fabrizi, *Libro della origine delli volgari proverbi* (Venice: B. & M. dei Vitali, 1526); Aloyse Cinzio de gli Fabritii, *Libro* (Milan: Spirali, 2007).

54 See his chap. 4, 'La satira contro il villano nella poesia popolareggiante. L'origine dello zanni della commedia dell' arte,' in *Saggio di richerche sulla satira contro il villano*, ed. Domenico Merlini (Turin: E. Loescher, 1894).

coasts in search of work, and there, with their rough ways and rustic dialect, made a comic space around themselves in the local society. 'They are Bergamasques, for the most part, these porters, but not from the city itself. These are the ones who live on chestnut meal and country fare, coming down into the world from the Clusone mountains. They carry nothing out with them, but when they return, what loads they carry on their backs. They are stocky and thick-skinned, and they can digest iron. The cheese they eat keeps them strong on their legs and strengthens their backs. It helps the brains of a few as well, but that's not the case for our porters. Still, they're not so clumsy when speaking up for their interests. One barb of their wit strikes a harder blow than all the chit chat rattling around in the mouths of the Florentines (lit. the hundred bits of conversation a Florentine always has in his sack). There is no place on earth without its flood of porters, but the only true porters are Bergamasques who can load boats and carry more than a camel.'[55] This is not an entirely unsympathetic portrait, but there is nothing here that rescues a race from the slights of stereotyping to the detriment of their learning and intelligence. That Florence had come to its fullness by beggaring Bergamo was a thesis awaiting a time when some imaginative mind would construct its antithesis.

The fuse for that inversion of affairs resided in the shrewd wit that had always been attributed to the Bergamasques. It simply had to be brought to function in the name of all Bergamasques against the pretensions of the Florentines; it had to be a collective endeavour expressed through a narrative event. Just who came up with the invention of the inter-city contest will remain somewhat moot because of the wild card represented by popular culture and Straparola's relationship to it; conceivably he found the present story ready-made. But the attribution of its origin to Straparola is encouraged by his familiarity with works containing its leading ideas.

Among the *novelle* and *facetiae* of Morlini (1520) is the story of the Ferrarese court fool Gonnella, who had travelled widely to test his acumen against the wits of various cities and nations. As the story goes, he had never measured himself against the Neapolitans, celebrated for their sagacity and shrewdness. Such became his mission and itinerary. As he approached the city, he met a woman working in the pear orchards who

---

55 Folengo, *Il baldo*, trans. (Italian) Carlo Tonna (Reggio Emilia: Diabasis, 2004), bk. XII, ll. 68–96 (my translation).

caught his attention by folding a leaf in the form of a letter and swallowing it. 'To whom do you send that letter?' asked Gonnella. 'To my asshole in block capitals' came the reply, which left the famous fool in a stupor. Further along, he met another country woman washing at a fountain with her dress hiked up over her hips showing her undershirt pinched between her buttocks. 'Say there, doesn't it feel like your arse is eating your shirt?' 'For Jesus' sake, you're way off,' she replied, 'it's my shirt-tail wiping my bum hole so you can do me the favour of kissing it.' This touch of vulgarity so shocked and frightened him that he revised his plans for testing Neapolitan wit and headed back to Ferrara, saying to himself, 'If the simple women of Naples are so full of such malicious retorts, what must the men be like?' 'This all goes to show that whether for vice or virtue, Neapolitans surpass all others the world over.'[56] When it came to the making of the present tale, a transfer of models seems all too apparent. If Morlini, by his invention, could shore up the credit of all Neapolitans by the tongue-strokes of low-lifers in the suburbs, Straparola could do the same for his own Bergamasques, folks with whom he might very well identify, being a one-time wanderer out of Caravaggio – another Lombard town – in search of work. This story also follows hard upon that of Papiro Schizza and the peasant's revenge, in which an ignorant, pedant priest imposes upon a young scholar with his pseudo-Latin, leaving the undeserving lad in humiliation until the tables turn and, in a real emergency, he can bring the priest to grief by citing his Latin back to him. What is learning if it disqualifies its practitioner from living efficiently in the real world? With Latin still on his mind, Straparola could easily adapt the experience of Gonnella near Naples to the arrival of the Florentines near Bergamo, a delegation that is led to believe it has already met its match in the Latin-speaking peasants of the Bergamese *campagna*. Moreover, just as the Neapolitans are celebrated the world over, the Bergamasques were assigned a 'safe-conduct' permit for world travel by the emperor.

---

56 *Les nouvelles*, trans. Fernand Caussy (Paris: E. Sansot, 1904), pp. 115–17; *Novelle e favole*, ed. Giovanni Villani (Rome: Salerno, 1983), no. 50, pp. 232–5. This story is by no means confined to Italy even as early as Morlini, for it appears in England in *A Hundred Merry Tales* by 1526 – telling not only of Gonella and the shirt between the woman's buttocks, but of the maiden who told the friar he could come and kiss where 'Bayard bites.' Ed. P.M. Zall (Lincoln: University of Nebraska Press, 1963), no. 23, p. 87.

Thereafter, the tables-turning Bergamasques became a new 'meme' or motif for comic exploitation. One example, potentially among many others, appears in the *Ecatommiti* (1565) of Giovanni Battista Giraldi, known among the English as Cinthio.[57] The story repeats the familiar facts, that the Bergamasques have big mouths but skimpy brains ('i bergamaschi hanno il becco grosso, ma lo ingegno sottile'), and that Tuscan is the most excellent and valued of all the languages of Italy, differing radically from the rude and graceless dialect in and around Bergamo. In preparation for the vignette to follow, Giraldi really lays it on to build up the irony. At the time of Leone de' Medici, when all virtue flourished, two of his servants were brought into his presence, one a native of Florence and the other from Bergamo, the latter a youth of quick wit but abominable speech, as with all men born in that country. When the Florentine gave him an order, repeating it three or four times over, the fellow just stood there doing nothing. The Florentine got into a snit, asking why it was that he could say a thing a hundred times and not be understood. 'How is it I understand you and you don't understand me, even if I say it ten times?' he asks. The sharp-witted Lombard replied to the effect that he was baffled that the other couldn't figure it out. Quite simply, 'he who speaks well is understood, and he who speaks badly, isn't. Thus, I clearly speak better than you do, because you comprehend and I don't.' This answer pleased Leone so much that he burst out laughing and told the Florentine that the other was completely right. You are indeed unfit to speak unless others understand you. Thereafter, he placed the Bergamasque in charge of various diplomatic missions and paid him handsomely into the bargain. Humour is constantly in search of opportunity, and those things that become stereotyped and commonplace are always subject to comic inversion. As matters stand for the moment, through the present story Straparola earns the patriot's badge as the maker of the battle between the nerds and the dolts, turning the tables to the benefit of his countrymen.

Those hearing the Italian version of Fiordiana's riddle understood immediately that masculine could become feminine when wheat or corn became flour, for 'frumento' and 'grano,' wheat and corn, are both masculine nouns, while 'farina,' flour, is feminine.

---

57 Giovanni Battista Giraldi, 'Un giovane Fiorentino riprende un Bergamasco' (How a Bergamasque gets back at a young Florentine), in *Gli ecatommiti* (Florence: Tipographia Borgha & Co., 1831), VII.2, pp. 320–1.

The Tenth Night

On all sides the beasts of the field, wearied by the labours of the day, were already seeking repose for their tired limbs, some resting upon soft feathers, some upon the hard and sharp-pointed rocks, some upon the swart herbage, and some amid the thick-leaved trees when the Signora, attended by her damsels, came forth from her chamber and went into the meeting hall where the company was gathered ready to listen to the next round of fables. Calling one of the servants, the Signora directed him to bring the golden vase, wherein they deposited the names of five of the young ladies, and then the drawing began. The first name to be chosen was Lauretta, the second Arianna, the third Alteria, the fourth Eritrea, and the fifth Cateruzza. But before the storytelling began, the Signora desired that after certain dances, Bembo should favour them with a canzonetta. Unable to come up with a sufficient excuse for himself, he began to sing in a sweet voice, while all sat listening in silence.

Song

> Love's ardour or love's chills I feel no more,
>   No more they make me fain,
> To ply you with my prayers in hope to gain
> The last, the sweetest boon you hold in store.
>   My spirit quails with fear,
> As to that hateful bourne I draw anear,
>   The bourne by mortals shunned in vain.
> And is this fruit the sweetest I shall find,
>   Enclosed within love's bitter rind?
> Shall I, when ended is my life,
>   No solace find
>   For all my weary days of strife?
> Shall there be granted me no rest benign
> Till I my trustful life for kindly death resign?

This sweet song of Bembo's greatly delighted all the listeners, and as soon as it had come to an end, Lauretta arose from her seat and began her fable in the following words.

X. Fable 1
Madonna Veronica Recovers
Her Stolen Jewels

LAURETTA

Finetta steals a necklace, a string of pearls, and other jewels from Madonna Veronica, the wife of Messer Brocardo di Cavalli, a gentleman of Verona, all of which Veronica recovers through the aid of one of her lovers, without her loss ever coming to her husband's ears.

Whenever I consider and reconsider the cares and perplexities that Fortune, day by day, sends our way for tormenting wretched mortals, I often conclude that no sufferings or sorrows can match those of a woman who loves her husband most loyally, yet without just cause is despised by him in return. For this reason, we should not be at all astonished if, at times, women as unhappy and miserable as those I've mentioned should employ all their powers to find some remedy for their unhappy states. And if by chance such ill-fated creatures should now and again inadvertently fall into some error, the husbands should not lay the blame on their wives but on themselves, seeing that in truth they are the ones responsible for the misfortune and shame that may overtake them. Such a fate as this might well have befallen a certain gracious lady of whom I'm about to speak, except that she was prudent and wise and, by her virtue and strength, she broke into pieces the arrows of unlawful love, keeping both her own honour and that of her husband unharmed.

In the noble and ancient city of Verona there lived not long ago Messer Brocardo di Cavalli, a man of great wealth and high reputation. Being unmarried, this gentleman took for his wife a daughter of Cansignorio della Scala by the name of Veronica. Although she was very beautiful, graceful, and modest, she did not win her husband's love, for as is often the case, he entertained another woman as his mistress. Because she was the delight of his heart, he took no thought of his wife. Madonna Veronica was sorely grieved, for she could not endure to think that such rare beauty as hers, which won the praises of all others, could be so despised and rejected by her husband. It chanced that this fair lady, having gone into the country to escape the heat of the summer, was one day walking all alone before the door of her house assiduously debating with herself the conduct and habits of her husband, considering how little he loved her and how common, vile, and filthy that strumpet was who had so dazzled the eyes of his understanding that he saw no better than a blind man. Lamenting thus to herself, she said, 'O, how much better it had been if my father had given me in marriage to a poor man than to one who is so wealthy, for then I would have spent my days in greater pleasure and contentment than I do now. What good are all these riches to me? What profits it me to go dressed in sumptuous clothes, to be decked out with gems, necklaces, pendants, and other precious jewels? Truly, all these trappings are but mirages compared to the delights that a happy wife enjoys with her husband.'

While Signora Veronica was dwelling upon these injurious thoughts, a beggar woman suddenly came across her path whose real trade was to steal anything she could find. She was, moreover, so wily and cunning that she could easily have cozened not only a lady in Signora Veronica's distraught condition, but any grave and prudent man she might have met. This woman, whose name was Finetta, no sooner saw the gentle lady absorbed in deep thought walking up and down in front of her house than she began to weave a plot against her. Approaching her, she saluted her respectfully and begged alms of her. Thinking of other matters than almsgiving, the lady repulsed her with an angry look. But the crafty and thievish Finetta was of no mind to go away. Peering earnestly into the lady's face and observing her sadness and sorrow, she said, 'O gentle lady, what ill can have befallen you that you look so full of care? Can it be that your husband leads you an ill life? Will it please you that I tell you your fortune?'

As soon as the lady heard these words, she imagined that this common vagrant had discovered the wound that was cruelly tormenting her, whereupon she began to weep bitterly, for it seemed to her as though she saw her husband lying dead before her eyes. Finetta, when she marked the lady's scalding tears and heartfelt sighs, her agonized sobbing and bitter lamentations, she said, 'What can be the cause of this piteous grief of yours, gracious Madonna?'

To this the lady answered, 'When you said that perchance my husband led me an ill life, you then laid bare my heart as with a knife.'

Finetta answered, 'Gentle lady, I only need to look a person narrowly in the face to tell exactly what her life has been. Your wound, in truth, is recent and fresh, and on this account can be healed without difficulty. But if it were of long standing and festered, it would be much harder to cure.'

The lady, when she heard the beggar woman discourse in this way, told her everything about the ways of her husband, minutely recounting his behaviour, the wicked life he led, and the evil treatment he gave her. When Finetta heard the whole of this pitiful story, she knew that her own plans were about to come to fruition exactly according to her wishes, or even beyond them. 'Dear Madonna,' she continued, 'do not grieve any more, but keep steadfast and of good cheer, for we'll soon find a remedy for your trouble. Whenever it may please you, I'll devise a method by which you may win the ardent love of your husband and cause him to follow you like a man possessed.' While they were thus conversing, they went into the bedroom where Madonna Veronica was accustomed to sleep with her husband. After they had both sat down, Finetta said, 'Madonna, if it is your desire that we get down to work on this matter, I'll ask you to send all the maids and servants out of the room to occupy themselves with the duties of the household. Then we can stay on by ourselves and do everything that is necessary for your case.'

After the servants had been dismissed from the room and the door closed, Finetta said, 'Now bring me the most beautiful of your golden necklaces, together with a string of pearls.' With that, Madonna Veronica opened one of her caskets and took out a necklace with a fine pendant and a string of oriental pearls that she handed over to Finetta. As soon as she had taken the jewels in her hand, the woman asked for a cloth of white linen, and this at once Madonna Veronica gave to her. Having then taken up all the jewels one by one, she made certain signs over them of a kind used by women in such trades and placed them separately into the white cloth. Next, in the presence of Madonna Veronica, she tied the cloth into a tight knot with the jewels inside, muttering her secret spells over it and making enigmatic gestures with her hands. Then, handing the cloth over to Madonna Veronica, she said to her, 'Madonna, take this cloth and with your own hands place it under the pillow upon which your husband sleeps. Once you have done this you'll see a wonderful thing come to pass, but be careful that you don't open the cloth until tomorrow, because if you do, all the jewels will dissolve and disappear into smoke.' After Madonna Veronica had taken the cloth with the jewels fastened inside and placed it under the pillow where Messer Brocardo slept, Finetta said to her, 'Let's now go straight down to the wine cellar.' And so that's where they went.

There, the crafty Finetta's eye fell upon a wine butt that had been tapped with a spigot, whereupon she said, 'Madonna, you must now take off all your clothes.' So the lady stripped herself and stood as naked as when she was born. This done, Finetta drew out the tap from the wine butt, which was full of good wine, and said, 'Madonna, put your finger into this hole and keep it well closed so that the wine doesn't run out, and be sure that you don't move from this place until I come back to you, because I must now go outside to make certain magical signs. Then all our work will be accomplished.'

The lady, who put full faith in everything Finetta said, stood there, all naked as she was, and didn't move, keeping her finger in the hole of the cask. While she remained without moving, the wanton Finetta went straight to her bedroom where she had left the jewels tied up in the cloth, untied it, took out the necklace and the pearls, and replaced them by filling the cloth with pebbles and earth. After she had knotted it up again securely, she put it back in the same place and immediately fled.

The lady waited for Finetta to return, standing stark naked with her finger thrust into the bunghole of the cask. But when, after some time had passed, she found that the woman did not come back and that the hour was now growing very late, she was seized with fear that her husband would come and find her there all naked and take her for a mad woman. So taking up the tap which lay by her side, she stopped the hole of the butt, put on her clothes, and climbed out of the cellar. A little time later, Messer Brocardo, Madonna Veronica's husband, returned to his house and saluted her with a good-humoured face, saying, 'Well met, indeed, my dear wife, comfort and solace of my heart!' When she heard this greeting, by then so strange to her as to seem unnatural, she stood dumbstruck, thanking God in her heart that He had sent this beggar woman to her, by whose aid she had found a remedy for her most weighty grief. All through that day and the following night as well she remained in loving dalliance with her husband, exchanging sweet kisses as if they were just newly married. Full of joy and merriment on account of the endearments that her husband bestowed upon her, Madonna Veronica told him the whole story of the passion and torment that she had suffered on account of her love for him and he, on his part, promised to treat her ever afterwards as his beloved wife, and that the misunderstanding of the past would never trouble them again.

When the next morning came and her husband had arisen from bed to go hunting, after the fashion of gentlemen of high estate, Madonna

Veronica went right away to the bed and lifted up the pillow. She took hold of the linen cloth in which the jewels had been placed and untied it, expecting to find the necklace and pearls. But instead she found it full of pebbles. When she perceived this, the wretched woman was utterly confounded and hadn't a clue what she should do, for in truth she feared that her husband would kill her should she tell him about her loss. Now tormented by fresh sorrows, the poor lady turned over in her mind one thing and another, unable to decide how she might contrive to get her beloved jewels back. At last she determined, as an honest woman might, to enlist the services of a certain gentleman who had for some time been courting her with longing looks. He was a cavalier of Verona, a gentleman of fine presence and a haughty spirit, famous for his prowess and his honourable descent. As with all others mastered by the pangs of love, he was so cruelly tortured by the flame that consumed him on account of Madonna Veronica that he could get no rest at all. For love of her, he spent much of his time in jousting and all kinds of martial exercises, and gave rich feasts and gallantries to the gratification of the entire city. But Madonna Veronica, who had given her love entirely to her husband, took little heed of him or his pompous displays, for which neglect the cavalier felt the greatest grief and sorrow that a lover ever knew.

As soon as the lady's husband had left the house, she went to the window and there espied, passing in the streets, this same cavalier who was so deeply enamoured of her, whereupon she called to him and thus cautiously addressed him, 'Good sir, you have told me so often of the burning and passionate love that you've always felt for me and feel now. I know that I, for my part, must often have seemed hard and cruel to you. But this humour of mine has not come about through any lack of love for you, but only my firm determination to keep my honour intact, which I value above all other things. Please, then, don't be astonished or offended that I have not at once assented to your ardent wishes, for the sense of honour that keeps chaste the wife of a dissolute husband is something to be greatly commended and held dear. Although you have wrongly judged me to be hard, cruel, and heartless towards you, I will not, for all that, refuse now to have recourse to you with all faith and confidence as to the fountain of my salvation. If, as a devoted friend, you will lend me help in my present time of trouble and give me your ready assistance, you may hold me in the future as one bound to you to dispose of as though I belonged to you.'

When she had finished her speech, she described to him in detail the whole of her misfortune. After he had listened to the words of his dearly beloved lady, the cavalier first of all thanked her that she had so graciously deigned to lay these commands upon him, promising her that he would not fail in his aid, while lamenting at the same time the mischance that had befallen her.

With that, the cavalier departed secretly. Then mounting his horse in the company of four trusty comrades, he went in pursuit of the woman who had taken flight with the jewels. Before evening had come, he overtook her at a ferry where she was about to pass over the water. Recognizing her by the description which he had been given, he seized her by the hair of her head and made her confess everything. With the recovered jewels in his possession, he returned to Verona full of joy, and when he had found a fitting opportunity, he restored them to Madonna Veronica. Thus, without allowing to her husband the slightest hint of her doings, she retained her honour without any spot upon her good name.

As soon as Lauretta had brought her fable to an end, the Signora made the sign for her to tell her enigma at that moment. So without further delay, the damsel gave it in these words:

> Fair and lovely is my face,
> Decked with every artful grace;
> With dames and maidens I abide,
> And day and night am by their side.
> A trusty friend I am always,
> For dust and heat I drive away;
> But, though I win them ease and joy,
> I murmur at my base employ.
> Forsooth, no path to honour lies
> In flouting gnats and wasps and flies!

This enigma was interpreted right away by most if not all of the listeners present to mean the fan that ladies carry in their hands. Then, to preserve the accustomed order, the Signora asked Arianna to start her fable, and so she began at once.

X.1 Commentary

This might be an uncharitable moment to pronounce upon Straparola's talents, for the story of 'Madonna Veronica' appears to be one of his weaker creations. Rua claimed that it was 'tra le peggiori delle *Piacevoli*

Notti' (among the worst of the *P. N.*).[1] That may have to be confessed, largely because of its occasional lapses in narrative logic and the disparate nature of its segments. It is a two-part affair, beginning with a beggar's ruse to prey upon a vulnerable lady by soliciting her participation in a spell-casting ritual. It is a scheme whereby the lady's jewels are brought out of safe keeping and the lady herself is detained in her own basement, naked, with her finger in the bung hole of a wine cask, all as a means for absconding with her personal jewellery. This little confidence game routine may well have been taken from a tale circulating in the popular culture, although contemporary traces of it are slight. The second part, that of sending a devoted admirer after the thief by vaguely promising favours, is more probably a literary borrowing, again on inferential evidence. All former editors have granted this story to Straparola's creative 'genius,' but there are grounds for thinking that it carries debts to folk and literary sources, even though readers such as Rua have not been enchanted by the outcome.

Of greatest interest in the story, perhaps, are the fraudulent practices put upon the vulnerable Veronica by the vagrant beggar Finetta, a woman of the streets who is not only a crafty thief, but an improvisatory fortune teller, self-imposed confidante, and specialist in amatory magic, amulets, and charms. Her ruse is an admirably creative invention of a kind best known to English readers through the revelations of Greene, Chettle, and the London playwrights concerning the stratagems of the rogues and confidence-game practitioners of the Elizabethan underworld.[2] Chettle's *Kind-Harte's Dreame* comes to its close with the tale of a travelling female thief, a 'walking mort' who, under the pretext of selling ribbons, convinces a rural couple that she can bring them great wealth through astrological magic if they send away the servants, set her up in a room equipped with quantities of money and goods, and agree to remain locked up in another room in the house to fast overnight while she conducts her magic rites. By the time they look for her the next day, she is

---

1 *Tra antiche fiabe e novelle*, vol. I, *Le 'Piacevoli notti' di Messer Gian Francesco Straparola* (Rome: Ermanno Loescher, 1898), p. 102.

2 Henrie Chettle, *Kind-Harte's Dreame* (1592), ed. G.B. Harrison (London: John Lane, The Bodley Head, 1923), pp. 62–5; Robert Greene, *The Notable Discovery of Coosnage* (1591), *The Second Part of Conny Catching* (1592), ed. G.B. Harrison (London: John Lane, The Bodley Head, 1923); Robert Greene, *Conny-Catching Last Part* (1592), *A Hee Conny-Catcher and a Shee Conny-Catcher* (1592), ed. G.B. Harrison (London: John Lane, The Bodley Head, 1923).

far away with their possessions. The parallels with the present story are loose but apparent. Its source was no doubt a local English folk tale, although it is not inconceivable that its narrative core and program of devices derived from a tale type known throughout Europe. That prospect has become familiar through an examination of the analogues to many of the other stories in the collection.

As for Finetta, there are parallel characters closer to Straparola, such as Melite in Leone de' Sommi's *Le tre sorelle* (1588); she is one of the many procuresses and sorceresses on the Italian stage. Melite serves as a matchmaker, but, like Finetta, turns to black magic to regenerate love that has gone cold. Her device is a wax doll with ritual power over the defector in a plot complicated by a second lover who bribes the sorceress to let him take the other man's place in bed. Meanwhile, Melite has made a reputation for herself by pronouncing spells in a neighbour's house with results that are attributed to her magic. In short, she earns her way by serving the amorous desires of her neighbours and pretending to powers that she herself admits are fraudulent.[3] In like fashion, Finetta promises to restore love by placing a sack of jewels under the husband's pillow as a charm, with the warning that the contents will 'dissolve and disappear into smoke' if the sack is opened too soon.[4] Is it a technical lapse on Straparola's part that the gems, in fact, turn to dirt and pebbles? Is it a flaw, as well, that the once credulous Veronica is not for a moment duped once she opens the bag, but knows her jewels have been stolen rather than transformed? Equally unaccountable is the sudden reversal of the husband's sentiments. Must we not then credit the power of Finetta's rigmarole? Veronica, herself, does not speculate. The second half deals with her exploitation of a lovesick gentleman conveniently on hand and ready for employment in the recovery of her jewels. He may be willing to earn credit with her in an honourable enterprise. But readers are keeping moral score in terms of what the lady offers by way of enlisting

---

3 *The Three Sisters*, trans. and ed. Donald Beecher and Massimo Ciavolella, Carleton Renaissance Plays in Translation 14 (Ottawa: Dovehouse Editions, 1993).

4 The story may have a remote basis in fact if Pirovano is correct in suggesting that Giacomo Cavalli of Verona is the Brocardo di Cavalli in the story. The Cavalli family was established there in the twelfth century, and the career of Brocardo dates to the first half of the fourteenth century. He married Costanza della Scala, through whose family he enjoyed high military and political connections and benefits. Fear of the loss of their favour may have been the greater incentive for the cavalier's about face. *Le piacevoli notti*, 2 vols. (Rome, Salerno, 2000), vol. I, p. 616.

his help – overtures she never intends to keep. It is an equivocal performance at best, for while Veronica continues to harp about her honour and loyalty to her husband, she invites her admirer to believe that, should he succeed, he might have his way with her. Straparola writes a story about the loss and recovery of jewels in order to avoid the wrath of an intolerant husband, but the unacknowledged story is about two men who, at the end, share entitlements to the same woman. The *récit* in this regard seems unfinished in light of a situation that, in other contexts, might put the Goddess of Love into a vindictive rage where unkept promises have been made in her name.

If these are the flaws Rua had in mind (he does not specify), it would seem that Straparola must stand responsible, now in the absence of specific sources to blame them on. But in the world of the humanists, with their heads filled with the fragments, touchstones, and plot scenarios of ancient and modern literature, acts of creation are seldom far removed from acts of memory, reconfiguration, and *contaminatio* – and that may prove so here as well. The dramatists creating plays throughout the sixteenth century under the aegis of the 'erudite,' or 'learned,' comedy sought to model their plays initially on the works of Plautus and Terence, absorbing from them not only plot fragments and character types, but notions of condensed time and concentrated space, qualities of dialogue, and simple 'ideas' through cognitive processes of memory, imitation, and transformation nearly impossible to diagram. In less acknowledged ways, the *novellieri* worked in similar fashion, a hunch that sent Rua in search of echoes.

He chose well in associating Veronica's cavalier suitor with Boccaccio's Federigo degli Alberighi from the ninth tale of the *Decameron*'s fifth day, and he came up with the word echoes to confirm the case.[5] Straparola says of his cavalier that 'egli per suo amore spesso giostrava, armeggiava e faceva feste e trionfi, tenendo tutta la cittá in allegrezza' (he, for love of her, often jousted and tilted, and gave feasts and triumphs, bringing pleasure to the entire city). Boccaccio, before him, had said of Federigo, 'acciò egli l'amor di lei acquistar potesse, giostrava, armeggiava, faceva feste e donava, ed il suo senza alcun ritegno spendeva' (so that he might win her love, he jousted, tilted, gave entertainments and donations, placing no limits on his spending). Once again Straparola had been reading

---

5 *Tra antiche fiabe e novelle*, vol. I, *Le 'Piacevoli notti' di Messer Gian Francesco Straparola* (Rome: Ermanno Loescher, 1898), p. 102.

Boccaccio in search of a few handy words to characterize his own forlorn suitor, or already had them in his memory. But the inspiration may go further than Rua imagined. To be sure, the present story is not a narrative adaptation from Boccaccio in the usual sense. Boccaccio's Giovanna is a widow; Federigo, her cavalier, has bankrupted himself in her service; the widow's child falls ill and asks for Federigo's falcon as a dying gift; and the mother is torn between asking for favours from a longing man and denying her son his dearest wish. In the end, the falcon is eaten, the son dies, and she marries Federigo. The differences are marked. Yet a common narrative 'idea' begins to take shape once the contrasting circumstances and events are pared away. What the two women protagonists share is the need to negotiate favours from suitors they cannot otherwise reward. Therein Straparola may have found the fuse for his own invention. The speeches of these two women are nearly synoptic as they manoeuvre themselves into positions for seeking services without compromising their honours. Giovanna offers to have breakfast with Federigo in the company of another lady in requital for all his lost efforts. She confesses that her past behaviour must have appeared heartless and cruel to him, but that a mother's anxiety for her son has driven her to seek his aid. Veronica begins in similar terms: 'I know that for my part I must often have seemed hard and cruel to you.' But she is more disingenuous in confessing to a secret love for him which she had hidden only for the sake of her honour. In a fashion similar to Giovanna's, she urges that her present need compels her to seek his aid as her only salvation. Their arts are decidedly comparable, although Veronica's gratitude is more daring in its hints of reward. The matter takes us to the heart of the humanist habits of imitation and memory, whereby the new is never far removed from the patterns and motifs of the most admired forebears. What Straparola devises in this fashion is far from a perfect story, whatever that may be, when readers are led to offer improvements of their own. But it is not without its 'idea,' its performative language, and its ethical crux, which may earn for it a bit more esteem than it has enjoyed heretofore. In sum, the story appears to be drawn out of a folk motif about a female trickster with an effective ruse brought to reversal by a reconstituted motif out of Boccaccio.

X. Fable 2
The Lion and the Ass Named 'Brancaleone'

ARIANNA

An ass escapes from his master, the miller, and by chance comes to a certain mountain where he meets a lion who asks of him his name, whereupon the ass, by way of an answer, asks of the lion his name. The latter replies that he is the lion, while the ass proclaims that his name is Brancaleone. Having then been challenged by the lion to give proof of his valour, in the end he carries off the honours of the contest.

The diversity of human affairs, the vicissitudes of time, the manner of life led by evil men, often bring it about that things beautiful seem ugly and that ugly things seem beautiful. For this reason, if it happens that anything in this fable I'm about to relate to you is found to be offensive to your ears, I ask your pardon, and that you reserve for some other occasion any punishment you may think I deserve.

In Arcadia, a region of the Morea that derives its name from Arcadius, the son of Jove – a land in which was first discovered the rustic woodland shepherd's pipe – there dwelled in times not long past a certain miller, a brutal and cruel fellow, so irascible by nature that very little provocation was wood enough to light the fire of his rage. This man was the owner of an ass with long ears and down-drooping lips, and whenever this donkey raised his voice, he would make the whole plain re-echo with the sound of his braying. This poor beast, on account of the stingy provender he got from the miller, both in eating and drinking, was no longer able to undergo the hard work of the fields or to endure the cruel beatings with the stick that his barbarous master was forever inflicting upon him. Wherefore, the wretched animal presented such a picture of lean and wasted misery that one could see nothing but his hide stretched over his miserable bones. One day it happened that the poor ass, exasperated beyond endurance by the many heavy blows that were rained upon him daily by his mean-spirited master and aggravated by the scant supply of food, took flight from the miller and wandered off bearing his pack-saddle still on his back.

The pitiful beast travelled a long way on the road, and when he was almost worn out with hunger and fatigue he came to the foot of a most delightful mountain – one that had little about it that was savage or wild, but seemed more like a fair and cultivated domain. Remarking just how green and beautiful it was, the ass determined to ascend it, there to spend all the rest of his life. While he was deliberating over the matter, he cast his eyes about on all sides to make sure that he was not observed. Not seeing anyone around who was likely to trouble him, he courageously climbed the slope and, with the greatest delight and pleasure, began to take his fill of the sweet herbage growing there, at the same time thanking God for delivering him from the hands of his wicked and tyrannical master, and for guiding him to this place where he found such abundant and excellent food for the sustenance of his wretched life.

While our good donkey was thus living on the mountain, feeding every day upon the fine grass, all the while with his pack-saddle upon his back, lo and behold a savage lion issued from a dark cave and saw him. Having looked at him for some time most attentively, he was greatly astonished that this beast was so arrogant as to climb his mountain without his licence or knowledge. Yet because the lion had never before beheld an animal of this sort, he was afraid to go near him. The ass, when he saw the lion, felt every hair on his body bristle and stand on end. Seized by this sudden fear, he left off eating and dared not stir.

Plucking up a little courage, the lion came forward and said to the donkey, 'What is it that you are doing here, my good friend? Who gave you permission to wander up into these parts? Who are you, anyway?'

To these questions, with a growing pride and arrogance of spirit, he answered, 'And who may you be yourself who ventures to ask me who I am?'

Greatly amazed at this retort, the lion answered, 'I am the king of all the animals.'

'And what may your name be?' enquired the ass.

The other answered, 'Lion is my name. But you, what do men call you?'

At these words, putting on his boasting airs, the ass said, 'I'm called Brancaleone.'

When the lion heard this speech, he said to himself, 'By his name, in truth, this animal before me may well be more powerful than I am myself.' Then he said to the ass, 'Sir Brancaleone, both your name and your manner of speech show to me clearly that you are more puissant and stronger than I am. Even so, I would be greatly pleased if we two should make certain trials of our prowess one against the other.'

With these words, the valour of the ass increased mightily and, having turned his rear end towards the lion, he said, 'Do you see this pack-saddle and the piece of artillery I carry under my tail? Well, if I were to give you a sample of its powers a spasm will take you.' As he said this, he gave a couple of kicks high in the air and at the same time let off a few crackers that were so loud that they sent the lion's brain spinning.

The latter, when he heard the resounding noise of the donkey's kicks and the cracking bombardment of his field-piece, fell into a fit of terror. But by this time evening was drawing near, so he said to the ass, 'Good brother, it is by no means my will that there should be any bandying of words between us, or that we should kill each other, seeing that there is nothing worse in this world than death. I would advise, however, that we both lay ourselves down to rest and when tomorrow comes that we meet. Then and there we will three times make trial of our strength and prowess. Whoever of us two shall prove himself to be the worthier in these encounters will remain the supreme lord and master of this mountain.' And so they agreed that it should be.

When the morning of the next day had come and the two competitors were duly met together, the lion, who particularly desired to witness some proof of the other's skill, said, 'Brancaleone, to say the truth, I've come to regard you warmly and I'll never rest until I've seen one of your wondrous achievements.' Whereupon they set out on their way, and as they journeyed together, they came to a certain gorge of the mountain, very wide and deep. The lion then said, 'Good comrade, the time is now come when we may see which one of us can best leap over this gorge.' The lion, who was very strong and agile, no sooner went up to the gorge than he found himself on the other side of it. Then the ass, presenting himself with a great show of boldness at the brink of the gorge, made an effort to leap it, but in the course of his jump he fell right into the middle of the abyss and there he remained suspended on a heap of uprooted timber so that his forepart hung down on one side and his hindpart on the other, thus leaving him in the greatest danger of breaking his neck. When the lion saw what had happened, he cried out, 'What is it you're doing, comrade?' But the ass, who for the moment had come to the end of his powers, made no reply. Whereupon, the lion, afraid the ass would die, descended into the gorge and went to his rescue. As soon as Brancaleone had been delivered from his pressing danger, he turned towards the lion with renewed arrogance and heaped upon him the most villainous abuse that one creature could use against another. The lion, at this, was confounded and amazed by what he heard and demanded of the ass the cause of this savage outburst, considering that, out of the love he felt towards him, he had saved him from certain death. To show just how truly he was angered, the ass retorted haughtily, 'What a wretched knave you are. You ask me why I'm abusing you? I tell you, you've robbed me of the greatest pleasure I ever felt in the course of all my life. You may have fancied that I was dying, but all that time I was enjoying the purest delight.'

The lion then asked, 'What was this great delight of yours?'

The ass replied, 'I had placed myself carefully on the top of that wood, with one part of me hanging on this side and the other on that side, desiring all along to find out for certain which part of me weighed more, my head or my tail.'

'Well, I promise you, on my faith,' said the lion, 'that in the future I'll not interfere with you on any account, for as far as I can see and understand, you'll surely become the lord and sovereign of this mountain.'

Thereupon, they once more set forth, and after a time came to a river, the current of which was wide and swift. Then the lion said, 'My good Brancaleone, I want both of us now to make an exhibition of our abilities by swimming over this river.'

'Agreed,' said Brancaleone, 'but I will ask you to take the water first.'

The lion, who was an expert swimmer, swam over the river with great dexterity, and, after he had crossed, he stood upon the bank of the stream and cried out, 'Comrade, now it's your turn to swim over.'

The ass, when he perceived that there was no way he could go back on his promise to face the trial, cast himself into the river and swam in such a way that, by the time he had arrived at the middle, he was so greatly hampered by the swirling eddies of the water that he was borne along, now with his head uppermost, and now his feet, sometimes sinking so deep into the stream that little or nothing was to be seen of him. The lion, looking upon this sight while turning over in his mind the insulting words of the ass, on the one hand felt that he dare not go to his rescue, while on the other he greatly feared that he would drown if he weren't helped at once. Standing there debating yes or no, he decided, whatever may happen, to go to his aid. So, plunging into the water, he swam up close to the donkey's side and seized him by the tail, dragging him along until he got him out of the water and safely on shore.

As soon as he found himself standing upon the riverbank and out of danger from the threatening waves, the ass flew into a violent passion and, all inflamed with rage, cried out in a loud voice, 'Ah, wretch that you are, and loutish knave – truly I don't know what keeps me from employing my artillery and letting you experience something you might not find entirely to your liking. You're the plague of my life and the destroyer of all my pleasure. When will I ever find another delight as great as the one you have just taken from me?'

Upon hearing this, now more overwhelmed by fear than before, the lion said, 'But my good comrade, I feared horribly that you'd be suffocated in the stream, so I went out to save you, thinking to render you a service that would please rather than offend you.'

'Don't say another word,' replied the ass, 'but first of all, there is one thing I want you to tell me. What gain, what advantage have you reaped by swimming across the river?'

'None at all,' answered the lion.

Then the ass, turning towards him, said, 'Now look carefully to it and determine, while I was in the river, whether I must not have found abundant diversion.' With these words he shook himself violently, and directly from his ears, which were filled with water, there came forth a great quantity of little fishes and other small water beasts that he showed to the lion, saying all along in a tone of grief and complaint, 'Now do you see what a huge mistake you've made? If you had only allowed me to go down to the bottom of the river, I would have had the greatest pleasure in capturing fish of a sort that would have amazed you. Therefore, take care in the future that you molest me no more, for if you do, we shall become foes instead of friends, and that would surely go badly for you. In fact, if at any time in the future I appear dead to you, don't give yourself any trouble on my account, because what may seem as death to you will only be life and contentment for me.'

Now the sun was already sinking beneath the horizon and making the shadows on the earth deeper and duskier when the lion said to his companion that the time was now come that they should retire to rest, with the agreement that they meet again on the following morning. And when another day had broken brightly, the ass and the lion met as they had duly covenanted. Then and there it was settled that they would go hunting, each in his own domain, and that afterwards, at a fixed hour, they would both return. Whichever of the two was then found to have taken the greatest number of beasts in the chase would be adjudged lord and master of the mountain. Forthwith, the lion went in search of game and in his hunting contrived to capture a great quantity of wild animals. The ass, meanwhile, having found a farmyard gate standing open, made his way in where he came upon a vast heap of maize stacked in the middle of the court. He went right up to it and ate such a huge quantity that his belly was ready to burst. After he had filled himself, he returned to the spot where he had agreed to meet the lion and lay down at full length, whereupon, from the pressure in his gut, his artillery fired, now opening, now shutting, like the mouth of a huge fish out of the river on dry land.

Seeing a chough flying through the air, the ass stretched himself out prostrate on the ground and, for not twitching a muscle, looked as good as dead. The bird, spotting the half-digested maize under his tail and his rump all spattered with shit, flew down and started to peck backward and forward until he stuck his head right up his butt. When the ass felt his hole getting pecked, he clamped his buttocks together and the chough, with his head still inside, had his life snuffed out.

A short time after this, the lion came back to the appointed place, loaded down by the prey he had captured. When he beheld the ass lying prone on the ground, he cried out and said to him, 'Have a look, good comrade. Here are the beasts of the chase that I've taken.'

The ass then said, 'Tell me now, in what fashion did you contrive to capture them?' and the lion at once recounted to him the manner of venery he had followed. But the ass, breaking in upon his discourse, said, 'What a fool and witless loon you must be! You've half killed yourself with fatigue this morning, ranging around the thickets, the woods, and mountains, while I've never moved from this same place. As I lay upon the earth, I managed to catch such a vast quantity of choughs and all sorts of animals with my buttocks, as you can see, that I dined in abundance. This one here, which got stuck in my arse, is the only one I have left. It has been reserved in your name, which I beg you to accept as a mark of my high esteem.'

At hearing these words of Brancaleone, the lion was more stricken with astonishment than ever before. Having accepted the gift of the chough out of the respect he had for the ass, he took it and without uttering another word returned to his own prey. Then, as he was making his way at a fast lope through the forest – not without a certain fear in his heart – he met a wolf, who was also going along at a goodly clip. The lion then said to the wolf, 'Goodman wolf, where are you going all alone at such a pace?'

The wolf replied, 'I'm tied up with the execution of a certain business that is of the greatest importance to me.'

Hearing these words, the lion sought to know what this business might be, but the wolf, as if he were in terror of his life, begged to be let go and not further delayed. Then the lion, perceiving the great peril into which the wolf was about to run, urged him not to go forward along that path, 'for,' he said, 'a little further on you will most certainly meet up with Brancaleone, a most fierce and dreadful animal, one who carries a certain piece of artillery under his tail that goes off with a mighty explosion; he is ill fated indeed who comes within its fire. Besides this, he bears upon his back a certain thing made of leather which covers the greater part of his body. He is covered with grey hair and works all manner of wonderful deeds; he is a thing of terror to all those who come near him.'

But the wolf, who perceived clearly enough from the account given by the lion what manner of animal this was, cried out, 'Good friend, I urge you not to be afraid, for surely this creature you speak of is nothing more nor less than a donkey, the vilest beast that nature ever made and one fit for nothing other than to carry heavy burdens and to be well beaten with a stick. In the course of my life, I alone have eaten more than a hundred of them. So let us go on together with assurance, good friend, and you'll witness the proof of all I say.'

Then said the lion, 'Good friend, I've no mind to go along with you, but if you feel that you must keep on this path, go in peace.'

With that, the wolf once more replied that there was no reason why the lion should be afraid, and the lion, when he saw that the wolf stood firm in his contention, said, 'Because you wish so earnestly that I should be your companion in this enterprise, and because, moreover, you give me full assurance that we shall run into no danger, it seems to me that it would be more prudent for us to approach him with our tails well knotted together so that when we have come into his presence there will be no danger that one of us will run away leaving the other in his power.' So after they had tied their tails tightly together, they went out looking for Brancaleone.

By this time, the ass had once more gotten up on his four feet and was cropping the grass. He saw the lion and the wolf while they were still far away and immediately he fell into such a fit of terror that he debated whether he should stay or flee. But the lion, who had pointed out Brancaleone to the wolf, said, 'There he is my trusty friend. Look he's coming towards us. Let's not linger here for if we do, both of us will surely die.'

The wolf, who by this time had seen the ass and recognized what manner of beast he was, said, 'Let's stand our ground here, my friend. Set your mind at ease, for I assure you that what we're looking at is a plain and simple ass.'

But the lion, whose fear seemed to grow greater every time he caught sight of Brancaleone, turned tail and took to flight, and while he was thus fleeing through rough brambles and jumping over one thicket and another, a sharp thorn struck him as he was leaping and tore out his left eye. When he felt the prick of the thorn, he at once imagined it to be caused by a shot from that terrible cannon that Brancaleone carried under his tail and, coursing all the while at the top of his speed, he yelled to the wolf, 'Didn't I tell you how it would be, old pal? Let's fly for our lives. Don't you see that he's already shot out one of my eyes with his field-piece?' And quickening his pace at every moment, he dragged the wolf along with him through sharp-piercing brambles, over rugged stones, through thick woods and other desolate places until at last the poor wolf, all mangled and shattered, gave up the ghost.

After running some great distance, the lion, thinking that they had by this time come to a place of safety, said to the wolf, 'Good ally, it seems to me that we might now untie our tails.' When the wolf made no answer, the lion looked towards him and saw that he was dead. Stricken with amazement, he said, 'Alas, didn't I tell you the truth when I said that he would kill you? See what has happened to us by going to meet him? You have lost your life and I have lost my left eye. But it is better to have lost a part than the whole.' Then, having untied the knotted tails, he departed, leaving the dead wolf behind. Thereafter, he dwelt in rock caves while the ass remained lord and master of the mountain, upon which he lived joyfully for many years. It is for this reason that nowadays asses are always found inhabiting civilized and cultivated regions, while lions occupy deserted and savage places, insofar as the common beast, by his fraud and cunning, proves himself to be the master of the ferocious lion.

The fable that Arianna recited in most ladylike fashion now came to an end. To be sure, it was somewhat indifferent in matter and without much sap. Nevertheless, the fair and honourable company did not withhold their due meed of praise. To keep the same order that had been so diligently observed on all the other evenings, the Signora immediately after commanded her to set forth her enigma, which, opening her lips, Arianna supplied in the following manner:

> Rough, long, and round am I to sight,
> Yet ladies find in me delight;
> They take me with a laughing face,
> And find for me a fitting place.
> They handle me in featly wise,
> And put me where my business lies.

> Next prick and pinch me, till I'm fain
> To do their will once and again.
> Now, ladies, if this thing you tell,
> 'Tis plain to me you know it well?

This enigma offered by Arianna won warmer praise than her fable did because it occasioned more laughter, and what's more, it was interpreted by the men in a somewhat lascivious sense. When she saw that all expositions of it went wide of the truth, the damsel said, 'Signora, what my enigma is intended to describe is the staff upon which our ladies embroider with a needle lace or any other delicate work. It is round and thick, and they have to hold it between the thighs when they are at work with it. They turn it, handle it, prick it with their needles, and do with it whatsoever they will.' This subtle interpretation was highly praised by the whole company, whereupon Alteria, as soon as she saw that all were silent and waiting for her, rose from her seat and thus began.

X.2 Commentary

'Brancaleone' is a human creation that holds up a mirror to our own species in a double projection of our natures upon the animals of the world both wild and domestic. The beast fable, after all, entails both an anthropomorphization of those animals through projecting upon them human emotion, thought, and language and, inversely, a representation of human nature through the emblematic codification of their own animal endowments, temperaments, and signature behaviours. The lion king of the fables can speak and roar, organize his court, become jealous of rival courtiers, and shred the victims who are a part of his natural food chain. This deployment of the animal kingdom has given rise to a genre of tales in which animals as protagonists are epitomized as themselves in accordance with their idiosyncratic animal traits, while at the same time receiving an overlay of human wishes and desires, will and volition, and a capacity to speak in languages intelligible to humans. The conventions underlying such *récits*, in the abstract, are complex beyond all satisfactory explanation, for they ask us to endorse as real, and in highly plastic ways, things not only contrary to nature, but constantly vacillating in significance between their animal and humanized natures. Yet our own instinctual kinship with animals, and the ease with which we attribute to them understandings well beyond their ken, enables even children to translate those conventions into empathetic representations of 'higher' socialized animals without any ontological confusion whatsoever, and, moreover, to draw morals through analogous application.

Salient among such 'semiotic' beasts are the lion and the donkey, traditionally associated with prowess, kingship, and autonomy on the one side and with drudgery, gratuitous chastisement, and dull recalcitrance on the other. The one is deemed regal and glorious while the other is deemed menial and common, as the wolf repeatedly confirms. In beast fables, these traits are routinely confirmed by act and outcome; such animals are doomed to enact the 'allegories' inherent in their natures and endure their fortunes. The fatalism inherent in such endowments is applied by analogy to the humans deemed their counterparts: donkeys will always bray, whatever they seek to say; asses who speak will always give themselves away. We know how to map these things, especially upon others. Nevertheless, even in the human-like negotiations among such animals, there is a place for ruse, the political power of language, fraud, and illusion whereby hierarchies may be broken down, jump-starting the wheel of fortune – a human process we are amused to foist upon animal actors apt to assume such roles: wolves, foxes, jackals, crows, owls, and, paradoxically, donkeys. It is thus a challenge to invention to bring the lowly donkey to pre-eminence, making him the terror of lions, the king on the mountain, by generating tricks and effects out of his limited armoury of natural endowments: giving himself an imposing name, eating thorns, braying, kicking, farting, and talking both big and menacingly. By stretching conventions, the lion may fear that which is unfamiliar to him, while the donkey under duress may have no other recourse but to brazen it through. Both creatures fear their own fears, but by strategy the one employs its meagre survival programming to defeat the survival programming of a categorically superior animal. Therein, likewise, a fable is to be found that is particularly appealing to the would-be arriviste. For by arrogance, impertinence, intimidation, and rationalization, combined with the strategic use of its grass-fuelled artillery, a mere pack-saddle donkey, made strange to the kingdom of the wild by his isolation in domesticity, upon returning to the wild secures complete control over its pastoral paradise. He is the embodiment of oppression, caught between domestic cruelty and the food-chain world of tooth and claw who, by bluff and fortune, finds provender and peace. But he is also the impertinent upstart who defies natural authority. There is meaning for humans in the double transaction.

Well may we ask, nevertheless, whether the vicarious will to power of the meek is the sum total of the collective intentionality that sustained this story over untold generations, because the ass is always just an ass, and the lion, no matter how exceptionally craven here, is still a lion. That is why this story belongs to a tradition of remarkable instability, for the donkey in the skin of a lion is, by other lights, made the victim of his own donkey nature when compelled to bray at a passing she-donkey in heat. This easy feeder thus exposes himself to slaughter. So the story began. Readers drift with the conventions in both kinds of stories, the one in which the sophist, in conjunction with his basest animal attributes, prevails, whereas in the other the donkey thinking 'higher thoughts' is nevertheless betrayed by his own animal instincts. It would appear that the tales of self-betraying donkeys have little to do with the popular tale conveyed by Straparola, but simple tweaking can turn losing strategies into winning strategies, because the narrator desires it so. Beast fables are slippery that way.

Under structural inspection, Straparola's story is itself a compound tale made up of potentially separable parts. In the first, a donkey socializes with a lion, joining with him in a series of contests through which, by a succession of unexpected victories fashioned largely by bluffing verbal constructions, he demolishes the lion's self-confidence (ATU 1074). In the second, the lion, illogically terrified of the beast with whom he had recently fraternized, induces the wily wolf to have their tails tied together to prevent the more cowardly of the two from breaking and running from the sight of the now appalling donkey (ATU 118). By this means the wolf meets an untimely death, which only confirms the lion's conviction that the ass is a true terror. There is a hard lesson here about being unequally yoked with cowards; it is a different kind of story. Straparola's 'ideal' reader will accept both portions as parts of a continuous fable, but it will prove instructive to see how the reciters of later folk versions strive for an even greater integration.

A quick sketch of donkey stories, ancient and contemporary, will reveal just how versatile the creature's roles might become, for the donkey is also the epitome of contrasting characteristics from the submissive drudge to the kicking berserker, and from the beaten stoic and patient sufferer to the chatty sophist and treacherous adviser. Moreover, it is an uncouth beast, a creature lacking all class and refinement with its absurd hee-haw and intermittent methane production. All of these traits feature in stories that serve as ciphers for human nature, but only through a judicious selection of appropriate applications. Is there a human counterpart to the strategic lifting of the tail? Among the stories of the Buddha's former births that make up the *Jataka* – one of the oldest surviving collections of animal stories – is that of the donkey disguised as a predatory animal. A merchant had hit upon an economy measure by disguising his donkey as a lion before putting him to pasture in a neighbour's field. The watchmen, naturally, were terrified, and kept a respectful distance until one day a group of armed villagers came to inspect, whereupon the beast let out a sociable hee-haw that brought him death by cudgelling, leaving the merchant with a moral about the inability of an ass to assume a lion's nature or to resist the expression of his own. The story would appear to have little affinity with Straparola's, except that in closely cognate versions the donkey seeking to roar like a lion to impress a lion, although he fails, nevertheless strikes terror through the impressive cacophony of his own 'natural call' by dint of its unfamiliarity.[6] In that surprising effect, the strategy of the present story was, in a sense, born.

The donkey broken by overwork, as he is in the present tale, also first appears in a related version of this story in the *Hitopadesa*. This beast, now good for little, is disguised as a tiger and sent to feed in alien corn to fatten up. This guardian, however, is suspicious and disguises himself in a donkey's skin, which causes the first to come running to encounter his own kind. That too proves a fatal blunder.[7] This story is likewise told in the *Panchatantra* in which a dyer's mule had become so skinny that pasturing alone could save it. But the disguise as a beast of prey is fatally compromised by the social instincts aroused by the cry of a she-donkey.[8] Another dies by the arrow because of his braying, having taken the farmer for another donkey in *The Ocean of the Streams of Story*.[9] These creations were elaborated upon in the West in the name of Aesop. Variations emerged in which a donkey saw a lion's skin and desired to play king for a day. All was well until a fox came by and the silly donkey,

---

6 *The Jataka*, trans. Robert Chambers, ed. E.B. Cowell, 3 vols. (Delhi: Low Price, 1990), vol. II, pp. 76–7. For the donkey that tries to roar, see bk. II, no. 188, vol. III, p. 75.

7 *Hitopadesa*, trans. Charles Wilkins (1787) (Gainesville, FL: Scholars' Facsimiles & Reprints [1886], 1968), pp. 173–4; originally published in (London: George Routledge and Sons, 1886).

8 'L'âne vêtu de la peau d'un tigre' (The donkey dressed in the skin of a tiger) in the *Pañcatantra*, trans. Edouard Lancereau (Paris: Gallimard [1871], 1965), no. 8, pp. 297–8.

9 Somadeva, 'The Ass in the Panther's Skin' in the *Katha sarit sagara*, trans. C.H. Tawney, intro. N.M. Penzer, 10 vols. (Delhi: Motilal Banarsidass [1923], 1984), no. 121A, pp. 99–100.

deluded by his own disguise, sought to roar him into submission. In another, the donkey gets into a farmer's fields and when the wind blows up the corner of the lion's skin, the farmer comes to the truth of the matter and clubs him to death. In the English translation by John Ogilby the cosmographer (1651), the tanner's donkey makes itself king, frightening away all who see him except the tanner himself who spies his long ears. The donkey tries threats of danger and death, much as Brancaleone bullies the lion in the present story, but his owner merely ties him up and takes him away.[10]

Just where and when Straparola's more particular version of the story originated as a folk tale, or how the donkey came to be called 'Brancaleone' (one who paws lions), is a question admitting of no definitive answer. There are many potentially false leads, for the name 'Brancaleone' had been current in heraldry since the time of the crusades, and there were semi-historical personages of that name. But there is corroboration, though sparse, that Straparola's tale was at least somewhat widely in circulation by the early sixteenth century. That evidence resides, for the moment, in a story entitled 'Eyn Fabel von einem Löwen und Esel' (The fable of a lion and donkey) in *Schimpf und Ernst* by the barefoot friar Johannes Pauli.[11] In this tale, the lion king convenes a grand assembly to pass the crown to his son. The animals enter into a lengthy debate about who should rule, how to avoid tyranny, and whether the donkey and the lion should not share power. Thus the fox and hound, as orators, bring the contrasting creatures to their famous contest of leaping over the river. When the donkey is forced to swim to shore he is ready with his answer as he shakes little fish out of his ears. All agree with the fox that a lion could never perform such a feat. During the hunting contest, the lion tears about in the woods while the donkey snoozes until a raven, taking him for dead, sits on his mouth to peck out his eyes. Thus, he hunts with a mere snap of his jaws and again wins the contest of esteem so that by such ruses he becomes king. By dint of this

---

10 'Of the Same Asse and his Lyons Skin' in *The Fables of Aesop*, illus. Wenceslaus Hollar (London: Thomas Warren for A. Crook, 1651), no. 70, p. Dddd2. See also Erasmus Alberus, *Die Fabeln* (1534, 1550), [*Tugent und Weissheit* after 1565], ed. Wolfgang Harms (Tübingen, 1997), no. 21; and Martin Luther, *Werke*, 60 vols. (Weimar: Hermann Bühlaus, 1909), vol. 26, p. 547.

11 Johannes Pauli (1450–1520), *Schimpf und Ernst* (Hildesheim: Olms, 1972), no. 744, vol. II, pp. 35–7.

single story, collected before 1520 (the year of Pauli's death), and published in 1522, Straparola's story has an established predecessor. But given their differences, there seems little likelihood that the borrowing was direct. Once again, it would appear that a popular tradition had produced the variants during the time that separated the authors, not to mention the space between Germany and Northern Italy; more plausibly Pauli and Straparola drew from a common provenance. That one deals with king selection, the other with the right to rule a feed lot is a matter of emphasis, for both rehearse the three-part contest and the ironic verbal tactics whereby a donkey assumes power. Also distinguishing Straparola's is the add-on episode of the knotted tails, absent in Pauli, as well as the peculiar variation on the fox stories in which the protagonist hunts by playing dead in order to attract predatory birds. The choughs in the present tale that descend to feed on the grain mixed in the faeces of the beast and find themselves snuffed out between its nether cheeks may be Straparola's own scatological elaboration, although even this image is by no means entirely new. As early as 14,000 BC, an ibex is depicted on the head of a Paleolithic spear-thrower looking back to see two birds perched on an extruding turd.[12]

Mention may be made in passing that the fable of the 'Donkey King' attracted the seventeenth-century satirists as a political frame to be filled out with diatribes against the governmental and institutional irregularities of the age. The Protestant Wolfhart Spangenberg from Strasburg wrote his *Esel-König* as an exotic tale about how the kingdom of the four-footed creatures collapsed, how the crown was placed upon a donkey, and how he ruled in a wonderful manner at the risk of life and limb. Throughout is to be seen the familiar design, but the thrust of the work, in fact, is a diatribe against the Rosicrucians.[13] In those same years, Latrobio, in his *Il Brancaleone*, lays out the political education of a donkey, with lessons in political brutality, prudence, and the art of dissimulation. In this grand allegory of political power and Machiavellianism, he draws upon the fable for principal events in the lives of the lion and the ass, such as the contest in crossing the water. Straparola's tale has, within a half-century, become part of a tradition demonstrably so well known that its intertextual dimensions could be deployed and received as current

---

12 Brian Boyd, *On the Origin of Stories: Evolution, Cognition, and Fiction* (Cambridge, MA: The Belknap Press of Harvard University Press, 2009), pp. 81–2.

13 *Esel-König* (Ballenstet [Strasburg]: Papyrio Schönschrifft, [1625]).

cultural coin.[14] That context was supplied, presumably, by the popular tradition, but the many editions of the *Piacevoli notti* throughout the preceding half-century undoubtedly played a significant role in disseminating the foundational materials upon which these satires were built.

That folk material corresponding very closely to the story told by Straparola was current in his day and part of a tradition known throughout Europe is given further support by the closely cognate tales gathered in the nineteenth century. Giuseppe Pitrè collected a 'Brancaliuni' with nearly all the familiar features found in Straparola, but duly adjusted and reapportioned over the years by Sicilian folk humour.[15] This donkey, lank and lean, is abandoned by its owner and left for dead. But with easy provender, he once again becomes fat. Then the wolf approaches and the ass is compelled to improvise with his terrifying name and then to demonstrate his cannon, which he pronounces to be fatal to wolves. So they strike a deal that if the donkey provides him with birds to eat, the wolf would bring cabbages. And so it came to pass that by playing dead, in the manner of Straparola's donkey, he catches birds to offer to the wolf on the following day. The wolf and donkey in flight from the approaching farmer generates an impromptu leaping contest that leaves the clumsy donkey suspended over a fence. When the wolf returns to help him down, the ass's farting sends flying pellets that injure his leg. The donkey thereby gains a mighty reputation in the wolf's eyes as a most dangerous and formidable animal. Then the wolf meets up with a lion and recounts his

---

14 Latrobio (pseudonym for Giovan Pietro Giussani), *Il Brancaleone* (Milan: Giovanni B. Alzato, 1610), ed. Renzo Bragantini (Rome: Salerno, 1998). There were other editions of this work, in Venice in 1607, and in Milan, 1682, in which Antonio Giorgio Besozzi also seems to have had a part. See the work attributed to him entitled *Il brancaleone: Overo l'idea della prudenza, favola morale politica* (Venice: Giovanni & Varisco Varischi, Fratelli, 1617). This elaboration upon the popular fable maintains all the familiar motifs right from the first encounter between the lion and ass in which the lion asks the ass's name and is impertinently asked his own, whereupon the ass replies in improvisatory fashion, that if the other is 'Lion' then he is 'Brancaleone' (the clawer of lions). Only a much closer inspection than is possible here could determine the degree to which these popular works influenced the development of the later folk narratives in this tradition. See also G.C. Croce, *Le astuzie di Bertoldo e le semplicità di Bertoldino*, ed. P. Camporesi (Milan: Garzanti, 1993), xxxi, pp. 24–6, 84.

15 *The Collected Sicilian Folk and Fairy Tales of Giuseppe Pitrè*, trans and ed. Jack Zipes and Joseph Russo, 2 vols. (New York: Routledge, 2009), no. 271, vol. II, pp. 745–7.

adventure, but when they return to the scene, the terrified donkey once more raises his tail and fires in his defence. The wolf, now lame, must be dragged away trembling by the lion; the episode is redolent of the attached tails in Straparola. And so the ass liberates himself from danger, grows fatter still, and returns to his master, once more fit for labour. The story has migrated considerably from its Renaissance roots, but the motifs have been faithfully retained from the use of the intimidating name to the asinine flatulence, the failure to leap over obstacles reconstructed as an act of pleasure, and the tandem flight in which the wolf gets the worst of it. The variants themselves are proof of a long-standing narrative configuration. It remains the story of the lowly beast of burden who, by its cumulative ruses, fashions itself into a creature more redoubtable and formidable than lions or wolves. The first line of entertainment is this playful inversion of the conventional animal coding.

An equally charming variant was collected in Corsica by J.B. Frédéric Ortoli entitled 'Harpalionu' (Superior to lions). A lion happening by sees a donkey braying in a field, something he had never seen before. Impressed, he approaches to demand his name. The story's title contains his reply, making the lion think he had met his equal in the animal kingdom. So they enter in league against all the other animals. The ass's awkwardness in crossing rivers he explains away as a fishing expedition with his tail, but that he had let the giant fish go to keep from drowning. Stranded on top of a wall, he claims he is weighing himself as in the present story. The finale is a wall-breaking contest, which the donkey wins with ease, restoring his credit. But the clincher is the ass's ability to eat thorns, which so impresses his co-ruler that the donkey is made king of lions.[16]

The repertory of tricks whereby a weak but audacious underling convinces a creature of might that he is the stronger and more worthy to rule is the common denominator among the many variants of the tale, some of which are otherwise so transformed as to seem at a glance unrelated. One such is 'The Herd-Boy and the Giant,' a Swedish tale in which a shepherd boy, by craft, defeats an ogre first in a squeezing contest

---

16 *Les contes populaires de l'île de Corse* (Paris: Maisonneuve, 1883), pp. 133–7; see also
   Friedrich S. Krauss, *Sagen und Märchen der Sudslaven* (Leipzig: Friedrich, 1883),
   part I, no. 2; republished as *Tausend Sagen und Märchen der Sudslaven* (Leipzig:
   Ethnologischer Verlag, 1914).

and then in a throwing contest.[17] The giant, like the lion, is so deceived that he takes the boy into service. This is a dangerous arrangement, because the boy is called upon again and again to perform in accordance with his reputation for great strength. But in every instance the lad deceives the ogre into thinking he had done his part such as carrying a tree trunk or thrashing grain in the dark by rationalizing away his failures as achievements of another kind. Before the ogre becomes utterly fearful and attempts to club him to death in his bed, the boy's premonitions lead him to put a butter churn under the covers, so that the beating leaves only spattered cream in the place of his brains. In a final eating contest the boy wears a hidden pouch that he stuffs and then slits open as though it were his stomach to prove his prowess. When the ogre does the same, he dies of his wound and the boy takes away the ogre's treasure as his own. Just how it relates to the 'lion and the ass' tradition is a matter of parallel structures, for the tricks are different in nature and execution, despite the common ending. This story, in fact, has something of a steady tradition of its own, with analogues as far away as Persia. Sir John Malcolm collected the tale in Isfahan for publication early in the nineteenth century. A ghoul – one of the lower demons and not very bright – was fooled by Ameen Beg, one of the city's clever and intrepid citizens, who met the creature in the Valley of Death and brazenly challenged him to a squeezing contest for which he had come prepared by placing eggs and salt in his pockets. With the egg he made the rock appear to give off liquid and, with the salt, to crumble in his hand. Impressed, the ghoul makes ostensible amity and invites him home, there to put him up to tasks such as fetching water in a bag that twenty men could not carry. By feigning an even greater feat, that of digging a canal from the stream to the cave, he tricks the demon into carrying his own water. When the ghoul takes flight in fear and meets up with a wolf, the latter lures him back, only to be shot straight through the head by a musket ball, which so terrifies the ghoul that he abandons his entire treasure to the intruder. This is a clear reference to the mule's artillery and the wolf's disastrous fraternity with the lion. The story is indeed remote, yet reveals much

---

17 Benjamin Thorpe, *Yule-Tide Stories: A Collection of Scandinavian and North German Tales and Traditions* (London: Henry Bohn, 1853), pp. 245–9. Other folk tales in this vein include Adalbert Kuhn, *Märkische Sagen und Märchen* (Berlin: Herbig [1843], 1937), pp. 289–94; republished by (Hildesheim: Georg Olms, 1973); and Sven Nilsson, *Skandinaviska Nordens Ur-invånare* (Stockholm, 1838–43), no. 4, p. 31.

about the migration of motifs and the emergence of cognate traditions, both upholding the thematic order of a presumed common ancestor.[18]

Returning to the more direct descendents of the story under investigation, of which there are potentially many more, we may conclude with the Spanish tale of 'El burro y el león' (The donkey and the lion). Once again a lean and aging donkey finds himself in the pasture of a lordly lion and must brazen his way through the situation by conducting himself as the lion's equal or superior by talking back and improvising alternative constructions of his apparent failures in leaping fences – he is weighing himself perched on top – or in hunting for game. As in Straparola, the donkey fills his paunch and falls down under his own weight, whereupon three crows alight, taking him for dead; with minimal effort he slays them and has them ready for presentation to the lion. The story rolls on to the prescribed ending in which the donkey reigns over his betters by ruse and verbal bluffing.[19] The record of Brancaleone tales in the Renaissance is relatively slight, but the four or five presented here provide evidence enough to propound a popular Brancaleone tradition that predates the sixteenth century. Moreover, it would appear that by the early seventeenth century, satirists could count upon a widespread familiarity with the tale sufficient to serve as a referential context for their literary elaborations. 'Brancaleone' is Straparola's only foray into the traditional beast fable, a subgenre of the popular tale that had enjoyed a history of its own beginning with the tenth-century *Romulus*. The relationship between Pauli and Straparola suggests that both were dependent upon the sprawling oral culture that almost certainly fostered this story and, by its unique means, produced the variants later recovered by ethnographers in many parts of Europe.

18 'Story of a Ghool' in *Sketches of Persia* (London: John Murray [1827], 1845), chap. 16, pp. 184–9.
19 Aurelio M. Espinosa, *Cuentos populares españolas*, 3 vols. (Madrid: Aguirre, 1946), vol. I, pp. 575–8.

X. Fable 3
Cesarino the Dragon Slayer

ALTERIA

Cesarino di Berni, a Calabrian, departs in the company of a lion, a bear, and a wolf, leaving his mother and sisters behind. Coming to Sicily, he finds the king's daughter about to be devoured by a dragon. By the aid of his three animals, Cesarino destroys the beast and, having rescued the princess, wins her for his wife.

In turning over the records of ancient and modern history, I have noted that prudence holds a place as one of the most illustrious and worthy virtues with which human beings are endowed, for the man who uses prudence correctly may call upon his past experience to discern matters of the present, and with mature guidance provide for the future. Wherefore, seeing that I have to take my turn at storytelling this evening, I will give you a little fable that has been recalled to my mind by the one recently told by Arianna, a fable that is neither laughable nor long, but that may still in some measure lead to your amusement and profit as well.

In Calabria not long ago there lived a poor woman of low estate who had an only son called Cesarino di Berni, a youth of great discretion, and one endowed more richly with the gifts of nature than with those of fortune. One day, Cesarino left his home and went into the country, and having come into a deep and thick-leaved forest, he made his way to the centre, enchanted by the verdant beauty of the place. Continuing along, he came upon a rocky cavern in which he found in one place a litter of lion cubs, in another a litter of bear cubs, and in another a litter of wolf cubs. Having taken one of each, he carried them home and with the greatest care and diligence brought them up together. In the course of time, the animals came to be so much attached to each other that they could not bear to be apart. Besides this, they had become so tame and gentle with the members of the household that they did no harm to anyone. But seeing they were wild animals by nature and domesticated only by chance, and that they had now attained the full strength of maturity, Cesarino would often take them hunting with him, always coming back laden with the spoils of the woods and rejoicing at his good luck. By such hunting, Cesarino supported both his old mother and himself. After a time the old woman, marvelling at the great quantity of game that her son always brought home with him, asked him how he managed to entrap so fine a spoil, whereupon Cesarino answered, 'With the animals you have so often seen, but I'm urging you never to reveal this to a soul, for fear my companions will be taken away.'

Before many days had passed, it happened that the aged mother met up with a neighbour of hers whom she held very dear, not merely because she was a worthy and upright woman, but because she was kindly and obliging as well. As they were talking of this thing and that, the neighbour said, 'My friend, how is it that your son manages to take such great quantities of game?' Then the old mother spilled all she knew, after which she took her leave and returned home.

Scarcely had this old biddy parted from her neighbour when the husband of the latter came in, whereupon the wife went to meet him with a joyful face and told him all the news she had just heard from the gossip next door. The husband, when he had learned how the matter stood, went right out to find Cesarino and, falling in with him, asked, 'How is it, my son, that you go so often a-hunting and never offer to take a comrade with you? Such behaviour is hardly in agreement with the friendship that has always existed between us.' When he heard these words, Cesarino smiled a little, but made no answer, and on the next day, without saying a word of farewell to his old dam or to his beloved sisters, he left home to seek his fortune in the wide world, taking with him his three animals.

After he had travelled a very long distance, he came into Sicily, and there he found himself one day in a solitary and uninhabited spot in the middle of which there stood a hermitage, which he approached. After entering and finding it empty, he and his three animals settled themselves down to rest. He had not been there very long before the hermit came back, and when he entered the door and saw the animals lying there, he was overcome with terror and turned to run. But Cesarino, who had watched the hermit's approach, cried out, 'My father, don't be afraid, but come into your cell without fear, because all these animals you see are so tame and gentle that they will do you no harm at all.' The hermit, assured by these words of Cesarino, went into his humble cell. Now

Cesarino, who was completely worn out by so much travelling, turned to the hermit and said, 'My father, have you here by chance a morsel of bread and a drop of wine that you can give me to bring back a little of my strength?'

'Assuredly I have, my son,' replied the hermit, 'but perhaps not of as good a quality as you may desire.' Then the hermit flayed and cut up some of the game he had brought in with him and put it upon a spit to roast. After setting the table and spreading it with such poor food as he had at hand, he and Cesarino ate their supper cheerfully together.

When they had finished their meal, the hermit said to Cesarino, 'Not far from this place there lives a dragon whose poisonous breath destroys and annihilates everything around, and there is no one in the country who can oppose him. So great is his devastation that before long all the peasants of the land will be forced to abandon their fields and resettle abroad. Over and beyond this, it is necessary to send him every day the body of some human victim to devour, failing which he would destroy everything both far and near. And now, by a cruel and evil fate, the one chosen by lot for tomorrow is the king's daughter, who in beauty, worth, and goodness excels every other maiden alive, for there is nothing about her that is not worthy of the greatest praise. Truly, it is a foul fortune that so fair and virtuous a maiden should thus cruelly perish, being so pure and free of offence.

After listening to these words of the hermit, Cesarino replied, 'Don't let your courage fail you, holy father. Such evil will not befall us, for in a very short time you'll see the maiden set free.' The next morning, just as the first rays of dawn appeared in the sky, Cesarino made his way to the place where the dreadful monster had made his lair, taking along with him his three animals. Once there, he beheld the king's daughter already present to be devoured by the beast. He went directly towards her, found her weeping bitterly, and comforted her with these words: 'Don't weep or lament, my lady, for I have come here to free you from your peril.'

But even while he was speaking, behold, the ravenous dragon came forward with a mighty rush from its lair, with its jaws wide open and ready to tear into pieces and devour the delicate body of the beautiful maiden, who was overwhelmed by fear and trembling in every limb. Stirred by pity, Cesarino took courage, urging the three animals to attack this fierce and famished monster, whereupon they grappled with him so valiantly that they forced him to the ground and slew him. Then Cesarino took a bare knife in his hand, cut out the tongue from the dragon's throat and placed it in a bag, which he stowed away with great care. Without saying a word further to the damsel whom he had delivered, he returned to the hermitage, giving an account of the deed to the holy father. When he understood that the dragon was veritably destroyed, the young maiden set free, and the country liberated, the hermit was nearly overcome with joy.

Now it happened that a certain peasant, a coarse and grasping rogue, was passing by the spot where the dead body of this fierce and horrible monster lay stretched out. As soon as he caught sight of the savage beast, he took in hand the knife he carried at his side and cut off the dragon's head, which he placed in a large bag he had with him and made his way towards the city. Going along the road at a rapid pace he overtook the princess on her way back to the king, her father. Joining company with her, he went as far as the royal palace, where he led her into the presence of the king, who nearly died from a surfeit of joy as soon as he saw his daughter back safe and sound. Gleefully this peasant snatched his hat from his head and addressed the king, 'Sire, I claim by right this fair daughter of yours as my wife, seeing that I have delivered her from death.' Having thus spoken, the peasant, in testimony of his words, drew out of his bag the horrible head of the slain monster and laid it before the king. When he beheld the monster's head, once so fierce, but now an insignificant thing, and considered in his mind how his daughter had been rescued from death and his country freed from the ravages of the dragon, the king gave orders for a celebratory triumph and a sumptuous feast, to which all the ladies of the city were invited. A great crowd of these, splendidly attired, came to congratulate the princess for her recent liberation from death.

As they were preparing all these feasts and triumphs, the old hermit happened to go into the city, where news came to him of a certain peasant who had slain the dragon and was to have the king's daughter in marriage as his reward for her liberation. Hearing such news, he was heavily grieved. Putting aside at that time any thought of seeking alms, he returned immediately to his hermitage to tell Cesarino what he had just heard. Aggrieved by this turn of events, the youth brought out the tongue of the slain dragon showing it to the hermit as reliable proof that he himself had destroyed the wild beast. When the hermit had heard his story and was fully persuaded that Cesarino was the slayer of the dragon, he found his way into the presence of the king and there, removing his ragged cowl from his head, he began to speak, 'Most sacred majesty, it would be a shameful thing if a malignant, rascally fellow, one for whom a hole in the ground is all the home he deserves, should become the husband of a maiden who is the very flower of loveliness, the example of good manners, the mirror of courtesy, and richly dowered with every virtue. It is even worse when such a rogue seeks to win this prize by deceiving your majesty in claiming for truth the lies issuing from his throat. But I, who am most jealous of your majesty's honour and eager to be of service to the princess your daughter, have come here to make manifest to you that the man who boasts of having delivered your daughter is not the one who slew the dragon. Therefore, O most sacred majesty, open your eyes and ears and listen to someone who has your welfare at heart.'

When he heard the hermit's bold declarations, the king was certain that his words were those of a faithful and devoted subject and credited them fully. He then gave orders at once that all the feasts and celebrations should be countermanded, directing the hermit to reveal to him the name of the man who was the true rescuer of his daughter. Wishing for nothing better, the hermit replied, 'Sire, there is no need to make any mystery about his name, but if it is your majesty's wish, I will bring him here into your presence, where you will see a youth of fair aspect, graceful, seemly, lovable, and gifted with manners so noble and honest that I have never yet met another to equal him.' The king, who was already greatly taken by this picture of the young man, bade the hermit to bring him as soon as possible into his presence. Leaving the king's palace, the hermit returned to his dwelling and told Cesarino what he had done.

After taking the dragon's tongue and putting it in a pouch, the youth went into the king's presence, accompanied by the hermit and the three animals, and kneeling reverently on his knees, he said, 'Most sacred majesty, the fatigue and the labour were indeed mine, but the honour belongs to others. I, with these three animals, slew the wild beast in order to set your daughter at liberty.'

The king replied, 'What proof can you give me that you really slew this beast, given that another man has brought its head to me, which you see suspended here?'

Cesarino answered, 'I do not ask you to take the word of your daughter, whose testimony alone would assuredly be sufficient. I will simply offer to you a token, the nature of which no one can contradict, to prove that I and no other slew the beast. Examine carefully the head you now possess and you will find that the tongue is missing.' With that, the king had the dragon's head examined and found, indeed, that it had no tongue.

Cesarino then put his hand into his bag and pulled out the dragon's tongue, one of such enormous size that its like had never been seen before, thereby revealing clearly that he had slain the savage beast. After hearing his daughter's confirmation, in addition to seeing the tongue, along with various other proofs, the king ordered his retainers at once to take the villainous peasant out and strike his head from his body. Then with great feasts and rejoicings, they celebrated the nuptials of Cesarino and the princess.

When the news reached the youth's mother and sisters that he had slain the wild beast, rescued the princess, and had taken the damsel for his wife, they resolved to travel to Sicily. Taking passage by ship, they were quickly carried there by a favourable wind and received most honourably. But these women were not long in the land before they grew so envious of Cesarino's good fortune that they began to think only of how they might bring about his downfall. Their hatred increased day by day, until they were determined to have him secretly murdered. After considering in their minds several deadly stratagems, they decided at last to take a bone, sharpen the point, dip it in some venom, and place it point upwards in Cesarino's bed so that when he tossed himself down to rest, in the manner of young people, he would give himself a poisonous wound. Having so determined, they went to work immediately to carry out their wicked plan. One day, when the hour for retiring had come, Cesarino went into the bedroom with his wife, threw off all his clothes and his shirt, lay down on the bed, and pierced his left side with the sharp point of the bone. So severe was the wound that his body right away swelled up with the poison and when this reached his heart he died. When the princess saw that her husband was dead, she began to cry aloud and weep bitterly, the noise bringing the courtiers running into the chamber where they found Cesarino dead. Turning the corpse over and over, they found it inflated and black as a raven, for which reason they suspected that he had been killed by poison. When the king heard what had occurred, he ordered that a thorough investigation be made, but finding no clues, he abandoned the search. Together with his daughter and the whole court, he mourned him deeply, ordering that the body of Cesarino be buried with the most solemn funeral rites.

While these stately obsequies were being carried out, the mother and sisters of Cesarino began to fear that the lion, bear, and wolf – once they found out their master was dead – might scent out the treachery that had been used against him. So taking counsel with one another, they hit upon the plan of sealing up the ears of the three animals, which they managed to carry out. But they did not seal up the wolf's ears completely, so that he was able to hear with one of them a little of what had transpired. After the dead body had been taken to the sepulchre, the wolf said to the lion and the bear, 'Comrades, it seems to me that bad news is circulating.' But these two, whose ears were completely stopped, could not hear what he said, so that when he repeated his words, they understood him no better. But the wolf went on making signs and gestures to them, at last making his meaning clear that someone was dead. Then the bear set to work with his hard, crooked claws digging down into the lion's ears deeply enough to bring out the seal. Then the lion did the same to the bear and the wolf.

As soon as they had all got back their hearing, the wolf said to his companions, 'It seems to me that I heard men talking of our master's death.' Seeing that he no longer came to visit and feed them as he usually did, they held it for certain that he must be dead, whereupon they all left the house together and came straight to the place where the body was being borne to the grave. As soon as the priests and the others who were assisting at the funeral saw the three animals, they all fled, as did the men who were bearing the corpse, while others of greater courage stayed to see how the affair would end. Without delay, the animals began to work diligently with their teeth and claws. Before long they had stripped the grave clothes off their master's body and, after examining it very closely, they found the fatal wound. The lion said to the bear, 'Brother, now is the time we need a little of your stomach grease, for by anointing our master's wound with it, he'll recover.'

The bear answered, 'There is no need for another word. I'll open my mouth as wide as I possibly can. Then put your paw down my throat and bring up as much grease as you need.' So the lion put his paw down the bear's throat – the bear drawing himself together, meanwhile, so that he could thrust it far down – and when he had extracted all the grease he wanted, he anointed his master's wound with it all around, inside and outside. When the wound had become somewhat softened, he sucked it with his mouth, and then thrust into it a certain herb, the virtue of which was so potent that it immediately began to work upon the heart and in a very short time rekindled its fire. Little by little Cesarino recovered his strength and was brought back to life.

When those who were standing by saw this marvel, they were struck with amazement and straightway ran to the king to tell him that Cesarino was restored to life. When he heard these tidings, the king went to meet him, accompanied by his daughter, whose name was Dorothea, and they embraced and kissed him with all the joy they felt over so unexpected an outcome, leading him back to the king's palace amid feasting and rejoicing.

The news of Cesarino's resurrection soon came to the ears of his mother and sisters, to their great distress. Nevertheless, pretending to be overjoyed about it, they went to the palace to join in with the rest. But as soon as they came into Cesarino's presence, a great quantity of blood suddenly issued from his wound. Upon seeing this, they were struck with confusion and their faces went pale. Growing suspicious of their guilt, the king told his guards to seize them and put them to the torture. Once done, they confessed to everything, whereupon the king commanded that they be burned alive. Cesarino and Dorothea lived long and happily together and left children to rule in their stead, while the three animals were tended with the utmost care and affection until they died in the course of nature.

When Alteria had come to the end of her story, she gave her enigma in the following words without waiting for any further instruction from the Signora:

> I bear myself a woman's name,
> A brother's presence near I claim,
> I live only by his death,
> I die, and he regains his breath.
> Our way together never lies,
> From my pursuit he always flies.
> Swifter than a bird's my way,
> No man ever made me stay.
> At supper time you'll find me near,
> Although no portion of your cheer.
> Birth and death are with me ever,
> Yet they hurt or harm me never.

Alteria's enigma was so clever and ingenious that no one could lay claim to the least notion of its meaning except she who had recited it. So when she saw that they could not bring their wits sufficiently together to disentangle it, she said, 'My enigma, ladies and gentlemen, is intended to represent the night, which has a woman's name, and has a brother who is called the day. When the day dies, the night is born, and again, the night being dead, the day revives. She and the day can never go on their course together. She flies like a bird, never suffering herself to be captured. And again, she is always with us at supper time.'

Everyone was pleased at this pretty interpretation of the subtle enigma, and it was declared by all to be a work of great learning. But in order to prevent the present night from flying away and being overtaken by the day, the Signora gave the word to Eritrea to go on with her story at once. Gaily the damsel began to tell the following fable.

X.3 Commentary

The story of Cesarino is one of the oldest and best established of all the European folk tales. It tells of the boy who wins a bride by rescuing her from a menacing, poison-breathing monster. In that profile of events, he participates in an archetypal narrative of conquest over a beast that is subject to a wide range of allegorical and mythological interpretations. Because this story resembles so closely the ancient myth of Perseus and Andromeda as well as that of St George killing the dragon, it might be said that 'Cesarino' carries in its narrative 'genes' all the mighty weight of those two noteworthy traditions. Moreover, merely in terms of its motivic components, the story 'remembers' not only all tales in which a princess is rescued from a dragon, but all those in which an imposter claims the deeds of the hero, all those in which animal helpers fight on the hero's behalf and convey to him the means for bringing him back to life, and finally all those in which invidious family members, jealous of the hero's success, seek to slay him. Just how many *idées forces* are embedded in these motifs and how profoundly they incorporate the mentalities of human communities in remote ages is good work for folklorists and anthropologists. Can this story not be about service to an 'out' community in order to win a foreign bride, or the revision of religious practices involving human sacrifice implicit in the heroic rescue of the victims, or the monster as the protector of virginity that must be ritually slain before the girl can pass from her father's house to that of her husband? This is to say nothing of the slaying of apocalyptic beasts as humankind's spiritual archenemies. At a lower mimetic level, this is a folk tale with romance overtones in which a young outsider gives comfort and encouragement to a girl facing death by offering to be her champion, risking his life for hers, and so gaining her devotion and love. The socialized behaviour of the hero must distinguish him from his rival, who is eager to enjoy the favours of the princess without committing himself to her protection or well-being. Thus, Cesarino's story may also be an emblematic courtship that overwrites the impression that the bride is mere booty for services rendered to the state. Implicitly, delay shapes hearts and necessitates a second deliverance. The curious sequel to this fairy tale is perhaps less intuitive as the hero falls victim, not to a wicked witch, but to his own jealous mother and sisters – relatives who live at court through his accomplishments and bounty, yet are prepared to slay him. This is not only a tale of exogamous wooing, but of managing the insidious forces within the family. How these contrasting motifs might have come together will become clearer as the investigation of the story's composition unfolds.

Because Ovid's *Metamorphoses* is so ready to hand, there is perhaps little need to rehearse in detail the famous tale of Perseus and Andromeda, in which Straparola's work may have found its remotest origin. A few salient features are that Perseus was born to Zeus and Danaë, making him half divine, half mortal.[20] As a warrior and adventurer, he had gained for himself, early in his career, a head of mass destruction, that of the deadly Medusa, which could be looked upon only in a mirror. He carried it with him everywhere, covered, but ready for display in the presence of his enemies when all other battle tactics failed. She was better than Excalibur. The first victim was Atlas, turned to a shaggy mountain after an ill-advised glance. His crime: withholding hospitality from the passing hero, fearful for his golden apples. Then on a fly-over, Perseus saw Andromeda ready to pay the penalty for her mother's big mouth, who had been boasting ill-advisedly of her daughter's beauty. Andromeda had been chained to a rock in the place were the dreaded sea monster roams when Perseus swooped down from the skies to hear her story. She told it to him, weeping. There was a touch of vanity in his reckless decision to render his services, but there was also a kingdom in the dowry. His battle manoeuvre was to dive at the beast from above and stab for the heart. Then, as though a spell had been broken, the girl's shackles fell away, Perseus saved the royal house, and desired Andromeda as his reward. The problem was that Phineus had a prior claim to her and started a factional war that entailed slaughter on both sides until Perseus

---

20 Ovid, *Metamorphoses*, trans. Rolfe Humphries (Bloomington: Indiana University Press, 1961), bk. IV, line 604–bk. V, line 249, pp. 100–14. For a thorough study of this legend and its influence on Western literature, including the dragon-slayer stories combined with the two-brothers folk tales examined below, see Edwin Sidney Hartland, *The Legend of Perseus: A Study of Tradition in Story, Custom and Belief*, 3 vols. (London: David Nutt, 1894).

gave him a dose of the Medusa – a sight he managed to avoid until the hero began swinging her about like an imminent projectile. Phineus is then turned to stone in a pose immortalizing his cringing fear, much as the brothers are turned to stone by witches in many of the folk-tale versions of the 'Cesarino' group. Phineus is the potential model for all the interlopers who seek to deprive the hero of the fruits of his valour – marriage to the homecoming princess.

By Ovid's time, the myth is already far from its original moorings on its way to becoming romance. Who is Andromeda that she should compel love? In the *Metamorphoses*, she is already an expression of the male fantasy of having to wife the girl whose life is indebted to him. Dragon killing, in this regard, is both a way of dealing with the crisis of chastity, the abandonment of paternal protection, and the bonding of the couple in an asymmetrical relation of service and gratitude. Little import, then, that the story may have arisen in Syrian mythology in which a sun-god figure on a white horse kills the sea monster, Tiamat, or that Andromeda is a stand-in for Aphrodite or Ishtar, or a lecherous sea-goddess, naked and chained to a rock by the hero for his own protection after killing the monster. In that rendition, the dragon is the guardian of the siren, just as, in the *Emblemata* of Alciati, the dragon is the custodian of chastity.[21] Ovid's story comes into focus when it is realized that Andromeda's mother is Queen Cassiopeia, who offended the sea goddesses in boasting of her daughter's beauty, causing them to send their champion to destroy her. It is all a catty tiff in the boudoir, but it gave rise to one of the great archetypal motifs (or paralleled it, or emanated from it): that of the dragon-slaying hero. Moreover, it is about extended family dynamics and dynastic survival, for Phineus was the king's brother and thus the girl's uncle; such was the man who claimed Andromeda at the wedding banquet. Tellingly, in many of the subsequent folk-tale versions, the dragon

---

21 Andrea Alciati, 'Custodiendas virgines' in *Emblemata* (Antwerp: ex officina C. Plantini, 1581), no. 22, p. 104. This is Pallas with a dragon at her feet, the custodian of virgins, so that to slay the beast is to clear the way for sex, an act of violence that allows the transfer from one state to another – the fire-breathing hymen. Virgins are associated with sacred woods and shrines, also guarded by dragons, because, as Alciati says, love places snares on every side. The dragon represents the difference between easy and difficult conquests, or bride-winning through masculine valour. Yet the girl must also seek freedom from jealous dominance or from being bartered as a prize for martial services rendered. Thus, the social prolongation of the story – the delays tantamount to a period of testing and preliminary devotion. The folk tales and later romances take this issue into further consideration.

slayer returns just in time to interrupt the wedding of the princess to a usurper of his own valorous deeds, whether a slave, a passing coal merchant, or an opportunist household menial. As early as Ovid, everything is in place: the passing hero, the maiden destined for devouring by a (fire-breathing, poison-spewing, dart-wielding, mean-jawed, omni-fantasy) monster, the glorious fight, the promised reward, the craven rival, his destruction, and the power transfer from the older to the now stabilized younger generation. But there will be a problem with the occidental genesis theory when it is seen that all the parts are equally in place in Eastern tales, some of them going back to the India of the sixth century.

After Ovid, the story's trail then fades for many centuries, for the 'dark age' folk tale has left no record, and St George does not meet a dragon with certainty before the early thirteenth century. To be sure, Ovid was known throughout the Middle Ages, both maligned and moralized. Hence, what began in myth may well have flowed directly into legend, for with a bit of Christian tweaking, St George was as good a man for damsel delivery as Perseus, albeit with a much reduced libido. Nevertheless, the origin of the legend remains moot. Medieval culture had its own quota of 'native' dragons and their killers from Saxo's Frotho and the dragons of *Beowulf* to the beasts and heroes of the *Bjarka Saga* and the *Tristan* (before 1210) of Gottfried von Strassburg (ll. 8942–11,236), in which the hero wins Isolde by slaying the dragon ravaging the countryside. Not only did they know the myths of Jason, Cadmus, Hercules, and Apollo, but tales from the ancient Middle East, all of which had ways of sifting down into vernacular cultures. In the words of Jonathan Evans, 'One of the vexed questions in the study of medieval dragon lore is that of the relationship between learned, classical, and sacred traditions ... and indigenous, vernacular traditions emerging through oral transmission. The diversity both of the sources of dragon motifs and of the genres, themes, and linguistic and national traditions within which these motifs were elaborated in the Middle Ages has led Lutz Röhrich to conclude that no single unifying formulation can possibly summarize medieval folklore related to the dragon.'[22] Such is the crux in tracing tales like 'Cesarino' to remote sources. Straparola's creation is first indebted to a folk tale, the prototype of which is best thought of as an amalgamation of indigenous, mythic, biblical, ancient, and oriental elements introduced

---

22 'Dragon,' in *Medieval Folklore: A Guide to Myths, Legends, Tales, Beliefs, and Customs*, ed. Carl Lindahl et al. (Oxford: Oxford University Press, 2002), p. 101.

through the mental play of the raconteurs. Inversely, however, we have at this juncture three superimposed narratives (a myth, a legend, and a generic folk tale) linked by the prospect that all three are derived from a once-in-the-history-of-the-world story, because it is too particular in its details to allow for multiple genesis in different times and places. In light of that hypothesis, it may be said that Straparola's essentially popular story bears in its make-up not only a Greco-Roman myth, but a Christian legend, and an Eastern tale as well.

To avoid controversy, it may be allowed that the story of St George is both the life of a true martyr and the legend of a saint garnished with myths whereby he is made more than 'a good man "whose deeds are known only to God."'[23] The 'historical' George was a soldier in the Roman army at the time of Diocletian, born to a Christian mother. When he received orders to carry out the persecutions in Asia Minor or Palestine, he tore them up, for which deed he was imprisoned and ultimately martyred. His Christian ascendancy was in the regions of the Eastern Church, with iconographical evidence going back to the seventh century. The earliest text concerning him is Georgian and dates to the twelfth century. But the centre of his veneration seems to have been Cappadocia, with evidence dating back to the eleventh century. Just where and when he acquired the legend of dragon slaying is work for specialists, for while some think his story arrived from the Eastern Orthodox world with the Crusaders (who made a mess of the place in the thirteenth century), others think that the overlay from romance or the folk tale was made in the West and travelled eastward. Duncan Robertson believes that the dragon motif was transferred to St George from the life of St Theodore Tiro, which merely removes the question of origin to a different saint.[24] However that may prove, there can be no doubt that the dragon legend was in place by the time of the writing of the *Speculum historiale* of Vincent of Beauvais and the *Legenda aurea* (The Golden Legend) of Jacobus de

---

23 Donald Attwater, *The Avenel Dictionary of Saints* (New York: Avenel [1965], 1981), p. 148.

24 The Bollandists agree with this assessment. This warrior saint, martyred in Pontus, was, before St Mark, the patron saint of Venice, where he is still associated iconographically with dragon slaying. Duncan Robertson, *The Medieval Saints' Lives* (Lexington, KY: French Forum, 1995), pp. 51–2.

Voragine, in circulation by 1265. It was this latter account that gave the story its wide circulation throughout Europe in the later Middle Ages.[25]

According to Jacobus, George encountered his dragon in the city of Selene in Libya, where, perhaps merely coincidentally, the drops of the Medusa's blood during Perseus's pass-over were said to have spawned poisonous serpents.[26] Victims appointed to the monster's chops were chosen by lot and George arrived when it had fallen upon the king's daughter. Thoughtfully, the girl had already been dressed as a bride for the beast's delectation. George offers his services and, in a manner redolent of subsequent folk versions, he is cautioned away by the girl, as Perseus is warned by Andromeda, but he refuses to leave her. The dragon then emerges from the lake, although not much of a fight ensues, for with the help of a the girl's girdle, invested with the power of chastity, the beast is subdued and led in all Christian docility back to the city. There George makes strategic use of its terrifying presence, for with the zeal of a true missionary he converts the entire city to Christianity by force. Only then was the dragon killed and a church built, from the altar of which welled up healing waters. The story captured the medieval imagination. As the dragon took on the characteristics of the seven-headed beast of the apocalypse, brought to the world's attention by John of Patmos in his *Revelations*, 12:4 and 17:3–4, more and more saints adopted the ritual of dragon slaying as warriors and warrioresses against the forces of Satan. Among them are Saints Mercurialis, bishop of Forlì, Julian of Le Mans, Veran, Bienheuré, Crescentinus, Margaret of Antioch, Clement of Metz, Quirinus of Malmedy, Donatus of Arezzo, and Leonard of Noblac, ora pro nobis. From folklore to legend or from legend to folklore, the story of St George participates in a circulation of materials presumably important to the formation of the oral tradition from which Straparola borrowed the substance of the present story.

The history of a legend that links Perseus to St George is sufficiently complex without factoring in the close counterparts to the story type to be found in Eastern sources. The following paragraphs will make a necessary leap from the saint's life to the folk-tale type, a version of which is told by Straparola. Poised between them are such tales as those of King

---

25 On the widespread influence of this work, see Margaret Aston, *Faith and Fire: Popular and Unpopular Religion, 1350–1600* (London: Hambledon Press, 1993), p. 272.

26 Jacques de Voragine, *La Légende dorée*, trans. Teodor de Wyzewa (Paris: Perrin, 1920), no. 59, pp. 226–32; *The Golden Legend*, trans. William Granger Ryan, 2 vols. (Princeton: Princeton University Press, 1995), no. 58, vol. I, p. 238.

Parityagasena from Somadeva's *Ocean of the Streams of Story*, in which the queen gives birth to heroic twins after consuming two magic apples, one of her own, and one intended for a second wife. They too, as in the European folk tale of the 'two brothers,' have recourse to a supernatural power should they find themselves in trouble – the goddess Durga, the giver of the apples. When they are falsely accused of intended rebellion by the slighted second wife, they flee on swift horses. Constant adversity dogs them, including the deaths of their horses, but in time the goddess supplies the elder with a magic sword. Like Perseus and St George, he comes upon a cursed city with a terrible Rakshasa or demon at the gate. When the boy delivers battle to Yamadanshtra, king of the demons, the severed heads continually grow back until he severs them a second time. The virgin under the demon's care falls in love with the hero; she is the younger sister of the beleaguered ruler of the city. When the fight is won, she does the proposing, the marriage is celebrated immediately, and the younger brother takes up residence with them. But as in the present story, there is more to follow concerning marital strife, a second woman, the near destruction of the magic sword, and the liberation of the elder brother by the younger. He goes on a journey, makes representation of their plight to the goddess Durga, and she releases the hero from a spell while restoring the beneficent sword. As will be seen, the Straparola tale is a departure from the more typical version of the combined 'two brothers' and 'dragon slaying' motifs, being closer in spirit to the domestic threat posed to the hero in the Eastern story type, initially by his father's second wife, and then by his own wife and a second woman. The option to be held in mind is that the folk tale to emerge from the Perseus–St George tradition was further diversified by the early arrival in Europe of some form of this Eastern model, and that the version borrowed by Straparola was more closely aligned to this recessive type, rather than to the more dominant 'two brothers' type.[27]

------

27 *The Ocean of the Streams of Story, Somadeva's Katha sarit sagara*, trans. C.H. Tawney, ed. N.M. Penzer, 10 vols. (Delhi: Motilal Banarsidass [1923], 1984), vol. III, pp. 263–76. See George William Cox, *The Mythology of the Aryan Nations*, 2 vols. (London: Longmans, Green & Co., 1870), vol. I, p. 162. There is a related tale in the *Tooti Nameh* that involves the surreptitious consumption of a magic bird. In both stories it is the dragon-slayer hero, alone or with his brother. For the deed they are sent into exile. Férîd the dragon slayer in this story marries a princess, but not the one delivered from the dragon. *Tuti-Nameh: Das Papageien Buch aus dem Turkischen*, trans. Georg Rosen, 2 vols. (Leipzig: Brockhaus, 1858), vol. II, p. 291. In another Eastern version two brothers flee their father's house where they were mistreated by

In those same years in which Straparola was writing, dragon slaying had become a nearly *de rigueur* component of the heroic romance, so that by the time Edmund Spenser came to the writing of his Book I of the *Faerie Queene* in the 1580s, he had a substantial repertory to draw upon. Luigi Pulci had enough of the tradition by the 1480s to indulge in touches of caricature and parody. His *Morgante* (1478, 1483) demonstrates that the matter of Cesarino was simultaneously in full circulation in elite culture. Fiorisena, the ravishing daughter of a brother-murdering father, King Corbante of Carrara, was on the verge of appeasing the hunger of the region's wasteland-maker when the three sworn heroes, Rinaldo, Oliver, and Dudòn, happen along. The girl is sweet fifteen and innocent as Cordelia, although she was about to pay for the sins of an older generation, insofar as her uncle and the prince were dead by foul play and nemesis demanded its due. A land once fertile was now barren and the three heroes from the ancient Matter of France (the Carolingian cycle) appeared to jest their way into battle, teasing each other over who was to get the girl (see the commentary on 'The Three Brothers,' VII.5). This dragon was endowed with both poison and fire, and Dudòn went down first, while Oliver got badly scorched and fainted dead away, his fist stuck in the beast's mouth while feeding it a gauntlet. Rinaldo, meanwhile, gives the coup de grace. All the while, their companion lion looked on from afar without shaking its mane. When Oliver came to, he was overcome with love after a second glance at Fiorisena and started to sicken again even as he healed, like Timias over Belphoebe in a counterpart passage of the *Faerie Queene* (III.v.42–3). The matter of romance receives prolongation; Rinaldo cedes his interest, and then asks the Saracen King Corbante, after declaring his Christian identity, whether he and his people wished to be baptized. With that he turns preacher, now styling the beast of ancient mythology as the emissary of God to urge them to repentance, à la St George. A mass conversion follows. Such is the cognizance on Pulci's part of the religious and secular profiles of the

---

a stepmother. They overhear two birds boasting that whoever eats them will become king and first minister. After killing and consuming them, the younger, destined to become king, arrives in a country where a princess is promised to the slayer of the menacing rakshasa. After his victory, he falls asleep while a sweeper takes the monster's heads in search of reward. Needless to say, the hero makes his return in time. Flora Ann Steel and R.C. Temple, *Wide-awake Stories: A Collection of Tales Told in the Punjab and Kashmir* (Bombay: Education Society's Press, 1884), p. 138.

dragon-slayer narrative, whether nourished by or nourishing the parallel traditions of the folk.[28]

More immediately, Straparola worked with a folk narrative already well established and circulating in diversified and regionalized forms by the middle of the sixteenth century. It included, characteristically, the magic birth of the hero, the circumstances that impelled his wandering, the gathering of animal helpers, enchantments, and cures by magic potions – features known in folk tales in all parts of the world. At its core, the tale featured the full legacy of Perseus, George, and Rinaldo, and the themes that inevitably arise when heroes kill dragons, which are desecrators of land and devourers of women. Through acts of empathy, valour, and cunning, on a reduced scale, his hero would likewise earn his rewards, both political and matrimonial, in the manner of the complete gentleman.

'Cesarino the Dragon Slayer' is, in effect, two folk tales in one. At the centre is the familiar episode of the hero's arrival at a royal city in mourning over the imminent death of their princess, doomed to be devoured by a beast ravaging their countryside and demanding human victims. This is 'the dragon slayer' tale (Type 300), represented by Straparola in all its customary component parts. But the second tale traditionally encircling 'the dragon slayer,' namely 'the two brothers' (Type 303), is barely recognizable. Cesarino should have a brother who detects his distress through a magic sign, repeats his complex journey, meets his wife, and even sleeps in her bed while respecting the sanctity of their union, before rescuing him from the evil enchantment. But Straparola's source had already wandered from the more conventional form of the story, a regional variation perhaps influenced by the Eastern sources mentioned above, with its closest analogues in the Spanish forms collected in the early twentieth century. Nevertheless, in a remote sense, the tale replacing the rescue by a second brother – that of rescue from death by treachery through the magic ministrations of his helper animals – performs a similar structural and thematic function.

Stith Thompson stated in *The Folktale* that 'if one wished to study the ways in which a tale in the course of centuries becomes scattered over the whole of Europe he could do no better than to direct his attention

---

28 *Morgante: The Epic Adventures of Orlando and His Giant Friend Morgante*, trans. Joseph Tusiani, intro. Edoardo A. Lèbano (Bloomington: Indiana University Press, 1998), IV, ll. 40–69, pp. 60–70.

to [these] two closely related folk tales.'[29] Each began as a separate tale, but when the 'two brothers' type was adapted to surround the far more ancient tale of dragon slaying, it provided it with its own conditions concerning the birth, departure, and equipping of the hero, and set him up for a closing adventure involving his brother[s] and his helper animals. The two folk-tale types, namely the 'dragon slayer' story alone and the same story coupled with the 'two brothers' frame, then competed with each other until the frequency of the compound story eventually doubled that of the simple 'dragon slayer' type. Both forms have been extensively studied, beginning with Kurt Ranke's penetrating 'Die zwei Brüder: Eine Studie zur vergelichenden Märchenforschung.'[30] He identified some 770 versions of 'the two brothers' type, and 368 of 'the dragon slayer' type, to which another 100 had been added by the time Thompson wrote about them in 1946. Because 'the two brothers' type incorporates the dragon-slaying episode, this brings the number of such tales collected in the nineteenth and twentieth centuries, principally in Europe, to well over eleven hundred. Of these, merely a handful can be sampled to illustrate the curious ways in which Straparola's tale takes on a kaleidoscopic relationship to the motifs and details in subsequent stories, and to show by comparison the kind and quality of choices represented by the makers of Straparola's source.

For the folklorists, the question of remote origins in ancient legend and mythology is of secondary importance – a matter of sheer speculative consideration. For them, the 'Cesarino' group is the successor to a prototype that can be retro-engineered through a frequency analysis of a

---

29 *The Folktale* (Berkeley: University of California Press, 1977), p. 24. Thompson provides a table of the distribution of these two stories by geographical region. The numbers of variants are determined, not by the absolute number available in each country, but by the number of versions collected by various ethnographers. Nevertheless, they do indicate a relative frequency of occurrence, that, for example, the story was far better known in Finland than in Greece, and that of the 143 Finnish versions, 141 were of 'the two brother' type, and only 2 were of the 'dragon slayer' type, while in Lithuania the opposite was true. Curiously, only 14 such stories of 'the two brothers' have been recorded in France, but that is due to the lack of collectors in many regions of the country. While Ireland and Scotland are well represented, England has none. Italian folklorists have reported a goodly number, 27 of 'the two brothers' type, one of which should be Straparola's, and 14 'dragon slayer' tales (p. 27).

30 'Die zwei Brüder: Eine Studie zur vergleichenden Märchenforschung,' *Folklore Fellows Communications* (Helsinki, 1934), no. 114.

large sampling of surviving versions. The moment and place of origin that is of interest to them concerns a work already in full possession of its oral characteristics and 'popular' design. Ranke located the birthplace in the north of France, the tale's genesis coming at a date sufficiently early to account for references in northern sagas of the fourteenth century. He is not concerned with potential hagiographical or popular Eastern influences. Basile's version (1634), 'Il mercante' discussed below, serves for him as that which is closest to the prototype. It provides an important contrast to the version recorded by Straparola, for given the diversification they represent, the generic type had to have appeared many years prior to both.

Straparola's tale is perhaps best compared with 'the two brothers' type because it too has a two-part structure, one of them encircling the dragon-slaying episode. But because it has wandered from the oikotype to a considerable degree, it is best to begin, at the risk of some prolixity, with a profiling of both types. In the generic form of the 'dragon slayer' type, the young hero sets out from home after his parents' death, often leaving a sister with the house. He, like the boy who inherits a cat (XI.1), may inherit barnyard animals that he exchanges for clever dogs to accompany him. Straparola's hero goes into the forest where he finds litters of lions, wolves, and bears, from which he takes one of each to raise as future travel companions. Like the dogs, they are noteworthy for their loyalty, obedience, prowess, and human-like intelligence. This hero may likewise receive a magic wand or weapon in exchange for favours rendered. Cesarino's meeting with a hermit who serves as local mentor and messenger may derive from such episodes. The hero then arrives at a royal city in mourning, learns of the seven-headed dragon, meets and comforts the princess destined for sacrifice, then goes about his work severing all the heads, preventing them from being reattached, and collecting their tongues. Rather than accompanying the princess home, however, he continues on his adventure-seeking way, but not without specifying the moment of his return, telling the princess meanwhile to keep his accomplishments secret. A spy, whether a court official, a coachmen, a blacksmith, or a peasant, now cuts off the heads of the slain dragon and returns with them to court, there to claim the princess in marriage. This imposter must threaten the princess to keep her quiet, yet submit to the time delay she imposes and await the wedding celebrations, which are, of course, broken off by the hero's return. Often the returning champion will stop at an inn and send his dogs to court with notes demanding banqueting food from the royal kitchen in order to win a bet. The princess, recognizing the dogs, then informs her father, who calls for the hero, inspects the missing tongues, arranges for the death or exile of the imposter, and weds the true couple. There the story ends, so that if Straparola's source adds a lengthy coda concerned with the death and resurrection of the hero, it does so entirely on its own, or by analogy with the 'two brothers,' while in effect making use of none of that story's particular features.

'The two brothers' type, by contrast, contains a far more elaborate opening device. A poor fisherman catches a speaking fish that begs for its life, only to explain how its parts should be employed to magic ends. By feeding one morsel to his wife, another to his dog, and another to his horse, this man finds himself with twin sons, twin dogs, twin horses, and even twin swords. The lookalike boys establish magic means for knowing if the other meets with misfortune: 'life signs.' Then the first sets out with horse and hound. After an undetermined number of preliminary adventures, the hero at last comes to the mourning city and performs the dragon slaying necessary to win the princess in the same fashion as described above. But no sooner have the newlyweds retired to their quarters than the hero looks out the window and sees a mysterious phenomenon, a strange light, a beautiful woman, or an enchanted forest that lures him to the hunt. Always his wife warns him, always he undertakes the adventure, meets an elderly witch, falls prey to her solicitations, and is turned to stone, along with his dog and horse. Then his brother notices the sign and sets off, tracing his footsteps right to the palace of his wife. Always he deceives her, but always he keeps his brother's honour, often by placing a sword between them in the bed, or wrapping himself in a separate sheet. Then he too sees the lure and follows the lead until he confronts the same temptations. He, however, resists the witch's blandishments and machinations, uses his animals to threaten her, forces the liberation of his brother, and sometimes seizes her magic potion. Then she is killed and the two begin their return trip. In some 20 per cent of the stories, there is a jealous brother motif when the liberated brother suspects his liberator to have slept with his wife along the way and kills him.[31] This adds a secondary episode, for upon discovering his error

---

31 This statistic is Thompson's, *The Folktale*, p. 28. Ranke did not consider this to be an original part of the story, but it is an early motif, nevertheless, for it occurs in Basile's 'Il mercante' (The merchant) in *Il pentamerone*, trans. Richard Burton (London: Henry and Co. [1634], 1893), Day I, Diversion 7.

from his wife, he returns to resuscitate his brother, often using the same means by which he had himself been revived. Typically, this has to do with severed heads and their replacement. There remains but a triumphal entry, confusion over their identities, and the wife's ability to know her own true spouse.

Basile's Seventh Diversion of the First Day of his *Pentamerone*, the story of Cienzo the dragon slayer, is important in confirming at an early date the formula that is so often met with in the nineteenth century, for despite his extreme stylizing, it remains a complete relation of the 'two brothers' type surrounding the rescue of the doomed princess.[32] In that regard, it offers no comfort to those who would make Basile one of Straparola's followers, for clearly this narrative arose through his own fieldwork among the folk. The version he found is much closer to the supposed prototype from which Straparola's is so pronounced a departure. Nevertheless, it has its own particularities. A merchant has two sons – they are practically twins, so much are they alike – but the eldest gets into a fight with the king's son, largely in sport, and biffs him over the head. For this bit of lese-majesty his father gives him up for lost, assuming the king would be out to settle scores. Thus, the hero is sent into exile and challenged to make good on his own if he could. Upon his departure, however, he is given the requisite magic horse and dog, which places him back into the traditional story. There is a wonderful meditation upon the delights of Naples as the hero bids adieu to his city – a bit of sportive Basile run wild. The next episode derives from 'the boy without fear' tradition (see the commentary to IV.5) in which Cienzo finds himself sleeping in an abandoned house where he is awakened by strange presences and is lured down to a cellar where three grotesques are lamenting the loss of their treasure, half of which, in the process, has become his. That portion, however, he delivers to the owner of the house and moves on to new adventures. For a sequel, he rescues a fairy from being ravished by a highwayman, but refuses her invitation to follow her to her palace to receive his reward. Only then does he arrive in the city of mourning, where he pledges his skills in the defeat of the seven-

---

32 *Il pentamerone: or The Tale of Tales (Cunto de li cunti)*, trans. Richard Burton (New York: Boni & Liveright, 1927), I.7, pp. 52–63; *The Great Fairy Tale Tradition*, ed. Jack Zipes (New York: Norton, 2001), pp. 366–74.

headed dragon, a silly fairyland beast with wings and claws. Princess Menechiella arrives with a large train of women, all of them weeping and tearing their hair as though the beast were a monster bridegroom to whom the girl was about to be delivered. The fight once begun, the monster reveals its knack for rubbing the stumps of the severed heads on a nearby herb with the virtue of making the heads grow back on. After distancing the heads from the necks and collecting the tongues, the boy gathers some of the healing weeds for himself for future use. Then he takes to the road in search of new adventure, oblivious to the prospects of a reward. But when Cienzo hears of the king's proclamation, and that a peasant was likely to marry in his place, he begins to kick himself for letting his fortune slip away so easily. So he writes the princess a long letter, carried by his trusty dog, asking her to speak to her father. The magic horse, meanwhile, simply bites on its own bit. With the missing tongues in his possession, Cienzo wins his case; the peasant is condemned to death, but the hero asks for his pardon. Then, with the nuptials barely over, the 'two brothers' episode resumes with a glance into a nearby window, where the hero sees a sex siren, enemy to marriage, who captivates and ensnares him by the glamour of her hair. This is remote from the witch who attaches the dog and horse with magic hair and turns the hero to stone, a substitution perhaps of Basile's own invention, but it serves a similar function. We know we are still in the right story when Meo, his younger brother, by occult means finds out that Cienzo is in trouble and requires his help. He follows the exact trail of adventures until he encounters Menechiella, yet keeps a sword's width away. Then he spies the siren in the adjacent house, receives the same admonition not to go, but knows what he must do. Once he is there, the dog attacks and swallows the witch and Cienzo is liberated from her spell. The jealous brother inset follows with Meo's beheading, but thanks to the dragon's herb, the heads of brother, dog, and horse can all be replaced, the party can return, their father can join them, and Cienzo can be celebrated as the bad boy who made good after all. The tale of bride selection is emboxed by the tale of brotherly devotion. Basile, with minor substitutions, maintains the requisite symmetry.

Thereafter, the history of this tale leaps forward three centuries, with representations in regions as diverse as Japan and Canada, where the Ojibwa have preserved a version no doubt taken over by the French. The future destiny of the story in Italy may be sketched in by references to a few gathered up by the great nineteenth-century collectors. Vittorio Imbriani repeats the version found by Gherardo Nerucci in the mountains of Pistoia, 'Il mago dale sette teste' (The seven-headed wizard).[33] This story follows the prototype summarized above with the fisherman whose special catch, when ritually apportioned, produces upon his wife, his mare, and his bitch the three brothers with their respective horses, dogs, lances, and guns. The first to depart leaves behind a bottle that would grow cloudy should he encounter trouble. The fearsome seven-headed wizard to be dispatched had the nasty habit of eating all persons he encountered in the king's garden. The boy asks to try his luck in battle because he had seen the princess, had fallen in love with her, and desired her as his reward. When the cannibal magus emerges at noon the earth shakes, and all seven of his jaws are agape as he seeks the princess. The dog joins in the fray, and with the heads severed, the princess tells the hero to bring proof of his conquest. While he is back at the hotel changing clothes, a wretched cobbler stakes his claim with the seven heads. The princess calls him a liar, but the wedding is declared. When the boy returns, he is barred entry and thus employs his clever dog, which heads first for the princess's lap, then yanks the tablecloth off the table, banquet and all, and makes a run for the inn. They try a second supper a week later, and a third, until the dog's owner is arrested. Then he makes his belated appearance with the testimonial of tongues. The post-marital

<hr>

33 *La novellaja fiorentina con la novellaja Milanese* (Milan: Rizzoli, 1976), pp. 375–87. Gherardo Nerucci, *Sessanta novelle popolari montalesi*, ed. Roberto Fedi (Milan: Rizzoli, 1977), no. 8, pp. 61–72. Another in this tradition was collected by Carolina Coronedi-Berti: 'La fola dèl pescadôur,' in which a great fish explains how his parts will give birth to three sons, along with dogs and horses. These three boys wander the world with dog, horse, sword, and money, and Grimèl rescues the king's daughter among his several adventures. *Il propugnatore, studii filologici, storici, e bibliografici* 8, no. 2 (Bologna: Gaetano Romagnoli, 1875), pp. 465–73. These motifs become subdivided between two stories in Angelo de Gubernatis's *Le novelline di Santo Stefano*. In no. 17, 'I tre fratelli,' the events are reversed, for the three brothers go out one by one with horse and dog, and the first two meet a witch on a cold mountain who turns them to salt. The third goes to their rescue. Thereafter, one of them engages in the liberation of a beauty in peril of being devoured by a seven-headed beast. When this inset tale is completed in the traditional way, the entire tale is deemed complete. In the following tale, no. 18, 'Il pescatore,' the story begins once more with the capture of a two-headed eel that, when consumed according to formula, brings the fisherman two swords, two dogs, and two sons. They set off on their respective adventures and the first one comes to disgrace while the second rescues the princess, defeats the imposter, and presents the tongues in proof of his claim. Only then does he receive a sign of his wayward brother's fate and rescues him from an enchanted castle after a long search; (Turin: A.F. Negro, 1869), pp. 40–1, 41–2.

episode is a hunting expedition in the forest primeval, where a little old woman seeking warmth comes into the cave where the youth is sheltering himself from a storm, and by her magic means turns him to stone. This motif is redeployed in many of the stories of 'the three brothers' (see the commentary to VII.5). The denouement is brought about by the offices of the lookalike brothers, the third one succeeding where the first two had failed, according to the traditional model.

In 'I tre cani' a peasant brother and sister find themselves alone in the world. The brother, with his three dogs, engages in multiple adventures loosely related to the tradition, one of which is the combat with the seven-headed sea monster whose tongues he severs in hopes of marrying the king's daughter. When a brute moves in on his territory, he temporizes while his dog plays havoc with several wedding banquets. Thereafter, he delivers proof of his claim and displaces his rival.[34] This version shares many features in common with the previous tale. In 'I tre cani mara-vigliosi,' a peasant drives a bargain for three dogs, to his wife's great annoyance. How did he expect to pay debts with dogs? (The sister in the previous story had argued in similar terms against the exchange of their sheep.) So she cuts him loose to wander the world with 'Runs like Wind,' 'Tears up Everything,' and 'Door and Chain Breaker.' (One assumes, erroneously, that future episodes will correspond to their names.) At last the hero comes to a town where bells toll in mourning. The intended victim is a princess offered in marriage to anyone who could eliminate the insatiable beast demanding her for supper. After a grand procession to the seaside, with princess and parents present, the dogs attack the sea monster and prevail. A triumphal entry follows and the peasant eventually becomes king.[35] All of these except the last are in the tradition of 'the

---

34 Giuseppe Pitrè, *Novelle popolari toscane*, ed. Laura Regina Bruno (Palermo: ILA Palma, 2005), vol. I, pp. 73–80. This story is from Siena. In the edition published in Palermo by Edikronos in 1981, see pp. 10–20.

35 Isaia Visentini, *Fiabe mantovane* (Rome: E. Loescher, 1879), no. 15, pp. 85–9. The dogs are 'Corri come il vento,' 'Sbrana-tutti,' and 'Rompi-porte e catene.' This story with the creative names for the three dogs was popular in many regions. There is another to follow in this collection, no. 19, 'Sangae di pesce,' which does follow the 'two brothers' pattern, beginning with the miracle births of the brothers after their parents consume parts of a talking fish. The dragon killer travels with horse, dog, and lance. A third brother, in this case, manages to kill the witch who has taken the first two in thrall. *Fiabe mantovane* (Bologna: Forni, 1968), pp. 104–10. Domenico Giuseppe Bernoni records one from Venice, 'La bestia de le sete teste' (The beast with the seven heads), in *Fiabe popolari veneziane* (Venice: Fontana-Ottolini, 1873),

two brothers.' All incorporate the dragon slaying. Together they provide
a profile of the variations admitted by the story type. None approximates
the roles of the mother and sisters in Straparola, the death of the hero
by poisoning, or his resuscitation by his fighting animal companions, nor
are those companions other than dogs and horses. In Italy, the Basile
type prevails and the Straparola variant seems to have vanished.

---

no. 10, and Georg Widter and Adam Wolf another entitled 'Drachentödter'
(Dragon-slayer) in their *Volksmärchen aus Venetien* (Leipzig: E.A. Brockhaus, 1866),
no. 8, in which the dogs are named 'Forte,' 'Potente,' and 'Ingegnoso.' The
prominence of these animals coincides with the centrality of the three tamed beasts
in Straparola's story. There are two further versions from the south in Laura
Gonzenbach's *Sicilianische Märchen* (Leipzig: Wilhelm Engelmann, 1870), no. 39,
'Von den Zwilligsbrüdern,' and no. 40, 'Von den drei Brüdern,' vol. I, pp. 269–72
and 272–80. The first is a classic retelling of the 'two brother' type. In the second
the hero is absent for 7 years and 7 months, carrying the tongues with him all that
time before he returns to claim his bride, leading to a lengthy development of the
second part, the distraction by a bright light on the neighbouring mountain and
the encounter with a wicked witch. Finally, there is a truncated version from the
central mountains in which the hero with his three dogs is ordered out of the house
by his father, as in Visentini's tale above. He goes into the mountains, finds a castle,
masters a giant, and liberates all the hidden and enchanted animals scattered
throughout. Antonio de Nino, 'Tavoleone,' in *Usi e costume abruzzesi*, vol. 3, *Fiabe*
(Florence: G. Barbèra, 1883), no. 36, pp. 194–7. Another from this same region was
collected by Gennero Finamore in *Tradizioni popolari abruzzesi* (Lanciana, 1882),
no. 12 (not seen). Yet another from Liguria, 'Le monstre à sept têtes' (The monster
with seven heads), appears in James Bruyn Andrews, *Contes ligures, traditions de la
rivière recuellis entre Menton et Gênes* (Paris: Ernest Leroux, 1892), no. 49, pp. 230–4.
This story is in fact widespread. 'The Three Dogs,' one example representing
potentially many throughout Europe, appears in Benjamin Thorpe's *Yule-Tide
Stories: A Collection of Scandinavian and North German Popular Tales and Traditions*
(London: Henry Bohn, 1853), pp. 175–92. This story is from Westergötland,
Sweden. This boy trades his hogs for dogs, angers his mother, then sets out on the
road with his performing dogs to earn a living. He comes to the mourning city and
gains his entry at court through his performing menagerie. There he hears of the
plight of the three princesses and the threats of the Mountain-troll. The victor in
this case had a choice of brides. His dogs are 'Quick Ear,' 'Hold,' and 'Tear,' and in
the fight they will perform according to their names. 'Quick Ear' has skills like
those of the brother in 'the three brothers' type who can detect small noises from
afar or locate lost objects by special skills. This enemy is not a dragon but a giant on
horseback, and the dogs shred him in no time. The damsel from the first fight is
treated with 'decorum and purity of heart,' as her sisters will be. A second and
a third giant must also fall to recover the other two damsels. The third giant,
however, is so friendly that he puts the boy warrior off his game by having him send
his dogs away on fetching missions. The boy cedes the contest, asking only to say a

Little is added to the story of the fisherman and the magic begetting of his questing sons in the version collected among the Walloons. One of the boys carries out the dragon slaying and after his marriage sees the light from his bedroom window that draws him into the clutches of robbers from whom he must be rescued by his brothers.[36] Many of the familiar features are elaborated in 'Le roi des poisons,' which, once again, tells of the fish that inseminates wife, horse, and dog and thereby produces three sets of triplets, each son with an orange tree as his life sign. The dragon slayer takes the condemned princess on horseback with him to meet the beast, and the combat lasts three days before he can dissever the last head from its neck. The city saved is now Paris. The dog hides the tongues, a thief steals the girl, the dog steals a turkey from the king's table, the princess follows the dog to its master, the interloper is quartered, and the principals are married. Then the hero sees the strange light or fire and is drawn into danger, calling the two brothers into action. This story is French and thus from the country of presumed

---

Pater noster and play a bit on his pipes. That brings the dogs running. On the way home, the hero is deceived a second time, and two rogues take the girls home in his place, leaving him for dead in the forest. Now the dogs perform acts of healing by washing and licking the boy's wounds. When the prenuptial festivities are in progress, the hero makes his way back. Once again he is invited in to entertain with his dogs, the three princesses recognize him and rush to greet him, the truth comes gushing out, the hero is known by the girls' rings sewn in his hair, and the two frauds are expelled. This story also makes prominent the animal helpers much as they are employed in the Straparola story.

36 *Les contes populaires Wallons*, ed. George Laport (Helsinki: Svomalainen tiedeakatemia, 1932), no. 303, pp. 41–2. Emmanuel Cosquin, 'La bête à sept têtes' (The beast with seven heads), in *Contes populaires de Lorraine*, 2 vols. (Paris: F. Vieweg, 1886), vol. I, pp. 60–81. This story includes the magic fish, the blood of which breeds sons, dogs and horses, lances, and a life sign system. When the adventures begin, the first brother is bewitched into a pollywog. The second is turned into a toad after making all the same mistakes. The third begins cutting off the dragon-witch's heads. After the fifth is gone the witch restores the two brothers, then loses her last two heads. To win the princess, the victor must show the seven tongues, the villain is a coal merchant, and so the story runs along. The hero turned husband is lured out of his house when he sees a brilliant chateau shining with gold. In other tales, as Cosquin points out, it may be a ploughman beckoning at the door, or, in the Serbian version, a burning mountain, or a great light on a mountain, as in the Sicilian version collected by Laura Gonzenbach, no. 40, or a house on fire in the Russian and Flemish versions. Cosquin, vol. I, p. 79.

origins – a very representative version.[37] The same story is known in the Tirol as 'Die drei Fischersöhne' (The fisherman's three sons). After a year and a day the wife has three sons, the bitch three pups, and the mare three foals, but the luckiest one, he who wins a princess, does not have to slay a dragon for her. In the sequel episode, the new husband looks out a window and is induced to explore a magic castle. Only the third brother knows how to deal with the wicked witch and liberate the other two. Then all three return to confront the baffled wife. To complete matters, the father joins them, each brother receives a castle of his own, and more joy could not be known.[38]

The best known tale of the present type from the German-speaking world was published by Jacob and Wilhelm Grimm in their *Kinder- und Hausmärchen*: 'Die zwei Brüder' (The two brothers).[39] This is a long story that contains all the now familiar parts, but which offers them in much altered forms. The two brothers are contrasted morally and economically, one an evil-hearted goldsmith, the other an affable broom-maker. When the latter finds a gold feather in the forest, the goldsmith not only buys it, but demands to have the bird, knowing that to consume its heart and liver would lead to the production of gold coins on a daily basis. Here

---

37 Michèle Simonsen, *Le conte populaire* (Paris: Presses Universitaires de France, 1984), 85–95, based on a version collected by Geneviève Massignon, *Contes de l'Ouest*, 1953, from the Brière. See Mette Rubow, 'Un essai d'interprétation du conte "Le roi des poissons,"' *Fabula* (1982), pp. 1–2, in which the story is traced to the myth of Perseus and Andromeda.

38 Christian Schneller, *Märchen und Sagen aus Wälschtirol* (Innsbruck: Wagner'schen Universitäts Buchhandlung, 1867), no. 28, pp. 79–82. This story bears comparison with 'Der Sohn der Eselin' in Ignaz and Joseph Zingerle's *Märchen* (Donauwörth: Buchhandlung Auer, 1931), no. 39, vol. II, p. 403. In this tale the hero collects travelling friends, including a giant, in a long introit before coming to the dragon slaying. That segment entails a confrontation first with a dragon with five heads, another with seven, and yet another with nine. In each case the tongues are gathered. Then his three giants betray him, marry the three princesses held captive in the castles of the three dragons, and leave the little smith to get free from the golden palace. Once back in the royal city, he shows the king the bag of tongues and then a general melee breaks out in which he must dispatch all three of his one-time companions before choosing the prettiest of the three wives for himself.

39 (Göttingen, Dieterich, 1857), no. 60; trans. Jack Zipes, *The Great Fairy Tale Tradition* (New York: Norton, 2001), pp. 374–89. Johannes Bolte and Jiří Polívka offer numerous analogues to this tale in their annotations, including two long versions from Hessen and several from Italy beginning with Straparola's, which they call 'Die trauen Tiere' (The faithful animals); *Anmerkungen zu den Kinder- und Hausmärchen der Brüder Grimm* (Hildesheim: Georg Olms, 1963), vol. I, pp. 528–39.

are bits of the copper, silver, and gold feathers tale, the fisherman's sons' tale with the consumption of body parts to magic ends, and the gold coin tale, such as 'Adamantina' and all its cognates (V.2). But when the poor brother's two sons manage to eat the parts by accident and become the magic bird's beneficiaries, the uncle is furious and has them driven into the world as devils, each with a gun, a dog, and a life object in the form of a knife that would rust should the other brother be in trouble. Curiously reminiscent of Straparola's tale as no other, the boys acquire on the way five animal helpers, neither horses nor dogs, but hares, foxes, wolf pups, bear cubs, and lion cubs. They separate at the crossroads and it is the destiny of the youngest to deliver battle to a virgin-consuming dragon to spare a king's daughter. After comforting her, he locks her inside a church. This seven-headed affair is a sociable one, for he asks the huntsman what he is doing there and warns him away to safety. After some flame-throwing and proto-chemical warfare, the hero severs three heads, then three more, leaving the last to be torn off by his helper menagerie. Then he carries the princess out of the church to see his handiwork, whereupon she places collars on all the helping animals, and then the pop-up lovers discuss their wedding. In time they fall asleep together, the spying marshal appears, kills the hero, cuts off the dragon's heads, threatens the princess to declare for him, and takes her home. She maintains the lie, but asks for a year's reprieve from the wedding, no doubt believing her hero was still alive. Again, in a fashion closer to Straparola than any other version, the hare goes to a special mountain in search of a healing herb, and so, by his loyal animals, the hero is resuscitated, albeit not without passing through the error of having his head replaced backwards, as in the fearless boy tales (commentary to IV.5). For a gloomy year, the hero now travels as an entertainer with his animal troupe, until at last he remembers the princess, and on the day of her wedding to the dastardly marshal he sends his hare as a messenger to the princess, who knows him by his collar. The Grimm tale repeats the long scene at the inn to which the animals bring parts of the royal banquet to their master. Through contact, recall, a royal entry, a trial of the marshal as royal theatre, and his quartering among four oxen, the first part is brought to a long spell of happy times. But the second brother is waiting and watching the knife blade. The lure is an enchanting forest and the deceptions of a white doe, leading to a witch in a tree who descends to neutralize the animals and then turn them, hero and all, to stone. This rescuing brother places the chivalric sword between himself and his brother's wife, follows the lead to the forest, induces the witch's ploys, but resists by shooting her with silver buttons to get around her invulnerability to lead. This brother also loses his head on the way home, the victim of jealousy, but when the error is revealed, the hare returns with the root of life. The formula is worth the repetition because this, of all the tales, is what Straparola's tale might have been had his source not been so eroded and altered. This is a tale in which the animal brigade contrives to bring their master back to life. That this operation can be integrated easily into the 'two brothers' type rebuilds the link between Straparola's tale of nefarious family females and the statistically more traditional tale of brotherly rescue.[40]

But as the next few stories reveal, the particular motifs that make up the Straparola version of the story did not die out after all. A rendition of considerable interest for our purposes came to light in Spain through the fieldwork of Aurelio Macedonio Espinosa. 'La princesa encantada' is, in fact, one of many variants known throughout Spain that tells of a royal daughter who is saved by the passing hero from a serpent with seven heads. Particular to this telling, however, is the framing tale of a disloyal mother who drives the hero into the world and, in the end, in

---

40 Further versions from German-speaking areas include: Johann Wilhelm Wolf, 'Das Schneiderlein und die drei Hunde' (The little tailor and the three dogs) in *Deutsche Hausmärchen* (Göttingen: Dieterich'sche Buchhandlung, 1851), pp. 9–15. In this curious version, the hero collects his helper animals at the outset much in the Straparola manner, but he must behead them in order to liberate the king and his two daughters, a throwback to the motif of the enchanted animal in which higher beings are incarcerated – as in the liberation of the frog prince or the pig prince (II.1). Other versions occur in Paul Zaunert, *Deutsche Märchen aus dem Donaulande* (Jena: Diederichs, 1926); Karl Müllenhoff, *Sagen, Märchen und Lieder der Herzogthümer Schleswig-Holstein und Lauenburg* (Kiel: Schwers, 1845), pp. 416–20, and (Hildesheim: Olms, 1976); Heinrich Pröhle, *Kinder- und Volksmärchen* (Leipzig: Avanarius & Mendelssohn, 1853), I, no. 5; Elizabeth Lemke, *Volkstümlisches in Östpreussen*, 3 vols. (Mohrungen: W.E. Harich, 1884-87), vol. II, pp. 147–50, and (Hildesheim: Olms, 1978). This fanciful story tells of the child-challenged queen who downs magic fish at the same time they are eaten by her chambermaid and the cat. This 'cat prince' conducts adventures against a twelve-headed dragon and then a fifteen-headed one. Thereafter, the story departs from the type under investigation. A version from Greece, but published in German, appears in Johann Georg von Hahn's *Griechische und Albanesische Märchen* (Leipzig: W. Englemann, 1864), no. 22, vol. II, pp. 114*ff.* Max Lüthi, in *Once upon a Time: On the Nature of Fairy Tales* (Bloomington: Indiana University Press, 1976), pp. 47–53, provides an analysis of the type in his chapter 'The Dragon Slayer,' based principally on a study of a Swedish tale in which the two brothers are named Silberweiss and Lillwacker, and on an Austrian tale recorded in 1916.

collaboration with her daughter, contrives to poison him. In Spain, the hero is characteristically accompanied by two dogs with magic powers, and it is through their offices that he is resuscitated. Thus, while the Grimm tale remembers the wild animals of the forest taken from their litters and raised by the hero in Straparola, the Spanish stories remember the treachery of a mother and sister who replace the actions of brothers. This group gives further assurance that Straparola employed a folk model, and that his model participated in a subgroup that preserved its place in the subsequent oral tradition.[41]

Two analogue tales in the annotations by Benjamin Thorpe to his Swedish story of 'The Three Dogs,' outlined above, are of equal interest for their employment of the helper animals as magic healers. In the battle against the third and final giant – a story in which there are three princesses to be rescued – the giant tricks the boy into sending his dogs out on missions, leaving the hero unprotected and vulnerable. One of their goals was to fetch the flask of healing water or water of life. When, on the way home, the hero is again betrayed and left wounded in the forest, the dogs, through their own intelligent initiative, complete the quest for the water, along with healing leaves and flowers of strength, all of which are brought back to restore their master. In another version, the young hero's inherited sheep are exchanged for dogs, and these, after many adventures, find themselves face to face with the sea serpent, Turenfax, to which a maiden is annually sacrificed. The lot had fallen upon the king's daughter, who had to be conducted to the monster's island by boat. The dogs are at the centre of the action, detecting, reacting, and fighting. Once the victory is gained, however, this hero, too, continues on his way, his dogs now sporting collars given to them by the princess. They will serve for purposes of identification when they interrupt the wedding festivities a year later. To complete matters, once the rights of the hero

---

41 *Cuentos populares españoles*, 3 vols. (Madrid: Aguirre, 1946), vol. III, pp. 9–26. Stories in this same general tradition were also known in the Basque country; see Wentworth Webster, *Basque Legends Collected Chiefly in the Labourd* (London: Griffith and Ferran, 1879), pp. 87–94. This story features the miraculous fish, the birth of three sons, three horses, and three dogs; the life sign is a boiling well behind the house. The monster to be slain has seven heads, the princess wears seven dresses from each of which the hero clips a small part, the villain is a coal man who finds the heads, and as an imposter he is burned. The post-marital distraction is a mysterious chateau. The hero is bewitched, the second brother comes to his rescue, and the wife must choose her true husband from the lookalike pair.

are re-established, the imposter dragon slayer is fed to the three dogs. The tongue-cutting feature is absent and these dogs are not the wild beasts of Straparola, but their place in the action is prominent.[42]

Further afield, stories of the conquest of seven-headed dragons are known in Cambodia, Persia, India, East Africa, and the Mediterranean. In Japan, a man appears at a household in mourning over the imminent loss of a daughter to a seven- or eight-headed sea monster. This hero woos the beast out of the water with sake, rather like the tactics employed in stories of the Costanza group to lure the wild satyr (commentary to IV.1). Then it is slain, the Mikado's sword is removed from its tail, and the maiden is married to the vanquisher.[43] Among Turkish tales is that of 'The Forty Princes and the Seven-Headed Dragon.' Now it is the youngest of forty who kills the dragon and follows one of its rolling heads down a well, where he is introduced to a magnificent underground palace with forty damsels rejoicing to hear of the dragon's death. The structure of this narrative is guided by a father's interdiction, in the manner of 'The Disobedience of Salardo' (I.1), not to sleep beside a well, not to approach a caravanserai, and not to linger in the desert. The first adventure follows from sleeping beside a well. The second entails yet another combat with a seven-headed dragon larger than the first – always the labour of the youngest, who is the only one who stays awake. When, in the desert, a new beast approaches, the youngest gives to the others his keys to the damsels as well as to the treasure won from the second beast, and remains to do battle alone. This fight comes to a draw and the dragon offers a complete truce if the young hero will undertake a mission to China to retrieve the Padishaw's daughter. Now begins the tale of 'the giant's egg' that contains the secret to his life, except the dragon's soul resides in three magic doves. The Padishaw's daughter wheedles his secret from him, the hero goes in search of the birds and, with the help of a magic horse, secures his safety and his love. Once home, however, he is in

---

42 *Yule-Tide Stories: A Collection of Scandinavian and North German Popular Tales and Traditions*, trans. Benjamin Thorpe (London: Henry Bohn, 1853), pp. 189–92.

43 Sir Grafton Elliot Smith, *Evolution of the Dragon* (Manchester: Manchester University Press; London: Longmans, Green and Co., 1919), p. 212. The same or a closely related version is told about Sosano-no-Nikkoto, who arrives at a house in mourning where seven of the eight daughters have already been consumed by the dragon. This hero likewise takes sake to the seashore to get the beast tipsy before cutting off its eight heads. A sword is found in the dragon's tail, Sosano marries the girl, and a temple is built in their honour. Félix Liebrecht, *Zur Volkskunde* (Heilbronn: Henninger, 1879), p. 70.

trouble, for the fortieth damsel awaits him, and thus his two brides must agree to share him, each having him six months of the year.[44]

Coming full circle and to a conclusion, the traditional story of 'the two brothers' was carried to Canada and somehow taught to the Ojibwa peoples, who incorporated the tale of the seven-headed dragon into their own cultural landscape.[45] Each son has the traditional magic dog and horse, and even the sword that turns rusty should the other be in danger. 'Golden Boy' features intrude when the venturer's fingers dipped into water turn to silver. The monster to be dealt with is an eight-headed Manitou, which is killed with the help of the horse and dog before the victorious hero wraps the tongues in a handkerchief. These are presented to the girl to give to her father for safe keeping. The blacksmith, meanwhile, lays claim to the girl and there is to be a four-day dance before the wedding. When the boy returns, this imposter is thrown into the sea. The lure from the window beginning the second part is a mysterious blue flame; the princess gives her warning. The hero meets a white-headed old woman in a longhouse who ties the dog with a magic hair and touches the boy's feet with a cane, resulting in his death. Then the second brother swings into action, meets his sister-in-law incognito, follows the flame, meets the old crone, but sicks his dog and horse on her instead. With the juice from a bottle, he brings brother, horse, and dog back to life, endures slaughter at the hands of his jealous beneficiary, and is himself resuscitated by the happy juice. Thus, they head for home until paths lead them again in opposite directions. This tale from so far away is as close to the oikotype as any in France, where, according to Kurt Ranke, this folk tale type was thought to have originated. Perseus is far from Libya.

Nevertheless, the story does make a kind of round trip, for a complete version was reported to a European folklorist from the Djurdjura mountains of Kabylie in Algeria. It tells of two brothers, Ali and Mohammed, who plant fig trees as life signs. Mohammed takes his falcon, dog, and horse and arrives at a city where a serpent is fed the daughters of its denizens in order to maintain the flow of its water. After his victory, Mohammed disguises himself as a beggar, but the princess, destined to be his wife, has one of his sandals, so that, in the fashion of Cinderella,

---

44 Ignácz Kunos, 'The Forty Princes and the Seven-Headed Dragon' in *Turkish Fairy Tales and Folk Tales*, trans. R. Nisbet Bain (London: Lawrence & Bullen, 1896), pp. 143–53.

45 See www.firstpeople.us (Health and Wellness website), Native American Legends.

he is detected, married, and made king. Later, while out hunting, he enters the domain of an ogress. She attaches his animals with a magic hair and the hero ends up in her entrails until Ali reads the signs, follows the traces, and discovers her whereabouts. She is killed by his horse, his falcon pecks out her eyes, and the dog rips open her belly to liberate Mohammed. Ali then watches two tarantulas fighting, the one resuscitating the other with a herb; so instructed, he is able to restore his brother to life.[46] The resuscitating herb of fighting animals goes back to the *lais* of Marie de France. This story is yet another of the presumably thousands known throughout the Old World in which brothers, remarkably born and equipped, seek adventures, one of them destined to follow closely in the footsteps of Perseus, only to blunder in a way that necessitates rescue by the other. All parts of the story may have Eastern origins including even the ancient Greek myth, and various two-part versions of it have been circulating in the West for more than half a millennium.

In sum, Straparola tells a folk tale with mythic overtones in a variant version that branched off early from the main narrative type and that survived down to the early twentieth century in Spain. Such was the type current in the part of Italy where Straparola was collecting, as distinct from the region where Basile collected some 85 years later. The story is rich in thematic possibilities to the degree that dragon slaying, princess rescuing, and maternal infanticide are rich. Straparola, in keeping with the nature of the folk tale, offers no allegorical clues. What you hear about is what there is. But the human mind is an allegorizing machine in its quest for meaning, reducing actions, relationships, causes and their effects, rewards and punishments, to categories of understanding. In that regard, even the most naive of fairy tales upholds the faith that such stories are riddles firmly grounded in the quasi-sacred nature of things. So many stories compulsively remembered about girl-devouring dragons and the boys who slay them on their way to a romance closure after errors, rivals, and delays can only be thought to have attained such popularity by encapsulating a profound truth, whatever its ultimate utility.

---

46 Joseph Rivière, *Recueil de contes populaires de la Kabylie du Djurdjura* (Paris: Laroux, 1882), p. 193.

X. Fable 4
The Diabolical Testament of Andrigetto di Valsabbia

ERITREA

Andrigetto di Valsabbia, a citizen of Como, being in articulo mortis, makes his will, leaving his soul to the devil, together with those of his notary and his confessor, and then dies, doomed to hell.

There is a well-known proverb that a bad end awaits every bad life, and for this reason it is far wiser to live piously, as a good man should, than to give loose rein to one's conscience or unthinkingly follow an unrestrained will, as did a certain noble citizen who, as the end of his life approached, bequeathed his soul to the enemy of mankind only to die in wickedness and despair – in keeping with the will of divine justice.

In Como, one of the lesser cities of Lombardy, not far distant from Milan, there once dwelt a citizen named Andrigetto di Valsabbia. Although he was richer than any other man in Como in goods and heritages, land and cattle, he paid so little heed to his conscience, whatever the matter, that he was ready to rise early each morning to engage in some new form of wickedness. His granaries were filled with all sorts of wheat and fodder, the product of his farms, and it was his custom to peddle this to the poor peasants and other souls in misery instead of selling it to the merchants or to those who came with money in their hands. He was not induced to this course of action out of compassion for the poor, but by design to cheat them of the little bits of land still remaining to them, thereby always seeking to achieve his end, which was, little by little, to have all the surrounding land in his own possession.

During one particular year, it happened that the country was afflicted by a terrible famine, so that in many places men, women, and children died of hunger. For this reason, peasants from all the neighbouring parts, both from the mountains and from the plains, went to Andrigetto, one offering to let him have a meadow, another a ploughed field, and still another a tract of woodland in exchange for wheat and other provisions to fill their present needs. The crowd of people around Andrigetto's house, coming from all parts, was so great that one might well have believed that the year of jubilee had come.

At that same time in Como there lived a notary named Tonisto Raspante, a man most adept in his calling, and one who surpassed all others of his trade for his skill in wringing the last coin out of the peasants' purses. Now one of the laws of Como forbade a notary to draw up any instrument of sale unless the money for the purchase was first counted up in his presence and in the presence of several witnesses. For this reason, Tonisto Raspante, who had no mind to get himself into legal difficulties, more than once had remonstrated with Andrigetto when the old usurer had required him to draw up contracts of sale that were contrary to the statutes of Como. But Andrigetto would heap foul abuse upon him and even threaten his life if he persisted in his refusal. Because the usurer was a man of influence and a leading citizen – one, moreover, who assiduously visited the shrine of San Bocca d'Oro – the notary dared not contradict his will, but drew up the illegal contracts as he was commanded.

Just before the customary season when Andrigetto went to confession, he sent to his confessor enough food and drink to supply a sumptuous feast, together with enough fine cloth to make stockings both for himself and his servant, telling him that he would be appearing on the following day. Because Andrigetto was a man of wealth and eminence in the city, the priest took due heed of these words, and when he saw his penitent approaching he bowed to him dutifully and prepared to receive his confession, whereupon Andrigetto knelt down to accuse himself of divers transgressions, at last stumbling upon the sin of avarice, which in turn brought him to reveal in detail the history of all the illegal contracts he had made. Now the priest, who had read enough to know that such contracts were unlawful and usurious, most respectfully took Andrigetto to task, pointing out to him that it was his duty to make restitution. But Andrigetto received this interference with an ill will and replied to the priest that he didn't know what he was talking about and that he'd better go and learn his duty. Fearing then to lose the generous gifts that Andrigetto sent, should the usurer resort to some other confessor, the priest forthwith granted him absolution and a light penance, at which point Andrigetto thrust a crown into this hand and departed with a light heart.

It came about, soon after, that Andrigetto was afflicted with a disease so severe that he was given up by all the physicians. His relations and friends, seeing by the report of the doctors that his malady was incurable, urged him to make his will, to settle his affairs, and to confess himself in the manner of all good Catholics and Christians. But he was so committed to his avarice, to thinking night and day only about how he could pile up more wealth, that he refused to consider his death. He thrust away from him all those who talked of such matters, preferring to have his prized possessions brought to him one by one so that he might delight in holding them. Yet his friends continued to press him on the matter, so to make them happy he had them call in Tonisto Raspante, his notary, and Brother Neofito, his worthy confessor, so that he might confess and settle his worldly affairs.

When the two of them arrived they saluted him, 'Messer Andrigetto, may God give you health. How indeed are you feeling? Be of good spirits and have no fear. Your health will be restored.' But the sick man replied that he felt much worse and that he therefore desired to make his will and to confess. Then the priest, turning his discourse to matters of faith, admonished him to be mindful of Almighty God and to bow to His holy will, by which means he would regain his strength. But Andrigetto directed them to bring in seven men to witness the making of his ultimate and nuncupative will. When these had arrived and had presented themselves to the invalid, he said to the notary, 'Tonisto, how much do you charge for every will you draw?'

'The law allows us a florin,' Tonisto answered, 'but we receive sometimes more, sometimes less, according to the wish of the testator.'

Then Andrigetto went on, 'Look, here are two florins, which I give to you on condition that you set down everything I direct you to write.'

The notary agreed to these terms. Invoking the name of God, he inscribed the year, the month, and the day, according to the manner of his calling, and began to write in the particular terms of such documents: 'I, Andrigetto di Valsabbia, being of sound mind though infirm of body, bequeath and recommend my soul to God my Creator, whom I thank with all my heart for the many benefits which He has showered upon me during this life.'

But Andrigetto, interrupting him, said 'What is it that you have written there?'

Whereupon the notary replied, 'I have written this and that,' and told him word for word what he had set down.

Then Andrigetto, in a raging passion cried out, 'And who told you to write in such terms? Why do you not keep the promise you made to me?

Now write down what I tell you – I, Andrigetto di Valsabbia, infirm of body but sound in mind, bequeath and recommend my soul to the great devil of hell.'

When they heard these words, the notary and the witnesses stood aghast and, turning to the testator, said to him, 'Alas, Signor Andrigetto, what has become of your good sense and your ordinary prudence? Surely these are the words of a madman. Only maniacs and the depraved use such terms. Put an end to your folly, for the love of God, and sin no more against your good name, which will bring scandal and disgrace upon your entire family. Remember too that all those who, until now, have considered you a wise and prudent man will set you down as the most wicked and mischievous traitor nature ever brought forth should you cast aside your well-being and salvation. For indeed, if you thus despise your own profit and welfare, how much more will you despise the profit and welfare of others.'

In answer to this, Andrigetto replied, his anger now raging as hot as a burning brazier, 'What? Haven't I commanded you to write exactly what I shall tell you, and haven't I paid you beyond the expected fee to set down exactly what I say?'

'Yes, sir,' replied the notary.

'Then put down the things I tell you,' said the testator, 'and not things I've no interest in.' The poor notary, who was always on an empty stomach, seeing the savagery of his humour and afraid he would die of rage, wrote down all that his mouth ordained. Then Andrigetto said to the notary, 'Write this – "*Item*, I leave to almighty Satan the soul of Tonisto Raspante my notary, as well, so that I may have him for company when I depart from this world."'

'Ah, Messer Andrigetto,' cried the notary, 'you are doing me a great injury, putting this affront upon my honour and good name.'

'Go on with your writing, miscreant,' cried the testator, 'and don't give me any more trouble than I have right now. I've already paid you much more than you deserve, so go to the devil and write what I say: "For if he had not been so ready to endorse and compose thus many unlawful and usurious contracts, but had driven me away from there, I would not find myself in such a maze at the present hour. Because he set more value upon my payments to him than upon my soul or his own in times past, I once more give and commend him to Lucifer."'

The poor notary, fearing that even worse things might befall him, wrote down all the foregoing words. Andrigetto continued. 'Write now – "Item, I bequeath the soul of Brother Neofito, my confessor, to be tormented by thirty thousand pairs of devils."'

'What's this you say, Signor Andrigetto?' interrupted the priest. 'Are these the words of a sober man such as you have always been taken for? Good God, take back what you've said. Do you not know that our Lord Jesus Christ is merciful, with arms of pity always open, provided that the sinner is convinced of his offences and acknowledges his transgressions? Therefore, repent of the grave and egregious sins you have committed and pray God for His mercy and He will plentifully pardon you. The means are at hand and you have yet time to restore what you have of other men's goods, for if due restitution is made, God, who is all merciful and wills not the death of a sinner, will pardon you and receive you into paradise.'

But Andrigetto replied, 'Wicked and apostate priest, destroyer of my soul and of your own as well, full of greed and simony as you are! Fine counsel this is to give at such a time. Write, notary – "I consign his soul to the centre of the pit because if he had not been such a pestilentially avaricious hypocrite, he would not have been so ready to absolve me from my sins, and then I would not have committed so many offences, nor would I find myself brought to this present state." What? Does it seem honest and fitting that I should now strip myself of my wealth, ill-gotten though it is, and leave my children poor vagabonds? No! Keep such counsel as this for those whom it may profit. I have nothing to say about it. And, notary, write this as well – "Item, that I leave to Felicity, my mistress, my farm in the village of Comachio so that she can have all the food and clothes she needs to be able, now and then, to take pleasure with her lovers just like she has always done, and that at the end of her days, she comes to me in the pit of hell to be tormented eternally along with the three of us. As for all my other goods, personal or otherwise, present or to come, I give them to my two legitimate sons, Comodo and Torquato, exhorting them to waste nothing of my estate in paying for masses or matins, vigils or *de profundis* on my behalf, but rather to pass their time in gambling, wenching, drinking, brawling, fighting, and in all other wicked and detestable activities so that my goods, having been badly gotten, may, in a short while, be spent in the same way, and that my sons, when they are finally destitute, may hang by their throats in despair. This I declare to be my last will and I call upon you all to witness it."'

When the will was written and executed, Andrigetto turned his face to the wall, and, with a roar like that of a bull, gave up his soul to Pluto, who had long been waiting for it. Thus, the wretched and sinful man, unconfessed and impenitent, made an end to his foul and wicked life.

When the self-confident Eritrea had brought her story to a close, the whole company stood amazed at the folly, or rather the malice, of the wretched Andrigetto, who thought it better to be the devil's slave and foe to his own race than to repent of his sin. And because the night was already somewhat advanced, Eritrea, without tarrying for the Signora's orders, proposed her enigma.

> I am supple, round, and white,
> A good span's length will gauge me right;
> If ladies to their service bind me,
> Searching and alert they'll find me.
> Give me but place, and lend a hand,
> I'll enter and I'll take my stand.
> But touch me not, on mischief bent,
> Or dirty fingers you'll lament.

'It seems to me, Signora Eritrea, that your enigma can only mean the consigning of a soul to the devil,' said Bembo with a sly look, 'but be careful not to put the devil in hell, for then a conflagration may ensue.'

'I have no fear of that,' said Eritrea. 'Besides, my enigma has in no way the meaning you give to it.'

'Then expound the true meaning at once,' Bembo continued, 'and put an end to our perplexity.'

'Willingly,' said Eritrea. 'It signifies simply a tallow candle, which is white, round, and not very hard, and if it's set up in the lantern, which is feminine in gender, there's plenty of room for it to stand. And finally no one ever yet handled a tallow candle without getting dirty fingers.'

Now the crowing of the cocks proclaimed that midnight was already long past, so the Signora made a sign to Cateruzza to complete the night, the tenth of their pleasant entertainment, by telling some graceful story and witty enigma – which met with no delay because she was always more ready to talk than to keep silent.

X.4 Commentary

In 'Andrigetto's Strange Testament' an avaricious and heartless usurer and land baron pronounces his own damnation. At the time of his death, contrary to expectations of eleventh-hour regrets and confessions, he dictates a solemn testament in which he consigns not only himself to the devil, but his accomplices in crime, namely, the very notary taking down his words and the father confessor called in for the extreme offices. He includes them, not only because they have been collaborators in his crimes – the notary in signing fraudulent deeds and transfers, the priest in giving him easy penance for fear of losing donations – but because he wishes to replicate his little society in hell. In this mode, he bequeaths his farm to his mistress where she can continue her whoring until death, ensuring that she too will follow him and complete the quartet in Hades. Through this perverse testament he burlesques his own death, settles scores, owns up to his many crimes, and boldly faces the chastisements in the afterlife fit for so confirmed a reprobate. The anecdote is amusingly dramatic, for the unwilling notary is compelled to inscribe his own damnation in order to keep his fee, which in turn obliges him to honour the final wishes of the dying. There the narrative comes to a close, but the historical, parodic, even existential innuendoes take time to settle in. Giuseppe Rua called this story 'una tra le più interessanti delle *Piacevoli notti*' (one of the most interesting of the *Nights*), and Joël Gayraud 'la plus virulente des fables de Straparole' (the most caustic and scathing of all the fables) in its denunciation of hypocrisy and venality.[47] Andrigetto, in this parodic performance, has made himself trickster to his own soul, a proto-Faust, a mocking prankster to the end, an unconscionable villain, a heroic atheist, and a depraved materialist, whose gesture is both a satire on all men of his class and attributes, and a perversely consistent assertion of an antagonistic personality.

At the close of the Middle Ages, tales of self-damning usurers were in wide circulation and may have been familiar to Straparola's early readers. It was a profession easy to malign, not only because the Church forbade it for its lack of charity, but because many had been its victims, gouged by high rates, or imprisoned for default in payment. The portrait of the usurer coincided with that of the avaricious man, the absolute materialist devoid of spirituality, even though he kept its outward forms, like Chaucer's famous Pardoner. One way of marking this hypocrisy was in crediting to him abusive uses of the liturgy, as in 'The Usurer's Paternoster.' In a phrase-by-phrase parody of the Lord's Prayer, the usurer would ask for greater profits by more devious means in a manner indifferent to the

---

47 *Tra antiche fiabe e novelle*, vol. I, *Le 'Piacevoli notti' di Messer Gian Francesco Straparola* (Rome: Ermanno Loescher, 1898), p. 87; Giovan Francesco Straparola, *Les nuits facétieuses*, ed. Joël Gayraud (Paris: José Corti, 1999), p. 629.

sacred or holy. From the prayer of the money-lender to the mock testament there is some formal distance, but they belong to a common end, employ the same company of protagonists, and share similar functions.

'La patenôtre de l'usurier' makes an early appearance in the French *fabliaux* of the first half of the thirteenth century. The author names his source as a sermon preached in Paris by the Englishman Robert de Corson (d. 1218).[48] No doubt this cleric derived the exemplum in turn from a collection of such materials for preachers. It tells of a usurer obsessed with security and with cheaters within. He bars all his doors, wakes up his wife and daughter to stand guard, and goes off to church, where he must be seen from time to time for appearance's sake. Along the way he repeats the familiar prayer, interlarding the lines with his own worldly fears, ambitions, and desires for greater wealth. He curses the Jews for taking away his business, blames the church for many lost opportunities for gain for which reason he consigns all priests to Hell, accuses his own wife and daughter of stealing from him, counts his keys, and gives nothing to the Church. In brief, the lines of the prayer are juxtaposed with his rambling wish list of material ambitions in a manner oblivious to irony or blasphemy. Such was the satiric formula. In a related form, the Paternoster was exchanged for the Credo, but it comes to the same ends, while Frischlin in his *Facetiae* has the Lord's Prayer corrupted by a bird catcher while mending his nets who, with each new flaw he discovers, sends everything to the devil.[49] The blasphemous employment of religious texts by an apostate soul provides a model for the spirit of Andrigetto's ironic testament, but there were also models for the inverted testament, as well, although the survivors are relatively sparse.

Luca Lossius, the prolific sixteenth-century rector and music theorist from Lüneburg, left a telltale poem published by Otto Melander in his *Jocorum atque seriorum* about the usurer confronted by imminent death who calls his wife to write out his last will and testament, just as Straparola's usurer calls in the notary. He tells her that he has been the servant of Satan and that soon he will cross over the Stygian waters in deserved payment for his fraudulent ways. He then compels her to write that she

---

48 Corson was an English cardinal who went to France in 1212. Giuseppe Rua mentions in passing the existence of further poetic versions of the 'Paternostre a l'usurier' in the 'lauda' of Jacopone da Todi, the sermons of Roberto da Lecce, and in a moral *novella* by Pauli, *Le 'Piacevoli notti' di Messer Gian Francesco Straparola* (Rome, 1898), p. 88.

49 Nicodemus Frischlin, *Facetiae selectiores* (Strasburg: Bernard Iobini, 1600), p. [151].

too will cross the waters with him as collaborator in his crimes. The frightened woman calls in the priest to dissuade him from his foolish resolutions, whereupon the usurer turns on his confessor, declaring that because he was party to all his crimes, he too must follow him across the river into Hades.[50] That Straparola knew this precise example may be doubted, but that he worked from a related model is certain, one perhaps in circulation among the folk narrators who had already carried out some of the local adaptations. Between the two versions, we could venture to posit a popular tradition called 'The Testament of the Usurer,' beginning with a portrait of the man and concluding with the dictation of a will in which he damns both himself and his associates, proposing they form a little society together in hell. Of this projected tradition, once again Straparola's may prove to be the earliest version in the literary record, reflecting the tale in its generic form.

Just how much Boccaccio could have known of the usurer's testament in formulating the story of Ciappelletto in the *Decameron* (I.1) is open to debate, for the second half is taken up with the arch-sinner who makes a hypocritical confession at the time of his death and afterwards becomes a saint.[51] But as the story opens, certain parallel features are in place. Ciappelletto is a notary who is remarkable in his depravity, for he is a maker of false documents, a liar under oath, and a gleeful troublemaker who works in collaboration with the wealthy merchant and moneylender Franzesi. When the merchant's end approaches with debts still uncollected from the Burgundians, he thinks of his wily notary as the only man likely to be able to collect them on his behalf. Once in Burgundy, however, he too falls ill and his hosts send for a priest to hear his last confession. The story now takes a new turn as Boccaccio splices on an entirely different form of terminal burlesque. This once vicious man feigns a sensitivity to sin of the most delicate kind, agonizing over peccadilloes to such a degree that the confessor takes him for a holy man and so reports him, arranging for a sacred burial. But up to that point, we have the tale of two wicked men, the usurer and the notary, on the brink of death, the second of whom squanders away his last opportunity to secure his salvation through an act of sincere contrition; it is the performance of a damned soul. The suggestion is that the Florentine's first

---

50 *Jocorum atque seriorum* (Frankfurt: Wolfgang Hofmann (Parthenius), 1626), vol. III, pp. 168–9.
51 Giovanni Boccaccio, *The Decameron*, trans. J.M. Rigg, 2 vols. (London: Privately Printed for the Navarre Society, ca. 1900), vol. I, pp. 22–33.

tale is a variation on the usurer's testament and a clue that the source
that shaped Andrigetto was in circulation a full two centuries earlier. If
it proves true, however, it is to suggest more about Boccaccio's narrative
sources than has been acknowledged heretofore by the leading scholar
in the matter, A. Collingwood Lee.[52]

Just how pointed this satire may have been is matter for historical
investigation. Andrigetto and his associates are assigned to the city of
Como situated at the south end of Lake Como some fifty-five kilometres
north of Milan. This is considerably west and to the north of Caravaggio,
where Straparola grew up, and even farther west of the valley north of
Brescia from which Andrigetto takes his name, Valsabbia. There is no
certainty as to who made this assignment of names and places in the
telling of the old story, but along the way, the profile of the diabolical
usurer has been imposed upon a man, fictive or real, who expropriated
the land of the peasants during lean years by supplying them with tem-
porary sustenance. Parcel by parcel, they signed over to him, through
the offices of the notary, now this meadow, now that field. The processes
employed were illegal, but the unscrupulous trafficker in real estate
silenced Tonisto Raspante's protests with threats to his life. The economic
and social effects were no doubt similar to those of the enclosures movement in England in much these same years, namely, of expelling the
rural populations from their villages and forcing them into the cities as
vagabonds. This adaptation of the satiric testament may reflect the social
conditions motivating the raconteur from whom Straparola borrowed
his materials.[53]

Andrigetto's portrait is that of the avaricious or acquisitive man,
possessed by a humour beyond the recourse of spirituality or compassion.
Just as Volpone in Jonson's celebrated play visits his gold as in a shrine

---

52 *The Decameron: Its Sources and Analogues* (New York: Haskell House, 1966),
    annotations to I.1.
53 Ruggiero Romano paints the dire circumstances of the northern Italian peasantry
    at mid-century, partially as the result of new owners more desirous of gain at the
    cost of peasant labour than the old landowners. The appropriation of land by
    devious legal means was but one of several woes. *Tra due crisi: L'italia del rinascimento*
    (Turin: Einaudi, 1971), pp. 54*ff*. See also Angelo Ventura, *Nobiltà e popolo nella società
    veneta del '400 e '500* (Bari: Laterza, 1964), p. 337, who describes the landholding of
    the Brescian peasants, which diminished from two-thirds of the rural territory in
    1442 to less than a quarter of it by 1591. Such a usurer as the protagonist of the
    present story is described by Emmanuel LeRoy Ladurie in his *Les paysans de
    Languedoc* (Paris: Flammarion, 1969), p. 142.

where he may see his saint, Andrigetto's misplaced values are summarized by his worship at the shrine of San Giovanni Boccadoro. In effect, the entire device of the *novella*, the perverse employment of sacred forms to secular and sinful ends, is contained in the ironic allusion to the saint of the Eastern church, San Giovanni Crisostomo (patriarch of Constantinople), as the patron of money or gold. Crisostomo, or 'golden mouth,' referred initially to his remarkable rhetorical powers, but in its translation into Bocca d'Oro, it came to be associated with a comic application that goes back at least as far as Boccaccio and Sacchetti, and no doubt earlier. In Boccaccio's story of an inquisitor who terrifies a rich but innocent victim into paying a bribe for his freedom (*Decameron* I.6), that bribe is referred to as 'a liberal allowance of St. John Goldenmouth's grease, an excellent remedy for the disease of avarice which spreads like a pestilence among the clergy.'[54] That same ironic application can be found in the anonymous *Chiose dette del falso Boccaccio (Inferno)* dating to 1375.[55] There were established prayers to San Giovanni Boccadoro as intercessor in the fourteenth century that, themselves, may have given rise to parody in the age of Boccaccio, thus nourishing the tradition of inverted Paternosters and burlesqued testaments, as in Jacopo Passavanti's *Lo specchia della vera penitenza* (1355).[56]

This story may prove to be Straparola's most palpable hit at all those who would sell their souls for material gain or prey upon the helpless and needy without scruple. His protagonist in kind is seen as jesting his way into hell through the instrument of his own testament, taking with him the souls of his accountant, his priest, his mistress, and his two sons to boot, destined by their evil ways to keep him company. That he is no Faustus in the making seems apparent, and yet Joël Gayraud sees in him 'a quality of nobility in the evil that forms the archetype of the "grand

---

54 Trans. J.M. Rigg (London: Navarre Society, ca. 1900), p. 49. See Franco Sacchetti, *Trecentonovelle*, ed. Valerio Marucci (Rome: Salerno, 1996), no. 14. Masuccio of Salerno in the sixth of his *Novellino* also makes reference to the saint in relation to a bribe, this time demanded by a bishop who had caught a priest and a prior among the nuns. Their condemnation to the flames was commuted to a monetary fine 'through the working of the greedy humour of San Giovanni Bocco d'oro,' now signifying bribery and the money paid in such transactions. Trans. W.G. Waters (London: Lawrence and Bullen, 1895), vol. I, p. 97.

55 Ed. William Warren Vernon (Florence: Piatti, 1846), chap. 13, p. 144.

56 Ed. Filippo Luigi Polidori (Florence: Le Monnier, 1856), dist. III, chap. 4, p. 64. See also Domenico Calvaca, *Specchio de' peccati* (1340), ed. Francesco del Furia (Florence: All' insegna di Dante, 1828), chap. 11, p. 98.

seigneur méchant homme" (the great lord of wickedness), the ultimate hero according to de Sade. He is a being who believes no more in the Devil than he does in God, and his testament is that of an atheist, a final jest that allows him to take delight – and us along with him – in the terror he has aroused in his heirs.'[57] Straparola would have meant this if he had thought of it. But of course we know that hardly matters.

---

57 Joël Gayraud, ed., Straparola, *Les nuits facétieuses* (Paris: José Corti, 1999), X.4.

X. Fable 5
Rosolino's Confession for Love of His Son

CATERUZZA

Rosolino da Pavia, a murderer and a thief, having been captured by the officers of the Podestà, is tortured, but confesses nothing. Yet afterwards, when he sees his innocent son put to the question, he straightway confesses, whereupon the praetor grants him his life, but banishes him from the country. Rosolino becomes a hermit and thus saves his soul.

No one can fully appreciate the ardent and tenacious love a father feels towards a morally upright and circumspect son except the man who has children of his own, for the father not only strives to give the child everything that may be necessary for his bodily sustenance, but will often put his own life in jeopardy, even shed his own blood, for the advancement and enrichment of his son. This saying I'll prove true through the short fable that I now propose to tell you. And given that this story will move your pity rather than your laughter, I think it will prove valuable for its instruction and learning.

In Pavia, a city of Lombardy famous both as a seat of learning and as the place where the most holy body of the venerable and divine Augustine is buried – that smiter of heretics and radiant lamp of the Christian religion – there lived, not long ago, a certain lawless and wicked man, a murderer and thief, one prone to every evil deed. He was known to men by the name of Rosolino. Because he was a rich man and the head of a faction, many of the citizens followed and were subservient to him. Yet, whenever he took to the road, he despoiled, robbed, and killed men one after the other. Moreover, the entire region round about held him in great dread on account of his many followers. Thus, despite the many crimes of which he was the author and the endless complaints that had been lodged against him, still there was no individual citizen sufficiently courageous to prosecute him, for the countenance and protection he received from various rogues and wicked men was so powerful that the plaintiffs, much against their wills, were always compelled to abandon any actions they might have taken against him.

This man had one child, a son, who by nature was the complete opposite to his father. He led a pure life worthy of all praise. With soft and loving words, he would often reprove his father for his wicked and ungodly life, gently pleading with him to put an end to his nefarious career by picturing for him the yawning gulfs of peril in which he continuously lived his life. But in truth, the wise and dutiful admonitions of his son proved altogether vain and fruitless, in that every day Rosolino applied himself more assiduously to his infamous calling, so that every week it was reported that such a man had been robbed or that such a man had been killed. Now insofar as Rosolino was obstinately determined to persevere in his wicked ways, becoming daily more barbarous and cruel, it pleased God that he should at last be captured by the officers of the praetor and led back to Pavia securely bound. Being brought before the judges, he was accused of all manner of premeditated wickedness, but all the charges brought against him he impudently denied.

After the praetor had heard him out, he soon after commanded the officers to bind Rosolino with strong chains and throw him into prison, at the same time directing that he should be carefully watched, and that for his sustenance he be allowed no more than three ounces of bread and three ounces of water a day, all of which was seen to with diligence. At this point there arose a great contention among the judges whether or not they should now condemn him upon the charges against him. But after a considerable period of wrangling, it was decided by the praetor and his court that Rosolino should be put to the torture, by such means hoping to extort a confession from his lips. When the following morning had come, the praetor commanded his officers to bring Rosolino before him. Once again he laid before the prisoner the charges against him, and once more he received a complete denial. Seeing the humour that he was in, the praetor gave orders that he should at once be bound for the strappado and hoisted into the air. But, although Rosolino's frame was several times cruelly shattered by the tormentors, they were unable to make him confess anything concerning his offences. Quite to the contrary, he yelled at them with incredible courage, heaping all manner of abuse upon the praetor and his court. He declared them all to be dogs, thieves, knaves, and villains, and that all of them deserved the gallows a thousand times over for the wicked lives they had led, and for the injustices they brought about as administrators of the law. Not satisfied with this, he claimed of himself that he was a man of worth and a good life, and that no one in the city could justly bring any charge against him.

After repeatedly taking the severest measures with Rosolino and leaving untried no form of torture that might force a confession, the praetor realized that he could extract nothing from the prisoner, for Rosolino stood as firm in his resolve as a firmly built tower and mocked all the efforts of his torturers. This caused the praetor considerable distress, for although he was certain of Rosolino's guilt, he couldn't condemn him to death without a confession. During the night, thinking about Rosolino's stubborn will and determination, he realized that the prisoner had earned his freedom by showing no signs of guilt under torture and that he could not legally be subjected to further torments. Therefore, he determined to assemble his court to propose a new course of action, which I'll now explain to you.

On the following day, when the court had met, the praetor addressed the other judges, saying, 'Excellent and learned sirs, verily the courage and firmness of Rosolino, the accused, is very great, but we must not forget that his villainy is greater still and that he would rather die under torture than confess to any of the charges made against him. Therefore, if you are all of a mind with me in this, it seems expedient that, as a last resource, we should try out a new method, which is this: let us send our officers to bring in Bargetto, Rosolino's son, and then, in the presence of the father, put the son to the torture. When Rosolino sees his innocent son in the hands of the tormentors, he'll confess his crimes readily enough.'

The praetor's proposition won the approval of the rest of the court. Therefore, he commanded that Bargetto should be seized, bound, and brought into his presence. When this was done, Bargetto was haled before the praetor and accused of trumped-up charges. Innocent of all such crimes, the youth answered that he knew nothing of the matter. Hearing this, the praetor immediately had him taken to the torture chamber, where, after he was stripped naked, he was put to the question in the presence of his father. Rosolino, seeing that they had taken his son a prisoner and were about to deliver him up to torture, stood in amazement, his heart wrung with grief. With Rosolino present all the while, the command was given that Bargetto should be hoisted up into the air, where again the praetor put many questions to him. But being entirely innocent, the youth had no idea what answers he should give. Then the praetor, feigning great anger, said, 'I will soon let you know what I mean,' and with these words he ordered that Bargetto should be strung up even higher.

The miserable youth, now feeling the sharpest pain and anguish, cried out in a loud voice, 'Have mercy, Signor Praetor, pity me, for I am innocent and have committed none of these crimes.'

Hearing him weep and lament in this fashion, the criminal magistrate said, 'Confess immediately and don't let yourself be torn into pieces like this. We know everything from beginning to end, but we desire to hear the facts from your own mouth.'

To this Bargetto answered that he had no knowledge of what the praetor was talking about and that there was no truth in the charges made against him. With that, the praetor, who had already instructed the chief torturer as to what he should do, made a sign to let Bargetto fall without any mercy from the top down to the bottom. Bargetto, in light of the judge's words, and of the agony he suffered in his arms, feeling that he could no longer endure any torture sharper than what he was then enduring, decided to confess to any crime they might charge him with, even though he was entirely innocent. So he cried out, 'Sirs, let me come down and I will confess everything in full.' Then, when the cord had been relaxed little by little, and Bargetto stood once more in the presence of the praetor, the court, and his own father, he confessed that he had indeed committed all the crimes that had been laid to his charge.

As soon as he heard the false confession of his son, Rosolino took counsel with himself concerning what had been done, and at last, stirred by his love for his son, and by the spectacle of his innocence, said, 'Sirs, I beg you not to further torture this son of mine, but to let him go free, for he is innocent and I am guilty.' Then, without being put to the question further, Rosolino confessed all of his crimes.

The praetor, after he had listened to the confession of Rosolino and had it written down and ratified in its entirety, yet still curious to know the cause that had led him to confess, said to the prisoner, 'Rosolino, you endured the sharpest torture with great courage and for a long time we were unable to extract any confession from you. But as soon as you saw your son, Bargetto, put to the question and heard his confessions, you changed your mind and, without being put further to the torture, you confessed all your crimes. Now, God give you grace and have mercy upon your soul, I'd gladly know what the reason was for this change of purpose.'

'Ah!' replied Rosolino, 'is it possible that your worships cannot discover the reason?'

'In truth, we can't,' replied the praetor.

Rosolino then said, 'If it is a true fact that you don't know, then I'll tell you, if you'll deign to lend me your attention. You, noble sirs, merciful and humane men and lovers of justice, you have seen the exhibition in open proof of my endurance under torture. But this was no cause for amazement, for at that time you were merely torturing a dead body. But when you put my only son to the question, then I felt you were torturing something fully alive.'

Then said the praetor, 'You must be a dead man yourself if you say that your flesh is dead.'

'No,' replied Rosolino, 'I am not dead, nor is my flesh dead, but living, because when you put me to the torture I suffered nothing because this flesh that you now see – the same you tortured a short while ago – is not my flesh at all, but the flesh of my dead father, decayed and already fallen to dust. But when you began to torment my son, you tormented my own flesh, because the flesh of the son is truly and in fact the flesh of the father.'

When the praetor heard this reasoning on Rosolino's part, he was powerfully moved to grant him free pardon for all his offences, but because justice would not suffer that such great crimes as his should go unpunished, he decided to send him into perpetual banishment – not indeed because his wickedness deserved so light a punishment as this, but because of the love that, as a father, he bore to his son. When it was made clear to him how light a sentence had been passed on him, Rosolino lifted his hands to heaven and gave thanks to God, promising Him with many oaths to put off his evil ways and to live a holy life. Rosolino departed straightway from Pavia and took himself to a certain hermitage, where he spent the rest of his life in great sanctity, doing extraordinary penance for his sins so that, by the grace of God, he was held worthy of salvation, leaving a memory that from that time to this present day has been serviceable as an example for the good and as a warning to the wicked.

When Cateruzza's fable was finished, the Signora directed her to tell her enigma at once, which the damsel delivered with a most gentle voice as follows:

> In a flowering meadow green,
> A lovely gentle thing is seen;
> Gorgeous are its robes to view,
> Bright with yellow, green, and blue.
> It wears upon its head a crown,
> And proudly paces up and down;
> Its splendid train it raises high,

> And seeks its love with jealous cry;
> But gazing at its feet below,
> It shrieks aloud for shame and woe.

Cateruzza's enigma was understood by the greater part of the company to refer to the peacock, the bird dedicated to the goddess Juno, which, with its feathers studded with eyes and painted in various colours, gazes round about upon all and bears itself proudly. But when it beholds its soiled and muddy feet, it lets down its gorgeous tail and stands stricken with shame.

As soon as the enigma had been explained, all the company rose to their feet and took leave of the Signora, promising her that they would all return on the following evening according to their custom.

The End of the Tenth Night

X.5 Commentary

The substratum of truth that infuses this story is both banal and mysterious: fathers love their sons and are prepared to make sacrifices for them, even at the cost of their own lives. The point is simply illustrated here by a father who has been entirely oblivious to the suffering of others, including those he has murdered, yet capitulates at the prospect of seeing his son subjected to the same torture that he has successfully endured in silence. When the judge asks the reason for this ostensibly incongruous behaviour, the father replies that his own body is beyond reach by torture because it is but the dead flesh of his father, whereas his son's body is his own living flesh. In this way, the story seeks to identify that sense of care for one's offspring that is even greater than the care for one's self. In effect, while self-preservation is a powerful instinct, it may on occasion be trumped by the mental engineering that favours and prioritizes the interests of the subsequent generation. Richard Dawkins deals with that paradox of evolutionary selection and design through the concept of the 'selfish gene,' a perspective on human nature that reveals the precedence not of the individual in the 'survival of the fittest,' but of the offspring.[58]

---

58 Richard Dawkins, *The Selfish Gene* (Oxford: Oxford University Press, 1976); for discussions and critiques of this controversial work, see *Richard Dawkins: How a Scientist Changed the Way We Think*, ed. Alan Grafen and Mark Ridley (Oxford: Oxford University Press, 2006).

We are all survival machines labouring under the delusion that we are protecting the 'I' of consciousness and the body with which it is affiliated, while in fact, through our selected traits, we are emotionally organized to foster our genetic futures. In that regard, the father is more alive in the son than he is in himself. Family relations and bloodlines may be understood as never before in light of this particular imperative. Love is merely a loose metaphor for the built-in adaptive mechanisms of the brain that override personal advantage with dynastic considerations.

Contemporary stories illustrating this precise principle are sparse and scattered, and only one, borrowed directly from Straparola, comes close to replicating his narrative order. There are, of course, many stories of sacrifices made for dear friends or beloved spouses, but the quality of motivation is subtly different. Valerius Maximus tells of the father who, as a lawmaker and ruler, had to deal with divided commitments when it came to enforcing a law of his own making upon his malefactor son.[59] The crime was adultery, which carried for punishment the destruction of both his eyes. The father, in good Roman fashion, determined that justice must be carried out, despite the outcries of the people against such unnaturalness and such a deplorable disfiguration of the crown prince. Yet by applying the principle that the eyes of a father are virtually those of a son, and those of a son tantamount to those of a father, justice might be served if the ruler volunteered to sacrifice one of his own eyes in the place of one of his son's. This story concerns the contest between the public and private man, between mercy and justice, yet it is resolved through that special bond between a father and son that modifies the principle of pure self-interest. Be it noted that in this story, an innocent father spares a guilty son, whereas in the present story a guilty father spares an innocent son. Comparatists may wish to ask whether that makes a difference regarding the emotional disposition under investigation. The narrative of Valerius Maximus was replicated in the *Gesta romanorum*, and thus made widely current in the Latin West.[60]

As with so many of Straparola's tales lacking apparent literary sources, the question remains moot concerning 'Rosolino's Confession': is it is an adaptation from a popular tale, an innovative reworking of a remote

---

59 *Memorable Deeds and Sayings: One Thousand Tales from Ancient Rome*, trans. Henry John Walker (Indianapolis: Hackett, 2004), bk. VI, chap. 5, ext. 3, p. 221.

60 'Of Praise Due to a Just Judge,' in the *Gesta romanorum*, trans. and ed. by Charles Swan and Wynnard Hooper (London: Bohn, 1876; reprint, New York: Dover, 1959), no. 50, pp. 86–7.

source such as the *Gesta* story, the transcription of an unidentified source, or his own creation? Similar stories written after the publication of the *Notti* are of little help because their exact relationships to Straparola are obscured by the many departures and narrative variations. Tomaso Costa's *Il fuggilozio* (1596) contains a story that may well have employed 'Rosolino's Confession' as a model.[61] Now father and son are in prison together for a serious crime, making both equal before the prospect of torture. The father instructs his son to remain silent, to endure a brief nuisance and thus save himself from a cruel and vindictive death. The father then endures his torment with impassive resolve. When it is the son's turn, however, the judge insists that the father attend. As anticipated, his pain is so great in seeing his son's suffering that he calls for a halt and confesses everything. (Because the two are accused together, we might ask how a father's confession would exonerate his son, but we must assume that the father accepts sole responsibility.) The judge is perplexed that he should endure so much in silence, yet make a full confession to spare his son. The answer is redolent of Straparola's, that to torture a father touches only his flesh, but that to torture a son is to torture his father, both body and soul. Costa's story thereby illustrates again the particular empathy and love felt by a father for his son that exceeds all other relationships. That *Il fuggilozio* was in Straparola's debt is most likely, while in Fortini's case, there is less probability.

Pietro Fortini wrote his *Piacevoli e amorose notti dei novizi* at the Villa Monaciano outside Siena no later than the mid-1550s, for the work was in print by 1557.[62] It is conceivable that he knew this story from the second volume of the *Piacevoli notti* published in 1553, but if so, his debts have been largely dissimulated. He tells of a loving and devoted couple whose tranquillity is troubled by an insistent young lover. Anton Luigi solicits, ignores negative responses, lurks, and ultimately threatens violence to the lady's husband. Fiordespina leaves the house with a weapon in hand, and, in defence of her husband, slays the young man. Husband and wife are apprehended by the magistrates and accused of his murder. Fiordespina is the first to endure a round of torture, a futile means in her case to exact a confession. But when she realizes that her husband is destined to suffer the same ordeal, she confesses the truth of her crime

---

61 Ed. Corrado Calendo (Rome: Salerno, 1989), bk. VIII.19, pp. 596–7. *Il fuggilozio* was
    first published in Naples in 1596.
62 Ed. Adriana Mauriello, 2 vols. (Rome: Salerno, 1995), vol. II, pp. 1305–12.

to spare him the torment. The 'Governatore' is amazed by her resilience, asking how she could remain so constant during her own tribulation only to confess after. She speaks of pity and the true love she feels for her husband, her equivalent of the feeling of a father for his son. But their case is ultimately less urgent, for, as is only right, Anton Louis's father emerges to blame his son's death on the tyranny of love, thereby exonerating and pardoning the young couple. Yet this narrative retains something of Straparola's design and the signature question about sparing those we love from the torments we ourselves have endured. An even lengthier version of this story is created by Niccolò Granucci in his *La piacevol notte et lieto giorno* (1574).[63]

Straparola's story goes on to deal with a dimension of justice not present in these cognate versions. The father's confession condemns him, but the judge, captivated by this gesture of paternal sacrifice, opts to spare his life. That susceptibility in a man whose conduct has been consistently psychopathic is read as a prelude to expiation and redemption. Justice demands that his malefaction be paid for, but mercy commutes his death sentence to banishment. Already a kind of transformation has taken place, for the father is not only grateful for leniency, but intends to lead a life of penitence thereafter that will win him a place in heaven. Implicit here is a saint's life in the making, a Robert the Devil who undergoes a profound transformation, inaugurating a new life of penitence for earthy crimes in relation to divine justice. The sudden surge of pity for a suffering son is the first step in a full religious conversion.

---

63 (Venice: Iacomo Vidali, 1574), Nov. XI, pp. 132r–5v.

The Eleventh Night

The shadowy night, the healing mother to the world's fatigues, had already fallen, and the wearied beasts and birds had gone to rest when the gentle and amiable company, putting aside all heavy thoughts, made their ways back to their customary meeting place. After the damsels had danced various steps in keeping with the prescribed order of their festivities, the vase was brought out. The first name to be drawn from it was Fiordiana's, followed by Lionora's, then Diana's, Isabella's and lastly Vicenza's.

After their *lironi* had been brought out and tuned, the Signora gave the word to Molino and the Trevisan to sing a *canzone*, which they performed without delay.

Song

The soft enchantment of your face,
Your beauty and your dainty grace,
Your eye, which neither coy nor bold,
   Can work its roguish spell,
And, pretty thief, keep close in hold
   My life, my death as well.

To lures like these I fall a prey,
They charm and bind me 'neath their sway,
And vanquishing by their radiance quite
   I willingly own thy power,
And kiss my chains by day, by night,
   Until my dying hour.

Lives there a man from pole to pole,
So base and churlish in his soul,
So barbarous and dour a wight,
   Who, might he once be blest
To gaze upon your bosom bright,
   Where love hath made his nest,

Would fail to turn from hot to cold,
Now chill with doubt, now overbold

> With strong desire to call thee dear,
>   And yet be doubtful still,
> If burning hope or chilling fear
>   Could wake the keenest thrill?
>
> Whose breast, now soothed with love's delight,
> Now vexed with doubts that burn and bite;
> Would not each hour send forth anew
>   Its sighs their tale to tell –
> Sighs which might soften and subdue
>   The lion fierce and fell?
>
> Nor all impatient would implore
> Both men and gods whom men adore,
> The heaven, the earth, the shining stars,
>   The ocean deep and vast,
> To end forthwith these cruel wars,
>   And give him peace at last?

This sweet and lovely song, sung by Molino and the Trevisan, greatly pleased the entire company. Its charm and pathos were so strong that it brought soft tears from the eyes of that certain person to whom it was most particularly directed. And then, in order to begin at once the storytelling for the evening, the Signora asked Fiordiana to commence, who, making her due salutation, told the following story.

XI. Fable 1
Costantino and His Wonderful Cat

FIORDIANA

Sopriana dies and leaves three sons, Dusolino, Tesifone, and Costantino, the last of whom, through the aid of his cat, gains the lordship of a powerful kingdom.

It is no rare event, beloved ladies, to see a rich man brought to extreme poverty, or to find someone who, from absolute penury, has mounted to high estate. Such good fortune, I heard tell, came to a boy in dire straits, who rose from beggary to the full dignity of a king.

Once upon a time in Bohemia there was a woman named Soriana who lived in great poverty with her three sons, one of them called Dusolino, another Tesifone, and the third Costantino Fortunato. Soriana had nothing of value in the way of household goods, with three exceptions: a kneading trough that women use in making bread, a board used in preparing pastry, and a cat. Borne down with the heavy burden of passing years, Soriana saw that death was approaching and on this account made her last testament, leaving to Dusolino, her eldest son, the kneading trough, to Tesifone the pastry board, and to Costantino the cat. When the mother was dead and duly buried, sometimes neighbours nearby would borrow the trough or else the pastry board as they happened to need them. Knowing that the young men were very poor, some repaid them with a cake, which Dusolino and Tesifone ate by themselves, giving none of it to Costantino, the youngest brother. And if he happened to ask them for something, they would tell him to ask his cat, who would give him whatever he wanted, leaving both boy and cat in a state of miserable privation. But in reality this cat was enchanted and had magic powers. Feeling compassion for Costantino and anger at his two brothers because of their cruel behaviour, she said to him, 'Costantino, don't be discouraged, for I'll provide for your well-being and sustenance, as well as for my own.' Whereupon the cat sallied forth from the house and went into the fields, where she lay down and pretended to be asleep. This she performed so cleverly that an unsuspecting rabbit came up close to where the cat was lying and was immediately seized and killed.

The cat then carried the rabbit to the king's palace, where, meeting some of the courtiers standing about, she told them that she wanted to speak to the king. When his majesty heard that a cat had begged an audience with him, he urged them to bring her into his presence. Asking her then what her business was, the cat replied that Costantino, her master, had sent a rabbit to the king as a present, begging him that he graciously accept it. With these words she presented the young hare to his liege, who was pleased to accept it, asking at the same time just who this Costantino might be. The cat replied that he was a young man without equal for his virtue and good looks. Upon hearing this report, the king gave the cat a kindly welcome, ordering the best meat and drink to be set before her. When she had eaten and drunk her fill, the cat most dexterously filled the bag in which she had brought the young hare with all sorts of food while no one was looking that way, then took her leave of the king and carried her bounty back to Costantino.

When the two brothers saw the pleasure with which Costantino ate his food, they asked him for a share, but he paid them back in their own coin by refusing to offer them a morsel, his good fortune unleashing in them an ardent envy that continually gnawed at their hearts. Now although he was a good-looking youth, Costantino had suffered so much privation and distress that his face was covered with scabies and ring-worm causing him much discomfort. So the cat one day led him down to the river and washed him and licked him so carefully with its tongue from head to foot, and tended him so well that in a few days he was freed of his ailment. Meanwhile, the cat kept up her presentation of gifts at the royal palace in the manner already described, by which means she sustained her master.

Yet after a time, the beast grew weary of these trips to and from the palace, fearing meanwhile the impatience of the king's courtiers in the matter. So she said to Costantino, 'My master, if you will simply do what I tell you to do, in no time you will find yourself a rich man.'

'And how will you manage this?' asked Costantino.

Then the cat answered, 'Come with me and don't trouble yourself for a thing, because I've got a foolproof plan for making a wealthy man of you.' Then the cat and Costantino positioned themselves on the bank of the river near the king's palace, and with that, the cat told her master to strip down to nothing and throw himself into the river. That done, she began to cry and shout, 'Help, help, run, run, for Messer Costantino is drowning!'

It happened that the king overheard the cat's cries, and bearing in mind what great benefits he had received from Costantino, he immediately sent some of his household to the rescue. After Costantino had been dragged out of the water and dressed in worthy garments by the attendants, he was led into the king's presence, who welcomed him heartily and enquired of him how it was that he fell into the water. Given his state of agitation, Costantino didn't know what to say. But the cat, right there at his elbow, answered in his stead, 'I should explain to you, O King, that some robbers found out through a spy that my master was taking a heap of jewels to your majesty as a gift. Thus, they ambushed him and robbed him of his treasure, seeking at the same time to murder him by throwing him into the river. Thanks only to the aid of these gentlemen he has escaped death.'

When the king heard this, he gave orders that Costantino should receive the best of treatment. Seeing him to be handsome, wise, and very rich, he made up his mind to bestow his daughter Elisetta upon him as his wife and to endow her with a rich trove of gold, jewels, and sumptuous raiment.

When the nuptial ceremonies were completed and the festivities at an end, the king instructed them to load ten mules with gold and five with the richest garments, therewith sending the bride to her husband's house, accompanied by a great entourage. Now when Costantino saw himself so highly honoured and loaded with riches, he was in a dire quandary over where he should take his bride, for which reason he again took counsel with his cat.

'Master, don't worry yourself over the matter,' said the cat. 'I'll take care of everything.' So as they were all riding along merrily together, the cat left the others and rode hurriedly on ahead. Once the company was far behind, she came upon certain cavaliers to whom she addressed herself, 'Ah, you poor chaps, what are you doing here? You'd better leave as quickly as you can, because there's a hoard of armed men coming along this road who will surely attack and rob you of everything. You can see them coming up over there; just listen to the noise of their neighing horses.'

Overcome with fear, the horsemen said to the cat, 'So what shall we do?'

The cat answered, 'It would be best for you, if they should ask you whose men you are, to answer boldly that you serve Messer Costantino, and then no one will molest you.' The cat then left them and rode still farther ahead, coming upon great flocks of sheep and herds of cattle. There she told the same story and gave the same advice to the shepherds and drovers in charge. Going on even farther, she spoke in the same way to anyone she happened to meet.

As the cavalcade of the princess passed along, the gentlemen who were accompanying her asked of the horsemen they met the name of their lord, then of the herdsmen who the owner might be of all these sheep and oxen. The answer given by all was that they served Messer Costantino. Then the gentlemen of the escort said to the bridegroom, 'So, Messer Costantino, it appears that we are now entering your dominions?' To this he nodded his head in token of assent, answering all their interrogations in a similar manner, so that all the company, on this account, judged him to be enormously rich.

In the meanwhile, the cat had ridden on and had come to a fair and stately castle that was guarded by a very weak garrison; so the cat addressed the defenders in the following words, 'My good men, what are you doing? Surely you must be aware of the ruin that is about to overtake you?'

'What ruin are you talking about?' demanded the guards.

'Why, before another hour has gone by,' replied the cat, 'your bastions will be swarmed by a great company of soldiers and you'll all be cut to pieces. Don't you hear the neighing of the horses and see the dust in the air? Unless you've a mind to perish, take my advice, which will free you from all danger. If anyone should demand of you whose castle this is, say that it belongs to Messer Costantino Fortunato.' When the time came, the guards answered just as the cat had instructed, for when the noble escort of the bride arrived at the stately castle and certain gentlemen enquired of the guards the name of the lord of the castle, they answered that it was Messer Costantino Fortunato, so that when the whole company had entered the castle they were most honourably lodged.

The lord of this castle was a certain Signor Valentino, a very brave soldier, who, but a few days previously, had left his castle to bring back the wife he had recently espoused. But as ill fortune would have it, on the road a certain distance from the place where his beloved wife was abiding, he met with an unhappy and unforeseen accident that immediately deprived him of his life. So Costantino Fortunato retained the lordship of Valentino's castle. Not long after this, Morando, king of Bohemia, also died, and by acclamation the people chose Costantino Fortunato for their king, seeing that he had married Elisetta, the late king's daughter, to whom the kingdom belonged by right of succession.

In this way, Costantino rose from an estate of poverty, in fact beggary, to become a powerful king. He lived long with Elisetta his wife, leaving children by her to become the heirs of his kingdom.

This fable, told by Fiordiana, gave great pleasure to the entire company, but in order not to waste any time, the Signora gave her command for the riddle, which, in a sprightly and ready spirit, the damsel related as follows:

> Through a flowery garden gay,
> A red and a white rose run always;
> Unwearied ever along they fare,
> And sparkle bright beyond compare.
> There stands in the midst an oak-tree tall,
> From which twelve branches spring and fall;
> And every branch from out its store
> Gives acorns four, and gives no more.

Among the company, no one was found who could interpret this obscure riddle, for although one person affirmed it to mean this and another that, yet all their solutions were faulty. Wherefore, Fiordiana, perceiving that her enigma would likely remain unsolved, said, 'Ladies and gentlemen, through my enigma I intended to shadow forth the planetary system, which may be compared to a garden full of flowers, namely, the stars. Through it there runs a red rose, which is the sun, and a white rose, which is the moon. By night and by day, these keep their courses shining bright and illuminating the universe. In the middle of this system is planted an oak, which is the year, having twelve branches to typify the twelve months. On each branch grow four acorns, the four weeks.'

When the listeners heard this – the real solution of Fiordiana's clever enigma – they all gave it the highest praise. Then Lionora, who sat in the next seat, without waiting for further command from the Signora, began her story.

XI.1 Commentary

The story of 'Costantino' is universally known as 'Puss in Boots.' It tells of a 'fairy' cat that, by means of subterfuge and intimidation, raises his 'master,' most popularly known as the Marquis de Carabas, from pauper to prince. The story type was made famous through its retelling by

Charles Perrault in 'Le maître chat, ou, Le chat botté' (The master feline, or the cat in boots).[1] Thereafter, it was spread by chapbooks, translated into many languages, and absorbed by generations of young listeners nestled in laps or snuggled in beds. Less known is that two literary versions predate Perrault by 60 and 145 years respectively, and that, with very little doubt, the eldest of the two, the present story by Straparola, was his source.[2] That, by rights, makes the mysterious author from Caravaggio the original 'maker' of this tale, an achievement that further contributes to his status as father of the modern fairy tale. But the widespread circulation of this story in forms remote from those by Straparola or Perrault and the telltale traces of former story types buried inside the Straparola recension argue, at the same time, for its existence at least somewhat before the mid-sixteenth century, modifying Straparola's part to that of quasi-maker and proto-folklorist. The disposition of the narrative carries all the features of the oral tradition, manifesting both the accretions and deletions by which the story of a helper cat achieved a formulaic identity that would appeal to popular tastes. The success of the generic story in its multiple manifestations was amply demonstrated by the folklorists of the nineteenth century, who collected versions generated independently of Perrault and the chapbooks in all parts of the Old World from Siberia to the Philippines and from Indonesia to Africa.[3] Some twenty variations were collected in Italy alone, testifying to its circulation, region by region, throughout the peninsula.

That the story enjoyed wide circulation before Straparola is further supported by the near certainty that Giambattista Basile, for his story of

---

1 In Charles Perrault, *Histoires ou contes du temps passé* (Paris: Claude Barbin, 1697).

2 Pierre Saintyves in *Les contes de Perrault et les récits parallèles* (1923) (Paris: Robert Laffont, 1987), pp. 386–7, examined the version by Basile, declared that many were deceived in thinking him Perrault's source, and then declared that the story was of necessity assembled from dozens of versions of the popular folk tale, forgetting that there is no indication that Perrault did fieldwork in collecting the sources of his tales. Because Saintyves was interested in mythological speculations and origins, he was not concerned with filiation and stemma research. He is right about Basile, but failed to consider Straparola, whom he cites on minor points in the study. That he 'overlooked' this attribution is probably due to his own disingenuousness.

3 Stith Thompson specifies that (ATU) type 545B survives in many versions, including those in which a girl is the central figure, which was given a type designation of its own: type 545A. He confirms, moreover, that it was carried to the New World by colonists. *The Folktale* (Berkeley: University of California Press, 1979), pp. 58–9.

'Cagliuso' (1634), relied upon a folk source differing significantly from that which nourished the pages of the *Piacevoli notti*.[4] It tells of only two sons, named Oraziello and Pippo, the first inheriting a sieve, the second a cat. Oraziello makes a good living, while Pippo is on the edge of starvation and regrets his inheritance. That regret becomes the cat's motivation to take measures literally to save its skin. This is the first of several features not found in Straparola. This cat, for a start, goes fishing, then follows in her gift-giving to the king with ducks, partridges, and pheasants, none of which she captures by pretending to be dead. She is more independent from her master and more rhetorically adroit than Straparola's cat. This feline does not risk the drowning-and-rescue scene by which the young initiate gains a royal wardrobe and an invitation to court, but works by report alone. Once at court with the boy, she must keep him silent and well behaved for fear he will spoil the entire enterprise. The reticence or clumsiness of the hero figures in many other recensions, but not in Straparola or Perrault. When the banquet is over and the master is sent off to bed, the cat remains to do damage control and to make suggestions about a match with the princess. Basile's king is altogether more suspicious of the boy and his purported wealth than in the present tale, and while he does not set up tests to expose the boy's lack of class and breeding (as in many related stories), he does send out a fact-finding expedition concerning the boy's wealth. In the familiar way, the cat must dupe him by racing ahead to intimidate all the locals into claiming allegiance to Lord Cagliuso (Pippo's assigned name, meaning youth). In Straparola's tale, the marriage takes place first and the test of Costantino's wealth arises only when he must take his new bride to his own castle. In Basile's version, there is neither castle nor the death or disposal of its owner. That is a significant omission. Basile's king grants the marriage merely on the strength of the replies from the harvesters and hunters. The rest of the story is taken up with the cat's own deception after doing so much good for his master. The creature goes so far as to feign its own death, only to hear that there would be no golden urn or royal burial as promised. Rather, she is treated to an undignified defenestration of her corpse. This motif, entirely absent in Straparola, is also well represented in many of the folk tales gathered later. Taking tally, it seems clear that Basile was not dependent upon Straparola, but found his own version, one in which

---

4 'Gagliuso,' in *Lo cunto de li cunti* (Naples: Ottavio Beltrano, 1634–6), II.4; trans. Sir Richard Burton (New York: Boni & Liveright, 1927), pp. 135–40.

the cat is more imperious and the boy less willing and grateful. Ingratitude, in fact, becomes his dominant theme, as it is in many cognate tales. Of the two, it may prove that Basile's source was the more representative in terms of the folk tradition, the features of which will maintain their identities in subsequent tales.[5] To reiterate the main point, if Straparola was not Basile's source and yet their tales were essentially of the same type, then a highly diversified folk tradition can alone account for their genesis, that diversification entailing many years of development and substitution.

In the absence of any clear indication that Perrault did fieldwork of his own, Straparola's tale, by default, becomes his source, and not improbably so given the many editions of the Louveau-Larivée translation available to Perrault, as it was to the Contesse d'Aulnoy, the Chevalier de Mailly, Thomas-Simon Gueulette, and others. Thus, the present tale supplied the prevailing version in the modern world, minus a few vestigial features that Perrault thought pointless to maintain. Those deleted features include Costantino's vengeance against his resource-hoarding older brothers (precisely as in such stories as 'The Three Brothers,' VII.5), his sickly condition that the cat heals by licking his face and body (just as in 'Biancabella,' whose serpent sister licks her into beauty, III.3), the feigning of death to trap game (as in the stories of Reynard the Fox), and the cat's sudden disappearance as soon as the princess and the pauper tie the knot (Perrault grants the cat a title, just as the Wild Man who helps the hero to a princess is married to her sister in 'Guerrino and the Wild Man of the Woods,' V.1). These vestiges of related story types

---

5 Nancy Canepa underscores the profiling of the hero, unique to this telling, as a 'dim witted' youth and something of a social liability, bringing his benefactress to wonder why she should labour to make him a royal bridegroom. The final speech on ingratitude is enhanced by Basile, no doubt a reflection of his own career deceptions. But the motif is widely known in the folk tradition. This cat, as it were, disposes of magic by relying on cunning to bring the desired social advancement. As the story passes from the folk to the court, the question of ambition and betrayal inevitably comes to the foreground. *From Court to Forest: Giambattista Basile's 'Lo cunto de li cunti' and the Birth of the Literary Fairy Tale* (Detroit: Wayne State University Press, 1999), p. 145. Concerning the boy's awkward, even stupid, answers at court, Basile may have known of alternative versions in which the boy makes continual reference to his riches at home, feigning a grandee's indifference to the riches around him at court. Stith Thompson in *The Folktale* (Berkeley: University of California Press, 1979), p. 59, goes so far as to say that the boy 'always' remarks that he has better things of his own. But this can hardly be true. In Straparola's tale he says nothing at all.

and the total absence of heroic feats on the part of the initiate hero in winning the princess (in contrast to Cesarino who, with the help of animals, wins a princess, but only by killing a seven-headed dragon, X.3) will serve as important points of reference in a further analysis of this tale. The largest problem to settle is precisely why Straparola should designate the cat 'enchanted,' yet provide it with no magical powers, why it should be a female cat, which Perrault, alone, makes masculine, and why the cat adopts Costantino in particular as the object of its persistent devotion. The story has in fact found its winning new formula largely in relation to what it no longer tells, but which the logic of the story would seem to require. Animal helpers, after all, do not offer their services in any such tales seen heretofore without favours first rendered to them, whether in liberating them from imprisonment (Livoretto, III.2 and Guerrino, V.1), preserving their lives (Pietro, III.1), or settling their arguments (Fortunio, III.4). There is something in this tale, even by Straparola's time, that has been 'overwritten.' The cat may have used magic powers to achieve its ends, or even have been an imprisoned human whose intelligence is speaking through the animal, an enchanted princess, perhaps, seeking liberation (see Biancabella, or the Damsel and the Snake, III.3), or even more plausibly the spirit of the boy's own mother who, through the actions of the cat, continues to nourish and promote her youngest son in a harsh world. To reread the present story as a revenant mother facing the contingencies of her environment in the interests of her son is to give the story a very special new meaning. But in the 'modern' fairytale that emerged through the efforts of Perrault, these features, already suppressed by Straparola's time, became mere structural innuendoes.[6]

Before turning to sources and buried mythologies, we may ask what kind of story it has become simply as a felt quality of experience, or a conveyer of social messages and meanings. For a start, it is a tale of rising

---

6 There is a revealing discussion of this precise topic in William Baldwin's *A Marvelous Hystory intitulede Beware the Cat* (London: William Gryffith, 1570), p. 16. One Master Sherry states that 'indeed ... it doth appear that there is in cats as in all other kinds of beasts, a certain reason and language whereby they understand one another. But, as touching this, Grimalkin I take rather to be an hagat or a witch than a cat. For witches have gone often in that likeness.' A discussion follows concerning the ability of Pythonesses to send their spirits into dead men's bodies, as well as demons, and so they debate the question of witches inhabiting other creatures. They make passing references to cats as the traditional hosts of persons metamorphosed into animals, no doubt reflecting the folklore values of the times. That many of the later

fortunes full of puerile wish-fulfilment as ostensibly innocent as any such tale can proffer. It addresses in brief some of the abiding themes of the race: how to deal with bullies, especially when they are older brothers, how to steward sharply limited resources, how to take advantage of opportunity, and how to set one's sights on the highest goals. It is the business of the fairy tale, in this instance, to fulfil fancy and grant success by eliciting the easy sympathy we extend to the helpless, by assigning the dubious means of self-advancement to auxiliaries, and by having the benefits bestowed upon a passive hero. Meanwhile, to reach her goals, the cat has perfected the arts of bluffing and intimidation. She usurps entirely the role of the initiate. Carefully chosen for her feline nature, this creature is a hunter by trickery and a practitioner of feints and fraud.[7] She has four objectives: get herself attached to a master, keep him healthy, attractive, and in prospects, gain his entry into the echelons of privilege, and style him as a youth of means and influence. It is only in creating a 'prince' out of an ersatz son that she can also 'rise.' Not surprisingly, subsequent raconteurs have seen in this story the portrait of the ambitious mother forcing her child to perform like a social puppet for her

---

versions in the 'puss in boots' tradition feature transformations of the cat into human form at the end suggests the preservation of an ancient tradition of cats so possessed, whereby they take on human interests and intentionalities. Straparola's story form and verbal hints intimate its origins in a story of this type.

7 Jack Zipes in his introduction to the tale in the *Great Fairy Tale Tradition from Straparola and Basile to the Brothers Grimm* (New York: Norton, 2001), p. 390, states that because the cat is feminine in most of these tales, it is indicative that 'Constantino [*sic*] and Caglioso need feminine intelligence and guidance to rise in society.' It is good of him to give this story a feminist twist, but the compliment seems backhanded. The cat, in these terms, serves *in loco parentis*, and hence must be a mother figure to be efficient in guiding 'her boy.' She is the one to stand up for him with shrewd social logic; what mothers won't do to help their sons get ahead, including staging a false drowning, intimidating the locals, and serving as a marriage go-between. But it is up to each female reader to decide whether this cat is the ideal representation of female intelligence and social strategy. Perrault resolved the problem by declaring the cat masculine, thereby realizing more openly what was formerly implicit, that the cat functioned as a squire or a cavalier in its own right, providing the nineteenth-century illustrators with an occasion to create sartorial hyperbole in the form of a flamboyant feline musketeer – Gustav Doré in particular. This, in turn, led to an emphasis on the fashioning of a false-aristocrat through sartorial trappings (even the cat demanded boots), and the gentle satire of class markers in clothes, manners, and titles, not to mention chateaux.

own vanity and vicarious aggrandizement. Of these four principal episodes in the narrative, two by Straparola's time are conducted almost as afterthoughts, namely, the initial pact between hero and helper and the healing of the child. A fifth – finding vital sustenance – is likewise muted when the captured game is taken to the court to curry influence rather than to feed the boy. Early narrators have, in fact, condensed two motifs into one, for now the cat must steal food for her master when leaving the court and through this means briefly settle the score with the two brothers before moving on to the two extended episodes far better known to readers. The first is a form of subterfuge in which the cat tells the master to feign drowning so that, by having him rescued by the passing king, the cat can verbally fashion him into a victim of robbery and a frustrated bearer of gifts to his majesty. The second episode is a form of bullying in which those along the road, soon to be encountered by the royal procession, are told to declare for Lord Costantino or face brutal consequences. We might call this the Mafioso ploy of soliciting payment for protection from dangers largely consisting of reprisals for non-payment. By these tactics, the boy is supplied with virtual wealth and virtual social status. These two transactions, in whatever form they are expressed, constitute the defining core of the fable.

To moralize further upon the matter, however, is to hold that getting ahead is best accomplished by creating social illusions using fraud and by ingratiating oneself into high society, there to employ assumed manners, borrowed clothes, the reports of flunkies, and sex appeal to turn the head of an heiress. Bruno Bettelheim claims that to hold up such tales to ethical standards is to miss the point entirely, insofar as '*Le Chat botté* does not propose a choice between good and evil, but makes the child believe that even the weakest can succeed in life. After all, what is the use of deciding to be good if one feels so insignificant that one is afraid of never becoming anything at all? These tales have no moral intention; they want to give assurances that one can succeed, which is an existential problem of great importance. First you have to approach life as a winner.'[8] The morality will come later, perhaps. But for the record, this cat is a bounder *sans scrupule*. It is the simple ingenuity of the cat in bluffing kings and commoners and in killing ogres that has won audiences

---

8 *La psychanalyse des contes de fées* (Paris: Robert Laffont, 1976), p. 27 (my translation); see *The Uses of Enchantement: The Meaning and Importance of Fairy Tales* (New York: Alfred A. Knopf, 1976).

everywhere.[9] The once 'enchanted' or 'magic' cat of Straparola has become a verbal trickster and social climber, excused for her means by the logic of the fairy tale. The many other meanings latent in the tale can only be teased out by investigating its variant versions and by pursuing its generic types and original forms. Straparola provides but one version of what the story was in the sixteenth century, with its own vestigial hints at former versions already in the process of disappearing. From existing variants, the scholar may seek to create filiations leading back to the earliest forms. This is by definition a grand exercise in comparative morphologies to which the 'puss in boots' tradition has been subjected.

The followers of Vladimir Propp, in particular, have sought to find not only the 'forme internationale' or oikotype of the story by statistical means, but a sense of its original form. These are two related objectives, the first constituting the most typical form, according to the greatest frequency of each of the contributing motifs, and the second the original story from which all subsequent variations are derived. This can be a laborious form of investigation as demonstrated by Paul Larivaille, who devoted a lengthy study exclusively to the 'puss in boots' type in nine variant forms – three literary, namely Straparola's, Basile's, and Perrault's, and six oral, including five Italian versions, four of which will be described in the following pages.[10] He first subdivided the versions into twenty-one narrative components, each of which was then assessed in terms of frequency, selecting thereafter each numerically dominant unit to compose the generic version of the story, the 'international form.' Propp was careful to distinguish between this composite form and the Ur-form, yet the bias in his method was to assume that frequency indicated dominance and longevity, and that hence many such features must have issued from

---

9 And as Jack Zipes has eloquently pointed out, it gets far worse when Walt Disney gets hold of the story and turns it into a barely disguised autobiographical whine disguised as a young boy's underdog triumph in stealing the princess from her tyrannical father, just as Disney had to fight to prevent hostile takeovers from the industry bosses of entertainment America. In the process, the cat is reduced to a toddy accomplice, albeit a manipulator of illusions by which the boy is brought to unmerited success. For Zipes, in the process Disney succeeds in destroying the integrity of the folk tale entirely. *Fairy Tale as Myth; Myth as Fairy Tale* (Lexington: University Press of Kentucky, 1994), pp. 81–4.

10 'Perspectives et limites d'une analyse morphologique du conte: Pour une révision du schéma de Propp,' *Centre de Recherches de Langue et Litterature Italiennes,* Documents de travail et prépublications, Université de Paris X, Nanterre, no. 2, 1973; new and revised edition 1979, with charts and graphs.

the foundational version. Larivaille's reconstruction suggests that the original helping animal was a fox, and that the dominant means for attracting the king's attention was the borrowing of a money-counting basket in which a gold coin is placed when it is returned, as though by accident. By this trick, the protagonist is deemed rich beyond measure. Such reconstituted narratives imply a full inaugural version subsequently damaged by deletions and inferior substitutions, marginalizing the idea that they may have been creations built up from the inherent narrative possibilities within single elements. One calibrates backward to the most representative rather than forward to the most accomplished, as achieved through trial and error. But in the evolution of the folk tale, both principles appear to function simultaneously, which entails value judgments concerning what is early and late.

Working methodically through these materials according to Propp's schema, Larivaille describes the oikotype as follows: the replacement of the hero by an animal that alleviates his hunger; the provocation of curiosity at court about the boy's riches and social position through the giving of gifts; the borrowing of a container for measuring gold and silver that is returned with a coin inside; the king's invitation to the youth to visit the court; and the accident on the way that entails the king's rescue. At this juncture, the hero is given aristocratic raiment and the king expresses a desire to confirm the youth's status by visiting his domains. The helper animal's solution is to cajole all those it finds along the route into declaring in favour of the hero. Then a castle is procured at the last moment by killing or incarcerating the rightful owner and duping the attendants into proclaiming the story's hero as their master. (The last stratagem of the wily cat, in Perrault's account, is tricking the ogre into transforming himself into a mouse, which the cat consumes in the manner of Lattanzio and his master, VIII.5). The hero then marries the princess. Such a statistical reconstruction may serve among existing versions as a basis for comparison and measuring deviations. But the sampling, in terms of the actual number of versions collected by ethnographers, numbering in the hundreds if not thousands, is very limited. Moreover, the method selects only the dominant features from existing tales, passing over the recessive but perhaps telltale vestiges of former versions in the process of being marginalized and suppressed as the story progresses and changing social environments diminish their contexts. Latest versions may not prevail by their statistical loyalty to original motifs, however, but may emerge from innovations that transform or discard earlier motifs around the central narrative formula or fabula.

Moreover, that Straparola's is the oldest surviving version does not mean that it is closest to the Ur-type. Cognate tales then in existence contained more atavistic features: the fox, for example, that surely predates the cat. Straparola's source tradition had already accommodated tastes in modifying the helper animal and in suppressing the final episode in which the hero is accused of ingratitude, or in which the cat demands to be beheaded as a prelude to self-transformation. In spite of these adaptations, his tale preserves trace features suppressed by Perrault that give clues to former versions. Initially, this was not a story about social climbing, but about fighting for food. The brothers inherited implements that, by their lending them out, brought them sustenance and an opportunity to mock their miserable and excluded younger brother. Their position: 'Let the cat bring him food as our sieve and kneading trough have done for us, for such is his legacy.' As mentioned already, the cat settled that score by stealing food from the royal court, after capturing game in the manner made famous by the foxes of folklore and beast fable, namely, by playing dead and waiting for the game to come to them. The jealous brothers now find themselves gnawed by envy. At the same time, Costantino is disfigured by privation and troubled by a blotchy scurf. The cat tends to this condition as a prerequisite to his appearance at court by washing her master in a river and licking him over his entire body. These telltale features, though much reduced, are potential conveyors of ancient patterns.

It would be supererogatory to dwell on the antiquity and wide diffusion of stories about animals that achieve their ends by playing dead, particularly as a strategy in their search for food. But a few examples are in order to show the ubiquity of this motif and how it came up for brief representation in the present tale. There is the story in the *Panchatantra* at the end of the second book in which the friends – a deer, a crow, and a mouse – work together to free a fourth friend, the turtle, from the hunter's cords. The deer feigns death on the road, with the crow gently pecking at him for effect. When the hunter approaches, putting aside his load, the crow flies off and the deer leaps to life, while the mouse chews surreptitiously through the turtle's cords.[11] In a second story collected by J.F. Campbell on the Island of Skye, two foxes meet a fisherman with a cartload of herring. The one tells the other to run ahead and play dead.

---

11 Visnu Sarma, *The Pancatantra*, trans. Chandra Rajan (London: Penguin Books, 1993), p. 263.

The carter, delighted to find such a fine animal, throws him on the load. The fox then begins to toss the fish out of the wagon to make a feast with his friend.[12] For the story's medieval currency, there is the tale of the death-feigning fox in a Latin bestiary from the twelfth century in which the hungry creature besmears himself with red mud to resemble blood and then lies on his back holding his breath in order to attract carrion birds. As soon as they alight, he seizes and devours them.[13] The legacy of Reynard the crafty fox with his cunning and amoral feeding instincts is fixed as a vestige in Straparola's story, one in which the hunger motif and the fox as helper presumably originated. The fox is motivated by the primal instincts pertaining to rudimentary survival, and it is his quest for food by trickery that may well prefigure the entire development of the story of the helper cat, which, as a domestic creature ever so slightly attached to a master, employs the fox's cunning for his benefit.

To this ancient motif is added that of the healing and beautification ritual. The boy is taken to a river for cleansing and then licked to wholeness by the cat. In this role, she resembles the mysterious Samaritana, who, as Biancabella's sister transformed into a serpent, makes her the most beautiful of all her gender by bathing her in milk and roses and licking her thoroughly. She is cast as a chthonic creature of extraordinary powers who arrives at a moment of dire need following a period of estrangement. This primitive element carries suppressed memories of deep mythological significance, for just as the serpent sister is enchanted and seeking to escape her reptile form to recover a human self, the 'fairy' cat may at one time have been a melusine, an enthralled princess, or a departed soul. Such a being can only live vicariously through an alter ego, seeking to create the circumstances under which the spell might be broken. This mythic strain is superfluous to a story of arrivisme by sharp social intelligence – the future of the 'puss in boots' type – but Straparola's 'fatata' (enchanted) cat is a trace element of former incarnations. His story still lingers upon matters of sibling rivalry, competition for food, and the reliance upon the totem animal of the clan for help in times of distress. Licking the hero back to health is the only manifestation of the cat's magic powers – powers thereafter entirely irrelevant to the story.

---

12 *Popular Tales of the West Highlands* (London: Alexander Gardner, 1870), vol. I, pp. 286.

13 *The Bestiary: A Book of Beasts*, ed. E.T. White (New York: Putnam, 1954), pp. 53–4, from the Cambridge University Library MS. 11.4.26.

Strangely absent or muted in the 'puss in boots' tale is the means for acquiring the auxiliary helper. The cat may be grateful, but the cause of that gratitude is unspecified. That lack is underscored by the number of animal-helper tales in which success alone depends upon charity and relief to creatures in distress, who in turn bestow upon the hero a variety of critical benefits. The tale of 'Le petit bossu' collected in the Lorraine by Emmanuel Cosquin is a classic example of that entire class, in which two unworthy elder brothers refuse help to others and find themselves destitute, while the third, performing many charitable acts along the way, including the burial of a debtor by paying his creditors, receives a fox as his counsellor and benefactor, an animal who feeds him miraculously, teaches him all the secrets for his initiation into palace society and his introduction to a princess, and rescues him from a murder plot perpetrated by his brothers.[14] That the fox performs functions similar to those in the 'puss in boots' group may be grounds for positing an ancient association from which the present type is a major departure.

From such dark roots, we may presume that the far lighter tale of the intrepid cat came into being through substitutions motivated by taste and audience favour. Diminution of the tale of the three brothers to an opening frame was equally germane. Likewise, how to dispense with the owner of the desired castle was a new challenge to narrators, for Costantino and his successors required a domicile. The tradition inherited by Straparola could do no better than have the owner conveniently meet an unfortunate accident as he went to fetch his new bride, leaving the wedding banquet in place for the intruders. Basile left the episode out altogether. In other tales the owner is vilified as an ogre, burned in an oven, locked in a pit, disposed of by magic, or killed outright. Perrault solved the matter by making the owner the stock fairy-tale ogre who can transform himself into animals. As a lion he forces the cat to take to the rooftop in his clumsy boots, while as a mouse, the anthropomorphized cat reverts to its animal instincts to gain a castle. Even children understand conventions, although I leap ahead in terms of readership, for there is no indication that Perrault himself was writing exclusively or even primarily for children (a fact overlooked by Bettelheim). That the cat is more than a quadruped with whiskers is remembered in Straparola only in the word 'fatata' (magic or enchanted). Written over entirely is the

---

14 Emmanuel Cosquin, *Contes populaires de Lorraine*, 2 vols. (Paris: F. Vieweg, 1886), no. XIX, vol. II, pp. 208–22.

person within the cat awaiting the rupture of the enchantment that will enable her to return to an original self. Such tales exist. In one, the cat's head is severed at its own request and a prince is liberated from a spell, a remnant of a tale of imprisonment and liberation.[15]

The folkloric heritage of this story is truly vast and can be outlined here only in the most cursory way. To collect and analyse even a portion is work of monographic magnitude. Yet, arguably, they are all valuable witnesses to the multiplicity of strains, including those that predate Straparola and Basile. Here are a few. 'La Golpe' is a Tuscan tale in which a woman named Rosa has a lazy son. One day she gave him a black chicken and warned him not to slaughter it because it would bring him good fortune. When the poor old lady died, the boy had nothing else to eat. So he set off on his travels and met a golpe that wanted to eat the chicken, but the boy refused. The chicken then went to work for them, enabling them to cross dangerous rivers, gain access to castles, and speak to kings, until the boy's fortune was made.[16] In a story from the Abruzzi called 'Barone Caiuso,' a father dies and leaves everything to the older son. The younger has only his 'tigna,' or cat, to which he confides all his woes. The cat assures him that he will become a baron and they retreat to the country where they have a little house. When midday comes and they have nothing to eat, the cat brings in food. But then the cat demands a pact that whatever the boy has to eat he must also share, to which the boy agrees. From that time forward, the cat calls him Barone Caiuso. She then goes to the emperor's palace to steal a huge diamond ring, which she places on her tail. Then she announces the Barone's intention of marrying the princess and displays the ring to the court. The king asks about the Barone's other possessions and the cat tells of lands and palaces. Then it sets off to inform all those along the way that they must report the owner of their fiefs and castles to be Caiuso. The king and princess arrive to meet the Barone while the cat hides under the table. Now doubting its master's gratitude, the cat plays dead in the garden. With the news, the Barone tells the gardener to throw it into a trench. The cat jumps up like a tiger, telling the boy that if he has any courage he will need it, for she then leaps in through the window, strangles him, and throws him into the ditch. Then the princess, the king, and all who

---

15 Stith Thompson, *The Folktale* (Berkeley: University of California Press, 1979), p. 58.

16 Giuseppe Pitrè, *Novelle popolari toscane*, ed. Gino Cerrito (Palermo: Edikronos, 1981), pp. 76–85.

are with them return to sleep in their own beds. Singularly evident in this version is the pact demanded by the serving animal and the revenge for ingratitude, the one spelling out the conditions of service, the other the failure of the hero to recognize in the benefactor a complex and dangerous personality, or to assume his own obligations in a social economy ultimately based on reciprocity.[17]

A Florentine tale, somewhat decayed it would seem, is nevertheless full of revealing hints. In 'Re Messemi-gli-becca-'l-fumo' there is a dying man who leaves three sons. The elder two depart to seek their fortunes. The youngest stays home with his cat and together they hide in the cellar. The cat then leaves to forage for food and returns with an entire meal. The palace is near, so the creature approaches and begins to howl. She reports that her master has fallen into a ditch and needs clothes. The wish is granted, but these she returns the next day, reporting at the same time to enquiries that her master is rich and a gentleman. Another day she repeats her caterwauling and asks for a bushel for counting money, returning it with a gold coin stuck in the bottom. When it is noticed, the cat says to keep it for the trouble, that to her master it is nothing. When the boy hesitates over visiting the king, the cat threatens to scratch him. Then she takes out a magic wand and dresses him royally. We must, at this juncture, ask no questions about ways and means; the story has become a reckless pastiche. Rumour spreads of the young gentleman's arrival and he is royally greeted, but in a private moment the cat must instruct him concerning his wretched table manners, and again when the boy remonstrates as an unwilling participant, the cat demands silence and threatens the claw. The boy asks for his rags again and is bullied into compliance. The beds are made up with rough sheets. It is a test, for no aristocrat would sleep in them. But the cat detects the ruse, forces the boy to sleep in an armchair, and howls her displeasure throughout the palace. The king is satisfied! A second test over the condition of a fine bed is then imposed, for it must not look mussed even if slept in by a true gentleman. The cat is again wary and administers the claw to get the desired results. On the strength of it all, the marriage is proposed and the cat, still answering on the boy's behalf, agrees to the offer. After a month of celebrations, the king invites himself along for the return

17 *Usi e costumi abruzzesi*, ed. Antonio de Nino, vol. III, *Fiabe* (Florence: G. Barbèra, 1883), no. 53, pp. 267–70. For a comparative text from this same region see 'Ju fatte de Dun Giuvanne de Lupine,' in *Tradizione popolari abruzzesi*, ed. Gennero Finamore (Lanciano, 1882), no. 46.

trip to the young king's realm. Once again the magic wand is employed to create roads, villas, palaces, and servants to shout long life to the newlyweds. In due course, the cat states that death may be near and asks what would be done with its remains? There was weeping and promises of a gold and silver casket. In a year's time, the cat went through all the rooms defecating and retching, leaving a terrible stench everywhere on the carpets – on anything of value. When the palace denizens awoke the next day to find such reeking devastation and a dead cat to boot, they hurled the beast into the Arno. Then presto, the boy found himself again in his cellar, destitute, although still with his bride. But she didn't stay for long and the boy was left to die of hunger and regret. In this telling, the cat becomes a bossy mother, then a sadistic social-climbing guardian, and the boy an unwilling accomplice. His debts are accumulated against his will, and when the cat kicks the bucket, the boy's wish comes too true of longing for the comforts of the cellar. Not only does this story 'remember' a great deal of its originating motifs, but transforms them into an anti-*Bildungsroman* concerning table and bedroom manners, wolfing food, and such little shibboleths that separate the washed from the unwashed. It is all about ingratitude with a twist, and this line of raconteurs seems really not to like cats.[18]

An altogether different variant turns up in Sicily entitled 'The Dealer in Peas and Beans.' It combines the projection of future wealth on the basis of a trivial object, as in the stories of dreaming vendors who begin with milk or butter, computing imaginary profits until they imagine themselves rich, just before dropping the initial commodity and losing everything. In this story, the poor chap who finds a bean that sets him dreaming of vast harvests and future riches goes so far as to make enquiries about warehouses long before he has planted anything. His stair-stepping process begins to take on the profile of our present story when he discovers that the warehouse owner's daughter is free and that he can go a-courting in borrowed clothes until he sufficiently impresses

---

18 Vittorio Imbriani, ed., *La novellaja fiorentina con la novellaja milanese* (Milan: Rizzoli, 1976), pp. 138–50. There is some discussion over the meaning of the title, which contains words for 'king, My Lord (perhaps), catches, and smoke.' Imbriani laments that Liebrecht, the German translator, did not get it right with 'König Schikt'-mich-ihm-pickt-den-Rauch.' The French translator of the story, René Basset, in *Contes populaires berbères* settled on 'Le roi Happe-fumée' (Paris: E. Leroux, 1887); new ed. 2008. This story appears in Marc Monnier's *Contes populaires en Italie* (Paris: Charpentier, 1880), pp. 254–62.

her family and strikes the marriage bargain. Then, turning spendthrift, he squanders the dowry on parties and clothes until the family becomes alarmed. When the moment of reckoning comes and the mother and daughter demand to see his estates, he takes more money to buy pronouncements in his favour from those along the road. Then, most improbably, he comes to a grand palace into which he is invited by a mysterious princess who turns it over to him because she is the fairy bean he has kept so faithfully in his pocket. It is a strange creation of consolidated and adapted motifs, revealing the recombinant features of the folklore repertory.[19] The helper is absent; the day-dreaming protagonist arranges it all for himself, with a cameo appearance by a grateful fairy in the role of 'the grateful dead.'

As a final sampling from Italy, there is the story of 'Count Piro' collected in Sicily by Laura Gonzenbach, telling of a pauper's son who received for his legacy a single pear tree with the wondrous property of bearing fruit the year round. A passing fox, in the dead of winter, was pleased by the tree and asked for a basketful. When the boy wondered aloud what he would then eat, the fox promised him a fortune in return and the offer was accepted. The fox took the pears to the king, who likewise was astonished, considering the season. That was the opening for the fox to boast of the owner's remarkable wealth and fortune. When the king offered to send a gift in return, the sly fox refused, saying it would be a slight. After another basket, he asks for the hand of the princess on behalf of his master. There follows a dinner invitation, the boy's

---

19 From Giuseppe Pitrè's 'Padron di ceci e fave' in his *Fiabe*, translated as *The Collected Sicilian Folk and Fairy Tales of Giuseppe Pitrè*, by Jack Zipes and Joseph Russo (New York: Routledge, 2009), no. 87, vol. I, pp. 387–91; retold by Italo Calvino, no. 154 of his *Italian Folktales*, trans. George Martin (New York: Pantheon Books, 1980), pp. 553–6. The next tale, no. 88, 'Count Joseph Pear' (vol. I, pp. 391–6), is in the same vein and closely related to the tale collected by Laura Gonzenbach. A passing fox pleads for its life, urging the boy protecting a pear tree not to shoot. His reward would be a princess. Her life spared, she is good to her word, first collecting game to take to the king in the name of 'Count Joseph Pear.' The fox then asks for a scale from the court to weigh money, from which she extracts her share. With this, she outfits her ward to give him an aristocratic appearance. The marriage and departure for the imaginary castle follow in rapid order, with the fox out ahead. When he meets the oggress, he induces her into a well and takes her castle in the nick of time. The couple settles down to domestic bliss until Joseph starts throwing dirt at the fox's head, who then threatens to expose to the wife her husband's humble origins. That was a blunder, for little Joey crushes her skull to shut her up, and then they live happily ever after.

consternation, the ordering of a special suit for him on credit, and a horse on similar terms. The fox in this tale also insists on doing all the talking. The banquet transpires, more pears are sent, and an affirmative answer is given to the marriage request. The boy then asks incredulously where he will take the girl, and the story pursues its customary course. The king departs with a large retinue, while the fox runs ahead to prime the populace by intimidation. His last feat is to enter the castle of an ogre and his wife, terrify them with reports of imminent attack, and urge them to hide in a bake oven; what must follow, follows. This fox too demands a beautiful coffin for all he had done and then plays the trick of feigning death to gain a reading of the future. Count Piro fails the test by treating the poor beast miserably, but this fox forgives the slight as a mere slip of the tongue. He lives on for years and at his death receives a very fine casket indeed.[20]

From the Caucasus there is the story about Boukoutchi-Khan and the fox, in which a bushel basket is borrowed from the Khan in order to count imaginary money. A coin is left in the bottom when the basket is returned, and by such means the pauper gains the prestige and status required to marry a princess.[21] A Norse tale entitled 'Lord Peter' presents a strange variation, for as the Lord is feasting the king in the troll's castle, the cat delays the troll's entry by telling him a long story about bringing in the winter rye. The cat informs his master that the only reward it seeks is to have its head severed. This is clearly the spell-breaker, for when the deed is done the cat becomes a beautiful princess with whom Lord Peter falls in love. It was the troll of the castle who had bewitched her and now she had her own castle back. Earlier in the story this intrepid feline, princess or not, could jump onto the back of a reindeer and demand that it head for the palace or have its eyes clawed out. Such is the magic of the beast fable that animals can favour their indwelling human side or their primal animal nature.[22] There may also be a cat in every princess.

---

20 The tales cited here for the most part involve cats, but as stated, in terms of frequency, the helping animal is more often a fox. For the Awares of Mongolia, the fox is the trickster of choice, as it is for the Greeks. See Émile Legrand, *Recueil de contes populaires grecs* (Paris: Leroux, 1881), pp. 20*ff.* In a Nubian version it is also a fox that asks for an elaborate funeral.

21 *Awarische Texte*, ed. Anton Schiefner (St Petersburg: Akademie der Wissenschaften, 1873), no. 6, p. 54.

22 George Webbe Dasent, *Popular Tales from the Norse* (New York: G.P. Putnam's Sons, 1888; reprint, New York: Johnson Reprint Corp., 1970), pp. 295–302. Geneviève Massignon reports that oral versions of the tale are rare in France, perhaps because

In 'Graf Martin von der Katze,' collected in the Tirol, a poor father, dying, leaves his two sons a bench and a cat, telling the boys to go their separate ways to avoid strife. This nourishing cat would march into houses to steal food before the eyes of the astonished onlookers and fetch clothes in the same manner. Thereafter, the boy, now well clad, was to call himself Count Martin of the Cat. When they came to a plain, the cat (who is female) began to ask who the fields belonged to, hearing mention of this Graf and that. At last they arrive at a castle, where the cat inveigles both the Graf and his wife into the cellar, where they are slain. Then she makes her master the new proprietor before going throughout the region announcing the death of the old and the installation of the new. Life was splendid, and remained so, even when the new Graf's brother came along with his bench and was installed in a palace of his own, without ever recognizing the identity of the donor. Then the cat, feeling its end drawing nigh, requested a beautiful monument. But while performing the mock death test, she heard the master say, 'Is that ugly animal (abscheulich Tier) finally dead?' followed by the recommendation to throw her into the yard. With that, the cat leaped up, accused him of ingratitude, and disappeared. This master repents in time, so that when the cat finally dies, he has her buried in a church with a fine stone telling of her services (although the stone is no longer to be found and no one remembers it!).[23]

In the Scandinavian version entitled 'The Palace That Stood on Golden Pillars,' two children are abandoned by their bickering parents, having for their sustenance a cow and a cat. The girl takes the cat and goes her way. To relieve their poverty, the cat feigns a robbery, placing the naked girl in a tree, then reports the condition of the 'princess' at court. Straparola's device is clearly manifest. The girl is clothed and

---

they have been displaced in the popular culture by the all-pervasive influence of 'Mother Goose.' Nevertheless, a few do occur, including one from the Poitou, which may or may not be several generations removed from its origins in Perrault. The cat initially steals black puddings and wine and shares in the spoils. Moreover, the cat itself is married briefly to a rat before escaping the curse and becoming a young man. At the same time, parts thought essential to Perrault are missing. *Folktales of France*, trans. Jacqueline Hyland (London: Routledge & Kegan Paul, 1968), pp. 96–8.

23 Christian Schneller, *Märchen und Sagen aus Wälschtirol* (Innsbruck: Wagner'schen Universitäts-Buchhandlung, 1867), no. 43, pp. 122–4.

treated with dignity, claiming now that she is royalty in her own right. The suspicious queen mother sets up tests of her breeding to verify her assertions, while the cat offers caution and instruction. The prince now wishes to visit her palace, and now the girl is certain to be caught out in her deceit. But the cat will also settle this in her favour by riding out ahead of the royal party to establish the Princess of Cattenburg in her own domains. Finally, they make themselves at home in the golden-pillared castle of an absent giant. Upon his return, the cat infuriates him by blocking the keyhole with a loaf of bread until the owner falls and splits most conveniently into pieces.[24] Then the wedding could safely be solemnized with all the material trappings in place, following which this cat wanted for nothing. Much of the familiar core story is replicated, but the protagonist is now a young girl whose career is identical to those of her male counterparts.[25]

One of the few tales reputedly of the folk that echoes Perrault directly and thus Straparola indirectly is 'Der gestiefelter Kater' (The boot-

---

24 Pierre Saintyves (pseudonym for Émile Dominique Nourry, 1870–1935) makes much of this episode as a demonstration of sun worship and seasonal strife in which the ogre, as a winter figure, in falling backwards must see the sun and hence be shivered like ice upon hitting the ground. Just why the winter palace stands on golden pillars, however, may be a problem. *Les contes de Perrault*, p. 399. There are other versions that play nicely into the hermeneutics of the mythographers. Two such are included in the *Narodnyja russkija skazki*, the second of which features a white palace captured by the fox that was once inhabited by the serpent king Uhlan. The creature is driven from his domicile by the threat of an imminent visit by King Fire and Queen Lightening. The serpent hides in an oak tree, which is then set on fire – the victory of the sun god over the dragon of winter? Ed. Aleksandr N. Afanas'ev, *Narodnyja* (Moscow: Grechev, 1873), vol. IV, pp. 10–11. A White Russian recension follows the same plan in which the parents of the princess are Thunder and Lightening. It is the girl's parents who dispatch the evil snake. E.R. Rumanau, *Bielorusskii Sbornik* (Vitobsk: G.A. Malkina, 1886–), vol. III, pp. 226–7. These appear to be genuine fusions of prince-maker fairy tales with seasonal agon myths. The folk mind is an alembic fit for strange experiments.

25 Benjamin Thorpe, *Yule-Tide Stories: A Collection of Scandinavian and North German Popular Tales and Traditions* (London: Henry Bohn, 1853), pp. 64–75. There were many such tales collected through the region of Westergötland (Västergötland, S.W. Sweden), including one in which the intrepid animal is a dog still connected to the magic tradition mentioned in a word by Straparola but otherwise forgotten. This creature, at the end, begs to be beheaded, whereupon there emerges a young prince who then marries the ward he had so successfully elevated socially and materially. The hero's beheading of the beloved guardian animal is the final act of reciprocity and faith.

wearing cat), which was first published by the Grimm brothers in 1812.[26] These three sons inherit a mill, a donkey, and a cat, and when the youngest complains that a pair of gloves is the best he will ever have from his legacy, the animal begins to speak, making promises and requesting a pair of boots. The first ruse is to go hunting with a grain sack and therewith catch partridges that none of the other hunters could catch (the equivalent of the pear tree in winter). The king is pleased by the cat's largesse, so pleased that he opens his treasury to the creature to fill her sack. This episode replaces the death-feigning ruse of Straparola. Now the miller becomes a count and the cat is just getting started in the get-rich-easy game. After a few more hunting exploits, the boy is sent bathing in a lake as the king is about to pass. The clothes of the famous count are reported stolen, confining him to the freezing water until the king brings him replacements from his own wardrobe. So tricked out, he is ready to meet the princess. Then the cat goes on the road to reshape public opinion concerning the count's holdings, uttering the usual threats for non-compliance. Only the sorcerer's castle remains to be gotten, which the cat appropriates by challenging him to shape-shift into a creature small enough to be gobbled down. The rest follows the template set out by Perrault.[27]

Perrault's version, following Straparola, remains the form in which it is best known today. WorldCat (provided by the OCLC Online Computer Library Centre Inc.) contains no less than 2898 entries for the title 'Puss

---

26 Jacob and Wilhelm Grimm, *Kinder- und Hausmärchen* (Berlin: Realschulbuchhandlung, 1812), no. 33; see also *The Great Fairy Tale Tradition from Straparola and Basile to the Brothers Grimm*, ed. Jack Zipes (New York: Norton, 2001), pp. 402–5. In studying the tradition of this story, Johannes Bolte and Jiří Polívka offer an extensive bibliography of 'puss in boots' analogues, beginning with Straparola's, which they could not have read attentively, calling it the scantiest and least sufficient ('dürftigste') of versions. Given their rich contribution in general, however, they can be forgiven this grim and abusive blunder! *Anmerkungen zu den Kinder- und Hausmärchen der Brüder Grimm*, 5 vols. (Hildesheim: Georg Olms, 1963), vol. I, pp. 325–34.

27 The Grimm tale was not the first creation in Germany bearing the title *Der Gestiefelte Kater*. Ludwig Tieck borrowed the story from Perrault to create a remarkably successful theatrical elaboration upon the fairy tale in which he deals satirically with the social enormities and eccentricities of the late eighteenth century. Hinze the cat is a lord, a citizen, and a huntsman who must sometimes claw his ward, Hanswurst, to comply with court expectations. The play constantly calls attention to theatrical fiction and illusion; characters even complain about the parts the author has given them. *Der gestiefelte Kater* (1797), ed. and trans. Gerald Gillespie (Austin: University of Texas Press, 1974).

in Boots,' including Metro-Goldwyn-Mayer's Home Entertainment version (2005). Most of these are illustrated children's books. Yet there is, as yet, no full-length scholarly comparative study of the story type in its multiple settings and manifestations. Just how many variants have been collected from 'the folk' by world ethnographers is difficult to estimate. The above sampling is only from the best-known collections, and yet, for our purposes, they suffice to reveal the diversity that is tolerated by the generic formula of a pauper made rich and royal by the machinations of a clever helper animal, whether fox, cat, chicken, jackal, or gazelle. Many of those stories may well carry vestiges of former incarnations in which the helper animal is either enchanted or represents the totem or tutelary animal of a tribe or clan. There is the sense, as well, that the primal survival instincts at the outset of the story are socialized or translated into social ambition in search of status and wealth. Beast fables have always managed to overlay animal instincts with an ethos of contemporary society. Stated otherwise, despite the displacement towards the familiar world of snobbish and upwardly mobile guardians who play the game through their wards, the fable adheres through its emblematic structure to a representation of humankind's primal condition. That condition is survival under duress, and while the laundered nursery versions may paint a scene of innocent hope and a fantasy-fulfilling rise to power, the folk traditions and their earliest literary manifestations tell principally of rivalry, cunning, and the unscrupulous survival of the computationally adaptive, followed by dull ingratitude.

This story in the twentieth century – apart from the hundreds of children's book versions – begins to lose its identity. A version collected at mid-century in the Poitou begins with the three prince's sons, who all wish to marry their cousin. It is no other than the story of 'The Three Brothers' (VII.5). Each must ride out to find the largest and most precious piece of cloth, which is tantamount to the gift quests of the three who rode out to find the most remarkable example of anything designated. The third son is a dullard who has no clue how to proceed, but receives the help of a talking horse who carries him to the ruined castle of the cat. This cat, like Costantino's, feeds the boy with his paws and provides him with a box full of splendid cloth. Seeing the youngest win aroused anger in the other brothers and the prolongation of the contest. The next quest is for fine hunting dogs, and this challenge the third son, with the help of his wonderful cat, is able to meet by pulling fine dogs out of an egg, where he can also return them. The third quest was for the prettiest girl, and the cat supplies her by having its own head cut off.

In this way, the young lad breaks the spell and delivers the captive princess, then takes her home dressed in white satin trimmed with precious stones. When the boy is assigned the cousin, he now refuses her, marrying the cat instead who had helped because the others had despised him. It is a strange recollection of the brotherly rivalry with which the Straparola tale begins, and a reminder that an enchanted prisoner is speaking through the cat all along. Even as the story collapses, its primitive elements come to the foreground.[28] But now it also belongs to a separate type: marriage to an animal (as in II.1). Not only does it relate to the brothers who dispute a single woman by performing feats in her honour, but to the quest for rare objects, and the deliverance of a princess from enchantment.

The story of 'Bertuccio' to follow (XI.2) is in the grand tradition of 'the grateful dead,' which, despite its very particular identity, shares certain traits with the present story. At the outset of this commentary it was stated that there is no transparent reason why the cat should perform so consistently and self-sacrificingly on behalf of a boy to whom it is not indebted for favours. In the Danish story 'Det fattige Lig' there is no cat. Rather it is a dead man, beholden to a young boy who had given all he had to pay for his funeral and burial, whose ghost later joins the boy as his mentor to help him style himself a prince. He furnishes him with clothes and intercedes on his behalf in active ways until he wins a princess and the means to keep her. The grateful phantom belongs to a different story tradition, but may express his gratitude in ways resembling those in the present story.[29]

What then of the origin of the 'Costantino' story type? Or rather, on the presumption of the story's great antiquity, what does it tell us about the mentality of our ancestors? The very question is now somewhat suspect. Through analogy and pattern assessment, the story may be superimposed on all manner of ancient rites and liturgies. Pierre Saintyves (Émile Dominique Nourry) began his quest for the tales' origins by reviewing a rather conventional version in Swahili. 'Sultan Doraï' reveals just the kinds of substitutions to be expected when such stories are

---

28 'The Piece of Cloth,' in *Folktales of France*, ed. Geneviève Massignon, trans. Jacqueline Hyland (London: Routledge & Kegan Paul, 1968), pp. 89–92.
29 *Gamle Danske, Minder i Folkemunde*, ed. Sven Grundtvig, 3 vols. (Copenhagen: Iverson, 1854), vol. I, pp. 77–80.

regionally displaced.[30] The helper animal is now a gazelle, which finds
and carries a diamond to the sultan, asking for his daughter in marriage
to Doraï, whom the animal has styled a sultan. In the traditional way,
the arriviste hero, made out to be the victim of theft, is royally dressed;
the boy is presented at court and the marriage follows. Then the gazelle
most improbably goes off to slay a huge seven-headed dragon and seize
its rich holdings. It too intimidates the locals and installs the newly-weds.
When, at last, the gazelle falls ill, the young Sultan refuses to visit, sends
atrocious food, and treats the creature with all the disdain of a snobby
parvenu. The princess tells her father, who is scandalized, and when the
creature dies, the retainers of her father's court arrive to provide it a
proper funeral. Thereafter, the princess returns to her own house and
the false sultan, in punishment for his ingratitude, finds himself back in
the miserable conditions of his childhood. Saintyves fixed upon this story
as a prototype for the entire tradition.[31] It was clear to him that the totem
animal dangerously maligned in death and celebrated by communal
mourning was the very essence of the story's origin and its most antiquar-
ian feature, clinching for him the Afro-genesis of the entire 'Puss' tradition.[32] This is one example among many through which he identifies
the pristine elements of liturgy, the instauration of kings, and the worship of tutelary animals. He does not for a moment consider that mis-
sionaries and traders had been in Zanzibar for centuries and had taken
their stories with them, just as the French deposited so many of theirs
among the North American aboriginals. The presentation of the diamond and the closural gesture of returning the ungrateful protagonist
to his original misery proceed directly from the tradition maintained in
the Abruzzi in the story of 'Barone Caiuso' outlined above. Saintyves's
general thesis was that all such stories are about 'l'instauration d'un roi'
(the king's renewal), through the agency of the totem of the clan, its

---

30 Edward Steere, *Swahili Tales as Told by Natives of Zanzibar* (London: Bell and Daldy,
   1870), pp. 12–137.
31 *Les contes de Perrault* (Paris: Robert Laffont [1923], 1987), pp. 387–91.
32 Emmanuel Cosquin is convinced that all these tales originated in the East and that
   the relationship between heroes and helpers derived from the levelling factor of
   Buddhist metempsychosis, whereby human souls found themselves embedded in
   animals and seeking expression, in the manner of beast fable characters. The
   principal marker of the 'puss in boots' type is the boy's ingratitude and the superior
   charity expressed towards humans by members of the animal kingdom. Therein, for
   Cosquin, lies the meaning of these tales. *Contes populaires de Lorraine*, 2 vols. (Paris:
   F. Vieweg, 1886), vol. I, p. xxxi.

destruction of an opposing ogre, and the enforcement of royal homage to the totem animal of the tribe.[33] But in such matters there will never be agreement because mythographers and source historians work by different criteria. By projecting ancient ritual into the thematic patterns, mythographers may assume great antiquity for these stories. In keeping with the filiation process of the historico-geographic folklorists, however, the search comes to a halt in the sixteenth century, for once again Straparola provides the prototype, even though it was not the only one in circulation, as the Basile variation reveals. Those variations emerge as the story is adapted to speak to the conditions of being human as felt by contemporary audiences, so that if ancient rituals are embedded in the structures, they must also replicate patterns of experience meaningful to all subsequent generations of auditors. Therein resides a particular challenge to those who would carry these stories back to the dawn of literary history.

But Saintyves's analyses concerning the great antiquity of this tale aside, there are reasons to think that it dates back to the end of the Middle Ages. Because of the many versions of the tale surviving in the nineteenth century in which there are trials of gratitude at the end, fox helpers, episodes of playing dead, overtones of enchantment, ritual beheadings, and transformations of the cat or fox into a prince or princess, the portion of the bride quest by ruse presented by Straparola would appear to be but a fragment of a longer and more complex tale; by the sixteenth century it was already in the process of transformation through episodic simplification and the domestication of the facilitating animal. The founding tale may well have been a close cousin to the tales in 'the grateful dead' group, in which the revenant helper was sometimes a fox (XI.2), as it often was in the tales of 'the three brothers' group (VII.5). This story hints at an intriguing relationship to a more generic originating tale, but the exact nature of the Ur-type remains speculative. The version that Straparola inherited was a modified recreation of his own age, calculated to do particular and innovative kinds of social work, such as underscore the social advancement of a pauper in a quasi-fairy tale setting and dwell upon the devious outfitting of an upstart aristocrat following marriage to a princess under false pretences – a story type that would enjoy an extensive future. Still, it is and will remain an odd 'fairy tale,' for there are no fairies and no magic, only a bounder cat, and no

---

33 *Les contes de Perrault* (1923), pp. 408–9.

heroes by merit or deed, only a half-willing ward. Pietro the Fool has more agency than Costantino; at least he wishes the princess to get pregnant if only out of spite. Costantino answers no skill-testing questions, but has riches thrust upon him without enough courtesy in many versions to say 'Thank you.' In that regard, it challenges us to rethink what offices fairy tales perform, and whether certain tales deemed central to the genre genuinely merit their membership. A boy from poverty has been advanced to riches, and that alone may prove sufficient. Concerning this tale, I hear protest in its defence, but my case has been made for this story's oblique relationship to the 'fairy genre.'

XI. Fable 2
The Grateful Dead, or Bertuccio and Tarquinia

LEONORA

Xenofonte, a notary, makes his will and leaves to his son, Bertuccio, three hundred ducats, of which the young man spends one hundred in the purchase of a dead body and two hundred in the ransom of Tarquinia, the daughter of Crisippo, king of Novara, whom he afterwards takes to wife.

There is a common proverb which teaches us that those who perform kindly acts can never be losers. That this proverb is true is clearly shown by what happened to the son of a certain notary. For, although his mother cautioned him repeatedly about spending his money foolishly, in the end both mother and son were satisfied.

In the castle of Trino in the Piedmont there lived in times of yore a notary, a discreet and intelligent man called Xenofonte. He had but one son, named Bertuccio, then fifteen years old, who was by nature more simple than sage. It happened that one day Xenofonte fell ill, and seeing that the end of his life was drawing near, he made his last will. According to this instrument, Bertuccio, his lawfully born son, was appointed his heir – which was the natural thing to do – but with the condition that he should not be permitted to enjoy the full and independent possession of his estate before he attained his thirtieth year. In mitigation of this, however, he expressed a wish that when Bertuccio attained the age of twenty-five, three hundred ducats of his wealth should be handed over to him with which to trade and barter.

After the testator's death, when Bertuccio's twenty-fifth birthday had come, the young man demanded of his mother, who was the executrix of his father's will, that she should hand over to him one hundred ducats from the above-named sum. The mother, who could not deny his request, seeing that it was according to her husband's intentions, at once gave him the money, begging him at the same time to employ it with prudence and judgment, using it only for some gain to himself whereby they might be able to keep a better household. Bertuccio replied to his mother's request that he would not fail to put the money to a use that would satisfy her.

Having received his money, Bertuccio set out on his travels, and as he journeyed along, he one day encountered a thief who had just slain a merchant on the public highway. Although the poor man was quite dead, the robber continued to beat and wound the body. When Bertuccio saw what the ruffian was doing, he was moved to great pity and cried out, 'Heh, what are you doing, my good man? Can't you see he's already dead?'

Whereupon the highwayman, with his hands all stained with blood, cried out in an angry voice, 'Get out of here as fast as you can, for your own good. If you don't, something terrible is going to happen to you.'

Bertuccio replied, 'So, my friend, would you be willing to hand the corpse of this dead man over to me? If you let me have it, I'll pay you well for it.'

The highwayman said, 'How much will you give me for it?'

'I'll give you fifty ducats,' replied Bertuccio.

'That's a pretty small sum of money, compared to the value of the corpse,' continued the robber. 'But if you really want to have it, it's yours for eighty ducats.'

Bertuccio, with his kind and charitable nature, at once paid out eighty ducats to the thief. Then hoisting the dead body onto his shoulders, he carried it off to a neighbouring church and there had it honourably buried, at the same time leaving the balance of the hundred ducats to be spent in sacred offices and masses for the repose of the murdered man's soul.

Bertuccio, now stripped of all his money and having nothing in his purse to live on, went back home, and when his mother saw him approaching, she deemed that he must have made some money, so she went out to meet him, and to enquire how he had fared in his trading. 'Very well,' he replied, whereupon his mother rejoiced greatly, giving thanks to God that He had at last endowed her son with intelligence and good sense.

Then Bertuccio said, 'My mother, yesterday I traded so well that I saved your soul and mine as well. Now, whenever our souls may take flight from these mortal bodies, they will go directly to Paradise.' And then he told her everything that he had done from beginning to end. As soon as his mother heard what he had to say, she was overcome with grief and reproached him bitterly for his folly.

Before many days had passed, Bertuccio once more approached his mother and asked her to give him the rest of the three hundred ducats that his father had bequeathed to him. The mother, who was not able to gainsay this request, cried out as one in despair, 'Here are your two hundred ducats. Take them and do your worst with them, and never come back to this house again!'

To this speech Bertuccio answered, 'Good mother, don't be afraid, but put yourself in good spirits, because this time I'm going to act in such a way that you'll be fully satisfied with me.'

With that, having taken his money, her son departed and, after travelling a short distance, he came into a certain wood where he happened to meet up with two soldiers who had just captured Tarquinia, the daughter of Crisippo, king of Novara. Between her two captors there had arisen a vigorous dispute as to which of them had the strongest claim to her. Drawing near, Bertuccio said, 'Brothers, friends, what on earth are you doing? Are you going to slit each other's throats over this damsel? If you'll hand her over to me, I'll give you a reward in return that will surely satisfy you both.' Then the two soldiers left off their wrangling and demanded of Bertuccio how much he'd be inclined to give if they promised to leave the girl at his disposal. His answer was two hundred ducats.

Having no idea that Tarquinia was the daughter of a king and, moreover, fearing death for what they had done, the soldiers took the two hundred ducats, dividing it equally between themselves, and left the damsel in Bertuccio's keeping. Greatly delighted that he had delivered the maiden, the boy went back to his home once more and said to his mother, 'O, mother, you'll have no cause to complain about me this time, saying that I've wasted my money again. Remembering what a solitary life you lead here, I've purchased this girl with the two hundred ducats you gave me and brought her home to keep you company.'

When his mother comprehended what her son had done, she felt that this last quirk of his was just about all she could bear. Turning on him, she began to assault him with bitter words and harsh reproofs, wishing all along that he was lying dead at her feet, because from her perspective he was nothing more than the ruin and disgrace of the house. But given the boy's gentle disposition, he didn't let his anger flare up over his mother's words. To the contrary, he tried to comfort her, affirming that he had done this entirely out of love for her so that she might no longer live such a lonely life.

The king of Novara, when he discovered that his daughter was missing, sent out a great number of soldiers in all directions to see whether they could gather any news of her, and after they had diligently searched throughout the entire country, the news was brought to them that a maiden was living in the house of one Bertuccio da Trino in the Piedmont whom he had bought for the sum of two hundred ducats. Whereupon, the soldiers of the king made their way immediately towards the Piedmont and, upon arriving, sought out Bertuccio, enquiring of him whether a certain maiden had fallen into his hands.

To this Bertuccio replied, 'It's true that some days ago I bought a young girl from certain robbers into whose hands she had fallen, but I have no idea who she may be.'

Where is she now?' asked the soldiers.

'She's in the keeping of my mother,' answered Bertuccio, 'who loves her as dearly as if she were her own child.' When they had gone into Bertuccio's house, the soldiers found the princess there, but because she was now meanly dressed and her face thin and shrunken from the many sufferings and hardships she had undergone, they scarcely recognized her. But after they had gazed upon her for some time and duly read over her features, they were assured, from the description given of her, who she must be, declaring that truly she was Tarquinia, the daughter of Crisippo, king of Novara, greatly rejoicing all the while that they had found her.

Bertuccio, convinced of the truth of what the soldiers said, then spoke up, 'Brothers, if the girl is really the one you're looking for, take her at once and conduct her to her home, for I'm content that she should go.'

Before she left, however, Tarquinia placed a command upon Bertuccio that if at any time news should be brought to him that King Crisippo was about to give his daughter in marriage, he should immediately get himself to Novara, and that when he came into the presence of the court he should raise his right hand to his head to let her know that he was there, declaring in the end that she had resolved to have him for her husband and no other man. Then, having bidden farewell to Bertuccio and his mother, she took her way back to Novara.

The king, as soon as he beheld his daughter, now that she was thus restored to him, wept copiously for joy and, after many endearments and fatherly kisses, he enquired of her how it was that she had been lost. Weeping the while, the damsel told him all the circumstances of how she had been captured by robbers, how these had sold her, and how, after all her perils, her virginity had been preserved. A short time after her return to her father's court, Tarquinia recovered all her beauty and became plump, fresh, and lovely as a rose. So King Crisippo let the report be spread abroad that he wished to find a husband for his daughter. As soon as this news came to the ears of Bertuccio, he immediately took the road towards Novara, mounted upon an old mare that was so lean you could easily count all the bones in her body.

As the good Bertuccio was thus riding along, equipped in a very scurvy fashion, he encountered a noble cavalier, richly equipped and accompanied by a great train of followers. With a merry face, the cavalier addressed Bertuccio, 'Where are you going all alone, my friend?'

'To Novara,' replied Bertuccio.

'And on what business are you bound?' asked the cavalier.

'If you'll hear me out, I'll tell you why I'm making this journey,' said Bertuccio. 'Three months ago I delivered the daughter of the king of Novara, who by ill luck had been captured by robbers. I ransomed her from their hands with my own money. Before she parted from me, she placed me under a command that as soon as I should hear the report that her father was about to give her in marriage, I should immediately go to Novara, and that once I arrived at the royal palace, I should lift my right hand to my head as a sign of my presence. She told me, moreover, that she would take no other man for her husband but me.'

'But the truth is that I'll get there long before you will and I'll win the daughter of the king for my wife, because I'm far better mounted than you and dressed in richer and more sumptuous apparel.'

Then said the good Bertuccio, 'Go on your way, my lord, and good luck go with you. I'll rejoice at your good fortune as though it were my own.'

As soon as the cavalier saw how naive and simple the young fellow was, he said to him, 'Well, give me your clothes and the mare you're riding and accept in exchange this charger of mine and my rich clothes, then ride on to Novara and good luck go with you. But there is one condition, that when you return to me here, you'll give me back not only my clothes and horse, but half of whatever you may have won for yourself.' Bertuccio answered that he agreed to all these terms.

Bertuccio then mounted the noble horse, richly dressed in the clothes of the cavalier, and rode on to Novara. Having entered the city and reached the royal palace, he saw Crisippo the king standing on a balcony and looking down into the piazza. The king, when he noticed this handsome and well-favoured youth so nobly mounted and accoutred, said to himself, 'Ah, would to God that Tarquinia, my daughter, might be inclined to marry this young man, for then I'd be mightily content.'

After this, he went down from the balcony into the audience chamber, where there were gathered a great number of the high nobility who had come to look upon the princess. By this time Bertuccio had dismounted from his horse. Going into the palace, he stationed himself among the humbler folk congregated there. King Crisippo, seeing that a very large number of gentlemen and cavaliers had now come together into the hall, requested that his daughter be summoned into his presence, and when she came, he addressed her, 'Tarquinia, as you can see, a great number of noble gentlemen are here assembled to demand of me your hand in marriage. Now look about you on every side and consider well which one of all those you see here pleases you best, and when you have decided upon one in particular, he shall be your husband.'

Tarquinia, as she walked through the hall, caught sight of Bertuccio, who held up his right hand to his head in the manner she had prescribed, and she knew him at once. Then, turning towards her father, she said, 'Sacred majesty, if it be your pleasure, I will take none other, but only this man for my husband.'

Thereupon the king, who desired this to happen as much as Tarquinia, answered, 'Be it as you will.' And before the company dispersed, the king caused the nuptials to be celebrated in the most sumptuous and magnificent fashion, to the great contentment and delight of the bride and groom alike.

And when the time came for Bertuccio to conduct his new spouse home, he mounted his horse and, having come to the place where he had first met the cavalier, he found him still waiting there. The cavalier right away accosted him, saying, 'My brother, take back this mare of yours and your clothes, and give me back my horse and garments, together with half of whatever you may have gained since we parted.'

With good grace Bertuccio gave up the horse and the accoutrements that belonged to the cavalier, and besides these, handed over to him half of the gifts the king had bestowed upon him. But the cavalier said, 'You have not yet given me half of all that is due to me, seeing that you have not shared your wife with me.'

To this speech, Bertuccio answered, 'But in what way would it be possible to divide her?'

The cavalier said, 'Can we not cut her in half?'

Then Bertuccio replied, 'Ah, my lord, it would be too great a sin and shame thus to slay such a woman! Rather than so wicked a deed should be done and she be killed, take her entirely as your own and lead her away, for I have already received benefits enough from your great courtesy.'

When the cavalier perceived what a simple and kindly nature Bertuccio had, he said to him, 'O, my brother, take everything that I have, for all that you see here belongs to you. I give you full possession of my horse, of all my clothes and my treasure, as well as my share in this fair lady. For now you must know that I am none other than the spirit of that man to whom you gave honourable burial after he had been slain by a highway robber, and on whose behalf you caused so many masses and other divine offices to be said for the welfare of his soul. Therefore, as recompense for the great services you have done, I hand over to you everything I have, at the same time announcing to you that for you and for your good mother as well, mansions are prepared for you in Heaven above where you will dwell in perpetual bliss.' Having spoken these words, the spirit of the cavalier suddenly disappeared.

Bertuccio returned home rejoicing, taking with him Tarquinia his bride, whom he presented to his mother, giving her at the same time a daughter-in-law and a daughter. The mother, having tenderly embraced Tarquinia, accepted her as her daughter, rendering thanks to the supreme Deity who had so beneficently worked on their behalf. And thus I declare at the end, as I did at the beginning of my story, that we shall never lose anything by performing an act of kindness to another.

As soon as Lionora had brought her fable to an end, she turned to the Signora and said, 'Signora, by your leave I will conform to the rule that we have observed from the beginning.' So with a gracious smile, the Signora asked her to recite her enigma.

> I tell of one who succour gave
> Another one from death to save;
> In these our days we sadly own,
> Such kindly deeds full rare are grown.
> Because Life battles ever with Death,
> Men chide thereat, and waste their breath.
> First hid the meaning was, but soon
> Revealed the purpose of the boon.
> Life sat upon a branch above,
> And gently giving love for love,
> Drew back from death the one below,
> Her kindly shield from bitter foe.

A great dispute arose over the real meaning of this cleverly conceived enigma, but there was no one keen-witted enough to hit the mark. So the prudent Lionora gave the interpretation in the following manner: 'By the brink of a clear gushing spring there stood a thick-leaved tree, in the high branches of which was a bird's nest full of lovely nestlings, over which the parent bird kept careful guard. It happened that a youth who was passing by below caught sight of a serpent that was about to climb up into the tree and killed it with his sword. Then the youth was taken by a strong desire to drink water from the nearby fountain, whereupon the mother of the nestlings he had saved from death befouled the water by casting down the dirt from her nest, which she did over and over again. The youth was mightily astonished by what he saw. Then drawing up some of the fountain's water, he gave it to his little companion dog to drink and straightway the beast died from the poisoned liquid. Then the youth understood how his life had been spared on account of what the bird had done.' Lionora's superb interpretation of her subtle enigma won high praise from all the company, and especially from Diana, who, without any further persuasion from the others, began her fable in the following words.

XI.2 Commentary

Straparola's tale of Bertuccio, a kind-hearted and naive boy who purchases for burial at his own charge the corpse of a man slain by robbers, incorporates a widespread and age-old narrative motif known generically as 'the grateful dead.' That defining act of charity may be performed under many circumstances, but traditionally it leads to self-impoverishment and ensuing disapprobation, eventuating in the successive hardships from which the hero finds relief only through the kind offices of a stranger who is revealed in the end to be the revenant spirit of the buried man. This is the simple, defining quid pro quo that is sometimes a complete story in its own right, although it is more often integrated into compound tales of questing or bride selection in which the re-embodied soul plays a vital supporting role while paying back its debt. Thus, the motif informs dozens of romances and hundreds of folk tales, all of them based on the solemn religious belief or necessary convention that the dead may sometimes assume bodies after death to involve themselves in beneficent or malevolent ways in the lives of those with whom they (whether alive or dead) had former affiliations. This narrative motif proved highly versatile in furnishing the guiding helper so often required by the logic and traditions of the folk tale. That is, a soul of the dead performs what helping animals, good fairies, or wild men do for the initiate hero in many a cognate tale. Those heroes' activities include competing in tournaments, searching for the water of life, marrying a princess, solving riddles, or slaying dragons and ogres. Because the protagonists in 'the grateful dead' group are rendered destitute by their largesse, they find themselves in dire need of good counsel, habiliments, and equipment in order to succeed. In each instance, story logic requires that those auxiliary supporters are in some way attached to the hero, are in debt to him, or stand to profit by his deeds. Many of Straparola's tales proffer examples of this relationship, as in the case of Livoretto counselled by his horse (III.2), Guerrino by the wild man (V.1), and Costantino by his cat (XI.1). In these stories, the ghost of the dead man, variously re-embodied, serves in these capacities. The motif of 'the grateful dead' as a narrative 'idea' was destined to enjoy a long history, for not only was it known in antiquity, but it was prominent in several of the chivalric romances dating to the late Middle Ages. Prior to these romance applications, the plot type had already diversified itself into several folk-tale traditions, one of which is represented quite faithfully by Straparola in the present tale – that which combines the motif of the grateful soul (E341) with the ransom of a princess from robbers who is returned to her father's house (ATU type 506B). As with most of Straparola's folk sources, all that can be known of their prior existences must be distilled from their amplifications and adaptations in literary genres such as saints' lives and *fabliaux* as well as jest books, romances, and *novelle*. Thus, our particular interest in Straparola, for he is, in essence, the first to have trusted in the wisdom and talents of the folk to tell a good story *tout court*. Even the close resemblances between his tales and those collected from oral sources in the nineteenth century tend to confirm that appraisal.

The conventional moral attached to this story, expressed both at the outset and at the end, is that acts of kindness never go unrewarded, and that in such an economy charity is both a duty and a source of credit towards future benefits. Moreover, the story holds that we live in a providential world sometimes administered through the interventions of the deceased. The entire religious system of the ancient Romans was based precisely upon this principle, that the sprits of ancestors found peace only through the duties rendered them by the living, coupled with their capacity after death to tangibly torment the faithless as well as aid the faithful.[34] In the present story, the boy naively reports to his mother that

---

34 Still one of the best accounts of the household rites, cults, and national institutions emanating directly from this deep-seated belief in the hovering souls of the dead and their lingering agency is that of Numa Denis Fustel de Coulanges in *Le cité antique* (1864), most recently republished by Cambridge University Press (2010), and in English as *The Ancient City: A Study on the Religion, Laws, and Institutions of Greece and Rome* (Gloucester, MA: Peter Smith, 1979).

the money spent on the body of the deceased was well spent, for it guaranteed the salvation of their souls. The mother, a complete pragmatist, gave up her son for lost as a competitor in the material world, for she had turned over to him a part of his inheritance in expectation of immediate material advantage and betterment. But the boy had intimations of a system of charity attached to transcendental values and forces, little knowing that souls of the dead were potential mediators. He had honoured the ancient and sacred obligations of the living towards the dead, arising from a profound belief in their entitlement to respect and a decent burial, an essential charity insofar as they were no longer able to negotiate their own futures. In the ancient world, truces were often declared following battles to permit the gathering of the dead for proper ceremonies, while the prevention of those rites was considered treacherous and reprehensible. The imperative to bury the dead with full rites appears to be the ethical motor that drives the entire story tradition. The boy ultimately prospers because he responds spontaneously and intuitively to that obligation. The tale, in that regard, epitomizes the deep and acutely human dilemma regarding self-interest in the marshalling of material resources versus empathy for the helpless, the maligned, the destitute, and the dead. In his naivety, Bertuccio is an example of saintly self-mastery in giving all he had on two occasions to succour others in distress without expectation of compensation.

His two acts build a strange fairy tale in which the soul of a dead man aids the hero in his romance quest after making a gentlemen's pact that all winnings would be divided equally between them. This innocent and equitable arrangement is later interpreted as a half-interest in his bride as well, who the protagonist must agree to cut in half or give up entirely in order to keep the bargain. Thus, the twin stories are joined, and 'the rising tale' from poverty to prosperity culminates in a micro-romance completed only when the dead man prevents the ritual murder of the bride, cedes all to the young hero and former benefactor, and disappears into death, at last at peace with the world of the living. The bride-severing motif is redolent of other tales concerned with the equitable division of persons for whom there are mutual attachments (see the commentary to 'Share and Share Alike,' VII.4). As will be seen in the survey to follow, the narratives featuring 'the grateful dead' motif need not conform to the Straparolan strain, although the present tale is, in its way, representative of one of the major currents of the folk tale – that of the spendthrift knight who recklessly bankrupts himself in compelling causes and thus lacks all hope of chivalric prosperity until a mysterious man aids him in his poverty. In the Straparola group, the story type is brought down to the mercantile (or lower) class level in which a boy goes into the world, buries a dead man, rescues an incognito princess, takes her home, returns her to her father, then upgrades his social status with the help of a stranger in order to recover his beloved.[35] The story profile and many of its narrative parts are richly represented in the subsequently collected folk tales of the Old World.

The motif may well have found its origins in far simpler anecdotes about the dead, who were thought to pay back debts to the living, as in the story of Simonides recounted by Valerius Maximus in his *Memorable Deeds and Sayings*. Upon landing on a foreign shore, Simonides found an unburied corpse and had it interred at his own expense. His plan was to set sail the following day, but a premonitory dream dissuaded him, a dream to his mind unquestionably sent by the soul of the deceased. The gods proved kind in his case, for those who insisted upon leaving perished in a storm before his eyes, thereby confirming his conviction. Such a conviction might be explained away as a mere supposition incited by recent events, but otherwise it confirms an underlying sense of reciprocity in the world order upon which the entire story tradition is based.[36]

---

35 Stith Thompson in *The Folktale* (Berkeley: University of California Press [1946], 1977), pp. 50–3, provides a brief overview of the 'grateful dead' motif as it appears in a variety of folk-tale types. Former historians of the motif have failed to see its versatility as an element incorporated into other tale types, but nevertheless set about the task of grouping under subheadings the main traditions in which it appears. Among them were Sven Liljeblad in *Die Tobias geschichte und andere Märchen mit toten Helfern* (Lund: P. Lindstedt, 1927), and Gordon Hall Gerould, *The Grateful Dead: The History of a Folk Story* (London: David Nutt, 1908). Thompson, by oversight, places Straparola's tale among those involving a tournament by which the bride is to be won, connecting it to the chivalric romance tradition going back to twelfth century France (probably too early by a century), and concludes that the tale 'hardly exists in oral tradition at all' (p. 52). Many elements of the Straparola tale resemble the narrative profiles of these romances, as described in the following pages, but there is no tournament; the princess is not won in that manner. She had already lived under Bertuccio's roof and had given him a sign whereby she would know him when he appeared at her father's court at the time of her betrothal to another. Finally, the recognition scene, the boy's two acts of charity, including rescuing a maiden from robbers, and other features of the story are abundantly represented in subsequent folk tales.

36 Valerius Maximus, *Memorable Deeds and Sayings*, trans. Henry John Walker (Indianapolis: Hackett Publishing, 2004), bk. I, 'Dreams,' Foreign Stories 7.3, p. 31. A Jewish version told centuries later is little more than an adaptation of the simple Simonides design, for there is no bride quest or other romance elements, but the

Indebted souls of the deceased will seek to aid their benefactors in times of equal distress.

The story form inherited by Straparola found prior expression in the chivalric Middle Ages in such tales as *Richars li Biaus, Lion de Bourges, Dianese, Rittertriuwe,* and *Sir Amadas,* each a testimonial to the existence of the folk tale upon which portions of its structure are based. The thirteenth-century romance *Richars li Biaus* tells of the many quests of a young knight, illegitimately born to a princess and abandoned in the woods, where he is found by a baron who raised him and later sent him into the world as an itinerant fortune-seeker in the tournament circuit of western Europe.[37] In the process, Richard 'the nameless' becomes Richard 'the handsome' (*biaus*). It is not until well into this sprawling and episodic tale that we find the present motif embedded. The hero is destined to compete for the proud daughter of the King of Montorgueil (Pridemountain), who is to be awarded to the victor of the tournament. But before he arrives, he enters a hostel, where he sees the body of a knight lying on two beams – a corpse five years unburied by reason of an unpaid debt of 3000 pounds to the host of the inn. Richard gives all he possesses to the greedy man to procure for the knight a suitable burial and in return receives from the innkeeper a pitiful mount on which he

---

simple quid pro quo of help for help. The young hero is carefully instructed day and night in his father's house from the Holy Word and becomes wise. But the father is concerned that he becomes equally sage in practical matters and clever business practices. That alone would make his heart glad. When the boy leaves Jerusalem for Constantinople he sees a man in chains, but is told not to meddle in Turkish secrets. The man was a Jewish merchant once in high esteem with the sultan who had now fallen from power and had been put to death. The boy asks the sum owing and arranges for the burial of the body. On the trip home there is a terrible storm. Alive but destitute, while weeping on the shore, he sees a white eagle, which speaks to him, takes him on its back, and returns him to his house in Jerusalem. Then he sees a man in white cloth who tells him not to fear, that he is the dead merchant who had already appeared to him as a plank and a bird, and that he would enrich him in the future if he kept the laws of Moses. It is a story of the obligations among co-religionists. Micha Josef Bin Gorion, 'Der dankbare Tote' (The grateful dead), in *Der Born Judas: Legenden, Märchen und Erzählungen* (Wiesbaden: Insel-Verlag, 1959), no. 319, pp. 739–42.

37 *Richars li Biaus, Roman inédit du XIIIe siècle,* ed. C.C. Casati (Paris: A. Franck, 1868). This same story is retold with minor variations as *Lion de Bourges,* for which, see *Manuscrits François de la bibliothèque du roi,* ed. Paulin Paris (Paris: Techener, 1840), vol. III, no. 1; *Lion de Bourges: Poème épique du XIVe* siècle, ed. William W. Kibler (Geneva: Droz, 1980). For a comparison of the two works, see Heinrich Wilhelmi, *Studien über die 'Chanson de Lion de Bourges'* (Marburg: R. Friedrich, 1894), pp. 43–63.

proceeds to the tournament. He is met along the way in a forest by a white knight who lends him his charger after they swear fealty to each other. Richard is fortunate in the games, winning many contests, yet he generously returns the forfeited booty to his defeated opponents. In the evenings there is feasting and an attractive girl begins to favour the victorious champion. When he is at last thrown from his horse, the white knight comes to his rescue, as he will in future episodes until the prize maiden is won. Once she is securely in his possession, however, Richard is reminded of his obligation to share all proceeds. Good to his word, though with sore regret, he offers his bride to the white knight for his many services. Only then does the mysterious friend explain that he is the dead knight, whereupon he bestows upon Richard all his worldly possessions and disappears, pronouncing the reassuring dictum that 'no noble deed is ever lost in the eyes of God.' The implications for our story are clear, for this inset piece, ensconced in a romance predating Straparola by three hundred years, follows a common narrative order, itself perhaps literary in origin, but ultimately based on a folk legend of the destitute fortune seeker abetted by a revenant knight with whom he enters into a pact to share the spoils of the games; such an adaptation would appear to push that specific tale's origins back to the early years of the second millennium.[38]

Several cognate romances, undoubtedly interrelated, confirm the place of the motif in the literature of the late Middle Ages. In *Rittertriuwe*, Count Willekin von Montabour on his way to a tournament was moved by compassion to spend all he possessed to pay the debts of a dead man whose body had been abandoned in the dung of a horse stall. Proceeding on a borrowed mount, he meets a stranger knight who lends him a proper horse for the joust if he agrees to split his earnings. Victory and marriage follow, and then the reckoning, when the stranger demands the wealth or the bride. Graf Willekin offers all his possessions and leaves in tears

---

38 With these romances, there is evidence not only of the early currency of 'the grateful dead' motif or theme, but of the tournament stories in which the hero is helped by the dead man's ghost. This is also a distinct type to which the Straparolan tale has been attached (see two notes above), but that, in fact, differs in several respects. Straparola's tale belongs rather to the rescued princess type, which is also subdivided between rescue from robbers (the present story) and rescue from slavery, culminating in an *anagnorisis* scene using signs, such as hand gestures (the present story), or tokens, such as rings or bits of embroidered cloth, whereby the hero is recognized by the liberated princess.

whereupon the stranger calls him back, revealing himself as the ghost of the dead man. In *Sir Amadas*, jousting is seen almost as an addiction as the venturer knights slowly impoverish themselves in travel and equipment in the pursuit of the big prizes. Sir Amadas, generous to a fault, sets forth to recover his lost fortunes by the only means he knows. He comes to a chapel with a woman inside who is weeping over a reeking corpse, that of an overly generous merchant whose creditors had stripped his house. Sir Amadas renders himself destitute in restoring her goods and burying the body at his own charge. Unable to keep his retainers, distressed and alone, he utters a long lament. Then he meets a stranger. They speak of a king and his fair daughter and the means to win her. Princely regalia is provided and they agree to meet later to share the profits between them. Many adventures ensue before the knight errant wins the princess and half the kingdom, and further time passes before the white knight comes to the palace asking for hospitality and his share in the spoils that now includes a wife and child. They were to be cleaved in half, as in the judgment of Solomon, but the denouement is that of a wraith satisfied and prepared to retire to eternal peace, leaving all to his one-time benefactor.[39]

---

39 *Rittertriuwe* is in Friedrich Heinrich von der Hagen, *Gesammtabenteuer*, 3 vols. (Stuttgart: Cotta, 1850), no. 6, a fourteenth-century poem in 866 lines, vol. I, pp. 105–28. *Sir Amadas* is found in *Early English Romances in Verse*, ed. Edith Rickert (New York: Cooper Square, 1967). This poem is an English middle-north metrical romance dating to the thirteenth century. In fact, it predates *Rittertriuwe*, and may predate *Richars* as well. George Stephens, its nineteenth-century editor, believed as much; his edition is entitled *Ghost-thanks; or, The grateful unburied; a mystic tale in its oldest European form*. Related to this work is *Sir Degarre*, found in the Auchinlech MS., ed. John W. Hales and Frederick James Furnivall, *Percy Folio Manuscripts: Ballads and Romances* (London: N. Trübner, 1867–8; reprint, Detroit: Singing Tree Press, 1968) no. III, pp. 16–48. There is a substantial number of studies on, and anthologies of, these late medieval romances. Some fifteen early representations of the *Märchentype* occur in *Erzählungen des späten mittelalters und ihr weiterleben in Literatur und Volksdichtung bis zur Gegenwart*, ed. Lutz Röhrich (Bern and Munich: Francke Verlag, 1967), vol. II, pp. 156–221, and commentary, pp. 438–6. Röhrich is in agreement that these tales go back to antiquity and originate in folk beliefs about the liberation of the soul that is possible only after proper burial and ceremonies, coupled with beliefs concerning the ability of the souls of the dead to help the living. See also Reinhold Köhler, 'Die dankbaren Toten und der gute Gerhard,' in *Kleinere Schriften zur Märchenforschung* (Weimar: Felber, 1898), vol. I, pp. 5–20; and Max Hippe, *Untersuchungen zu der mittelenglischen Romanze von Sir Amadas* (Braunschweig: G. Westermann, 1888).

Edmund Spenser may have been loosely indebted to this romance tradition for the story of Sir Sanglier and the Squire in his fifth book of the *Faerie Queene*. These men, disputing the possession of a lady, find themselves in the presence of Artegall, who must judge the truth of their claims and determine which of them is the lady's true lover. He employs the technique of Solomon in offering justice to both by severing the woman with a sword. It is little more to the point, for our purposes, that there were, in fact, two women, one alive and one dead, each to be severed – the one alive having been stolen from the Squire by the savage Wild-Boar knight. When Sir Sanglier consents and the erstwhile weeping Squire wishes her spared, Artegall condemns the former as the lady's murderer. The story, as a whole, is of a different order from the present one, and yet the phantom benefactor in the tradition of 'the grateful dead,' in demanding the severing of the wife, elicits one of two responses: acquiescence to the mutilation in the name of friendship, or tears and the sparing of the lady's life in the name of love. At the centre of both stories is the cleaving of the beloved wife as a test of the protagonist's conflicting values and obligations, and the prospect of tears as the double pledge of truth, both to love and to oaths made among men.[40]

Among the stories supplemental to *Le novelle antiche*, dating to the early fourteenth century, is the *novellino* of Dianese. It is the same story (with minor variations) of a spendthrift knight who is making his way to a tournament to compete for the king of Cornwall's daughter (Cornovaglia); the hero is already indebted to a friend for his equipage. He too encounters a stinking corpse lying in front of a church, that of an indebted knight. He turns over all but his horse to pay the creditors. Further along, he meets a merchant who will supply him with noble trappings in exchange for half of his earnings in the jousts. He does well enough in winning a lady and half a kingdom. Upon his return, the two men settle up and Dianese keeps only the lady. But the merchant overtakes him, divesting himself of his worldly goods in the hero's favour.[41] This is the work of a

---

40 *The Faerie Queene, Book Five*, ed. Abraham Stoll (Indianapolis: Hackett Publishing, 2006), V.i.13–30, pp. 11–16.

41 'Di messer Dionese e di messer Gigliotto,' in *Le novelle antiche dei Codici Panciatichiano-Palatino 138*, intro. Guido Biagi (Florence: G.C. Sansoni, 1880), no. 154, pp. 190–8. This has been separately edited by Alessandro d'Ancona and Giovanni Sforza as the *La novella di Messer Dianese e di Messer Gigliotto* (Pisa: Tipografia Nistri, 1868). There is an early Swedish version in which the protagonist is Pippin, duke of Lorraine, who buries a poor widow's husband, then makes the

master storyteller who closes with the merchant's celebration of the hero
of perfect honesty and self-mastery in a crescendo of sobriety and piety.
This story and its literary cognates are clearly indebted to a story tradition
characterized by the same core narrative as that collected by Straparola
more than two centuries later, except that Straparola's hero is also called
upon to ransom and care for the princess he is later to win through an
elaborate selection process. There is no tournament, but rather a romantic
reunion for which the dead man supplies the princely trappings.

The antiquity of the story type is demonstrated by its adaptation and
disfiguration in *The Book of Tobit,* to be found among the books of the
Christian Apocrypha.[42] It deals with the duty of tithes, the sacred right
of the dead to burial, as well as the poisoned maiden. Tobit, the father
of Tobias, buries by night at his own expense a dead body lying in the
street. Later Tobias, in the company of his kinsman Azariah, makes a
journey to collect money for his father. Far from home, he is introduced
to the beautiful Sara, whom he desires in marriage, even though seven
of her former bridegrooms had already forfeited their lives to her deadly
charms. Azariah, the angel Raphael in disguise, gives some useful advice
and offers his spiritual powers. By burning the heart and liver of the fish
that Tobias had captured on the way (his would-be animal helper), and
by prayer, the demon Asmodeus is driven out of Sara's body and bound

---

wager to share earnings with a man he meets along the way. He too is forced to
offer his bride or his kingdom to the stranger before having all restored by him
as the ghost of the dead man. *Ett Forn-Svenskt Legendarium,* ed. George Stephens
(Stockholm: P.A. Nordstedt & Son, 1858), vol. II, pp. 731*ff.* The source is medieval,
perhaps as early as the thirteenth century; its precise relationship to 'Dianese' is
in need of examination. Their close affinity is nevertheless manifest. See also
Novellino e conti del duecento, ed. Sebastiano Lo Nigro (Turin: Unione tipografico-
editrice, 1968), no. XVIII, pp. 402–9, which also contains a transcription of the
Panciatichiano 32 manuscript (1330–40).

42 'Tobit,' in *The Septuagint with Apocrypha: Greek and English,* trans. Sir Lancelot
Charles Lee Brenton (Peabody, MA: Hendrickson Publishers [1851], 1986). This
book of the Old Testament Apocrypha was never accepted into the Jewish canon,
but was adopted by Christians at the Council of Carthage in 397. It survives in some
30 manuscripts in five languages, the Greek versions almost certainly written in
Egypt in the second century. But many scholars believe the work to be older, from
further East, and to have been composed in a Semitic language, with estimates
going as far back as the second or third century B.C. One might wonder whether
those present at the council in 397 would have been so enthusiastic if they had
known that the Holy Spirit disseminated His plenary inspiration among the dozens
of folk raconteurs who begat this yarn.

by the archangel. This is a version of the toxic-maiden tales in which the bride, through rites and quests, is freed from a venomous curse.[43] Upon their return, the blind Tobit is cured by the gall of the same magic fish. Azariah, meanwhile, is offered half the wealth he has helped them gain, but then reveals his true identity and disappears. Clearly evident is the mysterious helper in a bride-quest tale who cedes his part in the winnings. But the story is garbled in several ways, for according to the folk tradition, that role should have been played by the soul of the dead man, who, in a related way, should also have helped Tobias capture the elixir of life. But the transmutation into a religious fable of an angel casting out demons no doubt accounts for the story's survival among the books of the apocrypha. The potion able to cure blindness is proof that by so early a date, the story of the grateful dead was attached not only to a bride-quest tale ('the monster in the bridal chamber' or 'the toxic maiden'), but to a form of the water of life tale in which sons seek a healing potion for their father ('the two brothers'), the successful one helped by an animal containing the soul of the dead.[44] Even though this narrative is a clumsy adaptation – Azariah the helper is not the soul of the dead, nor does he expect a share in the spoils – its principal elements are clearly derived from a tale made known by its hundreds of successors, for accepting the postulate that no such configuration of motifs is ever likely to arise twice, there is near certainty that the folk tradition that

---

43 The generic tale, of which this is a corruption in order to reflect Hebraic values and demon possession, is called 'the monster in the bridal chamber' (ATU 507B), in which bridegrooms are killed one after the other when a dragon enters the room, or issues from the princess's mouth. These tales also begin with the ransoming and burial of a corpse, gaining for the hero a helper able to dispel the toxins or vanquish the demon by killing it outright, or treating the body of the princess in which it dwells. The motif of separating the princess by the sword as a settling of a pact may have originated in the dissection of the princess to liberate her from the monster. This is, in turn, related to the breaking of an enchantment by beheading various animals in which humans are held captive. In certain of the stories the dragon is inside the woman, necessitating that a micro–dragon slaying be enacted by severing the heads as they appear from her mouth. In this regard, *The Book of Tobit*, though the earliest of the literary manifestations of the tale of 'the grateful dead,' is, in its other folk affiliations, remote from Straparola. It is an early adaptation of the 'monster in the bridal chamber' type.

44 Gordon Hall Gerould in *The Grateful Dead: The History of a Folk Story* (The Folk-Lore Society, 1907; reprint, Nendeln: Kraus Reprints, 1967), pp. 46–75, provides an outline of the many variants of the poison-maiden tradition, which is a specific branch of the folk tale.

gave narrative instruction to *The Book of Tobit* is the same that informed the medieval romances discussed above and all subsequent versions.[45]

It would be supererogation to dwell here on the theme of the poisonous bride, abandoned by Straparola, his sources, and the whole of the early romance tradition. But it appears to represent a deep-seated fear in almost symmetrical relation to the compulsive fear of corpses and the necessity of burying dead bodies. The curse of the dead is accompanied by the curse of the fatal bride, necessitating the magic rights whereby the female body is made fit for local habitation.[46] But the motif was by no means extinguished from the folk record by Straparola's time. George Peele's *The Old Wives' Tale*, first published in quarto by John Danter in 1595, and written no more than a half decade earlier, is a curious amalgamation of folk-tale motifs that are staged as the dramatized representations of tales told by the matrons of the labouring classes to while away the long evenings. Among them is the story of Eumenides the wandering knight and his love for Delia. Erestus, the mysterious senex of the cross (ways), pronounces such enigmatic lines to Eumenides as 'Bestow thy alms, give more than all, Till dead men's bones come at they call' (ll. 516–17), a foreshadowing of the role of the grateful dead. In a moment of despair, with but a few scattered pence to his name, Jack, who is now but a ghost of himself, reminds the hero of his expense in burying a poor man and asks to be his servant. He then runs ahead to the inn to command their

---

45 *The Book of Tobit, a Chaldee Text from a unique MS. in the Bodleian Library*, ed. Adolf Neubauer (Oxford: Clarendon Press, 1878). Neubauer dates the text to the time of Hadrian, p. xvii.

46 The motif of the poisoned maiden is an open invitation to the mytho-psychological hermeneutes to furnish us with major insights into the 'primitive' perceptions of the dangerous female, with all the attendant male fantasies concerning basilisk eyes, death-dealing beauty, castration worries, and biting vaginas to be dispelled prior to cohabitation. Why not? The stories are, after all, about something. Not to be resisted here is mention of Machiavelli's *Mandragola* (ca. 1518), in which the would-be seducer of the beautiful Lucrezia convinces the sterile couple that they will have children only if the wife agrees to consume prepared mandrake root, despite its unfortunate property of killing the first man to make love to the recipient. Thereafter, the husband and wife are brought to agree to the murder of a detoxifying male agent chosen at random in the streets, by prearrangement to be no other than the lover-doctor. That it is all a ruse does not discount the reference to Lucrezia as the toxic maiden who by congress fatal to the lover is alone made fertile. Strange fantasy; brilliant play. You can read all about it in *Renaissance Comedy: The Italian Masters*, ed. Donald Beecher (Toronto: University of Toronto Press, 2009), vol. II, pp. 101–62.

supper. Jack then fills the knight's purse with money by magic and asks if he will go halves in all he earns on his journey, and with that they shake hands. Along the way, Jack gives counsel and arranges for the breaking of the conjurer's magic glass that keeps a multitude enthralled, including Delia's brothers. After Eumenides has met and won the lady for whom he has travelled so far, Jack demands his part: 'Why, then, master, draw your sword, part your lady, let me have half of her presently' (ll. 1028–30). Delia has herself been liberated of a potion given to her by the evil Sacrapant, an allusion to the poisoned maiden, and in a parallel episode, two sisters proceed to the well of the water of life. The hero, in offering to sever his beloved, passes the test and Jack recedes into a shade. Among so many fragments is to be imagined the complete tale of the questing knight, the crossroads, the mysterious companion, the provisions for winning a princess, her detoxification, the pact, the near severing of the bride, and the revenant's release.[47] Peele's play is a rare testimonial to the currency of the tale in England as part of the popular culture – tales told by the likes of Madge on winter evenings.

Straparola's tale is not that of a wandering knight but of a simple boy under a widowed mother's guardianship who tests her son's financial acumen by giving 'talents,' as it were, from his inheritance to see what returns he might bring with them. That social level also has Latin literary antecedents, as in Story 474 of Jean Gobi's fourteenth-century anthology of vignettes, *La scala coeli*, which features Nicholas, the only child of a widow. He is sent out with fifty pounds to do business, but he spends them entirely upon the restoration of the church of St Nicholas. With another one hundred pounds he redeems a sultan's daughter. His mother is furious and sends him away with the desire that he never return. The sultan's daughter, precisely like her Straparolan counterpart, neither identifies herself nor seeks to return home, but supports the two of them with her embroidery. When Nicholas sets off to sell her handiwork in Alexandria, she even warns him to keep far from the palace. Nevertheless, in due course her work is recognized, she is sought out and seized,

---

47 'The Old Wives Tale,' in *English Drama 1580–1642*, ed. C.F. Tucker Brooke and Nathaniel B. Paradise (Boston: D.C. Heath and Co., 1933), pp. 23–37. For a study of the play's folklore, see Sarah Lewis Carol Clapp, 'Peele's Use of Folk-Lore in *The Old Wive's Tale*,' *University of Texas Studies in English*, 6 (1926), pp. 146–56. The play is also in the third volume of *The Life and Works of George Peele*, ed. Charles Tyler Prouty (New Haven: Yale University Press, 1970), and in numerous anthologies of Elizabethan plays.

and the young hero is left forlorn. But she sends to him by stealth a bit of her work, hinting at how they might escape by sea. The two stories are rejoined when St Nicholas himself, in gratitude for the boy's initial sacrifice, provides the ship. In this manner, the order of the narrative is maintained as an episode in the life of the saint. Even so, the substance of an underlying folk tale closely cognate with Straparola's remains visible.[48] The group featuring a ransomed princess seems to have developed in parallel with the poisoned-damsel group, but according to Gordon Gerould there are no versions showing a transition from one to the other.[49] The separation of the two from the 'home' type took place well before the fourteenth century.

This version of the story enjoyed a long career in England as a chapbook, beginning presumably as a Renaissance ballad or broadside bearing some such name as 'The Factor's Garland' or 'The Turkish Lady.'[50]

---

48 Jean Gobi, *La scala coeli*, ed. Marie-Anne Polo de Beaulieu (Paris: Édition du Centre Nationale de la Recherche Scientifique, 1991), pp. 362–3. Much of this story is replicated in the sixteenth-century Portuguese tale by Trancoso in which a merchant's son buys relics of a Christian saint in Fez, which renders his father furious. But he continues to redeem the bones of saints from the hands of infidels on subsequent trips (which he also sells for high prices). Then he ransoms a Christian girl who embroiders in cloth her story and asks the hero to take it to the king of England. She is returned to her family, but the hero mourns her loss. Two minstrels accompany him to the English court and through music they reveal the hero's presence (the equivalent of the hand signal in the present story), and aid him further in winning a tournament. These minstrels were the saints of the ransomed bones. But many of the conventional parts have now been transformed. Tournaments, saints' lives, and the Straparolan narrative of the boy and the liberated princess are joined together. Gonçalo Fernandez Trancoso, *Contos e historias de proveito e exemplo* (Lisbon [1575], 1693), pt. II, conti 1, pp. 45r–60r.

49 *The Grateful Dead: The History of a Folk Story* (London: David Nutt, 1908), p. 117.

50 *The Factor's Garland in Four Parts* (Edinburgh: Printed and sold by R. Drummond in Swan-Close, 1746). If Gerould's initial orientation in his study of 'the grateful dead' story tradition is an examination of 'the poison damsel' fables, for Karl Josef Simrock it is an inquest into the 'maiden ransom' stories. They represent two major streams of tales in which 'the grateful dead' framing and helper mechanisms have become traditional. There are, of course, many 'maiden ransom' tales without this mechanism, including all of the St George and the dragon-slaying stories. Simrock's is the first major investigation into the type, based mostly on Germanic sources such as 'Der gute Gerhard.' Hippe (see the note above on 'Sir Amadas') extended the range of sampled materials and came far closer to a sense of the 'Ur-type,' namely, the 'grateful dead' motif disentangled from all the surrounding material. *Der gute Gerhard und die dankbaren Todten: Ein Beitrag zur deutschen mythologie und Sagenkunde* (Bonn: Adolf Marcus, 1856).

The story remained in circulation until the early nineteenth century. An English merchant, after squandering most of his estate, joined a merchant embassy to Turkey. There he paid fifty pounds to bury the body of a Christian abandoned in the streets, then liberated a Christian slave and made her his housekeeper. When he enters the court of her father wearing a waistcoat of her embroidering, however, the prince recognizes his daughter's work and promises her in marriage to the man who should return her. But the merchant is betrayed and cast overboard by the ship's captain. The old man who rescues him in a small boat bargains in return for the merchant's firstborn child. In later years, that promise is kept – the distraught but loyal father offers up his child – whereupon the old man's identity is revealed as that of the corpse buried at the merchant's expense.[51] This textual tradition is an afterglow to Gobi, but represents the tale without the overlay of the saint's life. Meanwhile, its relationship to Straparola is not far removed, for the substitutions separating them through the operations of folk narrators are well within calculation. The romance element has driven the amalgamation of motifs – the intervention of the dead and the long-suffering courtship of a royal maiden. That nucleus is already clear in Straparola.

Mention must be made in passing of two further exemplifications of the story type before turning to the after-life of the folk tale: *Olivier de Castille et Artus d'Algarbe* and *Jean de Calais*. *Olivier* is a French prose romance written before 1472 and first printed in Geneva in 1482. Three contemporary manuscripts survive in Paris, Brussels, and Ghent. The work was translated into English for publication by Wynkyn de Worde

---

51 A nineteenth-century folk tale from the Germanic world bears many of the same features, telling of the merchant who sends his son to trade in the East, warning him never to buy human flesh. In Turkey, however, he sees the body of a black slave and buries it at his own cost, which so angers the father that he vows never to send him again. On a second mission, he sells the ship to free a woman with whom he returns. They have a son. Then, other adventures befall the hero, while the soul of the black man hovers in the background mistaken for a devil. When the child reaches his twelfth birthday, the devil appears at midnight at the tower window threatening to take the boy, only to explain that he is the tutelary soul of the black man buried in Turkey. The correspondences are striking. Johann Wilhelm Wolf, 'Des Todten-Dank,' in *Deutsche Hausmärchen* (Göttingen: Dieterich'sche Buchhandlung, 1851), pp. 243–50; republished (Hildesheim: Georg Olms, 1972).

in 1518.[52] The Spanish translation became the basis for Lope de Vega's play *Don Juan de Castro*, published in his *Comedias* in 1623, with a sequel entitled *Las aventuras de Don Juan de Alarcos*. The work features a compound plot that integrates 'the grateful dead' with 'the two brothers' in which one brother reads the distress of the other in a vial of water and, as in the combined 'dragon slayer–three brothers' group (see 'Cesarino,' X.3), must avoid sleeping with his lookalike brother's wife. Talbot, his friend, dies in Canterbury and is buried at Olivier's expense. He becomes the tournament knight who fosters the hero in later times. When he demands his half of the spoils, Olivier too raises the sword over his wife's body to keep the bargain. Leading up to that finale is the double imprisonment through which Olivier and Arthur, close childhood friends, come to each other's aid. This is among the most elaborate of the integrations of 'the grateful dead' motif into the open-ended structures of late medieval romance, drawing together elements, in eclectic fashion, from several of the folk traditions.

Jean de Calais, despite its many concordances with the Straparola tale, must be given cursory treatment, given its many published variants. Characteristic of them all is an act of charity on the part of the son of a rich Calais merchant who buries the corpse of a man killed by dogs. He then ransoms two slave girls and marries one of them. He is separated from her and helped by the ghost to reclaim her. In later years, in accordance with the letter of an initial agreement between man and ghost, the latter returns to claim his half of the couple's son. When the boy is given up, the bond is complete, the hero's loyalty is praised, and the child is restored.[53] In the version by Angélique de Gomen (1723), based on the

---

52 Of the first English edition, only one copy survives, most recently edited by Gail Margaret Orgelfinger, *The hystorye of Olyver of Castylle* (New York: Garland, 1988), but known to me in the edition printed in London by Blades, East and Blades for the Roxburghe Club in 1898. The translator was Henry Watson. The original French work is available on microfilm, but seems to enjoy no modern edition, although a critical edition was made of it by Danielle Régnier-Bohler as a dissertation for the University of Paris-Sorbonne, no date given. For the Spanish edition, see *Text and Concordance of Historia de los nobles cavalleros Oliveros de Castilla y Artus d'Algarbe* (Burgos, 1499), ed. Ivy A. Corfis (Madison, WI: Hispanic Seminary of Medieval Studies, 1996). The most accessible English version is taken from the German translation of the French by William Leighton and Eliza Barrett, *The History of Oliver and Arthur* (Cambridge, MA: Riverside Press, 1903).

53 Among the many early editions is *Histoire de Jean de Calais sur de nouveaux mémoires* (Liège: F.J. Desoer, 1789).

Histoire fabuleuse de la maison des rois de Portugal, the slave girl rescued is the daughter of the king. As she is being returned, the hero is betrayed by a treacherous general. Only through many adventures, with the help of a revenant companion, are the lovers reunited. In the seventh version of the ten considered by Gordon Gerould, the hero is a boy whose mother is angry with him for squandering his money on burying the dead and ransoming girls.[54] This protagonist marries the girl, then goes to Portugal with her portrait, a handkerchief, and a ring to prove her identity. This boy is likewise thrown overboard by a general, but he swims to an island where he is counselled by a fox. The transformation is telling, for it draws this story structure into close proximity with all those in which foxes, cats, even bears, become the representative forms of the grateful dead. The fateful bargain is now driven with an animal, so that once the boy prevails, it is the fox that demands its part, then retreats into the shades of death. This story remains in the Straparola group by dint of its conflation of the burial of a stranger and the rescuing of a maiden followed by the application of benefits from the first tale towards the completion of the romance.

The story type represented in the *Piacevoli notti* finds representation in after years in all parts of Europe and beyond, as distinct from 'the water of life' group ('the two brothers'), 'the poisoned maiden' group, 'the tournament champion' group, and those in which synthesis and *contaminatio* begin to blur the categories. These folk tales, as catalogued by Gordon Gerould in his bibliography, number in the hundreds, and potentially in the thousands, having as their only common denominator the burial of an exposed body and the return of its ghost in aid of the benefactor. Collectively, they provide a lesson in the compository capacities of the folk mind and the recombinant potential in story memes. One similar to Straparola's in design nevertheless manifests the many features of a local culture. In an Icelandic tale, Prince Thorsteinn has wasted all his resources and must abandon his realm to seek his fortune in the world.[55] With all that remains to him, he pays a rich sum to prevent creditors from disturbing the peace of a deceased man by beating on his grave. Further along, in the castle of a giant, he liberates a princess hanging by her hair, then loses her to Raudr, one of her suitors, who sends

---

54 Gordon Hall Gerould, *The Grateful Dead* (London: David Nutt, 1908), pp. 99–101.
55 *Icelandic Legends,* ed. Jón Arnason, trans. George E.J. Powell and Eiríker Magnússon (London: Longmans, Green and Co., 1866), pp. 527–40.

Thorsteinn out to sea in a rudderless boat. Exposure on water is a feature
in common with the *Olivier* and *Jean de Calais* groups, as well as the hidden signs by which the hero lets the princess know of his return. He had
been rescued by the ghost of the dead man who returns him to the palace, where he takes lowly employment in the stables under the tutelage
of his helper. In the end, Raudr, as in the 'dragon slayer' stories (X.3),
is punished as a treacherous interloper and the girl is handed over to
the partner she desires. This is a folk tale that conceivably reflects literary
sources, but may as easily be an adaptation of the folk tradition that
remained current through those same centuries.

Coming now to the hundreds of tales collected in the nineteenth and
early twentieth centuries, there are many ways to turn. Of principal interest is the survival of the Straparolan type, sustained by folk raconteurs
in parallel with the many others dealing with the questing brothers, the
youngest helped by a white fox or bear in gratitude for the boy's former
sacrifices, as well as the tales of poisoned maidens and tournament
knights. There are even versions that take on the shape of the wild men
stories who act as helpers to their young benefactors, as well as those who
resemble the fox or cat helpers in tales in which an impoverished ward is
clothed and equipped, as in the preceding tale of 'Costantino Fortunato.'
In a Danish version, a boy pays all the money he possesses to bury a dead
man. He is later joined by another youth – the form taken by the ghost –
who becomes his companion and advises the boy to style himself a prince,
provides him with the requisite clothing, and helps him win a princess.[56]

Of the many that I read, I have chosen the following four to represent
the range of variations upon the theme of the boy sent into the world to
manage his resources who bestows all instead for the burial of the dead
and the rescuing of maidens. In a story told by Turkish gypsies, the three
sons of the king enter the world, the two elder boys building ships and
shops, while the youngest pays for the marriages of poor girls. He then
buys a dead body to protect it from the abuse of creditors. This dead
man follows him directly, becomes his guide, and finds for the prince
a beautiful girl, although a dragon comes out of her mouth – clearly
another poisoned maiden. As the dragon's sundry heads appear, the

---

56 Svend H. Grundtvig, 'Det fattige Lig' (The poor corpse), in *Gamle Danske Minder i
Folkemunde* (Copenhagen: n.p., 1854–61), pp. 77–80.

companion cuts them off one by one. The prince becomes the first of her husbands to survive the night. Ultimately the two companions come to the matter of sharing the spoils and the prince sees no equitable solution but to sever the girl with his sword, whereupon the dead man calls out to desist, having seen in the intended gesture his kindness repaid.[57] This tale shows a considerable degree of *contaminatio* in beginning with the king's three sons who learn skills or professions, as in 'The Three Brothers' (VII.5), giving way to the burial and rescue features in common with Straparola, leading to the poisoned-maiden plot, before concluding with the kindness contest. Clearly, the types were known concurrently within single cultures and were subject to amalgamations of many kinds.

The second, from Pröhle's *Kinder- und Volksmärchen*, is rather more familiar, despite its many imaginative substitutions.[58] A merchant's son leaves home and finds himself involved in a number of strange adventures. He encounters a wounded man on the plains who later dies in hospital, the hero covering all his expenses. Then he rescues two young women victimized by a robbery at sea, and on the way home places a ring on the hand of the more beautiful of the two. Upon his arrival, he incurs the wrath of his father, but the boy's relationship to the girl survives and a child is born to them, whereupon it is revealed that the mother is the daughter of a king. With that turn of events, the boy finds himself once again in his father's favour. When the young husband decides to visit the girl's father, however, she agrees only if he follows her specific instructions, providing him in the process with a red silk banner bearing her name. This he was to wear aboard the ship and place high on the mast upon his arrival. The king is thus alerted and welcomes the young man to his court, where he is lavished with gifts for the return trip with an invitation for the entire family to come to court. On the second voyage, however, the first minister throws the husband overboard, makes a false declaration, and lays plans to marry the sorrowing wife. The hero makes his way to shore, sleeps off his fatigue, and is awakened by a huge form

---

57 Francis Hindes Groome, 'The Dead Man's Gratitude' in *Gypsy Folk Tales* (London: Herbert Jenkins [1899], 1963), pp. 1–4.

58 Heinrich Pröhle, 'Die rothe Fahne und der Ring der Königstochter' (The red silk banner and the king's daughter's ring) in *Kinder- und Volksmärchen* (Hildesheim: Georg Olms, 1975), no. 78; originally published in Leipzig (Avenarius & Mendelssohn, 1853).

asking the young man if he recognizes him. It is the revenant soul of the dead, to be sure, there to help him. By shining the light from his ring into the palace and spelling his wife's name, he is recognized and welcomed, the family is reunited, and the minister is quartered by oxen. This is the fate of the imposter in the 'dragon slaying' group (X.3). Although there is no contest over the spoils between the hero and the dead man, Straparola's story remains visible in the opening acts of burying the dead and rescuing victims of robbery, passing through the water rescue motifs of the romances, to the recognition scene by which the estranged lovers are reunited.

In a truly novel elaboration upon the motif, a young boy is sold to a pasha and thereafter wins the love and allegiance of his daughter.[59] There are objections, to be sure, and he is sent away to become a shepherd, but he remains near the palace, and the girl is able to give him her ring in a cup. When a second suitor appears – another pasha's son – the princess insists upon a period of trial. Both are sent into the world to seek their fortunes. The pasha's son wastes his in the city, but the shepherd boy meets an old man who teaches him how to make an eye-healing salve from monkeys' brains, with which he becomes vastly wealthy. Both suitors hasten back to court, accompanied by the old man, just in time to prevent the girl's marriage to a third. The ring becomes the object by which her true beloved is identified and the wedding is at last celebrated. Then the old man arrives to demand his half of the bride through physical severance. The hero agrees, but on what basis we may well demand. This mysterious helper professes to be God Himself who has come to the boy's aid because his father had sold him in order to pay for the burning lamp offered to a saint – a story redolent of those in which the hero offers money to rebuild churches dedicated to a saint. Low birth and high compete for the princess, and the one less favoured achieves his end, not only by winning the love of the girl, but by advancing his fortunes through skill and the aid of a divine being repaying an act of charity that, like Tobit to Tobias, has passed from generation to generation.

The final example of this widely diffused story comes from East Prussia, 'Of the Prince Who Escaped Hanging' (Vom Prinzen, der gehängt

---

59 Johann Georg von Hahn, 'Belohnte Treue' (Goodness rewarded) in *Griechische und albanesische Märchen* (Leipzig: Wilhelm Engelmann, 1864), no. 53, vol. I, pp. 288–95.

werden sollte).[60] This is the story of a boy cursed at birth by a witch; he was to be hanged when he reached the age of nineteen. When the boy comes to understand the silly precautions his parents have been taking on his behalf, he laughs and leaves home. He is captured by pirates and taken over the sea, meanwhile dreaming that he will find a body that he must bury. When he jumps ship in a strange land, this very circumstance comes to pass. Once in the city he takes employment with a merchant, marries his daughter, sets up a household, and lives happily until his nineteenth birthday. Then three black forms appear in his room and prepare to take him up – but there is a white form beside them – the buried man. So they all fight till the magic hour has passed and the Evil can no longer touch him. Then they all disappear. Two servingmaids have witnessed everything, happy to see the return of daylight and the arrival of their mistress. When it is known that her husband is a prince, she fears abandonment, but the prince reassures her of his love and they return to the land of his parents. Just how far we have come from the tradition reconfirmed by Straparola is manifest and beyond need of commentary; the variants speak for themselves. His was but one of the many folk tales in which the revenant as the helper of heroes engineers the reversal of fortunes.

A final and extensive gallery of tales attached to the motif of 'the grateful dead' is worth mention, namely, that of the brothers who go in search of a healing potion for their father and in the process become the enemy to the youngest, who is rescued by a totem animal inhabited

---

60 Elisabeth Lemke, *Volkstümliches in Ostpreussen* (Mohrungen: Harich, 1884), pt. II, pp. 88–92. See also Ulrich Jahn, 'Der Schiffer und die drei Königstöchter von Engelland' (The ship's captain and the three daughters of the king of England) in *Volksmärchen aus Pommern und Rügen* (Hildesheim: Georg Olms [1891], 1973), no. 34, pp. 182–9. In this story a shipmaster arranges for the burial of a man hanging from a gibbet with carrion birds hacking at his face. This man's ghost later rescues him after he is thrown overboard and reunites him with his wife. There are two further tales, both entitled 'Le mort reconaissant' (The grateful dead), nos. 26 and 41, bearing resemblances to Straparola's tale, in James Bruyn Andrews, *Contes ligures, traditions de la rivière recueillis entre Menton et Gênes* (Paris: Ernest Leroux, 1892), pp. 111–16, 187–92. In relation to the Grimm Brothers' tales, Johannes Bolte and Jiří Polívka have a great deal to add about the tradition of 'the grateful dead' stories in their *Anmerkungen zu den Kinder- und Hausmärchen der Brüder Grimm* (Hildesheim: Georg Olms, 1963): 'Der dankbare Töte und die aus der Sklaverei erlöste Königstochter' (The grateful dead and the king's daughter rescued from slavery), vol. III, pp. 490–517.

by the soul of a dead man grateful to the hero for his burial. This rescue
enables the boy to return to court with the water or potion he has struggled so arduously to bring back. These stories tend to build by accretion
and can be drawn out to considerable length by adding episodes of failure and further adventure, all under the admonishing eye of a guardian
animal. Those itemized in the bibliographical note attached here are
but a few of the many.[61]

In his version of 'the grateful dead,' Straparola has landed by choice
or chance upon a folk tale containing a representative example of one
of the most enduring of all story motifs. Its understated and workmanlike

---

61 Emmanuel Cosquin collected the story of 'Le petit bossu' for his *Contes populaires de
   Lorraine*, 2 vols. (Paris: F. Vieweg, ca. 1887), no. 19, vol. I, pp. 208–12, which provides
   a paradigmatic version upon which he bases his extensive historical commentary
   (pp. 13–22), one that begins in the study of 'the grateful dead' motif by Theodor
   Benfey in his commentaries on the *Pantschatantra ... aus dem Sanscrit*, 5 vols.
   (Leipzig: F.A. Brockhaus, 1859), vol. I, p. 221 and vol. II, p. 532. Another such tale,
   'Le merle blanc,' occurs in Wentworth Webster, *Légendes Basques*, trans. Nicolas
   Burguete (Anglet: Aubéron, 2005), pp. 247–52; originally, *Basques Legends* (London:
   Griffith & Ferran, 1877). The white bird that will heal the father's sight has many
   counterparts, as in the bird 'Drédaigne.' The fox is the third brother's helper
   against the treachery of the two older brothers, the ghost of the grateful dead man.
   For the quest of the bird 'Drédaigne,' see J.-F. Luzel, 'La princesse Marcassa et
   l'oiseau Drédaine' in *Contes populaires de la Basse-Bretagne*, ed. Françoise Morvan,
   3 vols. (Rennes: Presses Universitaires de Rennes, 1996), vol. II, pp. 131–43. In no. 7,
   'La princesse de Hongrie,' vol. II, pp. 155–69, the third son is again a hunchback
   rejected by the others who succeeds in his quest, buries a corpse, is served by a
   white-tailed fox as the ghost of the deceased, and eventually returns after many
   adventures. See also Gherardo Nerucci, 'La Regina Marmotto' in *Sessanta novelle
   popolari montalesi* (Milan: Rizzoli, 1977), no. 46, pp. 371–85. This is a particularly
   complex version about the multiple quests of the three sons of the king of Spain.
   Guillaume Spitta-Bey, 'Histoire du rossignol chanteur' (Story of the singing
   nightingale) in *Contes arabes modernes* (Leiden: E.J. Brill, 1883), pp. 125–36. Patrick
   Kennedy, 'The Greek Princess and the Young Gardener' in *The Fireside Stories of
   Ireland* (Dublin: McGlashan and Gill, 1870; reprint, Norwood, PA: Norwood
   Editions, 1975), pp. 47–56. Only the third son in this quest nurtures the fox and so
   gains the guide needed to overcome all the many complex obstacles in winning the
   princess, defeating his jealous brothers, and healing his father with the gold-
   feathered bird. In this tale the fox, beheaded, becomes a prince, as in certain of the
   'puss in boots' tales. It follows the stories of 'the three brothers' group associated,
   through the helper figure, with 'the grateful dead' group, except that in this version
   that motif has been dropped and the story drifts in a new direction. Johann Georg
   von Hahn, 'Der Zauberspiegel' (The magic mirror) in *Griechische und albanesische
   Märchen*, 2 vols (Leipzig: Wilhelm Engelmann, 1864), no. 51, vol. I, pp. 284–6.

presentation is certain assurance that it resembles the folk source from which it was transcribed, for there is no indication that it was distilled from any of the remote literary analogues. Nevertheless, those antecedent representations in the romances provide an equivalent assurance that the generic tale upon which Straparola based himself stretched back through the Middle Ages to antiquity, presumably in an unbroken chain of storytelling.

XI. Fable 3
Wind, Water, and Shame,
or the Gluttony of Dom Pomporio

DIANA

Dom Pomporio, a monk, is charged before his abbot with excessive gluttony, but saves himself from punishment by telling a fable that touches rather pointedly the weaknesses of the abbot himself.

It would have been my preference to have been excused this evening from the burden of telling a fable, because the truth is I can't recall a single one that's likely to please you. But in order not to break the rules we've been following so far, I'll do my best to tell you one that may at least be worth listening to, even though you won't gain much pleasure from it.

At a time now long past there lived in a famous monastery a certain monk who was of a mature age and a man of renown, but a huge eater. He even boasted that with no trouble at all he could down a well-fatted quarter of veal at a single sitting with a pair of capons tossed in for good measure. This formidable feeder – Dom Pomporio by name – had a deep platter that in jest he called his oratory of devotion, capacious enough to hold seven good ladlefuls of soup. In excess of his daily allowance of food, he would brim up this bowl, both at dinner and supper, with broth or soup and consume the lot without spilling a single drop. Besides this, whatever was left on the plates of the other monks, however much or little, was garnered to the glory of his oratory and consumed in sacred devotion. He didn't care a whit whether such provender was mushy and foul; not a scrap was unfit for his chapel, every one of which he devoured like a famished wolf. The other brothers in the monastery, seeing such unbridled gluttony and inordinate capacity, were scandalized by his vulgar and contemptible ways. But their frequent remonstrations, whether gentle or sharp, were to no avail. The more they busied themselves in trying to improve his unsavoury ways, the more scraps he heaped onto his prayer platter, oblivious entirely to their words of advice or blame. But I shouldn't forget to explain that this piggish monk had one solitary virtue: he never lost his temper. No matter how harsh the words his fellows might hurl at him, they never aroused in him the least spite or animosity.

Then it came about one day that the brothers carried an accusation against him to the father abbot, who, as soon as he heard the charges, had him summoned into his presence, where he said to him, 'Dom Pomporio, there has been placed before me the testimony of your fellow monks concerning your behaviour, which is not only a crying shame to you but a cause of scandal throughout the monastery.'

To this speech Dom Pomporio made his reply. 'Tell me the charges that my accusers lay against me. I'm the meekest and most peacefully-minded monk living in your monastery. I never interfere with anyone or cause any disturbance at all, preferring to spend my days in tranquillity. If I should happen to receive some injury at the hands of another, I bear my trouble patiently and never make a kerfuffle over it.'

Then the abbot said, 'But does this seem to you to be a decent and laudable thing? You have a certain trencher you use, not like a respectable monk, but like a dirty, stinking pig. Over and above your own allowance of food, you gather into it all the leftovers of the brethren, all of which you belt down without shame or a second thought, not like a human being who has sworn religious vows, but like some ravenous wild animal. Gross beast and useless lout that you are, can't you see that all the others in the monastery look at you like a buffoon?'

Dom Pomporio answered, 'So what's the reason I should be ashamed, good father abbot? Where in all the world is there any shame to be found nowadays, and who has any fear or respect for it? If you'll give me permission to speak my mind freely and without fear of consequences, I'll answer you. But if you refuse me this favour, I'll simply obey you and keep silence.'

'Well, say whatever you like,' said the abbot. 'I'm willing to listen to you.'

Dom Pomporio, reassured by these words, offered him the following. 'Father abbot, truly we are like those men who carry baskets upon their own backs, so that we can see what lies upon our neighbour's shoulders, but not what lies upon our own. If I had the chance to fill my belly with rich and delicate food in the manner of those who sit in high places, I'd surely eat far less of the stuff I now swallow. But seeing that I eat such rough and simple food, which is easily digested, it hardly seems shameful to eat a goodly quantity of it.' Now it was the abbot's custom, along with the prior and certain of his friends, to feast on choice capons, pheasants, and godwits. So taking good heed of the monk's words, and fearing that he might spread around what he obviously knew about the table kept by his superior, he excused him immediately, instructing him to feed in whatever manner pleased him best, telling him that it would be his own loss if he failed to discover the art of good eating and drinking.

At that, Dom Pomporio went out of the abbot's presence carrying his pardon with him. From that day on, he doubled his allowance, heaping his devotional platter with victuals of every kind. Nevertheless, the other monks kept on reproaching him for his monstrous appetite. So one day, in response to their censures, he mounted the pulpit of the refectory and in a witty manner told them the following tale. 'In times now long past it chanced one day that Wind, Water, and Shame all met together in the same hostelry. As they sat at meat together and talked of one thing and another, Shame said to Wind and Water, 'When, O brother and sister, have we ever met together before so peacefully as we are at this present moment?' Water answered, 'What Shame says is both reasonable and true. Only God above knows when we'll find another opportunity for our meeting. So in case I should want to find you again, my brother, tell me where your dwelling is.' The Wind said, 'My sister, if you should ever want to visit me and take your pleasure in my company, you need only to look in the middle of open spaces or in any narrow street and you'll find me in an instant, for I make my home in such places as these. And you, Water, where do you live?' Water replied, 'I dwell in the lowest-lying marshes and among the watercourses, and however dry and parched the earth may be, you'll always find me there. Now tell me, Shame, where is your home?' Shame said, 'Truly, I don't really know, for I'm a wretched creature rejected by everybody. If you look among the great ones of the earth and seek me out, you'll certainly never find me there, because they never choose to entertain me and only tell jokes at my expense. If you look for me among the people of low estate, you'll see that they're so debased that they care little for me. If you go in search of me among women, whether they're matrons, widows, or maids, you'll find your labour equally vain, seeing that all of these flee from me as from a mon-strous thing. If you seek me among monks, priests, or nuns, I'm to be found nowhere near them, for it is their custom to drive me away with sticks and stones. Hence it is that up to this hour I've not been able to find out a dwelling place where I can permanently reside. Unless I'm allowed to bestow myself with you, I'll be like someone deprived of all hope.' Wind and Water, when they heard this speech, were moved to great compassion and let Shame live in their company. But before many days had passed a great storm blew up and the wretched creature, tormented by both the wind and the water, and not finding any other place of rest, was overwhelmed by the sea and drowned. From that very time I've sought her in various places and I'm still looking for her, but I've found no trace of her, nor have I heard tidings of her from any man I've encountered. And because I've not been able to find her, I no longer give myself trouble on her account. I'll simply live the life that seems good to me and you can do the same, for in our time, Shame is no longer to be found in the whole wide world.

Although in her opening words Diana had led the company to expect little merit in her story, nevertheless it won the favourable notice of the assembly. But the girl was so free from ambition and had so little concern for praise of any sort that she launched at once into her enigma.

> As goddess great, and fair, and strong,
> Bears rule amid the mortal throng,
> No stranger sway than hers is given
> To any power of hell or heaven.
> Man hails her yoke with keen delight,
> Unmindful of the fatal blight
> She sheds on body and on mind,
> On play of wit, on impulse kind,
> On every grace from virtue sprung,
> On every fruit of brain or tongue.
> Wretched the pilgrim to her shrine;
> She strikes him with her touch malign,
> Dries up his blood till, fell and cold,
> Death comes and has him safe in hold.

The meaning of this enigma was divined, if not by all, by the greater part of the listeners. They declared this fair strange lady to be nothing other than gluttony, which weakens the bodies of all those who eat too much and uproots every sort of virtue, and is also the cause and source of death itself, seeing that the toll of those who die on account of gluttony is vastly greater than that of those who fall by the sword. Isabella, who was sitting by Diana's side, remarked that they had now brought the discussion concerning the enigma to a fitting end, so she at once began to tell her fable in the following words.

XI.3 Commentary

The parable of Wind, Water, and Honour socializing together is surely ancient, but just how ancient may be impossible to say. Francesco Petrarch was quoting it in the fourteenth century in his *Familiari* (Familiar letters): 'Lucam presbiterum placentinum, de suspitione.'[62] Straparola makes use of it as a commonplace, for his replacement of Honour with Shame would have been senseless to his readers had there been no conventional and widely received version in circulation as the basis for comparison. In both versions, the allegorized characters, at their parting, agree to meet again, but first they pose the simple pragmatic question about how they will find one another. The imaginative writer must now specify in the natural world where the essence of wind and water might be found, as in open spaces, mountain tops, the sails of windmills, and the leaves of trees, or in marshes, where willows and reeds grow, or the sea itself. But the defining 'lesson' is in Honour's oblique response, that once he is lost he can never be found again. Hence the uses of allegory: that as a 'friend' as well as a virtue, he can indeed be forsaken.

Straparola's gluttonous monk, seeking to liberate himself from the opprobrium cast upon him by his community for his Gargantuan eating habits, reframes the familiar apologue as a parable of Wind, Water, and Shame, in which the last of these is induced to explain to his companions that because no one in the wider world wishes to be associated with him, they must keep him in constant and close company or he will evanesce completely and never be found again. Therein resides the intertextual

---

62 'Letter to Lukas the Priest: On Suspicion.' *Le Familiari*, ed. Vittorio Rossi (Florence: G.C. Sansoni, 1933–42), bk. IX, letter 7, vol. II, pp. 236–7. In this version there are four travellers: fire, wind, water, and suspicion. They ask, should they become separated, how they might find each other. Fire assures them that where there is smoke, he will be there. The wind says to look wherever leaves and stalks are shaking, or where there are dust clouds in the sky. Water will not be far from where rushes are growing. But suspicion does not move about constantly like the others. 'Where I have once entered into a certain place, there I dwell.' Petrarch goes on to make a little allegorical homily out of each of the elements. In Straparola's tale, shame is forever lost, whereas, here, suspicion lodges itself and remains; either way, the structure of the little story is confirmed.

sport. In place of a lesson defining that strangely unquantifiable yet indispensable thing called honour, the noshing monk teaches his total indifference to the shame they would impose upon him, complacent in his present habits, calm in his resolution to continue, free as he is already from the threat of his superior whose fine feeding and hypocrisy have undermined his authority. Only those who assume a virtue for themselves are in a position to demand it of others. Thus, Dom Pomporio, in light of his little parable, will simply live as though shame does not exist.

This adapted parable serves in this instance as a quip or smart reply to those who would exercise collective control over a member of their group because of his inordinate eating habits. The explicit accusation is that he eats like a beast and that his portions are well beyond what was collectively held as appropriate, not to mention his equation of gourmandizing with prayer, whereby he turns his vice into sacrilege. The shame they would impose is the by-product of a social operation by which community members seek to enforce conformity according to collective notions of civility and propriety. That threat is easily mapped upon social reality by all who fear a bad reputation, ostracism, degradation in the eyes of their social set, and ultimately exile from civilized company. No threat is more instinctually felt, but just how that economy functions is a matter of some complexity, for it involves the inculcation of social norms including table manners viewed as a code to social ranking, questions of social reciprocity, of giving as well as receiving, such as taking a considered quantity of food from a limited supply calculated in relation to the numbers present. All such matters are brought to bear upon individuals through self-censorship, the active cultivation of good opinion, and the fear of remonstration if only through gossip – that means of communication by which groups referee individuals by shaping opinion around them. But it is peculiar to this monk that he has no such social pretensions. Hence, Dom Pomporio perverts an exemplum to generate a 'liberty' around himself, a free space in which he can pursue his compulsive feeding free of reproach, even to the point of making his trencher a substitute for the spiritual life. Food was for him a kingdom and a god; it could not be helped. The reversible parable, the smart reply, was his means for escaping the voices of obloquy and stigma.

Brother Pomporio was in the advantageous position, as a member of a religious community, of having membership by oath and vow, of having the silent approval of superiors, and of requiring nothing further from the world at large that would depend upon his table manners. The simple nature of his fare makes him even a dubious participant in the sin of gluttony, for in terms of quantity, where does the sin begin? He in fact recycles through his own digestive system the food that others would waste. In the end, it is an amusing anecdote, carnivalesque, and mildly subversive, for the friar delivers himself from the power of opinion and reprobation, as in 'The Widow's Broken Promise' (VI.3). That we live today in an age of obesity rights is well beyond Straparola's frame of social sensitivity – his tale is no cry for respect on the part of a 'man of difference.' We are still in the medieval world, in which food is not a marker of personal stress or low self-esteem, but of the debasement of the spiritual life, which compounds badly with liberationist dialectics. Brother Pomporio is more reliably a Renaissance grotesque bordering on the Rabelaisian order of comic inversion and negotiated licence that confirms rather than destroys norms.

The literary history of the saying that lays the foundation for this story may be difficult to trace simply because it belongs largely to folk wisdom. Who is most powerful of the three? Wind and water may be felt on mountain tops and seen in the sea, but honour, though without material trace of any kind, is yet the more powerful – proof of which is to be seen in the daily struggle to maintain it in every social act and in the devastation that ensues for all who lose it. Folk manifestations of 'Wind, Water, and Honour' are scarce in the English world, where the concept and its moral did not become a part of received culture, but it is known in Germany, and it is particularly well established in Italy. Giuseppe Pitrè collected two 'Il fuoco (vento), l'acqua e l'onore' stories in Sicily. In his main text (no. 274), water and wind boast all the good things they do, such as irrigating fields and turning mills, while honour is caught short in that department. But as an abstraction signifying a force over peoples' lives, honour scores a victory in the parade of prestigious principles. A second version, recorded in Pitrè's notes, is attributed to Gasparo Gozzi (1713-86) in which wind has now become smoke (related to 'fuoco').[63] Arturo Paoli in *L'acqua, il fuoco e l'onore, commedia in tre atti per soli uomini*, follows

---

63 Giuseppe Pitrè's *Fiabe*, trans. Jack Zipes and Joseph Russo, *The Collected Sicilian Folk and Fairy Tales of Giuseppe Pitrè*, 2 vols. (New York: Routledge, 2009), no. 274, vol. II, pp. 751–2, and p. 968 for the Gozzi version, 'Il fuoco, l'acqua e l'onore.' Pitrè found it, no doubt, in one of Gozzi's many publications: *Opere scelte* (Venice: Antonelli, 1832–3) might be a place to start, or *Favole, novelle e lettere*, ed. Giovanni Mestica (Florence: G. Barbèra, 1876), p. 2. These three elements, travelling together, agree that they need signs in case of separation. The first two cite their traces, but honour, once lost, is nevermore to be found.

suit in a play for a single actor, foregrounding the values of the parable.[64] A few more references to this motif in folk culture might include *A Sicilian in East Harlem*, in which the story makes an appearance in a chapter on 'Sicilian Folklore and American Comics,' the *Letture scelte* of Giovanni Lardelli, in which the characters enjoy a more elaborate social setting – Onore is described as a young man, spirited and lively, and de rigueur respected by everyone – and Joseph Freiherrn von Hormayr's *Taschenbuch für die vaterländische Geschichte*, where it is told as a fable of the author's childhood in which wind, water, and honour are playmates.[65]

---

64 Paoli, *L'acqua, il fuoco e l'onore* (Vicenza: G. Galla [1924]).
65 Salvatore Mondello, *A Sicilian in East Harlem* (Youngstown, NY: Cambria Press, 2005), p. 42; Giovanni Lardelli, *Letture scelte: Studiosi della lingua italiana* (Zurich: Orell Füssli & Co., 1883), no. 25, p. 36; Joseph von Hormayr, *Taschenbuch* (Berlin: G. Reimer, 1845), p. 48 (a paperback history of the fatherland).

XI. Fable 4
The Buffoon and the Stolen Veal

ISABELLA

A buffoon, by means of a pleasantry, tricks a certain gentleman and is cast into prison, from whence, on account of another jest, he is liberated.

There is a saying that is, for good reason, held in wide esteem, that a jester's tricks may sometimes please, but not in every instance. Seeing that I've been chosen to be fourth in the order of tonight's storytelling, I've been searching my memory for a fable, and the one that comes to recollection is about a certain buffoon who played a knavish trick upon a gentleman and how this gentleman tried to get his revenge, but could get no satisfaction because the jester simply put another trick upon him, and in that way even managed to get himself out of prison where he'd been sent for his former swindling.

Vicenza is well known to you all as a rich, noble, and splendid city – and it is the dwelling place of many men of brilliant parts. Among them was Ettore, a member of the ancient and noble family of the Dreseni, who far surpassed all his contemporaries in the elegance of his discourse and the loftiness of his mind, earning for himself a noble name that he left to his heirs. Truly, his gifts of mind and body were so great that he deserved to have his effigy carved as a marvel of art and workmanship, to be set up in the streets, piazzas, churches, and theatres of the city, and to have his name exalted with the most enthusiastic praise as high as the stars of heaven. So great was his beneficence, that it appeared as if no quality worthy of remembrance was wanting in him. His patience in listening was inexhaustible, while the answers he gave to any who might enquire of him were equally weighty. His fortitude in adversity, the splendour of his deeds, the justice and mercy of his decisions – in short, the whole range of his conduct – allowed it to be said that the great-souled Signor Ettore took the foremost place among the members of the Dreseni family.

One day it happened that a certain gentleman sent to this illustrious nobleman a quarter of very choice veal. The servant who carried the meat, as soon as he came to the palace of this great Lord, chanced to meet with a sharp-sighted thief. This latter, as soon as his eye fell upon the lackey with the quarter of veal, hastily went up to him and enquired of him who might have sent the meat he was carrying. After learning from the servant who it was, the knave ordered him to wait there until he had a chance to tell the Signor of the gift. Once inside the house, he began, in the manner of buffoons, to juggle somewhat and play the zany, waiting a while in order to fool both the servant outside and the master inside, but without dropping a word about the present that had been sent. Then he went back to the door and, in the name of the master of the house, he returned due thanks to the sender of the veal in terms entirely befitting the occasion, ordering the servant at the same time to follow him, inasmuch as Signor Ettore desired to pass the present on to a gentleman friend of his. In this fashion, he led the servant away most cleverly to his own house, where he found his brother, to whom he handed over the veal with the intention of having it cooked for his own dining. This done, they went their various ways, and the servant, when he returned home, gave to his master the thanks that had been offered to him in the name of Signor Ettore.

One day, not long after this, the gentleman who had sent the quarter of veal met Signor Ettore and asked him in the course of the conversation, as he might well do, whether he had found the veal good and well fattened. Knowing nothing of the matter, Signor Ettore demanded of him what veal he might be talking about, affirming that he himself had received no quarter of veal or third part either. Then the donor called his servant and enquired of him about the person to whom he had given the meat. The servant forthwith provided a full description, saying, 'The man who took the veal from me in the name of his master was a corpulent fellow with a merry eye, a big paunch, and a mumbling trick of speech. He told me to take the veal to the house of another gentleman.' By means of this description, Signor Ettore pictured in his mind exactly who the rogue must be, because the cheat in question was inclined to play a lot of tricks on him. So when he had the knave summoned before him, he discovered that matters stood exactly as he suspected. After taking the culprit to task, he sent him straight to prison, ordering them to clap his legs in fetters, indignant that such a disgrace and shame should have been put upon him by a trickster who had so rashly ventured to deceive him.

But, as it came to pass, the rascally juggler was not fated to spend even one full day incarcerated because in the palace of the judiciary, where this scoundrel was examined, there was, by a curious coincidence, a certain officer named Vitello or Calf. Either to pile up one offence upon another, or to discover some way out of his misfortune, the prisoner called the man over to him, wrote a letter to Signor Ettore in the following terms, and gave it to the officer to deliver: 'Gracious Signor, trusting in the generosity of your lordship I accepted the quarter of veal that was sent to you as a gift, and now in return for your kindness I send you, as a recompense for your quarter, a whole calf, and thus recommend myself to your favour.' Then he dispatched the letter by the hand of the officer, who promised to see it safely delivered in his name.

Without wasting any time, the officer went straight to Signor Ettore and handed the letter over to him, which he read right off, and then ordered his servants to lay hold of the calf that the prisoner had sent him as a present and to slaughter it. The officer, as soon as he heard the order given to the servants that they should take 'Vitello' and butcher him, quickly unsheathed the sword he carried at his side and, brandishing it naked in his hand and winding his cloak around his left arm, began to cry out in a loud voice, 'It is truly written that in the dwellings of the great wickedness rules supreme, but you shall never make veal of this calf unless you first kill and dismember him. Stand back, you knaves, if you do not wish to be dead men, all of you.'

Those who were standing round were astonished by this strange speech and behaviour, but even so, they were overcome by their urge to laugh. On account of this jest, the buffoon was set at liberty, showing that it was not without reason that the famous philosopher Diogenes declared how men should seek to avoid the envy of friends even more studiously than the snares of foes, inasmuch as the latter are evils plain to be seen, while the former, being secret and hidden, are far more potent for harm, because our fears are never aroused into watchfulness by their presence.

Here Isabella brought her brief fable to an end and for her efforts won no small praise from the honourable gathering. Then, to complete her task, she set to work on her enigma, offering it up for solution.

> Twofold are we in our name,
> But single-natured all the same;
> Made with skill and art amain,
> And perfected with bitter pain.
> Fair dames our service meanly prize,

> And poor folk like us large in size.
> To countless men we lend our aid,
> And never our hard fate upbraid;
> But when our useful task is done,
> No thanks we get from anyone.

'This enigma,' she said, 'signifies nothing other than the scissors that ladies use to cut thread. Among the poorer sort of people, such as tailors, shearers, barbers, and smiths, they are much greater in size than those used by ladies.' Isabella's pretty riddle pleased the listeners, who praised it loudly. Then Vicenza, who had been chosen to fill the last place of the present evening, thusly began the relation of her fable.

XI.4 Commentary

In this jesting tale consisting of a double prank, Straparola, through his narrative godfather, Morlini, may have connected himself to a bit of buffoonery and clever quipping that circulated widely in Turkey and the Near East at least as far back as the thirteenth century, there forming a generic story type that found its way into Boccaccio's *Decameron* in the mid-fourteenth as his fourth *novella* of the sixth day. Nasr-Eddin, at the court of Timur-Leng (Tamburlaine, crowned 1360), collected the farce of the one-legged goose at the same time that Boccaccio was putting the final touches on his collection of a hundred tales. Marcus Landau in his study of Boccaccio's sources states that this sketch, arising concurrently, 'kann ... schwerlich Boccaccio's Quelle gewesen sein' (can hardly be Boccaccio's source), but this is to overlook the fact that Nasr-Eddin, the court fool turned author, was likewise a collector, and that the tale, according to the several reporters Landau cites, was known throughout Turkey and had its origins in former centuries.[66] Boccaccio, in some manner, would seem to be in its debt. It is the story of the game bird with the missing thigh and the thief's smart retort that it was a one-legged creature. The story works best when it is a crane, for such birds do stand, while sleeping, on a single leg, but it has been told of geese and pheasants as well.

---

66 Marcus Landau, *Die Quellen des Dekameron* (Wiesbaden: Dr. Martin Sändig [1883], 1971), pp. 334–5. That quip can be read in the *Sottisier de Nasr-Eddin, bouffon de Tamerlan*, ed. Jean-Adolphe Decourdemanche (Bruxelles: Gay & Doucé, 1878), no. 75.

In a more rigorous historical sense, however, to say that this Boccaccian story is in any way connected to Girolamo Morlini's tale from the *Novelle* (1520) – which Straparola translates from the Latin and incorporates into the *Nights* – is a difficult call.[67] Both tales deal with cooked meat that is fully or partially stolen by a clever rascal (whether a household cook or a local rogue), a victim who intends harsh punishment for the swindler, and a clever quip or inventive trick that turns anger into laughter and wins the petty larcenist a pardon. But what is stolen and how, as well as the means for quelling the owner's wrath, are quite different. If Straparola's tale is viewed as a Boccaccian variant, it then inherits not only the Eastern sources, but an untold number of literary analogues derived from Boccaccio by which the tale is passed down to the nineteenth century. Without that connection, Morlini's production stands essentially alone without sources or analogues. If he employed Boccaccio, he cleverly buried all traces of debt. If he drew from the folk, his story is the only evidence of a contemporary tradition, apart from the now familiar prospect that what occurs in later centuries may well have had currency in former centuries. There the case goes cold.

Boccaccio's famous tale of the cook, Chichibio (VI.4), who is instructed to prepare the crane brought down by his master's hawk, begins somewhat in the manner of the cowherd Travaglino's tale in which Isotta prevails upon him to slay the master's bull with the gilded horns (III.5), for as Chichibio prepares the meat, his mistress drops by and demands a portion, the bird's thigh in exchange for her favours, or his sex life is over. Chichibio gives in, and when the bird is later served and he is questioned about the missing part, he replies that it is a one-legged crane. The master, not amused, the following day loads the culprit into a cart, takes him to the marshes, and defies him to point out such a creature in nature. The smart alec cook seizes upon the occasion to point out a group of cranes standing on one leg, whereupon the master goes up to them calling 'oho, oho.' Seemingly snared when the second leg descends and they all take flight, Chichibio replies that on the preceding evening the master had not called 'oho, oho' and that hence the bird did not put down its second foot. Amused by the sudden quip, his lordship could no longer pursue his vengeance and let the scoundrel go.

---

67 Girolamo Morlini, 'Excellentis condom [quondam] Ettoreis Carrafe' in *Novelle e favole*, ed. Giovanni Villani (Rome: Salerno, 1983), no. 7, pp. 40–5; *Les nouvelles de Girolamo Morlini*, trans. Fernand Caussy (Paris: E. Sansot, 1904), pp. 33–6.

This story found subsequent exposition in Sagredo's *Arcadia in Brenta* (there told of a cardinal), in Pauli's *Schimpf und Ernst*, no. 57, in Martin Montanus's *Schwankbücher*, no. 77, in *Tarleton's Jests and News out of Purgatory*, in Sansovino's *Cento novelle* (1561), Day IV, no. 9, in a *Fastnachtsspiel* by Hans Sachs, 1540 – there were many in those years – and sporadically thereafter down to 1900, as in Ballodoro's *Folklore veronese*. It also turns up in folk-tale collections from Hungary, Russia, Turkey, and further afield, these latter presumably still 'remembering' the Ur-tale, which required no refitting in fourteenth-century Florence.[68] The description of the tale heard in Hungary is of particular interest because the culprit is a Gypsy messenger who delivers a mutilated roast goose.[69]

At the risk of repeating the obvious, the jest functions differently in Straparola, for it is a quarter of veal that is stolen. When the buffoon lands in jail, he finds there a keeper by the name of Vitello (calf in Italian), who is sent with a letter to Ettore Dreseni, in whose name this entire anecdote is told, explaining simply that he (the robber buffoon) had indeed taken the meat, but that he was herewith returning an entire 'calf' in its place. The jest plays out nicely when the silly Vitello takes personally the command to slaughter the returned calf and decides that he must fight his way out – which sets the entire Dreseni household laughing. They recognize in a trice the joke that had been played on the simple messenger, as well as on themselves as an empty gesture of restitution, but Ettore accepts the filcher's wit in place of the goods. Are these

---

68 Giovanni Boccaccio, *The Decameron*, trans. J.M. Rigg, 2 vols. (London: Privately printed for the Navarre Society, ca. 1900), vol. II, pp. 82–4; Giovanni Sagredo, *L'Arcadia in Brenta* (1667), ed. Quinto Marini (Rome: Salerno, 2004); Johannes Pauli, 'Ein fasant soll nur ein bein haben' (A pheasant should only have one leg) in *Schimpf und Ernst*, ed. Johannes Bolte, 3 vols. (Berlin: Herbert Stubenrauch, 1924), no. 57, vol. I, p. 48; Martin Montanus, 'Gartengesellschaft' in his *Schwankbücher* (1557–66), ed. Johannes Bolte (Hildesheim: Georg Olms, 1972), chap. 77, pp. 335–7; 'The tale of the cook and why he sat in Purgatorie with a crane's leg in his mouth,' in *Tarleton's Jests and News out of Purgatory*, ed. J.O. Halliwell (London: Shakespeare Society, 1844), p. 78; Francesco Sansovino, *Cento novelle scelte* (Venice: Sansovino, 1561), IV.9 (from Boccaccio); Hans Sachs, *Der koch mit dem Kranich* (The cook with the crane), 1540, in *Fastnachtsspiele*, no. 121, vol. III, p. 225; Arrigo Balladoro, ed., *Folklore veronese* (Bologna: Forni, 1969).

69 This is reported by A.C. Lee in *The Decameron: Its Sources and Analogues* (New York: Haskell, 1966), p. 178, from L.L.K. writing in the *Temperance Reciter*, 10 ser. xi (29 May 1909), p. 438, who heard it in Hungary before 1870. Lee goes on to cite an entire page of additional references from Bolte's annotations to Montanus, who is listed in the preceding note.

the same story? On a different note, there is the difficulty for the English translator of working without an equivalent for 'Vitello' as a proper name. English may have Bird as such, but not Calf, while the French translator of Morlini could make do with Petitveau (Littlecalf), for in this case, the wit does not rely on the unique nature of the animal, as in the case of the crane, but a pun on a name in a prepared practical joke.[70] The story recurs in even more streamlined form in the Sicilian folk tales about Firrazzanu the buffoon who, when his master asks for 'humpbacks,' meaning a type of partridge at that time scarce in the markets, the prankster promises them and then rounds up twenty hunchbacks to parade through the dining room in a way resembling the replacement of calf meat with Vitello the guard. But in other ways the analogy breaks down and the story fades.[71]

A brief relation concerning a play on vitellus, vitellio, and vitellione in a section on 'Youthful Pranks' in Agostino Nifo's *De re aulica* provides a hint that some anecdote may have been in circulation that Morlini could have adapted. Nifo's book, however, was published in Naples in 1534, some fourteen years after Morlini's collection, and hence may provide no more than a corroborating reference.[72] Whatever its origins, Morlini was keen to apply the story to a Neapolitan dignitary in celebration of his wit and clemency, namely, Ettore Carafa, cardinal and count of Ruvo, who died in 1511. It is related as a comic moment in his eventful life, thereby taking on the particularity of local history; he specifies even that the calf came from Sorrento, which undoubtedly meant something to contemporary readers. Straparola purportedly finds an Ettore of his own in Vicenza and simply takes over the wording verbatim in praise of him. Nowhere else in the *Nights* does he lavish such an accolade on any of his ostensibly historical subjects. That he chose what appears to be one of the great families of Vicenza might well suggest to those concerned with filling in Straparola's biography that he had a particular motivation for eulogizing the elite in that specific part of the country. The identity of

---

70 For further play in Latin on 'vitellio' in its several forms see Augostino Nifo, *De re aulica* (Naples: Ioannes Antonius de Caneto, 1534), chap. 85, fol. Giiir–Giiiv.

71 *The Collected Sicilian Folk and Fairy Tales of Giuseppe Pitrè*, trans. Jack Zipes and Joseph Russo (New York: Routledge, 2009), no. 156.5, vol. I, p. 559. The story is also nos. 115 and 117 of the *Cento racconti ... della città di Nola*, of Michele Somma (Naples: Coda, 1821; reprint Naples: Istituto grafico editoriale italiano, 2000).

72 *De re aulica ad Phausinam libri duo* (Naples: Ioannes Antonius de Caneto, 1534), chap. 85, fol. Giiir–Giiiv.

the Dreseni remained elusive until my colleague, Maurizio Ascari, proposed that Straparola had in mind no other than the Trissino family, insofar as the Sylva de Dreseno is the same as the Selva di Trissino; it was simply a variant spelling. Yet, perplexingly, Straparola kept the Neapolitan's first name, Ettore, to which no Trissino answers that can be determined.[73] Nevertheless, in this covert and second-hand praise of an unspecified member of this noble family, we may have a clue to Straparola's professional connections and place of residence, some 60 kilometres west of Venice in the heart of the Veneto. Should it prove true, it would be just about right in relation to his assignment of circumstances and uses of dialect in several of his other stories.

---

73 See Gaetano Girolamo Maccà, *Della zecca vicentina* (Vicenza: T. Parise, 1802).

XI. Fable 5
Frate Bigoccio Takes a Wife and Leaves Her

VICENZA

Frate Bigoccio becomes enamoured of Gliceria, and, putting on lay clothing, fraudulently marries her. Then, having gotten her pregnant, he forsakes her and returns to his monastery. When the superior hears of this deed, he causes her to be honourably married.

Dear ladies, I've heard it said many times that virtue is surely fated to come to ruin through persistent hypocrisy – a saying that is clearly illustrated by what happened to a certain monk who was taken by all to be a man of piety and wisdom. This very man, seized with love for a young damsel, ultimately married her. When his transgression was discovered, he was forced to do severe penance for it, while the young girl was honourably bestowed in marriage. All this will become entirely clear from the story I'm about to tell.

In Rome there once lived a certain Frate Bigoccio, born of a high and noble family. He was a very young man, furnished with many graces of person and gifts of fortune. By chance, however, this unfortunate youth became so hotly inflamed with love for a most beautiful young lady that, by reason of this amorous passion, he came perilously close to putting an end to his life. He could get no rest whether by day or by night. He grew ghastly and lean in appearance. Neither physicians nor drugs served him to any benefit. He took pleasure in nothing. Neither the hopes of youth nor the prospect of the abundant wealth he might hope to inherit gave him any solace. He allowed his thoughts to dwell on her, always in that same frame of mind, conjuring up now one fantastic remedy for his ills and now another. At last, he resolved to write certain forged letters addressed to the superior of his monastery demanding permission to leave the place. Having thus made up his mind, he set to work to concoct them, using false words to make them appear as though they came from the hand of his father, who was very sick and infirm. Such was the wording: 'Reverend father, forasmuch as it is the pleasure of God, the Supreme and All-powerful, to put an end to my life, and seeing that death, who is now very near to me, will not long delay in fetching me away, I have determined, before I take leave of this world, to make my last will and testament, appointing as my heir my only son, who has taken vows in the monastery of your reverence. Because there is left to me in my old age no other son but this one alone, whom I desire most earnestly to see once more and to embrace, kiss, and bless before I die, I beg you that of your kindness you will let him come to me with all speed. Otherwise, your reverence may be well assured that, dying in despair, I shall go straightway to the realms of Tartarus.'

The letter having been duly presented to the superior of the monastery and the sought-after leave obtained, this Bigoccio made his way to Florence, where his father lived, and after he had received from his father a goodly store of gems and money, he purchased for himself many costly garments, horses, and other effects necessary for the maintenance of a household. Then he departed for Naples [no doubt intending Rome], where he hired for himself a house close beside that of his beloved, attiring himself every day in some fresh suit of silken clothes of varied fashion. In the course of a few days he contrived to get on friendly terms with her father, inviting him several times to be a guest at his house, and there presenting him with sundry gifts. Continuing on for some time in this way, Bigoccio found a suitable and opportune moment for advancing his plan. One day, when the two were talking together after supper about various matters, and especially their business affairs – as men will do at such times – the love-stricken youth, in the course of their conversation, mentioned his strong inclination to take a wife. Furthermore, he said that, having ascertained his guest to be the father of an exceedingly fair and graceful daughter, and dowered with every virtue under the sun, it would give him supreme pleasure were he to win this fair damsel for his wife, firmly uniting himself with her in matrimony – all along declaring that he desired this union solely on account of the many excellent reports about her that he had received.

The girl's father, a man of relatively low condition, answered that his daughter was not of the same social rank and condition of life as Bigoccio. Moreover, he must bear in mind, in celebrating nuptials with her, that she was poor and he rich, she of plebeian and he of noble birth. Yet seeing how ardently set he was on having the damsel around the house, the father agreed to give her to him, not to fill a wife's place so much as a servant's.

To this Bigoccio replied, 'There's no question that so dainty a maid should come to me in the role of a servant, for in light of her many excellent gifts, she is worthy of a man of far nobler lineage than mine. However, if it is your pleasure to give her to me, not for a handmaid, but for my beloved wife, I'll take her gladly and I'll always bestow upon her that fellowship which is the due and lawful estate of a true lady.' In the end, the two companions came to an agreement and the nuptials were celebrated, so that Frate Bigoccio got for his wife the young maiden he so desired.

When the night-time arrived, husband and wife went duly to bed and in a short while, in the course of their mutual endearments, Frate Bigoccio noticed that Gliceria had put on gloves. So he said to her, 'Gliceria, take those gloves off your hands and lay them aside. It's just not right that you should be wearing them while we're in bed together.'

To this Gliceria answered, 'Oh, my good husband, I could never bring myself to touch a man at such times as these with my naked fingers.'

When Frate Bigoccio heard these words from his wife, he said nothing, but kept himself busy with the work of a bridegroom. The next evening, when the two of them were getting ready for bed, Frate Bigoccio secretly found some hawk's jesses with a lot of little bells attached to them. These he tied around his cock and got into bed without letting his wife see what he'd done. At once he began to caress, embrace, and kiss her, she wearing her gloves as on the preceding night. Because she had by now acquired a taste for the delights of married love, she placed her hand on her husband's member and discovered the jesses. Then she said outright, 'What's this thing I'm touching? It wasn't there last night.'

To this Frate Bigoccio replied, 'What you're feeling are jesses of a kind men use when they go hawking.' Then he tried to get into her arbour and plant his spade in the shady vale. But because the jesses were an impediment to its entry, Gliceria spoke up, 'I don't want those jesses contraptions.'

Frate Bigoccio answered, 'If you don't want jesses, well, me, I don't want gloves.' And so it happened that from this moment the pair agreed by mutual consent to cast aside both gloves and jesses. Thereafter they took much pleasure with one another, so that in the course of time Gliceria was expecting a child.

For the space of a year they lived together as husband and wife, and when the time of Gliceria's delivery was drawing near, Frate Bigoccio secretly laid hands on all the best and richest things in the house and fled, leaving his pregnant wife. Then, after he had put on his former habit, he went back to the monastery. His wife, meanwhile, having given birth to a son, waited for a long time in vain for the return of her husband.

It happened that Gliceria was accustomed to going from time to time to the chapel of the monastery to hear mass, and one day, by chance – or rather by the will of God who governs all things – she discovered that the friar who performed the office was no other than her husband, recognizing him immediately. With all the celerity she could muster, she went to find the superior of the monastery and told him, with the greatest care and circumspection, all the adventures that had befallen her, as I have already told them. The superior, when he had been informed of all the facts and had satisfied himself of their truth, at once he laid criminal accusations against Frate Bigoccio. After he had signed it, he sent it on to the general of the congregation, who in turn urged them to lay hold of the friar and make him do such a penance as he would remember for the rest of his days. From the monies of the monastery they then gave Gliceria a dowry and had her secretly married to another. They also took possession of the child and had it brought up at their own expense.

Here the gracious Vicenza brought her fable to an end, which all the listeners heartily praised without exception, finding in it much diversion, especially when they were told how the lady with her gloved hands discovered the jesses with the little bells attached. But because the hour was already late, the Signora directed Vicenza to present her enigma, which, without waiting for further instruction, she set before the company.

> From everyone I something take,
> But on myself no claim I make.
> Mark well my nature. If you gaze
> Into my face I mock your ways:
> For if you sorrow, I am sad;
> But if you smile, you make me glad.
> Because I tell truth from a lie,
> Men call me wicked, false, and sly;
> Strange saying this, but true I ween.
> So I, to let it clear be seen
> That truth nor honesty I lack,
> Will never tell you white is black.

Not a single person in the company had wit enough to say what Vicenza's enigma was designed to mean, seeing that the true sense was so carefully hidden under the rind. But Vicenza, like a sensible maiden, gave out the solution as follows in order not to leave it undiscovered. 'The meaning of my enigma,' she said, 'is the mirror into which men, and ladies as well, are wont to gaze. This same thing catches the likeness of everyone who looks into it, but not its own. It does not show you one thing for another, but shows you to be that which you are in truth.'

The enigma was indeed ingenious, as well as the solution. But because the whitening dawn was now beginning to appear, the Signora gave leave to everyone to go home to rest, with the understanding, however, that they should all return well prepared on the following evening, insofar as it was her wish that everyone of the company should tell a short fable, completed as before by an enigma. To this they all gave their assent.

The End of the Eleventh Night

XI.5 Commentary

An unsuspecting middle-class girl is swindled into marriage by a monk masquerading as a grandee, who, after taking his pleasure with her for nearly a year, absconds with all his goods and returns to the monastery, leaving her pregnant and implicitly destitute. Such a tale falls easily into the category of the knaveries of the clergy, a genre of fiction affiliated with fact that held a substantial place in the *fabliaux* and *novelle* of the preceding three centuries, featuring all manner of predation upon innocent girls and citizens' wives. Every such story addresses a common deviation of the religious life with greater or lesser sympathy: that despite their vows, the urgings of the flesh for many gained ascendancy over the spirit. In this story by Straparola, appropriated with variations from Morlini's *novella* 'De monaco qui duxit uxorem' (Of the monk who took a wife), the protagonist is described not only as noble, handsome, sociable, well built, and well-to-do, but the victim of a malady caused by erotic desire that nearly cost him his life. (The subtext is how such a fellow found his way into a monastery in the first place.) His symptoms baffle the physicians so that in near desperation he settles upon the sovereign cure recommended by physicians from Avicenna down through the sixteenth century: coitus. To that end, he will remodel himself as an eligible bachelor and engage in a therapeutic marriage. Morlini is careful to remind us that his condition is remedied by 'nocte dieque in venerem baccatus' (revelling in love night and day). Straparola extends the story by including the sub-tale of the gloves and jesses. These comic cross purposes replace Morlini's simple line just quoted. But this moment of intimacy and inventive social negotiation cannot offset the fact that the bridegroom is a self-serving cad who could use his monastic refuge to walk out on a wife and child to whom he had all the obligations explicit in his marital vows and implicit in his paternity. To be sure, the tale is an open critique upon the abuses of priests, and perhaps a covert recommendation for married clergy. But there is no indication that a married clergy would have made Bigoccio into a man of honour and responsibility. More ambiguously, this story is not only a mean trick laced with hypocrisy, but an expedient social manoeuvre driven by mental necessity, and quite simply a memorable social anecdote in the grand *comédie humaine* told as though it happened to real people in the city named. Just how much social and moral intentionality there is in this fable, as opposed to amusement over so brazen an adventure and its 'comic' reversal, is largely in the minds of beholders.

The translation out of Morlini is relatively faithful, although the opening circumstances are slightly abbreviated and the lovesickness details amplified. Moreover, Straparola's apprehended monk is made to do harsh penance, whereas Morlini's is directly expelled from the community.[74] Morlini's tale begins and ends in Naples, with a detour to Rome to procure the trappings of a gentleman. Straparola's begins in Rome and ends in Naples (Rome?), with a detour to Florence to Bigoccio's father's house to acquire his accoutrements. This would suggest a slip on Straparola's part in intending Rome but writing Naples, because that was what he was looking at in the original. To this brief and direct vignette, Straparola introduces the joke about the lady who does not want to touch her husband's privates with her bare hands on the wedding night, and who, for that reason, wears gloves. The husband expresses his displeasure by attaching hawk's bells to himself, thereby spoiling his wife's pleasure. Whether her motive was simple modesty, or disgust, or unworthiness because of her class is not specified. But surely the purpose of the anecdote is simply to bring into the imagination the absurd possibility of the entire scenario, and particularly that of erotic activity accompanied by the jingling of bells. This inset story comes from Antonio Cornazano's *De*

---

74 Girolamo Morlini, *Novelle e favole*, ed. Giovanni Villani (Rome: Salerno, 1983), pp. 178–81.

origine proverbiorum (1503), where it illustrates the proverb 'Chi fa li fatti suoi non s'imbratta le mani.' In Cornazano's telling, once the husband and wife come to a mutual understanding, the wife now puts her bare hands into action while repeating the proverb, 'whoever minds her own business doesn't get her hands dirty.'[75] Cornazano's ingenious invention of illustrating proverbs with stories is carried forward by Cinzio de' Fabrizi in his *Libro della origine delli volgari proverbi*, published in Venice in 1526, which likewise contains this story in book XIX, cantica 3, in illustration of the same proverb.[76] Whether Straparola improves on or misbalances the story with this accretion is up for debate, for it appears to add an entirely independent and comic motif to an otherwise moral story, humanizing the cleric who afterward coldly abandons his wife and child.

Just where Straparola's two sources (Morlini and Cornazano) found these materials is altogether more difficult to say. The story of the gloves and jesses reappears in the eleventh *novella* of Pietro Fortini's *Le piacevoli e amorose notti dei novizi*, but that it served as an intermediary version for Straparola is unlikely. Fortini lived in Siena, and died there too in 1562; his two extensive collections of stories were written before and after mid-century, but his were not published before the eighteenth century. That Straparola knew his works is hence inconceivable, but that Fortini could have known Straparola's is not entirely impossible. Otherwise, Fortini came to the idea on his own of incorporating the jest of Cornazano into an extended tale of a mother and daughter on the road to Florence, and a young man's proposal and marriage to the girl.[77]

---

75 This story originated in Antonio Cornazarno's rare *De origine proverbiorum* or (*Antonii Cornezani … de proverbiorum … adeo delectabile et jocosum variisque facetiis refertum*) (Milan: Pietro Martire Mantegazz, 1503), a copy of which I was unable to locate. This segment (but not all those in the original work) reappears in a work often attributed to him entitled *Proverbii di Antonio Cornazano in facetie* (Venice: Zopino [1518], 1523), a work that went through many editions in all subsequent centuries. It was also translated into English and French, the English as *Proverbs in Jests or the Tales of Cornazano* (Paris: Isidore Liseux, 1888), Proverb 6, pp. 103–13. The earlier work, *De origine*, is written in Latin verse, the latter in Italian prose, but what the exact relationship between these works is I cannot say. Straparola, in any case, potentially had either to draw upon because this proverb appears in both.

76 *Libro della origine delli volgari proverbi* (Venice: Bernardino e Matteo dei Vitali, 1526; reprint, Milan: Spirali, 2007), pp. 256–9.

77 *Le piacevoli e amorose notti dei novizi*, ed. Adriana Mauriello, 2 vols (Rome: Salerno, 1995), vol. II, pp. 964–82.

As close as we may come to a source or to an early analogue is the forty-second tale of *Les cent nouvelles nouvelles*, provisionally entitled 'The Married Priest.'[78] A clerk from Noyon (near Compiègne) was the sacristan in his local church. He was married with children, but his wife was difficult, and a pilgrimage to Rome became his pretext for leaving her. Once in Rome, he found work in the household of a prestigious cardinal and prolonged his stay, rising in the esteem of his employer. When the priest of his home parish dies, his replacement comes to Rome in hope of a preferment through his friend's influence with the cardinal, telling him at the same time that his wife had died in the plague. This lie gave to him the idea that he was now free to take holy orders and to claim the benefice for himself. When he returns to claim his post, however, whom should he meet but his wife, alive, well, and a bit crotchety after five years' waiting. Alarmed, the man sought out the bishop, who carried his case to Rome, and from cardinal to Pope, where, in council, it was decided that he could keep his new office provided that he live faithfully and perpetually at home with his wife and children. In this way, he was compelled both to remain resident in his benefice, solving one of the Church's great problems, namely, absenteeism, and a second, which is the duty of caring for the Christian family. In the minds of many, such a papal dispensation might set a precedent, but the story treats it as a one-off adjustment in relation to a unique case.[79] This story does not have a great deal in common with Straparola's except in the fact of the married priest, the surprising discovery of a wife, as opposed to that of a husband officiating at the mass, and the adjudication by the Church, in the one case allowing for a married priest, in the other case chastising him. This story was borrowed and enlarged by Pietro Malespini for his collection of *novelle* appearing in 1609, and was presumably the story on the same topic to appear in the anthology of tales by famous authors assembled by the saddler Nicolas de Troyes in his *Grand parangon* (ca. 1510), and by Lodovico

---

78 *The Hundred Tales*, trans. Rossell Hope Robbins (New York: Crown Publishers, 1960), pp. 184–7. *Les cent nouvelles nouvelles*, ed. Roger Dubuis (Lyons: Presses Universitaires de Lyon, 1991), no. 85, pp. 306–8.

79 This exception is proved by the rule asserted in the tale from MS. Harleian no. 463, fol. 18v; 'De muliere maritum suum inebriante' is also included in Thomas Wright's *A Selection of Latin Stories from Manuscripts of the 13th and 14th Centuries* (London: Percy Society, 1842), no. 65, p. 59, in which a husband is gotten drunk by his wife and sent to the local monastery to take the habit, on the principle that once in, he could not return to secular life, for the tale states that even if the monk was married, that bond was dissolved by the taking of vows.

Guicciardini in his *L'hore di ricreatione,* subsequently translated into English by James Sandford as *Houres of Recreation or Afterdinner,* London, 1576.[80]

A related story with a different thrust was created by Marguerite de Navarre for her *Heptaméron* (1512), also involving a friar who marries and then attempts to return to his monastery.[81] This *novella* arrived on the scene in its own place in the world some eight years before Morlini published his, allowing for a slight prospect of influence. An aging Franciscan and father confessor gives counsel to a prosperous parishioner seeking advice about the marriage of her daughter to a man of quality who would fit into their domestic situation, mentioning the substantial dowry she was in a position to offer. This old hypocrite thinks of a young, well-built, sociable, good looking colleague in his order who might fraudulently marry the girl, bringing to them respectively a great deal of sex and a great deal of money. The mother welcomes the recommendation and the young friar performs his part to perfection, by nights at home with his wife and by days at his duties in the friary. This continues for some time, until the women, one day, take a pious turn and go the Franciscans

---

80 Celio Malespini, *Ducento novelle* (Venice: Al segno dell'Italia, 1609), bk. I, no. 26, pp. 75r–6v. In this tale a notary becomes a priest thinking his wife to be dead. All transpires precisely as in the *Cent nouvelles nouvelles,* and it is the College of Cardinals that makes the dispensation, with the same understanding that should he ever be inconstant to his current wife, he 'dovesse incontanente perdere la cura,' must immediately lose his benefice. I am accepting from Robbins, editor of the English translation of the *Cent nouvelles nouvelles* (see the preceding note), p. 383, that this was also the story collected by Nicolas de Troyes as no. 151 in his *Le grand parangon,* because it is not included in the nineteenth-century edition by É. Mabille (1869), or in the twentieth-century edition by Krystyna Kasprzyk (1970). It may prove that no. 151 [Of the clerk who thought his wife was dead and became a priest, and then returned home only to encounter her alive] can only be read in manuscript in such a work as *Le second volume du grand parangon des nouvelles nouvelles,* Bibliothèque Nationale, f.fr. 1510 (in folio with 384 numbered pages from the 1486 ed.). Of the 180 stories, precisely one-third of them were from the *Cent nouvelles nouvelles* and another 56 from the *Decameron.* James Sandford translated *L'hore di ricreatione* in 1576, published in London by Henry Binneman, wherein this story is also to be found.

81 Marguerite de Navarre, *The Heptameron,* trans. P.A. Chilton (London: Penguin, 1984), no. 56, pp. 451–6; *L'Heptaméron,* ed. Gisèle Mathieu-Castellani (Paris: Garnier Classique, 1999), pp. 579–87. Henri Estienne published his *Traité preparatif à l'apologie pour Hérodote* in 1566, into which he incorporated a version of this story in chap. 21, 'De la lubricité et paillardise des gens d'Église' (Of the lechery and bawdiness of the clergy). This work was often republished as the *Apologie pour Hérodote,* one such (Paris: Liseux, 1879), this story in vol. II, pp. 12–15.

for mass, there to see the husband and son-in-law performing the holy rites. Uncertain whether to trust their eyes, they await him that night, and once in bed they pull off his nightcap to expose his tonsure, thereby confirming the scandal. The magistrates are called in immediately and both brown friars are left in expectation of harsh punishment. The core idea is decidedly present, that of a priest who defrauds a young girl by feigning an honest marriage, the eventual discovery, the exposure of lechery and greed, and the closing chastisement. The topic of lecherous priests was ubiquitous, but stories of married priests were less so. Nevertheless, the configuration of known stories suggests the existence of others featuring the motif, whether brought into existence by fraud or accident, perhaps in circulation in the oral culture. But in the specific literary examples given, a source for Morlini is not self-evident.

The Twelfth Night

The blithe and watchful birds had now fled before the approaching shadows of night, and the bats, enemies of the sun and sacred to Proserpine, had come forth from their customary dwellings in the caves of the rocks and were briskly wheeling their flight through the dusky air, when the honourable and courteous company of ladies and gentlemen, laying aside every troublesome and hurtful thought, merrily made their way to the accustomed meeting place. When they had all seated themselves according to their respective ranks, the Signora came forward to meet them, giving to each a gracious salute. Then, after they had danced several measures, exchanging amorous talk all the while, the Signora, as was her pleasure, commanded that the gold vase be brought forth. Having put her hand therein, she drew out the names of five of the damsels. The first of these was Lionora, the second Lodovica, the third Fiordiana, the fourth Vicenza, and the fifth Isabella. To these five, and to all the others as well, permission was granted to hold forth in complete liberty on any theme that pleased their fancy, on the one condition alone that the fables that they might tell should be shorter and more succinct than those of the preceding night. To this, in one accord and each on her own behalf, they readily agreed. Then, having made choice of the damsels whose duty it was to relate the fables of the twelfth night, the Signora gave a sign to the Trevisan and to Molino that they should sing a canzonetta. Promptly obedient to her command, these two took up their instruments, and having tuned them, sang with graceful art the following song.

Song

Since Time makes youth and grace and beauty vain
   And faster flies with every day,
Why tarry still my sorrow to allay?
For life and time together fade and fly,
And all our hopes are false and unavailing;
Vast our desire, but soon our days are fled,
   Wherefore in deep despair I lie.
Too late! Ah, cruel lot of mortals failing!

> Remorse will come; then you will mourn me dead,
> And blame your cruel words which worked my bane.
>   Then pity now my amorous pain,
> While yet your beauty shines, and I of love am fain.

The delightful song, sung so harmoniously by the Trevisan and Molino, greatly pleased the entire company, and everyone gave it loud, high praise. Then, as soon as the Signora perceived that all were silent, she directed Lionora, who had been chosen by lot to relate the first fable of the twelfth night, to begin her story. Whereupon the damsel, without delay, began in this manner.

XII. Fable 1
How Florio's Wife Cures His Jealousy

LIONORA

Florio, jealous of his wife, is cleverly fooled by her, and is thereby so well cured of his malady that they live happily together thereafter.

Again and again I've heard it said, dear ladies, that the cleverest strategems of art and science are helpless when pitted against the tricks of women. The reason for this is that at her creation, woman sprang not from the dry, barren earth, but from the ribs of Adam our first father. Thus, from the beginning they were made of flesh and not of dust, even though in the end their bodies, like men's, must come to ashes. Insofar as it is my duty to begin our pleasant entertainment tonight, I've decided to tell you the story of a jealous husband who, although he was always taken for a man well endowed with knowledge and good sense, was nevertheless duped by his wife, through which discipline he was suddenly changed from a fool into a wise man.

In Ravenna, an ancient town in the Romagna – the dwelling place of many notable men and especially of those skilled in medicine – there lived, in former times, a worthy physician from a rich and noble family named Florio. He was a sprightly youth and well looked upon by all, both for his gracious bearing and for his medical skills. As his wife, he took a very fair and graceful maiden named Dorotea. But after the nuptials, by ill luck it fell out that her great beauty caused to well up in his mind so great a jealousy and fear that someone would defile his marriage bed that he had every aperture of the house down to the smallest crack filled up with lime and mortar and, in addition to this, he fixed strong iron gratings over all the windows. He even went so far as to forbid anyone, however closely related by blood, affinity, or friendship, from entering his house. In short, the jealous wretch spent all his energy and thought keeping watch day and night to make sure that nothing could possibly sully the chastity of his wife or make her forgetful of her marriage vow.

Now, under both civil and municipal law it is held that those who are incarcerated on account of their own debts, or as a form of bail or security given to their creditors, ought to be liberated and discharged after a reasonable period of duress. Even malefactors and delinquents come under the same rule. But as far as this poor lady was concerned, it would nevermore be possible for her, in her long-enduring affliction, to cross the threshold of the house or to break free from her captivity, because her husband kept loyal varlets in his service to guard the house. He would have been entirely adequate for the task himself were it not that he also wished to go out from time to time for his pleasure. But far-sighted and cautious man that he was, he never left his dwelling without first searching every nook and cranny, closing down every means of exit, and with the utmost diligence bolting the windows and locking them with keys of the most cunning manufacture. Day after day, he spent his life following these cruel compulsions. Now this discreet and prudent wife, who was in truth the very mirror of virtue and modesty and might justly have been put on a level with the Roman Lucrezia herself, being moved with pity by these sottish delusions of her husband, considered carefully how she might best cure him of this grievous distemper. The chances seemed small to her, were it not for her faith in women's wits and what they might accomplish.

It came about that she and her husband agreed to go together on the following morning to a convent standing outside the city to make confession – the two of them dressed as monks. Having discovered a means for opening one of the windows, she could see through the bars of the iron grating a certain youth passing by in the street who had avowed his passionate love for her. Cautiously, she called out to him, saying, 'Tomorrow morning early you must go to the monastery standing just outside the town dressed in a monk's habit. I pray you to wait for me until you see me coming along with my husband, both of us clad in the same fashion. Then you must come towards me in merry spirits, embrace and kiss me, begging me at the same time to come and dine with you, showing yourself overjoyed at meeting me in so unexpected a way. As I've already told you, this is because my husband and I have agreed to go tomorrow, both of us dressed in religious garb, to confess ourselves at the monastery I mentioned. So be in good spirits and vigilant, and make sure that you don't fail to carry out these directions I've given you.'

As soon as she had spoken, the gallant youth went his way, and having put on monk's attire and laid in a good supply of all sorts of delicate foods and exquisite wine, he went to the monastery mentioned by the lady and made an agreement with the reverend fathers for the loan of one of the cells in which to sleep that night. When the morning had come, he had even more dainty dishes made ready for the feast over and above those already prepared. This business dispatched, he began to walk up and down before the doors of the monastery. Before many minutes had passed, he espied his lady Dorotea approaching, clad in the habit worn by the brothers, whereupon he straightway ran to meet her, putting on a joyful face like someone completely overcome by some unlooked-for and excessive happiness. Then he said, casting aside all fear, 'Ah, I leave you to think what a pleasure and delight it is to see you once again, dearly beloved brother Felix, given the long time that has passed since our last meeting.' Using such words, they embraced and kissed one another, bedewing one another's faces with imaginary tears. This done, he made both Dorotea and her husband his guests, inviting them to enter his cell. Then he asked them to repose themselves at the table, which was superbly spread – not a single thing missing that a man's heart could desire. Having seated himself by the dame, he kept pressing the choicest morsels upon her, kissing her most ardently between every mouthful. The poor jealous husband, by the novelty of such actions, remained completely astonished, dismayed, and painfully confused, seeing his wife, before his very eyes, being kissed and caressed by a monk. Neither could he swallow a mouthful of food, no matter how small, nor could he draw her away. Thus, the entire day was consumed in these pleasures and delights. Finally, the evening coming, the jealous husband requested that they take their leave, saying that they had remained too long away from their monastery and that of necessity they must return, a request that was granted only after delays and difficulties. Even then, there was further hugging and sensual kissing before they got away, the husband in a state of agony.

When they finally reached home, the jealous man immediately began to reflect upon how he had been the cause of all the ill and torment he had lately suffered, and how, after all, it was always labour lost on a man's part to strive against the deceits and subtle inventions of women. After a brief review of his conduct, he recognized his past folly and swallowed his defeat, following up his recantation by opening all his windows and knocking off all the bars and padlocks from the doors, so that in all the city there was no house more free and open than his. Thus, after abolishing all restraints and granting to his wife full liberty to go wherever she desired, he lived with her in peace, being cured of the grave and serious malady that oppressed him. Dorotea, for her part, now freed from her cruel imprisonment, loyally kept faith with her husband.

When the graceful Lionora had brought her diverting story to an end, one that commended itself fully to the taste of the company, the Signora gave the word for her to complete her task by setting forth her enigma, which she did without waiting for further direction.

> One day upon a bank of grass
> I came across a pretty lass,
> And something else I also viewed
> Of aspect rough and coarse and rude.
> Then took the maid a thing in hand,
> For such a purpose duly planned,
> And steadily to work she went,
> To carry out her fixed intent.
> She held, and would not let it go,
> But worked it smartly to and fro,
> Until it gave her, brisk and neat,
> A pleasant savour for her meat.

Although nobody fathomed the meaning of this enigma, the men began to laugh, while the ladies blushed somewhat and hid their faces. When she saw this, Lionora at once gave the interpretation, 'It is a pretty village girl seated on a bank of grass holding between her knees a large mortar, and in her hands a pestle. This latter she works lustily, crushing certain herbs to extract the juices from them, which she uses to flavour her sauce.'

The company received the solution of this difficult enigma with approbation, and when they had given over laughing, the Signora directed Lodovica to set forth her story, which she, to show her readiness, began at once as follows.

XII.1 Commentary

This story clings to the tradition of those in which, in honesty or lechery, a wife so defeats her jealous husband's precautions that he confesses to their futility, endorses his wife's freedom, trusts her integrity, and lives the happier for it. All such stories interface with those in which wives in love defeat every precaution in order to take flight, or accept lovers who practise all manner of subterfuge to gain entry. In stories of this genre, the ruses of ladies and their inamoratos are endlessly inventive and astonishingly efficacious. In the best of *beffe* (or tricks), as here, the duped husband is brought to collaborate against his own best interests. In disguising his wife as a monk to deter all such amorous attentions, he provides the means for a credible mistaken identity. The delight for the lady, the lover, and the reader is to see an unreasonably jealous man, deep in his humours, as it were, compelled to endure his worst fears. That it serves as shock therapy and a cure is the lady's risk, for he could have reacted with violence and anger.

The story is drawn from Morlini's *Novelle*, 'De viro zelotypo' (Of the jealous man who was tricked or mystified by his wife).[1] There are but subtle differences in detail. Morlini tells of a husband in a state of distress to see his wife embraced by a monk right under his nose, so exasperated that he could no longer eat. A single bite of bread, which was small enough, was lodged in his throat so that he was unable to get it either up or down. Morlini concurs in his little moral that extremes are wrong and that women are crafty, making all skill or knowledge futile in opposing them. Characteristically, Straparola adds a specific location, Ravenna in the Romagna, not far inland from the Adriatic Sea, south of Venice, and north of Rimini, a city famous for its fifth-century mosaics. Moreover, he names the players Florio and Dorotea (who later becomes Felix [Felice]), making the husband a physician. There are many literary descriptions of the measures taken by jealous husbands to prevent their wives from being seen or approached. One of the most afflicted of all such husbands is Corvino in Ben Jonson's *Volpone*, insofar as his overactive imagination is obsessed with fantasized scenarios of his wife's infidelity. He too threatens his wife with incarceration, with having windows walled shut, putting chalk lines on the floor that she must never cross, hanging a lock on her body, and forcing her to walk backwards. The irony of his situation is that he too is brought to pander his own wife, but this time against her own virtuous but futile resistance, forcing her into the room where she is nearly raped.[2]

---

1 Girolamo Morlini, *Les nouvelles*, trans. Fernand Caussy (Paris: E. Sansot, 1904), no. 30, pp. 79–81; ed. Giovanni Villani (Rome: Salerno, 1983), pp. 126–31.
2 Ben Jonson, *Volpone or the Fox* (1605), ed. David Cook (London: Methuen, 1967), esp. pp. 99, 117–21.

XII. Fable 2
The Simpleton's Blackmail

LODOVICA

A certain fool, having enjoyed the favours of a fair and gentle lady, is rewarded by her husband.

I had made up my mind to relate to you a fable of a different nature from the one I'm about to tell you, but the story we just heard from my sister here has caused me to alter it, because I'm keen to illustrate how it often happens that there are benefits from just being a fool, with the added warning that it's not always a wise thing to share our secrets with them.

In Pisa, one of the noblest cities of Tuscany, there resided in our own times a certain lady most graceful and fair, although discretion compels me to pass over her name in silence. This lady, although she was joined in matrimony to a gentleman of high family standing, great wealth, and widespread influence, had a passionate flame for a young man of the city, a youth as well endowed as the lady herself with personal and social charms. Every day around noontime, this lad was received into her house to put the weapons of Cupid into play – which they did with carefree and confident minds, both of them taking the greatest pleasure from their gentle sport.

Now it happened one day that a simple-minded fellow ran past the house, crying out at the top of his voice in pursuit of a dog that had just stolen a piece of meat from him and was making its escape down the street. A great crowd of people had joined in the chase, hooting, yelling, and making a noisy hullabaloo. The dog, mindful of its own skin and intent upon saving its life, found the door of the lady's house ajar and rushed into the entrance to hide. When the nincompoop saw the dog running through the door, he ran up, knocked violently, and began to shout as loudly as he could, 'The thief who's hidden in there, drive him out right now. Don't give shelter to whoreson dogs that deserve to be hanged.' By chance, at that same moment, the lady had her lover with her, and she could only think that all those people she saw below had come to take her inamorato away and publicly expose his offences. Suddenly she was overcome with fear that she would fall into the hands of justice and suffer the penalty prescribed by law for adulteresses. Quietly she opened the door and allowed the fool to enter. As soon as she'd closed it, she threw herself on her knees in front of this dunce and, in the manner of a suppliant, she begged and entreated him of his mercy that he would keep silent, offering herself to him to take whatever pleasure he might desire of her, provided that he would refrain from exposing her lover. Well the fool, as it turned out, was no idiot in these matters, for immediately he abandoned his miff and started to embrace her tenderly and kiss her, and in no time at all got down to playing the game with her that Venus loves. But hardly were they disengaged from their endeavours when the lady's husband came home unexpectedly. Knocking at the door, he called out that someone should come and open it for him.

Although this unlooked for calamity shook her profoundly, leaving her uncertain what course she should take, nevertheless, with a noteworthy and commendable presence of mind, the wife carefully stowed her young lover under the bed – baffled and half dead with fear though he was – and then made the dim-wit climb up the chimney to hide himself. With that, she opened the door to her husband, whereupon she lavished him with her tenderest caresses and adroitly wooed him to bed to take his pleasure with her. Since it was now the winter season, the husband, seeking to warm himself, called for a fire to be kindled. So the lady had them bring wood, careful to choose the greenest that could be found, hoping it wouldn't burn quickly. But the pungent smoke rising from the burning wood made the eyes of the fool in the chimney to smart. Then he began to suffocate, hardly able to draw his breath, so that, in spite of all his efforts to remain still, he couldn't refrain from sneezing.

When the lady's husband heard this noise, he peered up the chimney and spied out the fellow hidden there, at once abusing and threatening him in round terms, taking him for some lurking robber. But the simpleton yelled back, 'Aha, Signor, you've found me out, but you haven't discovered the gallant hidden there under the bed. It's true that I've had your wife, but only once, while as for him, he's done it in your bed a thousand times.'

When he heard the fool's words, the husband went berserk with rage, and looking under the bed he found the lover there and slew him that very instant. With that, the moron, who by this time had come down from his hiding place in the chimney, caught up a thick stick and began to yell at the top of his lungs, 'You've killed someone who owed me money. So by God, if you don't pay me the amount I've got coming to me, I'll lay charges against you before the judge and accuse you of his murder.'

The homicide stood for a time reflecting upon the fool's words. And in the end, when he saw that he had little chance of getting the better of the fellow, and that his own position was a perilous one, he shut the fool's mouth with a bagful of money. By this means, the ignoramus, simple-minded as he was, gained things that wisdom might well have lost.

As soon as Lodovica had come to the end of her brief fable, she carried straight on with her enigma without waiting for further orders from the Signora.

> Gentle dames, I go to find
> What aye to me is blithe and kind,
> And having found it, next I ween
> I set it straight my knees between;
> And then I rouse the life that dwells
> Within, and soon its virtue tells.
> As to and fro my hand I sway,
> Beneath my touch sweet ardours play –
> Delights which might a savage move,
> And make you faint through too much love.

The ladies, as they listened to this enigma, restrained themselves as best they could from laughing. But carried away by the sweetness and wit of it, they were compelled to give it at least the approving tribute of a smile. To be sure, some of them were inclined to censure the damsel for telling it and fault her for her immodesty. Wherefore, aware of the wounds being dealt to her honour, she hastened to explain, 'Those of you who have smutty and malign minds can only imagine things nasty and evil; it's you who have judged my words to mean something entirely foreign to my own conception of them. This enigma of mine is intended simply to describe the viola da gamba, for when a lady desires to play it and so give delight to her friends, she places it between her knees, and then, taking the bow in her right hand she moves this to and fro so that she can draw forth from her instrument those sweet sounds that truly at times make us feel faint and sick with love.' Having heard this solution of Lodovica's subtle enigma, all the listeners were fully satisfied and content, praising it highly. But in order not to lose more time, the Signora gave the word to Fiordiana to begin with some pleasant love story, exhorting her, at the same time, to follow the example of the others in the matter of brevity. Then Fiordiana, not muffling her voice behind her teeth, spoke as follows.

XII.2 Commentary

This situation is similar to several others already investigated in which lovers are stowed away in containers, garrets, or fireplaces when the husband arrives. It resembles those particularly wherein the presence of the two lovers, through the wife's quick thinking, is explained to her returning husband as the result of their enmity towards each other, one being made to brandish a weapon as he leaves the house in a vengeful rage, while the other, still in hiding, is made out to be his intended victim (see the commentary to 'Erminione and Filenia,' IV.2). But the present story takes its own turn when one of the hidden parties comes out voluntarily, accusing the other as the greater offender, while making an exit, leaving the married couple to work out their differences. Girolamo Morlini, Straparola's immediate source for this tale, may be the first to have introduced the simpleton chasing his dog who, through a burst of uncanny insight, makes his escape with payment after accusing the husband of murder. Apparently original to Morlini, as well, is the fortuitous entry this simpleton gains by talking about his dog in such terms that the guilty woman inside can only think that he knows her situation and has to be brought to silence by any means imaginable, including sexual favours. Straparola translates Morlini's *novella* no. 30, 'De stulto qui mulierem pulchram devenustavit' (Of the fool who dishonoured a pretty woman and received from her husband a tidy sum of money), with the usual degree of fidelity, localizing the tale in Pisa, but this time inventing no names for the characters. Where Morlini found the tale is uncertain, but by the beginning of the sixteenth century, the generic type had already achieved wide circulation, particularly in Germany and France. The prototype for them all may be the French *fabliau* 'De clerc qui fu repus deriere l'escrine' (Of the priest who was hidden behind a coffer), in which a priest and a lady are preparing for love-making when another of her lovers, a jolly valet, comes barging in and sits down to the food abandoned by the priest, who is now hiding behind a chest. The valet draws out his foreplay, to the priest's great annoyance, until the husband returns. He is told to hide himself as best he can while she lets her husband in and tries to get him to fall asleep. But the master, once inside, refuses to go to bed before he takes a meal. In a suspicious mood, he says there is someone here who wants to pay his supper, and the priest, thinking himself targeted, speaks out (but with a stick in his hand), saying that he would never pay more than half insofar as the other one hiding behind the table owes at least as much. Outraged but outnumbered, the doubly cuckolded husband couldn't utter a word as the two lovers made their escape. This story began its European diffusion at least as far back as the fourteenth century and found representation in a goodly number of jest books in England, France, and Germany before Morlini came on the scene. It remained in circulation down to the eighteenth century, notably in the collection of Grécourt's *contes*. In addition to the *fabliau*, versions in five of the following predate the sixteenth century: Nicodimi Frischlini's *Facetiae*, the *Cent nouvelles nouvelles* of the court of Burgundy, the *Deceyte of Women to the Instruction and Ensample of All Men*, the *Joyeuses aventures et nouvelles récréations contenant plusieurs comptes et facétieux devis*, the *Contes de Grécourt*, Othmar Nachtgal's *Joci ac sales*, Heinrich Bebel's *Facetiae selectiores*, and Malespini's *Ducento novelle*.[3] To all these might be added, for good measure, the *novella* by Masuccio in which Massimilla takes both a priest and a tailor as lovers. She makes a date with the tailor, but the rowdy priest breaks in and assumes his place as he hides in the garret. Then, as the priest prepares to 'send the Pope to Rome,' the tailor can no longer bear the affront, so he takes out

---

3 Jean de Condé, 'Le clerc qui fu reppus derriere l'escrin' (The priest who was hidden behind the coffer), *Nouveau recueil complet des fabliaux*, ed. Willem Noomen (Assen: Van Gorcum, 1998), vol. X, pp. 54*ff*; also *Recueil général et complet des fabliaux des XIIIe et XIVe siècle*, ed. Anatole de Montaiglon et Gaston Reynaud (Paris: Librairie des bibliophiles, 1872–90), no. 91, vol. IV, pp. 47–52. Nikodemus Frishlin, *Facetiae* (Amsterdam: Ianssonnium, 1651); *Les cent nouvelles nouvelles* as *The Hundred Tales*, trans. Rossell Hope Robbins (New York: Crown Publishers, 1960), no. 34, pp. 154–7; *The Deceyte of Women* (London, ca. 1557, 1661), no. 10; the *Joyeuses Adventures* (Paris, 1682), no. 26; Jean Baptiste Willart de Grécourt (1683–1743), *Contes* (en vers) in *Oeuvres complètes* (Luxembourg: [s.n.] [1743], 1802), vol. III, p. 212; Othmar Nachtgal (Ottomaro Luscinio), *Joci ac sales mire festivi* (Augsburg [Augustae Vindelicorum]: Symperti Rüff, 1524); Heinrich Bebel, *Facetiae*, ed. Gustav Bebermeyer as *Heinrich Bebels Facetien drei Bücher* (Leipzig: K.W. Hiersemann, 1931), vol. II, p. 99; and Celio Malespini, *Ducento novelle* (Venice: Al segno dell'Italia, 1609), bk. I, no. 90. For further works pertaining to this motif, see *Die Novellen Girolamo Morlinis*, ed. Albert Wesselski (Munich: Goerg Müller, 1908), p. 287.

his pipes and blows a note that puts the priest to flight, enabling him to resume where he had left off.[4] But of course this lacks the double hiding and the return of the husband. Clearly, the pattern established by an early *fabliau*, perhaps the one cited, captured the imaginations of the many early gatherers of *facetiae* and ribald tales, so that with variations it was passed along during a good five centuries. From among these, Morlini's editor, Giovanni Villani, has chosen the version in the *Cent nouvelles nouvelles* as his most probable source on the strength of the similarities in the final discovery scene; it is a reasonable choice in relation to what remains.[5] Morlini and Straparola figure prominently in the dissemination of this tale, honest borrowers that they both were.

Straparola's knowledge of musical instruments is both precise and ambiguous. Lodovica's enigma plays upon the spread-kneed posture demanded by such stringed instruments as the viola da gamba, a source of verbal sport and amusement, it would appear, from the inception of the instrument's popularity. By 1550, the viol was still a relative novelty in Italy, having come from Spain with the Borgias late in the preceding century, thereafter spreading rapidly to Milan, Venice, and Brescia, all of which became centres for their manufacture. However, Straparola does not say 'viola da gamba' per se, but 'violone,' which is the great double bass of the consort, the grandparent of the double-bass viol of the modern orchestra (the one with the sloped shoulders), and hence played standing up. Nevertheless, for the double entendre to work, an instrument held on the calves between the knees is clearly intended. That the position and motions involved in playing upon it carried immodest overtones is beyond doubt, given the reaction to the enigma by those present. Such punning was to have a long literary life. A favourite appears in Thomas Middleton's *A Trick to Catch the Old One* wherein old Onesiphorus Hoard boasts of his niece's talents, that in having 'The voice between her lips, and the viol between her legs, she'll be fit for a consort very speedily.'

Equally intriguing are the references to the instruments accompanying the singers during the entertainments at the outsets of Nights IX and XI, for on both occasions the lirone is named, which is likewise a bowed

---

4 *The Novellino*, trans. W.G. Waters, 2 vols. (London: Lawrence and Bullen, 1895), vol. I, pp. 79–86.

5 *Novelle e favole* (Rome: Salerno, 1983), p. 146.

instrument held between the legs while one is seated. But this instrument belongs to the lira family. Its nine to sixteen gut strings and flattish bridge enable the instrument to sound rich chords suitable for accompanying songs. The *lirone* barely survived the sixteenth century, although Monteverdi fancied it, and it has been revived in recent years as part of the early music movement. For Night IX, the five young ladies brought out 'their' lironi, whereas on Night XI, when the two men sang, 'the' lironi were produced and tuned. It is for musicologists to decide whether Straparola's plurals (indicating multiple lironi) hold musicological significance, for two or more of them played simultaneously cannot have been usual and may have sounded ethereal in the extreme.

XII. Fable 3
The Language of Animals
and Pozzuolo's Wife

FIORDIANA

Federigo de Pozzuolo, a man knowledgeable in the language of animals, is urgently pressed by his wife to tell her a certain secret, but in lieu of this he beats her in a bizarre way.

It is the duty of all wise and prudent men to keep their wives in due fear and subjection, and on no account to be induced by them to wear their breeches as gear for their heads. For if husbands are led to follow other courses than these, they'll surely live to regret it in the end.

One day, Federigo da Pozzuolo, a most talented and prudent young man, was riding towards Naples on a mare that was in foal, with his pregnant wife behind him on the crupper. At the same time, there was a young colt following its mother, which, when it had been left some distance behind on the road, began to neigh and expostulate in its own language, 'Mother, mother, please slow up, because I'm still young and tender, barely a year old, and I'm not able to keep pace with you.' Hearing this, the mare pricked up her ears, sniffed the air with her nostrils, and began to neigh loudly in response, 'I have to carry my mistress who is with child, and in addition to this I'm carrying a young brother of yours in my belly, while you, who are young and brisk, carry no load of any sort strapped to your back, and still you declare that you can't travel. Come on, if you wish to come, but if not, go do as you please.'

The young man, when he understood the meaning of these words – insofar as he was well skilled in the utterances of all the birds and animals living on earth – smiled somewhat, whereupon his wife, who was surprised by this, asked him why he was chortling. To this her husband answered that his laughter just came over him spontaneously, and that, in any case, if he were to explain the cause, she could be sure he'd lose his life on the spot, for without a moment's hesitation the Fates would assuredly cut the thread. Still the importunate woman wasn't satisfied, saying that it didn't matter what the cost, she wanted to know the reason for his laughter, adding that if he wouldn't tell her, she'd strangle his windpipe. Finding himself now in a dangerous and difficult position, the husband responded to her, 'Once we've returned to Pozzuolo and have set all my affairs in order, and made all the necessary provisions for body and soul after death, I'll inform you then of all you want to know.'

With this promise from her husband, the wicked and malicious hussy fell silent. But once they had returned to Pozzuolo, she suddenly recalled to mind the promise, and right away urged her husband to keep his word. Federigo responded that she must go at once and fetch the priest, for given that he must die on account of this matter, he was anxious first to confess his sins and recommend himself to his Maker. As soon as this was done, he would tell her everything. More willing to see her husband lying dead than to give up her pestilential desire, the wife went right out to summon the confessor.

At this moment, overcome with grief as he lay in his bed, Federigo heard his dog address a few words to the rooster, who was crowing aloud, 'Aren't you ashamed of yourself, crowing like that, you wretched and miserable cock? Here's our good master very near his last breath, for which you ought to feel sorrow and melancholy, but no, you just keep on crowing as if you were glad.'

The cock gave a ready answer to these words, 'And supposing that our master should die, what have I to do with that? Am I going to be charged with his death? That's his own business if he wishes to die. Do you not know what's written in the first book of the *Politics*? "The wife and the servant stand on the same footing." So if the husband is the head of the wife, it's her bounden duty to keep his customs and practices as the laws of her existence. I've got a hundred wives of my own, if the truth be known, and by keeping them in a state of fear, I make them all quite obedient to my commands, castigating first one and then another, and pecking them whenever I think they deserve it. Now this master of ours has only a single wife, yet he doesn't have any idea about how to manage her or make her follow his orders. So let him die as he must. Don't you think that our mistress will find herself another husband soon enough? It'll just have to happen, given that he's a man of such little account and so ready to give in to the foolish and unbridled will of his wife.'

Now when he had understood and reflected upon the words he'd just overheard, all at once our young husband changed his mind, feeling a deep gratitude to the cock for all he'd said. So when his wife returned

from fetching the priest, still impertinently desiring to know the cause
of her husband's laughter, he seized her by the hair and began to beat
her with so many hearty blows that he nearly left her for dead.

Now this fable was hardly pleasing to the ladies in the audience, especially when they heard about the sound lambasting that Federigo gave
his wife. Still, they were grief-stricken to learn how she would willingly
have been the cause of her husband's death. When silence at last returned, Fiordiana, to keep the order they had adopted from the outset,
propounded her enigma as follows:

> Once on a time I had a view
> Of what would have seemed strange to you.
> A damsel, working at her trade,
> Who now a roomy opening made,
> Now shut it close, then took with care
> Something a span in length and fair;
> Its name I know not. First within
> The space she thrust its point so thin,
> And then the whole, and worked away
> With merry eye and aspect gay –
> As you would say, were you to meet
> One plying thus with hands and feet.

This enigma that Fiordiana set the company to guess gave plentiful
occasion for jest and merriment forasmuch as the greater part of, if not
all, the listeners put a most immodest gloss upon it. But Fiordiana, who,
on account of the laughter that went around, perceived that the company
had judged evilly of her enigma, so she rose to her feet and said, smiling,
'Ladies and gentlemen, the sound of your merry laughter tells me plainly
that you imagine the sense of the enigma I've just told you to be indecent,
or should I say, flagrantly indecent. But, in truth, if you'll listen to me
attentively, you'll find there's nothing lewd about it, for indeed my
enigma is meant to display to you a graceful damsel toiling at her loom.
She works the treadles with her feet and with her hands she makes the
shuttle fly from this side to that through the space between the threads,
and pulls forward the frame of the loom in order that the weft may be
closely woven.'

All the company praised this flight of Fiordiana's wit, which they
assured her was more excellent than they had anticipated of her, and

then they launched into a merry discussion. But to prevent too much time from being taken up with chatter and laughter, the Signora made a signal to Vicenza that she should take her turn at telling a story, which, with a merry smile, she began soon after.

XII.3 Commentary

This is one of Straparola's most problematic creations, for it does not appear to be of a high level of narrative achievement. The plot, in effect, is a mere pastiche of literary motifs, each one representing an independent story type. The responsibility can simply be fobbed off on Morlini, whose *Novella* 71, 'De Puteolano qui animalium loquelam intelligebat' (Of Puteolano, who understood the language of animals), served as his source.[6] But that Morlini appears to have lifted it from a version then current of the first tale of *The Thousand Nights and One Night* – that in which the vizier seeks to dissuade his daughter Shahrázád from a deflowering that night and a beheading the next day – may give pause for reconsideration.[7] Nevertheless, the first impression is of a vestige of something finer that has been lost through the misadventures of transmission. A leading motif is the gift of understanding the language of animals, one bestowed with the injunction that the secret never be revealed. The tale then takes up the motif of the inquisitive wife whose insistent curiosity is pursued even at the cost of her husband's life. Thereafter, a kind of beast fable ensues as a dog and a cock discuss their master's plight, and the rooster mocks the man's despair unto death in light of his own magisterial control over his hens. Such words, overheard, lead to the taming of the shrew with a good thrashing. Superficially, the narrative trips along from cause to effect. But it passes through incompatible story

---

6 *Les nouvelles*, trans. Fernand Caussy (Paris: E. Sansot, 1904), pp. 151–3; ed. Giovanni Villani (Rome: Salerno, 1983), pp. 312–15. Straparola makes his usual nod to the realism of the *novella* in situating the action in Pozzuolo near Naples and changing the name of the protagonist from Puteolanus to Federigo de Pozzuolo.

7 'The Tale of the Bull and the Ass,' in *Tales from the Arabian Nights Selected from The Book of The Thousand Nights and a Night*, trans. Richard F. Burton, ed. David Shumaker from the Burton Club Edition (New York: Avenel, 1978), pp. 16–24. A point to be confirmed is that the 'Story of the Ox and the Ass' actually predates Straparola – and it does, for it occurs in the fourteenth-century Syrian manuscript of the first 271 nights, the oldest to survive, today in the Bibliothèque Nationale in Paris. It has been recently translated by Husain Haddawy, *The Arabian Nights* (New York: Norton, 1990), pp. 11–14.

clusters. Why would a man forgo his life to humour a wifely whim (or escape from her nagging)? Is the story not about a Samson who should have known better than to divulge his secret? How profound is the wisdom of the animals? Are these not several tales in one, none completed except the last, which is merely to discipline a shrew?

Just why Friedrich Wilhelm Schmidt, in selecting eighteen tales from the *Piacevoli notti* for translation into German early in the nineteenth century, chose to include this tale is a further point to ponder.[8] His commentary is devoted largely to early Eastern tales in which the comprehension of animal language plays a pivotal role. Such stories are legion. His conviction is that it was a sacred gift, bestowed by supernatural creatures, often in reward for favours, and that it provided a privileged insight into the mysteries of nature or at least into the profound wisdom of the animal kingdom, and hence must be kept in complete secrecy. (It certainly provides no insight into the nature of wives in this story.) As usual, with the arcane sciences, such gifts come with all the responsibilities of initiation into a privileged cult. Schmidt, whose homework was extensive in some things, was clearly drawn to the implicit mysteries and initiations that lurk in these symbolic episodes. Another dimension of the story plays upon a feature of the limbic system and the cognitive jags that produce laughter. The laughter function is irrepressible and semiotic – a hard-wired feature of the species. Whatever it is in itself, it serves to elicit curiosity in others; it solicits communal response around a common stimulus. It is thus a gesture that demands explanation on the assumption that he who laughs is sane and that the causes of laughter are communal. But it is sometimes an ambiguous sign, apt for expressing states of mind linked to ridicule or mockery as well as to insight, incongruity, or secret understanding. The satyr employs this curiosity-arousing gesture to his advantage in the story of Costanza (IV.1), provoking the king to demand those things he would otherwise least prefer to know. In that regard, the story is about emotions and self-betrayal on the part of the husband, as well as about paranoia and nearly fatal curiosity on the part of his wife. Thereafter, the story is preoccupied with the business of revealing secrets that carry death for the divulger. The motif takes in the dilemma of Salardo (I.1), who is instructed by his father never to reveal secrets to his wife – a more pragmatic interdiction that avoids

---

8 *Sammlung alter Märchen*, vol. I, 'Die Märchen Straparola' (Berlin: Duncker und Humblot, 1817), no. 11, pp. 323–9.

vulnerability to blackmail. The engine of reversal is a micro-version of 'The Nun's Priest's Tale,' that worthy Chaucerian contribution to the gender wars reduced to the dynamics of the barnyard, wherein the mortal secret is the cock's divinatory dream concerning his imminent encounter with the fox. He too is self-betrayed, this time by groaning in his sleep, an explanation for which is wheedled out of him by an importunate wife. That his pragmatic Pertelote reduces the mystique of his dream to a matter of repletion, diet, and laxatives nearly costs him his life. But the fascinating common feature is that both Straparola's Federigo and Chaucer's Chauntecleer are overcome by uxoriousness and therefore act contrary to their own better judgments. The management of a shrew through the rough discipline of 'The Right Handling of Wives' (VIII.2) leading to eternal domestic tranquillity is the final piece in the pastiche. It brings the entire tale to closure through an act of masculine brutality – apparently the best wisdom the animal kingdom could proffer under the circumstances.

The history of this story type covers many generations, according to Antti Aarne in his 'Der tiersprachenkundige Mann und seine neugierige Frau' (The man who knew the language of animals and his inquisitive wife), for it is known in nearly all regions of the old world from Java to Africa. In such a way it can be said to have forged a place in the collective consciousness.[9] The basic story is very old, for it is to be found in the *Ramayana,* the *Jataka,* the *Vitālapañchavimsati,* the *Tooti-nameh,* and the *Alf Layla wa-layla* (The Arabian nights) in closely affiliated designs. In the prototype from the *Jataka,* a king saves a snake's life and is given a charm that allows him to understand all sounds, with the caveat that if the spell is given out, he will be forced into the fire.[10] When the ants under the table talk about eating the king's honey drippings and fallen crumbs, he laughs. The flies talk of making love, but first of rolling themselves in the king's talc, and he laughs again. The queen asks why,

---

9 *FF Communications,* no. 15 (Hamina: [Suomalainen tiedeakatemia], 1914). This was one of some sixteen story types Aarne studied on a large-scale comparative basis over a number of years in the first decades of the twentieth century, thereby adding greatly to our understanding of the spread, continuity, and variations of the folk tale. Aarne found some twenty-five versions among the African tribes, and while it is known throughout Europe in the oral cultures, it is especially popular in Finland and the Baltic regions.

10 *The Jataka, or Stories of the Buddha's Former Births,* trans. H.T. Francis and R.A. Neil (Cambridge: Cambridge University Press, 1897), no. 386, pp. 174–7.

divines an occult talent, and demands to know the spell. He explains that to tell is to die, yet being in the power of women he prepares to enter the fire. Then the gods appear as a pair of goats to correct his foolish idea. They argue with the king's donkey about their respective lots in the manner of the ox and the ass. The goat explains that the self is dearer than all things and the king takes the lesson. He calls the queen and says that he is prepared to reveal the charm if she is prepared to undergo the rites, which is one hundred lashes to the back. To this she consents, but after three, her curiosity abates. This story precedes Straparola's by some 1800 years, yet it is the very same fable.

All the other stories about listening to animals and prospering from their insights are merely collateral to this specific type. There is no need to examine here the many tales of those who held this gift from Apollonius of Tyana and Melampus to Siegfried and Pope Gerbert.[11] A substantial amount of information on this topic appears in the commentary to 'The Three Brothers' (VII.5), insofar as the third brother acquires this skill during his 'apprenticeship' in the forest, a skill through which fairy-tale benefits accrue to all three. Bird songs and the prediction of future events such as the outcome of wars was a popular medieval motif.[12] Sercambi offers a charming variant on the fable in his 'Of Tadde Cristiano of Jerusalem and his Son Paolo,' which tells of a young man's passage through a death curse that comes due upon the completion of his eighteenth year. On his way to Babylon he meets a dragon that covers him with fire and knocks him to the ground but does not slay him. As he revives from this contest, the dragon begins to speak, quelling his fears

---

11 But perhaps I might mention one! In William Baldwin's *A Marvelous Hystory intitulede Beware the Cat* (London: William Gryffith, 1570), p. 21, the story is recounted of the bishop of Alexandria and his ability to understand the language of animals. There was much speculation about how he had mastered the art, whether through natural observation and diligence, natural magic, or purging his brain with medications. When seated at dinner, the bishop stopped to listen to the chirping of sparrows. The others asked what he heard, to which he replied that a quarter of a mile distant a grain sack had fallen and broken open and the birds were calling others to supper. When a messenger was sent, it was proved true. The question of language acquisition and the demonstration of comprehension through the knowledge of remote events communicated by the animals among themselves are features common to the story type, ATU 670.

12 See *Rosenöl, oder Sagen und Kunden des Morgenlandes* (Tübingen: Cotta, 1813), vol. I, p. 144, and the *Cabinet des fées*, ed. Charles-Joseph Mayer, 41 vols. (Geneva: Chez Barde, Manget, 1786–9), vol. 16, p. 146.

and assuring him that he has passed from death to life by the will of God. The boy then receives from the dragon the gift of speaking and comprehending the language of animals. Upon his return, he is able to heal Isotta, the king's daughter, who was possessed by a frog. He takes her to a lonely place, where the frogs begin singing to one another and in this way he understands their thoughts and negotiates her deliverance. The ending is that of the conventional fairy tale and in no way pertains to the taming of shrews.[13]

By contrast, there are many tales of taming spouses, a topic already treated in conjunction with 'The Right Handling of Wives' (VIII.2). Pauli tells one such in *Schimpf und Ernst* in the name of King Solomon, who instructed a man troubled by a wicked woman that words, herbs, and stones had virtues.[14] Perplexed, the man was nevertheless forced to quit Solomon's court. But when it came time to confront the shrew, he knew what to do. After attempting inducements to peace using words and herbs, he began casting stones until she grew docile and begged for mercy. We recognize Straparola's story in the outline, but see nothing of cocks and counsel, or the danger of divulging secrets. This is more essentially a cognate to his tale concerning 'The Virtue of Stones' (VI.5), but now no longer applied to an apple thief, but a recalcitrant wife.[15]

13 Giovanni Sercambi, *Novelle*, ed. Giovanni Sinicropi, 2 vols. (Bari: Giuseppe Laterza, 1972), no. 122, vol. II, pp. 539–48.

14 Johannes Pauli, 'Ein böss Weib tugenthafft zu machen' (A wicked wife made virtuous) in *Schimpf und Ernst* (1522), ed. Johannes Bolte (Berlin: Herbert Stubenrausch, 1924), no. 134, pp. 91–2. This example must represent literally dozens of wife-taming stories involving the throwing of rocks at the wife after exhausting the virtues of words and stones. These include *Fastnachtsspiele*, such as Hans Sachs's 'Das bös Weyb mit den Worten, Würtzen und Stein gut zu machen,' 1553, ed. Ludwig Tieck, in *Deutsche Theater* (Berlin, 1817), I [no. 19]; Georgius Macropedius, *Petriscus fibula iucundissima* (Cologne: J. Gymnicus, 1540), bk. III, no. 4; *Mery Tales and Quicke Answeres*, no. 80, p. 98; Boccaccio's *Decameron*, IX.9; Franco Sacchetti's *Novella*, no. 67, Abstemius, no. 91, several of which are included in the commentary to VI.5, above, 'The Virtue of Stones.' I believe this story also appears in some form in Joachim Camerarius, *Praecepta morum ac vitae accommodate aetati puerili* (Leipzig: Valentin Papa, 1564), p. 255, and in the second part of Bernardino de Busti's *Rosarium sermonum predicabilium*, first published late in the fifteenth century, and in Lyons by Johannes Cleyn in 1513, and in Hagenau by Heinrich Gran in 1500, in one of which p. 206 is the place to look.

15 Hans Sachs employs the motif in the fable of 'Da poes weib mit den stainen' (The wicked wife [corrected] with stones). This, like Pauli's, tells of a consultation with King Solomon that leads to the advice concerning words, herbs, and stones. Sachs

Aarne has argued for the wide diffusion of the present story type with its now familiar sequence of parts, but the only contemporary version with which Morlini's has a clear and demonstrable affinity is that which is found at the outset of the *Thousand Nights and One Night*, the vizier's tale of 'The Ass and the Bull.' They differ only in the animal conversations that provoke the laughter: in one, the bull and the ass discuss labour and provender, whereas in the other a mare disciplines her lagging foal. Both stories were known in the West as independent tales (the *Arabian Nights* version is given below).[16] It is routinely said that many stories from *The Arabian Nights* were in circulation in Europe by the late Middle Ages, particularly those from the first 280 nights contained in the fourteenth-century Syrian manuscript from which Galland, early in the eighteenth century, translated the first part of his famous edition.[17] Manuscripts from this early period are themselves assemblages of the many tales once circulating independently throughout the Arabic, Persian, and Sanskrit worlds. What is perplexing in the present case is that Morlini's tale shows so few signs of the accidents and substitutions that invariably accrue to tales orally diffused; there are no grounds for imagining how his version is a systemic reduction of an Eastern tale orally transmitted in the West. Conversely, that Morlini put his version together from the bits and pieces of the motifs listed above in a way that resembles the vizier's tale told to his daughter, Shahrázád, is entirely inconceivable. Hence, how he came by a version so closely resembling that in the *Arabian Nights* remains difficult to explain, for the collection was unknown as such in Europe at

---

elaborates in full comic fashion on the details of the wife who stomps on his herbs and calls him a spendthrift, or on the colours of the stones carefully chosen, and the question about whether the husband has become 'stone mad.' The first one he throws hits her in the head and a good romp through the house precedes the capitulation. *Sämtliche Fabeln und Schwänke*, ed. Edmund Goetze and Carl Drescher (Halle: Max Niemeyer, 1900), vol. III, pp. 167–9.

16 A farmer blessed with an understanding of the language of animals detected and corrected his ass's scheme for avoiding work, laughing the while at the beast's futile stratagems. His wife's curiosity thus piqued, the familiar plot ensues; she would know his secret and the cause of his laughter even if it meant his death. She accuses him of mockery, threatens departure, and weeps for vexation, despite his vow to Allah. Nagged to despair, he prepares to divulge and die, only to overhear his cock arguing with the dog, saying that the master could not rule over even one wife while he ruled successfully over many. Thrashing her with twigs would (and did) settle the matter. *The Thousand Nights Commonly Called The Arabian Nights' Entertainments*, trans. Edward William Lane, 8 vols. (New York: Frank S. Holby, 1913), vol. I, pp. 22–8.

17 See Robert Irwin, *The Arabian Nights: A Companion* (London: Penguin, 1994), pp. 63*ff.*

that time, and there are no single stories in the literary record approximating the present tale before the nineteenth century – stories, in any case, that appear to have originated in the Galland translation and its legacy.

Stories similar to Straparola's, but unlikely to have been based on it, appear often in the grand repertoire of the European folk tale. One of the most complete is to be found in Giuseppe Pitrè's *Sicilian Folk and Fairy Tales*. It contains the Eastern motif of the snakes or two vipers, in this case, that are eaten by mistake in the place of eels, thereby providing the farmer with the ability to understand the language of animals. As in the tale told in the *Jataka*, he could hear small creatures arguing over bits of fallen food. Because his skill was acquired by accident, however, a means had to be found for the animals to impose the death penalty should the farmer divulge his secret. Then the tale could move on. It includes the collusion of the guard dogs and wolves over killing the sheep, a motif popular in Serbian versions. Overhearing their conversation in the night, the farmer informs the shepherds, who in turn put the treacherous dogs to death. For this good deed, he earns a wife and mule. There follows the mother mule's reproof of her recalcitrant child, as in Straparola, which causes the farmer (through his special talent) to laugh and his wife to nag. They go so far as to call the priest in preparation for his death, but the story of the cock and the hens brings about the wife's lambasting, this time with a belt, just as the priest arrives to hear confession.[18]

Similar stories have been collected in Norway, India, Sri Lanka (when it was still Ceylon), Palestine, and Bulgaria, which I have read, and in

---

18 *Sicilian Folk and Fairy Tales*, ed. and trans. Jack Zipes and Joseph Russo (New York: Routledge, 2009), vol. II, pp. 767–70. This story was also translated by Italo Calvino as 'Animal Talk and the Nosy Wife' in his *Italian Folktales* (New York: Pantheon Books, 1956), no. 177, pp. 639–41. The Serbian tale, 'The Snake's Gift: The Language of Animals' begins with a snake rescued from a fire who takes the frightened shepherd into a snake's lair where, good to the promise given, he is granted the ability to understand not only animals but plants, although the latter do not say much in the story! The ravens do, however, pointing him to a buried treasure. The tale includes the dogs in collusion with the wolves, the horse criticizing the mare for falling behind despite her heavy load, and the shepherd's laughter that sets up the final sequence. The shepherd is lying in his coffin ready for death when he hears the story of the dog and the cock and reverses his intentions. Csedomille Mijatovies, *Serbian Folk-Lore* (London: W. Isbister & Co., 1874), pp. 37–42.

many other places from the Caucasus to Mexico, which I have not.[19] The stories all follow the generic pattern, the early presence of which, in European storytelling, is presumed simply by dint of the widespread circulation. In the Norse tale, the cock with his fifty submissive hens speaks to the dog and the woman is beaten into obedience with a stick.[20] The Indian versions are numerous, but usually involve food fallen from the king's table and the quarrelling among tiny animals as the provocation to laughter. The king prepares for death, intending to drown himself in the Ganges to satisfy the queen, but is 'converted' by two goats. He, instead, builds an altar where he strikes off the queen's head and burns her body.[21] A version collected in Palestine is altogether more in keeping

19 A version was collected in Corsica in 1955 from a ninety-year-old shepherd that combines the story of the three brothers, the youngest of which learns the language of animals (VII.5), with the story of the correcting of wives. When the little shepherd rescues a snake from a fire who is really a magician's son, he is granted his request to understand the language of animals upon a promise never to divulge its source. He finds a treasure by information he learns from a crow. But his wife grows curious and insistent, giving him no rest so that at last he prepares to reveal the secret and die. But his rooster, overheard, reforms his thinking, so he beats his wife with a whip instead. 'The Shepherd and the Snake' in *Folktales of France*, ed. Geneviève Massignon, trans. Jacqueline Hyland (London: Routledge and Kegan Paul, 1968), pp. 239–40. It is not a current story in France, however; only two versions are recorded.

20 George Webbe Dasent, *Popular Tales from the Norse* (New York: George Putnam's Sons, 1888), pp. lxxviii–lxxix.

21 A. Campbell, *Santal Folk Tales* (Pokhuria: Santal Mission Press, 1891), pp. 22–4. Andrew Lang collected another entitled 'The Billy Goat and the King,' in which the penalty for revealing the secret is petrification. The husband and wife quarrel for a long time, but again the protagonist's mind is altered, now by a he-goat who disciplines the nagging she-goat who has been trying to expose him to pointless danger. The nanny is butted by the billy and that settles that. Andrew Lang, *The Olive Fairy Book* (London: Longmans, Green & Co., 1907), pp. 211–15. Yet another is called 'Ramai and the Bonga' (the latter a kind of mischievous household spirit). These two characters come to terms over a favour done for the latter. Being granted the power not only to understand animals but to see bongas, Ramai could now protect himself from their pranks. This was the gift leading to the curious wife and all that follows. Cecil Henry Bompas, *Folklore of the Santal Parganas* (London: David Nutt, 1909), no. 157, pp. 393–5. H. Parker collected yet another for his *Village Folk-Tales of Ceylon* (London: Luzac and Co., 1914), no. 238, vol. III, pp. 258–60. Finally, Adolf Holtzmann, *Indische Sagen*, 2 vols. (Stuttgart: Adolph Krabbe, 1854), vol. II, pp. 258–9, collected the tale of the king who knew the language of animals and spirits. Once in the still of the night he heard a ghost and began to laugh. His mother demanded the cause and the king demurred on the grounds of essential

with *The Arabian Nights*, for it includes the negotiations between the ox and the ass, as well as the dog reproving the cock for mating with the hens while the master was in danger, and the cock's unflattering but wise reply. The husband chastises his wife by beating her in an inner room.[22] When all is said, the precise origin of Morlini's production in relation to a worldwide story type remains uncertain. There can be no doubt that he found the tale at the beginning of the sixteenth century in a form closely resembling that which occurs in *The Arabian Nights*. But the absence of any affiliated versions in the Renaissance literary record means falling back upon inferential assertions about a story that must have been in circulation, one that, through whatever means of diffusion, retained an unprecedented degree of fidelity to the Arabic oikotype.

secrecy. Then he went to the holy man who had caused him to laugh and told him about his mother's demands, all of which led to the instructions that produce the now familiar denouement. This work was also edited by M. Winternitz (Jena: Eugen Diederichs, 1921).

22 J.E. Hanauer, *Folk-Lore of the Holy Land: Moslem, Christian, and Jewish* (London: The Sheldon Press [1907], 1935), pp. 190–1. For a version from Bulgaria, see A.H. Wratislaw, *Sixty Folk-Tales from Exclusively Slavonic Sources* (London: Elliot Stock, 1889), no. 39, pp. 199–203.

XII. Fable 4
Of the Sons Who Disobeyed
Their Father's Testament

VICENZA

Concerning certain sons who were unwilling to carry out the terms of their father's testament.

The greatest folly men or women can commit is to indulge the dream of doing good after they've passed on to the next world, for which reason, in our day, obedience to the commandments of the dead is deemed of little importance, or of no importance at all. I've tested this matter over and over again because of my own situation, for of all the money I've inherited, I've only been able to obtain possession of a very small portion of it. And all this has come to pass through the fault of the executors, who, out of their desire to make the rich more wealthy, have only succeeded in making the poor even poorer – a contention you'll understand clearly from the arguments I'm about to offer.

I have to tell you that in Pesaro, a town in the Romagna, there once resided a certain citizen, a man held in high esteem and very wealthy, but at the same time loath to part with his money. Upon seeing that he had come to the end of his days, he made his last will and testament. Therein he appointed his sons – of whom he had many – as the general heirs of his estate, laying upon them the burden of first paying out of his wealth a very large number of legacies and gifts in trust. After the testator was dead and buried, and duly mourned according to the customs of the country, the sons assembled themselves together to confer over the course of action they should follow in the matter of the legacies that their father had bequeathed to religious causes for the good of his soul. These they found to be not only extensive but excessive, given that if they should engage themselves in carrying out the will in its entirety, these bequests would swallow up the entire estate. Their property would then prove an absolute loss rather than any sort of benefit.

Once they had fully debated the matter, the youngest of the brothers stood up in the meeting and made the following speech, 'You're all aware I'm sure, my brothers, that there is one thing truer than truth itself, if I'm allowed to speak in these terms, which is that if the soul of our father is engulfed in the abyss of hell and condemned to stay there, it will be altogether vain and unprofitable for us to pay the legacies he has left for the repose of his soul, given that there's no redemption for spirits in hell and no hope of ever coming back again for those who enter there. And if he should now be in the flowery fields of Elysium, where reigns perpetual and eternal repose, then assuredly he stands in no need either of legacies or of bequests in trust. Or if he has been sent to purgatory, there to be cleansed of his sins for a certain period of time, it is plain and clear to everyone that when the purifying fires have done their work, his offences will disappear and he will be entirely freed of them, in which case, again, legacies will profit him nothing. For these reasons, then, I would advise that – leaving the soul of our father to be cared for by divine providence – we should simply divide his estate right now and enjoy it for as long as we shall live, just as he enjoyed it during his lifetime, in order that the dead may not profit from it more than the living do.'

I add again, at the conclusion of this brief fable of mine, that it behoves us to do our good works while we live and not after we're dead, because these days – as I mentioned at the beginning of my fable – men keep little or no faith with the dead. The subtle reasoning of the youngest brother's speech won the approval of all the company, except Vicenza herself, who was personally affected by these matters. But in order not to stand before the assembly like the picture of grief, she ended her fable by setting an amusing and fetching enigma for the others to guess at, which goes like this:

> I come with gladsome voice and face,
> And close by you myself I place;
> Then leaning over you I bend,
> And something deftly down I send,
> Until it touches the fountain bright,
> In which I take my dear delight.
> And as I deep and deeper sound,
> The keenest, sweetest joy is found.

> But, strange! I come all brisk and gay,
> And silent, weeping, go away.

'This enigma of mine is intended to describe the maid-servant who, early in the morning and again in the evening, is in the habit of going to the well to draw water. As she goes there the buckets make a noise, and as soon as she arrives near the well she leans over it, and having taken the rope in her hand, she lets it down into the well with the bucket attached to it, always cheerful in her work. The deeper down she sends the bucket to reach the cool, fresh water, the more she is heated in drawing it up again. With all that, she puts the bucket into the well dry and clattering and draws it back up silent and dripping.'

The company judged this enigma to be a very pretty, for they couldn't contain their laughter. Then once it was finished, Isabella immediately began to tell her fable in the following words.

XII.4 Commentary

Straparola here translates Morlini's *novella* no. 27, 'De filiis' (Of the sons who, after the death of their father, chose not to keep his last wishes).[23] He adds the fact that it transpires in Pesaro in the Romagna. The story deals with the contrasting interests of the two generations, the father preoccupied with the future of his soul, the sons with the uses of wealth for the enhancement of the present life. Robert Browning highlights that conflict in the 'dramatic monologue' of a bishop lying on his death bed and speaking to his sons in anticipation of just such a betrayal, begging them to honour his last wishes, not so much for his prospects in the afterlife as to enable him to continue his revenge against an old enemy in having the more spectacular tomb ('The Bishop Orders His Tomb at St. Praxed's Church'). A part of him knows, however, that his pleas will fall on deaf ears because his sons are worldly and hedonistic and will spend the money as they wish. The son in Morlini's tale provides a counter-argument after the father's death, around which Straparola adds an ambiguous moralizing frame, which implies an assault upon the misplaced desire of seeking to exercise control from the grave, or even of trying to do good after death, through the imperatives associated with

---

23 *Novelle*, trans. Fernand Caussy (Paris: E. Sansot, 1904), pp. 74–5; ed. Giovanni Villani (Rome: Salerno, 1983), pp. 132–5.

last wishes. In the exemplum to follow, it is not so much that the deceased seeks to guide his sons' lives by limiting their inheritances, but to deprive them of such legacies altogether by giving his funds to religious organizations in the hope of gaining spiritual capital. Implicitly under assault in the youngest son's position (in Morlini it is the eldest) is the doctrine of the Roman church concerning indulgences whereby the soul's sojourn in purgatory might be abridged. Why make such a futile investment, he argues. If one goes to heaven, there is nothing further to desire, and if one goes to hell, no further negotiation is possible. Purgatory, he continues casuistically, will come to an end when all sins are purged according to purgatorial principles and God's will. By this rationale, he urges his brothers to ignore the old man's testament and to divide up the money among themselves.

Morlini's tale is merely an irreverent quip. By generalizing the arguments, however, Straparola creates an inverted exemplum pertaining to an anti-doctrine. Therein resides the crux that makes this little anecdote memorable. Moreover, it espouses an overt violation of the rights of the dying to determine the uses and apportionment of their estates, no matter how frivolous, inequitable, or futile. That right is not only a question of proprietorship, but governed and compelled by the honour due to ancestors and the dying. It was a legacy of former ages when the will of ancestors was an even more integral part of daily life. The entire moral structure underpinning the Roman Empire was based on the worship even of the recently dead that included active rites and prayers to appease, honour, and give comfort to their souls in the hope that they, in their hovering presence, might give support to the living. To defy their wishes ran the risk of alienating their goodwill. That superstition was preserved in the Christian belief that the souls of the dead enjoyed moments of liberty during which they might reappear to settle scores with those remiss in keeping faith through commissioning masses and seeking the intercession of the saints. Such beliefs provided a basis for discipline, for religious observances, and a sense of continuity through duty over generations. Reduced to a matter of conflicting intergenerational interests, however, the claims of the dead are compromised, including the legal force of the last will and testament. Straparola's generalizing over the legitimized greed of the cynical and pragmatic second generation intimates a microrevolution against tradition, authority, and the law.

Nevertheless, a note of objection is sounded by the narrator, Vincenza, who says that everyone in her social set is in agreement with the clever sophist except herself. But her reasoning seems not to be a matter of high-minded principle so much as personal pique. She too had been victimized by the broken faith of executors. This provides an additional layer to the tale, now in mapping her relationship to the argument. She says that executors had deprived her of entitlements while making the rich richer and the poor poorer. Apparently she was the beneficiary of a will, the proceeds from which had been redirected to her prejudice and disadvantage. Does that mean that she is comparing the greedy sons of a niggardly will with the greedy executors of a generous will, all of whom fail to keep faith with the dead? When she concludes that it is better to be charitable when alive rather than after death, is it because the money could have been given directly to her? There may be other constructions to be placed upon her words. How, exactly, does her position as an abused beneficiary stand in an oppositional relation to the story she tells? Readers will find their own answers.

Morlini no doubt made use of a medieval source, of which 'De patre et tribus filiis' has been suggested by Villani, his Italian editor. But while it begins with a deathbed scene with three sons deliberating over their inheritance, the question in the Aesop fable is how to divide it equally.[24] The father had left a mill, a goat, and a pear tree, and in their anxiety over the matter of equity, the three foolish sons speak of dividing the tree by its qualities, and of settling who should get the goat and the mill by telling the biggest lies, or offering proof of the greatest laziness (placing the story squarely in the tradition of 'The Three Idle Rogues' (VII.1). This story is but a hand-shaking cousin at best.

---

24 Morlini, *Novelle e favole*, ed. Giovanni Villani (Rome: Salerno, 1983), p. 27. The story is from bk. V, no. 13, of *Steinhöwel's Aesop*, ed. Hermann Oesterley (Tübingen: L.F. Fues, 1873); Caxton published this work in English translation in 1484, *Here begynneth the book of the subtyl histories and fables of Esope*, ed. Joseph Jacobs (London: David Nutt, 1889), bk. V, no. 13, 'Of the fader and of his thre children,' vol. II, pp. 172–5.

XII. Fable 5
How Pope Sixtus IV Made His Servant Rich

ISABELLA

Sixtus, the Supreme Pontiff, by a single speech enriches a servant of his named Girolamo.

The tales told so far by my sisters have been so charming and witty that I'm afraid I will fail to please you on account of the meanness of my skill compared to theirs. But because of this, I still won't fail to do my part in keeping up our pleasant custom, even though the fable I'm about to relate to you has already been told by Messer Giovanni Boccaccio in his *Decameron*. Still, it wasn't expressed there in the same way I propose to treat it here, seeing that I've added a few things to make it more acceptable to your tastes.

Pope Sixtus IV, a man of Genoese extraction, was born at Savona, a city on the seacoast. Before becoming pope, he was known by the name of Francesco della Rovere. In his youthful days he was sent to school in Naples, where, among his mates, there was a certain boy from his own country, a compatriot called Girolamo da Riario. Now this Girolamo was faithfully devoted to the young della Rovere, serving him continuously both while he was a schoolboy and afterwards when he became a monk and a prelate. When Francesco was raised to high episcopal office, this same man stayed on and grew old in his employ, always faithful in the discharging of his duties. When Sixtus was at last elevated to the highest pontifical dignity through the sudden death of Pope Paul, he kept the ordinary custom of turning over in his mind the names of all his servants and attendants, bestowing munificent rewards upon them sometimes to the point of excess – with the exception of this same Girolamo, who in return for his long years of faithful service, and for all his even greater love and devotion, received only forgetfulness and ingratitude as his reward. I can only think such a thing happened to him through some malice of fortune rather than for any other reason. Taking stock, this same Girolamo, overcome with grief and disappointment, longed to take leave of the pope and Rome to return to his own country. After he had dropped to his knees in the presence of His Holiness, the licence he desired was granted to him. But the ingratitude of the pope towards his old servant was in fact so great that he refused to give him either travel money, or horses, or servants for the journey. And furthermore – which was the worst blow of all – he required Girolamo to render a strict account of his stewardship in the manner of Scipio Africanus, who was induced to display in public to the Roman people the wounds he had received in the service of the state, only to find himself rewarded later with exile for his great deeds.

Concerning avarice, it has been said most truthfully that it works its worst evils when it shows itself ungrateful. After he had departed from Rome, Girolamo went towards Naples, but as he travelled along, not a single word fell from his lips until he came to a certain pond that lay by the roadside. As he was passing, the horse he was riding felt an urge to stale, then and there adding water to water as the beast eased itself. When Girolamo took note of this, he said, 'I can see just how much you resemble my patron, who does everything without measure, and so has let me go back home without a reward of any kind, only giving me his gracious leave and licence in payment for my long years of labour in his service. Truly, is there anything more miserable in the world than the man from whom benefits drop away and perish, and upon whom injuries of all sorts close round on every side?' The servant in Girolamo's company fixed these words in his mind, noting that with regard to patience, their speaker surpassed Mutius, Pompey, and Zeno. Journeying in this manner, they came to Naples.

Then the servant, after he had taken leave of Girolamo, returned to Rome and told the pope word by word everything that had happened, and Sixtus, when he had thought it all through carefully, told the servant to go back immediately to Naples with a letter ordering Girolamo to return and present himself before the pope under pain of excommunication. Girolamo, when he had read the pope's letter, rejoiced greatly and made his way back to Rome as quickly as he could. The pope, after Girolamo had duly kissed his feet, commanded him to present himself on the following day in the senate at the hour of the council after the trumpets had sounded. In the meantime, the pope called for the creation of two very beautiful vases of exactly the same size, in one of which he placed a great number of pearls, rubies, sapphires, and other precious stones and jewels of very great value, while in the other there was nothing but pieces of metal – each vase being filled to exactly the same weight.

The next morning, when the priests, bishops, presidents, ambassadors, and prelates had come into the senate house and the pope had taken his seat on the tribunal, he had the two vases brought into his presence. Then he called Girolamo before him and addressed the assembly in the following words: 'My dear and well-beloved sons, this man whom you see before you has been faithful and obedient to my commands beyond all others who have ever served me, and I cannot praise him too highly for the manner in which he has borne himself since the earliest years of his service. Wherefore, in order that he may now obtain the due reward for his devotion and no longer have occasion to complain of his fortune and of my ingratitude, I will give him the choice between these two vases, allowing him to be his own judge, taking and enjoying the one upon which his choice may fall.'

After hearing these words of the pope, Girolamo set about to choose one or the other of the vases, but the poor misfortunate creature, after long consideration, fixing first upon one and then upon the other, in the end – as his ill luck would have it – chose the one filled with pieces of metal. When the other vase was opened and Girolamo saw the great treasure that it contained, how it was filled with emeralds, sapphires, diamonds, rubies, topazes, and other kinds of precious stones, he was overcome with amazement and ready to die of vexation. The pope, observing how disappointed and grief-stricken the poor fellow looked, exhorted him to confess himself straightway, declaring that this thing must have happened to him as a punishment for sins he had neglected to acknowledge. Then, after Girolamo had duly confessed himself and received absolution, the pope imposed upon him a secret penance, which was that for an entire year he should come every day at a fixed time into the senate – a place unlawful to enter by any unauthorized person – where the private affairs of kings and states and of great nobles were debated. There, he was to whisper an Ave Maria into the pope's ear. Sixtus likewise commanded that every door at which Girolamo might present himself should be immediately opened to him and that he should have free and on-going access to the papal presence with all the attendant honours.

Therefore, when the next day arrived, Girolamo, without saying a word to anyone, went into the pope's presence, bearing himself in a worshipful manner, but having at the same time a certain air of presumption about him. Having gone up beside the seat of St Peter, he directly performed the penance that had been imposed upon him. As soon as he had finished whispering into the pope's ear, he turned and went out, bringing astonishment by what they'd seen to all who were present. Then the ambassadors wrote news to their sovereigns saying that Girolamo was the real pope and that all questions coming before the senate were dealt with and settled according to his will. By reason of this report, Girolamo very soon gathered together a great sum of money made up of the many gifts that were sent to him by Christian princes everywhere, so that in the whole of Italy no richer man than he could be found. In this manner it came about that by the end of his year of penance he found himself more than happy with his lot and the possessor of great riches. Next, the pope created him a noble of Naples and of Forlì, and many other cities besides. So Girolamo, from the low condition in which he was born, became distinguished and illustrious in the same way as Tullus Hostilius and David, who spent their youths in feeding sheep, while later in their lives, the one reigned over and doubled the extent of the Roman empire, while the other became the chief of the kingdom of the Jews.

As soon as Isabella's fable had come to an end, and in the manner they all desired, Molino rose to his feet and said, 'There was no need, Signora Isabella, for you to excuse yourself in any way at the beginning of your fable, seeing that it has far outdone all those which have been told this evening.'

To this Isabella replied, 'Signor Antonio, if I really thought you were telling the honest truth I'd be most elated, because in that case I'd have won the praise of him who is praised by all. But because you say this by way of jest, I'm content to remain in my ignorance, leaving the glory of success to my sisters here, who are of more brilliant parts than I am.' But in order that the discussion not be further prolonged, the Signora made a sign that Isabella should follow up right away with her enigma, whereupon the damsel continued, still elated by the praise she had received.

> Good sir, there was a time I trow,
> Which time is gone for ever now
> Wherefore the thought comes back to me,
> That once I something gave to thee
> Which I had not. Now I decline
> To give it, though 'tis really mine.
> Hard must it be for you to dream
> Of what I was, what now I seem

How once I had what now I lack.
Therefore into the streets go back,
And call on one who lacks it too,
And beg her give this boon to you.

Here Isabella brought her enigma to an end, and because it was full of deep mystery, it was interpreted by the company in various ways, although no one there fully grasped its meaning. When Isabella perceived this, she declared, with a bright and merry face, 'By your leave, ladies and gentlemen, I'll now explain the meaning of the enigma that I've just recited to you. In fact, it's intended to describe a lovesick lady not yet married who was altogether subdued by the love of a certain gentleman. But after she was married to another, she would have no more dealings with her lover, and on this account she persuaded him to take his way about the streets, seeking the love of those ladies who had no husbands.'

Isabella's skilful solution to her subtle enigma delighted the company no end, who praised it one and all. But now already the crested cock had announced the coming of the bright morning, so the illustrious company took leave of the Signora, who, with a joyous face, begged them all to return in good time to her house on the following evening, which commandment, with the best of grace, they all promised to obey.

The End of the Twelfth Night

XII.5 Commentary

Faithful service and the ingratitude of princes, a complaint overheard on the way home that gets back to the pope, the papal recall and the promise of reward, the choice between two equal vases, the harsh dictates of fortune and the imputation of unconfessed sins, the permission to whisper an Ave Maria daily in the pope's ear, and the rich shower of bribes, gifts, and esteem from those who interpret this privilege as proof of high political influence – such are the elements of this story that have been brought together from diverse sources to form a pseudo-historical moment in the lives of Pope Sixtus IV and his nephew, Girolamo Riario. The narrative design incorporates three distinct motifs. The first is the analogy between a ruler's imprudence in bestowing rewards upon the unworthy and the urination of a beast of burden into a puddle or river. This comparison is overhead by a retainer and reported to the ruler in question. Its interpretation is hardly difficult: the bestowal of rewards upon the unworthy is like the gesture of the animal adding useless water to water. But the sovereign found it clever enough to consider its author worthy of recall for reward. The second narrative motif contradicts the first, however, because the ruler now chooses to have that compensation determined by pure chance or fortune, which he is pleased to associate with providential will. The reader may well wonder at the logic or fairness of it all. Matching caskets or vases are prepared, one containing treasure, the other dross or worse, necessitating a choice, the outcome of which is determined by blind luck. In this gesture, the ruler subtly throws off any imputation of ingratitude, for merit is now to be determined by the good or ill fortune of the man who must choose. Should chance go against him, it may be said that to reward him goes against Providence, or that hidden vices or unforgiven sins have dictated his destiny. A third and more cynical motif then appears, cancelling the two previous ones. It is the trick of exacting bribes by masquerading as the court favourite. The illusion is created by asking for the simple favour of whispering in the king's ear in public. The privilege, at the same time, is the cheapest of means on the part of the ruler for rewarding his servant. The first story type relates reward to the wit, discretion, and service of the retainer. The second necessitates that rewards be determined by chance with overtones of providential intentionality. The third links reward to power politics, illusion, gifts, and bribes. These three motifs have independent origins, but given their common ends they are assembled sequentially to fashion a single tale. Nevertheless, their conflicting principles produce a logical dissonance that destabilizes meaning.

Each part has a history of its own. *Barlaam and Josaphat*, written around 800 A.D. by a Greek monk named Joannes Damascenus, channels the second of the motifs into the Latin West and subsequently into its vernaculars. Charles Swan, in the annotations to his translation of the *Gesta romanorum*, provides a version of the relevant passage from one of the earliest surviving Greek manuscripts of *Barlaam* (MS Laud c. 72 Bibl. Bodl.) in Oxford's Bodleian Library. The king commissions the construction of four chests: two of them covered with gold and sealed with gold locks, but filled with rotten bones; two of them smeared with pitch and closed with rough ropes, yet filled with precious stones and rich and savoury ointments. These he places before his nobles in an elaborate object lesson concerning the superficial choices of the outward senses and the more subtle choices made through moral insight. When his retainers universally choose the caskets of external gold, he makes his point by treating them to the horrid stench of carrion, filling them all with revulsion. Here in ovo are the contrasting contents of Pope Sixtus IV's vases, and the imputation of corrupt thoughts to those who are led by outward allurements to make ultimately deceiving choices. It is but a small extra step to have a man's life in service be weighed in these terms, making his moral purity the basis for providential choice. But the matter is a most subtle one, for in the asymmetrical outer dressing of the caskets, the lesson is in judgment, whereas for Riario, in contemplation of two identical vases weighing exactly the same, the choice is attributed entirely to divine will. Therein resides one of the great paradoxes of – and a nexus of logical slippage within – the Christian world order. What is the ethical significance of sheer chance in relation to moral values, the rewarding of faithful service, or divine will? The story of Barlaam and Josaphat was incorporated into Jacques de Vitry's *Exempla or Illustrative Stories from the Sermones Vulgares*, no. 47, and into book 14 of the *Speculum historiale* of Vincent of Beauvais, where this episode may be found in chapter 6.[25]

John Gower provides an interpretation of this story in his *Confessio amantis*. He writes of a king who submits two caskets to his grumbling courtiers, who in turn choose that which has the straw and rubbish inside. By this means, the king demands the cessation of their complaints

---

25 *Gesta romanorum, or Entertaining Moral Stories,* trans. and ed. Charles Swan and
    Wynnard Hooper (London: Bohn Library Edition, 1876; reprint, New York, Dover,
    1959), pp. 390–1. In the spiritual romance it is told by the hermit Barlaam to King
    Avenamore. See *L'histoire de Barlaam et Josaphat*, ed. Leonard R. Mills (Geneva: Droz,
    1973), or *Barlaam and Josaphat: English Lives of Buddha*, ed. Joseph Jacobs (London:
    David Nutt, 1896), pp. lxiv–vi, cvii. This work, long attributed to John of
    Damascene, is actually from the life of Gautama Buddha. The story makes its way
    from Greek to Latin in the eleventh century, and into French in the thirteenth
    century, with parts appearing in the *Legenda aurea*, gathered together after 1250.
    The *Exempla or Illustrative Stories from the Sermones Vulgares of Jacques de Vitry*,
    ed. Thomas Frederick Crane (London: Folk-Lore Society, David Nutt, 1890),
    pp. 18–19. See also Vincentius Bellovacensis (Vincent of Beauvais), *Speculum
    historiale* (Graz: Akademische Druck und Verlagsanhalt, 1965), bk. IV, chap.10,
    vol. IV, pp. 578–604. This story of the four chests is also represented in Jean de
    Condé's 'Dis dou roi et des hermittes,' in *Dites et contes de Baudouin de Condé et de son
    fils Jean de Condé*, ed. A. Scheler (Bruxelles: Devaux, 1866–7), vol. I, p. 67, and in the
    Roman de Girart de Rosillon, according to Thomas Frederick Crane in his notes to de
    Vitry's *Exempla*, p. 154. It is also told by Johannes de Bromyard, *Summa praedicantium*
    (Nuremburg: Anton Koberger, 1485), 'Honour,' art. iv, exemplum. See also Nicole
    de Bozon, *Contes moralisés* (ca. 1350), ed. Lucy Toulmin Smith and Paul Meyer,
    Société des anciens textes français (Paris: Firmin Didot, 1889), no. 84, p. 106.

because in their choosing amiss a higher power had indicated their lack of merit. Thus, he sidesteps imputations of ingratitude, for he had indeed risked great wealth in the unchosen vessel. The statistician might well point out that such a system of 'heads or tails' would very neatly cut the king's payroll in half, while blaming the shortfall on God's will. But the matter, of course, can never be worded in such a crassly pragmatic way.[26]

An intriguing adaptation of this motif appears in the *Gesta romanorum*. There the principle of merit as determined by chance or providence is applied even to the person to whom the goods belong by right and law. A carpenter, fearful of losing his accumulated gold, hides it all inside a log for safe keeping. But a flood rises and sweeps the log away, bearing it along for some distance before it is retrieved by a good and honest man who piles it away for firewood. When, by accident, he discovers its rich contents, he places the log in safe keeping until its owner comes forward. At last, the carpenter arrives in search of his treasure, which the householder admits to having. But he insists that his visitor submit to a ritual banquet in which three cakes will be served, from which he must make his choice. One contains earth, another bones, and the third a portion of his own gold. The carpenter selects, for its weight, the one containing earth, and then the one containing bones, while awarding the third to the householder. Such choices are deemed incontrovertible proof, by the host, that God does not wish the money restored and so the carpenter is not only disappointed but abused for his depravity and greed. His gold is then distributed to the poor, blind, and lame before his very eyes.[27]

---

26 John Gower, *Confessio amantis* in *The English Works*, ed. G.C. Macauley (London: Oxford University Press [1901], 1969), bk. V, ll. 2273–2390 [Tale of the two coffers], vol. II, pp. 9–12. Those deemed worthy of reward approached the king, only to learn that Providence (or pure chance) would decide the justice of their complaints. After making two identical coffers, one filled with riches, the other with dross, the king made a speech, boasting his fairness in the matter. He urged them to take counsel together and that Providence would provide, for which he was thanked by all on bended knee. But the disgruntled seekers chose the straw and stones and were compelled to leave, both empty handed yet satisfied.

27 Trans. Charles Swan and Wynnard Hooper (New York: Dover, 1959), pp. 189–90, and Introduction, no. 48, pp. xliv–xlvii. It is also included in Thomas Wright's *A Selection of Latin Stories from Manuscripts of the 13th and 14th Centuries* (London: Percy Society, 1842), p. 25. These stories lead in the direction of Ser Giovanni's tale in *Il pecorone* (1378), which becomes Shakespeare's *Merchant of Venice* with its famous casket-selection scene. See A. Collingwood Lee, *The Decameron: Its Sources and Analogues* (New York: Haskell House, 1966), pp. 297–8 on the sources of *Decameron* X.1 in the English *Gesta romanorum*, and pp. 304–6 concerning the stories about

This story was undoubtedly Eastern in origin, for there is a most pertinent version in *The Ocean of the Streams of Story*, Somadeva's *Katha sarit sagara*, a work compiled in the twelfth century in Persia, but from materials as much as six centuries older.[28] In the royal city of Lakshapura there lived a king of exemplary generosity who nevertheless left a certain petitioner in rags lingering night and day at his gate. Then he offered the man an opportunity to serve, which this beggar made the very best use of, yet nothing was given in compensation. Similar occasions followed to the same effect until, after six years, the king relented and took pity, employing particular means to test whether Fortune was ready to admit him. He had a citron crafted and filled with jewels from his treasury that he presented to the man in the presence of his chiefs and ministers. Thinking himself scorned, the beggar gave the gift to another beggar, until eventually it returned to the king's own hands as a mere trinket. Such bestowals were made several times amid great pomp and each time the object was taken for a bauble until it accidently fell and broke open. The man's own cynical thoughts had been his destiny. In both tales it is not the king's unwillingness to reward, but Fortune's inclination to maldispose, for when the citron dropped, all the people cried out that they too had been deceived, but that the king's conduct in the matter had been impeccable.

This story's most direct legacy in the West appears in the early-thirteenth-century supplemental stories to the *Novelle antiche* found in the Panciatichiano MS.[29] The vehicles of potential royal largesse are no longer citrons but large loaves of white bread, the one natural and the other baked full of gold coins. As in the Straparola tale, there is the random choice between identical appearing loaves, yet we are reminded

---

gold hidden in logs and the test by pasties. Other stories about refuse and gold baked into pasties include the *Chronicle of Lanercost* (1272–1346), ed. Herbert Maxwell (Glasgow: J. Maclehose & Sons, 1913) (not seen), Johannes Pauli's *Schimpf und Ernst*, ed. Hermann Oesterley (Stuttgart: Litterarischer Verein, 1866), vol. I: no. 326, p. 206, and commentary in vol. III, p. 293, and Valentin Schumann's *Nachbüchlein* (1559), ed. Johannes Bolte (Hildesheim: Georg Olms, 1976), no. 155a, p. 115.

28 Trans. C.H. Tawney, ed. N.M. Penzer, 10 vols. (Delhi: Motilal Banarsidass [1923], 1984), no. 69, 'The Story of King Lakshadatta and His Dependent Labdhadatta,' vol. IV, pp. 168–72.

29 *Novellino e conti del duecento*, ed. Sebastiano Lo Nigro (Turin: Unione Tipografico editrice, 1968), no. 11 of the MS. Panciatichiano 32, pp. 385–9; *Cento novelle antiche*, ed. Biagi (Florence: Sansoni, 1880), no. 147, p. 173.

of the Eastern tale insofar as the rich loaf, when bestowed, is taken for an ordinary one and sold for a few pennies to a fellow beggar – for there are now two protagonists, both blind beggars, who are constantly wrangling. The French king had taken a bemused interest in their arguing because it was over which leader would be victor in the war between France and Flanders. He who acquired the enrichened loaf in the end was, of the two beggars, he who had pronounced all along that Providence would decide the war, just as Fortune had granted him the material prize.[30] Fortune's role is alien, perhaps, to our sense of justice in matters of reward. But such a tale was one means for illustrating the inherent irony associated with this medieval *idée-force*. Fortuna was a law of sorts both of eternal ambiguity and of hidden order, for it represented at once the inscrutability of future events, sheer chance, a talent for seizing opportunity, a systemic exchange between prosperity and decline, and the mysterious workings of the divine will in human affairs. Thus, from 'blind fate' to hidden order and necessity, the notion of Fortuna, with its implicit symmetry of constant change, of rising and descending motions, taunted the 'pre-modern' mind, leading to just such tales as these in which Fortune is both intuition, opportunity, luck, ill-luck, and destiny, eternally known to God and sometimes to kings, but ever dark to the minds of lower mortals.

The third motif may likewise be said to have originated in the *Katha sarit sagara* of Somadeva. It is the 'Story of the Rogue Who Managed to Acquire Wealth by Speaking to the King.' This clever chap imagined the scheme on his own, disguised himself as a rich merchant, gained an audience with the king and asked for one favour, with the understanding that it would cost the king nothing, and that he would even go halves with his majesty should any profit accrue from the arrangement. That favour was merely to have whispering access to the king's ear on a daily basis. The king agreed. But for this schemer, it was not enough merely

---

30 There were several variations on this tale in circulation including 'De duobus caecis' (Of two blind men), which Thomas Wright found in the British Library's MS. Reg.7 E. IV. fol. 185r, and included in his *Selection of Latin Stories from Manuscripts of the 13th and 14th Centuries* (London: Percy Society, 1842), no. 104, p. 93. It tells of wrangling beggars overheard by the emperor, who are taken to court, where they are presented with identical-appearing loaves, one containing a capon, the other gold florins. Their dispute was over God's bounty versus that of kings. He who had faith in Providence chose the rich loaf. For the curious, the story is also retold by John Gower in his *Confessio amantis*, bk. V.

to murmur and walk, for he would, from time to time, turn and give meaningful looks to a courtier singled out in the entourage. Frightened by the attention, the courtier would beseech him for an explanation, and thereby learn that he had fallen under suspicion of infidelity, or some related failing. Then the king's confidant assures him that he will gladly intercede on his behalf – implicitly for a consideration it goes without saying. Naturally, bribes and rewards begin to flow and he becomes prosperous beyond all imagining. This was a scheme proposed by a crafty and fraudulent-minded wag who understood perfectly the vulnerability of courtiers and the false assumptions they would make about his proximity to the ruler and the intentionality of his glances.[31]

This Eastern story came to the West only a few decades after its appearance in the *Ocean of the Streams of Story* in the *Anecdotes historiques* of Etienne de Bourbon. There was something about it that tempted writer after writer to assign it to a specific historical context. Etienne states that a 'trottier' or messenger at the court of King Philippe Auguste demanded of the king as his sole reward for years of loyal service the privilege of whispering a paternoster in his ear on court days. When the others saw this singular familiarity, they honoured him and gave him their petitions to carry to the king. This material appears to have originated around 1260 in the *Tractatus de diversis materiis praedicabilibus*, a collection of sermon exempla in the manner of Jacques de Vitry.[32]

A prototype for the first motif may be traced conveniently to Busone da Gubbio's *Fortunatus Siculus o sîa l'Avventuroso Ciciliano*, a historical romance written in 1311. The Squire of the Fortress was adventurous if not always wise. He had served faithfully but was dissatisfied by his remuneration and determined to leave. The king was not pleased by his request, for he esteemed him greatly, but gave his consent together with a mule and 25 silver marks. When the squire came to a large river the mule stopped, and there, as the animal was urinating, the traveller made the famous comparison, observing that while he had received next to nothing, the grandees are made even richer by the king's largesse. This saying was

---

31 *The Ocean of the Streams of Story*, trans. C.H. Tawney, ed. N.M Penzer, 10 vols. (Delhi: Motilal Banarsidass [1923], 1984), chap. 66, no. 158, vol. V, pp. 186–8.

32 Etienne de Bourbon, *Anecdotes historiques, légendes et apologues*, ed. A. Lecoy de la Marche for La société de l'histoire de France (Paris: Librairie Renouard, 1876), part III, no. 200, p. 175; Stephanus de Borbone, *Tractatus de diversis materiis predicabilibus*, ed. Jacques Berlioz (Turnhout: Brepols, 2002–6), no. 414.

carried back to the king, who recalled him immediately. Then he gave him a great deal of money and he became a rich knight. With Busone, this anecdote remains complete in itself, revealing its once independent status – that a just and fair quip was worth a just and fair reward.[33]

Coming at last to the middle of the fourteenth century and to the *Decameron* (X.1), we encounter the first amalgamation of parts in a story that now tells of Ruggieri de' Figiovanni, a Tuscan-born adventurer who could find nothing sufficiently rewarding to do in his own native land.[34] He thus took arms, horses, and retainers and made his way to Spain to enlist in the service of King Alfonso. Loyal and long in his service, nevertheless the king granted castles, cities, and baronies only to the undeserving. Ruggieri, discontented, determined to quit his service. The king granted him a mule for his return home and allowed him to depart, but he sent a domestic along to hear what he might say along the way. This would prove to be a test of his character and nature, for after many conversations, the 'spy' heard nothing of reproach. Only when the mule staled in the river did Ruggieri make the famous comparison, which was duly reported back. Upon Ruggieri's return, the king greeted him warmly and asked for an interpretation of his dark saying concerning the mule and himself. The knight made no bones of it, but told him outright that his management of bequests was like mule urine to a stream, a misplacement of unneeded resources. Boccaccio's king now makes the transition from his own ingratitude to the imputation of misfortune, saying that the knight's own bad luck prevented him from offering compensation. This was riddle for riddle, so the king produced two chests to illustrate his point. In choosing, the knight would see whether it was the king or his own luck that determined his lack of remuneration. When he chooses the dirt-filled chest, destiny is deemed to have spoken and the story hastens toward its close with this double deception. Only then does the king trump fortune and grant to him the chest of riches, almost as an afterthought. Boccaccio has joined the motifs of 'recall by clever quip' and 'merit determined by hazard' by having the king shift from one

---

33 Busone da Gubbio (Raffaelli), d. 1349, *Fortunatus siculus* (1311), ed. George
   Frederick Nott (Milan: Giovanni Silvestri, 1833), bk. II, chap. 17, pp. 248–51. See also
   Fortunatus siculus, ed. G.F. Nott (Florence: Dante, 1832), bk. II, chap. 17, pp. 176–80.
34 *The Decameron*, trans. J.M. Rigg, 2 vols. (London: Navarre Society, ca. 1900), vol. II,
   pp. 314–16.

mode to the other. The *beffe* of the paternoster in the king's ear is still missing, and it was up to Morlini, or an interim writer, to realize the final accretion.

Morlini adapts Boccaccio to his own historicized fiction of injured merit in the person of Girolamo Riorio. Throughout his later career, Girolamo was an associate and political henchman for his uncle, Francesco della Rovere, the man who, in 1471, became Pope Sixtus IV. Both were born in Liguria, in or near Savona, the pope in 1414 and Girolamo in 1443. That Morlini applies these story motifs appropriately in assessing Girolamo's relationship to the pope is up for historical investigation. The younger man had not done badly in receiving the city of Imola as a dowry in 1473 in anticipation of his marriage to Caterina Sforza, while in 1477 he took the city of Forlì, which was left to him by papal consent. But in April of 1478, matters took a turn, for the pope attempted to consolidate his power by liquidating Giuliano and Lorenzo de' Medici in the Pazzi plot. Girolamo was not only directly involved, but stood to benefit materially by its success.[35] Lorenzo, however, escaped, wounded but alive. The plot's failure dashed all hope for gain and left Girolamo a marked man, whether or not his assassination at the hands of Orsi family members in Forlì was in any way motivated by past vendetta or only by the Orsi's immediate financial concerns and the aspirations of the city to free itself from a tyrant. That was in 1488, some four years after the pope's death. Following the Pazzi disaster, the pope had named Girolamo as the captain general of the Church. But for all that, Girolamo may have been a man rankled by injured merit. What is certain is that the inventions, sayings, and political manoeuvres employed in Morlini's 'De summo Pontifice Sixto' are literary motifs of several centuries' standing and current in a substantial number of late medieval and early Renaissance texts.[36] If Girolamo uttered complaints, they are here poured into a ready-made narrative matrix. Straparola's translation of this Latin text offers no substantive changes; he reproduces the tripartite story in its same proportions and design.

The story received some further attention, whether as a retelling of Boccaccio's tale in the *Decameron*, as in Nicolas de Troyes's *Grand Parangon*

---

35 On the Pazzi conspiracy, see Lauro Martines's *April Blood: Florence and the Plot against the Medici* (Oxford: Oxford University Press, 2003).

36 Girolamo Morlini, *Les nouvelles*, trans. Fernand Caussy (Paris: E. Sansot, 1904), no. 5, pp. 27–32.

des nouvelles nouvelles, no. 170, or as an event in the life of a particular ruler, as in the case of the emperor Sigismund. It was first told in his name in the *Chronica durch M. Johannes Carion vleissig zusamen gezogen meniglich nutzen zu lesen,* a story transferred to Duke Frederick Elector of Saxony and Kaiser Sigmund by Martin Luther in his *Tischreden* (table talk).[37]

---

37 Nicholas de Troyes, *Le grand parangon,* ed. Émile Mabille (Paris: A. Franck, 1869), no. 170; Johannes Carion, *Chronica* (Wittemburg, 1533), p. 2013v; trans. into English as *The thre bokes of cronicles* (London: S. Mierdman, 1550); Martin Luther, *Colloquia, oder Christliche nutzliche Tischreden* (Leipzig: Bartolomaei Volgis, 1621), chap. 38, p. 490.

The Thirteenth Night

Phoebus had already taken his departure from this land of ours and the clear brightness of the day was gone and faded, so that now the forms of objects no longer made themselves clearly apparent, when the Signora, having come out of her chamber accompanied by the ten damsels, went to the head of the staircase to give gladsome welcome to the gentle company that had already disembarked from their boats. When all had taken their seats according to their rank, the Signora said, 'It seems to me that tonight it would be well and becoming – after the customary dancing and performance of a song – for all the gentlemen as well as all the ladies to each tell a fable, because it isn't fair that the young ladies should bear this burden alone. If my proposal meets with the approval of everyone here, then each will tell a story, but on the one condition that it remains brief, so that, on this last night of carnival, you'll all have the time you need for your recitation. As the principal person among us, Signor the Ambassador (Giambattista Casali) should be in first place, and then, one by one, you should all take turns according to your degree.'

The Signora's proposal won the approval of everyone, and so after they had danced for a time, she commanded the Trevisan and Molino to tune up their instruments and sing a canzonetta, whereupon these loyal sons of obedience took up their lutes and declaimed the following song:

Song

The choicest gifts of beauty and of grace
    That mortal beauty ever knew,
Lady, kind Nature lavishes on you.
    When gazing on your lovely face,
Your bosom into perfect beauty swelling,
Where Love holds sway, proud of his ivory throne,
    I hear my fancy telling
That surely you were made in God's own place,
And sent on earth to honour us alone,
To bid us for our trespasses atone,
    And teach how far excelling
Our feverish life of heat and cold
Those glories are the blest in Heaven behold.

The song performed by the Trevisan and Molino delighted all the listeners, and they applauded it heartily. When it had come to an end, the Signora begged Signor the Ambassador to begin his story, which he, lacking in his manner all rustic incivility, took up at once.

XIII. Fable 1
The Huntsman and the Madman

CASALI OF BOLOGNA

Maestro Gasparino, a physician, by the virtue of his art, works a cure on certain madmen.

The task of fable-telling which the Signora has assigned to me is a daunting one, since, in my view, this activity belongs rather to the ladies than to us men. But given that my playing the raconteur is her desire and the wish of this honourable company, I'll set to work with all my strength to satisfy your expectations. And while I may not succeed to your total delight, I hope at the least to divert you somewhat with the one I'm about to tell.

In England there once lived a certain very rich man – the head of his family – who had only one son, named Gasparino, whom he sent to Padua, where he might apply himself to the study of letters. But this youth took little interest in learning about literature, and even less in putting out an effort to surpass his fellow students in the pursuit of wisdom, using most of his waking hours in card games and gambling, which in turn brought him into the company of dissolute companions devoted entirely to lascivious and worldly pleasures. All of his time, in fact, he spent in this course of living, and all of his money as well, so that instead of learning medicine and mastering the works of Galen, as was his duty, he studied the art of fine dining, table games and other recreations, seeking pleasure in all things which proffered delight.

After five years had gone by, he returned to his native country, where everyone who met him could see clearly that he had gone backwards rather than forwards during his course of study. While it was his desire to be taken for a Roman, all of his friends took him merely for a barbarian and a violent Chaldean. After a short while, he fell into such ill repute among the people of the city that men pointed him out with their fingers, making him the byword and gossip of the town. I leave to your imagination the grief his unfortunate father must have felt, who would rather have forfeited all his money and his daily bread as well than to have abandoned his proud ambition of making a man of distinction out of his son. Now in truth he was likely to lose them both. One day, hoping to assuage his tormenting grief, the father called his son to him, whereupon he opened the chest in which he kept his money and jewels and gave the boy – who was by no means deserving of such bounty – half of all his goods, saying to him, 'My son, take your share of your paternal heritage and remove yourself from my sight so that I nevermore see your face, for I would rather be a childless man than have a son living with me who, through his infamous life, brings nothing but shame.'

In less time than it takes to tell it, the son laid hands on the money and jewels, and in ready keeping with his father's injunction, got himself out of town. Having travelled a long way from home, he came one day to the outskirts of a forest with a mighty river nearby. On this spot he set to work to build a great house of marble, fitted with bronze doors. Then he caused the river to flow around it on all sides, cutting trenches and watercourses in such a way that he could make the water rise and fall according to his needs. In some of the trenches the water could be made to rise to the full height of a man, and in others it would rise up to a man's eyes, in others to his throat, and others to the breast, while in still others, up to the navel, the thighs, and the knees. To the side of each of these trenches he had an iron chain attached, and over the entrance door of this great house he set up a tablet with the following inscription: 'In This Place Madmen Are Cured.'

In due time, the fame of Gasparino's house spread abroad, becoming known to everyone. Then from various places madmen were brought there to be healed, and in such vast numbers that it might have been said to rain imbeciles. Once they arrived, the master of the place had them placed into the trenches according to the degree of the madness which afflicted them. Some of them he treated with blows, others with vigils and fasts, while others needed only to breathe the fine pure air of the vicinity, and thus, little by little, he returned them to their right minds. In the spacious courtyard before the entry door, as a custom, he kept some of the morons and other men of weak intellect whose wits had been deranged by sunstroke.

One day it happened that a huntsman passed by this place carrying a hawk on his fist, accompanied by a great number of hounds. As soon as the demented ones in the courtyard caught sight of him, they fell into amazement at the spectacle of a man riding with hawks and dogs. So one of them straight off began to question him about the kind of bird he carried on his hand, and whether it was a trap or snare to catch other birds, and just why he kept and fed it. The huntsman replied, 'This bird you see here is called a hawk, which, by its very nature, is rapacious. These other animals are dogs who seek out certain fat birds which are good to eat called quails. When they find them, this hawk captures them and then I eat them.'

All this the moron followed up with more questions: 'So tell me, then, how much did you pay for these dogs, and how much for the hawk, and how much for the horse that you're riding?'

The huntsman answered, 'I bought my horse for the sum of ten ducats, my hawk cost me eight ducats, and my dogs twelve. Besides this, they cost me twenty ducats a year to feed them.'

'Well then tell me,' said the fool, 'and tell me the truth, how many quails do you catch in a year, and how much are they worth?'

The huntsman answered, 'I take two hundred or more, and they're worth to me at least two ducats.'

Then the madman – who in this business was not devoid of some sense – raised his voice and said, 'You should go away as fast as you can, because you'll be taken for an idiot here. You spend fifty ducats a year in order to gain two, without taking account of the time you waste in getting them. Better run, for God's sake, run. Because if the master of this place catches you here, he'll put you straight into one of his trenches, where you'll be drenched and nearly drowned. Myself, I'm a poor idiot, but you're a bigger fool than I am, bigger, in fact, than the worst loon in the place.'

The fable told by Signor Ambassador won everyone's praise, although there wasn't much of a fable to it, being an account of the plain truth, in that as a rule, huntsmen surpass all others in foolery for not having enough to live on, yet waste their time and money in hunting. Not wanting to fall behind in his task as a storyteller, the ambassador then delivered a choice enigma:

> Say, have you ever heard them tell
> About a creature said to dwell
> Far in the East? Though full of guile,
> 'Tis conquered by a maiden's smile,

> And in her lap will listen tame –
> No lion, though it bears the name.
> Contented in her arms to die,
> Its horned head it carries high,
> And by its loving tears they say
> All poisonous bane is washed away.

This graceful enigma set by Signor the Ambassador gave the company no less delight than the fable he had told to them, for it presented to the minds of the ladies a suggestion of unknown delight, and although all guessed its meaning, yet not one of the company was disposed to declare it, but prudently waited until the Ambassador himself should unfold it. After a while, with a smile on his face, he declared that the answer was the unicorn, an animal that, although it is treacherous and immoderate, holds the estate of virginity in such high esteem that it will hide its head in a damsel's lap and let itself be killed there by the huntsmen. The Signora, who was sitting by the side of the Ambassador, now began her fable in the following wise.

XIII.1 Commentary

Straparola derived this story from Morlini's seventy-seventh *novella* entitled 'De medico qui curabat mente captos' (Of the doctor who treated the mentally deranged), which Morlini took from the second of Poggio Bracciolini's *Facetiae*, entitled 'De medico qui dementos et insanos curabat' or 'Insanus sapiens' (The wise fool). Poggio has no preamble concerning the dissipated son who brings his father to shame. He opens with a group of men discussing the outlandish costs and efforts, even the madness, of those who keep dogs and falcons to hunt birds. Then Paul of Florence breaks in with the story of the doctor who looks after madmen, painting the situation of the asylum before continuing with the interview between the huntsman and the inmate, thereby bringing the topic full circle. This Milanese physician had a pond in his courtyard full of stinking water in which he attached his patients by their feet at various depths, in accordance with their degrees of alienation, and left them to soak or pickle themselves. On this matter he says no more. Among those patients, there was one who had earned his freedom to move about the house upon threat never to cross the threshold. One day he sees a hunter passing with his hawk and hounds and asks the rider such questions as any fool might put to him: what is that you're on? what

do you have on your fist? how much did all that cost you? and how much
can you catch in a year? His indulgent interlocutor is thereby induced to
provide him with simple quantitative answers, setting up the fool's innocent reply concerning the disparity between the cost of accoutrements
and the value of the game, for which reason he fears the sportsman may
find himself in the madmen's pond, and right up to his chin. That this
gem is told with relish in the Latin of one of that age's outstanding
humanists merely adds to the spirit of the enterprise. Such drolleries,
collected or composed, were Poggio's pastime in the years just after the
mid-fifteenth century; they first came to print in undated editions going
back to 1470. Within ten years they were translated into French (by
Guillaume Tardif), and began their long history of circulation among
European persons of letters and wit.[1]

Morlini, we must presume, for want of interim variants to prove otherwise, added the preamble of the boy sent to Padua to pursue an education
where he lost both his time and money in keeping company with the
local scum ('gamins orduriers'). Straparola follows his source closely in
telling how his father cut him loose to end the ignominy of his presence,
how the son came to a vale where he had a house built as an asylum, and
how the surrounding canals furnished his outdoor trenches with water
in which he deposited his patients, fasting and watching, until some
inkling of sense gained their release. In such fashion many are cured
and Gasparino's establishment gained widespread fame. Many also wandered freely about the house, enabling one to conduct the conversation
with the passing hunter in which he mocks his hyperbolical expenditure

---

1 Guillaume Tardif, *Les facéties de Poge* (Paris: La veufve feu Jehan Trepperel, 1510,
  but translated as early as 1480). There have been several important subsequent
  translations of Poggio: by Jacques Lenfant, 1720, M.-P. Ristelhuber, 1867, Isidore
  Liseux, also in the nineteenth century, and Pierre des Brandes, in the early
  twentieth century. Ludovico Carbone's *Facezie* no. 73 is very similar to Poggio's, but
  Carbone wrote between 1466 and 1471, rather too late, it would appear, to influence
  Poggio. Inversely, Poggio's earliest publication of jests was about 1470, excluding
  influence upon Carbone. Hence, they are like the two brothers from Chios in
  Annibal Caro's *Gli straccioni*: 'two persons fused into one or a single one split into
  two.' Ludovico Carbone, *Facezie*, ed. Gino Ruozzi (Bologna: Commissione per i testi
  di lingua, 1989), no. 73, pp. 41–2. Carbone's countryside is near Florence and the
  house contains baths corresponding to the varying degrees of insanity. An inmate
  queries the good sense of a passing hunter of birds, given the elaborate trappings
  and intense endeavour employed in the pursuit of such mean ends. This vignette
  treats the hunter to folly not for his expense, but for the degree to which he makes
  a beast of himself to catch animals merely for sport in such disproportionate ways.

for hawks and hounds by associating him with the insane. Morlini's reweighing of the parts, his assertion of Gasparino's success, together with the fame of his clinic and its novel methods, qualifies the satire and divides the attention more symmetrically between matters of the clinic and matters of falconry.

Both issues invite reflection upon the means whereby vignettes lead to inferences and inferences to precepts. But how equivocal has the transition from exemplum to meaning become? Is the asylum builder a ne'er-do-well who makes good, a quack doctor who sees nothing of the inhumanity if not the absurdity of his treatments, or a folk genius who takes the direct approach to therapy, carefully classifying his patients and implicitly making fools of the medical establishment whose precepts he refused to study? Concerning the huntsman and his expenditures, at face value it is the fool-savant who has the last word in reducing the activities of the sportsman to the common logic of cost versus benefit. As a mental outsider, he is the optimum critic of all such ostensibly pointless prodigality. The *réflexions* in the Amsterdam edition of Poggio published in 1712 contain observations in kind, and I translate: 'The physician, which is to say a kind of man I wouldn't call crazy exactly, but who thinks he is wise, a man always looking out for himself who earns a lot by smelling and touching, a man who prognosticates, a creature who lives on corruption and who delights in disorder, a man, in fact, who often cures those who are in perfect health and almost always kills those who are sick. Madness is of all the maladies the most contagious. It attacks everyone from kings down to bricklayers and shepherds [depuis le scepter jusqu'à la houlette]. The madness of a certain prince is to outfit his subjects with the scrip of the beggar, thus to style himself the "King of Rogues." It is to exchange the captured game for a shadow, like the dog in the fable.' There is more to follow about Hylas and Harpagon in the same vein, giving assurances that for this editor and reader, Poggio's story is an unequivocal diatribe against the excesses of the medical profession. But such a harangue may speak more clearly of the world after Molière than of the world of Poggio. Despite the satiric overtones, nevertheless, Gasparino's tale also resembles a 'rising tale' from failure to success, although his story is not taken up again, once the interrogation of the hawker begins, and we do not learn whether Gasparino's father was ever brought to an altered opinion of his son.

As for the denunciation of hawkers, there is always delight in the wisdom of fools, in those insights that emanate from the logic of the simple, unequivocal observer distanced from polite conventions, the habituated excesses of daily life, and the unexamined practices of tradition. To be sure, there is no correlation between the expenses for the sport and its material gains, and laughter must follow from the fool's perspective; falconers everywhere must blush. But if the simple mathematics of the fool were to prevail, as perhaps they should, fashion must cede to bare essentials, expressive architecture to modest shelter, symphony orchestras to reed flutes, waltzing to hopscotch, banquets to bare staples, and bull-fighting to surreptitious slaughter far from the sight of vegetarians, rendering superfluous if not immoral much that constitutes the urbane, creative, ceremonial, and commodious life.

Tidbits from Poggio's *Facetiae* first appeared in England in a collection of *Tales and quicke answeres, very mery, and pleasant to rede*, in print by 1549, although the date is in dispute and may be as early as 1535. Among the contents is 'Of hym that healed franticke men.' The collection was reprinted in 1567 and undoubtedly had currency and popularity, although it was given a particularly high billing when, in 1814, it was published under the heading *Shakespeare's Jest-Book* and again by W. Carew Hazlitt in 1864 as *Shakespeare Jest-Books*.[2] The generic story, whether through Poggio, Morlini, or related literary or folk traditions, made a goodly number of appearances in the sixteenth century. Hans Wilhelm Kirchhof includes in his *Wendunmuth* (1563) 'Ein Narr is witzig worden' (A fool becomes witty), which tells of a doctor in Meyland who devoted himself to the curing of the mentally ill. He had in his court a pool of stinking water into which he placed his patients, the depths corresponding to their conditions. There was a poor chap with confused thinking who wandered about. When a hunter called in, he interviewed the sportsman

---

2 *Tales and Quicke Answeres very mery and pleasant to rede* (London: Thomas Berthelet, 1535?), pp. Eivr–v; or *Shakespeare's Jest Book*, ed. Samuel Weller Singer (Chiswick: C. Whittingham, 1814). G.S. Gargano suggested that Straparola was the source for this work, but the confirmed 1549 publication date makes that unlikely. 'Una problematica fonte shakespeariana: *Le piacevoli notti* di G.F. Straparola,' *Il Morzocco* 20 (November 1927), pp. 1–2, col. 5. His thesis was that much of the folklore in England derived from Straparola, who had in turn recorded it from the folk. The story is also found in *A Hundred Merry Tales and Other English Jestbooks*, ed. P.M. Zall (Lincoln: University of Nebraska press, 1963), no. 52, p. 283. It is very similar to Carbone's, but is clearly earlier and provides proof of the story's wide European circulation. This house has 'gutters' of varying depths for the patients. The 'fool' enquirer in this account discovers from the passing hunter that his costs are considerably higher than his returns, and hence he urges him to flee to avoid his fate in one of the deepest gutters.

about his hawks and hounds and made the now familiar calculations that allowed him to treat the falconer as an idiot.[3]

Of somewhat greater interest is Straparola's own version of the story translated out of the *Nights* by Humphrey Gifford and published in 1580 in a work entitled *A Posie of Gilloflowers,* as 'Maister Gasparinus a Physician, by his cunning, healeth fooles.' The name Gasparino, unique to Straparola, along with very close translations of three other works out of the *Nights* (IX.5, XIII.4, and XIII.7), leaves no doubt of this story's provenance.[4] The particular significance of Gifford's modest effort for students of English literature is the proof he provides of Straparola's currency in Tudor England. Moreover, his competence as an Italianist further supports claims regarding a Tudor penchant for the Italian language, beginning with the queen herself.

Gifford bestowed upon these four pieces all the charm and insight of a competent and representative Elizabethan stylist. His departures are modest and typical – an interpretative detail, strokes of colourful vocabulary, and quaint turns of phrase. He is a faithful translator, more faithful than most, for the Tudors were particularly given to *amplificatio*, phrase doubling, and moralizing for a start. But he does specify that sluices were used to control the river water, and that in this mechanical way the levels in the little pools were increased and diminished according to the depths desired for the classes of patients – a bit more than Straparola had worked out. He specifies that the bird was a 'sparhawk' (sparrow hawk) and the dogs, spaniels. The hunter, moreover, explains that he kills partridge, a large bird that is 'very delicate of taste.'

But more entertaining yet is the reversal of perspective, for a second look at Straparola will confirm that the good citizen who sent his son to Padua to study is, in fact, an Englishman, and that hence when the boy returns after his five years abroad, he returns to England. It must be

---

3 *Wendunmuth,* ed. Hermann Oesterley, 5 vols. (Tübingen: Litterarischen Verein in Stuttgart, 1869), bk. I, no. 425, vol. I, pp. 436–7. Similar versions of this story may be found in Rimicius's fables, no. 18, *Aesops Leben und Fabels: Nebst den ihm zugeschriebenen alten Fabeln und den Fabeln des Rimicius und Avianus,* ed. Karl Simrock (Frankfurt-am-Main: Winter, ca. 1866), p. 170; Gaudentii Jocosi [pseudonym], *Nugae doctae et inauditae* (Solisbaci: Buggelium et Seitzium, 1725 [farcical names such as 'sun-kissed']), p. 56; William Fennor, *Pasquil's Jests* (London: S. Stafford, 1604) in *Shakespeare Jest-books,* ed. W. Carew Hazlitt (London: Willis & Sotheran, 1864), p. 62.

4 *A Posie of Gilloflowers* (London: John Perin, 1580), posie 5; Humphrey Gifford, *Complete Poems and Translations in Prose,* ed. Alexander B. Grosart (For subscribers [40 copies], 1875), pp. 60–4.

assumed, too, that the wood near the river where he built his asylum is an English forest, that the falconer is of the same persuasion, and that the fools were of good English stock sent from all over the country. That some were whipped and some deprived of sleep, while others were granted relative liberty, might have aroused a unique English interest in light of practices then current in 'Bedlam' Hospital. Moreover, an English reader could not have failed to see the story from the perspective of those gentlemen who, at great expense, had risked sending their sons to the famous University of Padua, their university of choice given its location within the 'liberties' of the Venetian Republic. They would have appreciated from their mercantile-class perspective that Gasparino (hardly an English name!) had fallen to haunting brothels, bowling, dicing, and loitering in dissolute company. By Gifford's time, the grand (educational) tour had soured in the English mind, as Roger Ascham confirmed in *The Scholemaster* (1570): 'I take going thither, and living there, for a young gentleman that doth not go under the keep and guard of such a man, as both by wisdom can, and authority dare rule him, to be marvelously dangerous.'[5] And finally, this story may have found an 'English' resonance insofar as hawking had declined in those mid-Tudor years into a costly aristocratic sport and symbol of elitism. Space does not permit all that might be said about studies abroad, therapy and care for the mentally deranged, and the practice of falconry in Elizabethan England, but such topics are reminders that as works travel through translation, they also pass through nationally specific fields of culture and interpretation.

---

5 Roger Ascham, *The Scholemaster*, ed. R.J. Schoeck (Don Mills, ON: J.M. Dent & Sons, 1966), p. 59.

XIII. Fable 2
Diego, the Hens, and the Carmelite Friar

SIGNORA LUCREZIA

One Diego, a Spaniard, purchases a great quantity of hens from a peasant, and owing money for them, he plays a trick upon the peasant and a Carmelite friar at the same time.

The fable just related to us by Signor Ambassador was so fine and delightful a piece of work that I can't hope to follow it with anything of my own that merits one-thousandth as much as his. But in order not to fail in keeping my own proposition, set out at the beginning of our present evening's entertainment and thus before the tale told by Signor Ambassador, I will recite a fable showing that when it comes to malice and spite, the Spaniards surpass even the roughest boors.

In Spain there is a city called Cordoba, near which there runs a most pleasant stream called the River Bacco. In this town was born a certain Diego, a very crafty fellow and well-to-do in the world, but devoted entirely to trickery and fraud. This rogue one day wished to provide a supper for a few of his companions, but not having the necessary provisions, he cast about in his mind just how he might play a prank upon a neighbouring peasant and so make a feast for his friends at this poor fellow's expense – all of which he managed to pull off according to his desires.

Off our Spaniard went to the piazza to buy some fowls and there he met the peasant, who had a large quantity of hens, capons, and eggs for sale, for which he began to barter, promising finally to pay four florins for the entire lot. To this the peasant agreed. Having then hired a porter, Diego sent him directly to his house with the birds, but without settling up with the vendor, even though the peasant pleaded with him to pay his debt. Diego protested that he didn't have the money in his pocket, but that if he'd go with him as far as the Carmelite monastery where his uncle – one of the brothers – was living, he'd have the money for the hens paid out to him right away. So together they went to the place aforementioned. It fell out that in the monastery church there was a group of ladies assembled to make their confessions to one of the brothers. Diego, managing to get a word in with the monk, whispered in his ear, 'Good father, this peasant who has come here in my company is my closest friend, but he carries a lot of heretical notions around in his head. And even though he's pretty well off and comes from a decent family, he's not too bright upstairs and is often afflicted with the falling sickness. It's been three years at least since he went to confession, and now that one of his more lucid moments has returned to him, out of charity, fraternal love, friendship, and the ties of spiritual brotherhood that exist between us, I promised his wife to work it so that he'd come to confession. By reason of your good name and the fame of your saintly life, so well known in the city and all the countryside around, we have come to your reverence, begging you that of your supreme goodness and for the love of God you will patiently hear him and correct his faults.'

In reply, the brother said that at the present moment he was fully occupied, but that as soon as he had attended to the needs of these ladies – pointing to them with his hand – he would be quite willing to hear the confession. Then calling the peasant over to him, he urged him to wait a little, promising that he would be quickly attended to. The peasant willingly agreed to wait, thinking all along that what the brother said had to do with the money owing to him. Having done this, the crafty Spaniard went off, leaving the poor swindled peasant lingering in the church. As promised, as soon as the brother had finished the job of confessing the ladies, he called the peasant over to him, intent upon bringing him back to the faith. The fellow came over quickly enough, uncovered his head, and straight off demanded his money from the good brother. But the friar merely instructed him to go down on his knees, and that after crossing himself he should say the paternoster. When the peasant found out that he'd been tricked and cheated, he flew into a violent fit of rage and anger, looking up to heaven, blaspheming, and yelling out, 'Ah, what a stupid idiot I am. What have I ever done wrong to merit the brutal knavery of this wretched Spaniard? I don't want to confess. I don't want your absolution. I want the money he promised me.'

The good brother, who knew nothing about any of this, started in to rebuke the peasant: 'It's no lie when they said you're possessed by a devil and that you're totally out of your gourd.' Then he opened his missal and began an exorcism, as if he had some evil spirit to deal with. The peasant, who by this time was of no mind to take any more such talk, demanded with an even greater uproar to be paid the money promised him by Diego, declaring that he was not possessed, not a madman, but that he'd been cheated out of his few poor wares by that rogue of a Spaniard. Gibing and complaining in this way, he called upon the bystanders for assistance, and then he seized the monk by his hood and shouted, 'I'll never turn loose of you until you've handed the money over to me.'

Seeing how things stood and that there was no way of defending himself from the rustic, the good monk started to wheedle in a soft voice to excuse himself, saying that he too had been duped by the Spaniard. But on the other side, the peasant held on firmly to his hood, affirming that the monk had made a promise on his own account: 'Didn't you swear to me in so many words that you'd dispatch this affair of mine in a hurry?'

'I promised,' answered the brother, 'that I'd hear your confession.' While they were wrangling together, certain old men came along who set to work on the good monk's conscience, in the end constraining him to pay out to the peasant what the Spaniard owed him. Thus, that villainous blackguard of a Diego gave a sumptuous feast to his friends with the hens and capons, clearly illustrating how the malice of a Spaniard surpasses that of any other villain in the whole wide world.

Signor Ambassador, who paid the closest attention to this fable so marvellously told by the gentle Signora, then gave to it his warmest commendations, declaring that in the manner of her telling of it she had bested him completely as a storyteller – to which the entire company gave their universal consent. Then the Signora, taking note of such high praise, smiled merrily and said, turning her sweet face towards the ambassador:

> To my sire, the subtle breath
> Of life my mother gave – and death.
> I took being from his grave,
> And nurture kind my mother gave
> To me and to my brothers too,
> Till we to full perfection grew.
> Long together did we dwell,
> Until there came a foeman fell,
> Who many of us crushed and killed.
> Sure we with love and grace are filled,
> Since we give life and daily bread
> To him who snaps our vital thread.

Not one of the company succeeded in grasping the meaning of this enigma, although a long time was spent in commenting upon it, wherefore the Signora, seeing that no one was likely to hit the mark, said, 'Gentlemen, this enigma of mine means nothing more nor less than the wheat which is born from the grain, its father, and from the earth, its mother. The earth destroys the corn, and in destroying it the wheat is born, which the earth nourishes until it grows to maturity. The wheat lives in close union with its brothers, that is, the grains in the ear, until the day when the miller crushes out its life by grinding it in his mill. And so great is its benevolence that it gives life to him who destroys it.' The solution of the Signora's enigma won the praise of all and, when she had concluded it, Signor Pietro Bembo began his fable in the following words.

XIII.2 Commentary

This novelette will do little to improve Italo-Spanish relations, but then, roving Spanish mercenaries in the sixteenth century, according to the stereotype perpetuated in the comic theatre, did little from their side to improve those relations in that bygone century. There was a routine settling of scores in such caricatures. Morlini's Spaniard – from the anecdote upon which the present story is based – could have been at market anywhere outside of his own country, for he is constantly referred to as 'the Spaniard.' Straparola, in turn, maintains that designation throughout his text, in addition to naming him 'Diego,' but paradoxically he relocates the tale to the city of Cordoba in Andalusia, where he is preparing a banquet for friends, the cost for which he means to impose upon a local peasant. That he is now in his own country makes him no less mean-spirited, but the constant references to him as 'the Spaniard' make far less sense. It would seem that in adding concrete detail to this sketch, Straparola has actually detracted from its satiric intent.

The design of the *beffe*, or trick, enjoyed considerable popularity from the time it was launched in a thirteenth-century French *fabliau*.[6] This

---

6 A related tradition that comes from the East, in my estimation, differs enough from the design of the *fabliau* cited as the prototype of the present tale that I have chosen not to incorporate its long parallel history here. It is epitomized by the 'Lady's Seventeenth Story' in Sheykh Zada's *History of the Forty Vezirs or the Story of the Forty Morns and Eves*, trans. E.J.W. Gibb (London: George Redway, 1886), pp. 194–8. It tells of a group of swindlers, one of whom is challenged to go into town and buy a sequin's worth of sweetmeats without paying for them. There are common features.

allows that it may have been rehearsed in oral tales or lost literary versions even earlier. In substance it is simple. Make a purchase of goods, remove them before making payment, direct the creditor to a stranger described as an associate who will pay on the purchaser's behalf, put him in a queue and then disappear, leaving the two parties to work it out between them as best they can. Of course, if the 'stranger' is a professional who can be approached and taken into confidence in order to prepare an even more entertaining 'dialogue of the deaf,' all to the good: hence the aggravated cross purposes, one asking for money, the other trying to confess the creditor as a sinner and calling him possessed when he grows angry. Diego is the classic trickster at work, clever and perspicacious in preparing a full mental draft of the trick and then pursuing it on the basis of a sound understanding of human nature. Such tricks play on gullibility, trust, and then anger when the truth is perceived by the victims, all of which makes for an entertaining imbroglio of a rough and ready kind. For such roles, peasants, petty merchants, and priests were the victims of choice among nearly all the *novellieri*.

To be sure, the origin of this *burla*, or practical joke, can never be determined, but it turns up early in the literary record, as in the second half of 'Les trios aveugles de Compiègne,' a *fabliau* at least as old as the

---

The swindler goes to market, makes the purchase, and sends it home, paying with the sequin (a Venetian gold coin), then steals it back again. But the sequel is entirely different. The confectioner arms himself with jugs, disguises himself as a member of the band, asks his fellow thief if he has succeeded in getting the coin, then retrieves it from him and leaves him with the jugs to fill. The thief, realizing he has been cheated, goes back to the confectioner and there, impersonating the voice of his wife, sends him on a goose chase while he takes back the money a second time. There are several similar ploys as the coin goes back and forth until the thief gets right into bed with the confectioner and his wife and there whispers to the husband, asking where he had hidden the money, and so retrieves it for the last time, winning the applause of his *confrérie* of crooks. This is replicated in the *fabliau* of Jehan de Bove, 'Des trios larrons' (the three thieves), in which the three brothers steal a ham back and forth through similar ruses until they finally agree that there will be no end to it and that they should just share it together. The present tale begins as a scheme to avoid payment by tricking the creditor (as in the *History of the Forty Vezirs*), but it works itself out in such different terms as to constitute an entirely independent story tradition. For a fuller account of the 'three brothers' type, see the commentaries to VIII.1, 'The Three Idle Rogues,' and I.2 'The Stratagems of Cassandrino the Master Thief.'

thirteenth century.[7] In the first part a priest pretends to put a sizeable amount of money in the cup of one of three blind beggars. They return to Compiègne, there to dine like kings on their windfall, while the priest slips along behind them to see what will happen when the time of settlement arrives. The hubbub is intense when beggar accuses beggar and the host grows more menacing in his demand for payment. The priest then steps in, like the good Christian that he purports to be, and offers to settle the debt on their behalf – such virtue and goodness reaping the admiration and celebration of all who are present. Because, according to his report, the local *curé* owes this generous priest an equivalent sum, he directs the host to the church, where he will readily be paid. Meanwhile, he tells his valet to saddle his horse while he goes to the church, just before Mass, to inform the unsuspecting priest that a man sin-laden and mentally unstable will soon be approaching him for spiritual guidance. The extent to which priest and vendor carry their deaf recriminations, threats, and tantrums leaves little room for improvement. Indeed, this rather tight design permits little alteration except in the details, settings, and professions.

In the name of François Villon, in the *Repues franches*, the tale of the three blind beggars is adjusted to tell of a fish merchant who is sent to a confessional to be paid by the priest.[8] In *Les nouveaux contes à rire* it is a roasting chef who is tricked in similar fashion.[9] In the *Courier facétieux*, a peasant sells a piece of cloth to a thief, who sets up payment in the now familiar way.[10] The story was too good to be missed by Antoine le Métel, who duly included it in *Les contes du Sieur d'Ouville*.[11] The tale is altered

---

7 Cortebarbe, 'Les trois aveugles de Compiègne,' in Pierre Legrand d'Aussy, ed., *Fabliaux ou contes du XIIe et du XIIIe siècle* (Paris: Eugene Onfroy, 1781; reprint, Geneva: Slatkine Reprints, 1971), vol. III, pp. 1–18.

8 *Le recueil des repues franches* (by François Villon and his associates), ed. Jelle Koopmans and Paul Verhuyck (Geneva: Droz, 1995), no. 1, pp. 26–9. This title signifies 'the art of eating and drinking without making payment.' It was a collection made towards the end of the fifteenth century in Villon's style and to which he may have made a modest contribution.

9 *Les récreations françoises ou nouveau recueil de contes à rire* (Rouen: Pain, 1661), p. 261.

10 *Le courier facétieux ou recueil des meilleurs rencontres de ce temps* (Lyons: Paul Burckhart, 1647), p. 355.

11 Antoine le Métel, 'D'un qui subtilement attrapa un rotisseur' in *Les contes du sieur d'Ouville* (Amsterdam: H. Desbordes, 1732), vol. II, p. 47; *L'Élite des contes d'Ouville* (Paris: Chez la veufve Trabouillet, 1641), vol. II, p. 290; and *L'Élite* as edited by G. Brunet, 2 vols. (Paris: Librairie des bibliophiles, 1883), vol. I, pp. 267–9. This rogue buys huge quantities of food from a meat roaster, then takes the roaster's

slightly when the creditor is sent to a surgeon for payment. The rogue prepares the visit by telling the surgeon that he will soon be visited by a crazy or stubborn relative in need of an operation, and that he should proceed despite his protests. In *Le curé Arlotto*, a creditor is sent to an abbey, where he is beaten and blessed at the same time.[12] In the *Histoire générale des Larons* (sometimes *Larrons*) the swindler buys a piece of drapery and then takes the boy-merchant to a surgeon, who is told the lad is weak in the head. As the two argue, the goods are spirited away.[13] In *La bibliothèque de cour* (III.32) it is a woman who buys fabric, takes the boy working in the boutique along with her to be paid, but leads him to the hospital of Saint-Lazare, the celebrated asylum, saying privately to the orderlies that he is one of her own children who misbehaved and is in need of correction. This may be but a sampling, but sufficient to reveal that this trick received steady literary attention in France over five centuries, and was altered only in its circumstances, beginning with the farcical and ending with the downright cruel and sadistic. How the lure of a good story seeking ever more intense exploitation can intimate the regression of civilization!

The story makes a clumsy entry into the Italian *novelle* collections with an adaptation by Sacchetti; there the ruse is attributed to the prankster Gonnella, who is in need of hens for carnival. This famous fool dresses himself like a seigneur, enters a poultry shop, haggles to a price, and tells the vendor to send the capons with his errand boy while he goes with another to the bank. There he kills time until the boy tugs at his cloak, whereupon he spins about with a false tooth and strange airs, convincing the child he is no longer the same person. Upon returning to the shop unpaid, the boy becomes the victim of his master's abuse and recriminations,

---

valet to be paid by his 'uncle' the priest. Once at the church, he asks for prayers for the boy, whom he describes as tetched in the head and deluded into thinking that he is owed money by nearly everyone. Then he makes his escape.

12	Curé Arlotto, *Mots et facéties*, no. 92; *Facéties et bons mots*, ed. Étienne Wolff (Paris and Monaco: Rocher-Anatolia, 2003). This same trick is told in *Le nouveau Pathelin*, dating to 1474–85.

13	François de Calvi, *Histoire générale des Larons* [sic] (Lyons: La veufve de Pierre Bailly and Pierre Bailly, 1664), p. 20. It was first published in two parts, 1623 and 1625, and again in Rouen by Jacques Cailloüe (1639). See also 'A Tragi-Comedy acted by two theeves' in the *Histoire des Larrons, or the History of Theeves*, trans. Paul Godwin (London: John Raworth, 1638), chap. 3, pp. 18–28.

while Gonnella, shape-shifter that he is, is no longer to be found.[14] The two professions in the French collections, the priest and the surgeon, are combined into a double intrigue by Sabadino degli Arienti in his *Novelle porrettane.* Carletto goes in search of a cartload of wood, but on the way gambles away all of his money. He continues with the purchase, however, and leads his creditor to the piazza to be paid. There he meets the priest and conveys to him the usual conditions concerning his friend's depraved soul and his absence from the confessional for fifteen years. This draws to a close when the priest and the creditor finally understand they have been duped. But Carletto is found back at the market. Now he berates the priest behind his back, descrying his lack of morals and integrity, thereafter taking his creditor into a second situation, this time to the barber surgeon and phlebotomist. He tells the practitioner in an aside that the man approaching is his worker, in need of blood-letting – a fellow suffering from headaches and signs of madness – and that force may have to be used. Carletto now takes flight, while his creditor, despite nearly maniacal protests, is bled to the point of syncope. Just as the angry man seems a devil to the priest, he seems a madman to the doctor, in both instances merely aggravating his case.[15]

---

14 Franco Sacchetti, *Trecentonovelle*, ed. Emilio Faccioli (Turin: G. Einaudi, 1970), no. 220, pp. 675–7.

15 *Novelle porrettane*, ed. Giancarlo Bernabei (Bologna: Santarini [1483], 1992), no. 19, pp. 75-79. See also *Novelle porretane* [*sic*], ed. Pasquale Stoppelli (L'Aquila: L.U. Japadre Editore, 1975), no. 19, 'Piron dal Farneto,' pp. 92–8. This story has been translated into French by Marie-Hélène Poli as 'La charretée de bois,' in *Conteurs italiens de la Renaissance*, ed. Giancarlo Mazzacuratti and Anne Motte-Gillet (Paris: Gallimard, 1993), pp. 261–5. A related story appears in Giovanni Sagredo's *L'Arcadia in Brenta overo la melanconia* (Bologna: Giovanni Ricaldini, 1674), p. 340; see also the edition by Quinto Marini (Rome: Salerno, 2004), pp. 165–9. In this later and more elaborate version, there are four cheaters who negotiate for bread, meat, wine, and oil. The first goes into a bakery and claims to be sent by the count. He takes the shop boy with him to be paid by the priest. He drops the bread off with a colleague near the house of a gentleman, then takes the boy to the church. The second dresses as a Franciscan and goes to the Jewish quarter to order meat for the convent. He then tells the local confessor that he is to confess a boy who is light in the head. The wine and oil merchants are deceived in similar fashion, allowing the four rogues to make off scot-free. The last uses a sponge that soaks up oil, then fills the flask. When he pays with a false coin that the vendor refuses, he simply returns the flask but takes his sponge. Sagredo or his source has merely compounded similar episodes, one of the received methods for drawing out a good conceit.

By 1520, when Girolamo Morlini published his *Novelle* and thus the story translated here by Straparola, there were many versions in circulation. Whether he had a more proximate source is always possible, including one from the oral tradition. Others at this same time were taking their hand at refreshing the defining trick. Alessandro Sozzini (d. 1541) left a story translated by Thomas Roscoe as 'Two Capons for Nothing' in which a good and kind-hearted citizen went shopping for a couple of capons for his wife.[16] When he discovered that he had no money, he continued on his mission, agreeing to a price of five *livres*. Then he invited the merchant to follow him to the Church of San Martino, where they found the prior busily engaged in confessing a young woman. As these little details accumulate, it is to be asked if he is not simply giving novelistic amplification to Morlini's 'De Hispani qui decepit rusticum monarchumque Carmelitanum' (Of the Spaniard who cheated a peasant and a Carmelite monk) – the source of the present tale.[17] That the price and the number of years since that last confession were both five, the figure is repeated aloud in a way that confirmed expectations on each side. Moreover, the man tells the vendor that the capons are for the priest, strengthening by that much more his expectation of payment. A short episode is thus added when the priest invites the vendor to ransack his cell in search of capons. These two are less vitriolic in their reactions, but their story is much in the spirit of Morlini's.

Another who employed the *beffe* in his own way is Pietro Aretino in the *Cortegiana* (1525), handling it in a way that takes for granted its universal familiarity. Rosso says, 'I want to try that trick that other fellow like me played – he was pretending to be shopping, and he sent a fishmonger to a friar confessor. Everybody knows the story' (I.xv).[18] Rosso then puts on a cape and proceeds to recreate the trick in the marketplace, approaching a fishmonger in a manner suggesting that he was about to make the merchant the official supplier to a major household. This is a play,

---

16 See *Novelle di autori senesi* (Milan: Giovanni Silvestri, 1815), vol. II: *The Italian Novelists*, trans. Thomas Roscoe (presumed) (London: Simkin & Marshall, 1827; London: Septimus Prowett, 1825), republished in *Tales from the Italian and Spanish* (New York: The Review of Reviews Co., 1920), vol. III, pp. 210–12.

17 Girolamo Morlini, *Les nouvelles*, trans. Fernand Caussy (Paris: E. Sansot, 1904), no. 13, pp. 43–5; ed. Giovanni Villani (Rome: Salerno, 1983), pp. 66–71.

18 Pietro Aretino, *Cortegiana*, trans. J. Douglas Campbell and Leonard G. Sbrocchi, intro. Raymond B. Waddington (Ottawa: Dovehouse Editions, 2003), p. 68; the play was reprinted in *Renaissance Comedy: The Italian Masters*, ed. Donald Beecher, 2 vols. (Toronto: University of Toronto Press, 2007), vol. I, pp. 101–204.

and one of the wittiest, so there is a great deal of chatter, repartee, and colourful local allusions, drawing out the event. He then prepares the sacristan: 'Father, you see that poor wretch over there? [meaning the fishmonger] His wife is possessed, and she's doing crazy things down at the Luna. I beg you, Father, chain her to this column and in the name of God take this curse from her. She's got maybe ten spirits in her body, speaking every language under the sun, and the poor man is half crazy.' The sacristan and the fishmonger then speak at hilarious cross purposes, and Rosso congratulates himself, saying, 'The trickmaster himself couldn't have done it better.' The fishmonger, meanwhile, is tied up and beaten, calls the clergy a pack of sodomites and thieves, after which he damns 'Rome, the court, the church, everyone who lives here, and everyone who believes in it!' Aretino gets his usual satiric mileage out of such situations, placing his scurrilities in the mouths of others through the prerogative of the theatre, making his puppets speak as though of their own minds.

Till Eulenspiegel enacts the little farce according to the formula provided by 'The Three Blind Beggars of Compiègne' (Cortebarbe's 'Trois aveugles de Compiègne'), first by pretending to give money to twelve blind beggars and sending them back for supper and lodging, and then by leading the innkeeper to believe that the local priest had promised to cover their expenses. The mutual accusations of their falling out lasted for the rest of their lives, the priest saying he owed nothing, but only that he wished to free the man of his evil spirits, while the other constantly claimed payment of the debt.[19] Carlo Casalicchio, towards the end of the seventeenth century, retells the same farce about the purchased chickens and the merchant taken to the church to be paid by the priest.[20]

An imaginative variant was left by Bonaventure des Periers in 'De maistre fai-feu, qui eut des bottes qui ne lui coustèrent rien' (Of Mr Make-Fire, who got his boots for free). Because the hero had been insulted by

---

19 [Hermann Bote], *Ein kurtzweilig lesen von Dyl Ulenspiegel* (Strassburg: Johannes Grüninger, 1515); trans. as *A Pleasant Vintage of Till Eulenspiegel*, by Paul Oppenheimer (Middletown, CT: Wesleyan University Press, 1972), no. 70, pp. 177–80. This same *fourberie* or *Schwank* is also included among the *Facetiae* of Heinrich Bebel, *Henrici Bebelii, Facetiarum libri tres* (Amsterdam: I. Janssonium, 1651), bk. II, no. 126; see *Schwänke*, trans. Albert Wesselski (Munich and Leipzig: 1907).

20 Casalicchio (1626–1700), 'Astuzia di un ladro, in vero graziosa' in *L'utile col dolce* (1687) (Venice: Baglione, 1741), Centuria I, Decade ii, Arg. 2, pp. 35–7.

the bootmakers, he worked out his revenge in the following way. He commissioned two of them, independently, to create for him a pair of boots. Both craftsmen worked throughout the night and presented their creations early the next morning. First one arrives and is told that one boot is superb but that the other pinches and requires adjustment. As he returns to his shop, the second arrives and is handled in the same manner. Then the swindler flees town with one boot from each, leaving the bootmakers to come to terms with their losses.[21]

The extent to which this story lived an independent life in the oral literature of the folk and in how many places is matter for an independent enquiry. Yet there are indications that it also travelled by word of mouth and formed part of the European oral culture. In *The Collected Sicilian Folk and Fairy Tales of Giuseppe Pitrè* is to be found 'The Petralian' (a man from Petralia Sottana, a provincial town in Sicily). This cheat owes money to a man in Cefalù. When they meet after many years, he agrees to pay, but first needs to change his gold into cash in a certain shop. The Petralian goes in first and explains to the merchant that his timid friend outside needs a harness for his hernia, necessitating the utmost of diplomacy on the merchant's part. Once they are introduced, the creditor leaves and the two men work out their cross purposes in an amusing dialogue until the man from Cefalù realizes once again that he has been made a fool. And for that one example we may presume a thousand ancestors, for there is no living species without an unbroken link to the past.[22]

---

21 *Nouvelles récréations et joyeux devis*, ed. Louis Lacour, vol. II, *Oeuvres françoises* (Paris: P. Jannet, 1856), pp. 102–7. Also known as *Les contes ou les nouvelles récréacions et joyeaux devis* (Paris: Dentu Co., 1887), pp. 89–94. This same story is retold by Antoine le Métel, Sieur d'Ouville in *L'Élite des contes*, ed. G. Brunet, 2 vols. (Paris: Librairie des bibliophiles, 1883), vol. I, pp. 251–3.

22 Giuseppe Pitrè, *The Collected Sicilian Folk and Fairy Tales*, trans. and ed. Jack Zipes and Joseph Russo (New York: Routledge, 2009), vol. I, pp. 547–8. There is another collected by Carolina Coronedi-Berti, 'Fola de tri quartirù d'quatrein' in *Novelle popolari bolognesi* (Bologna: Tava & Garagnani, 1874), also included in *Favole bolognesi* (Bologna: Arnaldo Forni, 1981), no. 40, pp. 159–65. And there is yet another, collected by Téofilo Braga, *Contes tradicionais do poro Portugues*, 2 vols. (Lisbon: Dom Quixote, 1987), vol. II, p. 160, which recreates the entire jest in the confession box while the chicken thief sneaks away 'com o furto,' like a thief. This version derives from the *Arte de furtar*, attributed to Manuel da Costa, seventeenth century, which links it to earlier versions.

XIII. Fable 3
On the Liberality of Spaniards
and Germans

PIETRO BEMBO

A German and a Spaniard happened to be dining together when their servants got into a dispute as to which was the most liberal. In the end, it was concluded that the German was more munificent than the Spaniard.

The fable just told to us by our worthy Signora brings back to memory a certain dispute that arose from the envy kindled between the servants of a German and a Spaniard who happened to meet at the same table. Although this fable of mine is very short, nevertheless, many may find it entertaining and a source of pleasure.

One day by chance a German and a Spaniard, having arrived at the same hostelry, ate their supper together, being served with many fine foods of all sorts and in great abundance. While they were dining, the Spaniard handed to his servant to eat first a morsel of meat, then a bite of fowl, or some other tidbit. The German, by contrast, went on dining in silence, downing one thing after another without a thought for his servant. From all this, a colossal jealousy arose between the two hirelings. Initially, the servant of the German declared that Spaniards were the most liberal and considerate of men, a view with which the Spaniard's servant entirely agreed. Taking stock of the argument, when the German had finished his meal, he took up the dish with all the meat that was in it and handed it to his servant, inviting him to make a supper of it. Seeing that, the Spaniard's servant, now filled with envy at the good luck of his companion, reversed the opinion he had just expressed, and grumbled out these words: 'Now I know well that the Germans are liberal beyond all other men [giving as much at one time as a Spaniard gives in a thousand].'

This fable teaches us that no one is ever contented with his own lot. Messer Pietro Bembo, without any further delay, set his enigma as follows:

> I dwell in such a lofty spot
> That soaring wings can reach me not;
> Much help I give to feeble sight,
> Working alone by wisdom's might.
> I high exalt the soul serene,
> But never let my light be seen
> By those who claim too much of me.
> Oft am I made appear to be
> What I am not, just through the deed
> Of things that neither know nor heed.

'This enigma,' said Messer Pietro, 'simply describes the science of astrology, which must be conducted in some elevated place, up to which one could not fly even with wings.' As soon as he had finished the exposition of his subtly devised riddle, Signora Veronica rose to her feet and began to speak.

XIII.3 Commentary

This story might be thought of as a cameo performance by Cardinal Pietro Bembo, Signora Lucrezia's favourite, a man who, among his flirtations with scandal, carried on many amorous liaisons in his youth, had three children with Faustina Morosina and lived with her until her death in 1535, struggled with the Corner family, actively engaged in marrying his illegitimate daughter to Pietro Soranzo, and was targeted by the notorious fortune-teller Fra Aurelio in an effort to stop the wedding.[23] But as a cleric of the world, an authority on languages, the famed author of *Gli asolani*, and so much more, what tale would Straparola assign to him? The answer is this tale lifted from Morlini – something of an indication that he was not paying close attention to the relationship between his narrators as persons and the tales they tell, for this slight anecdote is barely worthy of so stellar a talent. Straparola takes a somewhat soft

---

23 Guido Ruggiero, *Binding Passions: Tales of Magic, Marriage, and Power at the End of the Renaissance* (New York: Oxford University Press, 1993), pp. 177–80, 213–17.

approach to the confrontation represented here between national types, insofar as in Morlini's version, 'De Theotonico et Hispano simul comedentibus' (Of the German and the Spaniard who dined together), the principals are drunk and arguing from the outset. But otherwise, with the exception of the last phrase, which Straparola strangely omits, our author follows his source most faithfully.[24] Implicit in their encounter is the Renaissance interest in national character and characteristics, which early specialists in such matters attempted to explain according to climates and temperaments as well as in terms of cultural predilections. Cornelius Agrippa of Nettesheim, in *Paradoxe sur l'incertitude, vanité et abus des sciences*, divides men as lovers according to their national constitutions. Hence, the German is cold, but warms to love gradually. Once in love, he pursues the lady with art and judgment, and withdraws his generosity when he grows jealous, while hiding his passion from others. This is in keeping with his northerly temperament in relation to the environment. The Spaniard, by contrast, convinces himself he is beloved, becomes impatient in his ardour, giving himself no rest, places himself in danger in pursuing enterprises to win the lady's favour, worships her, and in winning her grows jealous and threatens her, or in not winning her, torments himself to death.[25] This has little bearing upon the present story except in revealing the fashion during the age for segregating nationalities according to a complex set of correspondences pertaining to latitude, average temperatures, and generic temperaments that control the humours and passions. In the present sketch, the matter concerns generosity. The Spaniard doles out bits of food while the more stoic German eats in a manner indifferent to those around him, yet in the end shows the greater largesse in a single gesture, keeping signs of his liberal nature hidden till then. That Morlini is playing upon such matters is based merely upon the naming of their respective nations and contrasting their conducts. Mere suggestion may perform the rest. The phrase added in brackets in the text is from Morlini, in which it is explained that in a single gesture the German does more than the Spaniard in a thousand. But in terms of actual substance, calmly reflected upon, one might wonder over the distinction.

---

24 Girolamo Morlini, *Les nouvelles*, trans. Fernand Caussy (Paris: E. Sansot, 1904), no. 6, p. 32; *Novelle e favole*, ed. Giovanni Villani (Rome: Salerno, 1983), pp. 38–9.
25 *Paradoxe sur l'incertitude, vanité et abus des sciences* (N.p.: n.p., 1603), pp. 72–4.

As stated above, this is a minimalist tale, as though Bembo had taken the Signora at her word to keep the stories brief on that final night. In that spirit, we might pretend that a clever satirist was sporting with her in constructing the shortest of all possible 'stories,' whatever constitutes such a form, much as Sunday schoolers are proud to pronounce that 'Jesus wept' is the shortest verse in the bible. He offers characters, dialogue, conflict, reversal, and resolution in one of the shortest plots in all literature; everything is there. But while it may constitute brevity to perfection, it isn't quite narrative perfection in brevity, if you follow my drift, for a literary touchstone it isn't. There are no apparent sources for Morlini's sketch, leaving the prospect that it is entirely his own.

XIII. Fable 4
The Servant, the Fly, and the Master

SIGNORA VERONICA

Fortunio, a servant, endeavouring to crush a fly, kills his master, but saves himself from the gallows by a pleasantry.

My most handsome gentlemen, many times have I heard it said that misdeeds committed unwittingly do not carry the same blame as those done by intent. Thus, we look more lightly on the transgressions of yokels, children, and others of like condition than on those committed by more responsible folk. Since it's now my turn to tell a story, I'll relate the adventure of one Fortunio, a menial, who, in seeking to kill a horsefly that was annoying his master, inadvertently killed the master himself.

There lived in the city of Ferrara a rich grocer of good descent who had in his service Fortunio, a fat, good-tempered fellow, but who wasn't very bright. Now during the heat waves, this grocer was accustomed to lying down for a nap in the middle of the day, at which times it was Fortunio's job to keep the flies off with a fan so they wouldn't disturb the master. One day it happened that, among all the others, there was a truly bothersome horsefly that paid no attention to Fortunio's fanning and waving, but alighted constantly on the grocer's bald pate, biting him remorselessly. Even though it was chased away three or four times, it kept coming back to give fresh annoyance. At last the servant-lad, all upset by the temerity and persistence of the thing, rashly tried to kill it when it was about to settle again on his master's temple and suck his blood. Simple fool that he was, he caught up a heavy bronze pestle and, striking at the fly with all his might in an effort to dispatch it, he put an end to his patron instead. Now as soon as Fortunio saw that he had slain the boss and that he was now liable to trial and execution, he considered how he might best save his neck. At first, he thought about running away to safety, but then he fixed upon another scheme, which was to secretly bury the corpse. So wrapping up the dead body of his master in a sack and carrying it into the garden adjacent to the shop, he buried it. With that done, he went to the sheepfold and there chose a big old ram, which he took and threw down the well.

When the master failed to reappear at his usual hour in the evening, the wife's suspicion fell upon Fortunio, so she questioned him about her husband's whereabouts, but the fellow declared stoutly that he knew nothing about it. Then the good wife, overcome with grief, began to weep and to call aloud for her husband, but all in vain. She went to her family and relayed her sorrow to them, which led them to seek out the governor of the city to lay the crime upon Fortunio, demanding that he should be imprisoned, given the strappado, and put to the question in order to make him tell what had become of his master. Having put the servant into custody and tying him by a rope, the governor gave him the strappado as prescribed by law, for such was the nature of the charges against him. Unable to endure such torture, the boy promised rapidly enough to tell them everything he knew if only they would let him down. So they brought him before the judge and this was the clever tale he had ready to bamboozle them. 'Yesterday, Your Honour, when I was asleep near the well, there was a big noise that woke me up. It sounded like some giant rock being hurled down into the water. I was really startled, so I jumped up and ran to the well and looked down, but the water was all clear and I couldn't see anything wrong, so I turned to go back to the house. But then I heard the same sound in my ears a second time. I'm pretty darned certain it was my master who was trying to draw some water up from the well, but instead he must have fallen in. If we want to find out for sure, I think we should all head for the well and I can let myself down to the bottom to see what there is.' The judge was favourable to Fortunio's request, claiming that investigation is the surest proof and that no evidence can equal what is brought before one's very eyes. So he headed towards the well, inviting the whole assembly to follow. Not only the worshipful persons in attendance upon the judge went along, but also a vast crowd of the common folk curious to find out how the whole thing would end.

Then the guilty lad, obeying the judge's orders, went right down the well, and when he reached the bottom he pretended to be searching for his master's body in the water. But what he found was the carcass of the old ram that he himself had recently tossed in. Feigning his astonishment, he bawled up from the bottom of the well, calling for his patron's wife, 'O my mistress, tell me whether your husband had horns or not, because I've come upon somebody down here who's got an enormous long pair. Do you know if it might be him?' When the good wife heard Fortunio's question, she was so overcome with shame that she couldn't find a word to say for herself. Meanwhile, the bystanders were all waiting with their mouths open to lay eyes on this corpse with horns and to see whether it really was the body of the missing grocer. So when they hauled up Fortunio's old ram, they all clapped their hands and burst into peels of laughter. When the judge saw the state of affairs, he deemed that the booby was acting in good faith and absolved him of the crime, even though the grocer was never more seen and his good wife was left with the trick of the horns to her dying day.

There was hearty laughter among the men and ladies over the story of the old ram in the well, although their principal diversion centred on the wife's confusion caused by Fortunio's ploy. Then, seeing how the evening was advancing, with so many gentlefolk still to tell their stories, Signora Veronica delayed her enigma no longer, which ran as follows:

> In the ground my head is buried,
> Yet with care I'm never harried.
> In my early youth and fresh,
> White and tender is my flesh,
> And green my tail. Of lowly plight,
> The rich man's scorn, the boor's delight.
> The peasant on me sets good store,
> The noble casts me from his door.

This enigma by Signora Veronica won praise from all present, but while nearly everyone mastered its meaning, yet no one was willing to take upon himself the honour of divulging it, but left this task to the Signora herself. Noting the silence of the company, she said, 'Although my wit is slender, I will, if it pleases you, set forth the solution of my riddle to the best of my poor ability. It is the leek, which, as you all know, lives with its head underground and has a green tail, and is favoured less by lords than by labourers on the table.' After Veronica had explained her pretty riddle, the Signora entreated Signor Bernardo Capello, there present with us, to narrate one of his fables, counselling him to be brief, in keeping with the format agreed upon for the final evening. So clearing his mind of serious thoughts, he thus began.

XIII.4 Commentary

The Signora's request to Bernardo Capello, 'there present with *us*,' brings a pretty pronoun to the reader's attention. 'Us' would seem to include the author himself, lending support to his assertion in his opening letter that he had heard his tales from the ten young women and had copied them down verbatim. At the least, Straparola would seem to have remembered his fictive stance and is here giving it a bit more support. It is doubly intriguing in light of the small probability that a Bernardo Capello would have translated from the Latin and memorized a story by Morlini, much as Straparola's fiction would have us believe it of all the other reciters of these Latin tales. Moreover, this story contains some of the telltale words in Venetian dialect that dot the stories as much here as formerly, for example 'ventolo' for 'ventaglio,' the little fan used to chase flies from the master's face. Just such little details give assurance that Straparola, himself, was still at work – that he had not given up somewhere in book XI and abandoned the Morlini section to another compiler and translator.

Apart from applying the story to a rich grocer living in Ferrara, rather than to a perfumer in an undesignated place, Straparola follows Morlini in his twenty-first story with nearly precision fidelity.[26] It is the tale of a fool, and the moral to follow is that such beings can hardly be blamed for their shortcomings. Their clumsiness is excusable and their simpleminded wit tempers their faults – so opines Morlini. Where there is no malicious intent and deeds are inadvertently committed, there are no grounds for prosecution. The judge decides as much in assuming that Fortunio literally took the goat for his dead master, or at least that he was snoozing nearby when he heard it fall in. In most stories of this type, the fools are utterly foolish and require a mother or guardian to get them out of their scrapes. The Sicilian storytellers in the nineteenth century realized the problem and had the boy's mother throw the goat in the well, so that when her simpleton son identifies it as the missing person,

---

26 *Les nouvelles*, trans. Fernand Caussy (Paris: E. Sansot, 1904), pp. 58–60.

she can protest his idiocy and so baffle the legal system on his behalf – as mother's are wont to do for offspring of whatever proclivity. But Morlini and Straparola have complicated matters by creating Fortunio as a kind of idiot-savant, for it is the boy who comes up with the plan to throw the goat in the well, making him both a fool in the murder and a trickster in the escape from punishment. In fact, he is clever enough to mastermind the perfect crime by staging his own stupidity, beginning with the little drama in the well that plays out perfectly to his advantage. Like the false mage, Harisarman, in the *Katha sarit sagara*, who feigns to use magic to locate the horse he himself has stolen (see the commentary to XIII.6), Fortunio locates the 'master' he himself has dumped in the well.

To our presumed amusement, both parts of this simple tale turn upon errors of category or decontextualized reasoning, generating for us the impression of a brain limited to the simplest of causal logic and to the most elementary forms of assessment and identification. The comic smokescreen of imputing sexual infidelity to the grocer's wife serves, meanwhile, to buckle up the entire anecdote. Clearly such tales, with their broad humour, pleased raconteurs and their audiences for generations. The precise tale of killing the patron while swatting a fly *and* making him a post-mortem cuckold is a very particular performance limited to Morlini and Straparola (being without apparent sources or analogues), but it participates in a wider tradition concerning the antics of fools, conjoining two elements, the pesky fly, ATU 1586A, and the goat in the well, ATU 1600, the former of which has a substantial history as an independent motif.[27]

Stith Thomspon gives assurance that the tale of the fly on the brow of the victim soon to be slain 'goes back to Buddhistic sources,' was 'popular in the medieval literary collections,' and is 'occasionally' found in folklore from Iceland to Indo-China.[28] The examples to follow, roughly in chronological order, represent the growth of a literary tradition that at some point, early or late, spread into the world of the folk.

The *Panchatantra* offers an inaugural version (ATU 163A), even though the stories set down by Vishnu Sarma in the third century BC undoubtedly had even more remote sources. Near the end of the first book he

---

27 It also figures in Thompson's Motif Index, J1193.1. *The Folk Tale* (Berkeley: University of California Press, [1946] 1977), p. 189.

28 Thompson, p. 189.

illustrates the caveat never to place your trust in fools. Once there was a king who settled down to sleep, asking his pet monkey to keep watch over him. When a bee came along and threatened to sting His Majesty, the monkey made every effort to drive it away. Exasperated by failure, he sought to smite it with the king's sword, thereby splitting the king's head in two. All those around His Liege awoke and began screaming at the monkey for the blockhead he was. But ostracism was as much as they could demand, for he was simply a brute beast. This little apologue establishes the form for the many renderings to follow and may serve as a prototype to the entire tradition.[29]

The variants in the East need not detain us overlong, but several have been gathered by Max Müller in his *Chips from a German Workshop*.[30] One such is that of the carpenter stung by a mosquito. When his son is called in to dispatch it, he takes his father's axe, but in his attempt merely divides his father's head, to which the Bodhisatta, looking on, observed, 'better an enemy with sense than such a friend.'[31] In the *Anwar i Suhaili* or *The Lights of Canopus*, the Persian version of the *Panchatantra*, the gardener, while asleep, is watched over by a trained bear who throws stones to ward off the flies. Aesop's fable ('Calvus et musca') about the bald man who smacked his own head to his considerable discomfort in seeking to dispatch a fly bears only a distant relationship to the present tale, but it was known throughout the Middle Ages and Renaissance down through the translation into English by William Caxton and after.[32] Other versions of the story include those to be found in the *Romulus*, and the exempla from the *Sermones vulgares* of Jacques de Vitry in which

29 *The Panchatantra*, trans. Chandra Rajan (Harmondsworth: Penguin, 1993), pp. 183–4.
30 *Chips from a German Workshop*, 4 vols. (New York: Appleton-Century, 1887), vol. II, pp. 229–30. The *Anwari Suhaili* was translated by Arthur Wollaston as *The Lights of Canopus* (London: John Murray, 1904). See also Auguste Loiseleur Deslongchamps, *Essai sur les fables indiennes et sur leur introduction en Europe* (Paris: Techener, 1838), pp. 43–4.
31 The story is from the *Makasa-Jataka*, no. 44, 'Ekanipātā,' in *The Jātaka*, trans. Robert Chalmers (Cambridge: Cambridge University Press, 1895), vol. I, p. 247.
32 See Léopold Hervieux, ed., *Les fabulistes latins depuis le siècle d'Auguste jusqu'à la fin du moyen âge*, 5 vols. (Paris and New York: Franklin, 1893–9), vol. II, *Phèdre et ses anciens imitateurs*, Phedrus, no. IV.31, p. 54.

the man swats at the fly on his own brow.[33] Further instances of this popular tale turn up in Johannes Pauli's *Schimpf und Ernst*, no. 673, and in Lutheran circles.[34] Concerning the combined configuration of events advanced by Morlini and Straparola, no predecessors are known. The fly and the inadvertent murder ineluctably must be traced to the Sanskrit, but the composite tale, for the nonce, remains Morlini's creation.

Straparola's *Nights*, rather soon after its publication, was translated into French and German, and in those editions all of his materials were placed into wider circulation. Straparola made his way to England in an altogether more restrained fashion, but this story was one of four chosen by Humphrey Gifford for inclusion in his *Posie of Gilloflowers* (1580).[35] The circulation of this work seems to have been rather limited and its influence confined; even when it was edited in the nineteenth century with a full historical introduction, its press run was limited to forty copies. The story appears in the collection without title and is referred to in the index as 'A second story of a foolish servant.' The translation is entirely faithful, yet introduces those colorations of style for which the Tudor translators were justly famous. Two samplings must represent the totality. 'Amongst the other flyes there was one so importunate, that not waying the bush of fethers, wherewith she was stricken often, with her sharpe sting would never lin byting the balde pate of his maister, and having beene three or foure times to anoye him, would still profer to come againe.' Such was the fly about to be assassinated with the heavy brass pestle. Following the court scene we read: 'And behold as the wicked fellow by the commandement of the Maior descended into the well, & sought for his maister in the water, he found the goate which he before [had] throwne thereinto, and ther with cried out to his mistresse (which was amongst the rest of the company) saying, hoe, mistres; tel me, had your husband any hornes? I have found one here in this well, which hath a payre both greate and long, was hee ever your husband?'

---

33 Hervieux, ed., *Les fabulistes latins*, Romulus, no. II.13, vol. II, p. 195. Jacques de Vitry, *The Exempla or Illustrative Stories from the Sermones Vulgares*, ed. Thomas Frederick Crane (London: David Nutt, 1890), no. 190, p. 210.

34 *Die Fabel: Theorie, Geschichte und Rezeption einer Gattung*, ed. Peter Hasubek (Berlin: E. Schmidt, 1982), pp. 27–42.

35 *A Posie of Gilloflowers* (London: John Perin, 1580), posie 8; Humphrey Gifford, *Complete Poems and Translations in Prose*, ed. Alexander B. Grosart (For subscribers [40 copies], 1875), pp. 67–9.

Scattered allusions to the primitive story appear to have resurfaced in *Le sottilissime astutie di Bertoldo* (1606) by Giulio Cesare Croce, followed by the 'Naïveté d'un plaideur,' in the *Élite des contes du Sieur d'Ouville*.[36] In a court hearing, a simpleton complains that the flies have eaten the neighbour's milk that was under his care. The judge replies that he should have killed them. The fool seeks confirmation that such is allowed and the judge assures him that it is permitted anywhere and at anytime, at which point the peasant strikes one on the judge's face.

La Fontaine, in his *Fables* (1668), borrows from the Persian *Panchatantra*, or a closely related version, to retell the story of the bear and the sleeping gardener in 'L'ours et l'amateur de jardins' (The bear and the lover of gardens).[37] To the signature event of the fly and the blow, he adds a charming preamble on solitude and the making of the friendship between the lone bear and the lone gardener. But only half licked, this bear was short on the reasoning necessary to imagine provisionally the full consequences of dropping a massive stone on the gardener's nose to dispatch a fly.

---

36 The references to *Bertoldo* were given by Aurelio M. Espinosa in his notes to 'Juan Tonto va a vender miel' in *Cuentos populares españoles*, 3 vols. (Madrid: S. Aguirre, 1947), vol. I, pp. 476–8, taken from an edition published in Barcelona. According to the endnotes by Jack Zipes to *The Collected Sicilian Folk and Fairy Tales of Giuseppe Pitrè* (New York: Routledge, 2007), vol. II, p. 923, Bertoldino chases about after flies, but unable to defeat them, he calls his mother Marcolfa to help him. This, without further reference, he traces to *Bertoldo, Bertoldino e Cacasenno*, as well as to the *Piacevoli e ridicolose semplicità de Bertoldino*, but the name comes from the Solomon and Marcolphus tradition. Antoine le Métel, Conte d'Ouville, *L'Élite des contes* (Paris: Alphonse Lemerre, 1876), no. 5, pp. 5–6. Yet another version of this story occurs in the four-act play entitled *Vita pentimento e morte di Pietro Bailardo con Pullcinella …* (Naples: Francesco Saverio Criscuolo, 1852), Act II, sc. 5, in which a servant reduces to zero a fly on the nose of the sleeping 'padrone.' Pietro: 'O heavens! And the head of the padrone?' Bargello: 'It looked like a focaccia' (twisted bread).
37 Jean de La Fontaine, *Fables* (Paris: Lemerre, 1926), bk. VIII, no. 10, pp. 83–4. The story came to France in the seventeenth century in the translation by David Sahid d'Ispahan of the *Livre des Lumières* (Anwari Suhaili) by Al Vaez Hassain ben Ali, attributed to Bidpai (Pilpai) (Paris: Simeon Piget, 1644), p. 135. See Daniel J. Maher, *La Fontaine à la rencontre de l'Orient: L'influence du Livre des Lumières sur les Fables* (Ottawa: National Library, 1990; thesis, printed in 1989). 'The Solitary Gardener who formed a friendship with a Bear; illustrating the Ends of Incongruous Friendship' in *The Lights of Canopus*, trans. Edward B. Eastwick (Hertford: Stephen Austen, 1854), no. 27, pp. 180–3.

This generic motif was known in many parts of Europe in the nineteenth century, but in terms of frequency, it remained essentially an Italian story, for the versions to be collected there in printed collections are relatively numerous, representing the many more then being recited in Italian towns and villages. Jón Arnason gleaned the following version in Iceland. A tub full of butter had been stored away for safe keeping in the royal palace. But when the old couple rolled it home and opened it, they saw an empty container and the issue of a single fly. Taking the insect for the thief, the old carl and his wife set up a merry but futile chase until the pest settled on the old man's nose. But his wife's ensuing blow served only to relieve the old one of his life while shooing the fly to safety.[38] Aurelio M. Espinosa found a lode of such tales in Spain, one of which appears in his *Cuentos populares españoles* under the title 'Juan Tonto va a vender miel.'[39]

Coming now to Italy, Pitrè in his *Sicilian Folk and Fairy Tales* recounts the story of Giufà the fool who sold meat to the flies on credit. When they refused to pay, he went to the judge and was told he could kill them with impunity, which again led to the breaking of the judge's head.[40] Laura Gonzenbach, in a section dealing with this same local bumpkin, has a version of far greater interest, for in the tale of 'Giufà and the Shepherd,' the fool kills the pastor because he was singing in the night, having misunderstood his mother's instructions. They decide to throw their victim into the water tank, but then while Giufà is sleeping, the mother dumps in a dead goat instead. It was a brilliant ploy, for she knew her simpleton son would confess to the crime as a matter of course and be hauled before the judge. There Giufà says to his mother, 'Don't you remember that we threw him into the tank?' So the magistrates send Giufà in to drag out the shepherd. Once inside he asks the shepherd's daughter whether her father had horns, or wool, thereby forcing the girl

38 Jón Arnason, *Icelandic Legends*, trans. George E.J. Powell and Eiríkr Magnússon (London: Longmans, Green & Co., 1866), pp. 606–9.

39 (Madrid: S. Aguirre, 1947), vol. I, pp. 476–8. The fly swatting that also kills the person on whom the insect is perched is the first of several episodes involving the illogical and damaging literal interpretation of commissions and instructions, somewhat in the manner of Till Eulenspiegel.

40 *The Collected Sicilian Folk and Fairy Tales of Giuseppe Pitrè*, trans. and ed. Jack Zipes and Joseph Russo (New York: Routledge, 2007), vol. I, p. 660.

to admit it wasn't her father. The mother then confirms his unreliable idiocy and so he goes free. This is clearly the second part of the Morlini-Straparola tale, and for want of evidence to the contrary, may have been derived directly or indirectly from it.[41]

Straparola's tale falls under the aegis of anecdotes about numbskulls and idiots, even if such characters display savant moments. Fortunio is one of a class of simplistic, literal-minded lubbers who performs according to a certain form of half logic that is sure to produce laughter in a rather rough and hearty way. The comprehensive literature concerning the exploits of fools is vast indeed. He lives in his own hermetic world in which the traditional uses of objects do not instruct his consciousness. Such a protagonist may try to sell things to animals, send inanimate objects in search of others already lost, wrap up stones to keep them warm, make marks on a ship's rail when an object has fallen overboard so he can search for it later, attempt to send an animal to school, burn down the house to kill insects – the list is as long as the jest writers' minds were fertile. These characters typically follow figurative instructions to the letter, set up as specialists and make ridiculous predictions, or write ludicrous prescriptions. To be sure, such tales are a part of the oral culture, but it may prove that they are more typical of jest books and literary collections, thus accounting for the fact that the second part of Straparola's collection is in a sense more 'literary' than the first insofar as his materials are more frequently derived from written sources. But as Stith Thompson points out, not only is this material based on iterative

---

41 *Beautiful Angiola: The Great Treasury of Sicilian Folk and Fairy Tales Collected by Laura Gonzenbach*, trans. Jack Zipes (New York: Routledge, 2004), pp. 147–8. Thomas Frederick Crane, in *Italian Popular Tales*, ed. Jack Zipes (Santa Barbara: ABC Clio, 2001), pp. 235–6, provides another tale concerning the flies, the meat, the lack of payment, the judge, and the blow to his honour's face. A similar tale, 'La frittatina,' was collected by Vittorio Imbriani, *La novellaja fiorentina* (Leghorn: Francesco Vigo, 1877), p. 545, in which a housewife goes to the Commissario to complain of the flies visiting her omelette in the window. She is given not only permission to kill them but a weapon to do so, whereupon she breaks the commissioner's nose in her first attempt. Others were collected by Domenico Giuseppe Bernoni, *Tradizioni popolari veneziane* (Venice: Tipografia Antonelli, 1875–8), punt. III, p. 83, and Giuseppe Pitrè, 'Il matto' in *Novelle popolari toscane*, ed. Gino Cerrito (Palermo: Edikronos, 1981), no. 37, pp. 181–5.

and ancient patterns of humour, it has also 'directly influenced traditional storytellers and ballad singers.'[42] Hence, the interplay between oral and written cultures pertains here as well.

---

42 *The Folktale*, p. 196. Of the many stories of fools, a further example, 'Jouon Nesci,' was collected by Paul Sébillot, *Littérature orale de l'Auvergne* (Paris: G.P. Maisonneuve & Larose, [1898]), pp. 81–9 in the series *Les littératures populaires de toutes les nations*, vol. XXXV, in which the protagonist is sent to sell cloth in the market with instructions to beware of the fast talkers. So he sells it to a statue which, in refusing to pay, makes the boy angry, whereupon he strikes it and thereby finds a treasure. Many stories follow, including the killing of a louse with a hammer at the expense of his brother's life. This story relates to another collected by Rachel Harriette Busk, 'The Booby,' in *Roman Legends: A Collection of the Fables and Folk-lore of Rome* (Boston: Estes & Lauriat, 1877), pp. 371–4. This boy likewise sells linen to a statue, barters away gold coins as rusty nails, and yanks a door off its hinges merely to close it. The devices are all based on the same principle found in the present story of performing literally what the speaker intended figuratively or generally, relying upon the complex cognitive evaluations that generate appropriate and efficient interpretations on the part of those able to adapt words to situations in relation to goals, circumstances, and means. A final example, for our purposes, was included by Joseph Haltrich, 'Wie soll ich den sagen' (Well then, what should I say?), in his *Deutsche Volksmärchen aus dem Sachsenlande in Siebenbürgen* (Berlin: Julius Springer, 1856), no. 65, pp. 310–12. This fool is beaten for saying inappropriate things, whereupon he carries the moral from each situation forward to the next, only to discover that it is devastatingly inappropriate in each successive circumstance. The next selection is more of the same: no. 66, 'Suche nur, es gibt noch Dümmere' (The more you search, the stupider you get), pp. 312–15.

XIII. Fable 5
Vilio Brigantello, the Robber,
and the Fateful Sack

Vilio Brigantello kills a robber who was set in ambush to murder him.

A very famous poet has said that the man who takes delight in beguiling others must not cry out and lament if by chance someone should trick him instead. I have remarked that those who have an inclination to outwit their fellows very often, perhaps always, are themselves outwitted. Such a fate befell a robber who had made up his mind to slay a certain craftsman, but who was killed instead by his intended victim.

In Pistoia, a city in Tuscany between Florence and Lucca, there lived an artisan named Vilio Brigantello, who was very rich and possessed a great store of money. Nevertheless, this man pretended to live in a state of great poverty, precisely because of his haunting fear of being robbed. He dwelled alone, without wife or servants, in a small cottage that, nevertheless, was well furnished inside with all the things men find necessary for their existence. Yet to make it more apparent to others just how poor and beggarly he was, he dressed himself without exception in the commonest, meanest, and dirtiest attire possible. Meanwhile, he kept a strict watch over the coffer where he stored his coin. Vilio was very alert and a most careful craftsman to boot, but when it came to spending he was miserly and avaricious, allowing himself no better diet than bread, cheese, a little wine added in, and the roots of plants.

Still it happened that certain sly and cunning thieves, with good reason suspecting that Vilio was in possession of a sizeable sum of money, one night went to his cottage at the time they thought best for robbing him. Because they weren't able to open or break down the door with their crowbars and implements, and fearful at the same time that they might rouse the neighbours with the noise they made with their evil work, they settled upon a plan for tricking Vilio, thus arriving at their ends by another way. By chance among the thieves there was one who was well acquainted with Vilio, and who often put on a great show of friendship – so much so that now and again he had been invited back to his house for supper. These robbers' plan was to tie up the leader and guide of their band in a sack and make believe he was dead. They carried him just as he was to the artisan's cottage, where Vilio's friend went forward to ask with a certain urgency that he take the sack into his charge and watch over it until they might come back to fetch it, promising that it wouldn't be long. Vilio, after listening to his feigned friend's importunities and suspecting nothing of what was going on, without objection let them take the body into the house. Meantime the robbers had made a plan among themselves that as soon as Vilio was sound asleep, their leader would get himself out of the sack and, after killing the artisan, he would lay hands on all his money and any of his effects deemed worth the taking.

So the sack with the robber inside was hauled into the cottage, while Vilio carried on busily with his craft, working close to the candle. Now and then he cast a glance towards the sack in which the robber was hiding – as those who are suspicious and fearful by nature are inclined to do – and it seemed to him as if there was something stirring inside the sack. With that, he got up from his seat, quickly snatched up a myrtle-wood stick thickly studded with knots, and brought the cudgel down upon the skull of the robber to such good effect that he instantly killed him, turning a feigning corpse into a real one. The thief's associates awaited his return until daybreak, and seeing no sign of him imagined that he had fallen asleep. More fearful of the approaching daylight, which was fast coming on, than they were for the safety of their friend, they made their way back to the cottage of the artisan and asked him for the sack that they had left in his charge the day before. As soon as Vilio had closed the door and barricaded it, he handed the sack over to them, addressing them in a loud voice, 'Yesterday, instead of a corpse, you brought me a live man in this sack, intent upon frightening me. But now, to frighten you instead, I return to you a corpse instead of a living man.' When the band of robbers heard these words they were dumbstruck. Opening the sack, they found in very truth the dead body of their trusty mate. Then, in order to pay due honour to their daring leader, with sighs and tears, they cast his body into the sea where it sank out of sight. In this way, the man who had planned to trick and deceive the artisan was himself tricked and deceived.

Such were the final words of Signor Bernardo's ingeniously told fable, one that amused all the listeners. The Signora thereupon asked him to follow up with his enigma according the rule, which he gave out as follows:

> From sire alone I sprang and grew;
> No mother dear I ever knew.
> But fate decreed that all must give
> Their fostering aid to make me live.
> Soon to bulk immense I grow,
> And o'er the world I spread and flow,
> And though to some I'm fierce and fell,
> Most men my praises loud will tell.

Many of the listeners thought they had divined the meaning of this graceful and scholarly enigma, but that belief proved to be ill founded, seeing that their understanding had in every case wandered far from the truth. Wherefore Capello, perceiving that the discussion threatened to be long, spoke up, 'Ladies and gentlemen, let's not lose more time over it, because the enigma I have set for you to guess means nothing other than games of hazard, which spring from a father alone, and are supported and nourished by all men. In a very brief space of time they have spread over the entire world, where they are welcomed and made much of, and in such manner that even though a man may lose on account of them, he does not for this reason chase them away from him, but continues to derive pleasure from their existence.' This explanation of the subtly conceived enigma gratified all the listeners, especially Signor Antonio Bembo, who was much addicted to play. But seeing that the hours of the night were passing, or rather flying, the Signora gave direction to Signora Chiara to begin her fable, who, having arisen from her chair and placed herself on a higher one – she being somewhat short of stature – at once began to speak.

XIII.5 Commentary

This is a most pleasant tale to annotate. It begins with a quotation from Petrarch's 'Triumph of Cupid,' which sets up the cruel irony of the tale, that those who live by the sword may die by the sword, or, in wording closer to Petrarch, 'he who takes delight in fraud must not complain if another tricks him.'[43] This follows in the tradition of tales and *novelle* written in illustration of proverbs or famous sayings. Again the story is borrowed, but the opprobrium can now be divided. Straparola, unapologetic for his literary larceny, has once again pillaged Morlini, this time in a nearly verbatim rendering of his twentieth *novella*, 'De cerdone qui insidiantem latronem eum interfecturum interfecit' (Of the artisan who tricks a thief, thus murdering his intended murderer).[44] But Morlini, with equal deviancy and little more craft, has cobbled the present vignette, in true humanist fashion, from two closely related episodes in book IV of Apuleius's *Metamorphoses* (The Golden Ass).[45] These two authors (Morlini and Straparola) deserve each other. The band of robbers returning from Thebes to their mountain stronghold had booty galore, but sad stories to tell of the loss of their three finest members. Having made enquiries initially about the local men of fortune within their zone of operation, they heard of a certain Chryseros, who took great pains to dissimulate his wealth, living alone in a small cottage, where he dressed in rags and slept nightly on his bags of gold. Their plan was to attack in the night, but their tools were to no avail and they could not arrive at their ends without making such noise as to wake the neighbours. Morlini, himself, is working nearly verbatim. At this juncture, however, he breaks with his source, continuing with the tale of the sack into which the gang had stowed their leader in the guise of a corpse. But that too will prove to be an adaptation of materials derived from the *Metamorphoses* a little further along. Apuleius, meanwhile, continues with an account of the leader's attempt to reach through a hole to unlatch the door from the inside. The suspicious householder, in this instance, sees the hand poking through and nails it to a post, thereby deceiving the deceiver. He then runs to his rooftop to alert the neighbours, forcing the thieves to a cruel option, either to abandon their comrade, to cut off his arm, or to flee without him. They choose the middle course, but the shock to

---

43 *The Triumphs of Petrarch*, ed. Virgil Burnett and Ernest Hatch Wilkins (Chicago: University of Chicago Press, 1962), 'Triumph of Cupid,' I.119–20; Petrarca, 'Trionfi,' in *Opere* (Florence: Sansoni, 1975), vol. I: 'ché, chi prende diletto di far frode / non si dê lamenter, s'altri lo 'nganna.'

44 *Les nouvelles*, trans. Fernand Caussy (Paris: E. Sansot, 1904), pp. 56–8.

45 Lucius Apuleius, *The Golden Ass*, trans. William Adlington (1566), ed. Harry Schnur (New York: Collier Books, 1962), pp. 92–103.

their comrade is too great; he is unable to keep pace with them, asks to be slain, then takes his own life, whereupon his companions, once more as in Morlini, honour the corpse and throw it into the sea. In a second and equally devastating episode for the thieves, they dress up one of their best in a bearskin and present the 'animal' to Demochares like a Trojan horse to be taken into his house. It was their intent that during the night their co-worker would slay the porter, unlock the doors to them, and so permit the pillaging of the house. All went according to plan, the bear still serving to keep any members of the household at bay, but in due course a group of servants came armed with clubs, spears and swords, accompanied by their mastiffs. The valiant thief, sewn into his hide, performs with brio for a considerable time, but he is hard pressed by every mongrel in the streets. Then a tall man comes at him with a spear and thrusts him right through the body. Both parts of the tale thus fall into place, drawn directly from Apuleius: the assault upon a man who feigns poverty, and who, suspicious by nature, turns the trick, followed by the sea burial; and the entry gained into a house by giving to the owner a container in which one of the thieves is hidden. From two episodes, Morlini makes one, barring any interim sources, exchanging the bearskin for a sack.

Given the probability of direct descent from a famous work of the second century A.D., there is little point in looking for motivic similarities in later stories, whether of swindlers or lovers gaining their entries in coffers and sacks, some of them clubbed nearly to death, as in II.5. This tale is, to be sure, about the trickster tricked, the huckster hoisted in his own halter (further examples of which include IX.3), and thus a form of heavy-handed justice, the punishment visited upon the culprit before he commits the crime. Thereby it becomes an exemplum to a saying, the truth of which will never rise above anecdotal demonstration: that tricksters will always be tricked in the end. More specifically, Straparola, for unspecified reasons, chooses Pistoia as the setting, a slight nod in the direction of verisimilitude no doubt, making the apologue into a robbery gone bad on the outskirts of a city between Florence and Lucca on the western side of Tuscany.

XIII. Fable 6
How Lucilio Finds the 'Good Day'

SIGNORA CHIARA

Lucietta, the mother of Lucilio – himself a useless, good-for-nothing – sends him out to find the good day. This he does, and returns home bearing with him the fourth part of a treasure.

I have always understood, gracious ladies, from the writings of the world's sages, that Fortune helps out those who are alert and help themselves and puts to flight the fainthearted and fearful. In demonstration of the truth of this saying, I'll tell you a very brief fable, which by chance may bring you a bit of pleasure and satisfaction.

In Cesena, an illustrious city of the Romagna, near to which flows the River Savio, there once dwelt a little widow, very poor, but of good repute; Lucietta was her name. This woman had a son, the most useless and dunderheaded loon that nature ever made. Once he'd gotten himself into bed he'd never get up before noon, and then, raising himself up, he'd gape and rub his eyes, stretching his arms and legs out of the bed like the worthless nincompoop he was. His mother was deeply vexed about all this because she had formed a real hope that this son of hers might prove to be the staff and support of her old age. In order to make a careful, vigilant, and accomplished man out of him, it had been her daily practice to instruct him as follows: 'My son, any diligent and cautious man who wishes to have a good day must rise up at the crack of dawn, insofar as Fortune stretches out her hand to help only those who are on the alert, and not those who lie about in bed. Only if you take my advice, my son, will you ever find the good day and rest content therein.'

Lucilio – for such was the boy's name – more ignorant than ignorance itself, failed to take in the meaning of his mother's exhortation. Considering only the shell rather than the kernel of her words, he roused himself from the deep sleep he was in and wandered out of the house. After he had passed through one of the city gates, he settled himself right back into sleep in the open air, stretching himself out into the highway, creating an obstacle to all those who were trying to get in and out of the city. On this very day, by chance, there were three men, citizens of Cesena, who were bound out of town on an errand, namely, to dig up a rich treasure they had discovered and carry it back home with them. In fact, they had already dug it up and were trying to transport it into the city when they found themselves face to face with Lucilio lying there on the road. At that moment, however, he was no longer asleep but awake and searching for the 'good day' as his mother had counselled him to do. As the first of the three citizens passed by Lucilio, he said to him, 'My friend, may you have a good day,' whereupon Lucilio answered, 'Aha, I have one of them,' speaking about the day. The young citizen, his head filled with thoughts about the treasure, attributed more meaning to the words than was intended – no surprise, of course, because, as someone wrote, guilty or suspicious minds always fear others can read their thoughts. The second citizen, as he passed Lucilio, saluted him in the same way, giving him the good day, to whom Lucilio replied that he had two of them, meaning that he now had two of the good days. The third citizen came close behind and in exactly the same way gave the good day to the fellow lying on the road. Whereupon Lucilio, now wide awake, got to his feet and said, 'Well, now I've got all three of them. So my plan has worked like a charm,' by which he meant his gathering of a few 'good days.'

When the three men heard Lucilio's last speech, they were frightened and terrified that this young rascal would go to the governor of the town and make public everything they'd been up to. So they asked him to follow them, telling him outright the whole story of the treasure and in the end gave him a quarter of it as his share. With his heart full of joy, Lucilio gathered up his booty and made his way back home, where he handed it over to his mother, saying, 'Good mother, truly the grace of God must be with me, because in following the orders you gave to me, I've found the good day. Here is money for you to take good care of so that it will serve our future needs.' His mother, joyful in the possession of the treasure her son had acquired, then encouraged him to always keep a sharp lookout in the future for the likely reason that he might just meet up with other good days like this one.

The Signora, when she perceived that Madonna Chiara's fable had come to an end, requested of her an enigma for the company to guess in order to keep unbroken the rule that formerly they had all observed. Then Chiara, whose mind entertained no ill thoughts, presented her riddle in these words:

> Full many beasts of every kind
> In nature's kingdom we may find;
> But one there is of tender mood,
> Of loving heart and spirit good,
> Which, when its sire grown blind and weak,
> With age his food no more can seek,
> Will guard him safe and feed him well
> Within a warm and cosy cell.
> So none may ever blame its greed,
> Or tax it with ungrateful deed.

'This enigma of mine is intended to manifest the virtue of gratitude in the form of the chough bird, for when its sees its father no longer able to fly on account of the weakness of old age, it shows its gratitude by preparing a nest for him and by giving him food for nourishment until the day of his death.'

Signor Beltramo, who was sitting near to Chiara, took note that his turn had now come to tell a story. Reluctant to wait for the Signora's command, he launched right in with a bemused and happy countenance.

XIII.6 Commentary

Straparola's tale of the lazy boy who finds a fortune by lying in the middle of the road and looking for a 'good day' is Morlini's *novelle* faithfully translated from the Latin.[46] Typical of his practice, he has exchanged the implicit Neapolitan setting for Cesare Borgia's one-time headquarters in the Romagna, the town of Cesena, situated just to the south of Ravenna and west of Rimini on the Savio River. This is still somewhat to the south of Padua, but certainly in the region traditionally associated with Straparola. The story turns on a double misunderstanding of language. Lucilio hears his mother's repeated admonition that if he is ever

---

46 Girolamo Morlini, 'De matre quae desidiosum filium ut reperiret bonum diem misit' (Of the mother who sends her lazy son to look for a good day) in *Les nouvelles* (1520), trans. Fernand Caussey (Paris: Sansot and Co., 1904), no. 29, pp. 78–9. *Novelle e favole*, ed. Giovanni Villani (Rome: Salerno, 1983), pp. 142–5.

to have a good day in his life he will have to get out of bed, look sharp, and keep his wits about him. The boy thought the collectable commodity was 'good days.' So when three thieves greet him in these terms, he begins to enumerate them as acquisitions. Meanwhile, the robbers think he is numbering them. Certain that Lucilio is onto their game, they take him aside, confess, and cut him in for a fourth of the loot – a good day, indeed. If the reader takes from such a yarn anything more than an amusing anecdote about the inversions of fortune, it would have to do with the power of guilt and the ambiguities of language.

The vignette is of interest because it is a significantly pared down segment of a more elaborate tripartite ancient Eastern tale that made its way into Europe, perhaps at the time of the Mongolian invasions, and subsequently became a part of Western folk culture. It is a dot on a vast but largely virtual stemma, insofar as the many versions collected in the nineteenth century entail the active dissemination of this story type throughout Europe during the preceding four centuries at the least, but from which there is but a sparse scattering of literary allusions. The Morlini-Straparola, single-episode reduction captures attention because it is proof positive of the tale's transmission and appears within a decade or two of its earliest surviving literary representations. Because the folk tale is somewhat fantastical in its expanded forms, it is not surprising that Renaissance anecdotalists would seize upon the salient episode, the inadvertent numbering of the criminals, and, in novelistic fashion, turn it into a real local event. What Morlini's comic portrait tells us about the folk tale then current is only that the numbering motif was a functional part. The 'good day' feature is apparently a late accretion, for in the literary record it remains unique to Morlini and Straparola, departing considerably from the Eastern *oikotype*, which tells of ambitious fools who style themselves as false sorcerers. In their cases, the accidental good fortune in catching the thieves saves them from certain death. Morlini places the emphasis on slothfulness and an unexpected rise in fortune – the dream of wealth without labour.

The most ancient version to survive may serve as a prototype. Therein a poor man or a fool chooses or is compelled to play the wise man, all-knowing doctor, or diviner who is called in to locate stolen property. Typically, he is incarcerated and given three days to come up with the answer, or he is invited to a banquet with three and four courses, and as he enumerates the days, or counts the courses, eavesdropping servants with guilty consciences, thinking themselves discovered, confide in him, tell where the goods are hidden, beg for secrecy, and offer bribes. The fool by such means is enabled to play augur and prophet, perform empty ceremonies, and locate the missing goods to the amazement of all. The imagined stemma connecting Straparola to this generic tale must include stepwise transformations and substitutions whereby the one evolves into the other, a process demanding many generations of oral and literary alterations. Moreover, the diversity of the allusions suddenly appearing within a couple of decades of one another at the beginning of the sixteenth century entails not only a spontaneous interest in the central motif, but a substantial period of prior circulation in order to arrive at such diversity.

For origins, we need look no further back than the *Katha sarit sagara* (*The Ocean of the Streams of Story*) by the Saivite Brahmin Somadeva, compiled for Suryamati, wife of the king of Kashmir around 1080, although it was without doubt collected from considerably earlier sources, including those assembled in Gunadhya's (Budhasvāmin's) *Brhat-kathā çlokasamgraha*.[47] In book VI of the *Katha* is the story of Harisarman, a poor and foolish Brahmin who worked for a prosperous householder. Slighted that he and his family were not invited to the wedding feast of his patron's daughter, he seeks revenge by stealing his horse and hiding it in a remote place. When the theft is detected and a search is launched, Harisurman's wife broadcasts her husband's remarkable skills in astrology and divination. By means of juggling with a map, he pretends to locate the horse at a point of crossing lines. When the horse is found, precisely where Harisarman left it, he gains instant renown as a wizard. (This is a hide-and-pretend-to-find-by-magic motif that has little currency in the Western relations of the tale.) His real challenge begins when gold and coins go missing and his master commands him to employ his skills in finding them. Sitting in his room behind closed doors, he begins to berate his tongue (jihvá) for boasting of such skills – at that point having no idea how to extricate himself. However, the culprits are the maid and her brother Jihva, so that when she eavesdrops outside the room and thinks she hears her brother's name, she enters, falls at Harisarman's feet, and divulges the location of the hidden treasure in exchange for secrecy. (This is a paradigmatic version of the counting motif and the reaction of the guilty.) Once again the Brahmin plays the seer before turning up the treasure in the garden. Such outstanding skills could not

---

47 *Katha sarit sagara*, ed. C.H. Tawney, 2 vols. (Calcutta: Munshiram Manoharlal [1880], 1992), vol. I, pp. 271–5.

but raise suspicion, so that ultimately he is tested merely to confirm the truth of his wizardry. His challengers place an object in a pitcher and defy him to name it. By marvellous good fortune, however, Harisarman's memory roams back to an episode from his youth when his father called him 'toad,' and so in pitying himself out loud by this pet name, fortune sustains him and he becomes a feudal chief, for just such a creature had been hidden in the vessel. (This motif occurs in many two-part Western versions, but not in Straparola.) There are now three elements to the story: the object hidden by the practitioner that he pretends to discover through augury or divination; the genuinely stolen article that is found when, as in Straparola's story, a phrase misconstrued by the thieves convinces them that their crime is known, bringing them to a confession; and a word uttered in despair when no answer can be imagined that doubles for the sought-after reply.[48] These three devices characterize and define the story type, singly or in sequence; they are the immutable motifs amid changing characters and settings.

A version of this story appears in the *Vetálapançavimsati* (The Twenty-five Tales of a Vampire) in which a magic gem is lost by the king's daughter.[49] This story becomes the source for another such tale in the Kalmouk *Siddhî-kür* of Ardschi Bordschi, in which the fortunate hero is now a physician who cures the sick khan of his evil spirits.[50] (This motif survives

---

48 Sages and astrologers were also suspect throughout the Middle Ages and put through various tests. In a famous anecdote, Louis XI, king of France, gave orders to have an astrologer thrown out the window. The astrologer was then called in to see if he could foretell the time of his own death, thinking to make him tell a lie. The astrologer answered merely that it would occur exactly three days before the king's own death, which deterred the king's plans. Karen Jolly, 'Medieval Magic: Definitions, Beliefs, Practices,' in *Witchcraft and Magic in Europe: The Middle Ages*, ed. Bengt Ankarloo and Stuart Clark (Philadelphia: University of Pennsylvania Press, 2002), p. 67.

49 This is a variation upon its correlate as one of the twenty-five vampire tales incorporated into *The Ocean of the Streams of Story*.

50 In *Sagas from the Far East: or Kalmouk and Mongolian Traditionary Tales*, trans. Rachel Harriette Busk (London: Griffith and Farran, 1873), pp. 55–62. The variations made to the tale are noteworthy. It begins with the lazy man driven out by his angry wife to earn something. After foolish exploits that cause him to lose everything, including his clothes, he takes refuge in the Khan's stables, where he sees the princess drop the bejewelled royal talisman; it ends up under a pile of dung. When he is discovered hiding in the straw, he pretends to be a great sorcerer and is taken before the king, where he is provided with a pig's head, which he then proceeds to question. The numbering game is remembered only in his eliminating as suspects

in the West in conjunction with other elements of the tale only in Lithuania.) This story in its southern and northern forms became an inevitable part of the larger debate concerning the conveyance of Eastern folklore into Western Europe, whether through the Mongolian invasions or through the southern trade routes and Byzantium.[51]

The European record of this story is so sprawling and diverse that a few examples must serve to outline a more complex history, including the many implicit phases that must have existed as living tales, but that can no longer be recovered. Straparola, through Morlini, once again provides a point of reference in the spreading stemma. Others from the period are scattered and varied, but testify to a widespread 'living' tradition of tales possibly involving lazy children who reap fortunes by chance through the counting routine, but more certainly about brazen fools who pretend to skills they do not possess, yet escape through luck reconstructed as occult understanding. One such appears in the *Facetien, drei Bücher* of Heinrich Bebel, first published in 1506. This is the story of the charcoal burner who goes to the king's court to locate the missing treasure. He, in counting off the limited number of days he has been granted to solve the crime ('Iam unus accessit'), inadvertently plays on the guilt of the servants responsible for the heist. The treasure once returned, the charcoal burner lives with honour and dignity for the rest of his days. This too is a one-episode version, scaled down from the full folk tale to a short anecdote, using the same counting feature as in Straparola, but otherwise differing in every circumstance.[52] Hans Wilhelm Kirchhof in *Wendunmuth* (1563) tells a similar tale of a charcoal burner who saw what

---

all the members of the court one by one. When the talisman is found by wandering about questioning the pig's head, the king is amazed and offers great rewards, but the protagonist settles for portions of meal and butter. His wife, incensed by the missed opportunity, convinces the khan by letter that he has also been healed of an invisible malady and so capitalizes upon her husband's reputation a second time. This is the fourth of the thirteen Kalmouk tales in the collection.

51 Emmanuel Georges Cosquin argues persuasively against the Mongolian entry theory in *Les Mongols et leur prétendu rôle dans la transmission des contes indiens vers l'occident européen* (Niort: G. Clouzot, 1913).

52 'De quodam carbonari' (Of a certain charcoal burner) in his *Facetien*, ed. Gustav Bebermeyer (Hildesheim: Georg Olms [1506, *Facetiarum libri tres*], 1967), no. 112, p. 85. See also Bebel's *Schwänke*, trans. Albert Wesselski (Munich and Leipzig, 1907), vol. I, pp. 96–7. Also *Facetiarum Heinrici Bebelii* (Tübingen: Ulrici Morhardi, 1550), pp. 53r–v, very similar in content to the version by Le Sieur d'Ouville described below, except the hero is a charcoal burner rather than a shoemaker.

a poor existence he led and decided to seek his fortune. He too ends up at court, pledging his life to find a lost article in three days, and saves his neck only when the thieves overhear him counting off the days in his room, thereby gaining the reputation of a soothsayer. The tale was decidedly current throughout Europe.[53]

Yet another from much these same years is contained in *Les cent nouvelles nouvelles* of Philippe de Vigneulles. When a poor cobbler living near one of the gates of Metz saw the fine life enjoyed by the men of arms with their horses and squires, he decides that he too will become a knight. A passing chevalier tells him to purchase all the trappings, then go to a place where he is unknown, present himself as a soothsayer, and boast of his powers to recover lost objects.[54] The knight was mocking him, but the cobbler took it all at face value. The affinity with the story in the *Katha sarit sagara* is readily apparent. When, in the new city, a young man comes to him to report a stolen treasure, he requests three days to prepare his answer. Three servants bring him his meals and, as he counts off the days, they are seized by their own guilt as though his words had placed the finger on them. In this way, the cobbler solves the crime, reaps his reward, and thereafter forswears the profession.[55] (A further version by Juan de Timoneda, first published in 1563, is summarized below.) Such is the profile of the early record of these tales.

---

53 'Ein Koler ist ein Warsager' (How a charcoal burner becomes a soothsayer) in *Wendunmuth*, ed. Hermann Oesterley, 5 vols. (Tübingen: Litterarischen Verein in Stuttgart, 1869), bk. I, no. 130, vol. I, pp. 160–2.

54 There are many such stories of low-lifers who are motivated to throw caution to the wind and plunge untrained into a profession in order to live the high life. Typically they become doctors or lawyers and find themselves in danger of death if they fail in their claims. All, true to form, come up with makeshift remedies and escape their fates, as in Giuseppe Pitrè's recounting of 'Il medico Grillo,' about a peasant who, seeing a prosperous doctor pass by, abandons his hoe in the field and goes off in search of the good life. By a turn of good fortune he cures the king's daughter (of a fishbone in her throat which she conveniently coughs up because he made her laugh). Thereafter, however, he finds himself the object of professional envy, driving him to riskier and more preposterous exploits. *Novelle popolari toscane*, pref. Gino Cerrito (Palermo: Edikronos, 1981), no. 60, pp. 264–9.

55 Philippe de Vigneulles, *Les cent nouvelles nouvelles*, ed. Charles H. Livingston (Geneva: Droz, 1972), no. 57, pp. 237–41. The closest analogue is Bebel's, but because de Vigneulles could read no German, any influence had to have been indirect. Another early version is to be found in Pauli's *Schimpf und Ernst*, ed. Johannes Bolte (Berlin: H. Stubenrauch, 1924), no. 818, vol. II, p. 433.

English examples are not easily come by, but one of the petty jugglers described by Henry Chettle in his *Kind-Hartes Dreame* (1592) employs the ruse of planting the missing object in a known place – in many of the later folk versions it is fed to a game bird – and then 'discovering' it as though by supernatural means. A wise man and his servant gain entry into a noble household. During the preparations for a banquet, the imposter magician slips into the parlour, steals a precious salt-cellar, and tosses it into the pond behind the house. Of this he informs his boy, who, when the hue and cry for the lost object is proclaimed, assures the household that his master, now playing scarce in his room, is their only hope. When the master and mistress of the house repair to the Mage, he feigns annoyance that they should pester him over such matters, being a man of higher things, but in the end consents to work his powers. After a suitable period of time, he informs them that one of their servants had taken it, but that he, by virtue of his arts, had compelled him to return it, having it cast into the pond to conceal the servant's identity. By this means, his name comes into 'rare admiration' and the owner pays him a substantial reward, while all the maids in the household come running to him to have their fortunes told. There is so much of the present story type implicit in this sketch, including the non-disclosure of the servant thief's identity, that Chettle's acquaintance with the continental tradition of tales is beyond doubt.[56] This part of the story goes back to Harisarman in the *Katha sarit sagara*, who hides the horse of his master, then, employing his wife to tout his astrological powers, gains his reputation as a wizard by 'locating' the animal. Nevertheless, other key narrative elements have been absorbed: the counting of hours and the guilty confessions.

A century later, the Sieur d'Ouville includes a version in his *L'Élite des contes* containing two of the three parts. It concerns a poor villager named Grillet, who is ready to play the prophet of lost articles for three gourmet feasts, no matter how dire the outcome. When a rich diamond belonging to a high-society lady is stolen by three of her own lackeys, the poor villager is ready to risk his life for three days' dining. As the days draw to a close, the servants overhear him saying 'Ah! Dieu merci, en voilà déjà un!' (God have mercy, there goes one already – meaning days), and then two, and three. Through a misconstruction of these words, the thieves are now certain he is party to their guilt. They turn

---

56 *Kind-Heartes Dreme,* ed. G.B. Harrison (London: John Lane, The Bodley Head, 1923), pp. 51–2.

the diamond over to the seer, he feeds it to a 'coq d'Ind,' then points out the bird and has it slain, producing the lady's jewel. But the dame's husband is less credulous and wants to put such prescience to a second test, promising a beating and the loss of the diviner's ears should he fail. He hides a cricket (grillet) between two plates and awaits the seer's answer. Baffled, the helpless hero laments aloud his fate, 'Hélas! pauvre Grillet, te voilà pris!' (Alas, poor Cricket, you're caught there!), but in accidentally naming the insect, he escapes with a good reward.[57] Emmanuel Cosquin noted the similarity between this story and a version he collected in Lorraine some three centuries later entitled 'Le sorcier.'[58] It tells of a villager, a lost ring belonging to the lady of the chateau, and the making of the false sorcerer who said he would locate it in exchange for three good meals. When the three cooks reveal their larceny and beg for mercy, certain they had been discovered, the sorcerer tells them to feed the ring to the big rooster in the courtyard. Thus, the cock is butchered and blamed, the robbers go scot free, and the hero reaps his reward. But there is a sequel, for he too is submitted to the *grillon* (cricket) test and escapes in the manner employed by D'Ouville. This correlation is perhaps best explained as a direct literary appropriation, for they are indeed similar.

A story with the same episodes in reverse order was also known in Sicily, the tale of 'Griddu Pintu' collected by Giuseppe Pitrè. This hero's name also means 'cricket,' and by lamenting his expected fate in the third person, he too solves the riddle of the hidden animal and establishes his reputation. He is then invited to find the queen's missing ring, and when the guilty servants confess after overhearing the fortune-teller talking to his trousers, they are told to feed the ring to a black goose.[59]

---

57 Antoine le Métel, Seigneur d'Ouville, 'D'un devin feint' in *L'Élite des contes du sieur d'Ouville* (Paris: Chez la veuve Trabouillet, 1641); ed. Gustave Brunet (Paris: Librairie des bibliophiles, 1883, a reimp. of the Rouen edition of 1680), vol. II, pp. 183–91; ed. Paul Ristelhuber (Paris: A. Lemerre, 1876), no. 63, p. 139.

58 *Contes populaires de Lorraine*, 2 vols. (Paris: F. Vieweg, 1886), vol. I, pp. 187–8.

59 'The Fortune-Teller' in *The Collected Sicilian Folk and Fairy Tales of Giuseppe Pitrè*, trans. and ed. Jack Zipes and Joseph Russo, 2 vols. (New York: Routledge, 2007), no. 167, vol. I, pp. 611–15. This is a far more elaborate telling, one that includes a black adder in the garden telling the peasant how to make his fortune, much as the chevalier instructs the cobbler in D'Ouville. It is a passing cavalier who puts Griddu to the test, taking him for a travelling huckster. And with each new success, he thanks his friend the black adder. Another captain wants to know whether his next child will be a boy or a girl and so the fortune-teller asks to see her. When he predicts that she would have one of each, he is kept in jail till the delivery, and his

Thus, Griddu Pintu comes through the ordeal a wealthy and respected man. A similar tale was collected in Mantua in which a poor peasant named Gámbara plays the astrologer, locates the king's ring after confessions, and has it fed to a turkey, leading to the amazing discovery when the animal is slaughtered. Then, in the second part he finds himself at a grand banquet that includes a rare plate of crawfish or small lobster. He is able to astonish once again by accident in lamenting his fate in a phrase that includes his name – Gámbara meaning crawfish.[60] From the top of the continent comes another version involving a charcoal burner who buys an old pastor's frock and becomes 'The Wise Priest and Prophet.' When the king loses a ring he is called in, with the threat of execution in the event of failure. He counts his three days of grace as they go past one after the other, which leads to the confession of the three valets and the stratagem of feeding the ring to one of the king's pigs.[61] And in *The Royal Hibernian Tales*, the hero, a false magician, turns up to locate a gentleman's stolen valuables and asks not for three good meals only, but three quarts of ale.[62] In counting these he exposes the

---

prediction turns out to be correct. In the episode of the queen's ring, he is placed in a room and the eavesdropping thieves hear him talking to his pants, saying 'It won't do you much good to go back and forth like that (drying in the heat), because tomorrow will see shit in those pants.' The culprits assume he is describing their fate. That leads to the success of the third episode with the slaughter of the black goose.

60 Isaia Visentini, 'Gambára' in *Fiabe Mantovane* (Bologna: Forni [1879], 1968), no. 41, pp. 188–91. The story is retold in Thomas Frederick Crane, *Italian Popular Tales*, ed. Jack Zipes (Santa Barbara: ABC Clio, 2001), pp. 253–4. Vittorio Imbriani included a similar tale, 'Re messèmi-gli-becca-'l-fumo,' in *Novellaja Milanese* (Milan: Rizzoli, 1872; Bologna: A. Forni, 1976), no. 10, pp. 138–45.

61 Peter Christen Asbjörnsen, 'The Story of the Charcoal Burner' in *Tales from the Fjeld: A Series of Popular Tales from the Norse*, trans. George Webbe Dasent (London: Chapman and Hall, 1874), p. 139.

62 (Dublin: C.M. Warren, n.d. but before 1887), pp. 57*ff.* Yet another occurs in Patrick Kennedy's *Fireside Stories of Ireland* (Dublin: McGlashon & Gill, 1870; reprint, Norwood Editions, 1975), pp. 116–19. A fagot-cutter grows jealous of the rich doctor, so he borrows a book and sets up shop as a universal healer and locator of lost articles. His reputation grows. When a gentleman loses a ring, he is sent for. He takes hair samples from everyone in the household and asks for eight days for the conjuring. Naming the remaining days prompts the thieves to reveal themselves, thinking they had been discovered. The doctor then professes to know all, the place of the lost article and the identity of the robbers, but qualifies that he is free to name only one or the other. The master takes the ring and the thieves go free. He too must pass further tests before he is released.

thieves, negotiates with them, and earns his reward. In all these tales, the mechanism of discovery is the same that is employed by Straparola. Its longevity as a comic device testifies to an intrinsic quality apt to amuse by its incongruity across centuries and cultures both as an accident that leads to unmerited success and as a lie detector that brings the guilty to work their own demise.

There are many others for the comparatist to consider. In a Lithuanian variant, the peasant who sets himself up as Dr Wiseman, as in the Eastern tales, must find a stolen horse and, as in the *Siddi-kür*, must also cure a princess of her disease. Only then is he called upon to perform the segment familiar from Straparola. As the 'Doctor' sits in his room ruminating, the thieves, fearful of his knowledge, listen under his window. Hearing him counting the passing hours, they are thereby deceived into making a confession. The persistence of the Eastern elements in this tale, including the Mongolian healing episode, gave Theodor Benfey the idea that the Mongolian raiders brought it with them.[63] A unique variation on the motif occurs in Heinrich Pröhle's *Kinder und Volksmärchen*. Once there was a woman who yawned three times before going to bed, and each one she numbered, 'Das war der Erste' (That was the first one), without realizing that thieves were listening at her window. When the third overhears her, he is convinced that the house is full of policemen and all three scamper away.[64] A more traditional version appears in the *Buen aviso y portacuentos*, in which Pedro Langosta, professing to be a sorcerer, finds himself with only ten days to locate those who have stolen the king's silver service. In a seemingly hopeless plight, he counts out the days and thereby snares the guilty servants. In due course, the plate is unburied and returned. The editor of this work assures us that the tale is known and recited all over Spain.[65]

---

63 August Schleicher, *Litauische Märchen, Sprichworte, Rätsel und Lieder* (Weimar: Böhlau, 1857), p. 115; new edition (Hildesheim: Georg Olms, 1975). Theodor Benfey, *Orient und Occident* (Göttingen: Dieterich, 1861), vol. I, pp. 374*ff.* Benfey considered this tale from Lithuania to be the most complete version of the Eastern story in the West.

64 'Die drei Gähner' (The three yawns) in *Kinder- und Volksmärchen* (Leipzig: Avenarius & Mendelssohn, 1853), pp. 129–31; new edition (Hildesheim: Georg Olms, 1975).

65 Joan Timoneda, *Buen aviso y portacuentos; el sobremesa y alivio de caminantes*, ed. Pilar Cuartero and Maxime Chevalier (Madrid: Espasa-Calpe, 1990), pt. II, no. 70, p. 179. This work was first published in Zaragoza and Medina del Campo in 1563 and in Valencia in 1564. A similar story some three centuries after Timoneda is that of 'Juan Cigare,' in Fernàn Caballero's *Cuentos, oraciones, adivinas y refranes populares*

One of the best known versions of the tale is 'Doctor Knowall' (Allwissend) in the *Fairy Tales* of the Grimm brothers.[66] All the elements are now entirely familiar. A peasant named Crabb grows envious of the doctor's comfortable life and decides to set up for himself with all the trappings and a sign over the door announcing the all-knowing doctor. This is in keeping with the earliest Eastern representations. He too is called in to locate stolen money, dines at the lord's table, and, with his wife by his side, numbers the dishes to her. Along the way, the crab in the covered dish is identified inadvertently as he refers to himself in the third person. With the four guilty servants in his power, he can play the wizard with his ABC book and pretend to great prescience. Reading therein, he also brings out a fifth thief hiding in the stove. Knowall ends up with a double payment from the thieves and from the lord.

This survey is arbitrarily brought to a close, and in a sense full circle, with a brief account of the 'Tale of Ahmed the Cobbler,' collected in the first quarter of the nineteenth century.[67] It is but one of many other non-European versions from as far west as Cairo and as far east as the Philippines.[68] There is reason to suppose that this more socially elaborate

---

è infantiles (Leipzig: Brockhaus, 1878), vol. II, p. 68. He too has but three days to discover who has stolen the king's silver plate or be hanged. Of the first servant to present himself he seems to say, 'Ah, by Saint Bruno, of three here is the first one,' referring to the end of his first day. After his reputation was established, he went out walking with the king, who told him to guess what he held in his hand. Juan named himself in a phrase of acknowledged defeat, but indeed it was a cigar in the king's hand. Another from the Iberian Peninsula was collected by Téofila Braga in *Contos tradicionais do povo Português*, 2 vols. (Lisbon: Dom Quixote, 1987), vol. I, pp. 205–6, in which the hero is also named Grillo, cricket, as in the Sicilian and French tales.

66 *Kinder- und Hausmärchen*, no. 98; *Grimm's Complete Fairy Tales* (Garden City, NY: Nelson, n.d.), no. 204, pp. 616–17.

67 Sir John Malcolm, *The Sketches of Persia from the Journals of a Traveller in the East*, 2 vols. (London: John Murray, 1828), chap. 20, pp. 212*ff.*

68 M.H. Dulac, *Quatre contes arabes en dialecte Cairote* (Cairo: Mission archéologique française, 1881–4), fasc. 1, pp. 55–112, no. 3, described by Dean S. Fansler in *Filipino Popular Tales* (Lancaster, PA: American Folklore Society, 1921), pp. 29–39. This collection contains a tale on the present motif, 'Suan Eket' (Suan's good luck). In the Arabic tale, two parts of the tradition are joined, the enigmatic counting overheard by the thieves and the concealment of an object that the practitioners, 'Grasshopper' (Garada) and 'Sparrow' (Asfour), must identify. Once again, in naming themselves in the third person, they produce the right answer. They toss thirty stones from the window marking the thirty days of discovery and thereby bring the thirty thieves to confession. There is likewise a Vietnamese tale in which the guilty porters are called Bung and Da (belly and gut). This story appears in the

version is built directly upon the tradition of the *Katha sarit sagara* and its Eastern descendants, now with marital contention and feminine social climbing driving the action. The cobbler lives in Isfahan with a beautiful wife, Sittûra, who compels her husband to become an astrologer to improve their standing, threatening divorce if he refused. He too buys all the appropriate accoutrements, in the manner of the Dr Knowall imposters, and announces his new skills in the marketplace. The king's jeweller approaches Ahmed because he had lost the richest ruby in the crown and wanted it back within six hours or he would arrange for the poor man's execution. The thief turns out to be the jeweller's wife, keen to have her husband slain in retaliation for the abuse she had received from him. But when her maid overhears Ahmed cursing his own wife for getting him into this mess, she assumes he is talking about her mistress, the jeweller's wife, and hurries home to tell her. The lady then begs him to spare her, and so they agree upon a hiding place for the money that he can pretend to identify by means of his art. In this way, he earns 200 pieces of gold and a great reputation. But his wife will never be satisfied and more clients arrive. Now it is a veiled lady who has lost a valuable necklace and earrings and is terrified her husband will find out. With words about her veil, Ahmed jogs her memory. Then the king's treasury is robbed, and Ahmed requests forty days to solve the mystery – his life once more in the balance. He chooses to escape, but his wife threatens to turn him in should he try. The forty days now correspond to forty thieves, who are already frightened by his reputation. As he numbers off his prayers 'This is one of forty,' one by one the thieves at his window hear their own indictment. So the entire group agrees to return the treasure and to pay a reward for Ahmed's concealment of their identities. This tale will not end, however, before the false prognosticator is offered a princess in marriage and his wife is disgraced in attempting to disgrace him as a collaborator with thieves. Although exposed for a fraud, the astrologer prevails and his wife falls from grace.

Straparola's story of the lazy boy who makes his fortune lying in the highway counting his 'good days' and thereby catching robbers is almost a byway to the traditional folk tale, having wandered far from the tripartite

---

Chrestomathie cochin-chinoise (a collection of Annamite texts) (Paris, 1872), fasc. 1, p. 30. For a saturation-level treatment of this narrative cluster, see Johannes Bolte and Jiří Pohlívka, *Anmerkungen zu den Kinder- und Hausmärchen der Brüder Grimm* (Leipzig: Dieterich'sche Verlag, 1913–32), vol. II (1915), pp. 402*ff.* They mention some 150 versions and variants.

prototype. Yet it testifies to the persistence of such narrative motifs as the counting routine and its misconstruction by those with guilty consciences. This too, in its way, is a rising tale, not by the help of fairies, but by dint of dumb luck and the accidents of language. It will have its ironic appeal to all who have been raised on the clichés of shopkeepers concerning early rising, the commitment to work, and the conflation of time with money. We are amused in spite of ourselves by those incapable of meeting even the minimal levels of such utilitarian ethics, yet who reap substantial benefits without effort.

XIII. Fable 7
Giorgio Hales His Master
before the Tribunal

FERIER BELTRAMO

*Giorgio, a servant, makes a contract with Pandolfo his master with respect to his
service and ends by summoning him before the tribunal.*

The illustrious gentlemen and the adorable ladies whom I see around
me have already narrated such a vast number of stories that it seems to
me there is hardly any material left to serve my needs. But so as not to
mar the pleasant sequence of entertainments, I'll give it my best effort
to tell you a fable that, although it may not shine with great wit, will at
least give you a little pleasure and diversion, as you'll soon see.

Pandolfo Zabbarella, a gentleman of Padua, was, in his day, not only
a brave and great-hearted soul, but a man of forethought. One time it
happened that he found himself in great need of a servant to attend
upon him. Not being able to find one exactly to his taste, at last he
engaged a fellow who, although outwardly he looked promising, in fact
turned out to be crafty and malicious. Ser Pandolfo asked him whether
he would be willing to come and live with him and be his servant, whereupon Giorgio – for such was his name – replied in the affirmative, but
with the condition that he should do no other service than attend to
Messer Pandolfo's horse and accompany him wherever he might go, seeing that he was unwilling to involve himself in any other duties than
these. Pandolfo assented to these terms and they were set down by a
notary in the form of an agreement under which each one bound himself
to observe the conditions, pledging as security all of his possessions.

One day, when Pandolfo was riding along a muddy and dangerous
road, his horse, by accident, slithered into a ditch and could by no means
be extricated, given all the mud. Pandolfo called aloud to his servant for
a hand, fearing for his life. But the servant merely stood and stared at

him, affirming that it was no business of his to help in such a case, seeing that their contract made absolutely no provision for it. Then, drawing the agreement out of his pouch, he began to read in minute fashion all the headings to see whether there was one that covered the present situation. Meanwhile, his master called out to him, 'For God's sake, my brother, help me now!'

To which the servant answered, 'Truly, I can't help you, for it would go against the terms of our contract.'

'If you won't help to deliver me from my present danger,' said Pandolfo, 'then I'll not pay you your wages.'

Giorgio replied to these supplications that he could not possibly cut his pay because he would thus render himself liable to the penalties set down in the agreement. It was only by good fortune that the master was helped out of his danger by wayfarers passing along the road, for on his own it would have been impossible to get free. On account of this adventure, they entered into a fresh agreement which they caused to be drawn up, in which the servant pledged himself, under threat of penalty, to give assistance to his master whenever he might be called upon and never to depart from him or leave his side.

It happened on a subsequent day that Pandolfo was walking with certain gentlemen of Venice in the church of St Anthony, but his servant now, according to the wishes expressed in the new contract, was almost rubbing shoulders with him and refusing to leave his side. The gentlemen and others around laughed out loud at this strange behaviour and were greatly amused by it. Miffed again, the master, after he had returned to his house, took his servant sharply to task, telling him that he had behaved in an ill and doltish manner in walking that way up and down the church, keeping himself so unnecessarily close without a whit of respect or reverence for his master or for the gentlemen who were with him. But the servant shrugged his shoulders, affirming that he had done exactly what he had been commanded to do, forthwith citing the conditions expressly written in their recently signed agreement. Given this turn of events, the master could only ask that they enter into a new contract by the terms of which the master required the servant to keep himself at a greater distance. Thereafter, Giorgio followed Ser Pandolfo about all day long a hundred feet in the rear, so that no matter how loudly the master might call or whatever signs he might make to him to come closer, the fellow refused to decrease the distance between them, but continued to follow his master at exactly the distance he was required to keep according to the agreement, fearing that by coming any closer he might incur the legal penalty prescribed therein. Irritated by his servant's stupidity and lack of sense, Pandolfo explained to him that the term 'distance' in the contract should be held to signify a space of three feet.

The servant, now fully enlightened as to the wishes of his master, then took a stick three feet in length and, placing one end of it against his own chest and the other against his master's shoulders, followed him about in this fashion. The townsfolk and the craftsmen of the city, when they looked upon this strange sight, laughed long and loud at what they were seeing, thinking that this servant must be some sort of idiot. But the master, who as yet didn't realize what the servant was up to in holding the stick between them, was most astonished to see all the passers-by gaping and laughing at him. As soon as he had discovered the reason for their merriment, he flew into a rage, berating his servant and threatening to flog him. But the fellow started to weep and lament out loud, excusing himself by saying, 'O master, you are in great error in seeking to beat me. Haven't I made a bargain with you? Haven't I observed your commands in every respect? When have I ever gone against the least of them? Here's the deed. Read it, and then punish me if you can find that I have in any way been lacking in my duties.' So just as before, the servant got the better of his master.

It happened that one day the master sent the servant to the butcher's shop to buy some meat and – as masters will sometimes do – in irony he said to Giorgio, 'Go on this errand and make sure that you don't spend more than a year over it.' So the servant, whose fault was in obeying such commands too literally, went away to his own country and there remained waiting for an entire year to pass. On the first day of the next twelve-month, he went back to his master with the meat in hand, leaving Messer Pandolfo stupefied, for he had forgotten long ago what he had ordered. He reproved the fellow for his absence, saying 'You've come back a trifle too late; a thousand times you deserve hanging for the thief you are. By God, I'll make you pay for all the trouble you've given me, you scapegrace rogue. Don't think you're going to collect any wages from me.'

To this Giorgio replied that he had carried out all the clauses of the contract between them and had obeyed all the commands it contained to the letter. 'Remember, good master, that you told me to be gone on my errand not more than a year and here I am, back on the very day. Therefore, you must pay me the salary that is due to me.' Thus it was, when the cause was carried before the tribunal, that the master was required by the sentence of the court to pay his servant the wages he had agreed to give him.

Although Signor Beltramo had been a little bashful in setting out the beginning of the story, the listeners were in no way dissatisfied with the fable he told them. Quite to the contrary, they praised it with one voice, begging him at the same time to set an enigma for them to guess. Not willing to disoblige so gracious an audience, he continued:

> Far in the sultry distant East,
> There dwells a gentle kindly beast;
> Its head is large, its body small,
> And patient is its mood withal.
> With eyes bent on the ground it goes,
> And from them oft a teardrop flows.
> I thus describe it clear and true,
> So you may keep its form in view;
> For whoso gazes in its eyes,
> Finds bane therein and straightway dies.

Signor Beltramo's graceful enigma was listened to with wonder by the assembly and no one grasped its meaning. The explanation then followed, that it was meant to describe a small animal called the catopleba, which goes always with its eyes fixed on the ground. This beast, though it is pretty to look at, should be regarded by men with great caution, because it holds death in its glance. Qualities like these may well be attributed to the devil, who urges on and cajoles a man, but afterwards kills him by means of some deadly sin that leads him to eternal death. As soon as the solution of this scholarly enigma was finished, Lauretta, who sat next to Signor Beltramo, began to tell her fable.

XIII.7 Commentary

Morlini's 'De famulo qui cum domino facit capitula' (The house-servant who accuses his master) is Straparola's narrative source for this tale and one that he follows closely in all essential matters.[69] In that regard, he renders his readers yet again the service of providing a sampling of Morlini's Latin anecdotes in the vernacular. The substance of the tale is the stuff of tricksters and *fourbes* of a kind that Till Eulenspiegel was later

---

69 Girolamo Morlini, *Les nouvelles*, trans. Fernand Caussey (Paris: E. Sansot, 1904), no. 74, pp. 161–3; ed. Giovanni Villani (Rome: Salerno, 1983), pp. 332–7.

to specialize in. He too was fond of tormenting his bourgeois patrons by taking their loose and figurative language in the most literal sense and then begging off on the basis of having followed instructions to the letter. Moreover, insofar as legal practice itself functions largely according to the exact statements of the law, the buffoon can go so far as to seek damages on the basis of such practices, once again illustrating the ways in which the law can be made an ass by its straitjacketed interpretations according to the letter. Such stories cut both ways, however, for they are reminders too of just how imprecise language can be, and how custom and concession alone allow for the mutual comprehension of the ironic and the hyperbolical, the figurative and the colloquial.

A few analogous antecedents deserve mention, not so much as potential sources, but as parallel examples of servants who torment their masters by following instructions over-scrupulously, a common feature of the humour then in appreciation. Antonio Cornazano offers such a sketch in his *De origine proverbiorum*, no. 4, 'La va da fiorentino a bergamasco.'[70] Another is found in the fourteenth-century 'Farce nouvelle tres bonne et fort joyeuse de Jeninot' (The excellent and joyful new farce of Jeninot), which features a man who desires a 'varlet' to serve him and thus improve his quality of living.[71] He plans with his wife how the boy will wait on them at table and conduct her to church. Then they hire Jeninot, who specializes in washing pots and speaking Latin. When they ask him to guard the house, he says he will chase it if it attempts to run away. They think he is a 'sot,' or fool, at least in his incongruous answers. Then the boy engages in a ridiculous routine with his cat, which he serves as a king. By degrees, through his calculated stupidity, Jeninot gains the upper hand so that the husband and wife wait on him and become his servants, dressing him when he says he can't dress himself, and feeding him. When he is told to take the wife to mass, he climbs on her back and tears her dress. Then he talks smut about his former master, climbing

---

70 *De proverbiorum origine* (Milan: Pietro Martire Mantegazz, 1503), reprinted in 1549 in Milan by Gotardo da Ponte. This rare work I have not been able to examine. The likeness between this work and Straparola's was proposed by Letterio di Francia in vol. I, 'Dalle origini al Bandello,' of his *Storia dei generi letterari italiani novellistica* (Milan: Francesco Vallardi, 1924), pp. 717–20; the story deals with the clever and astute servant who plays the 'loan game,' and seems to have been entitled 'Dove il diavolo non po metere el capo, gli mete la coda' (Where the devil can't put his head, he puts his tail).

71 *Ancien théâtre françois*, ed. Viollet Le Duc, 10 vols. (Paris: P. Jannet, 1854), vol. I, pp. 289–304.

on his lady's back and shaking her ass. In due course, the husband becomes annoyed and strikes him, and so Jeninot refuses to serve them further and demands his pay. There is a common profile in the misunderstanding servant who causes nothing but trouble, yet in the end demands and receives his wages.

In a related vein, Gonnella, the court joker and buffoon of the Estes in the early fourteenth century, became famous for similar kinds of behaviour. Franco Sacchetti tells of his exploits in a series of vignettes, in one of which he is told never to put foot on Este territory again. Gonnella goes to Bologna and loads up a cart with 'foreign' earth and makes his return, claiming his literal right to be there on alien ground, according to the letter of the command. The Marquis Obizzo d'Este is compelled to agree that he had been tricked. Gonnella's literal interpretations of other loosely worded commands gain new rewards for him through appeal to the courts.[72] Such tales of famous tricksters survived in the oral cultures of Italy down to the nineteenth century, as in the tales of Firrazzanu. Many of these were collected in Sicily by Giuseppe Pitrè, including 'Firrazzanu's Message,' in which the servant delays for over a week before telling his mistress that her husband wouldn't be home for supper that evening, because the master had said to, tell her 'at your convenience.'[73] Marcolphus employs similar tactics in his negotiations with King Solomon, as when he pulls down his pants and hides in a bake oven in a manner certain to attract the king's attention. When asked the meaning of this outrage, Marcolphus explains that because the king no longer wished to look him in the eye, by the letter of his wish he may still contemplate his nether parts.[74]

Significantly, this story was chosen to be among the four that Humphrey Gifford translated out of the *Nights* for the readers of his *A Posie of Gilloflowers*, there entitled 'Of one that hires a foolish servant and was served accordingly.'[75] That it tells of Pandolfus, a Gentleman of Padua, can leave no doubts concerning its origins, for it is a close translation of

---

72 *Il trecentonovelle*, ed. Emilio Faccioli (Turin: Einaudi, 1970), no. 27, pp. 67–9.

73 *The Collected Sicilian Folk and Fairy Tales of Giuseppe Pitrè*, trans. and ed. Jack Zipes and Joseph Russo (New York: Routledge, 2009), vol. I, pp. 560–1.

74 *The Dialogue of Solomon and Marcolphus*, ed. Donald Beecher (Ottawa: Dovehouse Editions, 1995), pp. 197–9.

75 (London: John Perin, 1580), posie 7; Humphrey Gifford, *Complete Poems and Translations in Prose*, ed. Alexander B. Grosart (40 copies for subscribers, 1875), pp. 64–7.

Straparola, with the usual stylistic flourishes that characterize the work of the Tudor translators. Thus, 'E cosí andati a giudicio, giuridicalmente fu costretto il patrone a pagar il suo salario al servo' becomes 'And hereupon they waged the law, and in conclusion the mayster was constrained to pay him his wages, whether he would, or no.' Gifford's translations are among the earliest representations of Straparola's work in England, along with the stories in Riche, Painter, Armin, and *Tarleton's Newes*.

XIII. Fable 8
Midnight Feast and Famine

LAURETTA

Gasparo, a peasant, having built a chapel, names it in honour of St Honorato, and puts a rector in charge of it. The rector and his deacon pay a visit to the peasant, in the course of which the deacon, without intending it, brings to pass a certain jest.

The vice of gluttony is a heinous one without any doubt, but it is nevertheless more tolerable than the vice of hypocrisy, because the gluttonous man only cheats himself, while the hypocrite, with his simulated actions, seeks to deceive others in appearing to be what he's not. All this was proved true in the case of a certain village priest who, by means of his own hypocrisy, suffered both in body and in soul, as I'll try to explain in just a few words.

Close to the city of Padua stands the village of Noventa, in which there once lived a certain peasant who was both rich and very devout. This man, out of his devotion to religion and to expiate the sins of himself and his wife, built a chapel which he named for St Honorato and endowed with a sufficient sum of money to name a priest as its rector – a man well versed in canon law. One day, on the vigil of a certain saint – but not one kept according the calendar of the holy mother Church – the rector called his deacon, and the two went together to pay a visit to their patron, Ser Gasparo the peasant, who had nominated him as governor of the chapel. You may decide for yourselves whether this was done to further his own affairs, or for some other cause. When the two arrived, the good peasant, wishing to pay them due respect, had a splendid supper prepared with roasted meats, tarts, and various other fine dishes, urging them to stay the night as guests under his own roof. But the priest declared that he could on no account take any food that day, seeing that it was a sacred vigil, thus pretending to keep a ritual that was in fact entirely foreign to him. He made a great show of fasting, refusing to touch a bit of the food his starving belly was crying out for. Seeing how it was, the peasant, unwilling to tempt him away from his habits of devotion, commanded his wife to put away in a cupboard the remaining dishes of food, the preparation of which was already begun, to serve the following day.

The supper finished and their conversation as well, they all went to bed in the peasant's house in two adjoining chambers: Ser Gasparo with his wife and the rector with the deacon. When midnight had come, the priest roused the deacon from his sleep and in a whisper asked of him where the good woman had put the tart that had been prepared for sup-per, for unless he could supply his famished body with something to eat, he would die of hunger. So the deacon, obeying his orders, got up from his bed, and little by little, turned his steps very quietly to the spot where the remains of the feast had been put away, and there he cut off a good slice of tart. On the way back, however, thinking he was going into the rector's bedroom, he went by accident into that of his host. Now because it was summertime when the sun is high in Leo, the peasant's wife, due to the great heat, lay stark naked on the bed, and from her nether mouth came the huffing of a lunatic. Deeming himself to be in the rector's room, the deacon said, 'Here, good master, take the tart you told me to fetch and eat it, if that's your pleasure.' With still more sighs from her other mouth, the deacon whispered that there was no need to blow like that on the tart, since it was already cold. But no heed was taken of his words as the puffing and blowing kept on. Growing annoyed, anxious as he was to get rid of the tart, the deacon began to feel about with his hands. Alighting upon something he took to be the rector's face, he put the tart down on the peasant wife's rear end. As soon as she was aware of something cold on her lower face, she awoke from her sleep and began to yell out, arousing her husband with all the noise to tell him something was wrong. The deacon, by this time, had now discovered his error and stole away quietly into the adjoining room, where the rector was lying. The peasant climbed out of bed and lighted a candle and started search-ing through the whole house. When he beheld the tart in its strange location, he was truly astonished, thinking it could only have come there through the agency of an evil spirit. So he called the priest and told him what had happened, making the poor man, on his empty belly, launch into the singing of psalms and hymns, having him meanwhile sanctify the house everywhere with holy water. When this was done, they all went back to their beds.

So just as I declared at the opening of my story, hypocrisy brings suffering both to body and soul, as it did to the priest's, who planned to feast on the tart, but had to continue fasting against his will.

All the gentlemen laughed heartily when they heard how the peasant's wife made puffing and blowing sounds as though she had been a pair of bellows, and how, because the tart was already cold, there was no need for her to blow on it. But in order that an end might be made of the laughter, the Signora gave the word to Lauretta to tell her enigma at once. Still laughing herself, she spoke as follows:

> Like a lofty house I stand on high,
> And yet no house in truth am I.
> Like a mirror all around I shine,
> And stand before the place divine
> Where you repair to kneel and pray
> That all your sins be washed away.
> I live, but with my vital fire
> I am consumed and soon expire.
> In every glorious shrine I live,
> And light to all who worship give,
> But frail and brief my life withal,
> I die if once to earth I fall.

This enigma, as set by the graceful Lauretta, was accounted a very scholarly feat. Not a single one of the listeners withheld high praise, asking her at the same time to carry on with its interpretation. Desiring nothing better, the damsel expounded it thusly: 'This enigma of mine describes the lamp that, when placed before the sacrament, sheds light over every part of the church. Day and night it consumes itself, adorning the sanctuary, although it is a frail thing, being made of glass.' As soon as Lauretta had finished the explanation of her riddle, Signor Antonio Molino, whose turn it then was to tell a story, began to speak.

XIII.8 Commentary

A Morlini 'novelette,' the sixty-eighth in his collection of *Novelle*, provides Straparola with this tale of a large-scale agricultural producer who had the means to build a chapel in honour of Santo Onorato.[76] He replaces Morlini's undesignated village setting with the town of Noventa, some seven kilometres to the east of Padua, confirming once again the impression that our author lived in this region and found amusement in relocating several of his tales to the Paduan *campagna*. In the process, Morlini's chapel to the saint is also borrowed, even though none such seems to have existed in Noventa. Just which saint by that name was intended is moot, in any case, for the most famous of them are to be assigned, respectively, to an island off Cannes, to Amiens (the St Honoré of the Parisian street and the famous cake), and to Canterbury.[77] None would seem to be of particular relevance to Morlini's peasant in the south of Italy or to Straparola's in the north. There is mention of a Santo Onorato who founded the Abbey of San Magno in 522, which I take to be the town a few kilometres to the south-east of Frosinone, and hence closer to Morlini country. It is, to be sure, a minor point.

The story makes use of four comic motifs: the hypocritical priest who would starve himself by day merely to look pious, yet pilfer food to satisfy his cravings by night;[78] the errors in the night whereby a holy man nearly ends up in the bed of the peasant's wife instead of his own room; the wife's heavy breathing interpreted as an attempt to cool the pie; and the deacon's deposition of the tart on the lady's rump, an act subsequently attributed to a demon. Posteriors taken for faces, mistaken bedrooms, and futile exorcisms are the stuff of good social comedy, if already a bit hackneyed by the time they get to Straparola. An examination of these motifs independently could spread to hundreds of stories: those of hypocritical priests, those of errors in the night (as employed by Henry Fielding in *Joseph Andrews*), and those in which strange events are attributed to the work of devils and demons. Chaucer's 'Reeve's Tale' comes to mind, in which two scholars find themselves spending the night with a miller, his wife, and their daughter. Cheated by the miller with regard to their grain, one of the students decides to seek repayment in the form of sexual favours from the daughter. When the baby's cradle is moved,

---

76 Girolamo Morlini, *Les nouvelles*, trans. Fernand Caussey (Paris: E. Sansot, 1904), pp. 131–2.

77 Donald Attwater, *The Avenel Dictionary of Saints* (New York: Avenel Books, 1981), pp. 172–3.

78 Dominic P. Rotunda refers to the motif as K2059.2, 'the priest who fasts only in public,' in his *Motif-Index of the Italian Novella in Prose* (Bloomington: Indiana University Press, 1942), p. 134.

the miller's wife then finds her way back to the second student's bed by mistake. Later, when the student in the daughter's bed returns to his own, he too is deceived by the cradle and crawls into bed with the host, to whom he whispers his exploits with the girl. That plot, in its own right, has several medieval analogues in French, Latin, German, and English.[79] But the medieval gathering of elements most resembling Morlini's tale is to be found in a *fabliau* by Gautier le Leu dating to the second half of the thirteenth century, in which there are mistakes in the night, an attempt to administer food from the wrong end, farting taken for blowing to cool it, and the mush all over the poor woman's ass, which she takes for her own excrement upon waking up.[80] How the story came to Morlini, whether directly from the *fabliaux* tradition or through oral intermediary versions, or whether the *fabliau* is itself derived from the oral tradition, is work for others to resolve, but it is important that the story type, ATU 1775, 'The hungry parson,' was widely known in later years, suggesting a long-standing oral tradition.

The story remained known among the folk in several parts of Italy during the nineteenth century. Giuseppe Rua states that he knew the story as a child in Brescia.[81] Giuseppe Pitrè collected a version in Sicily, which he included in his *Fiabe e leggende popolari siciliane*.[82] But the most elaborate of them is to be found in Imbriani's collection *La novellaja fiorentina*, about a priest and his boy, Marco, who come to an agreement that the first to become angry must pay the other 100 scudi. Multiple aggravations follow from each party in order to make the other angry, but neither takes the bait for a very long time. When they are invited to visit a recently married nephew, the two set off, playing tricks on each other along the way. Upon their arrival, Marco is given some chicken to eat, and when the priest asks for his share the boy refuses him and then refuses food on his behalf that was offered to him by his relatives. Then Marco says the priest is tired and wants to go to bed. The priest is angry to be sure, but of course denies it. During the night, he becomes so famished that he decides to raid the kitchen, but afraid of losing his way

---

79 For these texts see Larry D. Benson and Theodore M. Andersson, eds, *The Literary Context of Chaucer's Fabliaux* (Indianapolis: Bobbs-Merrill, 1971), pp. 79–201.

80 *Fabliaux: Französische Schwankerzählungen des Hochmittelalters*, ed. Albert Gier (Stuttgart: Reclam, 1985), pp. 180–91.

81 'Intorno alle "Piacevoli notti,"' in *Giornale storico della letteratura italiana* 15 (Turin: Loescher, 1891), p. 282.

82 *Fiabe e leggende popolari siciliane* (Bologna: Forni editore, 1969), no. 87.

in the dark, he ties a string to the bed. This string Marco detaches and ties to the bed of the nephew and his bride so that the priest will lose his way. On his return, now in the wrong bedroom, the priest stumbles over a shoe and tosses all the food into the faces of the newlyweds. They awake shouting 'Thief,' while the priest escapes by the window and breaks his neck. In this way, Marco comes into possession of far more than the 100 scudi, for he takes over the priest's house, gets married, and is probably still there.[83] The story has travelled considerably, but the gist of the old tale remains clear.[84]

---

83 Vittorio Imbriani, 'Il prete chi mangia la paglia' in *La novellaja fiorentini con la novellaja milanese*, ed. Italo Sordi (Milan: Rizzoli, 1976), no. 48, pp. 607–12.
84 For good measure, it was also known in Friesland, a version in which an arse is mistaken for a face and the person is told not to blow on the food to cool it down. J. van der Kooi and Theo Schuster, *Märchen und Schwänke aus Ostfriesland* (Leer: Schuster, 1993), no. 146.

XIII. Fable 9
Of Filomena the Hermaphrodite Nun

ANTONIO MOLINO

A certain damsel named Filomena, having been placed in a convent, falls into a grave illness. She is treated by several physicians and in the end is discovered to be a hermaphrodite.

The secrets of nature, most gracious ladies, are indeed mighty and numberless, nor is there in all the world a man who, by the powers of his intellect, can explain them all. I thought, for this reason, that I might tell you of a case that is not a fable, but that came veritably to pass a short time ago in the city of Salerno.

In this city of high renown, abounding with handsome women, there lived a certain gentleman belonging to the house of Porta. He was the head of a family and the father of one daughter – a girl then not quite sixteen and in the full flower of her beauty. This maiden, who was called Filomena, for her great looks was besieged by a flock of gallants, all seeking to marry her. But such attention she found irksome. Seeing that his daughter was in danger and fearful that some shame or other might ensue from all the daily provocations, her father decided to place her in the convent of San Iorio in the city of Salerno, not that she might take formal vows, but to put her under the charge of the sisters until such time as she should find a husband.

Now it chanced that while she was living in the convent, she fell sick with a serious fever, during which she was nursed and tended with the greatest care and diligence. At the outset of her illness, certain herbalists came to offer their help with the cure, making weighty oaths and pledges that they would bring her back to her former good health within a short while. But all their efforts were to no avail. Then her father sent for various physicians of great skill and experience, along with certain old women, all of whom promised to find a remedy for her malady and bring her back to health. Meanwhile, this gentle, pretty maiden was further afflicted by a troublesome swelling of the groin, which grew to the size of a large ball. This new ailment gave her such pain that she could only groan and lament. It appeared as though her final days were coming very near. Her kinsfolk, deeply moved by the young girl's miserable state, called in the best surgeons, men celebrated for their art. Some of them, after they had seen and examined the area of the swelling, prescribed the root of the marsh-mallow herb, well cooked and mixed with the lard of swine, to be applied to the place in order to alleviate the pain and swelling. Others prescribed different treatment, while still others denied the efficacy of any of the proposed remedies. But on one point they were all agreed, that at all costs they must cut open the swelling in order to remove the matter causing the pain.

As soon as they had come to this decision, they had all the nuns of the convent summoned, as well as various matrons and certain of the girl's relatives. Then one of the surgeons, a man excelling all his colleagues for skill, took his scalpel and made a light incision, and with the greatest dexterity cut through the swelling in the twinkling of a eye, perforating the skin. Everyone believed that blood and putrefaction would issue from such a wound, but instead a certain large member appeared of a kind longed for by women, but so disgusting to see. Now I'm telling you the sober truth and no fable, even though I still can't keep myself from laughing. All the nuns, stupefied by such a novelty, began weeping with grief, not because of the damsel's wound, or because of the distemper she had suffered, but for themselves, in that they would greatly have preferred for this event, witnessed by so many, to have happened in secret. Such a 'girl' they might have kept hidden among themselves, but now, for the sake of their good name, they would have to send her immediately out of the convent. The physicians who were standing by could only laugh as well, for now in a trice the young lady, restored to health, had become both a man and a woman. All this may look like a lie, but it is as true as reality itself, for I saw her afterwards with my own eyes dressed as a man, although having and enjoying both sexes.

The Signora, seeing that Molino's fable had come to its end in a burst of laughter, and taking note too of time's rapid flight, said to him that he should carry straight on with his enigma, according to the rules they had formerly kept. With that, Molino, not willing to keep the company any longer in suspense, offered this one:

> From a mother born alone,
> Other parent I have none.
> Unwilling to my mother's side
> I oft return, and there abide.
> I'm a strong and pungent wight,
> And some in me find great delight;
> Others hate me for the bane
> I bring to them, and loud complain.
> Thus my destined part I play,
> Working ever night and day,
> But children none, by fate's decree,
> Will ever take their life from me.

Not one in the group could imagine what the meaning of Molino's enigma might be except Cateruzza, who had been chosen to tell the next fable. 'Signor Antonio,' said the damsel, 'the obscurely devised enigma you have set for us to guess can only mean salt, which has no father, but has water for its mother. And to this mother the child will often return. Likewise, by its flavour it pleases some and displeases others.' [Having thus given her solution to the riddle, the damsel was silent for a moment, but noticing that no one else spoke up, she opened her pretty lips and continued with her tale.]

XIII.9 Commentary

Girolamo Morlini's vignette concerning the transformation of a girl into a boy by the surgical release of an enclosed phallus is so faithfully rendered here by Straparola that few substantive differentiations exist.[85] He keeps the city unchanged, but assigns the young lady a name and places her in the once innominate convent now assigned to the honour of San Iorio. This story is a sensationalist little anecdote, a fresh bit of gossip, yet prodigiously true, a medical event the author not only had witnessed, but that had made him laugh as he wrote about it, echoing the laughter of the several physicians in attendance who brought the transformation about. Communal laughter would appear to be a rather strange reaction

---

85 Girolamo Morlini, 'De hermofrodita' (Concerning a hermaphrodite) in *Les nouvelles*, trans. Fernand Caussy (Paris: E. Sansot & Co., 1904), no. 22, pp. 60–2; *Novelle*, ed. Giovanni Villani (Rome: Salerno, 1983), pp. 102–5.

to a surgical procedure, especially on the part of an audience composed of nuns, physicians, and relations witnessing something so unsettling as the presentation of a fully developed penis in place of the anticipated effusion of blood and pus. To be sure, some of the young ladies of the convent weep, but not out of empathetic concern. Rather, the public witnessing of this remarkable transformation meant for them that a masculine Filomena could no longer be kept in the convent for their secret pleasure. Meanwhile, the iconic male member has become a *coup-de-théâtre*, the centre of public attention as an object of amazement, desire, and perhaps ridicule. For most in attendance, its apparition has turned tragedy into comedy; what they had deemed a malady was merely a coming-out party. The laughter may signify relief that it is no worse for the girl, or it may express nervous anxiety over this ostensible lapse in the laws of nature, but fundamentally it is the laughter of dissonance resolved by the incongruous made manifest. As narrative fiction, the story's design is minimal, but its novelty or news value is incontestable, whether as a study in the bizarre, or as a bit of gossip involving a nice young girl from Salerno who got the surprise of her life.

Just how Morlini came by his story is not certain, but it makes an anecdotal contribution to the many stories in circulation during the early decades of the sixteenth century concerning sex changes and hermaphrodites. Among the anomalies of nature investigated by Renaissance scientists, this was one of the most fascinating and most discussed. Literature on the subject increased exponentially throughout the sixteenth and early seventeenth centuries, largely preoccupied with the stories of girls who, under a variety of circumstances and provocations, sprouted male members. Among the writers potentially known to Morlini was Raffaele Maffei of Volterra who, in his *Commentariorum urbanorum libri XXXVIII*, tells the story of a girl living at the time of Pope Alexander VI (1492–1503), who erupted into a male on her wedding day, a thing deemed miraculous at the time (without natural explanation).[86] The literature of antiquity included many such examples, but this is one of the earliest contemporary accounts. Giovan Battista Fregoso compiled a number of classical examples in his *Factorum dictorumque memorabilium*

---

86 ([Paris]: Joanne Parvo and Jodoco Badio Ascensio, 1511), 'Philologia,' bk. 24, fols. 259v–60v.

libri IX.[87] He tells of Lucius Cossitius, a citizen of Thysdritum in Africa, who was raised as a girl, but who became a boy on her/his wedding day. This story from Pliny the Elder is without doubt the source of Raffaele Maffei's 'witnessed' event. Ovid's tale of Iphis is likewise included, that of a girl raised as a boy by her mother to save her from a father's vow to slay any girl child born to him. When Iphis turned thirteen, however, her father chose Ianthé to become her bride, leading to a passionate love between the two girls. As the wedding date approached, however, the mother became desperate and called upon the goddess Isis for help. Then, we are told, the temple began to shake, and as Iphis left the sanctuary she began to take longer steps, lose her long hair and soft features, and assume a new mass of muscle. By the time she got home she was ready for the nuptials.[88] In these stories magic and medicine are juxtaposed. Just who Iphis was physiologically remains the acute question, whether a latent boy all along whose male member appeared, an undisclosed hermaphrodite (which contradicts the story), or a miracle of the goddess (which exceeds the laws of nature). This kind of metamorphosis would provide the model for several analogues in which a young woman becomes thereby eligible to marry another girl, or becomes a boy in order to avoid marriage altogether. To such a repertory, the present tale belongs.

Without doubt, tales of sexual transformation through the accidents of anatomy grasped the collective imagination; they combined voyeurism with medical speculation and the prodigious with natural causation. Straparola's account settles the matter of a latent penis as the completion of a hermaphrodite, but the controversy to which this vignette belongs was not to be so easily resolved. The story is attentive, moreover, to a final detail. In Filomena's change of dress, she opted to favour her new male identity, presumably to the complete repression of her feminine side – a choice she was compelled to make one way or the other, and to observe without exception, according to the law.

In designating his protagonist a hermaphrodite, Straparola's 'case study' does not completely avoid the contemporary controversy over sex changes, a transformation deemed possible by certain professional

---

87 (Paris: Pierre Cavellat, 1578), bk. I, chap. 6, 'De miraculis,' p. 40r. See also bk. I, chap. 5, and bk. VII, chap. 4. Giovanni Villani, ed., Morlini, *Novelle e favole* (Rome: Salerno, 1983), p. 102, cites *Factorum dictorumque* (Milan, 1508), IX, 16, 'De Carolo et Francisco Guarnis.'

88 *Metamorphoses,* trans. Rolfe Humphries (Bloomington: Indiana University Press, 1967), bk. 9, ll. 573–797, pp. 229–33.

observers in relation to the putative symmetry between male and female sex organs and the prospect that penises were hence merely inverted vaginas. (Straparola does not tell us the composition of Filomena's protrusion.) The notion originated with Aristotle who, at one point, opined that heat alone determined whether the genitals were thrust out of the body to determine the male, or held within the body to determine the female. Such a definition of sexual differentiation meant that females might be converted to males by simply increasing their body temperatures. Ambroise Paré assesses a young girl's sudden presentation of a male yard in these terms, and Montaigne follows suit in his *Essays*. But generally after the middle of the sixteenth century, there were few physicians who endorsed such an analysis, given the discrediting of organ symmetry through more precise anatomical investigations. Ironically, their progress in medical thought has not deterred modern cultural constructionists from imposing the one sex model upon the whole of the Renaissance as the dominant theory of sexual orientation, with all its attendant implications for sexual and genderal plasticity, indeterminacy, and the potential for self-fashioning.[89] Serious physicians later spoke of the procidence of the matrix as a prolapsus of the pelvic organs that resulted in infection and death, not as an extroverted vagina that becomes an operative male instrument.[90] They were equally aware of the clitoris and the irregularities that, on rare occasions, allowed women to use it for sexual penetration.[91] Hence, nothing in these mainstream and

---

89 Thomas Laqueur took this assessment of Renaissance sexuality as a received idea and from that assumption presumed for the era a lingering sense of orientational instability, because the symmetrical arrangement allowed that girls might become boys at any moment. The few reported cases by observers imbued with this Aristotelian notion have appealed to modern cultural constructivists by providing them with a presumed scientific basis for analysing the many examples of crossdressing in Renaissance imaginative literature as crises in identity. The idea of sexual symmetry was not endorsed, however, by the vast majority of serious medical philosophers of the age. The transformation applied, in any case, only to women, for there are no cases of males imploding into females; nevertheless, the anxiety has been extended to both sexes for purposes of cultural analysis. *Making Sex: Body and Gender from the Greeks to Freud* (Cambridge, MA: Harvard University Press, 1990).

90 Jean Liébault studied many cases of women with prolapsed organs and declared as a result the impossibility of a simple inversion into a viable male. *Trois livres appartenans aux infirmitez et maladies des femmes* (Lyons: Jean Veyrat, 1598), p. 448.

91 An apt summary of this entire discussion appears in the second chapter of Jacques Ferrand's *Treatise on Lovesickness* (1623), ed. Donald Beecher and Massimo Ciavolella (Syracuse: Syracuse University Press, 1990), pp. 230–1, with annotations, pp. 371–86.

often repeated medical observations gave much quarter to the idea of sex changes based on reversible organs.[92] These same physicians rehearsed the familiar case studies from both modern and classical writings to explain away such putative transformations either as the late appearance of the male sex organ in boys (even if they were mistaken for girls initially), as a tumescent clitoris, or as a case of hermaphroditism in which male and female anatomies are presented simultaneously. There were no other explanatory options available.

If Morlini and Straparola are genuinely concerned with the latent presentation of the second set of genitals of a hermaphrodite, they are not, in the strictest sense, concerned with a sex change, for hermaphrodites are of an entirely different ontological status; they possess both sexes at once. But this may be more than either writer reflected upon. Certainly in the popular imagination, and in opposition to the declared facts of the medical studies, the indeterminacy sometimes presented by hermaphrodites, combined with their capacity to choose the dominant sex and thus adopt their own gender, served to maintain their association with sexual instability and transformation. Hermaphrodites, in fact, epitomized all that pertained to ambiguous sexual behaviour, effeminacy in men or virility in women, epicenes, and related anomalies of nature. This in turn accounts for the laughter produced by the reversal, for in that laughter is all the anxiety concerning lapses from fixed sexual orientation, the immutability of nature, and the essentialist categories of male and female. Straparola's vignette could not, in its time, have escaped this contextual malaise.

Little had changed in the intellectual climate between Morlini and Straparola's publication in 1553 concerning this phenomenon, but in the decades to follow, numerous new studies and cases would come to public and professional attention. Amatus Lusitanus, in 1554, takes up the touchstone case of Maria Pacheca, who lived in a village near Coimbra.[93]

---

92 The last word in this regard, following many others, may be given to Sir Thomas Browne in his *Pseudodoxia Epidemica* (1646), where he states that the 'transmutation of sex is only so in opinion; and that these transfeminated persons were really men at first; although succeeding years produced the manifesto or evidence of their virilities.' He allows for hermaphrodites, but rejects all theories of 'inversion or protrusion' regarding sex differentiation. *The Works*, ed. Charles Edward Sayle, 3 vols. (London: Grant Richards, 1904), vol. II, p. 36.

93 *Curationum medicinalium centuriae quatuor* (Paris: Sebastianum Nivellium, 1554), centuria 2, curatio 39, pp. 78r–9r.

At the time her first menstruation was due, she produced a male member formerly hidden inside her body in the manner of Filomena, but she was not declared a hermaphrodite. Rather, with her new condition clear to all, she was rebaptized Manuel. He married after a long trip to India, but he never developed facial hair, we are told, and there is no record that the couple ever had children. Lusitanus leaves the matter unresolved whether Manuel was a late-developing male or a girl with a protuberance employed in masculine fashion. His concern was to confirm the reality of the sex changes recorded in antiquity.

Paré's section on 'Memorable Stories about Women Who Have Degenerated into Men,' in his much-consulted book *Monsters and Marvels* (*Des monsters et prodiges*, 1573), supplies one of the most discussed cases of the era, that of Germain-Marie who, until fifteen, had been taken for a girl.[94] But when she was out running and leaping, she ruptured ligaments and a penis appeared. She felt considerable pain and feared that her lower belly had burst. Her parents, amazed to be sure, called in the physicians, who agreed that she was no longer female. Rebaptism and a name change followed, together with the development of a complete set of masculine characteristics, including a stocky body and a heavy beard. Her 'case' is redolent of the present story. But Paré adopts the 'one sex' explanation – that heat had driven the female organs forth from the body in the form of a penis – but he does not investigate whether the new member was erectile and capable of ejaculation or urination. Paré was writing a vernacular book on prodigies of nature. In support of this case, he offers the account given by Antoine Loqueneux about a man by then some sixty years old, living in Rheims, who, at age fourteen, had changed from female to male. It happened while 'she' was in bed with a chambermaid and suddenly found herself sexually aroused. Her parents had her rebaptized as Jean 'by the authority of the Church.' Would Filomena be similarly rebaptized after choosing her male attire?

By the end of the century, the stories had accumulated and were treated as lore to be rationalized in terms of latent male development, abuse of the clitoris, or the fallen matrix; they no longer believed in sex changes of the miraculous variety, but many remained uncertain about

---

94 *On Monsters and Marvels*, trans. Janis L. Pallister (Chicago: University of Chicago Press, 1982), pp. 31–3. On this story see Patricia Parker, 'Gender Ideology, Gender Change: The Case of Marie Germain,' *Critical Inquiry* 19 (1993), pp. 337–64.

true hermaphroditism, in which both sexes were coexistent and viable. These included André Dulaurens, Jacques Ferrand, Jean Liébault, and Jean Riolan. It was Riolan who would engage in a polemic with Jacques Duval over the difficult case of Marie le Marcis, whose unique anatomical configuration, after extensive examination, left the courts undecided whether she was essentially male or female.[95] Riolan was entirely convinced that the member presented and retracted through a female fissure was a female appendage, whereas Duval argued equally forcefully in favour of a fully functional male yard existing in conjunction with the female parts. The case held more than a prurient or sensationalist interest for the general public, insofar as it fostered fantasies pertaining to deep-seated anxieties and troubling speculations. But the medical controversy was principally anatomical. Duval's argument concerning the latent development of the male component of a true hermaphrodite, such as it was implied in the case of Filomena, represented something of a medical milestone.[96] Tellingly, Straparola's (and Morlini's) medical anecdote preceded the Duval-Riolan controversy by sixty years.

In parallel with these medical anecdotes was a rich imaginative literature in which sex changes hovered between the medical and the magical. Two *novelle* written in Straparola's century that build their conflicts and reversals around the prospect of sexual transformation or the ambiguity permitted by the hermaphrodite are the second by Agnolo Firenzuola in his collection of *Novelle* (1548), and 'Of Philotus and Emelia,' in Barnabe Riche's *Farewell to Military Profession* (1580). In the first, young Fulvio falls in love with Lavinia, who lives in Tivoli and is married to a

---

95 *Traité des hermaphrodits, parties genitales, accouchemens des femmes* (Rouen, 1612), esp. pp. 327–40.

96 Dulaurens, 'Controverses anatomiques,' in *Toutes les oeuvres* (1600), trans. Théophile Gelée (Paris: P. Mettayer, 1613), pp. 224r–5r; Ferrand, *De la maladie d'amour ou melancholie erotique* (Paris: Denis Moreau, 1623), chap. 2; Liébault, *Trois livres appartenans aux infirmitez et maladies des femmes* (Lyons: Jean Veyrat, 1598), pp. 644*ff*; Riolan, *Discours sur les hermaphrodits, ou il est desmontré contre l'opinion commune, qu'il n'y a point de vrays hermaphrodits* (Paris: Pierre Ramier, 1614). For a discussion of these works, and of the controversy in general, see Donald Beecher, 'Concerning Sex Changes: The Cultural Significance of a Renaissance Medical Polemic,' *Sixteenth Century Journal* 36, no. 4 (2005), pp. 991–1016. On Duval in particular, see Kathleen Long, 'Jacques Duval on Hermaphrodites,' in *High Anxiety: Masculinity in Crisis in Early Modern France* (Kirksville, MO: Truman State University Press, 2002), pp. 106–36.

much older man. Fulvio's friend Menico comes up with a plan.[97] He tells Fulvio to dress as a woman and seek employment in Livinia's household by responding to her husband's advertisement for a maid. With his white skin, beardless face, and female looks – the first allusions to Fulvio as a kind of hermaphrodite – the disguise is a complete success. When the husband leaves for Rome and Fulvio, now as Lucia, is in bed with the lady, he becomes sexually aroused and Lavinia makes the discovery. Initially, she says nothing, but feigns sleep until she can repeat the test. She then looks in Lucia's eyes and sees signs of a transmutation. Lucia has undergone a sex change, which possibility the medical controversies of the age had sponsored in the popular imagination. Fulvio is then forced to reveal his entire stratagem in order not to be taken for an enchanted mutant. Thereafter, they become lovers and enjoy their secret life until Livinia's husband, Cecc'Antonio, begins harassing Lucia for sex and in his turn discovers that she is a male. Lucia explains the anomaly as a medical condition, namely, the very sex change imagined by Livinia. Lucia is no hermaphrodite, but fashions himself as such merely to recover his own masculinity. Justly suspicious, Cecc'Antonio makes outside enquiries, but his source of authority is none other than Fulvio's friend Menico, who begins to recite all the many case studies from Pliny and Battista Fregoso discussed above, making popular use of these cases to convince the old man, in the spirit of Machiavelli's *Mandragola*, that by keeping such a prodigy of nature he may obtain a male heir. Keen for a child, the old man is brought to encourage Fulvio's intimacy with his wife, who is soon pregnant and gives birth to a boy child. Thus, the lovers live under Cecc'Antonio's protection while he turns a calculated blind eye. There is no gullibility or confusion on Firenzuola's part, however, merely because Menico cites the medical literature. Fulvio is all along a confirmed male (as is the case in all male-to-female cross-dressing fiction) who pretends, on the basis of the medical record, that he too is a female who has undergone a recent conversion. The lore of sexual transformation had, by this time, become a factor in the collective imagination, and a means for duping the gullible.

---

97 *Novelle di Agnolo Firenzuola*, ed. O. Guerrini (Florence: G. Barbèra, 1886), pp. 34–53. This story reappears with modifications in Francesco Sansovino, *Cento novelle scelte da i piu nobili scrittori* (Venice: Francesco Sansovino, 1561), (which I read in the copy once belonging to the Pontifici biblioteca di Bologna), pp. 130r–6r.

Barnabe Riche makes use of a similar ploy in his complex and titillating story of a lookalike brother and sister.[98] Emilia is destined to be wed to an unwanted old man. To avoid her fate, she disguises herself as a boy and runs away, just as her brother, unannounced, returns to town. He is taken for his sister in male garb, intuits the nature of the situation, and for a lark decides to assume his sister's place, marry the old man, and then discover himself. Phylerno's situation (for such is his name) becomes even more interesting when he is put to bed with the old man's daughter by a former marriage, Brisilla, and finds himself in love. To convert himself from a girl to a boy for her sake, he begins to recite to her all the stories from antiquity concerning sex changes, assuring her of Venus's power to come to their rescue, as Isis did for Iphis on the day of her marriage. Then Phylerno invokes the goddess and feigns a trance, mumbling and gesturing in distracted ways, until he pronounces the transformation complete. He then invites the girl to manually confirm his newly minted sex, which she does to her great delight. In reality, of course, he merely becomes himself with Brisilla while maintaining the credibility of his female disguise. The marriage goes forward, Phylerno plays the virago by beating up the old man on their wedding night, then the two lovers put him to bed in the dark with a prostitute – a rather new interpretation of the bed trick. For the readers, the story confirms, not the plasticity of sexuality, but its misrepresentation through disguise and trickery. That may be a source of anxiety all its own, but the lore of sex changes is used only rhetorically, while the underlying sexuality of the characters remains fixed and determinant. On this score, the fiction writers were brighter than their medical counterparts, and the joke is on the recent critics who have sought to impose a limited and dissenting medical view upon the fiction of the age by treating it as a Renaissance norm.

While such stories may be read in relation to the controversy concerning sex changes that engaged the sixteenth century, and while there is evidence that the Morlini-Straparola tale of the hermaphrodite nun grew out of the tales of sex changes retrieved from classical writers, fictive fantasies of protagonists who shift back and forth from male to female through the powers of magic are also known in the Eastern tradition. One such from Somadeva's *Katha sarit sagara* called 'The Magic Pill'

---

98 *His Farewell to Military Profession*, ed. Donald Beecher (Ottawa and Binghamton, NY: Dovehouse Editions and MRTS, 1992), pp. 291–314.

shares common features with the story by Firenzuola.[99] A young man in love is given a magic pill by his master that enables him, by holding the globule in his mouth, to become a maiden in order to enter his beloved's house without being detected. By giving himself over to the care of the king, he is placed among the women. When the princess tells her new companion about her love for the youth who had saved her from the raging elephant, he identifies himself as that youth by removing the pill. His presence as a male evokes fear and shame, however, which the pronunciation of secret marriage vows alone can overcome. Thereafter he changes his sex routinely to become a female by day and a male at night. But when the minister's son falls in love with the hero in his female form and enters a dangerous state of lovesickness, it is determined that 'she' must acquiesce to save his life. The hero agrees, but buys time by demanding that the minister's son engage in a six month's journey to various shrines and holy bathing places. As the son's 'new wife,' he is thus taken into the household of the minister and there placed with the first wife

---

99 *The Katha sarit sagara or Ocean of the Streams of Story*, trans. C.H. Tawney, 2 vols. (New Delhi: Munshiram Manoharlal, 1992), Vitala 15, vol. II, pp. 301. This is but one of many related Eastern tales of sexual transformation. The idea of changing sexes may have originated in wishes made manifest through reincarnation and the return as the opposite sex in a new life. But the life situations that gave rise to those demands – seeking restitution for committed acts – were in due course brought into a single life through the involvement of the gods who were capable of conducting such transmutations. In the Turkish *Tooti-nameh*, a sorceress provides a sex change amulet to a lovesick adolescent that enables him to become a girl to marry the king's son in order that he can approach the princess and eventually flee with her as a man. Diya-ad-Din Nahsabi, *Tuti-nameh: Das Papageienbuch*, trans. Georg Rosen (Leipzig: Brockhaus, 1858), vol. II, p. 178. In the *Mahabharata*, a hermaphrodite child is born because Shiva promises that the child will be female and male. A daughter is born, but is raised as a son, as in the case of Iphis and Arescusa (Pliny). When the girl is married to another girl, the princess tells her father and he plans to launch a war to redress the insult. Then Yaksha takes pity on her in the forest and the two agree to exchange sexes, rescuing the girl from suicide and enabling her to fulfil her marital obligations as a male. *Mahabharata*, trans. Pratap Chundra Roy and Sundaribala Roy, 14 vols. (Calcutta: Bharata Press, 1884–96), sects. cxc–cxciv, vol. III, pp. 529–38. This story was still being told in Persia in the eighteenth century. See Izzat Ullah, *Gul-i Bakawali* in Garcin de Tassy, *Allégories récits poétiques et chants populaires* (Paris: E. Leroux, 1876), pp, 349–50, 372–4. See also Auguste Dozon, *Contes albanais* (Paris: E. Leroux, 1881), no. 14, p. 109; Johann Georg von Hahn, *Griechische und albanesische Märchen* (Leipzig: W. Engelmann, 1864), no. 58; and Heinrich von Wlislocki, *Volksdichtungen der siebenbürgischen und südungarischen Zigeuner* (Vienna: C. Graeser, 1890), no. 34, p. 260.

of the minister's son, to whom he tells the story of the goddess and her power to transmute women into men. Thus, while the son is away, the 'girl' for whom he pines turns himself into a man – that is to say, he returns to his original sexual identity – and sleeps with the rejected wife (much as Riche's hero is put to bed with Brisilla and performs in her presence a mock sex-change ritual whereby he equips himself as a male). Meanwhile, his Brahmin teacher goes back to the king to ask for the princess. The relationship between this story from sixth- to ninth-century Persia and those in the mode of Firenzuola and Riche with their similar narrative patterns and rhetorical employment of the cross-gendered disguise and ritual sex changes requires further investigation.

Straparola's tale, by comparison, is concerned with the drama of one such transformation as a physiological phenomenon in its own right, a tale that is not concerned with lovers and palace intrigue or the rites of magic. The common denominator, however, is the fascination with sexual transformation that marks these narratives, whether as fantasy or as empirical fact, and whether those deemed to be fact are real or putative in nature. The present anecdote accepts at face value that the heroine has produced a penis, that when the tumour is opened a female becomes a full hermaphrodite and functionally a male in her subsequent life. In this instance, the veracity of the tale is more than a pledge of its sincerity; it is also an assertion that what has been observed by a substantial company in real time and a real place is also medically and phenomenologically possible.

XIII. Fable 10
The Judgments of Cesare, Doctor of Laws

CATERUZZA

Cesare, a Neapolitan, after a long course of study at Bologna, completes his doctor's degree and, having returned home, files in advance all the court judgments he has heard to serve later as his own decisions.

There are three things, gracious ladies, that may be said to lay waste to the world and turn everything upside down: these three are money, hatred, and favouritism. The truth of this saying you will readily understand if you give a kind hearing to the fable I'm about to recite.

Lodovico Mota – as you may well have heard before now – was a far-sighted and wise man and one of the foremost citizens of Naples. Being unmarried, he took for his wife the daughter of Alessandro di Alessandri, also a resident of the city, and by her he had an only son whom he named Cesare. When the child was old enough to receive instruction, his father put him under the charge of a teacher to learn the rudiments of letters and afterwards sent him to Bologna to study civil and canon law. There he resided for a long time, making very little profit during his stay, even though his father, who was keen to make a scholar of his son, bought him all the books of the jurisconsultants of the canon law and of the experts in civil law, deeming that his son would be able to surpass all the barristers of Naples. He believed too that he would be in contact with the best clients and involved in all the important cases before the courts. But Cesare, although he was a much-studied young man, nevertheless lacked the essential groundwork of legal science and much of the knowledge pertaining to letters. Consequently, he failed to understand what he read, and the facts he had gotten by heart he could only mouth in a great show of impudence, most preposterously, and without any due order. Hence one of his arguments might contradict another, thereby revealing his ignorance. Constantly he would wrangle with his mates, taking the truth for falsehood and falsehood for the truth. Like an inflated windbag, he would go into the schools with his ears closed and there build his castles in the air. And because ignorant people never weary of repeating the saying that it is an improper and disgraceful course for the rich to spend their time in study, so Cesare – who was in fact well off – got little or no profit from pursuing the study of civil and canon law.

Nevertheless, being willing and ready to let his own ignorance come into competition with the learning of those who had not wasted their time and their lamp oil, but had studied long and diligently, he decided most presumptuously to apply for the doctorate. Presenting himself before the senate with this goal in mind, he took up the proposed points of dispute and set out to show his qualifications in public in the presence of a large assembly. But his arguments were all black for white and green for black, thinking that because he was blind himself, all the others around must be blind as well. Even so, by good fortune or the power of money, or by favouritism and friendship, his application was allowed and he was made a doctor of laws. Then, accompanied by a large company of esteemed persons, he paraded through the city to the sound of trumpets and fifes, returning home in vestments of purple silk looking more like an ambassador than a doctor.

One day, thereafter, this worthy magnate, dressed in his purple robe and velvet stole, prepared certain strips of paper and strung them together like a notary's file, and then placed them all together in a vase. While he was thus engaged, his father happened by and asked him what he was intending to do with the papers he was preparing, to which he replied, 'It is written, my father, in the books of the civil law that all judgments and sentences are to be numbered among matters of chance. Because I have studied the inner spirit as well as the letter of the law, I have made up these files at random upon which are noted down various judgments, all of which I shall deliver to the litigants before me without further troubling myself. Thereafter, by God's good will, your patronage, and your financial support I shall become a judge in the high court. Doesn't it appear to you, father, that I've investigated and solved this problem in a very subtle way?' The father, hearing these words, was nearly killed by sorrow. Turning his back, he left his useless son to his own ignorance.

Cateruzza's diverting story was received by the honourable company with the utmost of pleasure. After they had spent a few minutes in discussing it, the Signora directed her to continue on with her enigma, which she delivered without further coaxing.

> I trust I may not you offend
> In asking you, my worthy friend,
> Whether a certain thing you have
> Which lately in your charge I gave,
> Which straight you took and folded tight
> Between your left leg and your right.
> This I must know and know straightway,
> For much I grieve when 'tis away.
> Good friend, your wrath I understand.
> Fear not, for you shall hold in hand
> This thing which lies upon my thigh,
> Sways up and down, now low, now high,
> And galls me sore, and hangs behind;
> So take it when you are inclined.

When Cateruzza had finished, the listeners looked at one another, hardly knowing what to say. Perceiving that none of them understood the meaning, she offered this gloss: 'Ladies and gentlemen, stand no longer in suspense, for I'll tell you the meaning of my enigma right away, although I find myself scarcely equal to the task. There was once a young man who lent his friend his horse to ride out to his country house, which horse the friend sold. As the latter was on his way back, he was seen by the young man, who asked what had become of the horse, and finding no sign of it was most perplexed. His friend then told him not to get excited because he had the money safe in his purse from the sale of the animal – the purse itself rubbing his back side.' After Cateruzza, with her subtle wit, had revealed the matter, the Signora turned her glance towards the Trevisan, and in a modest way signalled to him to follow in the order of storytelling. His tale began without any wilful delay.

XIII.10 Commentary

At face value, this is a tale of a father's disappointment with his son. The boy has been sent to the best schools to study law, propped up with family money, but in the end proves himself an ignoramus and a discredit to the family. Those stories hold a profile of their own. He is not a prodigal but a nincompoop. But there is a second set of overtones, namely, that through wealth and influence, the boy has actually been granted a doctorate and has been sent into the world to practise as a judge. Thus, when it comes to handing out verdicts at random written on pieces of paper as a form of juridical *sortes virgilianae*, or bibliomancy, it is the public that is outraged by abusive accreditation, professional incompetence and charlatanry. The portrait of the incompetent judge epitomizes the helplessness of those who receive arbitrary treatment at the hands of unqualified and bungling professionals. Doctors and lawyers are particularly subject to such satiric profiling because they are trained to dispense healing and justice upon which very real happiness and well-being depend. Yet these persons enjoy a kind of privilege, prestige, and immunity that places them beyond recourse or recrimination, hiding behind the jargon and occult principles of their professions. A second line of satire has to do with the power of money and the influence that is gained through status. These are familiar complaints in all ages. Straparola's vignette was in wide circulation both before and after the publication of the *Notti*, particularly in France, where it appears largely in satiric works excoriating the abuses and enormities perpetrated by corrupt professionals.

Girolamo Morlini's *novella* no. 68, 'De jurista qui tenebat sententias in filzis' (Of the jurist who kept his verdicts in a notebook) provides the closest cognate to this sketch and is hence taken for its source.[100] Morlini's protagonist is the son of a Neapolitan gentleman who profits little from his training in law. Yet he had a knack for impressing people with his self-confidence, and he could recite all manner of principles and maxims, even though he applied them in no logical fashion, often claiming sheer falsehoods as truths. Nevertheless, he pursued a doctorate and succeeded, largely through intrigue and bribes, and graduated amidst fanfares and celebrations. He had kept a series of notebooks in which he wrote down a number of decisions and verdicts that he repeated tirelessly, and in this way, with family backing, he became a judge in the high tribunal. When his father asked him the purpose of these enumerated verdicts, he was told they were used to make pronouncements in current cases, essentially in random fashion, because he understood nothing of the letter of the law. When the father heard such folly, he turned his back and grieved. Straparola embellishes this sequence with specific details, perhaps of his own devising, perhaps derived from cognate sources –

---

100 *Les nouvelles de Girolamo Morlini*, trans. Fernand Caussy (Paris: E. Sansot and Co., 1904), pp. 146–7; *Novelle*, ed. G. Villani (Rome: Salerno, 1983), pp. 300–3.

details such as the vase from which the judgments are drawn, implying more forcefully than Morlini the arbitrariness of the judge's verdicts. That the anecdote applies to a student of law may be Morlini's innovation, one that Straparola follows and enhances by sending the boy to the famed University of Bologna. But the far greater number in circulation applies to physicians who hand out diagnoses and prescriptions at random on little pieces of paper drawn up in advance, accompanied by an ironic phrase to the effect that any good resulting from the paper would be the work of God alone.

Among the writers concerned with medical practitioners using chance remedies, both before and after Straparola, are Carlo Casalicchio and Poggio Bracciolini in Italy and, in France, Bonaventure des Périers, Richard de Romany, François Garasse, and Honoré Lacombe de Prezel. Poggio writes that in Rome it was the custom that if you wanted to consult a doctor you first had to produce a urine sample and two pieces of silver.[101] One of those physicians wrote various remedies on bits of paper that he tossed in a sack. When a urine sample appeared, he would pull out a remedy saying, 'Pray God that He has chosen the right one for you.' And so the health of his patients depended entirely on chance. The satiric intent is clear, for not only were there incompetent practitioners, but the entire discipline was deemed an imprecise art at best. Central to this anecdote is the preliminary writing out of prescriptions, the bits of

---

101 'Facetum medici qui sorte medelas dabat' (Of the physician who gave out prescriptions at random) in *Les facéties de Pogge, Florentin*, trans. Pierre des Brandes (Paris: Garnier Frères, ca. 1900), no. 3, pp. 252–3. Tomaso Costa, in *Il fuggilozio* (Naples, 1596), ed. Corrado Calenda (Rome: Salerno, 1989), bk. II, no. 18, pp. 115–17, builds a historical anecdote out of the generic sketch of the student who, sent to study with his father's money, makes nothing of his educational opportunities, but it lacks the satiric sequel of the fraudulent practitioner and the pronouncement of verdicts or remedies by hazard. A servant in the household of Cardinal Alessandro Farnese, a rich patron of the arts, himself became rich and sent his only son to Bologna with a considerable sum of money to pursue an education. After years of dissipation, the boy returned to Rome both indigent and unlettered. The father, convinced of his learning, sought his son's advancement in the cardinal's household. When asked about his specialization, the boy replied, 'Illustrious Monsignor, I have studied mostly in, how do you call it, let's say in theology, the middle of which, I must say, I can't remember very well, but the beginning and end, well, God only knows.' The cardinal, smiling at such insipidity, turned and said, 'Well, you'll have to make the middle appear, for without that, it's like a skull and a tail without a body.' Again, it is money that makes a man lazy and ignorant.

paper, the random selection, and the saying, stated with varying degrees of irony, to the effect, 'God help you because I can't' or 'The good that happens now is God's and the ill my own.' It would appear that the original version of this anecdote was, in fact, medical.

Carlo Casalicchio, in *L'utile col dolce, overo quattro centurie di argutissimi detti, e fatti di saviissimi huomini,* in later years added the moral that while we are commended to respect doctors, there are those, nevertheless, who, without study and observation, prescribe medications to the detriment of their patients. Providence alone can help them because the medications are useless. He then provides multiple examples of quackery, in which cases the recovery of the patient is nevertheless credited to the practitioner. The point could also be demonstrated inversely, as when an ignorant patient thought the power of the cure was in the paper rather than the message written on it, and thus swallowed it after dipping it in wine. Because in time he grew better, the prescription was non-essential. Healing is a matter of chance and not of medicine.[102]

Bonaventure des Périers tells the story of the law student on his way to Paris who is detained by an apothecary in a town near Cahors, then without a doctor. He told the student that good money was to be made there (insofar as the old doctor died rich), and that he could teach him the arts of medicine, in ten or fifteen days at the most, which consisted of a few sayings and following the apothecary's diagnostics.[103] All you have to do is look authoritative and learn a few prescriptions by heart. When the urine samples began to arrive, the young 'doctor,' by merely looking at the water, pretended to considerable knowledge of the patient – even the names of relatives and the numbers of children – through information supplied to him on the sly by the apothecary. Thus he gained credit. His success was based entirely on his air of self-confidence and show of erudition. This principle, Bonaventure tells us, was clearly understood by the Italian doctor who put a quantity of prescriptions in his pocket and drew them out at random, telling his patients, 'May God give you good, because better or worse is the way of the world.' Poggio,

---

102 (Venice: Nella stamperia del Baglioni, 1741), 'Centuria seconda dell'arguzie, decade seconda, arguzia sesta: "Casuale esser tal volta la sanità restituita all'infermo, e non opera della medicina"' (The health of the sick is often restored by chance and not by medical practice), p. 227.

103 'De l'escolier legiste & de l'apoticaire, qui lui aprint la medecine' (Of the law student and the apothecary who teaches him medicine) in *Contes et nouvelles, et joyeux devis,* 2 vols. (Cologne: Jean Gaillard, 1711), no. 14, vol. II, pp. 14–24.

presumably, is his source. The anecdote, thereafter, receives treatment in *Le carabinage et la matoiserie soldatesque* of Richard de Romany (1616), the *Jugement et censure du livre de la doctrine curieux* of François Garasse (1623), and the *Dictionnaire d'anecdotes, de traits singuliers* of Honoré Lacombe de Prezel (1787).[104]

That the story was still in circulation in Sicily at the end of the nine-teenth century as a feature of folk culture does not guarantee that it was part of the oral culture of the sixteenth century. Nevertheless, this one example must serve to suggest that this anecdote, as with so many of the others, enjoyed popular diffusion, and that many such existed in parallel with the literary renditions and even cross-fertilized them for indefinite periods of time. Poggio's *facetiae*, written after the middle of the fifteenth century, possessed elements of the popular culture, whether directly or indirectly obtained, so that even this anecdote in the following example collected by Giuseppe Pitrè may merely be closing the circle. A doctor, who was a complete jackass, wrote out prescriptions and stuck them in his pocket before doing his rounds. Then he would pull them out at random and say, 'God will grant the good, and may this help too. Then whatever will be will be' – the precise formula that concludes the sketch by Bonaventure des Périers.[105]

Other stories in this tradition take on features of XIII.6, 'How Lucilio Finds the "Good Day."' In the *Novelle popolari toscane* there is the story of 'Il medico Grillo,' who is one of three brothers hoeing in a field when a rich doctor rides by and he decides that he too, without any training, would like to take up the good life. When he heard that the king's daughter was ill and a high reward was offered, he answered the call, announcing himself as 'Dr Grillo.' There were heavy costs for failure. He rigged up an extraordinary set of pulleys, buttered her shoulders, and propped her up on all sorts of pillows until the princess began to laugh. When, for all this, the fishbone lodged in her throat came out,

---

104 (Drachier d'Amorny, anagram of Richard de Romany), *Le carabinage* (Paris: Monstroeil, 1616; Geneva: J. Gay, 1867), p. 38. François Ogier, *Jugement et censure du livre de la doctrine curieuse de François Garasse* (Paris: n.p., 1623), p. 392. This is the work of a fanatic, reactionary Jesuit who incorporates this vignette in his excoria-tion of all the abuses and enormities of his age. Lacombe de Prezel, *Dictionnaire de'anecdotes* (Paris: Lacombe, 1787), vol. II, p. 160.

105 'God will send help and this will do the rest' in *The Collected Sicilian Folk and Fairy Tales of Giuseppe Pitrè*, trans. Jack Zipes and Joseph Russo, 2 vols. (New York: Routledge, 2007), no. 251, vol. II, pp. 726–7.

he reaped the reward and gained a reputation. The jealous professionals then lodged their complaints and Grillo had to go from exploit to exploit to sustain his fame – all of which he managed to do by one silly device after another. All are tales of the remarkable success or escape of professional ignoramuses.[106]

106 *Novelle popolari toscane*, ed. Giuseppe Pitrè, intro. Gino Cerrito (Palermo: Edikronos, 1981), no. 60, pp. 264–9. Rachel Harriett Busk found the story of the peasant who wanted to become a doctor among the Roman raconteurs, which she included in the *Folklore of Rome* (London: Longman, Green & Co., 1874), pp. 392*ff.* One of the most amusing treatments of the accidental doctor compelled by circumstances to keep up illusions is Noël Le Breton, sieur de Hauteroche's *Crispin médecin* (1671), in which Crispin the comic valet, in the same fix as the lover-priest who is about to be castrated (The Priest and the Image-Carver's Wife, VIII.3), must play a cadaver on the dissecting table and contemplate being cut open before he finds himself, in the same clinic, impersonating Dr Mirobolan and prescribing to his patients in the most preposterous ways. *Crispin médecin* (Paris: J. Ribou, 1680), Act II, scenes v–viii.

XIII. Fable 11
The Novice's Night in the Barn

BENEDETTO OF TREVISO

A poor novice sets out from Cologne to travel to Ferrara, and having approached that city at nightfall, takes shelter by stealth in a certain place, where a terrifying adventure befalls him.

My dear ladies, fear is sometimes created from overconfidence, and sometimes from our spineless and cowardly natures, for by rights we ought to fear only those things that have a genuine power to work evil to others and to ignore all those incapable of producing harm. I want to tell you of a real adventure, not just a silly joke, that happened in our time to a certain poor novice – one that caused him serious misfortune. Having set forth from Cologne on his way to Ferrara, he passed by the abbey and along the high ground above the swamps of Rovigo, but when he reached the confines of the Duke of Ferrara's territory, black night had fallen. Although the moon was shining brightly, still the solitude and strangeness of the surroundings worked powerfully upon the poor chap's fears – for he was in fact little more than an adolescent and was mortally afraid of meeting his death at the hands of malefactors or from wild beasts.

As the poor fellow wandered along, not knowing where to go without having to pay, he saw a yard in front of him somewhat removed from the farmhouse. Making his way there without being heard or seen by anyone, he climbed up into a straw loft by a ladder conveniently placed against the side, and once he was up there, he arranged himself as best he could for a night's sleep.

But hardly had the novice settled himself down to rest when there also came up into the loft an energetic man with a sword in his right hand and a shield on his left arm. When the newcomer began to whistle softly, the poor monk in the straw, hearing this, thought he was discovered.

Every hair on his head stood up with terror, so crouching down still deeper in the straw, he curled up and lay as still as a mouse. Now the armed intruder, as it turned out, was a neighbouring curate, who was inflamed with love for the wife of the owner of the adjacent house. The novice waited for a while in tense anxiety, when from the house there issued a lady in her nightdress, very plump and pretty, who also made her way up to the loft. As soon as the priest saw her he threw aside his sword and shield and ran to embrace and kiss her, while on her side she was by no means slow to return his endearments. So they got themselves into the hay and, after lying down together, the priest took out the thing that men have, lifted up her nightgown, and without hesitation inserted it into the furrow.

Meanwhile, from up above the novice saw everything that was going on. Taking courage in his assurance that the priest hadn't come to do him any harm but to have his pleasure with his ladylove, he stretched his head out of the straw to see better what the lovers were up to. But leaning over too far, he lost his balance, because there was nothing but straw to support him, and fell down right on top of the lady and the priest, hurting them and whacking his own shin in the process.

Now the two lovers had arrived at the most beautiful part of the reckoning, but had not yet reached the completion of their masterpiece, when they saw the cloak and hood of the black brother. Then they were seized with terror. Thinking it must be some horrid night-walking ghost, they left behind both sword and shield and straightway took to their heels, trembling with fear. On his side, the novice, with his shin now broken and quaking all over, slunk away as best he could into a corner of the loft, burrowed a large hole in the heap of straw, and hid himself. Only then might the priest dare to return for the telltale sword and shield, dangerous to leave behind because they were known to everyone. Seeing nothing more of the ghost, he crept back to the loft, picked up his weapons and, in a state of apprehension, returned to his own house.

When the next day arrived, the priest wanted to get the mass over with early, leaving him time to dispatch certain private affairs of his own. He placed himself at the door of the church and waited for his clerk, who was to come and help him with the office. As he stood there watching, who should appear but the poor novice, who had abandoned his lodgings before daybreak in order not to be discovered and mistreated. As he came up to the church, the priest asked him where he has headed. 'I'm going to Ferrara,' came the reply. When the priest enquired further whether he was in a hurry, he replied that he wasn't, and that it would be all the same if he were to reach Ferrara by nightfall. Then the priest asked the young monk whether he would be willing to stop and help say the mass, to which the novice readily agreed.

The priest, noting that the young monk had on a black robe and that his hood and gown had sundry bits of straw clinging to them – began to suspect that he might be talking to last night's ghost, so he said, 'My brother, where did you sleep last night?'

To this the novice answered, 'I slept really badly on a straw stack in a place not far from here, where around midnight I fell down and nearly broke my leg.' When he heard these words, the priest was even more confirmed in his belief that the novice was the man he suspected him to be, and wouldn't let him go until he had revealed to him the entire situation. After the mass had been said, the novice dined with the priest and then went on his way with his broken shin. But before he got away, the host urged him to pay him another visit on his journey back, for he had gotten the idea into his head that the lady herself should hear the whole story from the lips of the young monk. But he did not return. Having been warned in a dream, he travelled back to his monastery by a different road.

As soon as the Trevisan's fable had come to an end and was duly praised, he launched straight into his enigma without any further loss of time.

> Its length and breadth shall I disclose?
> Upon my lap it nestles close;
> I stroke it and I hold it tight.
> To all around it gives delight.
> Fair ladies, is it strange to you
> It does its work correct and true?
> Though rapture sweet within may dwell,
> 'Tis passive till it knows me well.

'I would never wish, most gracious ladies, to suffer reproof from you on the score of impropriety for having brought forward in such an assembly as this anything that might seem offensive to your chaste hearing. But in truth, this enigma of mine is in no way allied to anything off-coloured, but rather to something that delights you and from which you take no small pleasure. My enigma, in fact, describes the lute, the handle of which is somewhat more than a span in width, while its body is designed to rest in the lap of the player, thus giving delight to all who listen.'

This clever enigma, as glossed by the Trevisan, was loudly praised by everyone, especially the Signora, who listened to it with great pleasure. As soon as the company had fallen silent, the Signora gave the word to Isabella to commence her fable, which she, being neither deaf nor mute, began.

XIII.11 Commentary

This little *récit* has all the ingredients of an anecdote worthy of memory: illicit lovers, a voyeur, a sudden accident that terrifies those caught *en flagrante délit* and puts them to flight, and in some versions a supper abandoned to the intruder who has fallen on top of them or startled them with the sound of an organ, trumpet, bagpipes, or drum in the middle of the night. Whether this began as a proper *novella* or as a historical anecdote is difficult to determine, but while Sercambi, in the late fourteenth century, fitted it out as a 'full' literary narrative, several in the fifteenth century reduced it to a vignette in order to assign it to a specific person, time, and place as a veritable event of recent times, often as told by one of the parties involved. In a sense, then, news that has been turned into fiction can always be reconverted to news, and what has been written can always be relayed orally from memory. Straparola, in the style of his telling, seems to favour the habits and proportions of the oral tale, although his *opusculum* may be assigned a literary source, given that he had so many to choose from. For this reason, this little production, with its literary antecedents and probable folk analogues, provides an ideal study group concerning the relationship between oral and literary cultures in the age of the *novella*.

If indeed Straparola derived his design from Girolamo Morlini, as we have been led to expect by his many concurrent borrowings, it has undergone major changes, insofar as Morlini's agent for the accidental fall is specifically from Sorrento, the wayward son of a gentleman who has lived a dissolute life in Naples and must be taken home bound hand and foot to receive enforced paternal instruction.[107] Unreceptive to any such guidance and discipline, however, this young reprobate escapes his father's household in the night. En route, he settles himself in a tower, nestles

---

107 Girolamo Morlini, 'Of a caitiff from Sorrento who unexpectedly deflowers a young
    girl,' the title translated from *Les nouvelles*, trans. from Latin by Fernand Caussy
    (Paris: E. Sansot and Co., 1904), no. 54, pp. 121–3; *Novelle*, ed. G. Villani (Rome:
    Salerno, 1983), pp. 246–51.

himself in the hay, and there hears the approach of lovers. His curiosity to observe the transactions below causes him to lose his place and fall on top of them, frightening the priest away. Then, rogue that he is, he deflowers the girl, timid and helpless, in what is tantamount to rape, before stealing the priest's clothes and later selling them in Naples. This is perhaps too brutal a tale even for the hearty Trevisan to tell, and in that spirit, Straparola makes the falling protagonist a travelling novice (resembling much more the *novella* of Philippe de Vigneulles), himself terrified of the night and fearful of the lovers until he divines their intent. Thus, despite the occurrence in Morlini, in this instance Straparola appears to have gone back to the folk, or to a French source.

Straparola's setting is in a remote farm in the region near the marshes of Rovigo just to the north of Ferrara. Rovigo, today, is the next train stop after Ferrara on the way northeast to Padua and Venice. That innovative detail adds one last hint that this region south of Padua as far as the Po River was a remote part of the author's stomping grounds. Also of distinct particularity is the subsequent meeting of the two clerics and the realization on the part of the local priest that the young novice was the monster in black who had terrified him during the preceding night. Likewise, the odd and apparently irrelevant shield and sword carried to the encounter by the priest and abandoned in the barn when he takes flight appears to be a vestige of an entirely distinct version, for it has no counterpart in Morlini.

Other antecedent depictions of interest, arranged chronologically, include those by Giovanni Sercambi (1328–1424), Masuccio Salernitano (Tommaso Guardati, 1410–75), Philippe de Vigneulles (1471–1528), Francesco Maria Molza (1489–1544), Marco Cademosto (fl. 1515–20), whose six *novelle* were printed in Rome in 1543, and Matteo Bandello (ca. 1480–1562), whose first collection of *novelle* appeared in print in 1554.[108] All of them carry motifs originally explored in several of the French *fabliaux*.[109] Nevertheless, their chronological arrangement offers

---

108 Albert Wesselski, ed., *Die novellen Girolamo Morlinis* (Munich: Georg Müller, 1908), pp. 303–5, offers further titles and an analysis of the sources.

109 An early tale collected by Anatole de Montaiglon and Gaston Raynaud tells of the poor clerk who is forced by poverty to return to his home country. On the way he begs shelter from the hostess of an inn and is turned away until he meets the host returning from the mill. Meanwhile, the hostess is spending her time with a priest and is nearly discovered when the two men enter, having hidden her lover in a manger (? croiche in Italian). Recriminations pass between the husband and wife,

no demonstration of linear influence or progress, whether from fact to fiction, or from primitive to sophisticated. In many ways, Sercambi's is the most accomplished and 'novelistic' of the lot.[110] Merendina, a jolly Florentine widow, spends too much time in the church of the preaching friars and finds herself accosted by Brother Bellasta, with whom in due course she agrees upon a time and place for a liaison. Meanwhile, Lamberto de' Monaldi goes to market on a mission for his father and there, meeting up with his comrades, joins in the gaming until he loses not only all of his father's money but his own clothes. Ashamed, naked, fearful of returning home, and hungry into the bargain, he takes shelter in the friars' church, where he climbs into the organ loft in the darkness of the night. Then the doors open, Brother Bellasta enters from the cloister and opens the door to Madonna Merendina, dressed in a black cloak and bearing a capon, three loaves of white bread, and a flask of muscatel. After their repast he begins his banter about putting his 'soldano in Babilonia,' no doubt in imitation of Boccaccio's Alibec, who placed the devil in hell. Lamberto, hearing everything, began thinking not only of Babylon, but of the cloak, the cape, and the capon, and decided to sound the organ. Hearing these terrifying notes, the friar takes flight to the cloister and the lady to her house, leaving the spoils to Lamberto, who then eats his fill and pawns the cloak and cape the next day to recover his losses and buy new clothes. That is as much of the story as most of his successors are willing to relate, but Sercambi continues with the friar's search for his clothes among the pawnbrokers, leading to the usurers' identification of the thief, the reaction of Lamberto's father, and the appearance before the podestà. Lamberto begins his defence merely by recounting the truth up to the moment at which the 'soldano' was to enter 'Babilonia,' at which juncture both the friar and the widow suddenly lose interest in the proceedings, withdraw their charges, and confess to the error of their accusations. Lamberto

---

leading to an exchange of proverbs between the men about the eternal verities of domesticity. In due course, the priest is discovered when the cradle or manger is to be tossed out the window. The story, nevertheless, lacks many of the key elements that make up the particularity of the present tale. But there may be others. *Recueil général et complet des fabliaux des XIIIe et XIVe siècles* (Paris: Librairie des Bibliophiles, 1872–90), no. 132, vol. V, pp. 192–200. See also Joseph Bédier, *Les fabliaux* (Paris: Bouillon, 1893), pp. 453–4.

110 'De vana lussuria' in *Novelle inedite*, ed. Alessandro D'Ancona (Florence: Libreria di Dante, 1886), no. 5, pp. 18–29. This story is not to be found in the standard editions of Sercambi's collected works.

then goes free and the lovers endure the shame meted out by their respective communities. With this prototype of the story before us, all those to follow can be examined as variations upon a typologized design. The 'ancient' story appears to involve the calculated sounding of an instrument by which the lovers are frightened and brought to abandon their food and clothes. Later variants emphasize the initial terror of the hidden voyeur and generate the reversal of the story by having him fall directly upon the lovers from a loft, necessitating the relocation of the action from a church or tower to a rotten old barn.[111] Two scenarios of potential transmission emerge, variations upon literary sources, and rewriting from a parallel folk tradition that may be independently responsible for each of the following versions, including Straparola's.

Masuccio's version differs in significant ways, yet it is entirely a part of the type.[112] His setting is a village near Amalfi, and his principals are a robust priest given to flirting, a jolly, coquettish carpenter's wife named Masimilla, and Marco the tailor, who is better at playing the bagpipes than he is at sewing. Following a festival at which the wife meets the tailor in the absence of her husband, they proceed to her little cottage in the hills. Just as their game of love begins, however, the pesky priest comes banging at the door and will not take 'no' for an answer. Because he was such a bruiser, intimidating both the wife and the tailor, she urges her first lover to climb up to the pigeon loft and hide himself. The priest is then admitted, and unceremoniously rushes into foreplay, biting and kissing Massimilla in anticipation of sending the Pope to Rome. When he had positioned her to that end, he declared outright, with his sword in hand, that the Pope was now about to enter. The tormented tailor in the loft at that point could no longer endure. Declaring that the Pope makes no such entry without music, he proceeds to blare away on his bagpipe while stamping on the planks of the floor. Fear seizes the priest and drives him straight out the door, leaving the field to Marco. He then

---

111 This is ATU type 1776, and Thompson Motif Index no. K1271.1. Of this particular story, Thompson states: 'Somewhat similar tales from fabliaux and jestbooks popular in eastern Europe but otherwise apparently unknown as folktales are two concerning discovered lovers. One of them tells how a man hidden in a roof sees a girl and her lover. He becomes so interested that he falls, and they flee and leave him in possession.' Stith Thompson, *The Folk Tale* (Berkeley: University of California Press, 1977), pp. 203–4. His unawareness of a folktale tradition fortifies the idea of a literary source for the present tale, although the point remains moot.

112 *The Novellino of Masuccio*, trans. W.G. Waters, 2 vols. (London: Lawrence and Bullen, 1895), no. 5, vol. I, pp. 79–86.

descends and finds the woman laughing, entirely prepared for the Turk's entry into Constantinople. With Masuccio, this tale remains a 'novelistic' enterprise, with its contrasting characterizations of the lovers and its double play on the comic euphemisms for sexual engagement, perfectly in line with this author's persistently anticlerical stance. The terrified traveller in the barn who tumbles down when the rotten timbers fracture is still to come. That appears in the following version of French provenance, which clearly has a bearing on the subsequent Italian renditions, including Straparola's.

Philippe de Vigneulles in *Les cent nouvelles nouvelles* tells the story of an apothecary who was caught in a storm and takes refuge in a mill.[113] There he overhears lovers and, while seeking a better view, falls from his perch when the rotten planks give way. Taking him for a devil, the priest and his ladyfriend break and run, leaving him the rest of their supper. Philippe de Vigneulles assures us that this is a true local event that happened to Jehan Regnault in his youth – an event he recounted on many occasions thereafter. Jehan was active as a cleric in Metz in 1505. Marco Cademosto tells the same story in his *Novelle*: an apothecary was hiding in a hopper (*tramoggia*) inside a mill when a priest arrives with a beautiful woman carrying wine and a chicken. When the hopper gives way and he falls down on them, they too take him for the devil and flee.[114] This same

---

113 Ed. Charles H. Livingston (Geneva: Droz, 1972), no. 49, pp. 211–13. Livingston mentions the versions by Morlini and Straparola, but also adds that it was widely known in Scandinavia, and that there are numerous versions in which the lovers are frightened by musical instruments, especially the tambourine. According to his research, there are many folk versions remaining to be discovered, allowing for a folk tradition that, as in the case of so many others, clearly reached back to the sixteenth century. No. 96 in this same collection is a related tale (pp. 379–83), this time involving a 'tambourin' by which the lovers are frightened and a long sequel in which the two brothers 'Pied Deschault' are introduced.

114 *Novelle* (Milan: [Giovita Scalvini], 1799; first edition Rome: Antonio Blado Asolano, 1544), no. 3, pp. 35–42. There is also the version in *L'Arcadia in Brenta* of Giovanni Sagredo, ed. Quinto Marini (Rome: Salerno, 2004), pp. 284–8. The setting is modern, referring to the war of the Mantuan succession, 1627–31. A trumpeter on his way home from the wars stops at an inn where the husband is away for the harvest and the mistress is looking forward to a night with her lover. With a full house, the musician is made to beg for a makeshift room, from which, as it turns out, he can spy upon the lovers. They play the game of Constantinople and the entry of the 'Gran Turco,' to which royal entry the trumpeter decides to lend music. When the lovers flee in terror, the silver cups are up for grabs – a larceny the hostess is later obliged to explain to her husband. When husband and

story was taken up by Francesco Maria Molza, who sends his 'Jehan Regnault' into Germany, where he was unacquainted with the language. His mission was to take food and wine to his seigneur's mistress. When, on the way home, he loses his direction, he finds an old mill, attaches his horse to a tree, enters with trepidation, and hides in a hopper, first making certain that it was not inhabited by a devil. Nearby there was both an abbey of monks and a convent of nuns, members of which sometimes met in pairs at the mill with food and drink to accompany their play. The young clerk takes one such couple for robbers, but his fears are assuaged when the monk lights a fire and he can observe them through the cracks. Then the wood collapses as he moves about to improve his view, the lovers part in separate directions, and he is left with the provisions. This telling is likewise treated as a true tale, for it is told by the protagonist himself upon his return, whereupon his audience laughs uproariously and repeats the story frequently thereafter.

These three versions appear to be of a group, but they clearly participate in a larger tradition with its many circulating variants: churches, mills, barns; hay, rotten planks, bagpipes; nuns, widows, wives; apothecaries, novices, and rogues. Authors are at liberty to claim historical veracity for their respective versions, and to provide their tales with local names and details. But in fact there is only one story with an invariable core of events that was passed along not only in written form, but orally, in keeping with Molza's closing remark that the story he had just told had already been embedded in the oral tradition for some time. Straparola's is a diminished version in comparison with several of those outlined above, but there is no certainty that he was responsible for making it so; that

---

trumpeter-thief meet the next day, the latter complains of being turned away and so is invited back for a supper where he is careful to make mention of the Turk's entry to keep the wife quiet. Antoine le Métel, Sieur d'Ouville tells the same story with minor variations. When the two lovers undress, he asks her the name of her special place, which she calls 'Constantinople.' To the same question he replies, 'The Grand Turk.' As she positions herself for the royal entry, the trumpeter blows as loud as lightening the advance and the retreat at once, for the lovers escape through a tiny window. The trumpeter later invites both the husband and the wayward wife to supper, where he openly displays the stolen plate. But when he is about to be accused, he reports that there is a mistake, for the plate had been given to him by the Grand Turk upon his entry into Constantinople, and with that, the wife assures her husband that he is mistaken and the accusation is abandoned. *L'Élite des contes*, ed. G. Brunet, 2 vols. (Paris: Librairie des bibliophiles, 1883), vol. II, pp. 286–91.

could have been the work of the folk artists from whom his version was derived.

Matteo Bandello's reworking brings the history full circle, for while his *novella* is the latest by publication date, it has the greatest affinity with Sercambi's. Arnoldo the trumpeter asks for a leave to return to France. In a hostelry he joins in the gambling and loses his entire fortune of 600 scudi, along with his clothes, hat, rings, and all.[115] Nevertheless, he keeps his trumpet. He makes his way to Paris on foot, encountering a number of adventures along the way, until he finds himself hiding in a room adjacent to a pair of lovers. At that moment he lets out a great blast from his trumpet which they take for the arrival of a devil. Thereupon, they scamper down the stairs, leaving behind their money and jewellery, and so the trumpeter becomes richer than he had been before. Straparola's historical vignette stands in stark contrast to this studied *novella* written by his contemporary. All these versions, in a sense, made their contributions to the repertory of motifs constituting the sum of the story's variants, a repertory that continued to grow as new imitations appeared. Yet in each reconfiguration, the same fabula is clearly in evidence. The story, with its incongruities, timely accident, fortunate fall, and coitus interruptus makes for masterly amusement and perhaps little more, for what didactic purpose can it possibly hold, or what virtue except its gemlike representation of the *comédie humaine* – a little holiday for the imagination?

---

115 Matteo Bandello, *Tutte le opere*, ed. Francesco Flora (Milan: Mondadori, 1966), vol. II, pp. 176–80.

XIII. Fable 12
The Healing of King Guglielmo

ISABELLA

Guglielmo, king of Bertagna, being grievously afflicted by a certain disease, causes all the physicians to be called to restore and preserve his health. One Maestro Gotfreddo, a doctor and a very poor man, gives him three maxims by which he rules his life and recovers his health.

All whose judgments lead them to successfully avoid everything that is noxious and to seek only things beneficial and profitable to them may truly account themselves born under a lucky star, or even more than mortal. But men of this kind, willing to conduct their lives by the best precepts, have been hard to find at any time and nowadays are scarce indeed. Yet it happened otherwise in the case of a king who received from a physician three rules for the preservation of his health, by which he regulated his life thereafter.

I think, no I'm certain, gracious ladies, that you've never heard the story of Guglielmo, king of Bertagna, who in his day had no peer whether for prowess or courtesy, and who was, for as long as he lived, the special favourite of Fortune. In a certain year this king fell seriously ill, but being young and courageous, he gave little thought to the disease. Yet, as he grew worse from day to day, things came to such a pass that all hope was lost of preserving his life. On this account, the king gave orders that all the physicians of the city should convene in his presence and openly offer their opinions concerning his state. As soon as the will of the king had been sent out, every one of the medical faculty, whatever his rank or status, went to the royal palace and presented himself before the king. In this crowd of physicians was Maestro Gotfreddo, a man of propriety and learning, but very poor, meanly dressed, and shod still worse. Because he was so badly clothed, he lacked the confidence to put himself forward among so many learned and illustrious men, but stood in shame behind the door of the king's chamber where he was hardly noticed, and there listened to all the opinions pronounced by the cautious and erudite doctors within.

As soon as all the physicians were in the king's presence, he said to them, 'Most worthy and excellent doctors, I have called you all here for only one reason, which is to learn from you the cause of the malady that afflicts me and to urge you to exercise all your skill and diligence in curing it by giving me the appropriate remedies to restore my health. And as soon as I am well again, you must provide me with whatever rules you deem fitting for the preservation of my future health.'

To this the physicians answered, 'Sacred majesty, to confer the boon of health is beyond our power. That lies only in the hands of Him who rules all things with a nod of His head. Nevertheless, we will endeavour, within our range of powers, to supply you with every remedy that may serve to restore your health and to maintain it once you have recovered it.'

Then the learned physicians began to dispute among themselves the cause of the king's illness and the medications they should prescribe for it, each one of them – as is the custom of the faculty – giving his own opinion, citing Galen, Hippocrates, Avicenna, Aesculapius, or others of the great doctors in support of his view. After their theories had all been aired, the king happened to look towards the door and caught sight of a shadowy form, whereupon he asked of them whether there was anyone present who had not yet spoken. They answered him that there was none. But the king, fully assured that he had seen someone, said, 'If I'm not blind, it's plain to me that there's something behind the door. Tell me what it is.'

To whom one of the learned doctors replied, 'Est homo quidam' (it's a certain man), jesting and making fun of the poor physician, forgetting that often enough art makes mockery of art. Then the king signalled to Gotfreddo to approach, enabling him to see that, though ill dressed, this man was in truth a physician. He came forward, trembling with fear, and bowed most courteously to the king, who, after inviting him to be seated with all due honour, asked him his name.

'Sacred majesty, my name is Gotfreddo,' came the reply.

Then the king said, 'Maestro Gotfreddo, you must have received information about my condition by listening to the disputations which these right worshipful doctors have made since coming into my chamber, so there is no need to retell the whole story. Tell me then what you have to say concerning my illness.'

'Sacred Majesty,' answered Gotfreddo, 'although I may justly style myself the lowest, least erudite, and poorest speaker in this gathering of luminaries, given my poverty and low esteem, yet in order to show myself obedient to your highness' commands, I will try with all my ability to make clear to you the origin of your malady, and to supply you with a regimen and rule of life, which, if you keep it, will maintain your health in the future. You should understand first, Your Majesty, that your infirmity is in no sense mortal, given that it doesn't arise from a defective constitution, but from some violent and invisible accident. This ailment will leave you as suddenly as it came upon you. So that you may recover your former health, I ask nothing more difficult of you than to watch your diet carefully, taking meanwhile a bit of cassia flower to refresh your blood. If you do this, you will be hale and hearty again in eight days. When your health has returned, you must carefully observe these three precepts if you wish to maintain your health for a long time. The first is to always keep your head dry. The second is that you keep your feet warm. The third is that in taking your food you follow the example of the beasts of the field. If you put these principles of mine into practice, you will be safe from harm – a healthy and robust man – for years to come.

The physicians standing around, when they heard the good advice Gotfreddo gave to the king concerning the governance of his life, all began to laugh so hard they were about to burst their cheeks. Turning towards the king they cried: 'Sure enough, here are the canons. These are the rules of Maestro Gotfreddo. Behold the fruits of his studies. Fine remedies, indeed. Fine provisions to offer to such an illustrious king!' And they went on in this fashion, mocking him.

But the king, hearing all the laughter and derision from the assembled doctors, ordered them silent and asked Maestro Gotfreddo to offer the reasoning behind his recommended course of action. 'My lord and king,' said Gotfreddo, 'these my superiors in learning, highly honoured men and greatly skilled in the art of medicine, have displayed their amazement at the rules I've offered for the regulation of your health, but if they would bring their sound and sober judgment to consider the causes of men's diseases, perhaps they would not laugh so heartily, but would be disposed to hear out the words of one who, with all due respect, is both wiser and more skilled than they. Don't be astonished, Sacred Majesty, at this proposal of mine, but set it down as a certain truth that all the infirmities that afflict men originate either from an excess of bodily heat, or from taking cold, or from a superfluity of noxious humours. Therefore, as soon as a man finds himself in a sweat from fatigue or great heat, he should immediately wipe himself dry in order that the moisture issuing from the body may not re-enter and produce distemper. Again, a man ought to keep his feet warm to prevent the damps and chills emitted by the earth from ascending to his stomach, and from his stomach to his head, thereby generating pains in the head, an unwholesome state of the stomach, and numerous other ills. What I meant by the example of the beasts of the field is that a man ought to eat only such food as is suited to his bodily needs, as do the animals, having no other reason to nourish themselves. We may take the example of the ox or the horse. If you offer either of these a capon, a pheasant, or a partridge, a bit of fine fat veal or any other meat, he won't touch it, given that this sort of food is not what his nature requires. But if you should place before him hay or other provender, he will fall to eating because the food is fitting for him. Again, give the capon, the pheasant, or the meat to a dog, or even to a cat, and it will right away devour it because it is appropriate food. On the contrary, these creatures will not touch the hay or the corn because it is not the diet they require as unfit for their natures. Therefore I beg you, O my lord, to give up eating all such food as is not suited to your habit of body and to take only the things that agree with your temperament. If you will follow these precepts, you will enjoy a long and healthy life.'

Gotfreddo's advice greatly pleased the king, who put his full faith in it and followed it closely. Dismissing the other physicians, he retained Maestro Gotfreddo close to him, holding him in high esteem for his virtue and worth. Thus, from being poor, Gotfreddo became a rich man – a well merited reward – and having been appointed sole guardian of the king's health, he himself lived happily.

Isabella brought her story thus to an end, a fable that delighted the entire assembly, pausing only briefly before offering her enigma.

> Marvel not, O lady fair,
> At what I now to you declare,
> For truth itself is not more true,
> Though it may worthless seem to you.
> One time, when pressed by danger fell,
> A friend I found who served me well;
> But had I not, with force amain,
> Sent him into his place again,
> I should have met my death straightway,
> And vanished from this world away.

For some reason the meaning of this enigma appeared to the ladies to be somewhat immodest, but in truth it was nothing of the sort, because under the husk there lay another sense different altogether from the way they had imagined it on the surface. It was as follows: a youth being chased by the sheriff's officers took flight and, as he was running, he saw the door of a house standing open. Then another man, to save him, pushed him into the house, closed the door, and shot the bolt into its place, namely, the hole it fitted into. If he hadn't reacted in this way, the youth would have been sent to prison.

Isabella had barely ended the exposition of her enigma when Vicenza, not waiting for the Signora's command, took her turn with the following discourse.

XIII.12 Commentary

Many are the stories in which ailing kings desperate for cures offer high rewards to anyone proffering a remedy, including his majesty with Adamantina's doll affixed to his posterior (V.2). But the present anecdote is so generic in nature as to render analysis in such terms superfluous. That it is a king suggests the beginning of a fairy tale or romance that could have involved a Helena or a Bertram, but it does not, and for that reason is something of a false lead. Rather, the vignette offers the simple satisfaction of seeing pretentious ignorance masquerading as smug erudition among professionals baffled by circumstances and dismissed in favour of modest observation and practice. The only hint of drama, still in fairy-tale fashion, is the invocation of a last-hope candidate hiding behind the door who must endure derision before his final exaltation. Even this humble practitioner is not without the conventional axioms and postulates of his science, however, and a detour of some scope might be undertaken to explain his principles of health by opposites (allopathy), applying heat to cold conditions and vice versa.[116] As a diagnostician, this down-home practitioner is remarkably certain that the symptoms of the king are not life-threatening; this is his boldest step. That his insights

---

116 Fundamental to Renaissance medicine was that all pain is caused by an excess of cold, heat, moisture or dryness, and that homoeostasis can be restored by correcting such excesses through precise counter-measures in precise degrees. Accordingly, it is stated that where there is moisture, it must be wiped dry in order to prevent its reabsorption into the body as a toxic element. In the words of Hippocrates, 'Opposites are cures for opposites.' See G.E.R., Lloyd, *Polarity and Analogy: Two Types of Argumentation in Early Greek Thought* (Cambridge: Cambridge University Press, 1966), p. 21.

prove correct in retrospect, the reader must accept at face value. The point of the story, however, is in Gotfreddo's prescription of a life regimen based on the fundamental directives of nature and moderation so that in eating appropriate foods the body might restore itself. In short, the king would appear to be suffering merely from an excessive lifestyle, which escaped the attention of the medical 'scholastics' in attendance. Such deflations of high science in the name of common sense were particularly acute in a period in which the helplessness of specialists was in sharp relief – witness their ineffectiveness in confronting both syphilis and the plague – often merely adding to the complexity and humbuggery invested in ever more esoteric and costly pharmaceutical and metallic preparations in order to keep up the reputation of their profession, all of which fostered the radical claims of quacks and mountebanks.

For this specific vignette, I have found no sources similar in substance and design. Straparola was hastening to a close in providing his designated young women and others present with short contributions to round out the final soirée in summary fashion, and may have supplied Isabella with an edifying intervention entirely of his own making.

Nevertheless, the tale has at its core one of the distichs of Cato, Book I, no. 26, 'sic ars deluditur arte,' which is subject to several interpretations insofar as 'art' signifies both learning and craftiness, hence that one man's better learning may make a mockery of another man's learning, that wisdom trumps former wisdom and, in our story, that the wisdom of the humble may sometimes make fools of the pretentiously wise, just as the cunning of one knave may surpass and mock the cunning of another. Thus, the maxim had floated free from Cato's precise original context, that 'whoever uses false words and is not a true friend in his heart should be treated in the same way so that one slight is deluded by another.'[117] There is a kind of symmetry in the correction of excess, namely, that it will be taken down by a rival employing the same means. This saying could, in its turn, become a principle of plotting, as in Boccaccio's *Decameron* VIII.7. There he echoes the distich in the story of the lady who left her would-be lover out in the snow only to be scorched by the sun on the roof of a tower when the scorned and vindictive youth takes the ladder away: 'spesse volte avviene che l'arte è dall' arte schernita' (often it comes about that art is mocked by art) which Straparola

---

117 'Qui simulat verbis nec corde est fidus amicus, / Tu quoque fac simules: sic ars deluditur arte,' *Disticha Catonis*, bk. I, no. 26.

clearly echoes in turn: 'che spesse volte aviene che l'arte dall' arte è schernita.' This little Decameronian citation, in fact, becomes the ideological motor of the present anecdote.

Finally, Donato Pirovano notes that Guglielmo, re di Bertagna might signify William I (ca. 1028–87), the conqueror of England (Bretagna) in 1066, or his son, William II (ca. 1060–1100), but admits that the name may also be entirely fictional.[118]

---

118 Giovan Francesco Straparola, *Le piacevoli notti* (Rome: Salerno, 2000), vol. II, p. 779.

XIII. Fable 13
How Pietro Rizzato Finds a Treasure
and Becomes a Miser

VICENZA

Pietro Rizzato, a spendthrift, is reduced to poverty. Then finding a treasure, he becomes a miser.

Prodigality is a vice that brings a man to an end worse than avarice, because the spendthrift devours not only his own substance but other men's as well, and when he is destitute, everyone scorns him. People want to distance themselves from him as though he were mad, an outlaw, or just to make fun of him. This is what happened in the case of a certain Pietro Rizzato, who, for all his reckless spending, ended up in total misery. Then by chance discovering a treasure, he became not only a rich man but a pinchpenny as well.

I must begin by saying that in Padua, a city most famous for its learning, in times past there lived one Pietro Rizzato, a courteous gentleman, handsome enough, and furnished with more wealth than any other citizen. At the same time, however, he was a spendthrift, continually giving to friends first one thing and then another – to each according to his condition. Because of this over-lavish habit of his, he had a great crowd of followers, and guests were never wanting at his table, which was heaped up daily with the finest and most costly foods. Among his acts of folly, there were two of special note, one of which happened on a day when he was travelling on the Brenta on his way to Venice in the company of other Paduan gentlemen. Noticing that his companions were amusing themselves, whether in making music or in other ways, one of them making music, the other in some different way, in order not to appear idle, he started playing at ducks and drakes by skipping coins across the surface of the river. The other was of a more serious nature. One day, while staying at his country house, it happened that a group of young men came to pay their respects to him. As soon as he caught sight of them, he set fire to all the houses of his staff in honour of their arrival.

Because Pietro was consumed with the desire to feed his appetites in all ways possible and to live the dissolute life to the full, in due course he found his wealth at an end and the company of all those friends who formerly paid him court dispersed. In the past, when he was enjoying his wealth, he had nourished up a great tribe of hungry familiars, but now that he was himself both hungry and thirsty, not a single one could be found who would give him food or drink. He had clothed the naked and now there was no one willing to cover his own nakedness. He had cared for those who were sick and now he called in vain for someone to relieve his infirmities. He had given loving entertainment to all, honouring them as best he could, and afterward he met nothing but frowns from his friends, who fled from him as from some contagious pestilence. And although the poor man was reduced to this bitter condition of poverty, being naked, ailing, vexed, and stricken with dysentery, he accepted with patience his miserable life, thanking God for having given him an understanding mind.

It happened one day that the wretched man, all dirty and afflicted with the itch, made his way into a ruined building, not for pleasure but merely to ease nature. While he was there, his eyes fell upon a spot in the wall fallen to decay through age, and in a large crack he saw the shining of gold. Breaking down the wall, he came upon a great vase of terra cotta filled with fine gold ducats, which he carried back to his house in secret. Then he began to spend again, not lavishly as before, but moderately and in strict accordance with his needs. His friends and close companions, who had courted him so assiduously in former jovial times, when they saw that he was once more a man of substance, automatically imagined that they would rediscover the same largesse they once knew. Seeking him out, they began to wheedle and flatter him, thinking they could again live at his expense. But their desires were not met, for they found him no longer a fool and a big spender – a man always lavishing his wealth and holding banquets. Rather, he had become not only prudent and careful, but avaricious. When these companions enquired how he came into so much money, he answered that if they sought wealth they would first have to evacuate their bleeding guts, as he had done, meaning that he who would find wealth must first pay with his blood. So all these friends and companions, as soon as they saw that it would not be easy to draw further profits from Pietro, abandoned him and departed.

This fable gave great pleasure to all the company because it showed openly that friends ought to prove their worth, not when the world goes well but when it goes ill, and that all sorts of extremes are evil. As soon as silence returned, the Signora commanded Vicenza to tell her enigma. No sooner had she heard these words than she produced this saucy little performance.

> Now, learned sir, I prithee say,
> What is it that is born today,
> Again tomorrow born? When dead,
> Beneath the earth it hides its head,
> But there not fated to remain.
> Short is its day of toil and pain,
> Early and guiltless oft it dies,
> No stain of sin upon it lies,
> And old or young, or large or small,
> We find them in our dishes all.

The entire company judged this enigma to be a very difficult one, whereupon Vicenza, like the discreet damsel that she was, explained its meaning in the following way: 'This twice born thing is the egg, from which there is born without intervention the chick. This has but a short lifespan and often dies before it has committed any offence, which is to say, before it has ever known the pleasure of its mate. Then again, whether they be big or small, fowls are good for our use.' This fair interpretation of a very difficult riddle was a cause of wonder to all the grateful company, not one of them withholding high praise for it.

And now, because the reddening dawn began to appear, and because the time of carnival had come to an end and the first day of Lent had begun, the Signora, turning towards the honourable company, her face brightly lit with pleasure, began to speak, 'I'm sure you all realize, you illustrious and honourable gentlemen, and you ladies most lovely and worthy, that we have now come to the first day of Lent. For this reason, it seems to me right that we should at once put aside the pleasure of our delightful conversation, our amorous dances, the lovely sounds of our angelic music, and our mirthful fables, now to attend to the health of our souls.' The gentlemen, and the ladies too, joined with her in this desire, expressing their agreement in words of high commendation. So without lighting the torches, because the broad daylight had come, in accordance with the Signora's request, they were to all get some rest, with the instruction that none of them should return to the meeting place except by request. The men, taking their leave of the Signora and of the young ladies, departed in holy peace, returning each to his own abode.

The End of the Thirteenth and Last Night

XIII.13 Commentary

The story of Pietro Rizzato is a rather anti-climactic conclusion to this sprawling collection, a moralizing vignette about improvidence and prodigality leading to penury and misery, followed by chance recovery and Pietro's conversion to frugality and thrift tending to miserliness. It is a brief but thematically pregnant sequence of events in illustration of diverse attitudes towards material plenty, the predation of associates styled as friends, and the strategic if not vengeful mind of a man made prudent or niggardly by experience. The vignette is equivocal in terms of its potential for thematic weighting: a lesson on prodigality; a lesson on the fickleness of friends; or a lesson on the vagaries of fortune. The gist of the tale is its double reversal, externally from adversity to prosperity, and mentally from profligacy to miserliness, through the school of hard knocks. Straparola maintains an exemplum-like minimalism, but as the select analogues to follow will demonstrate, the story is apt for elaborate embellishment and increased ambiguity of a kind that arises from compound circumstances and doublings.

Straparola is once again indebted to Girolamo Morlini, whose fifty-first *novella*, 'Asotus juvenis' (Of a prodigal who, having found a treasure, becomes a miser), relates the familiar tale of falling and rising fortunes, parasitic friends, and the formation of a scrupulous mentality concerning the management of personal resources.[119] The return of fair-weather friends – those who once fed on the protagonist's generosity but who fled in times of hardship – elicits from him the simple advice that henceforth if they wish to achieve wealth, they must sweat their own blood as he had been compelled to do both literally and figuratively. Straparola plumps up the central portrait by supplying the subject with a name, a trip down the Brenta in good times, and select examples of his extravagant behaviour,

---

119 *Les nouvelles*, trans. Fernand Caussy (Paris: E. Sansot, 1904), no. 51, pp. 117–18; *Novelle*, ed. G. Villani (Rome: Salerno, 1983), pp. 74–5.

such as skipping coins on the water or burning down houses in a gesture of welcome to his friends. At the point in the narrative where the despairing hero's fortunes change for the better, however, Straparola is content merely to translate, abandoning altogether his pretension to novelistic embroidery.

In a sense, the matter of sources begins and ends with Morlini, although the story type was cultivated in various forms by authors at work during the previous century. Poggio Bracciolini in his *Facetiae* provides a store of such anecdotes, including one on the present topic. Near the beginning of his collection is the troubling story 'About a Jew who by persuasion became a Christian.'[120] The basis of that persuasion is the scriptural nostrum that he who gives all to the poor will be rewarded a hundredfold. When the convert insists upon the literalness rather than the spirit of the words, the motive for the conversion is itself called into question. At first, he is welcomed into the Christian community with great celebration, but after his wealth has been disbursed, he finds himself alone in the fields in a state of sickness and misery, without a Christian soul to succour him. When the urge of nature takes him, he relieves himself, and in reaching for a tuft of grass, he finds a sack full of precious stones and so returns to material well-being. Then the Christians remind him of God's promises fulfilled in multiplying his wealth, but he reminds them only of his misery and of divine procrastination. This tale is likewise equivocal in signalling the grasping poverty of spirit of the convert, God's tardiness, or the rightful lack of celerity on God's part in rewarding the ungrateful, and the lack of Christian charity even within their own community. It is a more ironic instance of the mind resolved after enduring hardship.[121] If this is perchance Morlini's source, he strips it of its novelistic particularity and ethnic circumstances.

Tomaso Costo tells another in *Il fuggilozio* concerning 'The prodigal youth who, in seeking to hang himself in desperation, happens upon

---

120 *Les facéties de Pogge, Florentin*, ed. Pierre des Brandes (Léonce Grasillier) (Paris: Garnier Frères, [1900]), pp. 12–13.

121 A loosely related tale from much this same period, 'De viro amicos experiri volente,' occurs in the *Hecatomythium primum hoc est centum fabulae* of Lorenzo Abstemio (Laurentii Abstemii Maceratensis), published in *Aesopus Fabulae* (Venice: 1520), no. 85, pp. N3v–4v, in which the friendship of two men stands the test of adversity, while all others who had been lavishly received fall away in repudiation of their social obligations.

unexpected good fortune and thereafter becomes moderate and wise.'[122] The hanging motif attaches this simple vignette to all those more complex stories of fate and fortune in which a person in despair, in the very act of suicide, is confronted by sudden treasure – a story type destined to have a history of its own (already examined in conjunction with the story of 'Salardo,' I.1). The prodigal son of a rich merchant dissipates his entire inheritance. But the father, nearing death, gives his son a second chance, while warning him away from a little room that he must never enter unless his life has been reduced to the direst of necessity. The room, in fact, provides a third chance, although it was set up as an invitation to suicide, for it contains a rope suspended from a beam upon which there is a further store of wealth – a form of shock therapy to awaken prudence. To this place the youth resorts at last when friends desert him and he reaches his nadir. There he finds the noose and accepts suicide as his father's final legacy. But as planned, the weight of his body causes the roof to collapse and money to rain down, turning his sorrow into joy. Such are the means to his mental reform accompanied by new wealth after penury. It is a tale of redemption in a material world, less concerned with fortune or the betrayal of friends than with the wisdom of a father in caring for his offspring after death. The tale is central to our enquiry, however, because it stands at the crossroads among story types involving near death, sudden wealth, and the regenerated mind.

From the story of Costo we proceed by steps to the 'Strani & amirabili essempi casi della Fortuna' (Strange and wonderful examples of Fortune) in *L'hore di ricreatione* of Lodovico Guiciardini (as spelled on the title page). This sketch is concerned with the crisis and sudden reversal of fortune of Marcantonio Baristei, who, after losing 500 scudi in a maritime disaster, becomes so depressed by his impoverishment that he seeks to hang himself. But as he attaches the halter to a beam, he discovers 1000 scudi hidden there. Delighted by this turn of events, he leaves the noose (*capestro*) in its place and goes on his way. But when the owner of this money, unable to find it, sees the halter, he in his turn feels so much grief that without further reflection hangs himself.[123] The vignette now takes on a double turn of fortune around the same noose and beam, with a double reversal of moods, and a simple reflection upon the wondrous

---

122 *Il fuggilozio*, ed. Corado Calenda (Rome: Salerno, 1989), bk. VIII, no. 16, pp. 590–2.
123 *L'Hore di ricreatione* (Venice: Cristoforo Zenetti, 1572), p. 317.

productions of the goddess of inscrutable change. Meanings are shifting. This tale leads directly to the following story.

Giovanni Battista Giraldi Cinzio in his *Ecatommiti* (IX, no. 8) extends this story into a full *novella* that is translated by William Painter for inclusion in his *Palace of Pleasure*.[124] Care must be taken in assigning the order of influence, however, for the *Ecatommithi* was first published in 1565, the *Palace* in 1566 (the first 50) and 1567 (the remaining 34), while *L'hore* did not appear until 1572. Cinthio sets his story in ancient Carthage at the time of the Roman conquerors, so that the house in which the treasure is hidden changes hands following the outcome of the war in Scipio's favour. Philene is the young daughter of the mother who flees this house, leaving her treasure behind, with instructions to her child concerning its location and contents. The Roman soldier, noble yet poor, who occupies the house has a daughter about Philene's age named Elisa. Both girls are scorned for want of proper dowries by potential marriage partners whom they nevertheless love. Elisa in her despair discovers the treasure while attempting to hang herself from the beam, and in her generous way shares the new wealth with her father, who thereby gains status in the community, enabling Elisa to win her marriage. Meanwhile, Philene wends her way back to Carthage disguised as a boy, takes service in her old house, and at last attempts to find the hidden vase. Instead, she finds the noose hidden in the rafters and takes it for her destiny. Moments before her desperate life is to be extinguished, however, Elisa enters and rescues her, learning at the same time the truth of her family's prosperity. A long dispute follows because Elisa's husband will have nothing to do with charity, claiming that all has been forfeited to them through the fortunes of war. But the good Roman father sees things differently and offers to restore the full amount, whereupon Philene states that she would receive only that which he wished to bestow upon her as a gift. In the end, it is divided in half, and Philene is both adopted into the family as a daughter and married to her heart's content. The story concludes as a contest of liberality and a compound lesson in the ways of fortune. Yet it remains the story of despair, attempted suicide, and the reversal of fortune. To be sure, there is no longer the matter of profligacy and prudence. But given the story's origins, it remains a cousin to that which

---

124 William Painter, *The Palace of Pleasure*, ed. Joseph Jacobs, 3 vols. (London: David Nutt, 1890; New York: Dover Publications, 1966), pt. II, no. 11, vol. II, pp. 264–78. Giovanni Battista Giraldi Cinzio, *Gli ecatommiti* (Florence: Tipografia Borghi, 1831), IX.8, pp. 398–403.

appears in the *Piacevoli notti*. Yet for our purposes, we must turn back to the more minimalist designs of Morlini and his predecessors.

A potential source for Morlini, and hence for Straparola, is the story by Francesco Del Tuppo of the young man of considerable wealth who squandered it among his friends only to find himself both destitute and alone.[125] This protagonist, wandering, infirm, in need of a doctor, yet unable to pay, and weak from the loss of blood, comes to an old house where he takes shelter. There in his grief he sees a crack in the wall from which ducats come flooding down, whereupon his weakness and pain desert him. Then all of his friends return to congratulate him, whereupon he reminds them of their indifference to his misery, having left him to die, volunteering to them the following advice: 'If it is money you want, you can shit blood for it as I have been compelled to do.' This, for Del Tuppo, is the essence of the exemplum, that fair-weather friends may be justly reproved. His telling preserves the proportions of narrative already familiar from the related pieces by Morlini and Straparola. Morlini's *novelle* were published in 1520, Poggio's *facetiae* (the earliest editions undated) around 1470,[126] while Del Tuppo published his *fabula* in 1485. The model was current, for several writers displayed their individual talents in reshaping it in their own words from sources not easily determined. But it is Morlini who provides the funnel through which Straparola received this, along with more than twenty other *novelle*.

Along the way, Morlini's story was filled out with two anecdotes: skipping coins on the river for sport, and burning down houses in an extravagant display of welcome. These acts of folly were attributed to Jacopo da Santo Andrea, who is honoured with a three-line mention in Canto XIII of Dante's *Inferno*: 'O Jacomo,' it cried, 'of Sant' Andrea, / Why make a screen of me? What was the good? / Am I to blame for thy misspent career?'[127] The reference is cryptic, presumably because the story was so well known to Dante's contemporaries. The setting is the woods wherein the souls of suicides had grown up into trees. Two men appear, running from a pack of hunting hounds, one of whom is torn to pieces while the other hides behind a bush, which is mangled in the process and is now

---

125 *Aesopus vita et fabulae latine et italice* (1485), ed. Carlo De Frede (Naples: Associazione Napoletana per i monumenti e il paesaggio, 1968), pp. 401–2.

126 Pierre des Brandes, ed., *Les facéties de Pogge* (Paris: Garnier, [1900]), 'Introduction,' p. lii.

127 *The Comedy of Dante Alighieri the Florentine*, 'Hell,' trans. Dorothy L. Sayers (Harmondsworth: Penguin, 1949), p. 152.

speaking to the man cowering there: the Jacomo of our story. Giovanni Boccaccio provides illumination in his *Comento sopra la Commedia* (1373), telling of a man who had amassed wondrous riches that he then dissipated and squandered, his story thereby paralleling or even providing the initial fuse for the present tale. Boccaccio mentions the spectacle of the burning buildings, the ensuing poverty, the desperation, and the implicit suicide whereby Jacomo finds himself in this particular circle of Hell.[128] Cristoforo Landino elaborates upon the portrait in his *Comento*, a work first published in 1481. He says (and I translate), 'Once there was a nobleman of Padua from the chapel of Saint Andrea who was very rich but who squandered his wealth most stupidly. Among his idiocies was a trip to Venice on the Brenta in the company of other noble youths, during which, seeing that the others were amusing themselves in singing and playing music, in order not to look idle he started to throw coins one by one into the river. Another time, when a large group of young men were on their way to his villa, seeing them far off, in their honour he had all the houses and outbuildings of his farmers set on fire.'[129] (In Boccaccio's telling, it had been the villa itself.) Jacopo's is a parallel tale of profligacy and self-impoverishment, but Morlini's protagonist is reborn a miser, while Jacopo slays himself; thus the works part company. Nevertheless, the legacy of Dante finds partial recirculation in the borrowing of episodes, the completed process providing an example of the story-making process in action.

Of the many subsequent stories of material loss and recovery accompanied by a dose of self-knowledge, mention may be made of two, one of which may have a Straparolan connection. Thomas-Simon Gueulette is known to have borrowed liberally from our author for his materials. It is thus conceivable that the vignette included in the *Nights* provided the fuse for the story of 'Utzim-Ochanti, Prince de Chine' in Gueulette's collection *Les mille et un quarts d'heure, contes tartars* (1715).[130] Should that prove the case, however, it is only the generic pattern that prevails, for in this instance Gueulette had to spin the rest of his oriental fable from his fertile brain. Prince Utzim, desiring to leave the relative security of

---

128 Giovanni Boccaccio, *Il comento sopra la commedia*, ed. Gaetano Milanesi, 2 vols. (Florence: Successori Le Monnier, 1895), vol. II, pp. 350–1.

129 Cristoforo Landino, *Comento sopra la Comedia*, ed. Paolo Procaccioli, 4 vols, Edizione Nazionale dei Commenti Danteschi (Rome: Salerno, 2001), vol. II, p. 655.

130 (Paris: Libraires Associés, 1753); *A Thousand and One Quarters of Hours* (London: J. Tonson, 1716); ed. Leonard C. Smithers (London: H.S. Nichols, 1893), pp. 102–13.

his own realm to travel, beseeches and gains his father's permission. He takes along a considerable trove of wealth and six clever companions, each possessing a remarkable skill, such as exquisite painting, debating, mathematical wizardry, long-distance running, or musical performance. But the prince is a spendthrift along the way, seeking to impress all whom he meets with his nobility and largesse. He pays no heed to advice until his substance is exhausted and he is forced to live by the proceeds gained from the demonstrations of his fellows' skills. Their wealth somewhat restored, they make for home, only to be met by 200 robbers, who once more render them destitute. At last it is the prince who must make use of some profitable skill to their mutual benefit. Wandering alone he meets a funeral cortège, but fails to salute the deceased; this lands him in a brawl. His six friends come to his aid, and by degrees the companion with rhetorical skills is able to convince the inhabitants that being now without an heir to their throne, they could do no better than to crown Utzim-Ochanti, who had already impressed them by his doughty show of arms. Thus is his fortune reversed. At his nadir, however, he had sought to boast his nobility in a foreign city where no one would offer him a glass of water. Through such hardship he learned important new values. In the end, 'quite cured of the extravagance that had before made him so miserable,' the prince conducted all his affairs with prudence, although his adventures were far from over on his return trip to China. Those, however, involved treacherous and deceptive women and a second phase of his education.

The second work illustrates even more directly the universal features of this narrative type. 'The Heir of Lynne' is a Scottish ballad collected by Andrew Lang concerning a spendthrift laird who squandered his money and estate. He then found himself abandoned by all his associates and a beggar for bread on the streets of Edinburgh.[131] The ballad makes much of his grief, regret, and self-recrimination, and of the importance of preserving ancestral land. Only then does he think upon a 'bill' left by his father, to be consulted only when all hope seemed pointless. The paper tells of an old castle wall where there are hidden three chests of gold and silver coin. With this newfound wealth in his bread bag, he approaches the man to whom he had sold the estate, gets him in his cups, and extracts from him a reckless promise to restore his lands at a cheap

---

131 *A Collection of Ballads*, ed. Andrew Lang (Charleston, SC: BiblioLife, 2007),
    pp. 186–90.

price – a promise made on the assumption that the first laird's indigence was permanent. Then he opens his sack and pays out the sum, regains his title, and calls upon himself 'Christ's curse' if ever again he should commit such folly. And so this perusal of the literatures of the Eastern and Western worlds comes to an end, with the present editor calling upon himself a similar curse should he ever again take on a labour of such magnitude. Amen.